THE MIDDLE
OF THE FIRE

To

With sincere appreciation
for the inspiration you
transpired at the Eastern
Long Island Branch of
National Women's League

Rita Lamaya
Pres. 11/9/71

Books by Irwin R. Blacker

NOVELS

Westering
Taos
Days of Gold
Standing on a Drum

ENTERTAINMENTS

The Kilroy Gambit
Chain of Command
Search and Destroy
To Hell in a Basket

NONFICTION

Irregulars, Partisans, Guerrillas
The Old West in Fact
The Old West in Fiction
The Golden Conquistadores
Conquest
Prescott's Histories
The Book of Books
Hakluyt's Voyages
Directors at Work

JUVENILES

The Bold Conquistadores
Cortés and the Aztec Conquest

THE
MIDDLE
OF THE
FIRE

A NOVEL

IRWIN R. BLACKER

CHARLES SCRIBNER'S SONS · NEW YORK

FOR
Fishel and Rosa Gershevich
who introduced me to Israel

ACKNOWLEDGMENTS

The author is deeply indebted to many persons for their help: the officers of the Israeli Army and officials of their government in Los Angeles, Washington and Israel who gave of their time and their understanding; Dr. and Mrs. Jack J. Cohen, Moshe Davis and Mr. and Mrs. Harry Rosen, old friends, now residents of Jerusalem, who gave of their insights; and certain private individuals who were actual participants in the events which took place in the Old City, Aden and elsewhere, in particular Mr. Max Lapidus of Jerusalem and Col. and Mrs. Ram Rom of Givataimo. Their contribution can never be adequately acknowledged. However, any flaws in the background of this novel are the fault of the author and not of any of the kind people who helped him. Grateful thanks are also due to Bruce Carrick and Norman Kotker, my editors, and to Sylvia Weiner and Ethel Blacker who helped on the manuscript.

Transliteration of Hebrew and Arabic words varies greatly. I have adopted the most commonly used forms whenever possible. Israeli place names follow, for the most part, the form used by the Geographical Survey of Israel.

The Middle of the Fire is a novel. Its central characters are all fictional. Even though many of the incidents told here actually happened, the personal stories are not those of the Israeli participants in these events.

Book I
SPRING 1948

JERUSALEM, THE OLD CITY, SPRING, 1948

He wondered if he would ever know silence again.

Lying on the sloped roof of the old house, he felt the shock and the blast of the large guns which lay siege to the city. The fading sun reflected off a minaret less than a hundred meters away. Rolling onto his back, he could see the spire of the Church of the Holy Sepulchre. Three machine-gun slugs ripped the old stone coping beside his head. Inching back on the roof, he squirmed along the shelter of a wall. Then he dropped into an alley and, whirling about, brought his Sten gun up to rake the empty square at the alley's end. Five quick steps and he was in a doorway as the Arabs returned his fire. His shoulders against the heavy wooden doorway behind him, he scanned the doorway opposite. Calculating the ammunition he had in his Sten and his pocket, he decided he could not risk another sweep of the alley and dived across it without sheltering fire.

Looking upward, he saw he was under the shelter of an ancient vaulted arch which stretched over the alley. It was darker now. He could see no sun even though it was only late afternoon. He pressed against the dark wooden door behind him. Another burst of Arab gunfire. The sound of mortar fire somewhere in the distance.

Beyond the Old City, the Arabs were turning their frustration and wrath on the New City of the Jews. Zvi Mazon had no time to weep for his compatriots. He had enough trouble of his own. He had been inside the walls since November. It was now sometime in early May. He had no calendar. All he could be certain of was that it was spring and at the end of the alley the Arabs were preparing for another attack.

Suddenly he saw something pass him in the semi-darkness. Hurling himself down against the doorway, he waited for the shock. The grenade exploded within five paces of him. They knew where he was. They would not charge the alley until they were certain he was dead or at least alone. During the months inside, Zvi and his friends had taught the Arab mobs this much.

But he could not stay where he was. If not the last grenade, the next. He banged the butt of his Sten on the door behind him. Then he started to look

1

for another way out of his trap. A second grenade lobbed past him. Flat against the wall again, he heard the explosion and felt the warm air as jagged steel fragments splattered the wall. His Sten came up as he prepared to shoot the lock off the door. He heard a click. The old lock was being turned. Another grenade in the alley, and Zvi hurled the door open and himself inside and onto the floor beyond at the instant of the explosion. The metal ripped the air, splattered against the wooden door and struck someone standing in the doorway.

Without looking around, Zvi kicked the heavy door shut and came to his feet. No soldiers would risk crossing the open square at the end of the alley to pursue Zvi, but the Arabs were foolish fighters, and he knew they just might.

Ignoring the enemy for the moment, Zvi turned his attention to the room. It was small and dark and almost bare. Two tables against the far wall, books sprawled on them and a straight-backed chair. He did not smile as he realized that he had forced his way into one of the small *yeshivot* which marked the Old City for what is was: another world to him.

Looking down, he saw a young man on his knees in the corner. At first Zvi thought the *yeshivah bochur* was praying; then he realized that it was not prayers rocking the youth back and forth but the hole where the splinters of the grenade had torn into his chest. Making sure that the heavy door was locked, Zvi crossed the room, and forcing the young man to sit back against the wall, he knelt, rested his Sten across his knee, and inspected the wound. He was no doctor, but he had come to know wounds. The youth would not live.

Zvi's eyes locked with the stranger's.

"Why did you come?" the young man asked.

"You know," Zvi told him. He had heard the question before and resented it.

Then he heard someone enter the room and he grabbed his Sten. Heavy mortars continued to break the afternoon. An old woman was looking down at him and the youth. At that moment another grenade exploded in the alley. Zvi came to his feet, feeling ridiculous with his gun pointed at the old woman in the blue-black dress. "He was hurt," was all he could say. Then, almost blindly, he brushed past her and made his way through the building. As he expected, there was a courtyard at the back. A withered tree groped its way toward the light above. Cracked mosaics marked the floor of the court and a hen cackled at the sound of each shell striking the New City.

In the courtyard, Zvi slung his Sten over his shoulder and stood a moment as he tried to forget the old woman wailing in the room behind him and the young man with the blood on his dark, sleazy caftan. He wished he had a cigarette. He needed one. He scanned the roofs about the courtyard. Two flights up and across the roof. Another alley, but this one with a twist at the end and no Arabs raking it with grenades and machine-gun fire.

Taking a deep breath, he started for the roofs. Pulling himself over the first one, he surveyed the high ground overlooking the Old City. The British still held that. He did not think they would fire. It would depend on who the officer was commanding the height. Inching across the dirty stones on his belly, Zvi glanced toward the open square beyond the alley he had just fled. In the shelter of a stone wall he could make out the Arab machine-gun emplacement which had harassed him. He looked the other way and saw the Western Wall.

He could hear intensive rifle fire being exchanged on the outskirts of the New City, but Zvi was not aware of it.

The Western Wall. The Wailing Wall. The last wall of the Temple of Solomon, and beyond it the late sun glinting off the dome of the Mosque of Omar. There was the Wall before him, and he wondered what it meant. Solomon had built it and Herod had rebuilt it. The Romans had destroyed the Temple of which it had been a part. And except for those dark years when the early Christian zealots and then the Crusaders slaughtered the Jews who lived within its shadows, his people had made their way back to live and die within the shadow of that Wall. Men had wept here for sixty generations. Men had died to live within its shadow. The Wall. Irregular blocks of gray stone with small tufts of plants trying to grow in its cracks. A gray place. A grim place. A dark shadow. The wall which one of Hadrian's generals had suggested be saved to show the might of his emperor, and for his suggestion had been ordered to leap from it. The Byzantines had known and respected it. The Moslems of other centuries had granted the Jews the right to pray there. Neither the Turks nor the British had even allowed Jews to sit by the Wall, because that would mean possession. And now it was in enemy hands and no one was seeking its shelter for solace as so many had for so long.

Zvi Mazon's dark eyes seemed to recede into his square face as he stared at the Wall and tried to understand what it meant to him and why he was fighting in this Old City when all of his friends were in the south preparing to protect the Negev or in the New City preparing to defend the families living there. Who cared if Zvi Mazon died in this place? Who cared if the hundred men and women of Haganah or the fifty of Irgun — the underground — were able to hold out? Certainly not the Hasidim and the religious zealots who said, when their paths crossed his:

"Why did you come?"

"What are you doing here?"

"We want no State."

"When the time comes, the Messiah will come."

"Until that time leave us alone."

"Leave us alone."

Zvi half closed his eyes and squinted at the late afternoon sun beyond the New City at the other side of the high walls surrounding the Old. Rolling over, he tried to make out any movement near the Street of the Chain which bounded the Jewish Quarter. Nothing. He turned the other way toward the Dung Gate. Nothing. From where he lay, he could see sections of the high walls which isolated the Old City from the New. Within the walls, an area of less than one square mile held over twenty thousand Christians, Moslems and Jews. The center of three religious worlds all locked within the high walls rebuilt by the Crusaders so long ago.

His attention centered once more on the machine gun so poorly hidden behind the stone ruins of a small synagogue. A movement there. A head. His Sten came up. A young Arab boy rose from behind the machine gun to toss a grenade down the street. Zvi's fingers stiffened. He could not permit himself to waste ammunition now. There were twenty thousand Arabs in the Old City. He did not have twenty thousand bullets. In fact, he did not have twenty.

Edging back on the roof, he dropped to the street below. There was no one in sight. The high walls of the old houses blocked the sun, and it was as though he had passed in a single moment from daylight to twilight. Prepared to fire, he made his way through the known street and down another and into an alley. Two doors farther on, he stopped and turned about. There was nothing in sight except a small cart parked near a heavy wooden door. Zvi wondered where the peddler was and what he sold when the times allowed for barter. Resting the butt of his Sten on his hip, he entered the house.

Inside, a bearded soldier in his early twenties lay on a dirty mattress. He slowly came up on one elbow and smiled at Zvi. "There was news on the radio," gesturing to the battered wooden cabinet set against the far wall of the otherwise empty room.

Zvi nodded. "Got a cigarette, Avi?"

His companion, Avram Ben Ezra, shrugged. "I have not seen one for a week." Then he grinned foolishly. "Tomorrow, when the Messiah comes, we will all be given cigarettes from Virginia. There will be good wine and all the meat a man can want." He paused a moment and the grin departed. "When the Messiah comes."

Zvi knelt beside the mattress. "The others?"

"Out saving the city for history."

Zvi nodded, set his gun on the floor and, crossing over, poured himself a drink of warm water from a pitcher on top of the radio cabinet. Holding the greasy glass in his hand, he asked, "And the news?"

"Ben Gurion declared that we are a State. The nation has been reborn." There was awe in the soldier's voice. His lean, bearded face bobbed back and forth as he said once more, "The nation has been reborn."

Zvi did not smile when he said with humor, "Wonderful. But why did it have to happen in my lifetime?"

The sound of Arab mortar fire rolled over the city.

Avram explained simply, "We were reborn today."

Zvi nodded. Then, as though to change the subject, "They've got a machine gun set up near the Wall. Be careful if you have to go that way."

Slowly, Avram began to recite, "November, December, January, February, March, April and now May. And I am still alive. So, you can believe me, I am careful."

Both of them were smiling when the door opened and a woman neither of them had ever seen before entered. Avram looked to Zvi for an explanation, but Zvi shook his head.

"Looking for someone?" he asked.

"You are Haganah?"

Both men nodded. They were trying to decide whether or not she was pretty. It was difficult to tell in the dim light. She was almost as tall as Zvi, whom most men would not have considered to be very tall. She was slimmer than Avram, whom most men would have called lean in spite of his huge shoulders. Her black hair hung loosely about her shoulders. Her black dress was not cut as modestly as most of those worn in the Old City. But they knew she had to be from the Old City because the Jewish Quarter was completely cut off from the outside world. It was less than a hundred meters to the closest exit, but that hundred meters was directly under Arab guns.

"What do you want?" Zvi asked, assuming that his vague rank of squad commander made him in some way responsible.

"I can fire a gun," the woman said.

"You've used a gun?" he asked.

"I've seen a great many guns," she said flatly.

"And you would help us?" Avram was curious.

The woman nodded.

Zvi believed she was younger than he by several years. "Why now? Where have you been since the fighting started in November?"

The woman was silent for a time and then she said, "We have a State today. We didn't yesterday." Then, impatiently, "Do you want help?"

Nodding, Zvi conceded that why she was willing to fight did not matter. "We have very few guns to spare."

"You've some kind of weapon?" and it was clear that she did not care what kind she was given.

"We'll find something."

"What is your name?" Avram asked, deciding that it was time they accepted the girl.

"Dvora."

"Just that?" Avram asked.

"Dvora Rabsky."

"And you are not an Armenian who's going to tell the Arabs where we are and show them the way in?" Zvi was not as trusting as his friend, although he had already noticed the tattooed numbers on her wrist and recognized the Polish accent.

The girl remained silent.

"The Armenians said they would be neutral," Avram explained. "They've been photographing what we do and spying us out for the Arabs."

"For the Arabs and so many pieces of silver," Zvi added.

Avram, who was sitting up now, rubbed his right shoulder with his left hand. "Be careful, Zvi, or you will sound like a Christian." Then, as if he disapproved of the figure of speech, he repeated it, "And so many pieces of silver."

Ignoring him, Zvi told the girl, "Make yourself comfortable," at the same time gesturing to take in the empty room. "When we go out again, we'll contact the area commander and try to find you a gun."

The sound of heavy mortars rolled over them once more.

Sergeant Diyar al Ilm of the Arab Legion listened to the shells breaking over his head as he followed the British lieutenant through Zion Gate into the Old City. They had worked together for a month as the British officer and his men prepared to turn over to the Legionnaires those positions that the British were evacuating as well as all of the supplies which the British lieutenant and his superiors had decided they would not bother to ship out of Palestine. And now that the British flag was down and the country officially evacuated, there was nothing to prevent the two from making their final arrangements for the Arab Legion to enter the Old City.

Behind the two marched a dozen British soldiers, rifles slung over their shoulders as they walked through the Armenian Quarter in the southwestern corner of the Old City. Some of the Armenians gathered to watch the Tommies, others withdrew into their homes. The small detachment strode along the Street of the Inn of the Olive Oil. The young officer pointed out two Jewish barricades, three buildings where the Jews were known to have stored some supplies, and several different locations from which the Jews were prepared to protect themselves from the Arab mobs who for months had roamed wild in the streets.

"There." The British lieutenant, John Layton, paused to point to an old house with a domed roof of plaster. "There is a place where several Arabs approached last week and were shot at."

The sergeant marked the house on a street map he pulled from his pocket and they went on.

A shot struck the stone wall a foot above their heads.

Several men whirled, seeking the sniper. At the same time the lieutenant pivoted where he stood. He found no source for the bullet, and so he raised his arm and ran to the closest building in the Jewish Quarter with his men following. The door of the old house was locked and Layton waved for some of his men to open it. One stood back and fired his rifle at it twice, and then two of the men ran, shoulders forward, to break it down. The door swung open and Layton entered, Diyar al Ilm at his side and the soldiers after them. The British sergeant, who brought up the end of the column, sent two of his men back to watch the door, explaining, "I don't want to be trapped by any of these shit-eating Yids."

Finding the first rooms empty, Layton pressed his way into a bedroom. There an old Jew knelt in prayer, his wife and seven-year-old grandson beside him. Their heads were averted from the intruders.

"You, old man," Layton shouted.

The prayers continued.

Moving forward, the British officer swung his foot, kicking the old Jew over. "When I speak to a Hebe, I expect an answer."

The old man cowered, while the woman came to her feet, facing Layton and raising both hands.

Uncertain what she was going to do, one of the soldiers standing in the doorway fired his rifle. The woman spun backward as blood began to spurt from a hole in her neck. They watched while the old woman crumpled into a dark heap beside the cot.

"Nice shooting, soldier," Layton commended his trooper as he moved forward to stand over the old man. Frightened, the elderly Jew began to wail at the sight of his wife, whose features were no longer visible in the ooze of blood which covered them.

"They all wail," Layton explained to Diyar al Ilm, who nodded. Toeing the old man, the English officer asked, "Who shot at us out there?"

Unable to understand English, the old man did not know what was wanted of him. However, Judah Maginah, the small boy with a yarmulke on his head, who had been half hidden beside the bed, saw Layton's foot come back once more, and he jumped at the foot which was tormenting his grandfather.

Layton felt the impact of the boy's attack, but the child was light and the Englishman swung his foot back and forth twice to show his contempt for the assault. Then he fired the pistol into the top of Judah's head; as the boy spun backward, a second shot entered his right eye, splashing both his grandfather's face and Layton's shorts. Layton turned away with a nod to a corporal.

Diyar al Ilm was following Layton out the door when he heard the corporal's rifle. Neither the British officer nor the Arab sergeant had to look back to make certain the old Jew was dead. By this time the ten men who had entered the house were tearing up the rooms, ripping down the curtains, smashing the furniture and opening every cupboard and closet.

Satisfied his men would find no more than the two small pieces of jewelry one of them discovered in a battered coffee tin, Layton left. In the late afternoon sun which blazed the Street of the Inn of the Olive Oil, the British officer sighed. "I'm glad we're moving out of here. The whole place stinks of shit and Jews." He considered what he had said and added, "I don't know which is worse." Then, while they continued on toward the Street of the Chain, he gave his Arab companion a guided tour.

"The Hebes hold about four hundred fifty meters by about three hundred. I don't know how many men they have, but we do know that about fifty more came in in December. I don't think the terrorists total more than a hundred fifty." He watched one of his men stop to fire at a head which had appeared in a window. No sound followed the shot, and no one was sure a target had been struck.

Layton continued. "You have them completely surrounded within these walls and, as far as we know, there are about two thousand Jews, give or take a few—and you can take them, for all of me. And your people in the Old City must number about twenty thousand. With odds like that, you won't have much trouble."

A moment before there had been an exchange of rifle fire, but when the British appeared, it ceased. Several doors down the Street of the Chain, which was the northern edge of the Jewish Quarter, Layton pointed out a building. "I think Haganah are there. Zionists have most of this block."

Diyar al Ilm nodded and marked his map again.

"When do you plan to take over?"

The Arab shook his head. "Persons much more important than I shall decide that, Lieutenant." Diyar knew more than he was telling the Englishman; but then for two days he had been trying to learn exactly which heights the British would turn over to the Legion before evacuation was complete, and Layton had avoided answering.

Layton pointed out two carts parked in front of a Jewish house on the south side of the street. A moment later, four Tommies ripped the wheels off and set them rolling with a clatter down the street.

"Lieutenant," Diyar tried to find a way to approach his problem. "About the heights?"

The British officer continued to walk slowly down the Street of the Chain. He knew the name had some historic importance. If he were still in England, he would have looked up that fact. But now all he really wanted to do was get this sightseeing trip finished. "I don't know," he snapped. "Some of our men are siding with the Jews." He appreciated the shocked look on Diyar's swarthy face as the Arab's hand came up and grasped the heavy mustache for an instant. Layton knew he would never forget this nervous habit of his sergeant.

"The Jews corrupted them. I heard a pair of sappers sold the Hebes some guns and explosives a few months ago. One thousand American dollars." Layton spat. "Some bastards will do anything for money."

Sprawled on a roof looking down at the small British detachment, Zvi Mazon nudged the girl at his side. Surprised at the way she drew away from him, he reached out and pressed her head down. She rolled away from him and had to grab a ledge to keep from slipping off the roof into the street below where the British officer and his Arab companion had stopped to talk. Zvi recognized the suntan-cotton uniform, the stripes and the keffiyeh of the Arab: General Glubb Pasha's Legion. So far the Legion had not been seen in the Old City. Maybe this was no more than a casual visit.

Zvi glanced at Dvora as she edged toward him again. He was about to say something when she hissed between clenched teeth, "Don't ever touch me again."

Puzzled, but not particularly concerned with her problem, he said, "I could kill Layton, but we'd have a few hundred English soldiers ripping up the Quarter and tossing grenades into every house." As he spoke, the muzzle of his Sten lined up on the head of the British officer.

From their perch on the roof, Zvi, Avram and Dvora watched the detachment continue its tour. After almost ten minutes, Avram prodded Zvi with the butt of his rifle.

"*Nu?*"

Zvi nodded without taking his eyes off the Englishman. "Someday," he said simply.

"You should live so long," Avram said. "The British will be gone and you will have other things to worry about."

Zvi nodded again as he crawled back from the edge of the roof. The other two followed him. They were overlooking the courtyard of a house, and Zvi paused to rest. For months Zvi Mazon had roamed these roofs and buried his companions in the musky cellars beneath them. There had been many. Once he had had thirty men and women in his squad. Now he had fewer than ten. For six months they had lived under siege with the enemy trying to batter its way inwards. The Jewish Quarter was isolated and besieged within the ancient city of hills and narrow alleys, open stairways, house built against house, shop upon shop, cobbled streets twisting and turning, with synagogues, mosques and churches jammed within the confines of the Quarters: the Moslem to the northeast, the Christian to the northwest, the Armenian south of that and the Jewish in the southeast.

Zvi recalled the months of siege without enough water or food or arms, and most of all without enough men and women able or even willing to bear arms. Months of misery.

Zvi Mazon remembered his dead in that brief moment before he dropped from the roof into the courtyard, and wondered in which cellar he would be burying Avram. He never thought that he too might be buried.

As he recovered his balance, the others dropped into the courtyard beside him. Avram clutched his old British Enfield taken from the body of an

Arab assailant, and Dvora watched him make his way as though he expected an attack. Puzzled, she looked to Zvi for an explanation.

"They get into the Quarter more often than we like. A cellar. Over a roof. You fail to look, and there's a grenade coming at you."

Dvora did not react as she pressed against a wall and followed the men. Through an empty room to an alley beyond, down two crooked streets to a house higher than those surrounding it and into the house and past a middle-aged man in a prayer shawl and *tefillin* at prayer. Three flights of stairs and they were on another roof. Avram crawled out first, Dvora, then Zvi. There were five others on the roof already. Zvi surveyed the area to the north of the Jewish Quarter where the Christians and Moslems mingled.

It was almost dusk. There were lights in the northern section of the city. The colored windows of a church reflected off the polished stone of an old house, while the bright lights of several Christian shops lighted the Via Dolorosa. Zvi took in the sights below and rolled over to look at the others on the roof. Three of his companions were men no older than himself, and two were girls no older than Dvora. All were wearing trousers or shorts and shirts open at the collar. They had on heavy shoes, except for the girl with a scar over her left eye, who wore white cotton sneakers.

Moshe Gilead, his second in command, a slight youth of medium height with a straggling beard and a cap on his prematurely graying head, reported, "The Arabs have moved into most of the houses opposite. I think I killed one." He saw the expression on Zvi's face and added, "He was sniping through the window of the synagogue down there."

Zvi smiled. He was looking at Ruth Barovsky now. Wiping her hand nervously over the scar above her eye, she shook her head. She was almost pretty, slim, full-breasted and tanned from years of outdoor work on a kibbutz. "It was quiet on the street most of the day. Three Arabs tried to cross about an hour ago. They did not make it."

Accepting her report, he waited for the next. Fishel Warshow rubbed the back of his neck, revealing a tattoo on his wrist. He started to say something, seemed unable to and looked down at the lights of the Old City below.

Zvi looked past Fishel to the man lying beside him. "Five of them got into a house on this side," and the man pointed. "Fishel got into the house before any of us. And he came out alone." Dov Terivsky considered what he had said and continued. "There's been some heavy firing down toward the far end of the Street of the Chain. It may have been grenades."

Zvi confirmed this. "Grenades."

Dov was silent for a time and then asked, "Have we heard anything about more guns and ammunition?"

"And food and water and dancing girls," Zvi continued bitterly. Shaking his head in disgust, he snapped, "If we hear anything, you'll be the first to know. I won't keep it a secret."

Almost apologetically, Dov said, "It was just that . . ." And he shrugged.

Zvi reached out and clasped the young man with the thick glasses by the shoulder and drew him closer. He thought a moment and then said, "Avram tells me the radio says Ben Gurion declared us a State today." And he watched for the reactions of the others, who had been on duty through the daylight hours and probably had not yet heard the news.

Moshe Gilead pulled himself to his knees and started to say something when two rifle shots splattered against the stones beyond his head. Rolling over where he lay, Zvi knocked his friend down and at the same time came up with his Sten in hand, facing the semi-darkness of the Quarter below. The bullets could have come from anywhere. Except for the mortaring of the New City, there was silence, and Zvi relaxed.

"What does the news mean?" Dov finally asked.

"We're a State with a government and everything," Ruth said, and her voice sounded strange. It took Zvi a moment to realize she was crying.

"We're going to hold Jerusalem, aren't we?" Fishel asked hesitantly.

"Sure," Zvi said, "if the United Nations doesn't hold it, we will." He smiled at the worried look on Fishel's sensitive face. A musician, Fishel Warshow was Zvi's artist, the only one he had in his small squad. "I promise you, we'll keep the Wall," Zvi said, clapping Fishel affectionately on the shoulder.

The young violinist came to his feet in delight and started to dance over the roof. He had taken three light steps when a bullet struck his shoulder and sent him spinning toward the edge of the roof. Without thinking, Dov Tervisky threw himself forward, grabbed Fishel and slammed him down against the plaster dome. However, before he himself could drop, a sniper's bullet smashed through his brain, hurling him forward on his face. Dvora, the closest one to him, crawled over and looked down at the hole in the back of his head where the bullet had emerged. "He's dead," she said so flatly that Zvi wondered if she knew what her words meant. He stared at her while Avram ripped the shirt off Fishel's shoulder to reveal the hole where the sniper's bullet had torn cleanly through the flesh.

"Get him to the Hadassah station," Zvi ordered.

Avram nodded, and as he helped the musician through the window rising above the roof into the room beyond, Zvi scanned his small squad. "I think the rest of you had better stay here tonight. Keep one eye on the street and another out for snipers." He thought and then shook his head. "I was going to see the commander about a gun for Dvora," and he picked up Dov Tervisky's and handed it to the girl.

She looked at the old American Army .03 Springfield as though she knew what a rifle was before she slipped back the bolt far enough to make sure there was a cartridge in the chamber. Then she crawled back to where Dov lay on his face and started emptying the dead man's pockets. Finding what she wanted, she held up a handful of cartridges.

The others looked from the strange girl to Zvi for an explanation. He ignored them. "I'll be back in an hour," and then gruffly to Dvora, "Come on." She followed him until he paused at the window and looked back at the others. "Will you see that Dov is buried in the cellar?" Zvi asked, and then added, "Try to remember where we buried him. Someday we may have to tell his family." A smile crossed his face. "After all, we're a State now and have to do things formally."

"Mark it all down in triplicate like Lieutenant Layton," Ruth said angrily.

Zvi nodded, "Just mark Layton down." Then he and Dvora were gone.

At Misgav Ladach, the combination hospital and headquarters, there were half a dozen young men and women in the courtyard. A small radio was sitting on a table in the center of the flagstone yard where a young girl with short blonde hair and an upturned nose sat monitoring broadcasts from beyond the Old City walls.

Several of the men waved at Zvi. He paused beside the radio, and the operator looked up. "We're a State," she exclaimed.

"I heard." Zvi thought for moment. "What are we called?"

"Israel," the girl announced proudly.

"Israel." Both of them turned as Dvora repeated the name as though to see how it tasted on the tongue.

Zvi shrugged. "By any other name, we're still in trouble." His suntanned hand reached inside his shirt to scratch his stomach. "What else?"

"The Arabs are declaring war."

Zvi's head cocked to one side while he listened to an exchange of gunfire somewhere in the distance. "I'm glad you told me."

"The Egyptians say they are invading with two hundred thousand men."

Waiting for more news, Zvi remained silent. Dvora was at his side, listening to the report.

"The Arab Legion has eight thousand. The Iraqi are claiming they have two million who will fight. The Syrians ten thousand. The Lebanese have not said how many they are sending in."

A wry smile crossed Zvi's face. "The Legion and the Iraqi will come from the east. The Egyptians from the west and south. Syrians and Lebanese from the north." He chuckled. "Hell, Zella, now that they've got us surrounded, we know where they are." The humor left his voice as he asked, "The commander in?"

The girl named Hertzela nodded. "He's just heard something new about Finegold."

Zvi considered this before he started into the old building. Dvora followed. When they reached the door, she asked, "Finegold?"

Zvi looked at her puzzled, "You've been living in the Old City and you don't know Finegold?"

She shook her head.

"He sells things," Zvi explained. "Old clothes, old buildings, friends, Jews." A bitterness came into his voice, "He's the uncrowned King of Jerusalem. The British would give him a crown, but I think it would embarrass him."

"The British?"

"He works with them. Tells them things." His hand came out and he took her arm to lead her into the building. Suddenly, her rifle jerked up and she slammed the butt sharply into his side as she jumped away.

Dropping his Sten, Zvi clasped his side and stared at the girl. She was frightened.

"Don't touch me," she screamed, and Zvi saw the others in the courtyard were staring at them. Embarrassed and confused, he recovered his Sten and stalked into the house. A moment later she followed.

The room they entered was empty except for several large tables and a few chairs, a cot and an old street map on one wall. Standing before the map, a man in his early thirties stared at the two of them. He was shorter than Zvi. His British army trousers were tucked into high boots and he wore no shirt. Dvora noticed several scars on his bare chest. Ignoring them, she matched his eyes as he stared at her. Turning to Zvi, he asked, "Who is she, and how did she get in here?"

"Volunteered," Zvi explained. Then he went through the introduction. "Dvora Rabsky, Area Commander Benjamin Ezekiel." When neither of them spoke, he added, "She knows how to use a gun."

The commander nodded, not impressed. "You worked in the notions shop on Balfour Street." It was not a question, and the girl did not answer.

Uncertain what to make of the comment, Zvi changed the subject. "Dov's dead. Fishel's wounded."

The commander sucked on his lower lip as he nodded. "Finegold," he said after a time. "A British soldier stopped at his place this afternoon."

Zvi nodded, "And?"

"They asked him to meet them in front of his house in an hour."

"Them?"

The commander shrugged. "You and . . . " his head bobbed to indicate Dvora. "You'd better be on a roof above. I want to know what's going on."

Scratching himself again, Zvi smiled bitterly. "I'd thought the British had all left. Then I saw my old friend Lieutenant Layton, and now we're getting more visitors."

Ezekiel sighed. "They put on their big show. I heard it on the radio. The noble British governor-general bade us goodbye and even went so far as to shake hands with an Arab and a Jew before he took his leave at Haifa this afternoon." A smile crossed his ugly face, "He's got style, that one. His small whale boat was halfway across the harbor when he turned and saluted no one in particular."

Without asking, the commander poured three glasses of tea from a pot on one of the tables. Zvi set down his Sten and took a glass in both hands. Dvora held hers the same way. Sitting on the edge of the table, Ezekiel looked at them. "Sir Alan Cunningham. The last English proconsul of Palestine. He took East Africa from the Italians and almost lost North Africa to the Germans. Then he tried to keep us from leading our own lives in Palestine." He blew on his tea before he continued. "I sailed under his brother out of Alexandria. What a bloody place for an ensign in His Britannic Majesty's *naivy* to wind up."

Dvora did not know what to make of Ben Ezekiel's remarks, but Zvi knew him well enough to understand his superior was not feeling sorry for himself, but was instead aware of his own inadequacy. Only half joking, Zvi said, "You ought to be proud. It's been a long time since a Jew commanded troops inside the Old City. In fact, someday I'm going to take the time to look up how many years it has been since there was a Jewish army within these walls."

Ezekiel laughed. "Some army. One potter's son from Gadera who tries to act like an officer and a girl who sells needles and thread." He drained his glass and said almost sadly, "Get the hell out of here, find a roof and take a look at Finegold the Magnificent."

Nodding, Zvi set his glass on the table, picked up his Sten, and walked out. Dvora looked after him and then at the area commander.

"See that he doesn't get killed," Ezekiel said. "He is not bright when it comes to survival. He takes too many risks."

Fifteen minutes later Zvi and Dvora were stretched out on a roof overlooking the courtyard of Solomon Finegold. It was dark, but lanterns were hung about the yard and lights from the windows brightened the walls. Ten minutes passed and Zvi was getting ready to leave when he heard the sound of heavy boots marching down the street. The iron gate swung open and a detachment of British troops tramped across the yard. At the head of the small column stood a British colonel whom Zvi had never seen before, and at his side was Lieutenant Layton. At a snapped command from Layton, the column halted, faced right and stood in two rows, eight abreast, facing Finegold's door.

"Order arms!"

And the Tommies slapped their rifles as they set them to rest on the cobbled yard.

Zvi was more puzzled than impressed. In the past there had been little doubt that Finegold was cooperating with the British; he and his son were the only Jews allowed to traffic outside the cordon placed about the Jewish Quarter, and for twenty pounds they would buy a soldier a pack of cigarettes and for ten they would mail a letter. But the British had never formally called upon Finegold and his family before. From the roof, Zvi watched the British colonel look quizzically at Layton, and after an impatient moment, the young Englishman shouted, "Finegold!"

The paneled door swung open and Finegold stepped out, his son half hidden behind him. The Jew, whom the British recognized as theirs and whose own people rejected him, was about fifty, short and plump; his balding head reflected the light shining through the open door. The younger Finegold was shorter than his father and almost as fat. Both were wearing dark Shabbat suits and ties. They were obviously frightened by the attention they were receiving.

At a glance from the colonel, Layton stepped out, took the merchant by the shoulder and led him forward. A crop under one arm, the colonel grasped Finegold's hand and, to the surprise of the Jew, shook it.

Zvi strained to hear the conversation below.

"We are leaving officially," the colonel said, making clear what everyone in the world already knew. Holding out his hand, the colonel waited for the sergeant standing behind him to place something in it. For a moment the British officer looked at the object handed to him, and then he passed it to Finegold. "Eighteen centuries have passed since a Jew held the key to the gates of Jerusalem, and I am honored on behalf of His Britannic Majesty's government to give to you, Solomon Finegold, this symbolic key to Zion Gate."

Taken aback at what was happening to him, the merchant held the key at arm's length as though he were both frightened and awed by it.

Zvi noted the trace of a smile cross the English officer's face as he watched the sergeant hand a Sten gun along with a few magazines of ammunition to the younger Finegold. The colonel nodded approvingly, and Zvi knew that nothing was happening that had not been discussed and planned by the British.

"Our problems have been difficult in recent months," the colonel was saying. "I have done what I could. Others have done what they could. If things have gone wrong, it lies in the nature of the conflict of which we wanted no part. Your soldiers are brave, and I wish you good luck in what is to come." His hand was extended again, and he waited while the Jew fumbled the key from his right hand to his left. "Goodbye."

Finegold tried to say something, but he was so nervous that all he could do was nod, and only as the British were marching away did he call out, "God bless you. In the name of the people of Jerusalem, God bless you."

Then the charade was over. The British were gone. A moment later the courtyard was empty. Rolling over so that he could make out the silhouette of Dvora in the darkness, Zvi snarled, "In the name of the people of Jerusalem, God bless you, too."

The girl remained quiet.

Zvi lay looking up at the stars. Seventy years into the Common Era the Jews had lost the city and now the keys were given unto a Finegold. It was not an auspicious return.

Dvora and he rejoined the squad on the roof which overlooked the Street of the Chain. The others were asleep, except for Avram, who sat watching the empty street below. Once Zvi and Dvora were prone, Avram reported, "Fishel will be all right. Back tomorrow or the next day."

Zvi nodded in the darkness. "Anything happening?"

"A British colonel gave the Arabs down by the Wall another machine gun and a small case of ammunition."

Dvora's head came up, but before she could say anything, Zvi shook his head. "They've gone," and as far as he was concerned there was nothing more to be said about the British.

For a long time they were silent, and then Zvi said, to no one in particular, "I could use a cigarette."

Avram's weary head rocked from side to side. He smiled. "If you find one, I'll share it."

Zvi pulled himself into a sitting position. "Tomorrow." Then, as though the subject of a cigarette had never been raised, his head back as he stared at the dark sky above the city, he said, "I used to sit on the roof of my father's pottery in Gadera and watch the Bedouin gather at night in their tents, and the look of their campfires used to make me feel warm and comfortable." His voice dropped, "And now I see those lights out there and know I'm going to . . . " His hand came wide. "What in the hell do we know?"

Avram understood what his friend was trying to say. "Maybe we thought because we both tilled the same land, it would never come to this." The quiet kibbutznik wondered if he would ever get back to the land. During his years in Haganah, he had come to understand himself, and to his surprise, he had a talent for details. Thinking of this, he added softly, "It should never have come to this."

A harsh chuckle surprised both men, who turned to see what was amusing Dvora. "It always comes down to this," she announced. "We lived in a *shtetl* in Poland near Gbrodna. A *shtetl*—maybe fifty homes. Three Jewish families and our Polish neighbors. We plowed and planted when we were allowed to rent a piece of land. They plowed and planted. Cozy," she half snarled. "Once a Polish boy danced with one of my sisters. Once my father was given the honor to loan our neighbor five zlotys. It was all cozy until the trouble began and we were the Jews. They fought to defend themselves, but they fought also to tell the Germans where our three families were hiding in a ravine a hundred paces from our *shtetl*."

The two men could barely make out her words: "It always comes to this: there is no land small enough or bad enough for the Jews."

Avram felt sad at the bitterness in her voice. "How old are you?" he asked.

The cruel chuckle again as she countered, "You mean it's sad for anyone so young to be so bitter? *Oy*, to have lived here through the last ten years and have kept your innocence."

Neither man said anything because neither felt he had retained any innocence. Both had known the Arab terror of the late thirties and the terror of the postwar years. In between both had known the war.

No one spoke for a time, and then Avram said, "I don't think there is such a thing as innocence in this century."

This time it was Zvi who laughed. "Now that Avram's had his opportunity to be profound and you yours to feel sorry for yourself, let's get some rest."

Avram prodded the sleeping form of Moshe Gilead with the butt of his Sten. Once the other man was awake, he whispered in his ear and then followed Dvora and Zvi down from the roof.

An hour before dawn the squad was joined on the roof by an old man carrying a sack of bread. He counted out four loaves, left them on the windowsill between himself and Zvi's squad, and then he looked at the strangers and smiled. Before he could turn away, Avram crossed the roof and, patting the loaves, asked, "Where did these come from?"

"We found an Arab bakery. The baker had closed it and left." Then, as if it were important, "We didn't damage anything."

Avram smiled.

"They're back," the old man said.

Zvi moved closer and the others on the roof turned to listen. "Back?"

The old man nodded, proudly. What he knew was obviously important. His withered hand combed his long beard for a moment. "They are back," he repeated in a hushed tone.

In the distance, Zvi and his companions could hear a shepherd's pipe playing faintly.

Zvi decided to let the old man tell his news in his own way.

"A long time ago," the old man began, "when Titus decided to tear down the city, the rabbis threw the keys up toward the heavens and asked Him to keep them, and a great hand came down through the blue morning sky and a shepherd's pipe played David's song and He took the keys." The old man thought about what he was saying, and the awesomeness of it took him aback. His thin hand brushed away a tear as he continued. "They're back now. The keys have come back."

Zvi wondered how the story had reached the civilians, and if any of them could really believe the tight-lipped British colonel with the riding crop under his arm could in any way be construed as the Messenger of God.

However, he knew better than to argue or try to disillusion the old man. "I'm glad they are back," he said.

And then he heard Dvora smother a laugh, but the old man was already gone.

Waiting for Avram to break another loaf in half, Zvi turned toward the east where the sun was just beginning to reveal the morning. The hills which surrounded Jerusalem were lovely. Pink flowers growing in a garden on a hillside seemed brighter as the early light caught their color. Mount Scopus seemed to be at peace. The Mount of Olives was still in shadow, and no one looking at it would have believed there was war in Jerusalem. Zvi stared at the city. It had always looked grim, gray and drab to him. Nothing green grew within the walls. It was a dreary place, and not even the morning sun could make the city below the roofs anything but grim and gray.

He ate his bread slowly as he rested his back against a wall, his feet dangling down the slope of the roof. Before he had gone to sleep the night before, he had taken count of the ammunition they had. Less than a hundred rounds for the six of them. Seven grenades. He had sent Moshe Gilead to Ben Ezekiel to plead for more ammunition, and all Moshe had come back with was word that the area commander would try, would try, would try. The Palmach—those shock troops who had already become a legend—would break through the walls of the Old City and deliver them. Or at least they would take out the wounded and leave ammunition and reinforcements. Tonight. Or tomorrow night. Or the night after. The commander was certain. Moshe reported the story as it had been told to him, and there were those on the roof who believed it, and there were those who made a *berakhah*—or prayer—checked their guns and waited to see what the first day of independence would bring them besides hopes and promises.

They did not have long to wait. The morning opened with a shock.

A heavy barrage of rifle fire filled the streets below, splashed over the roofs, sought out windows. The squad flattened against the cracked plaster.

At the same moment, screaming hordes of Arabs emerged from the streets of the Arab Quarter and the Christian Quarter and ran toward the Damascus and the Jaffa gates. Zvi looked at Avram, and his friend stared back. It did not make any sense. The Arabs already controlled the walls and the entrances in and out of the Old City.

Then Zvi thought he understood. The Arabs were getting ready to welcome someone. Someone. A great many someones would march into Jerusalem now that the British were gone. Now that the British were gone, what was there in all of Israel that could stop the Arab countries from invading, except Haganah and Irgun, the two separate underground Jewish forces?

There was no reason for Zvi's squad to fire on the Arabs because they were not attacking the Jewish Quarter at this moment. Whatever the Arabs had in mind, it was not the occupancy of the Quarter. They did not cross the small streets and squares which had become the no-man's land between. However, when an eager Arab sniper thought he had a target, he let loose.

Morning turned into noon. Zvi went down to Misgav Ladach. Even before he asked, Ben Ezekiel announced that he had no extra troops and no extra ammunition.

"I just came to see how Fishel is," Zvi explained, and Ezekiel wiped the back of his bull neck with a dry palm. "The *hamseen*. All we needed was a wind off the desert now." Both of them looked around the courtyard. There were half a dozen young men of Haganah and three civilian volunteers. One of the civilians, an aged rabbi, was looking at Zella, who sat with the earphones on her head. The rabbi did not approve of what he saw and finally closed his eyes. The girl scratched her legs where the edge of her shorts revealed she was badly sunburned.

Neither Zvi nor the area commander said anything as they surveyed the courtyard. Two members of Haganah were sleeping near the entrance, their rifles beside them. Every few minutes one or the other would move so that he remained within the shelter of the crawling shadow created by the rising sun. The *hamseen* was in its third day now and they knew it was going to continue.

"It means we'll need more water," Zvi finally said.

Ben nodded. "Someday I'm going to fight a battle where I won't have to worry about water."

"I remember when we were coming into Tobruk, we said something like that. But as I think of it now, we had water in those days."

Ezekiel shrugged. "As the man said, 'everything can get worse,' but why does it always have to?"

Zvi thought for a moment. "At Tobruk we got a full canteen in the morning and we had a choice: did we wash with it first and then drink it, or did we drink it and not wash? After a time that was a tough decision."

The commander laughed. "I wish we had that problem now." He paused for a moment. "I'd make the decision for everyone: wash. Things are beginning to smell. There are more than a dozen bodies from the shooting near the Zion Gate last night."

Zvi waited to see where this was leading.

"They have to be buried."

"I'm going in to see Fishel," Zvi said, and when Ben Ezekiel did not press the matter of the burial, he left and, crossing over to Zella, asked, "What's the news?"

The girl looked up at him and shook her head. "I think they are going to turn Haganah into a national army."

Zvi looked at the sleeping soldiers and at the old rabbi, who now sat cleaning a German Luger he had found somewhere. "A real fighting army," Zvi said. Then, "What difference is it going to make to us?"

Zella brushed back her short hair as she smiled at him. "Two pounds a month pay."

A short burst of laughter and Zvi shook his head, "And all I'm really seeking is to be delivered." He became serious. "All my life I've heard how we were going to be delivered. And now I, Zvi Mazon, I am ready to be delivered."

The old rabbi looked up from where he sat. "Do not mock, my son. Do not mock the Lord."

Zvi nodded slowly. "I'm not mocking. I'm serious. I'm tired and I'm hungry and I'm ready for the Deliverance." Without another word he crossed the courtyard and went into the hospital. He was met at the door by a nurse who had been evacuated from the Hadassah Hospital on Mount Scopus.

"I'm looking for one of my squad," he said. She waited. "Fishel. He plays the violin." Knowing this was not quite what he meant, he added, "He was shot in the shoulder last night."

"He'll be all right," the nurse said as she wiped her perspiring forehead. "He left here about an hour ago."

Zvi was puzzled. "You're sure?"

The nurse opened the first two buttons of her shirt and rubbed her aching shoulders. "I'm sure. She thought a moment. "You've been through one of these *hamseens* before?"

"Yes."

"When do they end?"

"Sometimes you think they never will. Then one morning the wind is blowing from the other direction."

"Up at the hospital I planted some cyclamen. Do you think this will kill them?"

Shaking his head, Zvi apologized. "I don't know. I'm sorry." Then, "Did Fishel say where he was going?"

She thought a moment. "Something about the House of the Fish?"

"Thanks," Zvi said. He left, walked out of the courtyard and into a narrow street. Above, the louvered archway kept the sun off the cobblestones, and the pavement did not burn the soles of his feet. He stood for a moment with his Sten gun slung over his shoulder, while he tried to decide where to look for Fishel. "House of the Fish" meant nothing to him. He walked toward the center of the Quarter. Fish and the Catholics. There was a Catholic house near the street the Arabs called Khart al Yahud.

As he walked past synagogue after synagogue, Zvi wondered how many there were in the Quarter. He would have to ask Avram or one of the rabbis. He was approaching the Sephardic Synagogue when he heard music. Stopping in front of an old house from which the music was flowing over the street, Zvi saw the door was open; and when he entered, he found Fishel seated at an old upright piano. The Christian family to whom it belonged had been evacuated by the British months before. No one had been through the house except for Zvi's squad, looking to see if any food had been left behind.

Now, as he stood listening to Fishel play, he wondered how often the young musician had visited this house in recent months. Untutored in good music, Zvi remembered that he had seen pictures of Fishel on posters announcing concerts which Zvi had never had the money to attend. And here he was listening, even though it was an old piano instead of a violin. Haganah had its advantages. Suddenly Fishel was done. He turned about slowly toward his squad commander. A large bandage covered his shoulder where his shirt had been ripped away, but the bandage had been left loose enough for him to handle his weapon. Picking up the Enfield which lay on top of the piano, he followed Zvi out of the house, closing the door behind him. "This damned *hamseen* is bad for a good instrument. Dries the frame and tightens the action." He thought a moment, and then appealed to Zvi, "We could find a tub of water some place and put it under the piano—it would help."

"I'm sure," Zvi said, recalling Ezekiel's comment about water. "If we've time tomorrow, we'll come back and do it then."

They were crossing the Quarter toward their own post when it started. The first explosion came as a shock. For a moment neither of them knew what it was. Then there were four more, one right after the other. A house across the street suddenly shook and an old stone wall crumbled and fell into the street, blocking their path. Zvi looked up and saw a bedroom exposed and a little boy clinging to the edge of a floor two stories up. He started to run toward the house, but the child fell into the street before Zvi took three steps. The boy was dead. Two more explosions and Zvi yelled, "Let's get to the others."

They fled back down the street as another heavy mortar shell exploded meters from where they were. Families came running out of their homes, and the streets were suddenly filled with men and women. They looked up as the shells continued to fall on the Quarter. Grabbing the arm of the man nearest to him, Zvi shouted, "Get these people down into the Yohanan Synagogue."

The man looked at Zvi and then at his wife. She was pregnant and stood rocking back and forth in the street as she prayed.

"Get going!" Zvi yelled.

But the man, lean and taut, his beard shaking as his head bobbed, merely asked, "Why did you have to come here?"

Annoyed, Zvi grabbed the woman and turned her toward the street which led to the synagogue. "Go on, woman."

She looked at his hand on her arm and drew back. It was not proper for a strange man to touch her, and her husband threw himself at Zvi. Retreating before the assault, the young soldier yelled to Fishel, "Let's get out of here."

The mortar shells were falling more often now. One and then another only seconds apart.

Zvi and Fishel ran through the crowds. An old man wearing a shabby caftan rolled over and over on the ground as he prayed. Fishel paused to watch him. Then the stone archway that covered the street collapsed, dropping great stones over the old man.

Down another street—and more terrified people. Zvi tried once again to direct them to take cover, but a young rabbi shook his head. "It is His way."

In disgust, Zvi ran on.

Fishel stopped to push a little boy into the shelter of a doorway, and the two soldiers ran on. Another street and more mortar shells. Both men felt the Arab fire was seeking them out. Then they saw a building half a block away break into pieces and slip into the street. Climbing over the still-moving stones, they made their way to the building where the squad was stationed.

Fishel paushed to watch, and when Zvi reached for his arm, the musician pulled away. "The piano!" he screamed, and would have run back if Zvi had not folded his arms about him. Fishel struggled for a moment before he relaxed. Two mortar shells fell near them, but they were in the shelter of an archway which held.

"Let's get up to the roof," Fishel said. They scanned the street. Civilians were still standing amid the debris in awe and wonder at the immensity of the assault which was tearing their homes down about them. One old woman stopped her scurrying long enough to pick up a piece of bright blue tile. She looked up at Fishel and said dazedly, "It is pretty."

He nodded and followed Zvi into the house and up the stairs to the roof. As they emerged, Moshe Gilead looked back at them. "You've seen?"

"Couldn't miss it." And Zvi fell prone and crawled over to Moshe's side.

"They're not trying to come through."

"Yet," Zvi warned.

"Why didn't they do it before?" Ruth asked.

Without looking at the girl, Zvi said simply, "The British."

"Then even the British had some value," Avram said drily.

The mortar shells continued to rise from the Arab Quarter. They could follow their trajectory as they climbed high, arced only slightly, and then came almost straight down. The roof of the building next to where they lay was struck, scattering broken stone over them. Another explosion in the street below hurled broken cobblestones against their building. More explosions and walls collapsing. The first fire they saw was only five buildings away. At first they were only aware of smoke, and then the flames broke out of the lower windows to seek the sky. More mortars and more fires.

Somewhere a woman screamed.

Somewhere a child was crying.

Zvi thought he heard a shepherd's pipe.

The window of a synagogue splashed glass dust over a fleeing couple. Two young *yeshivah bochurs* knelt in the street and prayed. A moment later they were gone, and where they had been there was a hole in the pavement. The noise became unbearable.

Ruth Barovsky closed her eyes and prayed. She was trembling, and without realizing he was doing it, Moshe Gilead placed one hand on her shoulder to comfort her.

Zvi scanned the faces of his companions. The noise was getting to Fishel too, and he lay with his arms over his head. Avram stared numbly at the devastation. Only Dvora Rabsky did not seem to notice anything as she calmly rubbed her hand over the butt of the old Springfield rifle beside her, as though finding comfort in it.

A whine above them, and Zvi rolled over to shelter Dvora. The shell struck the corner of the roof on which they lay, and he thought the jolt he felt was from the explosion; and then a moment afterward he realized that Dvora had slammed the barrel of her rifle down on his hand. She was not looking at him, but at the hole blown in the roof. Ruth started to slide forward as the whole roof canted. Grabbing her by the waist, Moshe dragged her back from the edge, sat up and looked to Zvi for orders. Nodding, Zvi half rose and shoved Moshe aside as a sniper's bullet slammed into the stone wall behind them. "Let's get the hell out of here," he shouted.

Staying where he was, his eyes on the street below, Zvi waited until Ruth, Avram, Moshe and Fishel fled the roof. Then he turned and screamed at Dvora, "Get off this roof, you *meshugenah*."

Ignoring him, she continued to watch the street. An Arab exposed himself on a building across the way to snipe at a small boy running from a house. In that instant, Dvora's rifle came up and, without seeming to take aim, she squeezed off a shot. There was a scream and the Arab staggered to the edge of the roof on which he had been hiding. He turned in a last effort to keep from falling into the street, but his legs buckled and he slid forward and fell without a sound.

"Get off this roof," Zvi yelled again.

Dvora watched as the little boy disappeared into another building. Then she edged back, rose and climbed through the window into the room beyond. Only when he was sure that the others were under cover did Zvi move. Very slowly, he came to his knees. He paused, and when an Arab appeared in a window across the street, he squeezed off three shots. Satisfied that there was nothing more he could do on the roof, Zvi packed off through the window. Dvora was standing there, her rifle half raised.

"That was stupid," she said flatly.

Not caring what she thought, he grabbed her arm, spun her around, and shoved her toward the door on the far side of the room. When her rifle came up, he said softly, "Strike me with that again and I'll ram it up your ass."

Dvora hesitated an instant, and said, "Next time I'll shoot," and slowly walked out of the room. Zvi followed her. He was almost to the ground floor when he first smelled smoke. The house was on fire. When he reached the room at the foot of the stairs where the others had gathered, he could see flames flaring out a small hallway. He slammed a door on them.

Moshe grabbed his arm. "Where?"

Wiping his hot face on his sleeve, Zvi thought for a moment. "We'll stay here while you go next door. If it isn't burning, we'll join you."

Nodding, Moshe dashed down to the cellar to a tunnel that led to the house on the left. Zvi did not wait for his return, but moved to the front of the house, smashed what was left of the two small windows and took his place beside one of them. Ruth took a position behind the other. They could not leave the street unwatched.

Mortar shells continued to fall, but there was no one in the street any longer. Avram and Fishel knelt behind Zvi, waiting to take his place if they had to. Dvora looked about the room. An old sofa, a long table and several chairs. Crossing over, she opened a book lying on the table. A volume of the Midrash. The others watched as she flipped the pages.

"She never said a word all the time you were at headquarters," Avram told Zvi.

Shrugging, Zvi turned his attention to the street. His hand hurt where she had slammed the Springfield down on it, and he wondered if she were angry.

Moshe reappeared and waved for them to join him. Five minutes later they reached the house next door. A young couple with a child stood near the doorway as they entered. The husband, whom Zvi thought could not be more than twenty, shook his head.

"Don't come in here," he pleaded in a gentle voice.

Zvi was tempted to listen, but he knew he could not. There were too few houses which could give him a clear view of both the street and the square at the end of it. There was no spanning arch to block the field of fire here, and he had to stay.

"Take your wife and child and go someplace," he said. "The Yohanan Synagogue would be best."

"If you would only leave us alone," the woman protested.

Zvi was waving his squad to the windows as a mortar shell fell in the street just outside. Dropping to the floor, all of them waited for the explosion. The last fragments of window shattered across the room. When the woman turned her back to protect her child, a piece of jagged steel slashed through her neck. Zvi leapt to his feet and folded his arms about her and the child as she started to fall. The woman was dead. Separating her from her child, he held them both until Ruth took the infant and passed it to its father. Very gently, Zvi lifted the woman in his arms and walked out of the room, down a hall until he found a bedroom where he set her body down. When he looked around, he saw the young husband behind him.

"And you still won't fight?" Zvi asked angrily.

The young man shook his head. "You don't understand. None of this would be happening if we had waited for the Messiah. You brought this on us when you went against Him and did the things you have done."

Zvi looked at his bared arm and wondered how much of the blood on it was his own from the time he had been cut out in the street with Fishel and how much of it was the woman's. It did not really matter. His arm was beginning to hurt, and he knew he would have to do something about it. Appealing to the young man for the last time, he suggested, "Why don't you take your daughter out of here? The Arabs will have to come through this way."

But the youth was setting the infant on the bed beside its mother so that he could pray.

Dizzied by the heat and the noise and his own fatigue, Zvi closed his eyes and fled. When he rejoined the others, he found that they had already moved the scant furniture so that they could sit sheltered behind it. Moshe and Dvora were manning the two windows. Dropping behind an overturned table, Zvi held his bleeding arm out to Ruth.

She examined it for a moment before she pulled off one of her white tennis shoes and then her sock. Once the sock was wrapped tightly around Zvi's arm, she slipped her bare foot back into the shoe.

The house rocked as a shell landed nearby, but Zvi was not aware of the jolt as he wiped his hot face.

Ruth watched. "As if the Arabs weren't enough, we have to have a *hamseen*."

Avram laughed softly. "Maybe after all these years, they're turning the plagues back on us."

They took turns at the two windows through the rest of the day. The tempo of the Arab mortar fire did not slacken off as dusk approached, and when Zvi went outside into the courtyard behind the house, he could see that most of the Jewish Quarter was on fire. A sickening pall of smoke hung over the Old City. Flames could be seen in many places.

Zvi stood in the street, his lungs filled with the heavy smoke, his eyes tearing from the heat of the burning city and the *hamseen*. His shirt clung to his lean body, and when he reached inside to scratch his belly, he could feel his ribs. There were no civilians in the streets now. They had found their way into the synagogues. Zvi himself hoped the walls of the old houses of worship would hold against the Arab mortar fire which continued to fall.

When he arrived at headquarters, there was no one in the courtyard except Hertzela who still sat with the earphones on her head. She looked up at him, smiling. Then she saw the expression on his face—as though he had been weeping. Of all the young soldiers inside the Jewish Quarter, none was less likely to show deep feelings than Zvi Mazon. His hand came up and he wiped his face, revealing a bloodied woman's sock tied incongruously about his arm.

"Any news?"

"We've been recognized as a State. President Truman."

"Anything else?"

She shook her head. "I think the commander would want to tell you that himself."

He cocked his head to one side. "All the years you've loved me, and you won't even tell me one small secret?"

She smiled. "Loved you? I've heard girls saying for years that no one could love Zvi Mazon—he isn't the sort of man a woman loves." She thought about this, and added, "I could tell you many things women have said about you."

"*Nu?*"

Hertzela smiled as she began, "Well, there was a girl up near the Syrian border . . . "

But he was shaking his head, "Let's forget her."

"And there was one whose father owned an orchard near Kfar Etzion, who . . . "

He was shaking his head again. "Let's forget her too."

The girl smiled. "Are there any you want to remember?"

The explosion of a mortar shell less than a dozen meters away silenced them. After a moment, as though their conversation had never been interrupted, Zvi said, "Well, there was a girl named Hertzela Fishbein whom I met once in Tel Aviv after a long night of being chased by the British." And he was remembering how the two of them had hidden in an apartment of a friend of hers for three days and nights while the British combed the city for them. In those three days and nights they had become lovers and strangers. Now, as they listened to the Arab gunfire, both of them recalled only the moment when they had become lovers three years before and the fact that she had been married and widowed twice since.

Bending over, he kissed her forehead lightly. Then, without another word, he left her looking after him, a puzzled expression on her face.

Disappearing into the large room where Ben Ezekiel maintained his headquarters, Zvi found his commanding officer poring over a map of the Old City. Ezekiel remained stripped to his waist. Waving for Zvi to sit down at the table, he poured a glass of tea for his guest, and then with a gesture to take in his own dishevelment, he commented, "I know it isn't very military, and I intend to see that from now on we're military." A smile crossed his ugly face as his heavy cheeks seemed to puff. "And what have you got?" he asked, taking Zvi's arm. Slowly turning the arm from side to side, he inspected the sock which passed for a bandage. "Better have the nurse over at Hadassah look at it."

Zvi nodded. "That isn't what I came about."

Ezekiel laughed loudly. "Do you want the usual lies?"

Shaking his head, Zvi was about to say something, but the commander went on talking.

"There are two kinds of lies," he said. "There are those I tell my squad commanders and then there are those which I get from headquarters across town and merely pass on. You may designate which kind of lies you desire."

Breathing deeply, Zvi spoke quickly. "Food and some ammunition, and we can hold that sector forever."

A twitch of Ezekiel's mouth as he shook his head. "You don't know how long you can hold it because you haven't really tried yet. Don't give me any pep talks until you start fighting." He shook his head, "And don't make me any promises."

Startled at the bitterness in the other man's voice, Zvi asked simply, "If we haven't been fighting since December, what happens next?"

"They start coming over in tens of thousands. All you've had have been snipers and small gangs of roving, undisciplined Arabs. Now you'll find soldiers and planes and heavy guns and planned movement. Now you're going to find out what separates terror from war. And though terror may be more dramatic, war is somehow more final." He thought a moment and then apologized. "That was the right speech, but I gave it to the wrong man. You were in Italy, weren't you?"

Zvi nodded.

"Then you know what I mean."

Looking through several papers lying before him, the commander pulled one out and shoved it across the table to Zvi. He read the message quickly: *Haganah HQ, Jerusalem. Hold on at all costs. We will reach you tonight with supplies. Have your wounded ready for evacuation. We will bring reinforcements. Do not give up one meter of ground.*

Zvi looked up hopefully. The commander shoved another piece of paper across the table, explaining, "The one you read arrived today. Zella copied down this one yesterday."

Quickly scanning the earlier message, Zvi was startled to see it was identical; as he tried to understand what he was reading, Ezekiel pushed a third message toward him.

"And this one came the day before yesterday."

The words seemed to blur as Zvi read: *Haganah HQ, Jerusalem. Hold on at all costs. We will reach you tonight with supplies. Have your wounded ready for evacuation. We will bring reinforcements. Do not give up one meter of ground.*

Pushing his chair back, Zvi rose and walked over to the wall map. The outlines of the Old City were carefully marked and so was the location of the positions held by the Arabs and the locations held by the Jews. Inside the Old City, only the Quarter was in Jewish hands. And above it the heights.

The commander was at Zvi's side, one arm resting on the young man's shoulder. "No one is trying to fool anyone. They are doing the best they can." And then, as though he had to justify headquarters to this officer as much as to himself, he explained, "HO has almost a hundred thousand people over there outside the walls, and the roads to Jerusalem are closed. The Arabs hold Latrun and Kastel. We'll get them back, but to get them back, we're going to have to fight. And to fight for the New City doesn't leave anything for the Old."

Zvi nodded. He already knew all of this and somehow he resented someone talking to him as though he were a child being called upon to understand the human frailty of his elders. Turning to the burly officer, Zvi queried him: "Then I shouldn't expect anything?"

Shaking his head impatiently, Ezekiel contradicted him: "I said you could expect more fighting and this time of a different kind. And I didn't say the Palmach wouldn't break through tonight or tomorrow night or the night afterward." He let his voice drop as he concluded, "If they do, you can expect help of some kind."

A bitter smile crossed Zvi's face. "What you're telling me is that if I get to heaven, there's a chance I'll find angels."

The commander nodded. "The ifs equate." He smiled, "But you're not going to give up the notion that there's a heaven, and that if there is, there may be angels, and so keep equating."

A chuckle as Zvi said, "I was telling someone before we've already proved the theologians half right."

A questioning look crossed Ezekiel's face.

"We've found hell, which means that by some kind of logic, there must be a heaven."

Ben Ezekiel smiled. "I could turn some of the *yeshiva bochurs* over to you to dispute the point ... "

But Zvi laughed, "You know where to find us?" And when the commander nodded, Zvi left.

That night the enemy continued to drop mortar shells into the Quarter, and the fires continued to spread. No one tried to put them out, because there was too little water and to come out into the open would have exposed the firefighters to the heavy mortars and snipers. The fires ceased to burn only when there was nothing left to consume.

It was shortly before midnight when a loud voice shouted at them from the darkness: "Leave. Surrender. Give up your arms. Jews, you will be spared.

You will not be killed. *Inshalla. Inshalla.* Jews, surrender. You have been forgotten by your own people. We, your Arab friends, remember you. We will let you go back to the New City with your families. We will accept your surrender."

The voice was loud and almost soothing for the first moment, and then as it began to jar, Zvi realized the Arabs had parked a sound truck somewhere near the Jewish Quarter. At the same moment, he realized that the offer to surrender would reach all of the people who were hidden in cellars, wishing Haganah had never come, all of the people who would look to Finegold and his son for support, all of the *yeshivah bochurs* who believed that if they surrendered, *inshalla*, nothing would happen because that would be the will of God. The way of God. Zvi's Sten came up and he fired a burst across the street in the general direction of the sound.

Someone on one of the Arab roofs opposite returned his fire. The exchange started along the entire perimeter of the Quarter. Hoping that his own squad would have enough sense to save ammunition, Zvi smiled as the announcer tried to be heard above the constant crackle of rifle fire. And then suddenly the heavy machine gun at the end of the street opened fire, and with that the Arab sound truck fell silent. Only when the last words came garbled through the din did Zvi understand that the speaker had not been an Arab, but an Englishman. The voice had been Layton's. The British had gone, but Layton remained.

Zvi started to put his hand on Dvora's shoulder, changed his mind and snapped, "Come with me." He had his Sten in his hand again and was already making his way through the burned-out hallway. Old plaster had fallen when the lathes disappeared into the flames and the charred plaster rose as dust over their clothes. When they stepped outside, Zvi noticed that the black dress Dvora had worn when she joined him was now ripped, burned and thick with dust. In the wavering light from a burning building, he looked at Dvora Rabsky, trying to see her for the first time as a girl, a woman, not a soldier who held a gun and could shoot an Arab or smash the hand of a man who touched her. Her dark hair was longer than Ruth's and her eyes were so dark they did not even reflect the light of the fire behind him. Her figure beneath the tattered dress was better than that of any of the women Zvi had seen in recent months. Her breasts were firm, her shoulders squared in a kind of defiance. Her head was held high as she allowed him to look at her for a moment, and then in disgust, she spat at him. Startled by the spittle striking his face, Zvi pulled his hand back to hit her, and in that instant her rifle came up, pointed at his belly. A mortar shell landed nearby, throwing debris over them, but neither moved. Zvi became aware of how much control she had of herself when another shell crushed the side of the building behind her and she did not even glance backward.

With great effort, he brought up his arm and wiped his face with the clean bandage the Hadassah nurse had wrapped about it. When he was done, he said very softly, "Get back in there. Avram shouldn't be alone." He whirled and walked away down the street. A wall crumbled ten meters from him and he paused to let the dust settle before he continued on.

Twenty minutes later, the patrol completed, he returned to the post, his Sten slung over his shoulder and a bucket of water in each hand. Entering the sitting room, he found Avram at one window and Dvora at the other. Their rifles were resting on the sills. Avram turned and thanked Zvi. "And Layton's been broadcasting again." A wry smile crossed the face of the young farmer as he said, "He's generous. He'll give us our lives."

Zvi winked at his companion, looked at Dvora a moment and then went up to the roof with the second bucket. This roof was built with a line of large, squared stones along the front edge as though someone had planned a defense when the house was built five centuries before. Moving up to the row of stones, Zvi noticed for the first time that there were crenels every few meters. Taking a position behind one, he saw that the edges of the stones were beveled as in a castle or fortress so that a bowman could have a maximum sweep with his arrow and still be protected. Moshe, Ruth and Fishel were watching him.

Fishel crawled over to the bucket, dipped his hand into it, wiped his face with the water and then cupping his hands, drank. Over his hand he looked at Zvi balefully. "You forgot to chill it."

Ruth laughed softly and Zvi smiled. Sitting on this roof with his back against the stones, the lights of the burning Quarter throwing wild shadows over them, the gray smoke climbing, he felt comfortable with these people. He knew that there were other things he should be doing, but at this moment, he felt comfortable. He scratched his belly, thinking while he did so of Dvora's Springfield pointed at it only half an hour before.

"That girl Dvora," he asked. "Do any of you know her?"

Moshe shook his head.

Fishel shrugged. "She shoots well."

Zvi turned to Ruth, who was kneeling over the bucket. Her short hair hung in front of her eyes, and then, as her head came up, she brushed her hair back. "I don't know her," Ruth said, "but there's something wrong with her." Seeing Zvi waiting for an explanation, she went on. "Moshe brushed against her this afternoon as he was leaving the room and she swung her rifle butt into his side."

This much Zvi could have guessed. He was about to tell Moshe it was not personal. Instead, he asked, "Why?"

"How would I know?" Ruth answered with another question.

"Is she dangerous?" Moshe asked.

Zvi shrugged. "Somehow I suspected there might be some danger in this assignment when the commander who gave it to me told me his sister was pregnant and she said it was my fault."

The others smiled. All of them knew the aged commander who had selected the squad for duty in the Old City did not have a sister.

"I don't know about Dvora's problems," Ruth said softly, "but I've got some I'm willing to share." She thought a moment. "If I told the commander I was pregnant, do you think he would find another assignment for me?"

"Are you?" Fishel asked.

The others laughed.

"It could be arranged," Ruth assured him, and she smiled to see how much she had embarrassed him.

Zvi sat for a time watching Ruth take her place against the stone wall and stare into the street below. He did not think Ruth was pretty. There was something about her face that put him off. She lacked warmth. And there was nothing delicate about her. She stood erect and strong, taller than most women, and her figure, well revealed by the dirty blouse and tan shorts she wore, was full. Voluptuous was the word that came to mind. The first time they had met, shortly after his return from Italy, Haganah had given him a detail to patrol the Negev where it was thought the Egyptians were training for their eventual clash with the British. Ruth Barovsky had been assigned to him then. Though she was only about eighteen at the time, she knew how to live in the desert and how to take care of herself among the men she traveled with. Zvi recalled the time they had bumped into a British patrol and Ruth had kept the English back with a Bren gun until her companions stole the British petrol, refueled their own truck and escaped into the desert. She had used a gun well then. She used one well enough now. He had not seen her much in the years after he had left the Negev, and he was surprised when she was assigned to his squad destined for the Old City. He recalled that she had once told him her father had walked to the Holy Land from some *shtetl* in Russia.

Curious, Zvi asked, "When it's all done, Ruth, are you going back to Kfar Ata?"

The girl looked across the roof, her hand resting on the barrel of her rifle. She thought before answering, and then she smiled, "How are you going to keep them down on the kibbutz after they've seen Jerusalem?"

Fishel did not understand what she had said and looked to Moshe for an explanation, but the kibbutznik shrugged angrily.

"What's wrong with a kibbutz?"

Ruth smiled. "Nothing." Then, because she did not want to offend him, she explained. "I'm going to open a shop in Tel Aviv and design dresses to cover the broad bottoms of American matrons who want to patronize us."

The others did not know if she was serious, but Zvi did not really care. Crawling back from the edge of the roof, he told his companions, "Keep your eyes open. Maybe you'll see something come morning."

When he reached the bottom of the stairs, he found Ben Ezekiel waiting for him.

"Everything all right up there?"

Zvi nodded.

"Pull those two you have downstairs and follow me," the A/C ordered.

Zvi called for Avram and Dvora and the three followed Ezekiel. Half a block away they found two other squads waiting for them. As they crossed the Quarter, they were joined by others until they numbered more than twenty when they approached the southwestern corner of the Quarter. Here they stopped in the shelter of the entrance to a synagogue. Ben Ezekiel did not offer to explain anything. A heavy mortar shell struck a corner of the wall of the Old City. Fragments of stone filled the air for a moment, and then nothing. The Old City wall was more than three meters thick across the top and ten across the base. No single mortar was going to destroy it.

Zvi pushed closer to Ezekiel. "You asked for help?"

Ezekiel nodded without taking his eyes off the Old City wall, which rose less than a hundred meters from where they stood. "At noon today I told them by radio they had to help at once or we would not be able to hold out."

"And?"

Ben shrugged. "You will hold out at all costs."

Suddenly, there was a loud noise outside the wall. The rush of heavy trucks and heavy equipment. The Arabs guarding the battlement above Zion Gate began to fire. Heavy mortars were brought into play. Machine guns spat loudly, spilling bullets over the approach to the gate.

Now they knew why they had been brought here: the Palmach was going to try to break in. There was nothing they could do but wait to see if they would get through. Zvi saw more Arabs on the wall now, as well as more men scurrying out of small buildings and down the street to climb the wall above Jaffa Gate. Cases of ammunition were being hauled up onto the wall by the Arabs. And over it all the heavy gunfire smashing the night.

The firing above Jaffa Gate grew heavier as more Arabs joined the battle. The diversion at Zion Gate was abandoned.

Ezekiel did not move.

Somewhere a shout rose up from the other side of the wall. Zvi heard it over the sound of the firing and he knew there was no longer any sense in his waiting.

The shout again, from someone unseen on the other side: "Every man for himself."

And the Palmach's attempt ended in blood and failure.

Zvi shook his head. "And all they had to do was ask Finegold for the key."

The Arabs on the wall continued to fire. The Jews inside the Old City knew they were alone and would remain alone.

Afraid that their victory might encourage the Arabs to press his own defenses harder, Ben Ezekiel spilled his orders: "Go back to your posts. Hold your positions. I'll see if I can get them to try again tomorrow."

Zvi wished that somehow the man were more like other senior officers and could have shown one moment of comradeship, one moment to let the others know that he, too, felt the disappointment. This was not the British navy. The stiff upper lip was not needed here as much as a single word of friendship and hope. Instead, the area commander turned and walked off in the direction of Misgav Ladach.

If he ever commanded more than a squad, Zvi knew that he would remember the peculiar feeling of being lost which subordinates always felt because no one bothered to explain the situation as a whole.

Gesturing for Avram and Dvora to join him, Zvi started back to their post. Passing the Tiferet Israel Synagogue, they could hear the prayers rising from within. For once in his life, Zvi Mazon thought that he, too, might have liked to pray. No one had taught him how, and he did not think he had the time now to learn.

Approaching the old house from which they had departed about an hour earlier, Zvi told Avram, "The two of you go on in and take turns trying to sleep. Tomorrow won't be like today."

Avram asked him what he meant.

"It will be worse. I assure you, it will be worse."

"And where are you going?" Dvora asked Zvi so bluntly that he was taken aback, because in the few days she had been with the squad she had shown no interest whatever in the others.

His head down, Zvi looked at her. "Once when I was young, my father wanted to show me the Old City. He saved his money for months. The day we were to come, he fell ill. The money was spent on medicine." A shrug and a grin and he explained, "I'm going to take a tour of the city tonight."

He half bowed to Dvora, slung his Sten over his shoulder and started down the narrow alley. Avram watched him go and even smiled when he saw Zvi stretch his arms out wide so that he could touch the walls on both sides of the narrow street. The gesture was that of a boy, and Dvora shook her head, impatient with what appeared to her to be childish.

"And why not last night and tomorrow night?" she demanded.

Avram looked at her tolerantly. "He did not think he would get killed last night . . . and . . . well, who knows about tomorrow night?" He followed the strange girl into the room where they were going to spend a long time watching an empty street through a broken window. She gestured for him to rest while she took the first watch. Avram did not argue. He was weary.

Avram Ben Ezra was a kibbutznik, a sabra, born on the land his father and grandfather had farmed. Once, long ago, a stranger had sat down with one of the Rothschilds and explained that all the Zionists needed was a piece of land and they would farm it, build a new kind of community, the basis for a state. But to get this piece of land they would need money. And the Rothschild gave the stranger the money, but instead of going directly to Palestine, where he wanted to found his community, he went to Kiev. The year before the Cossacks had celebrated a victory and killed seventy-three Jews. Now that the Cossacks were losing a war, no one knew how many Jews they would have to kill to drown their sorrows, and so the stranger led the Jews who lived in the *shtetl* near Kiev westward and away.

Many months later they arrived in Palestine with the dubious blessing of the Turkish government. The Arab landowners joined together to see how much they could charge for a poor piece of land that edged no water. The purchase was made, the Rothschild money spent as promised, and the communal farm grew. Avram's grandfather died, as did all the men and women who had walked from the *shtetl* near Kiev, but their children and their grandchildren remained on the land.

Confident that he belonged, Avram slept soundly despite the mortars laying down their fire.

Zvi actually did not know where he was heading when he left the others. He did not expect a major attack in darkness, and there were several hours before dawn. What he really wanted to do was cross the line into the Arab Quarter. He suspected that something would happen in the morning. Ezekiel expected as much, though he certainly had not been specific.

As Zvi moved through the ruined Quarter, he was keenly aware that he had to find out what that "something" was. He passed a house he had been in days before when he had helped to bury the family killed by snipers. Two doors farther on, an ancient *yeshivah* lay in rubble in the narrow street. He paused to catch his breath and then climbed over the rubble into another alley. Beyond lay the Armenian Quarter, and he was about to make a dash across the narrow street when he heard something behind him. Whirling, he unslung his Sten and moved toward the sound. Silence and darkness. He waited. Silence. He thought for a moment that he could have been wrong, and then he knew he had to trust instincts built up during months under fire. Something had made the sound. It could have been rats. There were many in the Old City.

Slipping into the shelter of a doorway, he decided to outwait whatever or whoever it was. The heat of the night settled over him like a woolen blanket, and he felt himself choking. He wiped his face. The Sten held steady.

And the sound again, as if someone were trying to walk softly. And then silence. Zvi waited.

Finally, he saw a figure move in the darkness two doors back up the street he had just passed through. Taking a deep breath, he raced down the narrow street, his gun ready to fire, his hands tense, his breath held as he tried to be silent. The figure broke from a doorway and darted away from him. Three more steps and Zvi was on it. His Sten came up and he swung the barrel in a high arc, striking at the stranger's head. A crack as though he had broken bone. The figure dropped. Without a pause, Zvi grabbed it by the clothes and dragged it into the nearest doorway. A moment later several shots struck the alley, throwing sparks, steel and broken stone. Kneeling where he was, Zvi rolled the stranger over so that he could see who it was.

A woman in a black skirt and blouse. Young. Probably under twenty. Her face was narrow, her cheek bones high. In the faint light thrown from a burning building, he could see that she wore lipstick and her black hair was set in a fine coiffure. Puzzled, he ran his hands down her sides. She carried no weapon, not even a knife. His Sten across his knee, he fished through the pocket of her skirt. Nothing. Then he realized she was saying something. At first he did not understand what it was, and then he recognized the words were Arabic. He brought up his Sten. Her eyes were open now, and she was looking at him from where she lay.

"Do you speak English?" she asked.

Zvi kept his gun pointed at her head as he nodded.

"Are you going to kill me?" She did not appear to be afraid, though whether she knew it or not, she had reason to be.

He said flatly, "I haven't decided yet."

They stared at each other. Slowly the girl pulled herself to a sitting position. One slim hand rose to touch her head where he had struck. "You could have broken it," she said.

"I could have." Zvi was beginning to feel uncomfortable. It was possible that she had just lost her way, but he did not think so because the lines between the Jewish Quarter and the rest of the Old City were too carefully drawn by gunfire. Then he realized that that being so, someone on the Arab side of the line had held his fire while she crossed. And that could only mean she was a spy.

"Can you tell me why I shouldn't kill you?" he asked.

The girl shook her head.

"Then you did come to spy." It was not a question. She did not answer him. "You're out of purdah," he said.

The girl nodded.

"A whore?" he asked flatly, because he had never known an Arab girl this young who was not dressed in the traditional gown that covered her whole figure.

She laughed softly. "My name is Bedia Hassani."

Zvi did not know if this was supposed to mean something to him or if she was merely trying to be friendly.

She shook her head half in disappointment, half in annoyance at having to explain, "My father's the banker."

A smile crossed Zvi's taut face. "And mine is married to the Queen of the May."

She started to rise, but he kept his gun leveled at her throat and shook his head.

"You are either going to have to kill me," she said, "or you're going to have to let me go."

Her English was better than his own, and this embarrassed him. "Where did you go to school?" he asked, not knowing quite why he was interested and why it should make any difference.

"London," she told him.

Somehow, he knew he believed her. "Why are you here?"

The girl hesitated before she said, "To see what was happening."

Zvi's head shook slowly. "You're trying to tell me you just went for a walk and no one fired at you when you crossed into the Quarter?"

She nodded. "I gave the sergeant at the end of the street my watch and he agreed to see that no one fired as I crossed."

"The sergeant?"

"From the Arab Legion."

"Just a sergeant?"

The girl who called herself Bedia continued to smile. "The Arab Legion," she said again, and he could tell she was waiting for his reaction. When he showed none, she added, "The whole Legion."

"Why are you telling me this?" Not trusting what she was saying, but knowing it had to be true. The Legion had been under British command. It would continue to be, only now there was no British government to hold it in check. And Zvi knew that he had learned what he had been seeking—the "something" that was going to happen in the morning.

"And so you're spying for them?"

Again she tried to rise, and this time he shoved his Sten in her face so that she could not move.

"The lieutenant would be furious if he knew I was here," she tried to explain.

"Who?"

"Lieutenant Layton. He is a friend of my father's and he told my father he would look after me if my father let me come to the Old City."

Zvi wanted to laugh. The girl could be everything she claimed, but he was certain now that she was also Layton's doxy. "I could kill you and send you back to loverboy with a note around your pretty neck." He thought a moment, "And on that note I could write the names of the old men, the women and children Layton's had killed these past few months."

The girl's eyes did not waver as she said, "And you could sign it: a visitor to Deir Yassin," naming the Arab village where the Etzl terrorists had massacred over two hundred Arab civilians a month earlier.

Zvi slowly lowered the muzzle of his Sten as his other hand came up and grabbed her by the hair and drew her toward him. He felt himself shaking all over, and he did not know if it were anger, fatigue, or perhaps even some shame. He stared into the girl's face, and then he struck her across the cheek with an open palm so hard that the back of her head struck the stone wall and bounced forward. For an instant he thought he had killed her. However, her eyes met his. They were dark and angry. She did not cry out.

"I'll trade you Deir Yassin for Kfar Etzion," he said so low that he did not know if she had heard the name of the block of kibbutzim which had been destroyed with all of its people less than a week before.

Her hand came up to her face where he had struck her. "Kfar Etzion," she repeated. "Kfar Etzion," and he could tell that she was enjoying the name.

His Sten was pointed at her once more. "I'll give you two minutes to start down that street and disappear at the end of it," he snapped.

She glared up at him.

"Cross the street and stay out of the Quarter, or the next time you'll be killed." It was less a warning than a piece of information he wanted to be sure she understood. Again, he was surprised as she held out her hand for him to help her to her feet. Taken aback at the gesture, he drew her up. They walked out of the shelter of the doorway and started toward the end of the crooked street that led away from the Quarter. Near the end of it, she turned to him, "What's your name, Jew?"

"Zvi Mazon," he said proudly. "Be sure to tell Layton my name."

"I will," she said. "I will."

"Keep your head down and start running," he snapped as he put out his arm, took hers and pushed her on her way.

The Arab Legion attacked in the early morning. Entering the Old City through the Damascus, Herod and St. Stephen gates, they drove through the Moslem Quarter in the northeast section, the Christian Quarter to the northwest and cut off the Jewish Quarter by driving through the Armenian Quarter on the southeast. Their twenty-five-pound cannon on the hills north of the city began to batter the Quarter. With great effort, Ben Ezekiel was able to persuade the civilians to take cover in their cellars, in the subterranean synagogue of Yohanan ben Zakkai, and in the basements of the Batei Machseh, the housing complex near the city walls.

The Arab assault began along the Street of the Chain on one side of the Quarter; and on another side, it struck toward Misgav Ladach.

Zvi Mazon and his companions were being forced out of the house they occupied. The fire laid down by the heavy machine guns of the Legion ripped up the walls of their shelter. A platoon of Legionnaires raced into the street firing submachine guns and throwing hand grenades. The small squad held its ground as the grenades burst about them, returned the fire; and when the Arabs broke into the houses, they met them hand to hand.

Zvi saw the first Legionnaire enter the room he was in, brought up his gun and, firing twice, dove toward a hallway. Another Arab entered to be cut down by Dvora, and then she plunged into the hallway after Zvi. Three Legionnaires approached the window, one sweeping the room with his submachine gun as Moshe fell flat against the wall directly under the gun. A second Legionnaire dropped two grenades into the room and Moshe jumped over them, reaching the hallway as the first exploded. A jagged fragment of steel tore through his trouser leg. The Legionnaires tried entering the room again, but Zvi rose in the doorway, sprayed the window with his Sten and jumped back as another grenade was lobbed toward him.

Suddenly the room they were trying to hold exploded in their faces when the Legionnaires fired a Piat anti-tank missile through a wall. Abandoning the room to the enemy, Zvi waited in the hallway until the others joined him. They were about to withdraw to the next house behind when a small boy, his long corkscrew-curled payot shaking as he ran, scurried up. Tugging Zvi's arm, he shouted, "Ben Ezekiel wants you at the Ben Porat Synagogue."

Zvi knew now that the entire Quarter was under attack. If he pulled out of his present position, it would mean giving up the street which bounded the Quarter. However, he had to assume that Ben Ezekiel knew what he was doing. Gathering his detachment, he led it through the alleys and crooked streets to the synagogue school on the eastern edge of the Quarter. The Legion's heavy guns on the hills were ripping up the streets. Only the turning and twisting of the alleys, the rise and fall of the stone steps from street to street protected the squad. A wall collapsed behind them. An old man ran out of the ruins of his home and tried to tell them something, but they had no time to listen. Ruth paused over the body of a young woman, obviously pregnant, and when Zvi saw the woman was dead, he grabbed Ruth's arm and pushed her on. Two mortar shells landed where they had been standing.

When they neared the Ben Porat Synagogue, Lieutenant Layton's voice blasted at them from a sound truck. "Surrender or we shall repeat the massacre of Kfar Etzion. Surrender now. Cease fighting. The Arab Legion cannot guarantee the mob will not massacre every man and woman who continues to fight."

The Englishman's elegant tones carried over the din of fighting. The clear voice was so loud, Zvi almost believed it was on the street beside him.

Then they saw the synagogue and heard fighting inside. The Legionnaires had placed a machine gun on the wall near Dung Gate to cover the approaches. Zvi drew back into the shelter of a doorway and grabbed Avram's arm. "Keep their heads down," he shouted and started running toward the synagogue. When Avram opened fire with his Bren, pocking the wall about the heads of the Legionnaires, they ducked, and Ruth, Dvora and Moshe followed Zvi to the old building. They had just gone through the open doors when a grenade exploded in the street behind them. Zvi paused at the doorway to protect his squad, and when Moshe hobbled past, he saw that he had been hit. Leaping into the building, Zvi found three soldiers of Etzl fighting hand to hand with several Legionnaires. A British officer tried to fire the pistol thonged to his wrist, but when he brought it up, a young girl in tan shorts and torn shirt grabbed his arm and twisted it. An Arab soldier slashed at the girl's back with an unsheathed bayonet. Dvora fired, dropping him where he stood. The British lieutenant jerked back and fired once at Dvora, splintering a panel behind her. Zvi shot the Englishman without taking time to bring up his Sten. An Arab spun around to cover the doorway, but Fishel, too close to use his rifle, fell on him with his bare hands. The two locked for a moment, and then the Arab hurled the lighter man aside. Before the Arab could bring up his pistol, Avram cut him down from the doorway. There were only three Legionnaires left in the room. One of them backed into another room as he jerked a grenade from his belt. Before he could pull the pin, Ruth threw herself on the man, grabbed his arm, twisting him around and snapping his arm at the elbow. As the live grenade dropped to the floor, she jumped out of the room and slammed the door behind her. An instant later the grenade exploded, tearing the door off its hinges. When she looked into the room again, she saw that one of the Legionnaries was still alive and she shot him through the head.

In the entrance room of the synagogue Zvi and the others were now alone. The Arabs on the wall above the Dung Gate tried to reach them with machine-gun fire, but they were shielded by a stone wall.

"You," Zvi pointed to Dvora and Avram, "check out the rest of this building." Then he turned to Moshe, who was no longer able to stand. The lean-faced kibbutznik tried to smile as he said, "I'm glad I learned."

"Learned?" Zvi asked.

"The Legionnaires are not invulnerable." And his hand went out to indicate the bodies lying on the floor.

The three from Etzl—the Irgun Zvai Leumi—were already pulling their wounded out of the building. "Can we help you?" their commander asked Zvi.

"If you're going to Misgav Ladach, you can take this learned one with you," and Zvi pointed to Moshe.

Ruth joined them, and Zvi crossed the room to see how badly she was hurt. There was blood down the front of her tattered blouse, but she continued to clutch her rifle. A wry smile crossed her face. "I hadn't planned to get my discharge this way."

Zvi ignored her words as he ripped open the front of her blouse to examine the wound. The size of the bullet hole puzzled him. It was small and blood barely oozed out of it. When he looked up at her, she explained, "It was spent coming through a door."

"I'll give you your sock back," he said, reaching into his pocket where he had put the bloody sock after his arm had been bandaged.

Ruth shook her head and tried to hold up the front of her torn blouse, which exposed her large breasts. "I'll take your shirt," she told him.

Unbuttoning his shirt, he handed it to her.

By the time Dvora and Avram returned, Ruth was wearing Zvi's shirt and Moshe had departed with the other squad. Fishel was cutting the thong-tied revolver from the wrist of the dead British officer while Zvi was collecting the ammunition from the pouches of the dead. Counting out the cartridges, he decided they had come out ahead in this fight. "Will you get me that Limey bastard's battle jacket?" he asked Fishel.

The musician stripped the bullet-torn jacket off the Englishman's body and tossed it to Zvi, who was passing out the Arab ammunition and guns. Dvora accepted a Sten, and from the way she threw the bolt and checked the ammunition, he knew she was familiar with the weapon.

Zvi walked over to the body of the British officer. Young. Younger even than Zvi. His red wavy hair was wet with blood from the pool in which he lay. Kneeling, Zvi went through his pockets for some kind of identification. A wallet revealed only that Lieutenant Walter Spears had been transferred from British headquarters, Palestine, to the service of the Arab Legion on 14 May. This explained Layton's continued presence in the area. Knowing the orders might interest Haganah HQ, Zvi folded the mimeographed sheet and shoved it into his pocket.

The door to the street was still open. The heavy machine gun mounted on the city wall above Dung Gate continued to rip at the walls near the synagogue.

Reaching into Avram's grenade pouch, Zvi motioned for the others to wait. Taking a deep breath, he skirted a building, rounded a corner and emerged only a few meters from the machine gun above the Gate. An instant after he ducked back, bullets smashed against the wall where he had shown himself. Pulling the pin of the grenade, he zigzagged into the open street, hurled his grenade toward the wall and took refuge behind a heavy stone archway. A moment later the grenade exploded and the machine gun fell silent. Returning to the synagogue, Zvi led his companions back to their post.

Ben Ezekiel, catching up with his squad as it neared the corner, gave orders for the others to take a position half a block behind the original line bounded by the Street of the Chain, which had been overwhelmed by the Arab Legion. Then the A/C took Zvi with him to a meeting which was taking place at the ancient synagogue named after Yohanan Ben Zakkai. As they neared the synagogue, they could hear prayers rising from within and they paused to listen to the familiar ancient words. Mortar shells continued to fall over the area. And still the prayers rose.

"Whosoever prays in Jerusalem is like unto him who prays before the seat of the Lord," Ben Ezekiel quoted.

Zvi looked at the A/C in surprise.

"Don't belittle it," the stocky officer warned. "Too many people have believed in it and been willing to die for it for too long."

A shell crashed into a building a dozen paces away and old stones powdered.

"I didn't know you believed," Zvi said quietly.

Ben ran his palm over his balding head. "Me believe? I don't know enough not to."

They walked on together. The door of the synagogue was ajar, and Ezekiel led the way inside.

The entrance chamber of the synagogue is one of the four prayer halls. Once, long ago, when there were only nine Jews living in the Old City and they lacked a tenth for a minyan, they were joined on the Day of Atonement by an aged stranger, who gave them the necessary quorum for prayer. And when the prayers were ended, he was gone. And the nine men knew he had been the prophet Elijah, and so they named the first prayer room for him.

When Zvi and the area commander appeared in Elijah's chamber, the civilians in the room finished their prayer and waited for the two soldiers to speak. Ezekiel ignored them and walked into the next prayer room, called Kehal Zion—the Congregation of Zion.

The civilians had gathered from the other prayer rooms and they stood together, watching the two Jews who were strangers to them in a way that even the Arabs and English destroying their city were not strangers. These two men of Haganah were blasphemers. They had come to create trouble where there had not really been trouble for a long time. And in the Old City of Jerusalem time was measured in centuries and not days. The troubles of the Zionists had been only yesterday, whereas the peace with the Arabs of the Old City went back before memory.

Benjamin Ezekiel turned to face the old men, who still wore long caftans, and the young men in black suits and broad-brimmed hats. "You wanted to see me," the A/C finally said.

The several hundred men all seemed to nod at once while turning to Finegold, who had the key to Zion Gate on a string about his neck.

"We want to talk," Finegold blurted out, and then as if he had spoken too quickly and might not have retained his dignity, he repeated his words. "We want to talk, and that is why I have sent for you."

Ezekiel nodded and waited.

"We think you should know that if you do not make terms at once, we will." The short man with the pudgy face and manner of one anointed looked about him to be certain the heads of the other civilians bobbed in agreement.

"You can't," Zvi said so innocently that the others did not know what he meant.

"But we can, young man," Finegold said patronizingly. "We can. This is our city and this is our Quarter."

However, Zvi shook his head. "Israel needs Jerusalem. You can't give it up."

Finegold laughed softly. "The Arabs have broadcast that they will ensure our lives if we surrender. Can you say as much if we do not?"

Again, the heads bobbing.

"I've a wife and two children," said a man from Casablanca.

"It isn't fit for us to fight in the City of David," said another who had walked from Yemen.

"I came to pray here and die here. I did not come to be killed here," said a middle-aged man from Vilna.

Finegold waited until he was satisfied that they had made the impression he was seeking and asked again, "Can you assure our safety if we don't surrender?"

Taking a deep breath, Ezekiel slowly turned his back. After a moment, he swung about to face them. "The only thing I can assure you is that I will kill the man who does surrender." He paused to let them fully grasp what he had said, before he added, "And I will assure you also that I may have to kill anyone who talks of surrender." His broad palm came up as though to wipe his balding head, but instead it covered his face. His head went down and Zvi was aware that the man was close to weeping.

Then the A/C's head snapped up and he met Finegold's eyes. "Good men have fought and died to keep Jerusalem. They cannot have died in vain." He started to walk away when an angry rabbi from Warsaw grabbed his arm and swung him about.

"You heathen. You think you can say who lives and dies in God's city? You think you can say whose death has meaning? Why—"

The rabbi from Warsaw would have said more, but Zvi took the man's wrist and forced it off Ben's arm. Still holding the rabbi, Zvi said, "We did not come so that you could deliver a sermon. We did not come to dispute theology. We are soldiers. We have our orders. We will carry them out."

Drawing away, the rabbi shook his head. "Do you really believe 'only obeying orders' is an excuse?"

Though Zvi's hand came back, he held his blow, looked at his hand and let it fall to his side. "I believe what I am fighting for is good," he said.

The rabbi started to say something, but Ezekiel shook his head. "We did not come for disputations on the morality of war. Just remember that I am small and insignificant and mean enough to do what I have said." And he stalked out into the alley. When they were once more in the open air with the shells breaking about them, he told Zvi, "I hope we are right."

The *hamseen* seared the long afternoon. The brazen sky was gray with smoke. British cannon pounded the Quarter. In squads as few as two and three men and women, Haganah and Etzl held as much of the perimeter as they could. They had little ammunition. They had few grenades. Those civilians who were finally willing to cast their lot with the fighters did not know how to use either; and in the desperate madness which gripped the Jewish Quarter, fighting for that survival which in itself is victory, Benjamin Ezekiel found himself setting up small units to teach civilians how to hold a grenade and how to load and fire a pistol.

When he made the rounds of the few strongholds which were not collapsing under the pressure of the Arab attack, he found Zvi Mazon lying in the bedroom of an old stone house, firing his Sten gun one shot at a time as he selected his targets.

Ezekiel crawled across the floor to scan the ground below. A British half-track lay on its side, burning furiously. Scattered along what must have been its trail were the bodies of four Legionnaires. Looking to Zvi for a report, the A/C waited.

"Fishel. He crawled out on that," pointing to an arch which stretched across the street, "and dropped a lighted kerosene lamp like that one," and he pointed to the lamp on the table, "right into the vehicle." He smiled as he added, "I think their own ammunition did the rest."

Ben Ezekiel nodded. "I got ten new men today."

With obvious disbelief, Zvi rolled over on his side and stared at his superior.

"It was a trade," Ezekiel explained. "The Neturei Karta," naming the "Guardians of the City," the fanatic sect of Orthodox extremists to whom the entire idea of a Jewish State was heresy.

"Ten soldiers?"

Ezekiel shook his head. "Warm bodies."

"And what did you give up for them?"

"I agreed that none of the women fighting with us would enter a synagogue."

Zvi rolled over onto his back so that he could see the smoke which hung over the city. Ezekiel started to inch back toward the doorway of the bedroom, continuing to face his squad commander as he did so. "I have more messages which tell me we will be rescued." He smiled bitterly as his hand went wide to take in the Arab Quarter and the twenty thousand Arab civilians and the Arab Legion. "How many have you lost today?"

Zvi shook his head. "Moshe Gilead got hit in the leg. Avram's over in the next building with Fishel. Dvora and Ruth are downstairs." While he spoke, a burst of Sten fire shook the building. Zvi rolled back onto his belly, his gun up to cover the street. Another dead Arab lay beside the burning half-track. The uniformed figure was stretched out full length and at its fingertips lay a torch which continued to burn. Zvi and Ben stared at it. Each knew the Arabs wanted to blow up the building they were in.

"The needle-and-thread salesgirl," Zvi commented, knowing that only Dvora in the room below had a Sten.

Ezekiel nodded. A twisted grin spread over his face as he said, "Someday, when we have time, I'll tell you about her . . . " and his voice trailed off.

"What?" Zvi snapped, resenting a meaningless hint.

Shrugging, Ezekiel assured him, "It would not make any difference now."

Then he was gone. Zvi watched a band of Arabs approach the street across the roofs of the houses opposite. Smoke billowed upward from one of the houses. Most of the roof of another had been destroyed by shell fire. Reaching into his pocket, Zvi pulled out a grenade. Then he crawled toward the closest wall that could give him cover. Two gun bursts from the house where Avram and Fishel were posted did not stop the Legionnaires. One after another appeared on the edge of the roof opposite. Knowing they had no place to retreat except backward through the fire burning behind them, Zvi pulled the pin of his grenade and lobbed it across the street.

The Legionnaires saw it coming. One rose to grab for the spinning grenade and Dvora cut him down. Another turned to run and slipped through the hole in the roof behind him. A third came to full height and swept the rent front of the building where Zvi and the two women were posted. A single rifle shot from Fishel dropped the Arab into the street below. Then the grenade exploded. Two Arabs half rose and then collapsed. One crawled off the roof, dragging a bloody leg behind him.

"That's coordination," Zvi shouted so that the others could hear.

A mortar shell struck the house where Fishel and Avram were posted. The walls seemed to rise for an instant, and then they billowed outward as though the stones had been held together by something elastic. A moment later all was rubble.

Zvi half crawled and half ran out of the bedroom. Taking the steps two at a time, he reached the floor below just as Ruth and Dvora emerged from the room in which they had been posted. Passing the two women, Zvi continued to the ground floor, the girls following. Pausing only to make certain he had a clear passage to the rubble of the building next door, he raced across the closed courtyard and started to tear into the pile of stones heaped against the fragment of wall which remained standing. At that same moment the Legionnaires across the street realized that the house they had been attacking was no longer defended, and so they crossed the disputed street and occupied the house.

Throwing broken stones aside, Zvi shouted, "Avram! Fishel!"

Two bullets struck several paces away. From where she stood in the shelter of the building she had just left, Dvora swept the windows looking onto the courtyard with her Sten gun.

Hearing his name called faintly, Zvi continued to dig into the rubble. In one corner where the wall remained standing, he threw a beam aside, discovered two legs and, pulling with all of his strength, he drew Avram from the ruin. The Arabs continued to fire at them from the roofs across the street. The building which would have blocked their view had disappeared.

Ignoring the fighting going on about him, Zvi dragged Avram to the shelter of the building where Ruth and Dvora stood, and he dashed back to the rubble. The Arabs continued to fire cautiously because the girls returned the fire. One minute passed. Two. The exchange of fire was constant. A bullet struck Zvi's calf and he paused momentarily in his digging. He shook his head as though to clear it, and then bending over, he removed more stones from the heap. A hand appeared. It opened and closed. Zvi grabbed it. Disregarding the weight on Fishel, he braced his legs, pulled with all his strength and freed his companion. Dvora covered Zvi's retreat as he started for the shelter of the house in the row behind, dragging his burden with him. Ruth jerked a dazed Avram to his feet and followed Zvi.

When Dvora reached the others in the alley behind the courtyard, she found Fishel lying limp on the cobblestones, Ruth bending over him. The girl from Poland looked at the others, tossed Zvi's Sten at his feet, and said, "You're a fool," and then turned her attention to the area behind them where the Arabs had now crossed the street and were preparing to make another attack.

Zvi knelt where he was, ripped his trouser leg up to the place where the blood was flowing from his calf. He tore the trouser leg into two strips and tied them above his wound. When he was done, he turned to Avram.

"I'm going to have a headache," Avram said, as he rubbed his hand over the torn skin of his face and forehead.

"That's all?"

Avram nodded.

Zvi looked across Fishel's unconscious body at Ruth. She was running her hands over his arms and down his sides and legs. When she looked up, she reported, "Both of them are broken."

Trying to decide what he had to do, Zvi wiped his face, leaving a streak of dirt over his cheeks and nose. Ruth wanted to smile, but could not bring herself to.

Looking up at Avram, Zvi asked, "Can you carry him to the hospital?"

Avram nodded as he stared at the crude tourniquet about Zvi's calf. "I'll be back as soon as I can," he promised.

Ruth helped him raise Fishel from the ground onto Avram's shoulder.

She picked up the Sten gun and told Zvi, "You should go, too."

Shaking his head, Zvi started back to join Dvora, but he had not gone more than a few steps when she appeared in the courtyard.

"They hold that line of houses."

Zvi thought a moment before he said, "We'll give them the block and take a position across there," pointing with his gun toward the next street deeper into the Quarter.

The Legionnaires, not knowing that they had no opposition in the next line of houses, which were mainly rubble, took their time about attacking.

Zvi, Ruth and Dvora settled into the first house which gave them a field of fire covering the houses they had been driven from and the roofs beyond.

With his back against a wall, Zvi watched Dvora load a clip from a pouch she had taken off a dead Arab. Breathing deeply, he tried to relax, but he could not forget the manner in which she had written him off. "Why?" he asked. "Why was I a fool?"

Without looking at him, Dvora continued to load the clip. "You could have been killed as well as the two of us." She shook her head in disgust, "And you had no way of knowing either one of them was alive. As it is, only one of them is going to be of any more use." She spat over her Sten. "You risked three lives for one."

Ruth looked at Zvi from where she lay sprawled on a heavy table she had pushed up against a window. They had been in Haganah long enough to know how they felt without even discussing the matter. "Do you want to tell her?" Ruth asked.

Nodding, Zvi spoke softly. "I was sixteen, living with my father. I told a friend I wanted to join Haganah. A couple of weeks later one of the boys in school asked me if I would meet him that night. I didn't know what he wanted. But when I got to his house, he suggested we go for a walk. There was an old storehouse near the edge of town." He smiled "Gadera may be a big name in history, but it isn't much of a town. In the basement of the storehouse I thought I was standing alone, but then a light went on. I couldn't see anyone else in the room. I knew there were at least three men there. They started asking me questions. What did I want to do? Who were my friends? What did I do with my time?" He smiled as he recalled, "And then one of them—I never knew who it was—asked if I could keep a secret. I said I could, and he asked me to tell him one I had kept recently." Zvi was silent for a time. Then he continued, "That was a trap, because if I told him, it wouldn't be a secret. Later my classmate took me out of the building. I saw there had been men surrounding it. Three different rings of men, but in the dark I couldn't tell who they were. Weeks passed, and then my friend suggested we go for another walk. Down in another cellar there were more men. There was a table, a kerosene lamp, and in the light of the lamp a Bible and a pistol. That night I joined Haganah. And for the next two years I carried messages. When I was eighteen, two men who were friends of my father took me out to learn how to fire a gun." He half closed his eyes. "I've fired a good many since then. But what was most important was what we who fought together came to mean to each other. We learned to trust each other no matter what happened. We had confidence in each other. We believed. Even those of us who were not religious believed. No one was going to desert us. No one was going to let the man next to him down. No one was going to be left behind in a fight, even if he was dead."

Two shells struck a house nearby as the Legionnaires bracketed in on a school.

Dvora said nothing as she slammed the clip into her Sten.

Abruptly, Zvi asked, "Does a violinist need to use his legs to play?"

The Arabs were less active after dark. It was almost ten when Avram and Moshe found them, and they brought four loaves of bread, two pots of water and some broth made from grain. Sitting in the darkness, Zvi posted Dvora as sentry while he listened to Moshe tell the news he had heard at the hospital.

"The Russians may recognize us. The British claim we are going to be beaten. The Egyptians have invaded. The Syrians say they have invaded, but no one is sure about that. There is fighting in the Negev. Dov Joseph is still the military governor of Jerusalem, and Jerusalem is cut off from the rest of the country."

Zvi chuckled as he mopped up the last of the broth with a piece of bread. "That's going to put Finegold off."

The others laughed with him.

His dinner finished, Zvi sailed the old plate on which he had eaten against a building where it shattered, drawing fire from a machine gun not too far away.

Moshe laughed. "They're touchy."

Pulling himself to his feet, Zvi felt the sharp pain in his calf and flinched, glad that the others could not see his face in the dark. "I'll relieve Dvora," he said and slipped into the darkness. He had gone only a short distance when he dropped to his knees and called her name softly.

She answered from behind a broken wall and he crawled forward to her side. "There's some broth back there and bread," he said.

"And there's an *Ayrab* trying to crawl along that wall," she whispered, pointing to her left.

Zvi's Sten came up as he dropped beside her. His leg brushed hers, and he felt her stiffen and he inched away just in time to miss the sweep of her Sten barrel as it cracked down on the spot where his injured leg had been. The noise of her gun striking stone could be heard as clearly as a rifle shot. Zvi held his breath and waited. A moment later he saw a dark figure rise behind a broken wall. Dvora squeezed off four shots. There was a scream of pain and the sound of a man falling. Both of them crawled several paces to their right. "Go on, eat," Zvi whispered.

The girl shook her head and said softly, "There's going to be a moon tonight."

Zvi was about to ask what she meant.

"I'll leave you out here alone when I'm sure they can see you."

His stomach tightened at the flat way in which she had told him she did not care if he were killed. He started to grab her arm, thought better of it, and asked, "Why in the hell did you join us?"

After he had spoken, he knew he had been too loud, and again both of them crawled from where they lay. An instant later shots from rifles bracketed the place where they had been. He heard the girl snort at his mistake.

Then she said, so low that he had to lean forward to hear, "Why do you sabras all think the State belongs to you alone?"

Sighing, Zvi made up his mind that he would not argue politics with this girl in this place. He checked his gun. There was nothing more he had to say to Dvora Rabsky, even though he knew it was going to be a long night. He shut his eyes in the darkness and felt it overwhelm him. He thought about his friends fighting on other fronts. Wherever they were, they were not trapped in Jerusalem beside a girl who slammed at them with a rifle butt if they so much as touched her. Zvi thought about touching a woman. He hadn't had one in all the months he had been inside. Others might have. He did not know. All he knew was the dull fatigue and the sense of proportion which kept him on his feet when he was too tired to stand, kept him alert when his eyes wanted to close, kept a gun in his arms when the weight seemed more than he could hold.

Rolling onto her side, Dvora stared at Zvi's profile in the darkness. His eyes were deep set; his nose, straight at the bridge, broadened at the nostrils. His upper lip extending out above his lower gave him the look of a child, though his chin was firm. He seemed tense. She admitted to herself, resentfully, he was not afraid.

Half an hour passed before the two were joined by Moshe, Avram and Ruth, who took up positions on both sides of Zvi. Satisfied the others could manage without him for a while, Zvi edged back from the rubble. His leg was numb where he had been hit. Reaching down, he felt a sticky dampness.

The moon was low on the horizon, but rising. He wondered if they could be seen, if he should withdraw from this place, if . . . And he knew he was not thinking clearly. He had no right to withdraw.

"Moshe," he hissed.

Moshe crawled back to join him.

"I'm going to the hospital," Zvi explained, and then for fear he might be misunderstood, he added, "I'll be back in an hour. If I hear any firing, I'll be back earlier."

Moshe understood.

"And that Rabsky girl," Zvi said, "she hasn't eaten tonight."

Combing his beard with his fingers, Moshe suggested, "I'll take her to dinner at the King David Hotel."

Zvi slipped away into the darkness.

The nurses at the Hadassah Hospital bandaged his leg, changed the bandage on his arm and then let him see Fishel, who was lying on a mattress on the cellar floor.

The violinist smiled wanly at his squad commander. "I don't think I'll be of much use tomorrow."

Zvi nodded. "Let's put it this way: I won't count on you."

The slim, strong hand of the musician came out from under the sheet and covered his friend's. "Those girls," he said hesitantly, "they shouldn't be out there."

"I'll tell them," Zvi agreed.

Then, as he started to leave, Fishel called after him, "Zvi," and the young officer waited.

"That piano in the house, the one we were at . . . "

And Zvi Mazon nodded.

"Will you drop back there if you can and, maybe, put a bucket of water under it?"

"Sure. The first chance I get."

With a half salute to his friend, Zvi left the hospital and, crossing the courtyard, strode into headquarters. The room was lighted by a single kerosene lamp, and only Zella was there, studying the map on the wall.

"Will the Palmach come in?" he asked.

Zella smiled. "Just the way they did last night and the night before." She reached out and picked up copies of the messages she had recorded. "Or have you already seen these?"

The firing in the distance was heavier now, and Zvi wondered if he should rejoin his own squad. He stepped outside to listen. Placing her headset on the table, Zella joined him. The moon was high now, but much of its light was cut off by the smoke hanging over the Quarter.

"If we were on the walls, we could see the lights of the New City," she said.

Zvi put a hand on her shoulder and drew her to him. She did not resist and her head fell back against his chest.

"And if I were in the King David," he said, "I would order Cornish guinea hen."

"Your taste has improved."

Then they fell quiet as they listened to the heavy exchange of machine gun and rifle fire. It was coming from both the south and the west. "The Jaffa and Zion gates," he said.

"I told you that," she reminded him.

When he gently ran his hand down her side, he tried to make up his mind which route he would take in if he were commanding the assault on the wall. "If they come in Jaffa, they will have to fight their way through David Street and part of the Street of the Chain."

She turned to look at him. "The Street of the Chain?"

"I had to fall back from it today."

"And Zion Gate?" she asked.

"They'd come under fire," he said, "but we still hold the line at the Bazaar of the Jews."

His hand drew back and he slapped her bottom. "If Ben Ezekiel returns, tell him I've gone to Zion Gate."

Before she could object, he ran out of the courtyard as fast as his injured leg would allow. He knew there were at least a hundred meters already in Arab hands of the approach road from Zion Gate to the Quarter, and so he came to a halt in front of a small building on the edge of the Bazaar. From where he stood, he could make out the backs of the Arab machine-gunners on the wall. He wondered if his Sten could reach them and was about to try a shot when someone touched his shoulder. Whirling, he sprang back and brought his Sten to bear on Ben Ezekiel.

"Don't waste ammunition," the A/C admonished.

Zvi slung his weapon over his shoulder and turned so that he could watch the fight at the distant gate. "We could try to help them," he suggested.

At that instant a great explosion rocked the Old City, shook the ground under their feet and threw up a cloud of dust and smoke. From where he knelt, Zvi tried to see Zion Gate. He could see the battlement, the moon over it, and below, where there should have been only darkness, he could barely make out a breach, narrow, but a breach. Coming to his feet, he threw one arm about Ben Ezekiel and hugged the man. "They did it," he shouted.

Ezekiel did not take time to respond as he shoved Zvi against the door of the building and out of range of the machine-gun fire that swept the area. While Zvi was catching his breath, the A/C shook his head, "Don't I have enough trouble without your shouting invitations for more?"

In the shock from the explosion that blew Zion Gate, the Arab defenders of the battlement held their fire. That confused moment was long enough for the assault platoon of the Palmach to flow through the breach and take their first positions inside the Old City. In the twenty minutes that followed, the fighting about the Gate and on the street leading along the edge of the Armenian Quarter to the Jewish Quarter was furious, bloody and, for the Jewish shock troops, successful.

Once contact had been made, the Palmach commander accompanied Ezekiel and his squad commander through the winding alleys that led to Misgav Ladach. They were followed by troops carrying food, ammunition and guns. A few of the Palamach were left to hold Zion Gate and Moorpark Street.

At the Old City headquarters, the youthful brigade commander told Hertzela to radio his headquarters that he had broken through. Standing in his battle dress, his Sten gun slung over his shoulder, his deputy at his side, he directed the radio operator. "Tell them we have carried out the task and have reached the Jews of the Old City." And in a moment of jubilation and pride, he boasted, "Seventeen hundred souls have been saved."

Hertzela looked to Ezekiel for approval. He nodded, then poured tea for everyone.

The supplies were arriving now. Cases of food were stacked in the courtyard before their dispersal to cellars, cases of ammunition and grenades were taken directly to the posts scattered along the diminished perimeter of the Quarter.

Picking up his glass of tea and the kerosene lantern, the young Palmach commander walked over to the wall map and stared at the positions held by the defenders. It took him a few minutes to realize that the x-ed out city blocks had already been destroyed by shelling and fire, and that the circle connecting positions was really the perimeter of the Quarter. Turning to Ezekiel, the young man asked, "And that's all of it?"

The A/C was not ashamed. "I've been telling headquarters."

The youth picked at a scar on his face as he shook his head. "It's not exactly a Shabbat celebration."

"Did you bring in reinforcements?" Zvi asked.

The shock-troop commander smiled at Zvi. They had fought together on a beach the year before, holding off a British company determined to capture the immigrants coming off a sinking vessel from Naples.

"Mazon, what in the hell are you doing here?" The greeting was friendly. Warm enough to give Zvi some pride.

"You've got that wrong, Uri. It's 'What am I doing here in hell?' "

Ben Ezekiel looked from one to the other and laughed. "He's fighting."

At the explanation, the others in the room laughed too.

"Can you start getting our wounded out tonight?" the A/C asked.

The deputy commander of the Palmachniks agreed, and after finishing his tea, he left. Zvi stared at the map for a time and then walked out into the courtyard where a small detachment of the Palmach was moving the wounded from the cellars. Two men appeared, carrying Fishel on a stretcher which was no more than an old door, and for a short distance Zvi walked beside his friend.

He saw that Fishel was weeping. Placing a hand on the violinist's shoulder, he said, "You'll be all right."

"I'm going," Fishel sobbed without embarrassment.

A broad smile spread over Zvi's face. Reaching out, he squeezed Fishel's shoulder affectionately and smiled, "I hope everyone lets me down the way you did."

The first streaks of dawn appeared. When he entered the courtyard at Misgav Ladach again, he saw several strange doctors and nurses directing the traffic out of the hospital. One of the doctors, a survivor of the attack on the convoy from the Hadassah Hospital, was explaining to the defenders that he had only been able to bring a small supply of medicine. "The shelling is taking its toll," he said.

"How badly damaged is the New City?" Zvi heard one of the nurses ask.

The doctor, a famous surgeon from Marseilles who had spent five years in a concentration camp, shrugged. "How bad is bad?"

Passing the medical staff, Zvi entered the headquarters room after two signalers who had come in with the Palmach. One was a woman in her mid-forties, the other a girl no more than eighteen. He was looking over the younger one when he saw that Zella, standing near him, was watching the older signaler, who was checking out the radio.

Zvi asked, "You know her?"

Zella nodded, a kind of awe on her face and in her voice as she said, "Kineret Heschel. She dropped into Hungary for the British. After the war she organized the illegals coming out of Yugoslavia and Italy."

Zvi recalled the name now and wondered why so legendary a figure was now in the Old City. If he had time later, he would try to talk to Kineret Heschel.

Suddenly Zella handed him a slip of paper. "For Avram," she said. "His parents were both killed in a shelling."

Anger crossed Zvi's face, but there was nothing to say.

Ben Ezekiel joined them long enough to ask, "You want out now, Zella?"

When she finally understood, she shook her head. "Let someone go who has a family."

The Area Commander smiled at her affectionately. "Thanks." Hands on hips, he turned to Zvi. "You have two women in your squad. Go and ask if either one wants out."

The young commander hesitated. "And reinforcements?"

"Don't worry. As you heard Palmach announce, we've been saved." There was a touch of bitterness in his voice which surprised his two companions, who now turned to look at the youthful Palmach commanders who were picking up their weapons and starting toward the door. Everyone was aware now that the firing from the direction of Zion Gate had suddenly become heavy.

"What's wrong?" Zvi asked.

Ben Ezekiel shrugged. "It's no one's fault, but they made no arrangements for their own reinforcement."

"Oh, my God," Zella said softly.

"Better ask the women of your squad," the A/C suggested.

Zvi nodded and left. As he crossed what remained of the Quarter, he could hear the fighting at Zion Gate as the Arab Legion reacted at dawn to its defeat in darkness. The shelling of Mount Zion was stilled, but the mortar shells which had been falling for days still battered the Quarter.

When Zvi finally reached his squad, they already knew that the Palmach had broken through. Two strange middle-aged men sat with the detachment amid the rubble behind which they had taken up their position.

"Nachum Shemin and Joseph Ben Dur," Moshe introduced the men. "They just came inside."

Zvi introduced himself as he tried to evaluate the two. Shemin was probably fifty or older. There was the scar of a burn down the left side of his face. He stood taller than Zvi, but one shoulder was hunched up as though someone had pushed the bones together. He held a Sten gun comfortably in his hand. Seeing that the young officer did not know what to make of him, the older man tried to put him at his ease. "I fought with the Russians," he said. Then a smile broke over his battered face. "I must admit I was in tanks then."

Clapping the man on his twisted shoulder, Zvi said, "If they issue us tanks, I'll see that you ride in one." Then he turned his attention to the other man, trying to recall if he had heard the name Ben Dur before.

A rotund man, Ben Dur's sunken dark eyes met Zvi's. "I didn't fight with the Russians," he said flatly. "In fact," he continued, looking at the Enfield in his hand, "I never fired one of these before last week."

"Then what are you doing here?"

Ben Dur leaned back against a large stone. He was shorter than Zvi, his eyes were darker, his hair almost white. With a snort he shook his head. "I could say I was assigned, but that wouldn't be true. I volunteered." Then, as though the others would understand, he said, "I never saw the Wall."

When Dvora raised her head, Zvi saw the puzzled expression in her eyes. Obviously nothing could have meant less to her than the Western Wall.

"I understand," he said. Turning to Ruth and Dvora, he told them, "Ben Ezekiel said you can go out if you want to."

Ruth Barovsky, aware that all the others were looking at her, self-consciously brushed back her hair, revealing the scar on her forehead. The others waited for her answer, and it came as a question. "Are the rest of you being evacuated?"

Zvi shook his head.

"Then I'm staying," she said almost aggressively.

Proud of the girl, Zvi said, "Thanks."

He turned to Dvora Rabsky. "You came on your own," he reminded her. "You have no obligation to stay."

"I can take care of myself," the girl said ambiguously as she patted the gun in her hand.

Zvi thought that in spite of the anger always in her eyes, Dvora would have been considered beautiful by some. And then he wondered if it was, rather, because of that strange and angry look.

The battle taking place at Zion Gate could be heard more clearly now. At the same time that the fighting near and about the Zion Gate became heavier, the Arabs surrounding the Quarter began to press inward. Legionnaires completely replaced the irregular Arab volunteers who had begun fighting months before. Now professional and well-trained soldiers—most companies commanded by British officers—took over the assault.

From where his squad lay behind their rubble, Zvi could see the new pattern of attack emerge. The Legionnaires were not only trying to take each position held by Haganah, but they were also trying to link up their own forces by formidable drives which they hoped would cut the Quarter into smaller sections. The first of the new attacks was violent and pointless. Charging across streets, the Legionnaires dropped torches and Molotov cocktails as well as hand grenades into each house around the perimeter. However, they followed up their attack by systematically setting off heavy explosives and leveling the empty houses. When Zvi saw the first few houses destroyed by set charges, he knew the pattern of battle had changed. It was too well planned and organized to be Arab tactics. These were British tactics.

One house behind the Street of the Chain fell and then another and then another, and finally, even before noon, Zvi knew the one directly in front of him would be next. Leaving Moshe to cover the withdrawal, he fell back with the rest of the squad. Seconds later the last remaining walls of the building they had evacuated only the day before were demolished. From behind a low wall, Zvi saw the Legionnaires occupy the position he had just vacated. Laying down a field of fire, he and the others covered Moshe until he could reach them. Then he reorganized his defense.

Leaving the two women under the protection of the house they were going to hold, Zvi posted Joseph Ben Dur and Nachum Shemin in the ruins of houses on either side of the girls. Avram and Moshe were moved still farther out on the flanks. He stationed himself at the center of his line, in the house with the two women. He could command the street, which was little more than a twisting alley, and at the same time know that the ends of the alley were covered by Avram and Moshe.

Settling into place behind a stone wall in front of the house, Zvi looked up. He could not see the sun. He knew it had to be about noon, give or take an hour. Moshe had come up to report no movement on his end of the alley.

Glancing at Dvora, Zvi suggested, "Why don't you go into the house? Get some sleep until they attack."

The girl looked at him balefully. "Your concern for the morale of your troops is touching."

Moshe rolled over onto his side so that he could see her better.

Zvi found it difficult to hold his temper. "It's their physical condition that interests me," he snapped.

When Moshe laughed, "Her physical condition?" Zvi realized how foolish he had sounded and smiled at his friend. When he looked back at Dvora, he saw that she had not laughed and that her Sten gun was pointed at both of them. Zvi stared at the girl while he told Moshe, "I'm going to ask Ezekiel for more men and grenades. See that she joins Ruth. If you need help, I'll hear it." He rose, his eyes still on Dvora's gun.

"I'm sure you'll hear it," Moshe agreed. After Zvi had gone, Moshe turned toward Dvora. "What the hell's wrong with you?" And before she could answer, he added, "Zvi's the best commander we could have. Why do you give him grief?"

The girl's Sten did not waver from Moshe's stomach. She spoke so low he had to strain to hear: "I don't hate him in particular."

Moshe's stomach tightened. She watched him for several minutes, though he did not think she was really seeing him. Then without another word, she pulled herself to her feet and disappeared into the house where Ruth was posted.

By the time Zvi reached headquarters, he already knew there was nothing to be gained. The cobblestoned courtyard was almost empty, though fifty who had been wounded that day were lying in the shade of the hospital wing, and across the yard Hertzela was sitting at a table with Kineret Heschel. The older woman was operating the radio, and when Zvi approached, she glanced up, and Zella introduced them.

The fact that Kineret Heschel was a small woman, slim and delicate, surprised Zvi. He had always imagined her an Amazon, a figure to match the legend. Her slim hands turned the dial on the radio as she tried to pick up a broadcast from Damascus. Nothing but static. Zvi waited to hear if she had anything to report before he asked, "Did they all get out before it closed?" gesturing with his head toward the general direction of Zion Gate.

Zella nodded. "The Arabs closed in on them soon after you left, and they fled. We're cut off again." There was a finality about the way she said it.

The older woman's head came up angrily, and she removed the earphones. "Don't say 'fled,' " she snapped in a surprisingly deep voice. "They came as soon as they could. Their orders never told them to get killed hanging on." She shook her head almost in disappointment. "There are almost ninety thousand on the other side of that wall, ninety thousand who want to stay and see a State born."

Zvi looked to Zella for an explanation. She stared down at her hands for a time before she told him, "The Neturei Karta—the Guardians of the City—came in earlier. A dozen of them. They heard Kineret was here. They stood right where you are standing and they cursed her. Spat on her. Told her she was obscene. They said things I don't want to repeat. Dirt. Pornography. They called her *kurveh*." Her eyes matched Zvi's as she asked, simply, "What right have they to call Kineret a whore?"

Zvi shook his head in anger and was about to say something when Zella said, "One of them threatened to assassinate her."

Looking at the delicate features of the older woman, Zvi was embarrassed, though he did not understand why. "I'm sorry," he said.

All three of them were silent for a time, and then Kineret said, "You have to understand them. They take understanding. For centuries just such Jews lived here believing in something." A trace of a smile crossed her face. "They still believe in it. Never forget that. Then, over a century ago, our people came. People like us. And they threatened a way of life." She was openly smiling now, and Zvi was enchanted by her friendliness.

"It was a simple way of life. They studied and they prayed and every so often some of them went out into the world for *chalukah*. You and I might call them beggars, *schnorrers*, but begging for money to be holy all of the time became a business. They really don't know any other way. They go to Arizona, New South Wales, Paris and Shanghai. Any place there is a Jew." The smile broadened. "And there are Jews just about everywhere. And these people beg. Our coming changed that in some ways. We asked for help to help ourselves. And we asked for more money than they ever believed existed, and we got it." She was no longer smiling, but in that brief time when she had been, Zvi understood how she had achieved so much in so many strange places. He saw why few could refuse her anything.

She looked at her two companions. "You and you and I are threats to them."

Zella shook her head. "It was you they were most angry about. It was you they spat on."

The other woman nodded. "Only because I am older and have had the good luck and time to do more."

"If they come back," Zvi said, "I wish you would let me know." Then he asked, "Ben Ezekiel?"

"He's gone inspecting," Zella said. "And he told me to tell any commanders who showed up that they should be with their squads, that he has no more reinforcements for them, and that he will dole out the supplies as needed."

Grinning, Zvi said, "And that covers that." He nodded to the two women and started to leave. When he reached the alley beyond the courtyard, he heard someone behind him. Wheeling about, he saw Kineret Heschel.

She smiled. "You are jumpy."

Zvi nodded. "Too much coffee and too many cigarettes."

Her head cocked to one side as she smiled, "How long since you've had either?"

Feeling self-conscious about complaining to this woman, Zvi shrugged. "How long?"

He thought for a moment. "I had some coffee in January. I had a cigarette about two weeks ago." He almost blushed as he told her, "I bought it from Finegold for an American dollar I had saved from the war. A souvenir."

"Ben Ezekiel makes awful tea," she said. "I'm sure you've had your share of it."

Zvi's head bobbed. Then to his surprise, she reached into the pocket of her shorts and pulled out a package of Players cigarettes. When she started to press them into Zvi's hand, he shook his head.

"I'm not one of them," he said. "I don't live by *chalukah*. I don't take handouts."

Her deep-throated voice took on a tone of authority as she ordered, "Take these cigarettes, Commander."

And to Zvi's surprise, he took them.

"Don't you ever again say anything like that to me or anyone else in Haganah." Then, as though satisfied she had made her point, she explained, "This is an army of friends, not beggars."

Both of them fell silent while two British twenty-five-pounders dropped shells into the Quarter.

"Is there anything I can do for you?" Zvi asked.

She smiled. "You knew I wanted something?"

Zvi felt pleased that at least she didn't think him a total idiot. "For years I've been hearing and reading about you: Kineret Heschel in Romania, Kineret Heschel in Germany, Kineret Heschel in Yugoslavia. Kineret Heschel standing beside Ben Gurion in London."

"You make it all sound like a travelogue," she said pleasantly. "Don't believe what was written or most of what was said. We needed the stories so we could get help." She laughed brightly as she added, "You left out the Kineret Heschel on Hadassah tours throughout the United States speaking at ladies' luncheons and businessmen's dinners trying to raise arms and dollars." She laughed. "That was the really difficult work."

A mortar struck near them and she stepped into a doorway in time to avoid the flying debris.

Zvi smiled at her, still surprised that she was talking to him.

"Joseph Ben Dur is with you?" she asked.

"Yes," he said, not understanding how they had arrived at this question.

"Take care of him," she pleaded.

He tried to match up the image of the rotund, white-haired man he had met earlier in the day with this woman. "Take care of him?"

"He's a very . . ." she was struggling for a way to describe Ben Dur. Finally, she shook her head as though to brush aside her first words. "Once Ben Dur was a judge, a real judge in a high court. He had a wife and five children." She fell silent while she thought of the horror her words had conjured up in her own mind. "He only arrived here a few months ago."

And as she spoke, Zvi thought of refugees coming home to Palestine across the night beaches.

"He will be important to the State," she added.

"Then why is he here?"

"He wanted to come," she said, as simply as Ben Dur had said, *"I've never seen the Wall."*

"And that's why you're here?"

"Thanks for understanding, Zvi," she said, and she kissed his cheek. Then she stepped back and looked at him for a moment before she turned toward the headquarters courtyard.

He wanted to call after her and say that he did not want the responsibility. He had enough, but he did not know how to tell her that.

Sergeant Diyar al Ilm did not understand the Jews of the Old City. They did not die the way they had when he was young. As he stood in the entrance of the Talmud Torah several blocks south of the Street of the Chain and watched the defense against his detachment, he realized that something had changed. Glancing up at the sky, he could see the smoke hanging over the Quarter. That was as it should be. He heard the sound of the Legion's cannon and the whine of rising mortar shells splitting the afternoon. And that was as it should be. But the Jews in the house across the street were not as they should have been.

Puzzled by that which he did not fully understand, Diyar al Ilm hesitated to order the attack. The Jews inside would die, and this would be good. But he knew now that some of his own men would die, and this he had not expected. He looked about the Talmud Torah. Much of the building was of wood. Smiling, he entered, reached onto a shelf and spilled the books resting there across the floor. Picking up one, he flipped through it. He could not read. He had never been taught. However, he was not unhappy. Not every Arab boy had been promoted to sergeant in the Arab Legion. Striking a match, he lighted the pages of the open book, held it until the flames crawled upward and then tossed it among the other books. One lying open caught fire. Then another.

Satisfied that his work here was done, the sergeant walked outside. Taking his pistol from his holster, Diyar smiled as he waved his assault squad forward. They were bunched closely when a Jew leaned out of an upper story and dropped a grenade in their midst. Diyar ducked for cover. The grenade burst, and when he looked back at the house, he saw that all of his assault team lay on the ground. Some of them were still alive. The Jews inside the house did not bother to shoot them.

The sergeant briefed the men quickly, and then taking up a position behind one of the machine guns, he swept the upper windows of the house while the machine-gunner at his side swept the lower windows. At his yell, five men moved forward. One of them reached the house and dumped his grenade inside. Diyar watched the man duck below the window level as the grenade burst. Picking up a submachine gun from one of the dead, Diyar moved toward the house with the man who had thrown the grenade. They burst in through the door, their guns sweeping the room.

A single old Jew in a caftan lay in the corner.

Solomon Finegold did not believe in violence, he did not believe in war, and he did not believe in the Jewish State. All his adult life he had been telling his neighbors that the Zionists would only bring them trouble. And now that the Quarter was besieged, he felt justified in what he planned to do. In fact, as he told his wife and son, the British had made him the Mukhtar of Jerusalem in the same way High Commissioner Herbert Samuel had made Haj Amin el-Husseini the Grand Mufti of Jerusalem so many years before. And if he was the Mukhtar, then the Jews of the Old City should listen to him and not to the bald-headed commander, Ezekiel.

And finally, when he believed what he was saying, he left his house and walked through the shell-torn streets to Misgav Ladach to find the man Ezekiel. It was late in the afternoon. The cloud of smoke held over the city. The *hamseen* burned the man's face.

Some of the pietists stood aside as he walked from alley to alley. Some took off their hats and bowed, for after all, Solomon Finegold carried on a thong around his fat neck the keys which had been thrown up to heaven. The women smiled at him to show they appreciated what he did for them. Though if asked, most of them would have had difficulty explaining exactly what it was that Solomon Finegold did for them or their families.

When he arrived at Misgav Ladach, Finegold stood for a moment at the entrance of the courtyard. The shameless girl with the blonde hair and the goyish nose sat beside another shameless woman with earphones on her head. Finegold had never seen this woman before. She was small and older than her companion. There was a weary expression on her face and he hoped it was mixed with shame for the shorts she wore and the shirt which revealed the flesh of her browned arms. Finegold crossed the courtyard and was about to enter the headquarters when the older woman came to her feet and called to him, "Is there something you want?"

Annoyed at being addressed by a strange woman, he decided to ignore her. However, before he could enter the building, the woman came between him and the door.

"Is there something you want?" she asked again.

Finegold saw that she was shorter than he, that she carried a Sten gun like the one the British had given his son, and that her expression was almost friendly.

"Madam," he announced, "I am Solomon Finegold."

The woman looked down at his feet and then slowly her gaze rose to his florid face. "Isn't that nice."

Not knowing what he was to make of this, Finegold explained, "I wish to see that man Ezekiel."

"Do you mean Commander Ezekiel?"

The fat man nodded angrily.

With a trace of a smile the woman shook her head. "He isn't here."

Finegold had not expected the commander to be away from his headquarters. He had taken it for granted the ugly man would be waiting for him. Unexpectedly he offered, "I have some food."

A broad smile crossed the small woman's face, and for a moment he thought she was pretty. "Thanks. We can use all of the food we can get." She did not ask him why he had waited so long to tell anyone about his food. Instead, she suggested, "I'll send some men over for it if you tell me where they should go."

Taken aback at the boldness of the suggestion and realizing that she had failed to understand him correctly, he explained, "I have food for sale. Two cases of canned kosher beef and three dozen sacks of flour." He thought a moment and added, "My son has a Sten gun with ammunition which the British gave him. I'm willing to sell that, also." Then, before she could answer, he tried once more to make his point clearly, "At a good price, you understand."

Kineret Heschel slowly brought up her Sten gun and walked toward the short man with the florid face. Two steps and the muzzle was prodding his stomach.

Frightened, he backed away. "You don't understand."

Nodding slowly, she continued forward while he stumbled back, afraid and unable to turn away.

"I understand," she said. "There are always people like you." She continued to walk slowly forward and he continued to retreat.

"Always," she said again. Then, as though she were telling a tale to an idiot child, she spoke so softly her deep-throated voice was barely audible. "Once I was in a prison in Poland. There was a man who tried to give me his dinner if I would sleep with him. Once I was in prison in Hungary and there was a man who gave his two daughters to a Hungarian guard for an extra bowl of thin barley soup. And then he tried to sell the barley soup for the wedding ring a woman had hidden from the guards. Once we were bringing some illegals across the line into Italy and one of them tried to sell all of us out to the British for a passport and fifty pounds so he could go to Canada."

She continued to walk and Finegold continued to retreat. His back came up against the wall surrounding the courtyard, and moving a half step closer, she jammed the barrel of her gun into his fat stomach.

"I will tell you what happened to those men," she offered. "I ate the dinner of the man in Poland before the other prisoners castrated him. We spilled the barley soup the man had received for his two daughters and then we left him alone to hang himself. When his courage failed him, his companions helped. And the man who wanted a passport and fifty pounds from the British was sent to their camp in the hills in the middle of the night after someone warned the British a member of the Stern Gang was coming. They emptied a Bren gun into his gut."

She rammed her gun into Finegold's stomach as hard as she could.

Gasping, Finebold doubled forward over the hard barrel of the gun while Kineret Heschel stepped back, letting him fall to the ground.

Then, before he could say anything, she asked, "Where will we find this food?"

Solomon Finegold felt the cold barrel of the Sten on his neck, and he belched loudly from fear.

"Finegold, you said?"

He tried to nod.

"Where will we find the food, Mister Finegold?" And the gun jammed into his neck.

"At my house. In the basement. I'll let you have it cheap."

"You are going to give it to us, aren't you, Mister Finegold?"

The fat man who had the key to Zion Gate about his neck and who had been selected by the British to be Mukhtar of Jerusalem could not bring himself to agree. "Cheap," he offered. "What it cost me."

Kineret Heschel forced him flat on the ground with the gun at his neck and then she shoved the muzzle of the gun into his stomach once more to be certain he was lying flat and still, before she set her foot on his neck. Very slowly she applied her weight. "Please tell us you are giving your food to the community," she asked.

Finegold tried to nod.

"Louder," she said. "I can't hear you."

"I'll give," he gasped.

Her foot came off his neck and she stepped back. Hertzela stood beside her, shocked at the violence of the older woman.

"Did you hear?" Kineret asked.

Zella nodded.

Finegold wanted to rise, but he saw the small woman shake her head.

"Get some men from the hospital and find that food," she directed.

After Hertzela had left them alone, Kineret held out one hand to help Solomon Finegold to his feet.

Frightened by what she might do next, he moved toward the table where she was pointing.

"Be comfortable, Mister Solomon Finegold," she said sweetly. "We'll be together for a while. And when the others come back with the food, I know Commander Ezekiel will want to thank you." Her smile was kindly, her manner gentle as she asked, "Now, isn't it better to give than to receive?"

The British officer stood on a roof of the Arab Quarter and watched the Legionnaires attack a house several streets away. The young woman who stood at his side waited to see what he would say as his men fell before a burst of Sten fire. Bedia Hassani had been observing the famed Legion for several days, and though she knew little about war, she was not impressed. There was no question that the soldiers of Jordan's Arab Legion were the best in the Arab world, and she had expected them to win more easily from the Jews. The small skirmish she was now watching seemed to be costing more Arab lives than it should.

Lieutenant Layton, standing beside her, drew up the fieldglasses hanging about his neck so that he could watch the fighting more closely. Shaking his head in disgust as four more of his men fell, he pulled the glasses from around his neck and handed them to Bedia. She refused them and stepped back. "I've seen enough."

Laughing, Layton said, "He should have taken the house two hours ago." Then he added, "I should be down there."

"But you have reasons for not going."

He winked at her.

She thought his blue eyes looked like glass. "We'll both go through the house after it's taken," and she started for the window through which they would make their way off the roof. Layton glanced back at the battle, shrugged and followed her. Once they were inside the mosque and alone on the staircase leading down, he reached out, put his hand on her shoulder, and held her firmly.

The girl's head came back against his chest. His arms encircled her and his hand cupped her breasts. He kissed her neck and would have turned her about so that he could kiss her lips, but she shook her head and laughed softly. "Your men are waiting for you to lead them to victory."

The young Englishman realized that she was mocking him, and he clenched his hand tightly on her breast. She winced, but she made up her mind she would not give him the satisfaction of protesting.

Layton's hands fell away and he moved aside. "I'll lead them in," he announced. He looked at her twice as they descended the steps. Bedia Hassani was a bonus he had not expected when he transferred from the British army to the Legion. He had not met anyone like her before. He had known other Arab women in North Africa, and he had even flattened a Yid his men had once found in an empty house. But he had never met anyone like Bedia, and while she thrilled him, she also frightened him. He knew that at least part of his fear lay in the fact that she represented power. The son of a village clergyman from Kent, John Layton had rarely had anything to do with people who held power other than the duke who lived in his father's parish and to whom he had been expected to show deference. He had known a general or two in his military career, but obviously none of them as well as he knew this banker's daughter. When they reached the door of the mosque, he looked about, saw no one, and kissed her. She did not resist.

When they separated, she said simply, "I want to see you take that house."

Layton shook his head. "You would be in danger until we secure the street, and you father would have my head if anything happened to you."

She smiled sweetly at him. "The idea of my father having your head is a tired cliché, John. I don't think it would interest him."

When they reached his sergeant, Layton asked how many men were still able to fight.

The sergeant, a burly man with a heavy mustache, smiled at the banker's daughter because he knew who she was and her relationship to the lieutenant. "There are thirty men, sir. I've now used most of them."

Layton looked over the rubble of a wall toward the house where his men were fighting.

"How many Jews?" he asked.

"Possibly twenty."

Bedia cocked her head to one side and looked skeptical.

"If Miss Hassani will permit me," the sergeant said, "the Jews were able to get some men in the other night. They may have brought in as many as five hundred reinforcements."

Layton agreed. "They've decided to hold this Quarter, and Glubb Pasha has decided to take it."

Bedia looked from one to the other. "I thought the Jews were getting ready to throw everything they have at Latrun," naming the strong point the Legion held which blocked Jewish reinforcements and supplies from reaching Jerusalem from the coast.

Layton nodded. Then with a smile, he explained, "They spawn like rabbits."

He and Bedia laughed while the sergeant looked the other way. He could not express his disapproval of anything the banker's daughter or the lieutenant said, but he had difficulty in his own ʳ ᵢnd with the notion of an Arab girl from a fine family being so open, so frʳ ᵢdly, so like an English or a Jewish girl. It just was not seemly.

Layton became serious. "If you'll round up your troops, we can get this thing over with."

The sergeant saluted and joined his men who had taken cover two doors down the alley.

Bedia watched him go. "He's a good man," she commented.

Layton nodded. "Once the Jews had me pinned down. There were probably thirty of them and Diyar came out of a building and together we fought them off and made our escape."

Having heard the story from the sergeant, she tried to match the Jewish force of fifty he had mentioned with the Englishman's thirty. Being a banker's daughter, she had a great respect for figures and assumed that there might have been even fewer Jews. As she thought of the Jewish soldiers, the one she had met some days before in the alley came to mind, and without thinking, her hand went to the back of her head where she had struck it when he had thrown her against a wall.

Layton was thoughtful enough to notice her gesture and recall the story she had told him.

"I'll castrate that Hebe for you," he promised. "He was called . . . ?"

"Zvi Mazon."

Layton only had time to nod. The sergeant was back with his thirty men. And the lieutenant took charge. Bawling his orders, he explained his plan to take the house. Bedia listened with fascination.

Ten minutes later when the Legion attacked, she was not so sure. Twenty minutes later, he was able to get the first grenades into the house and the Jews inside ceased firing, but by that time there were seven dead Arabs along the approaches to the building and Layton's shoulder was bleeding. Satisfied that the enemy had at last been silenced, he returned to her.

Knowing she was expected to show her concern, she looked at his wound. The skin was torn away where his shoulder had hit a rough stone wall when he ducked to avoid a Jewish grenade. The wound could wait. Taking her hand, he led her into the house.

Inside the small room which overlooked the alley where they had started their attack, they found only a single body. Layton walked over and toed the limp figure over. An old bearded Jew with payot and a British rifle in his hand. Bedia looked from the unseeing eyes to Layton, waiting for an explanation.

"The rest of them must have fled," he told her.

They found no bodies in the rooms beyond. The Arab girl paused at the last door they opened: a small bedroom with an old bedstead. The sheets had been removed from the puffed mattreᵢ. Slowly she turned until she had seen every corner of the room. It was a ʳ ᵢean place, a poor man's home. Seeing a small book on a table, she walked over and opened it and read: "So David and all of the people returned unto Jerusalem . . . "

Surprised, Layton said, "You read Hebrew."

Though it had not been a question, she nodded. "I think we will need to know all we can about these people."

Layton was about to say that the Jews would be beaten in a matter of days and that the victors never needed to know the language of the vanquished, but she silenced him with the comment, "My father thinks so, too."

He turned from her to the sergeant. "Place your men outside around the house. I'll use it as a headquarters until we get our next orders."

Diyar al Ilm understood, saluted and left. A moment later Bedia and Layton could hear him loudly posting his men.

Smiling at the girl, Layton put out his hands and took her in his arms. She came readily. The blood ran from his torn shoulder and felt warm as it soaked her white silk blouse, and it felt even warmer when there was nothing between her bared breast and his wound as they lay on the mattress a few minutes later.

After their passion was spent, Layton stared at the ceiling and thought for the first time in his life he had found out how a war should be fought. The girl curled up at his side was wondering why the British officer had allowed the sergeant to lead the platoon against the house; and if, so long as she was saying thanks, she should not have said them to the man who had done the fighting.

For two days and two nights Zvi Mazon and his companions kept the Legionnaires at bay. Having given up the fifth building and block in three days, he was determined to hold onto the large, rambling house in which they were now barricaded.

Looking out of the shattered window, Zvi saw that it was dawn. He knew the Arabs would attack soon. He knew, too, that only the afternoon before, the Arabs had driven an armored car into the center of the Quarter, several blocks behind him. Wishing he had a cigarette now that he had shared those Kineret had given him, he walked back through the rooms. Though they had once been well appointed, the furniture was broken now, the upholstery torn, cotton puffing out. This had been the home of a wealthy family. Ruth sat hunched in a corner, a blanket behind her head for a pillow, her rifle across her knees. She was no longer plump. Her blouse and shorts were both ripped and dirty. The scar on her forehead was livid, the bandage on her shoulder bloody. He knew she should be in a hospital, but he could not spare her now. Slapping the back of his neck in anger, he remembered the times she had shown courage when all anyone had the right to expect of her was flight. He knew nothing would wake her except an enemy attack. Days and weeks and months and she had to be so weary her bones ached as his ached. Walking out into the hall, he climbed the staircase to the room above where Avram lay stretched on a floor, his arms folded behind his head, his dark eyes starting at the ceiling. He did not turn as Zvi entered.

"I hear they are cooking chicken soup with kneidlach down at Misgav Ladach," he said.

Zvi smiled. "And they are going to top it off with strudel made by a real Hungarian. And when we're done, we're going to smoke American cigarettes and drink Napoleon brandy."

A shell landed in front of the old Jerusalem-stone house, shaking the building and throwing glass splinters across the room.

"She said it would not last," Zvi sighed.

"Who told you what wouldn't last?" Avram asked, finally looking at his companion.

"This job. My mother told me years ago this was no way for a Jewish boy to make a living."

Avram snorted. "But you're going to be rich. Two pounds a month."

"What's an Israeli pound worth?" Zvi asked.

Avram wiped his face with a dry hand and shrugged. "Less than an English promise."

Satisfied that Avram was all right, Zvi went to the next room where Moshe Gilead sat at a woman's dressing table looking at a row of bottles. He held one open in his hand and sniffed. Looking up, he sighed. "I wonder who the wench was that came with this perfume." He offered the bottle to Zvi. "For your girl up there," gesturing toward the roof.

Zvi smiled. "Somehow, I don't associate Dvora Rabsky with perfume."

"Why not? She's pretty. Put ten pounds on her and she would be real pretty."

"The others?" Zvi asked.

"Nachum is asleep on the roof," and he smiled as he added, "with your friend Dvora."

Zvi did not smile as he thought of the incongruity of the pair he had stationed on the roof the night before. Nachum had said he had soldiered with the Russians. Zvi believed this, but the man had never soldiered with the Jews, because he kept waiting for orders, waiting for someone to tell him when to move and where, when to eat and what, when to fire and when to stop firing. As each day passed, he became more mechanical.

"And Joseph Ben Dur?"

Moshe opened and sniffed another perfume bottle before he answered. "Last night he went out."

Stunned, Zvi repeated what he thought he had heard. "Went out?"

Moshe opened the next bottle and touched the crystal top behind each ear.

Sighing, Zvi asked, "When and where?"

Rolling the small bottle between his thin hands, Moshe shrugged. "He said something about not wanting to be alone. Or was it he did not think she should be alone?" He thought a moment before he added, "I think he said both, but maybe he was confused."

Squatting on his heels in the middle of the bedroom, Zvi slowly rocked back and forth as he thought about the man who had been a judge and the woman who was a hero. After a time, he said, "I hope they're all right." He was about to say more when he heard a strange sound. Running to the window, he looked out. Nothing. Whirling about, he dashed from the room to the ladder which led to the roof. Climbing quickly, he emerged under the sky.

Dvora smiled wryly at him. "Raise a flag. We're going to be saved."

He followed her glance. An airplane. Small. No more than a Piper Cub. For an instant he lost it in the haze and smoke.

"There," Nachum pointed.

Zvi saw the plane once more. Now it was coming toward the Quarter. Low. Almost skimming the buildings. There were two men in it.

The Arabs began to fire. A bullet ripped through the wing. The small plane banked, rose several hundred feet. From its side something tumbled out, rolling over and over. A parachute blossomed. Beneath was a package.

Nachum started to come to his feet so that he could see better, and Zvi, swinging out his elbow, knocked the Russian back on the sloping roof.

The parachute slid slowly down the sky. For a brief time the haze hid it and then it was there again. The three watched silently.

Then Zvi cursed under his breath as he saw the course it was taking between the matzo factory and the Wall. "Right into their hands."

The plane was climbing higher now and with it their hopes.

Another chute opened and they turned to watch its descent. It was farther to the south and west. Zvi squeezed Nachum's shoulder. The Arabs were firing again. Suddenly they stopped. The Old City was silent as both the Arabs and Jews watched the parachute marking the sky.

Somewhere an Arab shouted. A moment later there were more shouts.

Half closing his eyes, Zvi said, "Outside the wall and theirs."

"That break the illusion?" Dvora asked cynically.

"Illusion?" Nachum asked.

"Our secret weapon. The pride of the Jews. The invisible air force isn't invisible and still isn't an air force." She laughed bitterly. "Only we could come up with that."

As disappointed as he was, Zvi wanted to tell her he did not need her commentary. "Don't sneer," he snapped. "They risked their lives to try that."

She looked at him tolerantly as she said, "I'm glad we don't risk ours. I'm glad we're all tucked in bed by Mama."

Suddenly Zvi shouted, "No one asked you here. You asked in."

The girl chuckled and Zvi came down on his knees before her. Afraid the young man would strike out, Nachum grabbed his arms. Shaking the Russian off, Zvi reminded the girl, "You were offered out."

"You make it sound as though I were crashing a party." Then she was not smiling any longer. "All of you think it's your country. A private place."

Moving back, Zvi shook his head as he sought to be reasonable. "I'm sorry. You're welcome to die here."

Two mortar shells struck nearby and he fell silent.

"They'll be along now," Nachum said.

He was right. A moment later the Arabs attacked.

Though all of them were tired, none could sleep that night. Zvi lay sprawled on a floor with his small detachment around him. Dvora cleaned her Sten with a piece of cloth she had torn from the hem of her dress while Moshe Gilead stared unseeing at her. Ruth lay nearby talking softly to Avram. The two older men who had joined the squad sat in a corner and watched the flashes of gunfire through a window.

Nachum picked at his beard with a nervous hand while Ben Dur slowly shifted his unfamiliar weapon from hand to hand.

It was Moshe who asked if anyone knew what day it was.

No one answered. After a time, Zvi asked without looking at Moshe, "You got a date?"

"No. I was just wondering if I've spent more time in the Quarter than I did in my mother's womb."

Ben Dur looked compassionately at the youth. "At least we can move around."

Moshe shook his head. "Not very far."

Nachum disagreed. "I spent ten months in a room once. Five paces by five paces. I got so I was able to walk from end to end in total darkness and know just when I came to a wall. I must have been slow-witted because it took me two weeks to figure out that if I walked around the edges of the room, I could take a twenty-pace walk without turning around. Things seemed brighter after that."

"You were alone?" Dvora asked.

Nodding, the Russian continued. "That was part of the horror. Ten months and nothing human but a hand coming in to pass soup and a hand coming to take out a bucket of shit."

Zvi rose to his elbows and stared at the Russian. "How does a man keep sane that way?"

Nachum explained. "I played chess. Ripped up my shirt for enough pieces to make two chess sets. Scratched the boards on the floor with the eyelets from my shoes."

"Two boards?" Ben Dur was curious.

The Russian nodded. "I played a move on a different board each day, because, playing both sides of the game, I tried to forget the plan I'd had the day before." He grinned, "It was the best way I could work it out to be honest."

Ben Dur nodded. "I'm not certain how honest that was, but I think you can be credited with trying."

Zvi looked at the older man. The onetime judge seemed intrigued by the Russian's plan.

Several hours later, Joseph Ben Dur made his way through the alleys toward Misgav Ladach. His full face was flushed; his white hair shone in the night. Carrying the Enfield cradled in his arms, he looked up at the sky. There were no stars. There was no moon. He could recall other nights when he had sought a light in the vast expanse. Satisfied now that he would always be disappointed, he ducked into the shelter of a doorway as a shell exploded in the street.

Continuing on his course, he knew his disappointments did not matter any longer. He had made his decision when he joined the Palmach and entered the Old City. In the months before, he had been confused. A wry smile crossed his face as he wondered if perhaps he had been confused for years. The sound of the cannon mixed with the sounds of a gavel, and through his once orderly mind ran the specter of himself sitting on the bench of the high court in Prague. He recalled the dark wood where his hand had rested through so many cases, the panel before him where a predecessor had scratched the single word: *patience*.

The sound of the gavel mixed with the sound of cannon and jackboots marching. The court had been in session when they came, the six soldiers and the thin German captain. The spectators in the court started to shout, but Judge Ben Dur had gaveled them down while the Nazis marched to the bench and announced he was under arrest.

When the prosecutor stepped forward and asked what the charge was, the German captain, taken aback at the impudence, hesitated a moment before he laughed. The defense attorney rose to object, and a Nazi soldier struck him across the forehead with the butt of his rifle.

This was the first violence Ben Dur had ever seen in a courtroom. He could still recall the heavy breathing of the spectators and the shocked expressions on their faces. Rising behind the bench, he delivered himself of his final statement as a judge:

"Above all, there must be a respect for the law. It is woven into the pattern of civilization, and to remove that respect would leave nothing. No civilized man will create violence in a courtroom or to a courtroom. No civilized man will ignore the due process of law, because it is the single thing which stands between peace and anarchy."

And while Joseph Ben Dur spoke, the German captain attempted to drown out his words with laughter. In frustration, Ben Dur had raised his voice to be heard. The others in the crowded court silently watched the grim spectacle of justice dying before their eyes.

"Ignore me as a person, but respect what I stand for. Respect the law which is the standard of liberty, the living symbol of the moral sentiments of good men."

The captain ceased laughing when he saw the spectators and even his own men were listening to the Judge. Pointing to Ben Dur, he shouted, "Arrest that Jew." And then as two of his men came around the sides of the bench, he told the other soldiers, "Shoot anyone who is still in this courtroom three minutes from now."

Through the dimness of memory Ben Dur remembered rising and telling the others to clear the court. Thrice he struck his gavel, and as the Nazi took his arm, he declared, "Justice is adjourned."

He had been younger then. He had had hopes then. Five times he had petitioned to see his wife and children. Five times he had been laughed at or beaten. Then the Germans had shipped him out of the country and he had heard war had begun. Poland had been invaded. Word trickled through the barbed wires of the camp that England and France were fighting. Months and years and camps and prisons, beating and hunger and death all blurred together to confuse his weary mind.

Even now as he walked through the Quarter, he did not know how he had survived or why. When there was peace again, he had returned to Prague. The younger Masaryk was the first to tell him that his family was dead. His wife and children had been hidden by friends until a colleague on the bench had told the Germans where and who they were.

Feeling that neither the bench nor Prague was for him any longer, Joseph Ben Dur had taken the underground route to Palestine. One long night, crossing over an Alpine pass, he had settled down beside the woman who was leading them. They had talked. Morning came, and he realized he had talked for five hours, and he realized, too, that he had not talked this way to another human being since he had adjourned justice.

He had not known then that the slight woman with the delicate face was a heroine. All he knew was that he, Joseph Ben Dur, exile and refugee, had been able to talk to her, and that he, Ben Dur, the fat little man who looked fifteen years more than his fifty, had been listened to with patience as though what he had to say concerned someone. *Patience.* The word scratched on the panel before him on the bench. *Patience*—the only way he believed anyone would listen to his confused words spilling out after the dark and dying times.

The woman had come to Israel with him on the old Italian coaster. She had crossed the beach with him and taken him to her small apartment in Jerusalem. For three months she had listened while he talked. They had eaten together; they had walked together, but they had never touched hands. However, when the fighting started, she left him to rejoin Haganah. And he had been lonely until she returned. When she did, he told her he was going into the Old City with the Palmach because he had never seen the Wall. She smiled patiently and understood. And she came with him.

However, he still had not seen the Wall. When he was a boy in Prague and his father had served in the cabinet of the elder Masaryk, he had seen an old print of the Wall in his father's study. It was a clear print of the high Western Wall with the solitary figure of an old Jew, a *tallit* draped over his shoulders, praying before it. Sometime, his father had said, sometime a good Jew should see the Wall. In the years that followed, the son forgot that he was a Jew. The Germans reminded him.

A mortar broke the night, but Joseph Ben Dur did not hear it. He approached Misgav Ladach and, entering the courtyard, he asked a young man where he would find Kineret Heschel. The youth pointed toward the headquarters, and inside Joseph found her seated at a table. Kineret rose and asked him if he wanted a glass of tea. He shook his head and waited. Kineret told her companion, a young woman wearing headphones, "I'll be back. Keep hitting them for supplies." She smiled at Joseph and they walked into the night together, across the courtyard and down a narrow alley.

They did not know where they were going. They did not care. For the first time since they had met in the Italian Alps six months before, he took her hand.

Surprised, she looked up at him.

And he, afraid that he had offended her, dropped his hand to his side.

Kineret reached out, clasped his pudgy hand in hers, and drawing him close, she kissed him.

Impulsively, Joseph tried to enfold her in his arms, and clumsily, he dropped his rifle to the cobblestones with a clatter. Embarrassed, he looked from her to the weapon until she put her hands on his shoulders and drew him to her once more. Then he kissed her, awkwardly and tenderly. They clung to each other.

When she finally stepped back, he told her, "I came to tell you I am going to the Wall tonight."

At first Kineret wanted to shout, "No!" She did not. They had never asked anything of each other. They had had very little to give each other except patience, understanding and companionship. At another time, in another place, these would have sufficed. However, here in the burning Quarter she had other responsibilities, and they both knew the truth of the matter was that he had been rescued too late. Only the clear sharp print of the Wall remained in his mind.

Taking him in her arms again as though he were a child, she said, "I can't go with you." She wanted to say more, to tell him he could go another time, when the Old City was conquered by the Jews, but she knew he would not accept what both knew would not happen. Like so many others, they would not say what they already knew—the Old City would not be held. "I can't go with you," she repeated.

"I know," he assured her. "These people need you."

They were walking northeast through the Quarter now.

"For me," he said, "it is different. Nothing I ever knew has any value here." He paused to watch the side of a burning house fall. "Nothing," he repeated.

Kineret wanted to argue with him, to tell him that sometime there would be peace in Israel, but she did not know how to say this to Joseph Ben Dur, whose story she had listened to through that long night in the Alps.

A shell struck nearby, and Kineret Hescehl knew it was too late to talk to Joseph Ben Dur about the law and his future on the bench. She knew there would be peace in time. But as much as she loved this sad man, she knew, as he did, he would never sit in judgment again, because in some way he had died with the world he had known.

Suddenly a figure emerged before them in the darkness.

"Who the hell is it?"

"Haganah," Kineret identified them both.

The stranger warned, "They hold the streets beyond."

"Young man," Joseph asked, "how many streets to the Wall?"

The soldier calculated and then said, "Five blocks over the roofs."

"I thought I counted correctly." And he explained, "I charted the route in my head froom a rooftop today."

"You can't go there," the youth said impatiently.

Ignoring him, Joseph handed his Enfield to Kineret. "There are four bullets in it someone can use."

She accepted the rifle. After she kissed him, he put his hand on her cheek and said, "Thanks."

When he started to go, the young soldier reached out to grab his arm, but Kineret pulled the youth away.

Fading footsteps and Judge Joseph Ben Dur was lost in the dark.

"He can't . . . " the soldier protested.

Proudly, Kineret disagreed, "But he can."

When morning came, Zvi and his companions watched the Arabs raise their flag over the great synagogue called the Churva—the Ruin, because this synagogue had been established amid the ruins of centuries-earlier destruction in Jerusalem. And they wondered in silence how many of their companions had died before they had allowed this landmark to fall. The Churva was believed by many to be the most beautiful of all the synagogues in the Old City. Almost a century before a school called Etz Chaim—the Tree of

Life—had been founded in the courtyard there. From this school great rabbis had been ordained. And many of them had scattered across Europe to preach of the Old City. For generations the courtyard of the Churva had been the center of the Ashkenazi world. And now on this morning their school and its synagogue were no longer Jewish.

And now as Zvi and his companions saw the Jordanian flag with its three horizontal bars of black, white and green, marked with a red triangle at the staff and a seven-pointed white star, flying over the Churva, they knew that it must once more be just a ruin.

All of Zvi's people had gathered on the roof of the house. They could see Arabs in the area below, but they did not fire, hoarding their ammunition against necessity.

Zvi looked at them. The livid scar down the side of Nachum's face quivered, but the Russian combed his beard with one twisted hand while he rested his other on his hunched shoulder. Ruth jerked her head back to settle the hair off her forehead and stood tensed and defiant and almost beautiful. Beside her, Dvora's dour face showed no emotion, and Zvi could not decide whether anything that had happened had in any way touched the girl. She remained coldly beautiful. Avram's eyes were set on the Jordanian flag, while Moshe Gilead knelt, and, picking up a piece of broken tile, threw it across the roof tops in a gesture of frustration and rage.

Suddenly, Arab machine gun fire swept the roofs, Arab shells poured into the Quarter, Arab half-tracks moved from hidden positions and poured heavy fire into the last Jewish strongholds. The entire Quarter shuddered. Zvi's small detachment held firm. They did not return the fire until the Arabs exposed themselves, and then they only fired when they were certain they had a target. Every grenade had to take out a squad or a vehicle.

Five minutes. And then ten.

The firing continued.

The shells slammed against their roof and part of a wall holding it collapsed. Finally, they were forced down to the ground floor.

Dvora set her Sten on single fire, aimed with care and made each shot count.

Ruth held her fire until an Arab stood within a hand's grasp, and then she squeezed off her last shot, saw him look up in surprise, shout something she did not understand and start to walk away. He had covered half the width of the street when his legs wobbled and jellied.

Nachum stood with his back against a wall and fired through the window, slowly, mechanically and numbly. Five shots and his Sten was empty. He was about to move forward so that he could use it as a club when Zvi tossed him one of his own remaining clips. The Russian nodded his thanks, rammed the clip into place and, bracing himself against the wall, continued to select his targets. A British face appeared ten paces beyond the window. The officer was moving slowly; and, tracking his target, Nachum brought down his game.

Avram and Moshe had remained on the roof, dropping their grenades whenever the Arabs gathered in groups large enough to justify the expenditure of so valuable a weapon.

Kneeling, Zvi kept his Sten to his shoulder. Once he fired at a bearded Arab who looked as old as Nachum. The man's face flushed red with blood before it disappeared from the window. Another time Zvi waited until a mustached youth ran toward him, bayonet in hand as though he wanted to grapple. Taking a deep breath, Zvi held his fire until he could see the thin line splitting the mustache, and as the face fell away, he could see that he had struck his target.

An Arab emerged from a house two doors down the street and ran toward them with a grenade in each hand. Zvi squeezed off a shot. The man paused and then continued his race. Dvora fired twice. The Arab fell and the grenades exploded in the street. When Zvi nodded his approval to the Polish girl, he received only an angry glare in return.

"You wasted a shot," she pointed out.

The machine-gun bursts again, and Zvi heard someone behind him gasp. Pivoting on his knees, he saw Nachum's head drop forward on his chest, the Sten fall to the floor and the old Russian suddenly rise to his full height, extend both hands as though he were trying to reach something just beyond his fingertips; and then he slammed flat across the floor.

For fifteen minutes more the Arabs continued their assault.

Then there was silence.

Not a sound to be heard but the loudspeaker demanding surrender and the shells falling from the hills beyond the city.

Moshe Gilead and Avram joined the others and for a moment all of them stared at the man with the scar on his face who had once fought in the Russian army. Zvi picked up the Sten, removed the clip he had given the man during the battle, shoved it into his belt and told Avram, "I'm taking him back."

"He's dead," Dvora snapped in obvious anger.

Wondering if the girl were deliberately trying his patience, Zvi nodded agreement. "And he will be buried." Then, as though he had to explain to her once more, "I do not leave my wounded and I do not leave my dead." The others looked at him; his voice was choked, his face in agony. Very slowly he crossed the room and knelt in front of Dvora. Their eyes at the same level and equally angry, he told her, "I saw a Jew the Arabs had taken one day. It was a long time ago. A man no older than Moshe here or Avram. He was lying face down in the dirt. His trousers had been ripped off. When we turned him over to see who he was, we found they had cut off his penis and sewn it in his mouth. And there was a woman . . . " His hand came up to brush away the image which hung behind his eyes.

When he saw that the girl did not even blink, he said, "I'm sorry for you." Starting to rise, he returned to his knees once more. There was blood on her blouse above her right breast. Zvi stared at it a moment. Then, as he reached out to tear the cotton blouse away, Dvora leapt backward. Like a frightened animal her lips curled, revealing her teeth. She started to raise her Sten, but Zvi knocked it halfway across the room with an open palm. The two stared at each other without moving until Ruth placed a hand on each of their shoulders and pushed Zvi aside. "I'll take care of her," she offered in a voice soft enough to quiet both of them.

"If she has to go to the hospital, send her." He rose to his feet. "I don't want to have to carry her later."

Through clenched teeth, Dvora spat at his feet.

Ignoring the girl, Zvi nodded to Moshe, "I'll be back as soon as I can," and he lifted the heavy body of the dead Russian and left the house by a rear door.

When he arrived at Misgav Ladach, he handed the body to one of the soldiers standing there and went in search of the area commander.

Inside the headquarters room, Ben Ezekiel sat over a street map. Kineret Heschel stood at his shoulder tracing the movement of the Arabs into the Quarter with her finger. From where she sat in the far corner of the room, earphones on her head, Zella returned Zvi's smile.

Kineret watched the two of them before she nudged Ben Ezekiel, who finally looked up.

"I haven't got any," Ben Ezekiel said with a cynical smile.

"And you're going to get more tomorrow," Zvi countered.

Pleased that the younger officer understood his problems so well, the A/C poured him a glass of tea. "And what else can I do for you?"

Zvi looked from Ezekiel to Kineret, surprised to realize they were about the same age. "Can you brief me as to what's going on?" Zvi asked almost ingenuously.

"Would it make any difference?" Ben answered with a question. He started to turn back to his map when he felt Kineret's hand on his shoulder. Looking up, he saw her nodding.

With a sigh, Ben Ezekiel rose. "The same promises. And there are more wounded. I don't know how many. Some say there are six hundred all told. I don't know if that takes in the wounded who should be in the hospital and are still fighting. We've buried the dead we could bury. I think there are about a hundred graves, counting the forty you dug." He half-smiled. "I heard about that. The Neturei Karta came here to protest your forcing their young men to help."

Zvi smiled.

"The last of the plasma is spoiled. We're out of machine-gun ammunition. I tried using some rifle bullets. They jammed the guns. I think there are about fifty grenades left in stores. I keep hearing about desertions, but I think it is men who have gone from one place to another and can't get back to their posts. The Legion has a dozen armored cars scattered through the Quarter now. We found some coffee. Four cans. You can have one if you want it."

Crossing to a small cupboard, Kineret took out a coffee tin and handed it to Zvi.

The A/C watched. "Don't say you left here empty-handed."

A grin broke across Zvi's weary face: "But you're telling me I should leave?"

Looking up at the woman beside him, Ben Ezekiel smiled crookedly. "I told you these young commanders aren't stupid. Green and eager to get killed, but not stupid."

She was about so say something when a soldier entered. The others turned to see a middle-aged man who had come in with the Palmach less than ten days before. He already showed signs of the fatigue which was wearing all of them down. His once chubby face seemed to sag and the shoulder of his shirt was ripped away.

"Can I talk to you, Ben?" he asked, uncertain what he could say in front of the others whom he did not know.

Ezekiel nodded, introduced the three with him and said, kindly, "What is it?"

"My uncle—he's Rabbi Mitzenberg—asked if you would meet with him and some of the other civilians at his house." The soldier's manner was hesitant as though he knew he was asking something no one wanted to hear.

"Yussel," the commander warned, "I'm not going to meet with even your uncle if he wants to talk surrender."

The man called Yussel nodded. "I told him that. He agreed: no surrender." Then as though he did not want to be misunderstood, he added, "You scared the shit out of them with your threat to shoot. They believe you mean it, Ben."

Pulling himself to his feet, the A/C looked around. Zella had the earphones in her lap now as though she was waiting for him to ask her something. He stared at her expectantly for a moment before she shook her head. There was no news.

Turning to Kineret Heschel, he asked simply, "Will you take command until I return?"

She considered this before she agreed. "Take Mazon with you."

And he asked Zvi, "Will you come?"

Pleased that Kineret had remembered his name, Zvi nodded.

Ezekiel checked the pistol in the holster at his waist and walked out of the headquarters with Yussel. Before Zvi could follow, Kineret put a hand on his arm.

"A few days ago when you sent Joseph Ben Dur back here for some food, he told me you were a good young officer."

Zvi waited to hear what she wanted to say.

"Ben," she said simply, "is going to need all of the support he can get now."

Not knowing just what good his support would be, Zvi smiled.

"He left us last night," Zvi said, knowing she would understand whom he was talking about.

"He went to see the Wall," she told him.

Wiping his hot face with his hand, Zvi tried to guess what that would mean with the entire area in Arab hands. "I'm sorry," he finally said.

But the older woman shook her head as though to brush off his sympathy. "It's what he came inside for."

Zvi noticed the crow's-feet about her eyes and wondered when she had last slept. "Of course," he said, and then walked outside where Ezekiel and the man called Yussel were waiting for him.

Walking beside the Area Commander, Zvi noticed for the first time that the burly man rolled from side to side with the gait of a sailor. Smiling to himself, he wondered if this was a habit Ben Ezekiel would carry with him all his life. And then he wondered how long that might be, partly because he liked the man and partly because his own life was so obviously linked at this moment with Ezekiel's.

They passed a gutted building and were moving on toward the next when Zvi recalled that this had been the house where Fishel had found a piano. He thought about the bucket of water the piano never got and would never need now. Zvi was suddenly conscious of the heat, and he wondered if it was because he was nervous. The Arabs did not frighten him as much as the meeting they were about to attend.

"Here," Yussel said, stopping before a small house at the end of an alley.

Taking a deep breath, Ezekiel wiped his bald head, nodded to the others and entered the house.

A middle-aged woman greeted them. She tried to smile at Yussel, who introduced his aunt.

"This way," and she led them into a small sitting room. A half-dozen men sat uncomfortably on chairs and a sofa. Zvi recognized all of them as leaders of the Old City. And he knew, too, that all were rabbis. Yussel started to introduce the civilians, but Ezekiel cut him short.

"We know each other. What I don't know is why we're here."

He accepted the glass of tea his hostess offered him. His host, a slight man in his early fifties, rose to offer the soldier a chair, but Ben shook his head.

With his companions on each side of him, the A/C waited for the civilians to start the discussion. An elderly rabbi from one of the older synagogues put his hand in front of his mouth as he cleared his throat, and the others turned to him. Bearded, with a small, pale face, Rabbi Harov was obviously the spokesman of the group.

"It is this way, Mister Ezekiel. We think we should make contact with the Arabs."

Ezekiel remained silent.

"They know us," the rabbi explained. "We know them." He shook his head, dissatisfied with what he had said. "No. We think we have to make some provision for our people."

Seeing that the commander remained silent, the rabbi paused, nervously picked at his nose, and then started to speak haltingly. "We have responsibilities. It isn't just our families. It isn't ourselves. It is our congregations. They depend on us. They believe we can do something for them." He paused once more to think about what he had said before he went on. "My wife's hungry. People come into the synagogue to tell me who's been killed and who's been hurt."

He leaned forward, hoping for some reaction from the man who stood staring at him.

"Maybe if you could just talk to the Arab commanders and see if they will let us take our people out."

To Zvi's surprise, Ben Ezekiel cocked his head to one side and said nothing.

A second rabbi, whom Zvi knew came from a Sephardic synagogue, said in a voice louder than necessary, "We know you have your orders. Your men have been brave." And then proudly, he added, "The young men from my congregation have fought alongside your men. They have been brave." The rabbi shook his head from side to side while he thought about bravery, and then in a softer voice he asked, "Does everyone here have to die?"

"That's right," a third rabbi agreed. Zvi looked at the gaunt face, trying to recall where he had seen it before. The last time he and Ben Ezekiel had met with the good citizens at the Yohanan ben Zakkai Synagogue.

"That's right," the man repeated angrily. "Does everyone have to die before you will admit that there are more Arabs, that they have food, that they have guns and other things to fight with that you don't have?"

Zvi started to answer him, but Ben restrained him with a hand on his arm.

The room was silent while everyone waited for Ezekiel to answer the question.

"Does everyone have to die?" He repeated it as though he had never thought about this before.

To their surprise, he crossed over to the window, pulled a heavy brocaded drapery aside and looked out into the street. Somewhere in the distance there was a fire fight. Two heavy shells exploded. They were far away, the sound was faint, and a moment later he heard a third explosion.

The others waited for him to answer the question. Zvi wondered what he himself would say if he had the Area Commander's responsibilities. He forced himself to look at the rabbis. Where he expected to see fear, he saw instead a firmness, a determination on each face.

The A/C let the drapery drop back into place and then swung slowly about. "Does everyone have to die?" he asked once more.

And Zvi realized that Ben Ezekiel had, indeed, thought about this question.

"I don't know," he confessed. "Once I would have said our living and dying ... " his face was contorted with concern. "And by our living and dying I mean all of us—once I would have said it was worth it if we could hold this place." He fell silent for a moment while he stared at the glass of tea in his hand. Then his head came up. "I don't know about the rest of you, but for myself, I can't imagine a Jewish State without a Jerusalem, all of it, without the Wall, without our right to come and go because these are a part of our world." He said again, "I can't imagine it."

To Zvi's astonishment, the homely man seemed almost handsome as he explained how he felt.

"The Jewish State," one of the rabbis said, "that's madness, heresy. You imagine what you want. When the Jewish people are reborn again, it will be when He decides, when the Messiah comes and He will give us Jerusalem and rebuild the Temple, and we will have the dignity which comes with having been good Jews and with having had faith."

Zvi listened to the impassioned anger of the old man whom he recognized as the spiritual leader of one of the smaller synagogues.

"I don't think we came to argue this point," Zvi snapped.

The others turned to look at the young man whom most of them had ignored earlier.

Ben Ezekiel smiled at his companion. And when the heads all turned toward him once more, he said, "No, we didn't come to argue politics." He sipped the tea, looking over the glass at the others. Zvi could see that Ben was trying to organize his thoughts.

"It does not matter now what you or I think about the Jewish State. Israel exists. The Arabs will have to become accustomed to that idea, and so will you."

The old rabbi started to dispute the point, but Ben Ezekiel shook his head. "If I thought we could hold this city, I would answer you," and he was speaking to Rabbi Harov. "Yes. If need be, until everyone was dead." He watched their shocked expressions and continued. "But I'm no longer confident we can hold the Quarter." A smile spread over his face as he speculated, "Given support—yours among others—and the material of war, I could hold this Quarter until the Messiah arrived, or at least until our descendants outnumbered the Arabs."

"But?" his host asked.

Ben Ezekiel nodded sadly. " 'But,' and therein lies the problem. I have no 'but' and so if all of you agree that any contact we make with the Arab Legion at this time will be no more than that—contact, and not a discussion of surrender—I will go along with that contact when the times comes."

The room was silent while the rabbis tried to evaluate what they had just heard.

"When the time comes?" the Sephardic rabbi asked.

Ben Ezekiel half smiled. "I know that is vague. Believe me, I know that." He shrugged almost imperceptibly. "I alone will have to make that decision. And when I am certain that we cannot hold the Quarter any longer, you have my word that I will cooperate with you in making contact."

Rabbi Harov stroked his heavy beard and then shook his head. "I cannot accept that. It doesn't tell me anything."

Zvi was startled to hear Ben Ezekiel laugh.

"If you want the exact hour, I can't give it to you." Then, to be certain he was not misunderstood, "The moment I think we no longer can hold the Quarter, the moment I think the next death would be for nothing, I will tell you." His face set as he concluded, "And that is all I will say now."

He crossed back to where his companions were standing, while his host said to Yussel, "Plead with him. Make him understand all of these deaths are for nothing. Men and women are dying before their time."

"No man dies before his time," Ben Ezekiel growled. He sighed and added softly, "So long as there has been the slightest chance of our holding the Quarter, no one has died for nothing."

Two of the rabbis started to speak, but the A/C's hand came up to silence them. "When the time comes, you will hear from me." He pivoted on his heel and walked out of the room. Yussel's hands came wide in a gesture of futility as he looked at his uncle. Then he trotted after his superior. Zvi bowed his head in a gesture of respect to the older men and followed.

Once the three were in the street, Ben Ezekiel stood very still for a long time, his head thrown back as though he were looking at something in the smoke-filled sky. "I won't fault them," he said. "They aren't wrong. But if there is any hope, any hope of keeping the Quarter, we stand."

When the A/C's head came forward and he stared down at the pavement, Zvi could see tears coursing down his leathered cheeks.

"If we have to talk," Zvi said, "use my deputy, Moshe Gilead. He was with me when we negotiated with Etzl. The two of us talked with them all night and they agreed they would hold those parts of the Quarter they were in. We divided and coordinated our responsiblities. When Moshe talks, people will listen."

"If there's any hope . . . " Ben Ezekiel said once again before he started walking back to his headquarters.

The next day was the worst sustained by the men and women fighting in the Old City. The Bethel section of the Quarter fell. All of the Street of the Jews shifted over into Arab hands, and by the end of the day more than one third of the Quarter had been lost.

For Zvi Mazon's detachment, the day was different from other days only in its intensity. The shelling continued. The battles from house to house continued. The only real change came about four in the afternoon when a small boy found them trying to hold a street in the northern sector.

Holding his hand to a bloody shoulder, the child told Zvi that Ben Ezekiel wanted him to take his people to the Yohanan ben Zakkai Synagogue as fast as they could run.

Sending Moshe to gather the others, Zvi started out with Dvora, dashing through the noisy streets, the twisted alleys, over the rubble piling high now. When he approached the synagogue, he found that only a single small street separated it from capture.

Throwing himself down on the cobblestones between two houses, he prepared to cover the few meters of ground. Dvora took up a position at his side, bringing her Sten to bear on the same few meters of ground. They could hear the Arabs screaming. They could hear the sound truck offering open passage to the New City. Rolling closer to Dvora, Zvi said, "I'm going in. I've got to see how many are there." And, coming to his knees, he dashed back down the alley and approached the synagogue from the rear. Bursting through a heavy door which stood ajar, he sprang into the building.

Faces turned in his direction. There were old men and women, children and *yeshivah bochurs.* They stopped praying and turned toward the intruder. Embarrassed, Zvi shrugged and walked through the building.

It had been here that he and Ben Ezekiel had first listened to the proposals for surrender. The building was below the level of the ground, and this might have protected it from the heavy shell fire. However, checking the windows opening onto the street, he knew nothing could keep the Arab Legion back. There were no more than three paces separating the closest Arab line and the synagogue. Three paces from the massacre the Arabs had been shouting about for days and weeks. Three paces from a bloody end to what Zvi estimated to be eight hundred people. Whenever an Arab exposed himself, Dvora laid down enought fire to drive him back. It took Zvi a few moments to realize that what was holding the Arabs in check was not Dvora's Sten or his own but that they were not Legionnaries, only part of an undisciplined mob.

Across the way an Arab appeared and then another. Then there were a dozen. Dvora fired several small bursts, and when three other guns started firing, Zvi knew that Moshe, Avram and Ruth had finally arrived.

What he did not know was where the other members of Haganah who had been assigned to this sector were located and why they were holding their fire. Swinging about, he faced the rabbi he had listened to the night before. The old man half smiled, a gesture that said, "I told you as much."

Nodding to indicate he understood, Zvi pushed through the group and strode out of the synagogue. He did not know why he had felt so uncomfortable inside the building and why he felt so much more relaxed at the prospect of fighting in the open air. He glanced back at the synagogue. The people there had expected either nothing or too much from him and he was too weary to sort out the problem.

He swung to the right and around the building in search of another detachment. There had to be another.

There was an alley between the synagogue and the next building. In other times the alley had led directly into the small street which now separated the Arabs from the Jews. However, the end of the alley was walled up now and Zvi felt safe for the moment. From where he stood, he could see three bodies lying on his side of the wall. One of them was a woman. Very slowly, he approached the three. There was a rifle beside one of the men, and he emptied its clip and chamber, pocketing the bullets. The second had two hand grenades, which Zvi pocketed also. Then he turned and stood over the woman. She was lying on her side. Blood flowed slowly from the place where her arm had been attached to her body. Zvi looked about without realizing what he was doing. Then, when he understood he was looking for an arm that was not there, he knelt and picked up the woman's rifle. An Enfield. Five bullets left.

He raised his head for an instant, forcing himself to look away. For the first time in days he remembered that he had been struck in the shoulder. That pain had somehow come to be lost in all the pain he felt. Dropping to his knees, his eyes still averted, he reached out and patted the dead woman's body. His hand came to rest on a rifle clip, which he shoved into his belt before he came to his feet. Walking away without looking at the woman again, he realized he had not noticed if she were young or old. All he knew was that she had fought until she was killed.

Several paces down the alley, he collided with Kineret Heschel. She held a Sten gun in her hand. Her face, usually in repose, was tense. She seemed older than when he had seen her accept the command from Ezekiel only the night before.

"Where are your people?" she asked.

He stared at her as though he had not heard her question, and both of them heard, as though from a distant place and another world, voices at prayer. And mingled with the prayers of the Jews in the synagogue were the shouts of the Arab mob.

"Your detachment?" Kineret asked more gently.

Zvi nodded. He wanted to tell her that he was glad she was with him, but all he could do was point down the alley.

Puzzled, the older woman waited until he led the way around the rear of the synagogue to the alley where his people had taken up positions.

"Avram," he called.

The tall man rolled over from where he lay behind some rubble.

"Bring our dead into the synagogue. There's a rear door off its hinges. Take it inside and put it over that window," gesturing toward the one opening onto the street.

Avram's head bobbed. Then he crawled back out of the line of fire. After he came to his feet, he asked, "Couldn't someone in there have done it?"

Zvi ignored him and concentrated on the buildings across the way, and Kineret answered, "They don't agree that the Lord helps him who helps himself."

Avram looked at the woman for a moment before he asked, "You're Kineret Heschel?"

Embarrassed by the awe in his voice, she nodded. "Do you want me to help you with that door?" reminding Avram that he should be somewhere else.

"No thanks," he said, and he reached out and put a broad hand on her shoulder.

She knew he was not trying to be familiar, and she closed her own hand over his. A moment later Avram was gone.

Zvi looked after him and then smiled at Kineret.

Kineret nodded, understanding the affection unexpressed.

And then the Arabs attacked. Not all of them. Just a few at first. Some were killed, some dropped wounded, and the rest were driven back. And then there were more. Zvi emptied his Sten gun from where he stood. Kineret emptied hers, took two grenades from her pocket, and when a cluster of Arabs appeared at the same time, she lobbed one grenade into their midst. Dvora brought down three men. As though by agreement, both Moshe and Ruth held their fire in case part of the mob made its way across the street. None did. However, in the twenty violent minutes in which they tried, more than two dozen died.

Zvi fished through his pockets for more ammunition, and when he found none, cursed. "One of us has to go back," he told Kineret, wishing that she would go if only because he did not want to command the detachment in which she was killed.

Brushing a lock off her forehead, she smiled. "You want to get rid of me."

Realizing that she understood and was not asking a question, he nodded.

She smiled and stepped closer to him. "I'll bring back whatever Ben can spare," she assured him. Handing Zvi the last grenade she possessed, she backed farther into the alley and disappeared.

Half an hour after Kineret left, Zvi received the ammunition she had promised. Passing it out among his companions, he waited through the rest of the afternoon for the Arabs to attack again. When darkness settled over the battered Quarter, he relaxed for the first time. An hour later he left for Misgav Ladach.

Zvi reached headquarters shortly after nine. He had not eaten since noon. There was food, but he was too tired to eat. His legs hurt and his shoulder throbbed. When he arrived at the courtyard, he sat down on the cobblestones and rested. He was sitting there with his gun across his lap when Zella joined him. Looking down at his weary face in the semi-darkness, she asked if he was all right.

Zvi smiled wryly. "I've been better."

"Are you wounded?" she asked impatiently.

He thought the honest answer was, "No." With great effort he pulled himself to his feet and started across the courtyard.

"How bad was it today?" he asked.

Matching his steps, she shook her head. "There was one time this afternoon when Ben tried to figure out how it was going." She paused and turned to face him. "In one twenty-minute period we lost four and had forty-two wounded." She pointed toward the hospital. "It's filled now. More than filled. They are lying on the wooden seats in the synagogue waiting for the doctors to get to them."

Zvi nodded and they continued walking.

"And you?" she asked.

Shrugging, Zvi posed his problem. "They could have taken us this afternoon. Overrun us and reached the ben Zakkai Synagogue."

"And?"

"They didn't. Eight hundred people, and they didn't come. I'm not sure why."

Zella noticed that his voice was slurred and that he was having trouble talking. He didn't seem to be aware of it.

Zella wanted to say something, wanted to tell him that he was not the only one who was tired, but all she could do was put one hand out and touch his arm, seeking some link to him.

Zvi forced himself to smile at her and half stumbled into the building and up the stairs. At the far side of the room, Ben Ezekiel stood beside Kineret, who was wearing earphones and listening to someone. After a moment, she looked up at Ben and shook her head. With an angry gesture, she removed the headset and slammed it down.

"They've postponed again?" Ben asked.

She nodded, and Zvi saw that she was as tense as when he had met her in the alley. "They've got other problems," she told Ben.

He poured himself a glass of tea and turned to Zvi, who stood across the room. "I've never thought we were high priority, but to be bottom . . . "

In a comforting voice, Kineret tried to explain, "They're mounting an offensive someplace else. And as they say, 'There are only so many troops.' "

Ben Ezekiel looked at her skeptically, "From where I stand, it's hard to see the broader picture."

The bitterness in his voice was so obvious that she laughed.

"You want something?" Ben asked, as Zvi and Zella joined them at the radio.

Taken aback at the A/C's bluntness, Zvi nodded. It took him a moment to comb out the word, "Help."

Ignoring Zvi, Ben asked, "Will you tell the company commander I have to talk to him?"

Picking up the headset once more, she passed on the message. For a moment she listened, and then she insisted, "He has to talk to the commander." Silence while she listened. Then Zvi saw that she was not listening to anyone any longer, but merely sitting with the headset in her hands. When she finally looked up, she said, "He won't talk to you."

"Why?"

"Maybe the Arabs will hear."

"I don't believe it." And it was obvious that this rejection disturbed him more than anything had in months. "I don't believe it," he said again. He walked slowly across the room, his glass of tea between his palms, his head rocking back and forth as though he were in pain. When he reached the door, he rested his head against it.

Zvi thought his commander might collapse, and he started to move toward him, but Kineret grabbed his arm and shook her head. The only sound was some static from the radio and a shell falling in some far place. Suddenly, Ben Ezekiel's head went back and he moaned—loud, shocking, painful. A man who hurt inside and out. His heavy frame shuddered and he swung about to face the others.

"You," he shouted at Zvi, "go tell the rabbis I will talk to them."

When dawn broke across the Quarter on 28 May, it looked like any other dawn of that month. There were no clouds. The sun was bright. The smoke hung low. The hot breath of the *hamseen* burned the air. And the sound of cannon shattered the morning.

However, Zvi Mazon knew that this morning would be different. The night before, his detachment had been relieved of its responsibilities for the Yohanan ben Zakkai Synagogue and another detachment had taken its place.

Zvi and his companions had been pulled back to the courtyard of Misgav Ladach. They had been fed, and they had slept through the first full night in months. Shortly after dawn, Zvi had been called in to the area commander's headquarters. Only Kineret Heschel was with them. No one was monitoring the radio. No one was listening for orders from the New City. Ben Ezekiel had made his decision.

When Zvi emerged, he gestured for his squad to join him, and started across the Quarter. The others did not know where they were going. And Zvi did not feel like talking. His huge shoulders hunched forward as he walked slowly through the debris. Twice he paused to wipe his face with an open palm, and once when he turned to look at Ruth, she thought his dark eyes had sunk even further into his head than usual.

They had walked several minutes when Zvi heard someone running behind him and, turning, he waited for Kineret. Her face looked lined and aged beyond her forty-five years. In fact, as she matched steps with Zvi and Ruth fell back, the younger woman thought for the first time that Kineret Heschel was an old woman. Glancing to her right, Ruth noticed that Dvora looked at none of those in the small column, her eyes fixed ahead on nothing in particular. "Any idea where we're going?" Ruth asked her, more to say something than to get an answer.

The Polish girl did not even shake her head.

Sighing, Ruth glanced back at Moshe Gilead. He was walking steadily; his usually tense face was screwed up as though he were trying to avoid a bad odor. She looked at Avram, who bobbed his head to let her know he was aware that she was looking at him, and for an instant she wanted to kiss his whiskered cheek. Months, and not a complaint. Months, and not a word that was not encouragement—and surely he was as weary as the rest of them. Her eyes went front again and she saw that Zvi was favoring his wounded shoulder, one hand resting on it, and his Sten cradled in his other arm rather than slung.

Turning into an alley almost blocked with rubble, Zvi paused before an old house. Then he took a deep breath as though what he had to say had to be said in a single moment. Suddenly he wheeled about and told the others that they were to follow Kineret Heschel.

Puzzled, Moshe asked, "You joining us?"

"I guess you could say that," Zvi told him.

"Where are we going?" Dvora demanded.

Looking at her patiently, Zvi half smiled. "Soldiers don't ask questions—and all that."

An angry look spelled her face for an instant, and then before she could say anything, Kineret started off through the alley and the others followed. Zvi watched them go.

Following behind Kineret, Ruth tried once more with Dvora. "He'd have told us if he could."

The other girl ignored her. Shrugging, Ruth dropped back to walk with Avram and Moshe.

Finding herself alone, Kineret paused long enough for Dvora to join her and then walked on beside the girl. "You've been here too long," Kineret said sympathetically.

"I didn't complain," Dvora snapped.

"And I didn't say you had."

Both were silent for a time and then Kineret said, "That young man, Mazon, he's a good officer."

The other girl shook her head. "He's not hard enough to be a good commander."

Surprised, Kineret asked, "And you've known good commanders?"

For a long time Dvora said nothing. They passed two homes which had been blown up by set charges days before. Then Dvora said simply, "I've known soldiers. Believe me when I tell you I've known soldiers."

Kineret believed her and she wished she had never asked the question.

They neared the end of an alley and saw a street beyond, larger than most. Drawing back so that they would not be seen, Kineret suggested to Moshe, "Better position your people so they can hold this alley if they have to."

Moshe Gilead stood for a moment evaluating the position. There was rubble enough to hide a small army. But the way across to the Arab position was guarded on its flanks by two other detachments. His rugged face set as he tried to understand what he was supposed to do. Carefully selecting his positions, he stationed Dvora, Ruth, Avram and himself where they could cover most of the street. He looked to Kineret for further orders.

She merely leaned against a building and waited. From where he lay sprawled behind a row of fallen stones, Moshe measured the woman against the legend. He had never thought of her as old, but now, calculating, he was shocked to come to the sum that made Kineret, indeed, as old as his mother would be had she lived.

Kineret looked back the way they had come as though expecting someone. And Moshe saw that her face was startlingly delicate, almost like a porcelain figurine a girl he had been living with had shown him in a shop window. The figurine he was going to buy her when his pay came through. Two pounds a month. He was figuring how many months he would have to work to buy a porcelain figurine with a face as delicate as Kineret Heschel's when he saw her move away from the wall she was leaning against; Zvi was approaching with two others. Strangers to Moshe. One of them was an old man, the other was younger, fifty at most. From their beards and the long black coats which they wore even in the *hamseen*, he guessed they were rabbis.

The others turned to look at the strangers. Zvi nodded to Kineret. She glanced at her watch and said, "There's no need to wait."

"And nothing to wait for," Zvi agreed.

The two rabbis prepared themselves. The old man drew a stick from his coat, held it for a moment and then looked at his companion. The other man nodded and drew out a stick almost as long. Moshe thought they were curtain rods, and he wondered what anyone wanted with curtain rods. When he saw the old rabbi draw out a bedsheet, Moshe came to his feet. He started to say something, but he saw Zvi shaking his head. The silence was broken by a sudden cry, and they all turned to see Ruth sobbing where she lay behind a fallen archway.

Avram pounded the stones beneath him with the butt of his rifle and looked away, not wanting to watch as the two rabbis poked their sticks through the ends of the sheet, held it up and started toward the open street. As though by a signal, a hush seemed to come over the Quarter, and yet Zvi was aware that not a dozen persons knew what was happening.

The two bearded men in caftans and round hats walked slowly, stiffly, nervously forward. Zvi held his breath waiting for the first Arab shot, waiting for the sudden burst of gunfire that would bring the pair down. He wiped his face with his hand, hunched his shoulders forward and set the butt of his gun into his hip. Waiting.

Then a scream, "They can't," and a shot.

A single shot. The older of the two rabbis faltered, drew himself up and limped on, wounded.

But Zvi was not watching him any longer. At the sound of the gun fired beside him, he hurled himself upon Dvora, wrapping her in his arms and wrestling her gun up so that she could not fire a second time. She struggled wildly, her teeth closing on his arm, her eyes closed as though she did not want to see. Her strong legs wrapped around him and she tried to hold him still while she forced his head backward to bash it against a shattered stone.

Then Kineret was astride both of them, pulling the two apart and shouting, "They've gone. Break it up. They've gone."

Throwing Dvora aside, Zvi started to come to his feet. He was not even looking at her, as he scanned the empty street. He did not see the Sten pointed at him or hear the girl hiss, "I warned you. I warned you." But he did hear the gunfire and he did feel the bullet enter his chest. He wavered for an instant, rocking back and forth in surprise and pain and then he pitched forward onto his face.

Before Dvora could fire a second time, Kineret kicked the Sten out of her hand and slammed the butt of her own weapon against the girl's head. Dvora slumped and lay still.

Dropping to her knees, Kineret shouted for Ruth, who was already running across the alley. Somewhere an Arab soldier fired. Not knowing what he was shooting at, Avram emptied his rifle in frustration and fury. By the time Moshe reached Ruth and Kineret, they had Zvi's shirt open. Ripping off his own shirt, Moshe shoved it into the hole in his friend's chest and appealed to Kineret with his eyes.

The older woman slowly shook her head. She came to her feet and stared at the empty street for what seemed a long time before she called Avram. "Take him back to the hospital."

The kibbutznik nodded and dashed into a nearby house. By the time he returned with a door, Kineret had sent Ruth back to her post, Moshe to his and was herself standing in the alley, Sten in hand, waiting for the Arabs to react. Kineret waved Moshe to one end of the door and stood quietly while the two men carried Zvi into the Quarter.

A short time after they had gone, Dvora rolled over. Her hands closed on the sides of her head.

Kineret dropped to her knees beside the girl, grabbed her by the hair and brought her own face down so that their eyes were locked only inches apart. "I should kill you for that," she said softly. Then, in disgust she seemed to throw the other woman's head aside. "He followed his orders," she explained.

But Dvora would not accept that. "I told him if he touched me again, I would kill him."

Slumping forward so that she had to brace herself with two outstretched hands, Kineret shook her head from side to side in anguish. "I'm sorry, child," she said. "I'm sorry."

An hour after Zvi Mazon had been taken to the hospital, Ben Ezekiel appeared at the point where the rabbis had crossed into Arab hands. The small detachment looked to him for word of its commander, but the A/C ignored their glances and joined Kineret. Resting her back against a wall, she listened to the shells which continued to fall on the Quarter.

"Nothing?" he asked.

"Nothing." And then she asked, "What prerogatives did you give them?"

Combing his thinning hair back with his fingers, Ezekiel looked at her. "I'm not exactly playing this from strength."

"That's not an answer," she said.

His twisted face broke into a wry grin. "Be patient. I have no answers."

"And Mazon?"

Ben Ezekiel looked about him. Avram and Moshe were back at their posts. Ruth and Dvora were at theirs. "She did it?" he asked with a gesture of his head toward Dvora.

Kineret was silent for so long a time that he started to repeat his question. "I heard you," she snapped.

"You know about her?" he asked.

Kineret nodded. "I've met them before." Then, shaking her head sadly, "Do you think time will change her?"

The A/C laughed. "You're asking the right person. I couldn't know less about her kind."

He would have said more, but someone was walking toward him from between two buildings on the Arab line.

Moshe came to his knees, his gun on the lone figure. Avram checked the clip of his weapon while Ruth cautioned, "Patience," to Dvora.

The aged rabbi. He approached Ben Ezekiel and handed him a note.

Slipping back from the exposed position, Ezekiel asked, "Your companion?"

"A hostage," the old man explained.

Ben looked to Kineret for an answer, "For what?"

Sighing, she shook her head. "Read it."

Unfolding the note, Ben Ezekiel read aloud: "We shall only discuss military matters with military men. Send an authorized representative of Haganah should you wish to surrender." The area commander turned the sheet over as though he were looking for more on the other side. "Signed: Abdulla el Tel, Commander of the Arab Legion Forces of Jerusalem."

"Give the man two chairs," Kineret said mockingly. For a moment she waited to see what Ben Ezekiel would do. However, he merely turned around slowly. The smoke hanging over the Quarter seemed to bother him more than the falling shells.

"I remember once," he said quietly, "I remember once at sea when the sky over the water was so sharp and clear that it seemed to cut into a person."

"What? What sky?" The rabbi was confused.

"I know," Kineret said, ignoring the rabbi. "Once in the mountains in winter there was a sky I knew I would never forget."

Then, as though the older man was not with them, Ben said, "I have no authority, you know."

She nodded, "I know."

Then, after a moment, she offered, "I'll go if you want."

Ben reached out and rested his hand on her thin shoulder. "There's no one I'd rather have out there talking to them, but I don't need to tell you about Arabs and women." He half smiled when he added, "And Englishmen and women."

They fell silent again and then Ben saw her staring at someone or something. Turning, he realized she was looking at Moshe Gilead.

"You know him?" he asked, remembering Zvi's suggestion.

She shook her head: "He's Moshe Gilead. Mazon thought enough of him to turn his command over to him."

A low and bitter chuckle from Ben brought the rabbi's and Kineret's heads up sharply.

"You say that as though there were options."

Kineret shook her head while she rubbed her cheek with the back of her hand. "You could send for someone else. And would you know if he could do any better?"

Taking a deep breath, Ezekiel raised his voice, "You, Gilead."

Uncertain what was expected of him, Moshe Gilead slipped back from the firing line and joined the others.

Ben Ezekiel handed the note in his hand to the younger man.

After he had read the note, Moshe looked up and waited.

The youth's straggling beard, his intense eyes and the nervous way he seemed to jerk his head forward gave his whole bearing a tautness that almost frightened the aged rabbi who stood watching.

"You want to talk to them?" Ben asked. "Mazon thought you could handle it."

To their surprise, the youth shook his head. "I'd just as soon go on fighting."

Ben and Kineret smiled, but the rabbi protested.

"We settled that matter last night."

Moshe looked down at the butt of the Sten which rested on the toe of his shoe. "If you want, I'll talk. I won't like it, but I'll talk."

There was a surprising warmth in Ben's face as he said, "Just remember, you haven't the right to commit us to anything. You will go and you will listen and you will come back."

Both men looked to Kineret for approval as though her opinion were important to them. She nodded, and then she shook her head suddenly, "We've forgotten something."

The others waited.

"Finegold," she reminded them. "Both the Arabs and the British will deal with him." Turning to the rabbi, she asked, "Did you only meet with el Tel?"

He thought for a moment. "There were others there," he said, surprised to find himself answering this woman.

"Any British officers?"

"None," but he was answering the commander now.

Ben thought about this a moment. "Did el Tel ever leave the room while you were talking?"

Baffled, the old man considered the question before he nodded.

Winking at Kineret, Ben agreed. "He went out for his instructions. You," he shouted so that Ruth, Dvora and Avram turned to look back at him. "One of you get Finegold."

Twenty minutes later the strange trio of Solomon Finegold, Moshe

Gilead and the rabbi crossed through the square which had become a no-man's land.

For four long hours Ben Ezekiel and Kineret waited at the entrance of the alley which opened out upon the square. Ruth was the first to move. She drew back from her post, rose stiffly to her feet and without looking to anyone for permission, she stood for a moment rubbing her legs with her hands. Then she slung her rifle and started back down the alley toward the center of the Quarter.

Kineret watched the girl go and when Ben Ezekiel looked to her for an explanation, she said, "Zvi Mazon. Someone has to tell them if he's alive or dead."

Ben did not even nod as his attention turned once more toward the square beyond the alley.

Two o'clock became three o'clock.

Ruth found Zvi lying on a mattress on the floor of the Hadassah Hospital. The plain-faced girl asked the nurse if she could talk to him, but the nurse was too busy to pay any attention to anyone who could walk into the crowded building. "There are two hundred wounded here. Talk to whomever you want."

And so Ruth folded her legs and sat on the floor beside her friend. Someone had thrown an old coat over Zvi's feet. His chest was bare except for a wide bandage. His eyes were closed. Finally, he rolled his head toward her and smiled. "It's all over?"

Ruth shook her head. "Ben sent Moshe to parley with them."

A look of pleasure crossed Zvi's face, but then he winced at the pain in his chest. He stared at the dirty ceiling for a time before he said, "Moshe will do what has to be done."

"He's very able," she said. The trace of affection in her voice surprised Zvi, and without turning to look at her, he asked, "You like him?"

"I barely know him."

Zvi tried to laugh but the pain in his chest caught up with him and he closed his eyes, biting his lower lip to keep from screaming. "The bitch," he finally said. "The stupid bitch."

Ruth waited until he was quiet again before she asked, "They took it out?"

"Yes."

"And what did the doctor say?" Her restless hand went to his forehead as she tried to wipe away the beads of sweat.

"I'll live," Zvi assured her. "I'll live." Then, because he could not understand, he asked, "Why?"

It took Ruth a minute to realize what he was asking. "I don't know," she admitted. "I think Ben knows something about her, and I heard Kineret talk as though she knew something." Ruth was silent for a time before she added, "But me, I don't know."

Zvi continued to stare at the ceiling. "From November to May, and now we lose it." And then, as though it was important to be on record, "I'd have been willing to fight on."

Ruth nodded. The crowded cellar with its smell of antiseptic and death blended with the heat and she thought she would gag. "I think if they had asked, we would all have fought on."

Zvi tried to nod, but the effort hurt and he said, "No one asked."

The two were silent as Ruth watched one of the doctors check the pulse of a man lying two mattresses away. Sadly, the doctor closed the dead man's eyes. Wincing, Ruth turned back to Zvi. "They will still be fighting in the New City."

"I know," he said. Then, because of the pain in his chest and the pain he felt at being shot by one of his own, he started to talk so he would not think of anything else. "How it's going, I don't know. One night I was with Zella and she got a news program on the radio and we heard the Arabs had Kastel and Latrun, that the Egyptians and the Iraqi and Jordanians and Syrians and Lebanese had all crossed the borders." He was quiet for a moment and then he continued. "I had not thought about that for days."

"There were other things to think about," Ruth reminded him.

"With Kastel and Latrun they control the roads to Jerusalem."

She nodded, but he was not looking at her, nor would he have cared if she had answered.

"It's such a small piece of land, and two thirds of the United Nations voted to give it to us and where the hell does Egypt get into the act or any of the other Arab countries? Where the hell do they get the right to say if we can live or die? They never owned this land. They never lived on it. Even the Palestinian Arabs came late, but they came and they were given a chance to have their own country, too. And now . . . " His voice trailed off, and she could see that he had worked himself up into hysteria.

In all the years she had known him, Zvi had not been the kind to argue politics or question the state of things. He was Haganah. He knew why he fought. He had never had to justify it to himself or anyone else. She started to rise, and his hand came out and held hers. Settling back, she waited to hear what he wanted of her.

"I won't go on," he assured her.

It took her a moment to realize he meant he would not talk about the justice of it any longer. "Moshe should have been back some time ago," she told him.

"He'll be all right." Then, as though it was important for her to know, he said, "Moshe takes understanding. He isn't like the rest of us."

Puzzled, Ruth waited for him to explain.

"His father came here about sixty years ago and they lost one farm after another. They joined a kibbutz where his sister was killed in the Arab raids of 1920. His mother was raped before they slit her throat in 1929. His father got a bullet in the back ten years later."

When he said nothing more, Ruth laughed softly, "Different? That's the autobiography of the country. If you don't get killed in one place you get killed in another." She smiled bitterly. "Sometimes I think there are people who don't like us."

Dropping her hand, Zvi placed his own on the bandage as though he could stop the pain. Very softly he said, "Moshe is different. Sometimes I don't think he feels, or even knows that the rest of us do." Then, as if he had to justify his fondness for his friend, "He's almost a genius, though at what, I'm not sure." A warmth covered his words as he said, "When you're alone with him, you feel sometimes there is nothing he can't do." He fell silent, and all the while Ruth hoped he would continue.

"You known him long?" she prodded.

Zvi's eyes were closed. "Long. Through the war together."

In the large room in the Armenian Quarter where Moshe Gilead stood with Finegold and the two rabbis, Abdulla el Tel, the Legion commander of the Old City, sat back in his chair listening.

"And we think that the Red Cross should arrange the transfer," Moshe was saying, uncertain why he was pressing this point beyond the fact that he feared for the lives of the civilians and knew that the Legion might not be able to control the mobs.

The slight Arab officer with the handle-bar mustache nodded and smiled. "You are in no position to think anything. I gave you until three o'clock to accept the terms and surrender." He glanced at his watch. "It is now four."

Moshe slammed his fist on the desk between them. "You bastard. You know damned well we were picked up by your own people after we left here." He snorted and threw his hands wide as he appealed not only to the others present, but, by raising his voice, appealed to the British officers in the next room. "Treaty. White flag. The amenities of war. They may be small, but decent and honorable men observe them. You held the rabbi here as a hostage. Then you dictated terms. Then you gave us a deadline." His voice was raised and he was shouting, "But did you stop your mobs from beating us when we tried to return to our own lines? Did you furnish us escort? Did you make any move to prevent mob action?" He pointed his cocked forefinger at the Arab officer, who sat unruffled at the obvious display of Jewish rudeness. "Did you in any way control the mobs?"

The short, wiry Arab rose to his feet behind the desk and touched the tip of his mustache much as he had seen British officers do when they did not want to appear flustered. "I did not bring you here to debate. I told you the terms of surrender. You may take them back or you may be released to the mob. The decision is yours." He glanced at his watch again. "You have until five. After that we will attack in full strength and I cannot—I will not—promise to control the mobs."

Moshe Gilead looked at the nattily dressed officer, and at his own hands for a moment. His hands shook and he knew it was as much anger as fatigue. His head came up and his dark eyes met the Arab's. "Damn you," Moshe said so that only the two of them could hear him. He picked up the surrender terms from the table and walked out. The two rabbis started to follow him, but when el Tel shook his head, sentries stepped in their way.

Less than an hour later Moshe Gilead returned. The foppish el Tel was waiting for him, confident that he would achieve what he wished.

The young Jew had the surrender document in his hand, and without formality, he returned it to the Arab. The two old rabbis and Finegold, who had been waiting, moved forward to see if it had been signed. With an angry gesture, Moshe Gilead turned on the three of them. "You don't speak for Haganah," he half shouted. They drew back and waited.

The Arab officer picked up the paper. "It isn't signed."

Moshe nodded. "The Red Cross," he demanded.

Abdulla el Tel half smiled as he tapped the edge of the surrender document against his thumbnail. Then he sat down once more behind the desk and penned a short note. One of the sentries took it out, and the men waited. Moshe felt the heat of the day and the fatigue of months overwhelm him, but he knew he could not yield to it now. There would be time, time later, time in an Arab prison camp. There would be time to wonder why things had gone so badly when all they wanted was . . . And then the sentry returned and handed el Tel another note. The Arab officer read it, and looking up, smiled broadly. "I have seen fit to think the matter over and you shall have a Red Cross representative present."

Ignoring the courtesies which might pertain between their ranks and his own defeated position, the young Jew snapped, "Write that into the agreement and then I will sign it."

El Tel's small head bobbed back and forth as he waited for his clerk to pen the requested paragraph. When the Arab secretary was done, Moshe Gilead snatched the paper and read it. Nodding, he took the pen el Tel offered him and signed in behalf of Haganah. A moment later, el Tel signed and then offered his hand in some kind of a gentleman's gesture. Moshe looked at the Arab as though he could not believe what he was seeing. He smiled slightly and turned to the two rabbis. "That is it. You have what you asked for, and we are a State without Jerusalem, a Jewish State without a heart." He started to say something else to them, felt foolishly sentimental, and turned to face el Tel. "When you talk to your masters, remind them the

Jews have been waiting a long time. We can wait as long as we have to for Jerusalem."

Ignoring the others in the room Moshe started for the door. An Arab sentry moved to block his path, but el Tel shook his head and Moshe emerged into the afternoon sun. It was done.

Several hours later the Israeli troops drifted into the square which the Arabs had selected as the gathering point. In all there were forty men and women carrying weapons. Some of them were weeping and not all of those who were weeping were women. Some paused to look at the Legionnaires who stood guard around the square. These were the enemy and in this moment they stood between the surrendering troops and the Arab rabble. Twice the angry Arabs behind the Legionnaires surged forward and twice they were driven back.

Ruth Barovsky dropped her weapon on the stack of weapons. There were fewer than a hundred rifles and most of these were from the First World War. The Arab sergeant in charge counted fifteen Bren guns, but he knew weapons well enough to recognize that five of these were damaged. When the last Sten had been dropped on the pile, he checked off the number 40. At the sergeant's side stood the British lieutenant Layton, Abdulla el Tel, who was the commander of the Legion in the Old City, and a woman who traveled with the British officer. Across the square stood the soldiers of Haganah. Very slowly el Tel began to count the enemy.

"Forty," he finally shouted. "Forty."

Layton nodded. His count was the same.

"Ezekiel!" el Tel yelled for the Haganah commander.

His bald head raised, one hand tucked inside his shirt, the sometime sailor sauntered almost insultingly across the square to stand in front of the victors. "You called me?"

"This was all the people you had fighting?" el Tel demanded.

Ben Ezekiel slowly turned and looked at the forty who stood together. Kineret tried to smile at him. At her side, Dvora and Ruth nodded and looked toward Moshe Gilead, whose head remained high.

"That's all all I had left," he admitted proudly.

"You dog!" the Arab officer snarled. "If we'd known this, we'd have marched in with sticks in our hands."

Ezekiel looked at the British officer, who nodded in agreement.

Through the Jewish Quarter, Arab Legionnaires were scurrying from house to house and room to room to be certain no one was hiding.

In another corner of the square the Jewish civilians were gathering— men, women and children. The wounded were being carried into the square on stretchers, doors and mattresses. The civilians who brought them carefully laid the group out in a long line at the direction of their own doctors, who would go into captivity with the less seriously wounded.

Ben Ezekiel watched the arrival of the wounded as he stood with the British officer. The woman holding Layton's arm seemed to be enjoying what she saw. For a moment Ezekiel watched her face. She was lovely, and he wondered who she was.

Now the doctors were going down the line of patients. Without waiting for permission, Ben Ezekiel joined them. Several of the physicians were Jewish, one was Arab and one represented the International Red Cross. They stopped beside each patient, knelt while the Arab doctor confirmed the wounds described by the Jewish doctors. Several times they disagreed over how serious a wound actually was, and each time they allowed the Red Cross representative to decide if the person was seriously enough wounded to be evacuated or slightly enough wounded to go to prison. As he listened, Ben Ezekiel noticed Abdulla el Tel walking among the civilians. Gesturing for Moshe Gilead to join him, he asked what was going on.

Moshe shook his head and trotted off to see.

Then Ezekiel realized there were people at his side. The British officer and the woman. He waited to see what they wanted.

"There is one of your officers," Layton said. "He tangled with Miss Hassani recently." Shaking his head in disapproval, he added, "Struck her, in fact. Which one of these men is . . ." And he looked to the woman for the name.

"Zvi Mazon," she said.

Ben Ezekiel shrugged. "He may be dead."

Several of the Haganah women had drifted across the square to join the wounded. Zella, Ruth and Kineret were among them. Ben saw the three women were standing beside Zvi Mazon, and he shrugged a second time.

Dissatisfied with the answer, Layton took the Hassani woman by the arm and slowly walked down the line of improvised stretchers. Twice the Arab girl paused and then shook her head. When they reached the three women standing beside Zvi's mattress, Layton asked, "Do any of you wenches know a man named Zvi Mazon?"

Before they could answer, Bedia Hassani looked down at Zvi, half closed her eyes and walked on, saying, "He isn't here."

Angrily Layton followed her.

The Jewish women looked at each other.

Across the square, Kineret saw Moshe walking back to Ben and she joined them.

"Well?" Ben asked sadly.

"They are taking everyone they can pass as able-bodied."

It took Ben a moment to realize what this meant. "The Zealots, too?"

Moshe almost smiled as he nodded.

"With the wounded, how many will they have?" Kineret asked.

Ben shrugged. He could see el Tel sorting out old men and boys from the group and sending them to stand beside the men of Haganah. "They'll have close to four hundred if they count that way."

Moshe nodded. "When they take us to Amman, they won't want anyone to think forty Jews held them off."

Layton and Tel joined them now. For a moment the Arab officer stood watching the doctors and then he told Kineret, "You can start moving the women and children and wounded out now. You will go through Zion Gate."

She looked at the mustached officer who spoke such brittle English and shook her head. Putting one hand out, she touched Ben Ezekiel's bare arm. He nodded. She tried to smile at Moshe, who shook his head slowly. Then, without a word, Kineret walked over to the line of stretchers.

A few minutes later, the wounded began the move toward Zion Gate. The Legionnaires were lined up shoulder to shoulder to protect them from the mob whose shouts and screams carried over the column. Many of the wounded were helped by the Arab soldiers. And once when some Arab civilians started to throw stones at the wounded, el Tel told his men to fire above their heads. Four rifle shots were heard, and then silence.

A few minutes later the women and children joined the line moving toward Zion Gate and New Jerusalem.

Ruth and Zella took their places in the column, walking beside Zvi, who was being carried by two Arab soldiers.

The young squad commander looked from one girl to the other. He tried to smile at them and failed. With a great effort, he raised his head and looked back at Ben Ezekiel and Moshe Gilead. A few yards behind them he saw Avram. He wanted to call and tell them he would see them again, but the men carrying his mattress turned a corner and all he could see was Dvora walking several paces behind. Their eyes met and he shook his head in disgust.

A pain that did not come from his chest swept over him and he wished he was going into captivity with the others. Somehow and in some way, he believed he was letting down his friends and companions. Someone took his hand. It was Zella. She tried to smile. Her head was high and he, had he been able, would have laughed at the way her nose was tilted upward.

Kineret dropped back down the line and was at his side for a moment. "You're going to be all right," she assured him.

Zvi nodded.

The older woman kept pace as the column moved between the Arab Legionnaires. "They've been decent," she said. "Courteous."

"I'm not going to break out in cheers," he told her.

Kineret looked at him, and then waving Zella and Ruth away, she took Zvi's hand herself. "Don't cheer. Just be thankful."

A wry and bitter smile came over his face as he tried not to scream at the pain in his chest which stabbed more deeply with every step taken by the two Legionnaires carrying his stretcher. "I'll say my *berakhot* another time," he told Kineret.

"And when you do," she said softly, "say one for the girl Dvora."

Surprised, Zvi started to raise his head, but Kineret's hand came up and forced him down again.

"At fifteen the Nazis used her as a field whore from camp to camp to camp in a trailer. You can say a *berakhah* for a girl who has had too many men touch her."

Then Kineret dropped his hand, gestured for Ruth and Zella to rejoin him and took her place at the head of the column as they were moving out of the Old City through Zion Gate.

With great effort Zvi raised his head and stared at Dvora walking behind him, and then he closed his eyes and tried to see Israel without the real Jerusalem, the Old City. He wanted to cry out to people that he was sorry, that he had not meant to lose it, that he had done the best he could. Zella was holding his hand and pushing his head down. Then he was being carried through Zion Gate to New Jerusalem. And he was sobbing along with the two young women at his side.

Book II

WINTER, 1949 SPRING, 1950

YEMEN, 1949-1950

The last place in the world that Major Zvi Mazon had expected to find himself was in San'a. No longer the capital of that wretched corner of the Arabian Peninsula which was part highland, part desert and almost all anarchic, San'a remained part of Islam's past. Though the other Arabian countries were peeking into the twentieth century—even if only through heavy veils—they were at least conscious that time passed. However, Yemen was not only avoiding the present; through all the years since the collapse of the Turkish Empire after the First World War, the Imams had fought hard to block out the influences of the West as well as the East.

And now Major Zvi Mazon of Zahal, the Israeli Defense Force, was in Yemen. Not officially though. In fact, as far as the Yemeni were concerned he was not of Israel or of its army. He was a stranger passing through the land. Under normal circumstances, he would have been robbed and probably killed for no other reason than that he was a stranger. However, a few months earlier the Imam had been asked by the British if the Jews of Yemen could leave. The Imam had read the question written out on the formal document which had listed all of his exalted ranks—Ambassador of the Image of Perfection, the Controller of Affairs, the Prince of the Faithful, the Luminary of Creation, the Dependent of Allah, and the Incarnation of the Ancient Virtues—and beside the question he had penned simply, "I will not prevent it."

Insofar as he was able, the Imam did not intend to prevent the exodus of his Jews, who wanted to join their coreligionists in the new State of Israel. Zvi Mazon knew, however, that this did not solve the problems the Jews would have with the Imam's followers.

As he squatted in the small guest house which had been provided him in the Jewish Quarter of San'a, he listened to the rabbi, or mori, as his people called him, explain the reasons why the flight from Yemen would not be easy. Zvi rocked back and forth on his heels and thought about what the real difficulties were going to be when he tried to lead the medieval Jews from San'a to Aden.

103

The hour was late, the night cold. The small dung fire burned low. Accepting the wine the old man handed him, Zvi explained for the tenth time that day that he would be ready to move in the morning and that he would meet the persons who were going with him outside the city.

The old mori listened and nodded, and again Zvi was not certain he had been heard. His Arabic was good, but San'an Arabic was different and was sprinkled with biblical Hebrew. Pulling himself to his feet, Zvi raised his glass of wine, said, "*L'chaim*," and emptied the glass, hoping as he did so that he would be at long last left alone.

The old man smiled. "I will go."

Embarrassed, Zvi grinned. "We will have many nights to talk."

The older man rose from the mattress spread on the clean floor of the almost bare room and, bobbing his head, withdrew.

Finally alone, Zvi opened his shirt and stood for a time staring into the dying fire. For over a month he had made his way north into Yemen, wandering off the roads to avoid the towns and villages, and for over a week he had been in San'a. He was certain the Arabs knew he was in the city, but he did not know why they were leaving him alone. Shaking his head, he thought about the simple comment: "I will not prevent it." That was all he had between the Jews and a pogrom. How would the Arabs react to an exodus?

Zvi walked to the small doorway of the guesthouse. The building, like most of the others in the *Qa'ul Yahud*, the Jewish Quarter, was a single room. There were a few two stories high, but these were the tallest, because the law allowed no Jew to build higher. Though cold night air struck his face, he did not bother to button the front of his tan cotton shirt. In the morning he would put on a robe and try to look like the others, but for tonight he was going to be comfortable.

His head went up as he stared at the dark sky. For reasons he could not explain to himself, there was peace for him in San'a. And he had known so little peace in recent years, he enjoyed it. His thoughts wandered back to the fall of Jerusalem and his months in the Hadassah Hospital before he was released to fight again. He had come out in time to join the last battle of that brief war; and somehow he had been one of the many who had become heroes. Moshe had done as well, and in his own way the quiet Avram had done even better as a staff officer. But then they had had to wait until they were released from the Jordanian prison camp.

Now as he stared at the dark sky, Zvi thought about his friends: Ruth, who had married a refugee from Poland, and Fishel, the violinist who had given a concert only the night before Zvi had left Lod airport for Aden. And last of all, before he turned to look back at the dying fire, Zella, whom he had married only six months before. He did not know if he loved her, but he knew that he needed her.

The fire was dead now. The room was dark. Without caring about his own safety, he strode out into the small alley and down its unpaved way through the Quarter. At night the rest of San'a was forbidden to Jews.

Zella. Thoughtful and gentle. Zella was back in school now studying to be a physician. He knew she would be a good doctor and work well with children. He wished he were with her now. There was a sound in the alley and he turned to see two men following him at a respectful distance. Waving to them, he assumed they were there for his own protection and he walked on.

He wondered where he was going and he laughed at himself. Time, only two brief years, had had its way with his wounds and they did not bother him much now. Time had had a way with his memories and they, too, did not bother him much now. But what time could not erase was the restlessness which had come over him in the months after the War of Independence. Moshe had joined Zahal with the comment that he would see it through until the State could defend itself without him. A few weeks afterward, Zvi had also signed up. He, too, felt the job was not finished. Yet, unlike Moshe Gilead, he told himself that he had his own personal reasons for joining. Zella wanted to go back to school, and that would cost money. He wanted to be free of the problem of finding a job and a new career. After all, he had been in the service of his country since he was fourteen and that was more than a decade ago. To start looking for another way to earn a living made little sense, when he already knew one and he was needed. Besides, the army had promised him that some of his years in Haganah would be applied toward retirement. Zvi thought he had worked it all out logically. And at the same time he knew that beneath it all lay his own restlessness, his own dissatisfaction with himself and what he had done. Though some had blamed the defenders of the Old City for losing the Quarter and the Western Wall, everyone had agreed that the junior commanders had fought well. And as far as the senior commander was concerned, few condemned Ben Ezekiel now that he was dead of dysentery and buried in a Jordanian prison yard.

He heard the footsteps closer now, and once again he turned about. The old mori's young son was beckoning for him to come back. Seeing that he had reached the end of the Quarter, Zvi nodded and slowly returned to the guest house.

Once there, he glanced at his watch. One o'clock and the Yemenite sentries were calling out the hour to each other as they did in most Arab cities. The room was dark and cold, and Zvi was thankful that he had a blanket. Rolling up in it, he hoped he would be able to sleep and that he would awaken early enough to be out of the city before dawn.

He closed his eyes and rested his head on his folded arms. He thought of Zella again. She had been married to soldiers twice before and they had died. He hoped he could keep her from becoming a widow again.

The call of the muezzin awakened him and for a moment as he lay on the mattress staring at the whitewashed walls, he tried to remember where he was. His hand went to the money belt about his waist. It was secure. Rising, he quickly dressed in the blue tunic which hung down to his bared shins, slipped into his sandals and hung a shawl over his shoulders. He hoped he was tanned enough to pass for Yemenite Jew. Reaching into the bag he had brought with him, he perched the small yarmulke on his head and slipped out of the house.

Striding down the single wide street of the Quarter, he went directly into the Arab section of the city. Though it was no older than the Jewish, it was dirtier. Walking past several of the large houses which he assumed were those of the wealthy, he wondered if the Koran set forth the same standards of cleanliness as the Talmud and the Torah.

Walking slowly, Zvi realized that for the first time in his life he was a part of a minority in an alien world. When he had made his arrangements to come north from Aden, he had been warned that there were restrictions on Jews: no riding of horses, camels, automobiles; no carrying firearms and no rights before the courts.

Before him now was the Grand Mosque, a strange, not quite square white building with two tall tapered minarets. He wondered how old the mosque was and then, believing that, perhaps, he should not be seen staring at it, he walked on.

He felt a tug at his sleeve and when he turned he saw a tall Arab wearing a bright yellow turban. The man's face was lean and long. From the girdle which held his lower skirt in place hung the large curved dagger which Zvi had come to recognize as a part of the Arab costume.

Uncertain what was expected of him, he decided to let the other man speak first.

"Yahudi," the Arab said, turning aside to spit.

Zvi did not know if he was supposed to acknowledge the statement that he was a Jew.

"The Imam said I was to help you." The Arab clearly did not like the Imam's decision.

Very slowly, Zvi nodded. "Can you tell me what the Imam asked you to do?" hoping that what he was saying was right, and comprehensible in his stilted Arabic.

The Arab considered the question before he said simply, "I am a nazan."

Zvi accepted the fact that the Arab was a regular soldier. Trying to be friendly, he offered, "And so am I in my country."

For an instant the Arab looked bewildered, and then without warning, he struck Zvi across the face with the back of his hand.

Startled at the blow, Zvi's fist clenched and he was about to strike back when he saw the Arab's hand settle on the handle of the dagger at his waist.

Trying hard not to show that the blow had both offended and hurt him, Zvi smiled.

A mistake to compare a Jew to an Arab. Acting as though what had taken place was normal, Zvi glanced at the Grand Mosque and decided that he might be paying the Arab a compliment when he said, "The Grand Mosque is beautiful."

The other man turned to look at the building. "It was built in the time of the Prophet."

Zvi smiled. "It reflects his wonders."

And now there was nothing more to say. The two stood in the street with people flowing by the suq on the far side of the square. There were crowds about the stalls, which Zvi noticed were larger than those in the Jewish Quarter. They offered fruit, cheap tin dishes, hammered jewelry, chunks of unwrapped mutton and brightly colored cloth.

After a time the Arab soldier said, "You are going south?"

Nodding, Zvi realized his movements were no secret.

"I shall see that you are safe for as long as I travel with you."

"May you be blessed," Zvi said, hoping again his stilted Arabic would cover the situation. And at the same time he accepted the fact that the Imam intended to see that he was watched with care.

Zvi walked on and the Arab walked with him.

The heat of the early sun brazed the street, shimmering the distance as through a haze. Walking quickly to get out of the city, Zvi approached the main gate. High walls surrounded the town and for a moment he paused to evaluate them. The walls were little more than rubble and mud—perhaps fifteen feet high—but at their base they must have been at least two paces thick. Glancing along the top, he could see that the turrets were crumbling and that they had not been maintained in many years.

"The Queen City of the World," the Arab at his side boasted when Zvi turned back to look at the city before he left it. "This was the capital of the Jinn."

"Beautiful," he agreed, impressed by the medieval splendor of San'a, which lay in a high plain surrounded by mountains.

"There," the Arab said, pointing to the east, "there is 'Ishan and beyond Mount 'Ishan lie the alabaster and marble quarries." He turned the other way and pointed to the mountains to the southwest. "And there beyond those mountains lie the silver mines and the mica." The man's pride in his country made Zvi almost like him.

"Blessed be the Imam and his city," and Zvi felt like a fool saying it.

They walked south from San'a and fifteen minutes later, Zvi saw the Yemenite guide he had hired in Aden running toward them. The man slowed his pace when he noticed the Imam's soldier and waited for the two to approach.

Zvi's guide was a middle-aged Arab, recommended by the American from the Jewish Agency who ran the refugee camp just outside Aden. His English was understandable and he seemed to know enough to help Zvi manage the next few weeks of travel.

Uncertain of the protocol, Zvi introduced, "Ali Harja, my guide," to the Imam's emissary, and to be sure the guide understood, he said, "Ali, I want you to know the Imam has given us an escort."

The Arab soldier shook his head slowly as he evaluated the older man. Ali Harja was shorter than either of the others and his right shoulder was slightly hunched. The dirty turban about his head had come loose when he ran and a part of it dangled about his shoulder. The heavy rifle he was carrying had been left behind by the Turks after the First World War. His dirty cassock hung almost to his ankles, and the girdle which held it was loose about his thin waist. Ali Harja was not very impressive.

"You work for the Yahudi?" the Arab soldier asked in disbelief.

Ali Harja shook his head. "I work for Maria Theresa thalers and I ride a horse."

The Imam's man obviously disapproved. "I am Abbas Marwan."

Zvi wondered if he or Ali Harja were supposed to recognize the name, but Abbas Marwan did not seem to care.

"The others?" the soldier asked.

Ali Harja smiled. "This way." And he turned to lead them through a small grove of trees. Zvi waited for the soldier to follow, but instead he saw the man start walking back toward the city.

Puzzled, Zvi watched him for a moment before following Ali. Five minutes later he saw the Jews. They stood together in several family groups. Zvi estimated at least three hundred. Later he would make a count. Now he just wanted to see what he had. There were young women and old. They wore leggings down to their calves and below them, red putties. Many wore high-heeled sandals, and Zvi wondered how long these would last on the march. Heavy looped earrings made of hammered silver hung from their ears. Though their faces were bared to the sun, they all had silken or cotton kerchiefs tied about their heads. More than a dozen were carrying babies. Some met his look evenly, some shyly. A few, he thought were beautiful, a few crones.

Surprised at how much these women looked like the images he had of harem wives, Zvi turned his attention to the men. They, too, varied in age from the very old to small boys. All wore multicolored turbans even though it was warm, and the billowing Arab cassock hanging down to their bared shins. These men were dark and lean and small. Any of them could have passed for an Arab, and Zvi guessed that many were descended from the Arab conversion of the sixth century.

Walking slowly through the different groups, Zvi patted one child on the head and another on the cheek. He shook hands with the older men and nodded at the younger. One young woman was sobbing and he tried to assure her with a few words that all would be well. Coming to a stop before the mori with whom he had talked the night before, he asked, "Is this all?"

The aged teacher nodded. "Others will come another time. Many have already left."

The last part Zvi knew. But he wished that none had remained behind because he did not know when, if ever, they would be allowed to leave. He smiled at the old man, clasped his arm affectionately and moved on to the mori's son. About Zvi's own age, he stood with two young girls, one holding an infant in her arms while the other stood proudly beside a small son.

"Your name is what?" Zvi asked, wishing he could drop the Arabic inversions now.

"Isaac Ben Aaron."

There was an assurance about this young man which Zvi Mazon had not found among most of the ghetto Jews of Yemen and he liked it. "You will help me?" he asked.

Isaac smiled and nodded.

The mori, who had been watching, offered, "My son is the best silversmith in San'a."

"Besides my father," Isaac said humbly.

Puzzled, Zvi looked from one to the other. "Aren't you the mori?" he asked the older man.

Proud of the designation, the teacher nodded. "I am a teacher, a preacher, a shochet who slaughters for his people, a circumciser and a judge. But my work is all honorary." Then to make sure the young Israeli understood, he added, "There were nine synagogues in San'a and I was not the only mori."

Nodding, Zvi moved on. Each of the families had large bundles in front of it, blankets and pots and bags of clothes. Though he was tempted to strip the weight down now, he decided to let time do it for him. Then he saw the books. Dozens of them tied together in stacks and with them the manuscript rolls of the sefer Torahs. He stared at these for a long time. Probably among the most ancient in the Jewish world. He hoped they would be able to bring them through, and then as he looked about and saw the eyes of the others on him, he knew if anything or anyone could reach Aden to the south, these books and scrolls would.

It took Zvi a moment to realize that the Yemenites' gaze had switched to something beyond him, and whirling about, he saw the Arab nazan who called himself Abbas Marwan and five other Arabs seated on stallions, silently watching him. They were dressed alike and each carried a rifle across his high, caparisoned saddle as well as a cartridge belt over his shoulder.

Zvi saw that Ali Harja stared first at the Jews and then at his compatriots. The guide was frightened; the Jews were, also. For the first time since he had left Aden, Zvi wished he was armed, and then with a shrug, he realized a single gun would not make any difference if these soldiers wanted to fight.

Ignoring the Arabs for the moment, Zvi called, "Isaac, let's get these people in some kind of order so we can start moving."

The Jews had difficulty taking their eyes off the nazanim, and for several minutes none of them stirred. Then slowly at the urging of Zvi and Isaac, they began to string out into a column. When he was satisfied that there was nothing more he could do here, Zvi raised his hand to begin the long march south. However, before he could call out, the aged mori raised his voice in prayer. After a moment, the others joined him, chanting in ancient Hebrew.

When they were done, Zvi raised his hand again, but he did not have time to call out before Abbas Marwan and his companions trotted into the column, breaking it into pieces, shoving the women and men apart with the rumps of their horses until it was no longer a column but a milling, frightened mass. A child cried out. A woman began to sob.

Zvi faced Abbas Marwan and waited to see what he wanted. The Arab dismounted, shoved his rifle across his saddle and approached the nearest Jew. Zvi closed the distance between them to stand at the man's side. The Jew, a middle-aged glassblower, put his arm about his wife and watched the Arab closely.

Spitting at the man's feet, Marwan kicked the bundle that lay on the ground between them. "Open it, Yahuda."

The Jew looked to Zvi for guidance, and when the Israeli nodded, the glassblower knelt and emptied his bag on the ground. Clothes, some papers, tools and a small leather pouch. The Arab toed the pouch and held out his hand. The glassblower looked at Zvi once more and again the Israeli nodded. For an instant Zvi was afraid the Arab would lose his patience and strike the man, but when the bag was handed to him, he ripped off the cord and dumped the contents into his palm. Maria Theresa thalers.

Throwing the pouch in the glassblower's face, the Arab explained, "You are not going to steal anything that belongs to the Imam."

Now Zvi knew what was going to happen.

An hour later, the Arabs were satisfied that they had all the money and all the jewels that the Jews had planned to take with them in their exodus. The small treasure, dumped into a large bag, was now slung over Abbas Marwan's saddle. The Arab smiled at Zvi Mazon. "The Imam will not prevent your leaving."

With difficulty, Zvi and Isaac re-formed the column and finally at midday they moved it out. Isaac walked at the head beside Ali Harja, who rode on a horse while Zvi stood off to one side.

As the last Jew turned to look at San'a for the last time, Zvi trotted to the head of the column and sent Isaac to bring up the rear. They had reached the road and started down it when the six Arabs galloped by on their way back to the city.

Moving slowly, the long column passed the Turkish fort to the south. It was little more than a ruin, and few even glanced at it as they passed.

The plain of Sanhan shelved off to the south before them.

The sun was high.

Looking back over his shoulder, Zvi Mazon saw the line stretching out farther and farther as family after family slacked off the pace. He slowed his stride even more, wondering as he did so how long it would take them to reach Haziaz.

After about fifty minutes, he raised his hand and motioned for the others to rest. Before he could suggest they stay where they were, the families gathered in small groups and slipped to the ground. Several children started to shy stones at a distant rock. One of the women came forward and offered Zvi a drink from a goatskin bag she carried on her shoulder. While he drank, he looked at her face. She was probably no older than he, but there were lines about her mouth and her cheeks seemed to sag. For an instant, as the sunlight struck her face, he thought she was lovely in spite of the fact that she was aged beyond her years. In a self-conscious gesture, she shoved the tassled kerchief back on her head so that the sun reflected off her long black hair.

Seeing she wore no ring, he assumed that she was not married.

Zvi heard Ali Harja chuckle and turned angrily toward the Arab, who knelt in the shadow of his horse. The hunchback's small head bobbed back and forth as though he were enjoying a joke. Embarrassed for the girl, Zvi returned the waterbag.

"Thanks," he said.

She half closed her eyes and nodded. "We will reach Haziaz tonight?"

Zvi shrugged. "We should." He looked toward the south. "It took me only two hours coming north."

"But now you don't know?"

His hand went inside his robe as he scratched his stomach. "I don't know. We're moving more slowly than I had thought."

The girl nodded again and returned to her place in the line.

He watched her for a moment, wondering what she would look like without all of the heavy wool outer clothes and strange leggings which revealed so little of her legs. The clothes were not really new to him as he had seen Yemenites since he had been a child in Palestine.

Then Ali Harja was laughing again.

With great patience, Zvi glanced down at the guide. "You find something funny?"

The Arab slapped the side of his neck to emphasize his enjoyment. "That one might be pleasant," he suggested with so obvious a leer that Zvi laughed with him.

However, Zvi did not laugh long as he saw the six Arab horsemen behind the column and looking down the length of it. He wondered what they wanted now. The sound of the refugees rose as they, too, became aware of the Arabs. Shaking his head, Zvi walked back through the families, smiling at one and then another. Passing the girl who had given him the waterbag, he smiled at her and moved on to join Isaac, who stood over his wives so that his shadow lay across them and the two children.

"What do they want?" the Yemenite asked.

Shrugging again, Zvi moved on to stand before Abbas Marwan. "Is there something else, nazan?" he asked, his hands resting on his hips as he stared up at the mounted Arab.

"I told you, Yahud, that the Imam wants you escorted. You will be escorted." Again the spittle and this time at Zvi's feet.

"There is little left to take," Zvi suggested.

For a moment he thought the Arab was angry, and then the trace of a smile crossed his dark face. "If there's nothing else, there are the women."

Not knowing how serious the man was, Zvi tried to smile. "I believe a man like Abbas Marwan can find all of the women he wants to warm his bed."

The Arab shrugged. "Nights are cold in the desert."

Not knowing what else he could say, Zvi glanced at his watch. Turning about, he called to Isaac, "Let's move on."

They walked on through the plain of cactus and small shrub plants. The soil was white, the plants green, touched with red blossoms. In the distance, Zvi could see more mountains through a bluish haze. Hearing someone at his side, he turned; Isaac had joined him.

"Did they tell you what they want?" the Yemenite asked.

Lying, Zvi shook his head.

"They aren't likely to kill anyone," Isaac reassured him.

Wiping the sweat off his forehead, Zvi wished he had not worn a turban. "Why?" he finally asked.

The Yemenite chuckled. "Superstition. Fools. They think if they kill a Jew his soul will cry out for revenge on the Day of Redemption."

Zvi nodded. This was a tale no one had told him. He wondered if Abbas Marwan and his companions had heard it.

Almost an hour later Zvi saw Haziaz in the distance. It was nothing more than a few huts, an inn and several open pens for sheep. It was almost four in the afternoon and growing cold.

As they approached the village, Zvi saw several men coming out to meet them. Moving rapidly, he closed the distance between, because if there were going to be trouble, he wanted it to be as far from the column as possible.

Before he reached the approaching strangers, the six nazanim, who had been pacing their horses behind the column, passed him in a flurry of hoofbeats and dust. Zvi signaled for Isaac to stop the others and he moved forward alone. A few minutes later Abbas Marwan galloped toward him.

"You will not stop here for the night," the Arab snapped.

"Where do we go?" Zvi asked, trying to be humble and not let his anger show.

The Arab brought his stallion to a halt only a hand's span from Zvi. "They do not want any Jews in their village tonight." he thought for a moment and then suggested, "There are some fields beyond the village."

Nodding, Zvi gestured for Isaac to start the column moving once more. It took him another hour to swing out to the east of the village and make his way to the fields beyond.

Before the column broke up into family groups again, he shouted for all of them to stay in close, and as soon as they were rested, he told the men he wanted to talk to them. Twenty minutes later, there were fires of camel chips and dried grass. Women were baking beans and slicing onions and garlic. The odor spread over the field as Zvi watched the families settle in, spreading out blankets and heavy squares of cloth. After a moment he realized that many of these were the same turbans the men had worn during the day. The children ran about gathering more dried grass and searching for more camel chips. The men were putting on their phylacteries and prayer shawls and gathering about the old mori.

Several turned to see if Zvi would join them, and when he did not, Isaac invited him.

"Thanks," Zvi said, "but someone must keep watch while you pray." Then, with a seriousness that startled himself, he added, "And pray for me, too."

Isaac gave him a glowering look and asked, "Did the Arabs tell you anything you have not told me?"

"Nothing."

The Yemenite seemed to doubt this as he waited for Zvi to say more. However, Zvi was already looking for Abbas Marwan and his companions. After a moment, he saw them in a distant field and he started toward them. He had gone only a few paces when the girl who had offered him the waterbag earlier in the day stepped into his path. He waited to see what she wanted now.

"The Arabs," she said softly so that no one else about could hear, "If they want a woman . . ." And her voice trailed off.

Puzzled, Zvi tried to understand what she was saying. "Yes," he snapped impatiently.

The girl's eyes met his. "I've worked in Arab households. A servant," she explained without apology.

When he still did not comprehend, she shook her head at his stupidity. "It would be best if they did not frighten any of the other women."

And then he half closed his eyes as his head fell back and he looked at her as though for the first time. He did not think she was a whore. Somehow he knew she was not. His hand came out and touched the sleeve of her heavy cloak.

"Thanks," and, aware how meaningless this was, he tried again. "They won't touch any women in this camp."

Her head fell to one side as she looked at him dubiously, as though neither he nor any other Jew could stop an Arab from doing what he wanted.

"Believe me," the Israeli assured her. Then, he brushed by and, crossing the fields between, he approached the nazanim who were squatting on the ground beside their tethered horses.

The six Arabs circled a fire. Their leader rubbed the back of his neck as he watched the Israeli approach and laughingly told his companions, "This Jew claims that he is a soldier in his own country."

Several snickered, but one thin-faced man with a large black beard said simply, "The Koran says: 'If thou meetest unbelievers cut off their heads, until thou has made a great slaughter amongst them.'"

Zvi ignored the comment. Standing beside the fire, he stared at the Arabs. At first he thought all of them were chewing tobacco; then he saw it was ghat.

In a high, thin voice one of the Arabs asked, "Does the Jew want some?" holding out a ghat leaf.

Zvi accepted the flat leaf and rolled it in his hand as he considered what the effect of this drug would have on the behavior of the Arabs. He had seen the leaf several times before. A small shrub with a small dark leaf, ghat blossomed without a seed. Spread by cuttings, it was grown over much of northern Yemen and was as important a crop to the Yemenites as wheat or corn. The fresh leaves were rushed into San'a and other towns and sold for as much as ten to fifteen rupees to feed a day's habit.

"Chew it," the generous Arab ordered.

Putting the rolled leaf in his mouth, Zvi was repulsed by the bitter taste.

"It is our sovereign habit," one of the soldiers boasted.

"The bounty of Allah," the man with the large black beard added.

Zvi smiled. "Mohammed forbade the drinking of alcohol. Would he not have forbade the chewing of ghat?"

Abbas Marwan laughed loudly. "It is one of the blessings of life that Mohammed never knew about ghat."

The others joined in the laughter while Zvi smiled broadly, trying to humor them.

The taste in his mouth was not unlike that of a bitter tea leaf and he wanted to spit, but the gesture could be misunderstood. The pleasure of ghat was in the juice, as no one swallowed the leaf itself.

The six men eyed him and Zvi realized after a moment that all of them were as exhilarated as if they were drunk or had taken a drug for its jolting effect.

"What do you want?" Abbas Marwan asked suddenly.

Zvi continued to smile as he tried to think of what he could say. Finally he asked, "We will need to use the cistern of the village tomorrow before we move on."

The Arab considered this and after a moment he nodded. "I will take in two people with waterbags."

Shaking his head, Zvi pointed out, "That would not be enough water for over three hundred people."

The Arab's eyes seemed to darken even though the light of the campfire flashed unsteadily across his face. Very slowly he held up two fingers.

Deciding that he had to find a compromise that would save the Arab's face, Zvi suggested, "Ten times the two will go in to the village," hoping that twenty bags of water would sustain them for the day.

Marwan wiped the dark juice from the side of his mouth and shook his head. "Eight times."

Satisfied that he had done the best he could, Zvi bowed his head, turned on his heel and walked away. Behind him he could hear the Arabs laughing. As he made his way across the field, the woman joined him again.

Matching her step with his, she waited for him to say something.

"Everything will be all right," he said, as though he had accomplished something.

She put out one hand and took his sleeve to slow his pace.

He glanced at her with a twinkle in his eye. "Ghat," he explained.

The young woman's laughter broke loudly over the empty field. "You know ghat paralyzes their manhood for hours."

"I've heard stories." He started to walk on and again she was beside him.

Shaking her head at what she considered his stupidity, she said bitterly, "It isn't always funny. Have you ever been locked up in a closet waiting for some fat Arab to overcome ghat?"

They walked for a time in silence, and as they approached the large camp, Zvi said, "I'm sorry."

The woman at his side paused to look at this strange Jew. He was taller than she, a foreigner even though he was a Jew, a leader because he had come to take them to the Homeland, a soldier, rumor reported, though she did not know what it meant to be a Jewish soldier, and he was handsome in a rugged, almost stolid way.

"Just get us to Jerusalem." Her voice was low. "The one thing I want is to see Jerusalem."

Sighing, Zvi turned to look at the scattered camp. He had asked the families to stay close together. His broad hands rested on his hips as he watched a black bat whirl down the sky and then disappear. A milleped crawled over his sandal. And when he moved toward the campfire, he kicked his way through some dried iris, faintly yellow in the night.

The woman watched him for a moment and then disappeared into another part of the camp. Zvi walked among the refugees. One old crone put a hand out to touch the edge of his cassock as though somehow this would bring her luck.

A few paces farther on, Isaac Ben Aaron rose from the ground where he had been squatting.

"You will eat with us?"

Taken aback that he had not even thought about eating, Zvi put out his hand and squeezed his host's arm.

The Yemenite introduced his two wives. One no more than sixteen knelt over a pot of Indian beans mixed with red pepper, garlic and onions while the other, whom Zvi thought at least two or three years younger, flattened pitah on a stone. The brown Arab bread was still warm when she handed him a piece. Thanking her, he started to eat it when he saw the disappointed look on Isaac's face. Without realizing what offended the other man, Zvi knelt beside the younger wife and dipped the folded bread into a small pot of boiled butter. Isaac watched his guest eat for a moment before he asked, "And you do not say a *berakhah* before eating and after?"

Zvi suddenly looked down at his hand and was embarrassed. When he looked at Isaac again, he said, "I have fought for Israel and my people. I am willing to travel far to foreign places for my people and what they believe. Don't expect me to pray, too."

After a moment the Yemenite took Zvi's hand and pulled him down beside the fire.

"You must think we would not fight?"

The two wives set a large bowl between the men and withdrew from the fireside, taking their children with them.

"Have your people ever fought?" Zvi asked.

Isaac tore off a piece of pitah and slopped up some beans from the pot. After a time, he said, "No Jew ever fought in Yemen." Zvi waited for more.

"Don't," Isaac said, "don't think all was bad in San'a. It was our home. We lived there for centuries, tens of centuries. We lived with the Torah, we lived with our families and our wives' families, and life was quiet."

The two men were silent for a time. A cricket rasped nearby.

"There were Jews in the world who led worse lives than ours. I don't know, but I believe it must have been true." Then as though what he had to say would astonish his guest, he added, "And we traveled."

Zvi's head came up sharply from the campfire he had been watching.

The Yemenite smiled. "There are few roads in Yemen we do not know. We carried pots and ironwork, jewelry and glass. We peddled the villages from the high mountains through the Hadhramaut. We were allowed to sleep in some of the inns.

"And we knew and never forget," Isaac continued.

"You knew?" Zvi was holding the pitah in his hand wishing he had something more to eat than bean stew and dry Arab bread.

"That there would be redemption, that we would go home, that the End of Days is more than a vague dream." He was silent for a time before he continued. "We never lost faith."

Accepting the implied criticism, Zvi picked up a peach and bit into it. The sweet juice trickled down his chin as he thought about the small piece of life for which these people had settled.

"Your people started coming to the Holy Land a long time ago," Zvi said, wondering how much of the Yemenite exodus was known by these people.

"Eighteen hundred and eighty by the Christian calendar," Isaac said. "My father's father's brother went then. They walked to the sea, and at Hodeida they sailed in dhows to the great canal, from these they walked to Alexandria where they worked as carriers and cleaners until they earned the money to sail to Jaffa and from Jaffa they walked to Jerusalem and by the time they arrived a third of the women and children were dead."

Wondering how Isaac knew all this, Zvi waited to be told.

"My father's father's brother sent a young man back to tell us about it."

Zvi stared at the peach stone in his hand and, overwhelmed with anger and shame, he hurled it into the darkness. What Isaac did not know and what Zvi did not intend to tell him was that the Ashkenazi Jews who had lived in Jerusalem would not believe those Yemenites were Jews and had kept them at arm's distance for generations. Isaac would have to learn about life in his own way.

Thanking his host for the dinner, Zvi rose to his feet. He was about to leave when Isaac looked up from where he sat. "Havah is not as bad as she pretends," he said tolerantly. "The women do not like her. And the men do not approve of her, but we try to understand."

"Havah?" Zvi looked down, puzzled.

"The woman you were talking to."

Waiting for the other man to say what was going to be said, Zvi shoved back the turban on his head so that the cold night air could reach it.

"There were Arabs who made her come to work in their homes. Some of them were kind and paid her for her work. Others did not. Some of them were good men. Others were not." And Isaac had had his say.

Zvi looked patiently at the Yemenite. "I will remember that some men are good and some men are not."

And Isaac's laughter followed Zvi through the camp as he went in search of his hunchbacked Arab on whose horse his own gear had been tied.

Ten minutes later Zvi located his guide outside the small village. When the Arab came slowly to his feet, Zvi explained, "I came for my things."

The Arab shrugged, indicating that Zvi could take care of the matter himself. For a moment Zvi almost felt sorry for this small, ugly man. He untied his gear from the horse's saddle, swung it over his shoulder and returned to the camp. As he walked, two small boys joined him. The taller, payot—long sidecurls—pushed behind his ear, asked, "Can I carry your baggage?"

Surprised at the generosity, Zvi started to hand the child his gear when he heard a woman laugh, "Give it to them and you will have none of it left by morning."

He recognized the voice of the woman whom Isaac had called Havah. Annoyed that she was following him, he handed his gear to the youth beside him and paused long enough to point toward a small rise to the east of the camp. "Set it there, *chaver*."

The two boys smiled and trotted ahead with the large bag between them. Zvi waited for the woman to walk at his side as he had already learned she would. Looking after the two boys in the darkness, she let her head fall back as she laughed again.

"Sheep are for shearing."

Zvi was too tired to argue with her now. He had been on his feet since he had first awakened in San'a. Now that it was dark he intended to rest. Ignoring the woman, he followed the boys. Havah walked silently beside him.

They made their way around the edge of the camp and were climbing the small knoll when she asked, "That Arab who works with you, you trust him?"

Zvi chuckled. "He gets paid when we get to Aden."

"And if we don't?"

"He cries for it." The Israeli thought about this and then added, "Or if there are those who think he sold me out, he gets his throat cut in the bargain."

They were on the top of the knoll now and Zvi's large bag lay open. Neither of the two boys was in sight. Dropping to his knees, Zvi checked over his belongings. Most of them were there. A camera was missing, but he did not mind. Several pairs of undershorts as well as socks were missing, but he would survive without these.

The woman stood with her hands on her hips smiling at him. "You've been sheared?" she asked.

Looking up at her as he spread his blankets, Zvi shook his head.

She dropped to her knees beside him and without a word carefully laid out the several blankets. When she was done, she turned on her knees and looked at him, her eyes only inches from his. "You'll be all right."

He waited for her to explain.

"The other women are wives or daughters . . ." And her voice trailed off.

"And you?"

"I'm Havah."

"I'm Zvi," he said, "but that doesn't tell you anything."

She nodded slowly as though what he had said was important. "You are leading our people out of the wilderness. You are taking us to the land He gave us. You are supposed to be a soldier." A smile crossed her face and even in the faint light of the sky he thought she must once have been beautiful. She looked old for her years now, and she was obviously as weary as he.

"I don't need any taking care of," he told her. Then as if it summed up everything he felt at this moment under this dark and foreign sky, he added, "I'm tired."

Havah laughed again, and Zvi wondered why everything seemed so funny to her. "You sound as old as the mori, but you aren't much older than his daughters-in-law."

Zvi wanted to protest, decided he was ready to sleep, dropped full length on the blanket and said, "If you will wake me in the morning . . ." He waited to hear the woman walk away. Instead, she jerked one of the blankets out from under him, spread it over him and then crawled under it, setting her body against his. One arm came over his side and she drew herself close to him. He felt her breasts soft against his back and knew the smell of incense as her arm tightened about him. Startled, he wanted to push her away. From what he had always heard, the Yemenite Jews were puritan, simple, moral, and he did not want to alienate them now that they were depending on him.

He started to turn, to say something, but she whispered, "Rest, you idiot. Rest. They don't like Havah, but they won't blame you for what she is."

He opened his eyes and saw the far horizon. For an instant he thought he should be up posting sentries, and then he remembered they would not be of much use. A few minutes later, he closed his eyes. The woman's arm about him relaxed and he fell asleep.

Later, he recalled having known her sometime during the night, but when he awakened in the morning she was gone and his gear was all packed in his bag except for the blankets in which he lay. He thought for a moment of Zella. When there was time he would worry about it. Now there was no time.

Throwing aside the blankets, he saw his sandals together beside them as well as his missing underwear and camera. Havah had been busy. Pleased that he did not have to thank her, he finished packing his bag.

Twenty minutes later they had the column moving again.

South toward Wa'lan.

The mountain peaks high, the winds cold, the earth barren. Then down into the Wadi Khabbah with the heat rising, the sun bright off the rocks. The dead river valley wild with loose stones and twisted rock.

The wind again, colder off the peaks, the dust rising and the sand shifting and suddenly the way down and a plain spread before them.

And the column crawling south with Mount Samarah behind them now and the winds dying slowly and the heat rising fast and the sweat of the long march.

Cold meals, cold beans and garlic eaten with onions and pitah.

The blankets thin and the women with their men huddled and comforted and the children crying from the cold or the heat.

And suddenly the land fertile after days of drought, suddenly the land damp and cool and the breeze gentle and the banana groves bright and orange gardens with walnut trees and the scent of almond.

South and fatigue setting in like an illness for which no one knows the cure and which each man fears to mention because it could spread like a contagion.

The Jews were leaving now. They had been in Yemen since the first Diaspora and possibly earlier. They had come to trade and remained. Others had followed in increasing numbers through the second and third Diasporas. And by the sixth century their religious influence was so great that some Yemeni rulers converted to Judaism, taking whole tribes into the new religion with them. What might politically have meant much to the Yemenite Jews was shattered by the jolting impact of Islam upon the Middle East, and with it the conversion of the Yemenites to the new religion which burned its way through the deserts and the highlands. When the first fanatic fires had died down, the country was Moslem with a remnant of Jews, who would always suffer because of that earlier conversion.

And yet to the Yemenites, their Jews were important. They were the craftsmen; they were the tradesmen. They worked and they served. And even the Koran directed the Moslems to have Jews to whom they could be kind. More important than anything else to the isolated peoples of Yemen, the Jews made their weapons and their jewelry. For the loss of such skills Zvi knew the Yemenites were going to demand recompense.

Past Khadir through the wadi with the high narrow walls, the deep gorge which funnels the hot winds like a bellows.

Into the plain of Jahran hard by the mud village of Ma'bar and the afternoon late, the water short and the women weary.

Zvi gestured for Isaac to break up the column, and now after five days which should have been no more than three he was going to stop for Shabbat. Zvi knew that he should be covering more ground each day, but he did not know how that could be done with the women and children walking so slowly and the Arabs denying them the use of the road for miles at a time.

Seating himself on a rock, he watched the families make camp. What had been difficult the first night was almost routine now.

Isaac was with his wives and the men were preparing for Shabbat. None bothered Zvi about this. After the first days few even noticed he was not with them at prayers. Those who did tried several times to bring him into the fold, but Isaac intervened, and now Zvi was left to himself. Off in the distance near the mud-hut village, he could see a small herd of goats. His hand went inside his cassock and he fumbled with his money belt. So far it had gone undetected, though he assumed that Havah knew he wore it. Pulling several small coins out of the pouch as he appeared to be scratching his stomach, he held them in his hand for a moment. Probably there would be better use for these coins later, but at this moment he knew what he wanted and what he thought the refugees needed.

Rising, he looked about the scattered camp. Several children paused in their play to look at the man who was not praying with their fathers. One of the women shook her head as she watched him stride by toward the small village. Zvi had gone only a few paces when he paused, looked around and then waved for Havah, who was building a fire for two old women, to join him. She ignored his gesture until the fire was burning and then she made her way through the camp at her own pace. He smiled slightly at her deliberate independence. Unlike the other women, she had pushed the shawl back from her head so that her long black hair could be seen. Her stride was long; and with her head up, he thought again that she was a good-looking woman. The short coat which hung loose seemed to reveal more than it covered; however, the haremlike pants which came half way down her calf covered her long legs. When she reached him, she set her hands on her hips and waited for instructions. It was the first time that he had ever singled her out in front of the entire camp, and now he was aware that all the women and children were watching.

Taking a deep breath and feeling like a fool, Zvi gestured toward the village. "There are sheep there. Take this and see if you can buy about a half dozen." Then as if he had to explain, "We're going to need all the strength we can muster to get through to Aden."

Havah looked at the coins in his open palm and then into his face. "Is this the best way to spend that money?"

"Damn it, I'm not asking your opinion. Can you bargain for those sheep better than I?"

Her loud laughter shattered over the camp, and the men, who had completed their prayers and were removing their phylacteries, looked up at the two.

In anger and embarrassment, Zvi waved for Isaac to join him. A moment later, his prayer shawl rolled under his arm, the silversmith crossed the field. Everyone in the camp was watching. "Can you buy some sheep for dinner tonight?" Zvi asked the silversmith. "I could," he explained, "but I'm not sure what one pays for things here, and we haven't very much money."

Isaac's hand ran down the length of his straggling beard as he thought about this. After a time he said, "The price of a lamb should be measured against passage through a village and so many miles of toll on a road."

Sighing as he tried not to see the smile on Havah's face, Zvi considered shoving the coins into a pocket, but instead he remained firm. "Are you going to buy them or am I?"

Isaac looked distastefully at Havah. "Let the woman try. If she does not do well, then I shall try."

Satisfied, Zvi held the coins out again. With a shrug, Havah accepted the coins and started off across the open field.

Scratching his stomach, Zvi kept his eyes on Havah, who was talking to the Arab shepherd. He hoped Marwan and his companions did not notice that money was going to change hands.

Isaac was speaking to him. "All the time a man is traveling he should be careful so that he does not break off the holy union and be left imperfect and deprived of the female. And he is good and safe so long as the heavenly mate is with him. And when he returns home, he should give his wife pleasure because it was she who helped him obtain the heavenly union."

Across the field, Zvi could see the shepherd culling sheep from the flock. Without bothering to look at Isaac at his side, he asked, "Who was the one who asked me to be tolerant of the woman called Havah and who told me her name?"

Isaac weighed the question before he answered, "Tolerance and dalliance are not the same thing."

Zvi laughed softly. "She is not married?"

Slowly, Isaac shook his head.

"She is not betrothed?"

Again, the Yemenite shook his head.

"Then there isn't anyone going to be hurt." But as he finished his explanation, Zvi lost his temper. Now he was looking at Isaac and his hands were on the other man's arms. "Don't preach at me and don't judge me. I've told you that before. And as far as she is concerned, she can sleep where she wants. You tell her that. You tell her that. You tell all of your people that for me." His voice was raised and he knew that there were many who heard him. His hands fell to his side and he looked about for the old mori. Not seeing Isaac's father, he told the son, "I imagine your father will want to do the slaughtering before sundown. As for me, I just want a piece of lamb when it's cooked."

Isaac shook his head sadly, "We thank you for the sheep which should not be purchased on the Sabbath, but if you think our people would put a woman in your blanket, I am disappointed; you offend us, you defame us and what we are." Before Zvi could say anything, Isaac's hand came up. "I had hoped you could at least try to understand us better than they," waving his hand toward Marwan and his companions.

Zvi looked at the proud young Yemenite, felt he was a fool and strode off toward the small rise where he had dropped his baggage and where he saw Ali Harja squatting beside his horse.

The small Arab spat as the Israeli approached, and without thinking, Zvi struck him in the face, knocking him backward. In an instant, the Arab came to his feet, dagger in hand. Zvi remained where he was. All the anger and frustration of the past few minutes welled over him and he was not going to retreat from this idiot, not now, not the way he felt. His dagger raised, the Arab moved slowly toward the Jew; however, as he approached, he came forward more cautiously, uncertain just what he should do. He had not expected the blow and he had not expected the Jew to stand his ground. When he came within reach, he slashed with a wide motion and Zvi, stepping inside the swing, grabbed the Arab's wrist and with a quick twist dropped the dagger to the ground. Placing one sandaled foot on it, Zvi held the little man up so that their eyes were level.

"Calm down or I will break your neck," the Jew said in an almost friendly manner. "I don't want to kill you, and you want your money." He waited to be certain he had been understood and then, "Never spit at me again."

Satisfied that he had made his point, he set the Arab down. "Now get out of here and be ready tomorrow when I call you."

Ali Harja glanced down at his dagger, but Zvi shook his head. "I'll keep that."

The Arab shrugged and wandered off, leading his horse.

Zvi did not know if what he had done to the little man's pride was going to cost the refugees more than he wanted to pay, but it was done and he would live with it.

He picked the dagger up. The hilt, set with cheap stones, revealed two dark spots, which meant that two stones were missing. Zvi shoved the dagger inside his cassock between the money belt and his bare skin. The weapon was cold, and he grinned.

Seating himself, he waited until one of Isaac's wives brought him a platter with several pieces of hot sliced lamb. He smiled at the young girl, thanked her and asked, "Is Isaac going to be all right?"

The child did not know what he was asking, and she looked at him for a moment as if he were stupid.

"Tell him I said that there shouldn't be any anger between us," he explained, and after she nodded and walked back to the fire where her husband sat with his other wife and the two children, Zvi wondered when he would stop speaking with all of the formality of the Arabs. An hour later he unrolled his blankets and spread them out on the ground. From where he squatted on the knoll he could see the small camp scattered over the field. There were fewer fires now and these were beginning to die. Some of the men sat in gróups and Zvi could hear them singing. The sounds and songs were both strange. He fell onto his back and stared at the sky. It was dark now. There were few stars. He could make out the sound of a bird in the distance. Then a large shape came between him and the stars, and when he started to rise, a foot on his chest pushed him flat.

Looking up, he recognized Abbas Marwan, and a glance revealed the other Arab soldiers.

Relaxing to show that he was not frightened by the Arab who stood astride him, Zvi waited for the other man to talk.

"We are going now," Marwan explained. "We have escorted you far enough. In the next day or two you should reach Dhamar. There you may find another escort."

A crooked smile spread over the Arab's face. "The Imam wished that none prevent your leaving. He did not say how you leave or with what."

Sucking in his breath, Zvi waited for the soldier to demand some kind of payment. To his surprise, Marwan stood aside and looked at his companions.

"Is there anything else we can do for the Yahudi?" he asked, a trace of mockery in his voice.

Only the older man with the heavy black beard acknowledged the question. "We could leave some of the women with good Arab sons."

The others picked up the laughter, but Marwan shook his head. "I can find better women than these and so can any Arab."

To dispute this would have been to deny the quality of Arab women, and so a few minutes later, Zvi watched the nazanim ride off in the darkness.

Slipping under his blanket, he wondered where Havah was. Usually she had joined him by this time. He wondered if he should remain awake and wait for her. However, he was weary and a short time later he fell asleep.

How long after he had fallen asleep he felt the boot in his side, he did not know. But the blow was sudden, sharp and shocking. Trying to roll over, he felt something at his throat. Looking up, he saw the dark face of one of the nazanim who had ridden away earlier in the evening with Marwan. Beyond him knelt the man with the heavy black beard who had said that Mohammed ordered the death of all nonbelievers. Without looking down, Zvi knew the man kneeling over him had a knife at his throat.

Zvi closed his eyes and to his surprise he was thinking of his wife for the first time in days. He hoped she was all right and he thought of the promise he had made himself that she would not become a widow a third time. It was a promise he had hoped to keep.

There was a sound behind the Arabs and both of them turned. The shadow of a woman emerged on the knoll.

Havah.

Before Zvi could say anything, the large, bearded Arab grabbed her hand and swung her flat on the blanket beside Zvi.

"I am willing to kill both of you," he said softly. Zvi wondered why the man was speaking in a whisper when he had nothing to fear.

Havah looked from Zvi's eyes to the knife at his throat and reminded the Arabs, "You took all that we had."

The younger man who held the knife smiled. "We have come to give."

And the thought rammed home in Zvi's brain as he recalled the offer one of them had made earlier. Through the fog that overwhelmed him now he was no longer sure who had made that offer, but he could still recall the words: *good Arab sons.*

Then the bearded soldier was pushing Havah down on the blanket, one hand over her mouth as he said, "Remember that if any Jew so much as touches an Arab, the Imam will allow me to kill him."

Zvi started to rise, but the knife at his throat moved forward and he could feel it sharp against his skin. Once he tried to raise his hand, but the young Arab shook his head and made a slicing gesture. Zvi felt the blood warm in his throat. He closed his eyes and tried not to listen to the sounds on the blanket beside him.

After what seemed hours, he felt the knife come away for an instant, but before he could move, he saw that the bearded Arab was holding the blade now. A short time later, he heard Havah sobbing softly. The two Arabs came to their feet, daggers in hand. The younger was holding the reins of the horses and he removed a rifle which had been lying across his saddle.

He bowed in a gesture of mockery. "I thank both of you."

The young Arab shoved his rifle back across his saddle, mounted and waited for his friend. The older man ran his hand down his beard, spat into the dirt beside Zvi Mazon and said, "I wonder what kind of an army you Jews have."

When he turned his back on Zvi to mount his horse, the Israeli leaned forward, grabbed the man's foot, hurled him away from the horse and in almost the same gesture, grabbed the younger of the two Arabs by the stirrup, twisting his foot so sharply, the four of them could hear the leg break. The Arab started to scream, but before he could, Zvi dragged him from his saddle. Hurling the man on the ground, Zvi sought the dagger he had taken from Ali Harja and fell on his victim, shoving the blade through the man's throat, cutting off any sound. Without waiting to see if he had killed the nazan, Zvi rolled over, just as the bearded Arab landed where he had been. Flaying wildly, Zvi caught the man's arm, half lifted him from the ground, snapping bones as he himself came to his knees. The Arab's dagger fell between them, and for an instant Zvi had the pleasure of seeing fear in the Arab's face. In that same instant, he drove his fist between the man's eyes, felling him. With careful deliberation, Zvi picked up the bearded man's own blade and drove it twice into his chest. And then Zvi lost control of himself. He started swinging his arm up and down, driving the dagger into the Arab's neck and chest time after time until he was so weary he slumped over the body.

How long he lay across it, he could not recall. When he finally pulled himself up, he saw the blank face of the younger Arab at his side and the body of the older one in front of him. He could not make out the features for the blood which covered them. Beyond the two, Zvi could see the horrified expression on Havah's taut face. He tried to smile at her. Then he looked down at his bloody hand and clothes and saw that he still held the Arab's dagger. Wiping it off carefully in the sand beside him, he shoved it inside his cassock.

Coming to his feet, he looked around. The campfires were all dead. There was no movement among the refugees. Zvi wondered if any knew of the horror which had risen on the knoll, assuming that if they did these people had been so long in bondage they would not make a gesture. He would bury his own dead.

Without looking at Havah, he dragged the older man off into a clump of bushes where he dug a shallow trench with his dagger. Twenty minutes later he buried the Arab's companion beside him without even removing Harja's blade from the man's throat. When he was satisfied he had done the best he could to hide his indiscretion, he wiped his hand and clothes and returned to the blanket. Havah was sitting up now, and he could tell that she had been watching him.

All Zvi could bring himself to say was, "I am sorry."

"You said that once before," she reminded him, "and you explained it was because you were not there."

He nodded. "I was here this time. I did the best I could."

The woman seemed to be satisfied that nothing could have happened other than what did. Very slowly, she came to her feet and started to walk away. Zvi took her hand, but she jerked it free and whirled back toward him.

"Isaac said you did not want me before. You don't have to want me now."

She was less surprised than Zvi when he went to slap her across the face, caught himself and snorted. They both stared at each other, and then she laughed. "Killing them would not have made you feel as good as that would have." Her hand came to her cheek, and as Zvi started to slip down on his blanket again, she joined him. Her hand reached out to cover his.

Zvi put his arms about her and held her closely for a long time and all the while he was wondering why he was thinking of his wife. They fell asleep in each other arms.

The journey from Ma'bar to Dhamar took two days. The way was easy, the road clear, the Arabs few. The first night they spent in a field and drew water from a stream. The second night as they approached Dhamar, several Arab soldiers came out on horses to look over the column. They sat on their high saddles in silence. And then, without a word, they raced back toward the city.

The climb to the town was difficult, the wadi beside it dry. The smell was of jasmine, clematis and myrtle. Acacia trees and cactus covered the fields. Tamarisk and laurel were bright.

Zvi stood beside the column, letting it pass as many turned to look at him. Some of the women smiled and some of the men. Isaac joined him and quietly waited for the last of the straggle. Then the two men followed.

They had spoken on the Sabbath as if nothing had happened between them. The night after the Sabbath, Havah had not come into Zvi's blanket. Nor did she come the next night.

A half kilometer from Dhamar the Arab riders returned. This time there was a well-dressed youth at their head. He left his men in front of the column to block its progress and waited for the leader to emerge. Half trotting, Zvi made his way forward.

The young Arab sat looking insolently down at the Israeli. Measuring the stranger, Zvi thought he had found someone different from others he had met in Yemen. There was not only an assurance about this youth, but from the way he moved and the way he was dressed with a European shirt and trousers showing beneath his cloak, Zvi knew this Arab had traveled outside Yemen.

"I have heard from the Imam," the young man said.

Zvi felt reassured and, nodding, waited to hear what this would mean.

"You will stop outside the city tonight. After your camp is made, you will be brought in and you and I will talk further."

He glanced at his wrist and to Zvi's surprise, there was a watch on it. "An hour," the young soldier ordered. And Zvi knew the other man was aware that Zvi was not a Yemenite.

The refugees fanned out over the field, making their camp among the cypress trees. It was almost evening. The sun was low and the high air cool.

An hour later two Arab soldiers led Major Mazon to Dhamar. Pausing for a moment before the gates, he looked at the double semi-circle of hills which surrounded the white city. The town had a reputation for being particularly unfriendly to strangers and a stronghold of the Imam's.

Zvi was surprised that some of the streets were broad with rows of trees planted down the middle. Most, however, were more typically Arabic, narrow, high walled with houses like fortresses along the outer edge of the city. The two soldiers wore skirts and turbans of indigo blue, and Zvi assumed the streaks of blue on their faces came from the sweated turbans, though he had been told some Arabs painted their faces in the belief that blue kept them warm and kept evil spirits away. One of the pair stopped, pushed back his headpiece and ran his hands through his black hair for a moment while he stopped to listen to the music flowing from a streetside café. A sudden stench filled Zvi's nostrils, and only after the Arab had replaced his headpiece did Zvi realize that according to Bedouin custom the man must have washed his hair in rancid, boiled butter.

They started on again but had gone only a few paces when a middle-aged Arab, bare-headed and out of breath, emerged from the café and grabbed Zvi's arm. Uncertain how he should react, the Jew looked to his guides. Neither of them said anything as they stopped to watch. Finally, Zvi shook the Arab's hand off his sleeve.

"What do you want?" he snapped, trying hard to control his temper.

"Girls," the Arab said ingenuously, as though there could not have been doubt about his needs.

Zvi cocked his head to one side and tried not to laugh as he asked, "Girls?"

Nodding, the portly Arab washed his face with a browned hand. "I used to be able to get Jewish girls. Young ones. The parents died and the girls were available for a price." Wanting to be sure that the Jew did not misunderstand, he spoke quickly and to the point. "I pay. I pay well. I need girls who can sing and girls who can dance. If they don't know how, I will teach them." And as he spoke, he broke into a dance, wriggling his pot belly with one hand set lightly on his hip to emphasive the femininity of his gesture. Three times he whirled about, wriggling as he turned, and chanted in an awesome voice. He finally came to a stop in front of Zvi and waited for the Jew to accept his offer.

Zvi stifled a laugh as he shook his head. "I haven't any dancing girls or singing girls."

But the Arab café owner was not to be put off so easily. "Moslem girls are not for cafés or for inns. It would be forbidden." Then, believing he understood the Jew better, he smiled. "I will pay well, and after they have learned how to sleep with the customers, I will pay even better."

Opening his hands wide in a gesture of futility, Zvi shook his head slowly. "I have nothing to sell."

The Arab would not believe him and appealed to the soldiers. "I used to be able to buy Jew girls. Why shouldn't he sell me some Jew girls now?"

The guides shrugged, reached out and, grabbing Zvi's arm, dragged him along after them. When Zvi looked back, he saw the fat café owner shaking his head sadly as though the world had betrayed him.

A few streets farther on, the two guides stopped and pointed to a large house which dominated the area.

"He is waiting for you, Yahud."

Nodding, Zvi entered the house. On the ground floor was a large stable. A dozen or more horses stood in well-kept stalls while sheep and chickens wandered about. Climbing the staircase, Zvi made his way up a hundred steps, wondering if there was something symbolic in the round figure. At the top he found a guard.

"In there, Yahud."

Taking a deep breath to restrain himself, Zvi entered a *majlis*, or large gathering room. There were only four small windows in the room though more than fifty men were there. The windows were closed and both the smell and heat struck Zvi in the face. The furniture was oriental-low divans covered like the floor with rugs and cushions. In one corner of the room a small fire burned in a recess in the wall. Most of the men were smoking water pipes; however, Zvi could see that many were also chewing ghat.

Deciding that he had more important things to do than change the pattern of Yemenite life at this moment, the Israeli scanned the room for his host. A thin, elderly man dressed in western clothes approached.

When they came together, the old man, who seemed to sway on his spindly legs, asked, "You are the Jew from the Holy Land?"

Zvi nodded.

"Come."

On the far side of the room, Zvi saw the youth he had met earlier. As the young Arab rose to his feet, Zvi noticed that he wore only European clothes now—a dark suit, a white shirt and a necktie. To Zvi's surprise, his host said in English, "This room is too warm for you?"

Puzzled at the interest in his comfort, Zvi did not know if he should complain or be stoical, though the room needed an airing and he would just as soon be away from these men watching. "It is not the cool air of Dhamar or the beautiful night of the city."

The young Arab's smile was almost friendly as he led the way out of the room onto a low roof. There were two torches set in niches and several rugs strewn about as well as two low divans. It took Zvi a moment to adjust his eyes to the light before he made out the figure of a woman standing against the far side of the roof. He could not see her face behind the veil, nor could he even guess her age as the shadows thrown by the torches left her in the dark. Half nodding, and at the same time hoping he was committing no breach of etiquette, he turned to his host.

The young Arab introduced himself. "I am the sayid. My father is the sultan of this city." Then as though he had to explain, "My father is ill now."

"I am sorry to hear that," Zvi said, wondering if his expression was not a presumption on the part of a Jew.

"Ajiam ibn Ali," the youth introduced himself.

"I am honored,"

"And you are Zvi Mazon of the Israeli army," his host said, leaving no doubt that he had his own information.

Zvi's eyes wandered to the woman who was watching them. After a moment he nodded.

"We can speak English," Ajiam offered as he gestured toward the nearer of the low divans and seated himself on the other.

"Can I send for something to drink?" Ajiam ibn Ali asked, smiling as he watched the Jew staring at the woman and trying not to be seen doing it.

Zvi shook his head and sat down.

"A Jew may drink alcoholic beverages in Dhamar," the Arab explained. "If I found an Arab drinking them, I would have him killed."

Not knowing if an answer was expected of him, Zvi remained silent.

The young man picked up a dagger from the floor near his shoe and tossed it into Zvi's lap. Startled, Zvi caught the weapon and held it up so that he could see it better. The hilt was set with cheap stones. The impressions were obvious where two were missing. For an instant Zvi held his breath as he recognized the blade he had left in the young Arab's throat three nights before. After a time he looked up at his host. "Is there something you want me to do with this?"

The young Arab laughed softly, apparently pleased with his theatrics. Glancing at the woman, he said, "He is a good soldier—control."

Realizing that his host was speaking in English to her, Zvi looked at the woman once more. However, the sayid brought him up sharply. "It will cost you one real for each Jew you take past Dhamar."

Wondering why he felt so warm when the night was cold and wondering, too, if the Arab was going to let the matter of the dagger go without further comment, he pleaded, "The nazanim who escorted us from San'a took what money we had."

A smile flickered across Ajiam's face as he nodded. "They thought they did. However, three nights ago you bought seven sheep—not very fat ones—for good Maria Theresa thalers."

Zvi tried to smile but failed. The woman edged closer, remaining in the shadow.

"And if I told you that was all the money we had?"

A guffaw this time as his host enjoyed the attempt to bargain. "I would say that I have evidence enough in that dagger and where it came from to kill you twice." He thought a moment and then added, "Three times."

Puzzled, the Israeli wondered what his third crime had been and then he realized how Ajiam ibn Ali knew so much about him. "The little man with the hunched back," he said flatly.

The Arab's head bobbed. "You insulted him."

Deciding he had little to lose at this moment, Zvi said bluntly, "I should have slit his gullet, emptied his entrails across the road to see what they forecast for the future and then fed them to the mountain cats." He hoped his words impressed the young Arab, but to his surprise it was the woman who laughed.

Ajiam turned toward her. "He talks as though he were a dangerous man."

She nodded.

His attention on the Jew once more, the sayid said, "One real a person times three hundred and seventy people. That makes three hundred and seventy reals." He thought about this and concluded. "That is a fair price because at Lahej the sultan will charge you three reals."

"And if I do not have it?" Zvi had to try once more.

The young Arab rose to his feet and smiled as he looked up at the night sky. He was still smiling when he looked down at the Israeli. "There are shopkeepers who need clerks, café owners who need singers, innkeepers who need women to sleep with their guests. They will pay for it."

Deciding he had bargained as hard as he could and had done the best he could, Zvi reached inside his shirt, pulled out a handful of Maria Theresa thalers and held them out. His host accepted them, computed the total and held his hand out for more. And twice more Zvi dug into the pouch.

When he was satisfied, Ajiam threw the money on the divan and turned to the woman, "And now that our business is done, I think we should enjoy some coffee."

The woman nodded and slipped onto the divan beside the sayid.

The torchlight caught her face now and in spite of the veil that covered it, Zvi though that somewhere he had seen her before. He looked at her gown. Arabic fashion and fine silk. She watched his glance as his eyes wandered over her, and he could tell that she was laughing at him.

A moment later without either of the Arabs sending for him, the thin old man in western clothes appeared with a servant carrying a tray with three coffee cups. The tray passed around and then the old man and the servant disappeared into the gathering room, taking the toll money with them.

When the three were alone again, the woman told Zvi, "You look better than when I saw you last."

Zvi scraped the back of his mind. The voice was familiar and so was the English accent, and then he remembered. "As you can see, I survived."

The woman laughed softly. "You do remember me?"

Zvi nodded, hoping he was not being too familiar.

Ajiam sat watching the two. "Bedia and I were at school together in England."

Again Zvi nodded.

132

The woman reached up and dropped the veil covering the lower half of her face. "You may remember you and I talked about school in England," she reminded Zvi.

His mind wandered through the haze of broken walls and shattered buildings into the Old City. "I remember," he said after a time.

Bedia Hassani smiled. Her small hand went out and closed over Ajiam's. "We were not only at school together, but we are cousins."

Zvi wondered why she was telling him this now. He certainly was not going to feel free to make any advances just because the woman did not belong to the young sayid. He was tempted to ask if Layton had also been her cousin, but recalling his position, he merely smiled.

"I think I should thank you," he said.

Ajiam looked from one to the other and waited for his cousin to explain what the Jew meant.

She smiled. "That last day when they carried you out?"

Zvi nodded. "If I recall, you were there as they went down the line asking for me."

Bedia explained to her companion. "The British would have killed him if they had known who he was." She fell silent and then added, "I didn't tell them."

Placing his hand affectionately on her arm, Ajiam asked, "Why would they have killed him?"

Zvi waited to hear what she would say.

A trace of a smile touched her lips as she dropped her head back and stared at the dark sky for a moment. "There was this British officer who thought that the young Jew should be punished for having expelled me from the Quarter."

Ajiam waited for her to continue.

Recalling how the Jew had struck her, Bedia continued, dropping her voice, "He—the Jew—let me cross back to our lines without killing me."

Ajiam looked at Zvi once more. His interest in the Jew was heightened. "Why did you let her go?"

Zvi shrugged, "Let me just say that I do not fight against women."

The young Arab smiled. "I'll remember that."

Uncertain what the sayid meant, Zvi said nothing.

"You are taking that rabble all the way to Aden?" Bedia asked after a moment.

"I am taking my people home," Zvi said softly.

Ajiam shook his head. "They'll never make it."

"I've got to try."

Bedia looked at the two men and again her head fell back. "I shall be in Aden in a few months. When I get there, I'll tell your people you tried."

Hoping to keep the irony out of his voice, Zvi smiled, "I would appreciate that."

Bored with the conversation now, Ajiam rose and ended it. "As the Imam said, 'I shall not prevent it.'"

Realizing that he was expected to leave, Zvi rose, smiled at Bedia and then at his host. "I thank both of you."

The woman noted the irony in his appreciation and laughed. "Wait until you get to Aden before you thank anyone."

Smiling a second time, Zvi waited to be excused.

The sayid walked away from them to the edge of the roof where he stood for a moment looking down. Bedia and Zvi watched him go and then stared at each other. No one said anything for a few minutes and then Ajiam swung back to the two. "The Imam knows how to deal with situations like this."

Puzzled, Zvi waited for the other man to explain.

"There are four thousand young hostages in Yemen. Most of them live in this city. The sons of men who might be important, and to the Imam 'important' means dangerous." Almost proud of himself, he added, "I am responsible for their safety."

The woman came to her feet now and, approaching her cousin, asked, "And what would you want with a Jewish hostage?" Zvi realized how the other man was thinking.

The sayid smiled at her, put out one hand and drew her to him so that she stood at his side, one arm about his waist. "You are clever," he told her. He looked at Zvi. "If I had a few dozen of your women as hostages, I could be assured there would be no more Arabs killed." He thought about what he had said and then, satisfied with himself, he added, "You Jews take care of your women, a warped set of values, but you will have to admit that it would be protection for me."

Bedia laughed more loudly this time while Zvi tried to think of a rejoinder which would not raise more problems.

He was only relieved when Bedia stopped laughing and reminded Ajiam, "He does not make war on women. Do we?"

The young Arab shrugged. "You think I should just let him go?"

"Do you give a damn about the Imam's dead nazanim?"

Both of them seemed to have forgotten the Jew.

"No," Ajiam admitted. "But I have taken money now to see that they cross my land without trouble. Why shouldn't I insure myself against them?"

Bedia considered this and then, with a broad smile, suggested a solution. "If you don't take the money, then you're free to let them pass, and whatever happens to them is not your responsibility."

Surprised, the sayid thought she was joking.

She nodded to indicate she was not.

"And just let the Jews go on with three hundred and seventy reals?"

However, Zvi, who was trying to follow the logic of the two, lost it when she explained, "You can give it to me and be free of your burden."

The Arab youth laughed. "You need the money the way your father needs banks."

However, she was not to be so easily dissuaded. "It is money."

The sayid thought about this for a moment and then shouted, "Araji!" A moment later the old man joined them on the roof.

"You," the sayid told him, "will see that this Jew gets back to his camp, and then you will turn the toll money over to my cousin."

Bewildered, the feeble courtier looked to his master for an explanation. "The toll money?"

Ajiam nodded and turned away, swinging Bedia with him so that they stood with their backs toward the servant and the Jew.

With a shrug, the old man led the Jew off. As the door closed behind him, Zvi heard the two young Arabs laughing, and he wondered what he had let himself and the refugees in for now that his host was free to pretend that the toll had not been paid.

Back at the Jewish camp, Zvi found his blankets laid where he had set down his bag earlier in the evening. However, before he slipped in between them, he sought out Ali Harja. The small Arab lay on his blanket with his head resting on the saddle of his horse. Kneeling beside the hunchback, Zvi slowly drew his fingernail across the man's throat. Awakening with a start, the guide opened his eyes in fright.

"It is only my hand this time," Zvi warned him. "If I hear that you have betrayed me a second time, I shall not warn you." And then realizing that he possessed a threat, he said almost kindly, "The sayid's cousin will be expecting me in Aden. If I do not arrive with all of my people, there are those in Aden who will be looking for you." He knew what he was saying was half a lie, but there was no way for the guide to know this. With a smile, Zvi patted the man's browned cheek, ending the gesture with a stinging slap. Satisfied that he had made his point, he returned to his blankets.

Isaac was waiting for him. "We shall be able to go on?"

"Of course," Zvi assured him, wishing he was as confident as he sounded.

The Yemenite's head bobbed, "We will have much to thank you for."

Zvi wanted to say that what he was doing was nothing, but before he could say anything, Isaac said, "We are glad you have come with us."

After he was alone again, Zvi wondered what the other man had meant. Later as he slipped under the covers, he was joined by Havah. The woman stood beside the blankets, dropped off most of her clothes, and then crawled under the blankets with him. And though Zvi knew Isaac would not approve of her being there, he was certain the young silversmith would be even more shocked to know Zvi's thoughts were on Bedia Hassani.

Almost anywhere except in the Arab world he would have thought the coincidence of their meeting great, but he knew enough about the Arab aristocracy to understand that most of it was interrelated from Syria through

Saudia Arabia and apparently beyond into the Yemen. However, as he fell asleep, it was the Arab girl with the imperious look he was thinking about and not her relatives.

South from Dhamar through Yarim to Manzil. Two days' walk through the high country, the sun brazen, the winds battering, the nights char.

And all the while, the Bedouin watching the long column.
The sheep keeping the road and the Jews turning aside.
And the sayid's men watching from their brown horses, remote expressions marking their faces with scorn.

Between Yarim and Manzil the Jews held the first burial. An old woman whose daughter had remained in San'a. The body was washed, the mori held services, and the grave was dug after paying an Arab farmer the price of two goats for a piece of land three paces by one.

And the column moves on through the planted fields, the smell of jasmine and the stench of dung.
To Manzil, where the local wise man warned his people against the plague of Jews descending upon them, and the column slept in the fields beyond the town.

For a time Zvi lay on his back and stared up at the sky and wondered when a bird had last crossed it and if somehow birds did not leave tracks.

A short time later Havah joined him. She stood looking at Zvi for a few minutes before she knelt beside the blanket. "You shouldn't be by yourself in the dark."

He rolled onto his side so that he could see her better. Though the night was dark he could make out the lines of her face, and he thought that she became more lovely each day they marched. A trace of a smile crossed his face as he wondered if he had been too long in the field.

He put out one hand and let it come to rest on the shoulder of the sheepskin cloak she had wrapped about her.

After a moment she moved next to him and they lay on their backs staring up at the stars.

Neither said anything for a long time, and then without looking at him Havah said, "We should have put more stones on the grave."

Zvi's thoughts, dragged away from the stars, dwelled for a moment on the lonely grave they had left behind. "We covered it," he reminded her, thinking that they had spent too much time piling stones one on another over the isolated grave.

"Did you bury your dead well in the Holy City?" she asked, and he realized that she was using the only thing she knew about him to make conversation.

Nodding, Zvi was on his side now, looking at her gentle profile. "Within sight of the Wall when we could."

A tone of reverence filled her words as she asked about the Wall.

Her nose was small and her cheekbones high, but Zvi saw that the full cheeks gave her the appearance of a large woman, and having known her for weeks, he would always remember her as small.

"The Wall?" she asked again as much to take his attention from her face as to start him talking.

"It's crowded in," he told her. "The Arabs have built their houses so close to it that you can really only get there through a stairway. But the Wall's high. Not as high as we would like to think, and there's the mosque overwhelming it."

"The mosque?" she was curious because no one had ever told her about the mosque.

"Omar's," Zvi explained. "Built a long time ago and it is as important to the Moslems as the Wall is important to us."

"But the Wall is older." She was not asking a question.

He nodded, but she was still looking at the sky and did not see him.

"The Wall is theirs now?"

Again Zvi nodded. "We lost it," and in the bitterness of these three words, Havah knew more about this soldier from the Holy Land than she had learned in the nights she had spent with him. This time it was her hand that went out. Entwining her fingers with his, she consoled him, "But it stands, and we can wait a little longer if we have to."

Zvi wanted to say that he had had enough of patience and nobility, but before he could speak, she whispered, "I'm going to see it sometime."

"You'll see it," he promised.

"There were others with you there?"

And he knew she merely wanted to keep him talking.

Almost pleased with the prospect, Zvi told her about his companions. "There was a girl named Ruth. She's married now. Another girl—Dvora. I never heard what happened to her. Another who operated the radio," and as he said it, Zvi realized that Havah did not know what a radio was and was not even interrupting him to ask. At that moment he decided the conservation had no meaning.

Reaching over, he pulled the blanket across both of them and lay with his arm under her head, one hand searching beneath the sheepskin cloak to the swell of her breasts where he gently kneaded the soft flesh. She did not look at him as she continued to stare at the dark sky.

Somewhere in the distance Zvi recognized the blather of a camel. Off beyond the camp he could hear the sound of sheep complaining. Cricket noise rasped through the field. And within the confines of the camp, he could make out the low voices of men and women talking quietly by the dying fires.

"Are you a rich man?"

His hand closed on a breast as he thought about the strange question. "No," he finally said.

Her head rocked from side to side. "There is a great store of treasure buried in Yemen's earth, but it is protected and only the man in whose name it has been kept can have it. The others will be killed if they try to take it."

Zvi's hand moved restlessly. "I'll remember that," he assured her.

"If you could find the treasure that was yours, you could have any number of wives," she reminded him.

Wondering if she knew he was already married, Zvi realized that to the Yemenite Jews, multiple marriage was a way of life so ingrained that his relationship to Havah, while not approved, was not viewed the same way it would have been in Israel. She had hopes, and so might the others for her. For a time as he lay running his hand over her firm body, he considered telling her about Zella.

His hand came away and he rested his head on his folded arms as he, too, stared at the night sky. Zella would probably be in their apartment at this hour. He wished he knew how many hours' difference there was in time. Maybe she would be sleeping. Maybe she would be studying. He had seen enough of her studies to know that he would not understand them. Biochemistry remained a mystery to him and always would. And yet, he was deeply concerned that Moshe and Zella were back in school and he was not. Even knowing that Havah would not understand what he was saying, he began to explain his concern. "If I get home again, I think I will go back to the university and study history." He shook his head from side to side. "It has been a long time. There was the school in Gadera where my father lives, and then a few months in a school on a kibbutz when I was training. Then an officers' school at another kibbutz in the Galilee. And then nothing. I am a bit of a fool." He might have said more, but a burst of laughter at his side brought him sitting upright.

Ajiam was kneeling on the edge of the blanket. "Gently, Yahud," the young Arab warned him.

The girl started to rise, but Zvi reached out and pulled her down, keeping the blanket over her. But he did not take his eyes off the sayid of Dhamar.

The two men stared at each other silently before the Arab held out his hand, "If you have any weapons?"

Zvi shook his head, keeping one hand on Havah's arm so that she would not move or attract attention.

"Then," the young Arab smiled, "we can talk."

Trying not to reveal both his surprise and anger, Zvi asked, "About what?"

Ajiam ibn Ali sat down, his knees pulled up before him and his arms encircling them. "We could begin by talking about my cousin."

Zvi did not say anything, afraid that whatever he said would be wrong, and assuming this young Arab nobleman had not come without his own soldiers.

"My cousin," Ajiam suggested a second time. "What happened between the two of you in Jerusalem?"

Shaking his head, Zvi decided he could not risk being trapped between something he might say and something the girl might have said. "We met one night. She was in the Jewish Quarter. I sent her back to her own lines." A smile crossed his face, "Lines may be a bit too formal considering the situation."

"And that was all?"

Zvi kept his hand firmly on Havah's arm, wishing that she was some place else. "That was all, except that she was not killed."

Slowly and with obvious impatience, Ajiam rocked back and forth as he considered this, "And because of that she asks me to be a gentleman as far as you are concerned?"

Seeing that the Arab expected an answer, Zvi said, "I'm sure I wouldn't know."

A short laugh as Ajiam said, "If it were any other Arab girl, I might not be thinking the same way." He waited for the Jew to comment; and when he heard nothing, he explained, "My cousin is known for her intelligence and her beauty, but she is not known for her virtue."

Zvi knew this was no time for him to say anything.

The young Arab remained patient. "And if there was anything between you and . . . " His voice trailed off.

"She walked back to her own lines. I think we talked for five minutes." He thought about this and shrugged. "It might have been five."

Ajiam was not satisfied, but Zvi could see there was very little room for him to press the argument. "This place you call Israel," the sayid began. "It is an affront to all Arabs. It will have to be destroyed."

Zvi knew the man was waiting for an excuse to attack, and as Zvi was in no position to defend himself or his people, he asked, "Have you been there?"

Ajiam shook his head at the unexpected question.

"Did you ask your cousin about it?"

Again the young Arab showed that he was uncomfortable. And at this moment Zvi realized that he must not make the man resent his answers.

"Your cousin knows a great deal about Israel," and to temper his own knowledge of the girl, he added, "I would assume, seeing that she was in the area during the war."

Ajiam continued to rock back and forth. "You don't know her well?" Zvi admitted he did not.

"Her father is the man who arranged the boycott of your country. He is rich enough to bring it down about your ears. He is my father's distant cousin."

Ajiam's arms came free from his knees and he drew a small jeweled dagger and began jamming it into the earth as he spoke. "My father's distant cousin has let his daughter travel where she wanted. He has let her become like an English girl or a Jew girl." And as he spoke, Zvi could see the Arab was looking at Havah, who lay still and frightened between the blankets.

Then somehow the notion came through to Zvi that this young man was in love with Bedia.

"She is lovely," Ajaim said after a moment, and Zvi did not know if the sayid was talking about Havah or Bedia and decided only to nod.

"Bedia Hassani is my father's cousin's only daughter," Ajiam said for no apparent reason. "Maybe that is why he allows her to do things no Arab girl should do."

Zvi remained silent.

Ajiam laughed. "Jew soldiers. I shall look forward to fighting you one day." He suddenly jammed the dagger into the ground between them. "I think I would enjoy it now, but she asked me to be a gentleman." A snort as he added, "I am not a Christian, and the concept of a gentleman is their own kind of hypocrisy. But," and pride came into his voice, "I shall act as an Arab who has given his word."

Believing this confrontation was done for the moment, Zvi asked, "Can I offer you some coffee?"

The Arab's eyes half closed. "I'm not going to become indebted to a Jew." His hand closed once more on the hilt of the dagger. Then with a nod the sayid said seriously, "We are guiltless of you and we are done with you."

Zvi watched the young Arab walk away into the darkness. Sighing, he slipped down into the blanket and rolling onto his face, he closed his eyes. He was asleep when Havah stretched the other blanket over him and, placing one arm across his shoulders, covered him for the night.

Below Yarim lies the vast flank of Jabal Sumara. The land slopes upward, twists, and the view spreads wide. There are the gorges deep, the horizons vague as mountain range spills into mountain range, each serrating the sky.

The road narrows as it hugs the mountainside. While the weak stagger in the thin air, the strong carry the pots, beans and holy books.

And then there is Sumara Pass. Beyond lies Green Yemen: valleys and fields, ravines and terraced mountains. Behind lies High Yemen: plateaus and wild rocky heights, larger fields of brown and yellow.

They left High Yemen behind.

Into the terraced mountains and down toward the green fields; however, darkness caught them on the mountainside.. They spent the night rolled up on the rock road, the children crying along with the wind and the men chewing their lips and wishing they could build a fire and all the while knowing that no fire would survive the sudden gusts.

In the morning they went on toward Ibb, stopping in an untilled field near the black tents of a Bedouin caravan.

Zvi Mazon watched his charges settle in, hoping all the while that the Bedouin would ignore them. He wished he could go farther, rest an hour and then move on, but the Yemenites were too tired to walk any more without a long rest. He watched a blacksmith gather dung for a fire as his three wives wrapped their children in blankets and set up the small stove they had hauled from San'a. The blacksmith's arms reminded Zvi of strong vines. The women paused in their work to watch the foreign Jew make his way through the camp. Shy, they averted their heads as he passed, and then one of them smiled at the others, "He will lead us there."

Catching her words, Zvi wished he were as confident.

The mori was helping his wives prepare a noonday meal, and Zvi wondered when these people had last eaten two meals in one day. Smiling to himself, he wondered when he, too, had lost the habit.

Standing on the narrow strip of land that separated the Yemenite Jews from the black tents, Zvi turned to look at the refugees once more. Most of them were barefooted now. The clothes they wore were torn and dirty. Many of the men no longer had the robelike shirts they started out with. Between the dirt and the thickets of the fields they had slept in, little remained of their clothes. And what they had looked more brown than blue.

Both the men and women were thinner than when they had left San'a. Zvi doubted if any of the women weighed eighty kilos. Glancing over his shoulder, he watched two young Bedouin shepherds driving their small flock to the far side of the migrant camp. Zvi wondered if he could strike a bargain with them. And yet, as he thought about it, he knew he had to conserve what little money was left.

From where he stood, the Israeli noted a middle-aged Jew trying to force pus out of a sore on his leg. Zvi tried not to watch. Most of the men had sores on their legs and feet, and he assumed the women were no healthier. He looked at his own legs. There were bruises from climbing, but his slacks had protected him, and his shoes were still intact, worn but usable. The middle-aged man slipped to the ground and held up his feet to his wife. Small green sores covered the soles.

Zvi's head went up to face the midday sun. It was warm now. The sun would help. He wished there were something he could do to help. When he looked back, he saw a young man he recognized as a weaver standing over the man with the blistered feet. Puzzled, Zvi watched the weaver roll a piece of torn blanket over his hand, reach into the campfire and draw something out. Then Zvi smelled burning flesh and heard the sick man trying to stifle a scream.

Without realizing what he was doing, the Israeli closed the ground between them. The smell of burnt flesh hung in the air as the Israeli looked from the burned feet to the weaver and waited for an explanation.

"It cleans it," the other man said. "It leaves healthy flesh and drives out the bad." As the man spoke, he clasped his hand over something hanging about his neck. In disgust, Zvi reached out and slowly opened the man's hand. An amulet of hammered silver in the shape of a scroll.

Others had gathered about the three. The sick man's wife had withdrawn a short distance behind her husband and waited to see what the foreigner would do next. Very slowly, Zvi released his grasp on the weaver's hand and let his own fall to his side. With great effort he met the man's startled eyes and then shook his head.

"There's got to be another way," he finally said.

It was the mori who explained, "We have always done things this way. An amulet. It is our way. It has sustained us."

Zvi swung toward the teacher whom he had come to respect. The mori looked older now. His hair stood out in all directions, stiff with dirt and sand. His dark eyes were withdrawn farther into his small head. The two stood trying to understand each other.

"Amulets?" Zvi asked. "Do you believe in amulets?" knowing the man was not talking about the mezuzah but primitive good-luck charms.

The older man nodded. "I believe." Then with a friendly smile, "What do you believe in?"

Zvi's head dropped back and he ignored the small group about him as he stared at the bright sky. "I don't believe in signs, in portents, in superstitions, in the tales told by the very foolish or the very old."

He stretched out his hand and clasped the mori's shoulder affectionately as he tried to be kind. "I don't belittle your faith. It is going to take all the faith of all of you for us to reach home."

"Don't put too much hope in our faith, for we are cursed," the old man said.

Later as he sat by the fire with Havah, Zvi asked, "What did the mori mean when he told me your people are cursed?" And even while he spoke, Zvi wished he could be less formal in Arabic.

The woman reached up, placed both of her hands on his and put them into her lap where she held them as she spoke.

"A long time ago, in the years when the *taj* was being lived . . . "

And it took Zvi a moment to recall that these people called the Bible *taj*, or crown.

"There was the great exile in the place called Babylon and God took pity on His people and the king called Cyrus and the prophet called Ezra said that His people should go once more to the Holy City, the city which He had given them. However, at that time there were many rich men who had lived in Yemen and they knew there were riches there and they did not want to go to the Holy Land." Her voice dropped for a moment as she seemed to be reflecting on the iniquity, but to Zvi's surprise, she reminded him, "Nights ago I told you that there was treasure in the Yemenite earth for the man in whose name it had been held."

Zvi tried not to smile as he nodded.

"The people of Yemen," Havah continued, "they would not hear what the prophet Ezra was telling them." She was quiet again, and Zvi knew he could not prod the simple tale from her and would have to wait until she thought it through. He was wondering if all the people in the camp knew the story, when she said, "If everyone had gone to Israel then, would there have been a Second Temple and would it have been destroyed?"

Zvi shrugged. "I'm sure I don't know."

Astonished that this foreigner whom everyone believed so wise did not know the answer, she was reluctant for a moment to continue and then it was obvious that she felt obliged to explain her people to him. Her small fingers closed more tightly on his as she dropped her voice even lower. "And then when no one came to Israel from Yemen, the prophet Ezra cursed my people." Her head fell back and Zvi could see that she was almost frightened. " 'Whosoever came not within three days, all his substance should be forfeited and himself be separated from the congregation.' " And having quoted the prophet, Havah's eyes locked with Zvi's. "And so the people of Yemen were without honor and without wealth and we lived apart from Zion." Then she dropped her head and hid it against Zvi's chest. The Israeli enfolded her in his arms and stared beyond her toward the fires.

Sighing, Zvi thought he now knew that he did not understand these people as well as he thought he had. A figure rose from among those by the fire and approached the Israeli. Zvi did not bother to rise. Nor did he put Havah aside. Rather, he closed his arms more tightly about her, resting one hand on the back of her small head to comfort her.

A moment later Isaac squatted beside the couple. Looking from the woman to Zvi, he asked, "Is she all right?"

Zvi nodded. "She just told me about the curse of Ezra."

The young Yemenite pushed his small cap back on his head and tried to smile. "All of our people have heard it often."

"And you think that was why there is hunger?" Zvi asked, trying to determine how naïve this man was.

Isaac's strong fingers closed behind his neck as he considered the question. "Many things have happened to our people since Ezra, and a few of these have been good. We have had our promises, our messiahs, but most of them were false." He shook his head and swayed from side to side as he asked, "How does one know when he is following a false messiah?"

Zvi shrugged and when Havah started to sit up, he held her head firmly against his chest.

"You see," Isaac said, "you don't know. But we have a way. We have not always used it, but we have a way."

"Well?" and Zvi was almost laughing because he had been tempted to say *nu*.

"One time there was a false prophet and a great mori wrote the Rambam," then, assuming this Israeli was truly ignorant, "the man who was called Moses Maimonides."

Zvi tried to keep a straight face.

"And the Rambam sent us a letter," a strange pride came into Isaac's voice as he said again, "To us. He sent the letter to us, the Jews of Yemen, and he told us to keep the faith and we would know when the Messiah came."

Suddenly, Zvi felt self-conscious as he realized that he was the man leading these people out of Yemen. However, he relaxed when Isaac continued.

"And now there is a leader named David in the Holy Land and he has sent for us."

"And until he sent for you?"

With great patience, Isaac explained as though to a child, "We lived in terror and hoped for a king of the Jews who would rule over Yemen; we prayed for it daily."

Deciding there was nothing he could say about this, the Israeli remained silent.

After a moment he sat upright and Havah drew away from him, looked at Isaac, rose and left the two men alone. Isaac looked after her for a moment and then asked, "Why don't you marry her?"

Taken aback at the suggestion, Zvi shook his head. "I can't. I'm married."

The answer baffled the silversmith. "What difference does that make?"

"I can't," Zvi repeated, not wanting to become involved with the problem of polygamy, which he knew these people would have to face once they reached the Holy Land.

Two days later they reached Ibb. The journey was fatiguing. They were moving more slowly. They paused twice to bury their dead. The first time they dug, they buried a child. The second time, an old man. But they pushed on along the hairpin road to the city set on a mountaintop. To the east was a large mountain massif from which flowed fresh water over the terraced mountain sides. The principal gate stood between two high circular towers which looked down the mountain. The heavy walls of the city had stood for centuries and as Zvi and his column approached, he could see that the walls had been maintained. Tall white houses made up part of the wall. Along its northern length were hundreds of Arabs who had come out to see the Jews. The large curved buttress of the walls broadened at the base, and near it the Jews came together in a group and stood looking up at the people of Ibb. Beyond the people they could see the tall minarets of two mosques. One of them was circular with white designs, while the other was whitewashed and octagonal. The paved stone slope which led to the northern gate was crowded with camels and horses, and Zvi assumed a caravan had just arrived. He stood with his hands on his hips looking up the slope and towers. He could hear shouting and he knew the Arabs of Ibb were trying to tell him something. Even though he could not make out what they were saying, he was able to guess. Turning slowly, he looked at his charges. The women and children were already sitting down along the roadside. Some of the men had moved forward to create a wall of shadow from the sun. Over to the east, Zvi made out an arched aqueduct running into the city. Somewhere along its base, he knew he would find water. He was trying to decide where he should take his people, when a man walked out of the crowd near the gate and down the slope toward him. The stranger wore a white Arab robe and a green turban. Sighing, Zvi took for granted that he would be told where his people would spend the night, and so he waited. A few minutes later the stranger greeted him.

"Mazon?"

Zvi nodded, aware that his clothes set him apart.

The stranger, small and olive brown as any Yemenite, stuck out his hand, "I'm Adam Ibn Shukr."

And the stranger was speaking modern Israeli Hebrew.

Speechless, Zvi grabbed the man's hand and shook it.

Neither of them spoke for a time as the stranger walked down the length of the column and smiled one at a time at the refugees. When he reached the end of the column, he swung back and looked at them, his small dark face beaming. "Don't worry," he said confidently. "We will see that you reach the Holy Land."

Then he put one hand on Zvi's arm. "The Agency sent me ahead."

Zvi almost wished the mori had taken the time to teach him how to pray because he wanted to say thank you. The Jewish Agency had been running the operation from Yemen through Aden to Lod airport to Israel, and it was the Agency which had sent Zvi to San'a. And now at last here was someone to help him.

Not wanting to feel too confident, he asked, "Your Arab clothes?"

"I put them on," the explanation was almost ingenuous, and both smiled. "I'm a sabra, but my father was from Zahran. It might help to pass as an Arab."

Zvi did not know where Zahran was except that it was in some vague area on the Saudi Arabian side of the border to the north. "Where do we spend the night and can we get some food?" Zvi asked without waiting for any more formalities.

At that moment a jeep raced down the slope toward the two Israelis. Panicking, the refugees ran back from the road into an open field before the dust settled. Ignoring the jeep and its occupants, Zvi shouted to Isaac, "It's all right. Calm them down."

One of the two Arabs in the jeep stepped out, and told the two Israelis, "You are under arrest."

It was already late in the afternoon when they entered Ibb. For several minutes after the arrest, the two Arab police tried to decide whether or not their prisoners should be allowed to ride, and to the satisfaction of the Arabs, it was Adam who suggested they walk in front of the jeep.

The crowd around the main gate stood back to let the Jews through. Some hooted. One man threw a stone, but when one of the police shook his head, no others joined in. The streets of Ibb were unpaved and narrow, and except for the market place, all the land within the walls had been built upon. The west side of the city stood on level ground which had been artificially built up, and as he walked through the streets, Zvi realized that this was why the city walls had been buttressed. Arabs gathered on rooftops and the small balconies to watch the two Jews enter the city.

Realizing they were the center of attention, Zvi and his newly met companion threw back their shoulders and walked with pride.

Finally, one of the Arab police ordered them to stop. Then he led the two into a small building and down a corridor to a whitewashed room where a middle-aged policeman sat behind a table. The officer who had brought the two withdrew and left them alone with the older man. Rising from behind the table, the Arab revealed a great girth. He was taller than most of the Arabs Zvi had met in Yemen and he was better dressed. Zvi wondered for a moment where he had seen the man before; and then, he brought his hand up to wipe his face and cover it. At that instant the other man was staring at him.

"You are both Jews?"

Zvi decided to let Adam answer as he knew the country and the language better than he.

"I am a Jew," Adam admitted. "And so is my companion."

However, before the officer could make a judgment about this, Adam added quickly, "We are traveling with the permission of the Imam. He knows we are here. He has said that we have his protection," handing the officer a slip of paper.

The Arab officer accepted the slip, tucked it unread into a drawer of the table and shouted. A moment later the two policemen entered.

"Throw these damned Yahudim into a cell."

Startled, Adam began to protest, but the Arab drew back his hand. "Do you want to make trouble?"

Very slowly Adam shook his head and followed Zvi out of the room. The two police escorted them into a small basement and just before they threw open a door and shoved the pair into a cell, Adam dropped three thalers. The Arabs did not wait for him to pick them up before they slammed the cell door closed with the Jews on the other side. A faint light revealed a slit in the wall far above them. Zvi slowly pivoted about. There were scars in the wall which he recognized as bullet holes. Two large iron bars jutted out on the far side of the cell, and Zvi looked to Adam for an explanation.

"You can get hung up on these if they feel like it."

The Agency man lowered himself to the dirt floor, shoved his legs out before him and folded his arms.

With a snort, Zvi asked, "What next?"

Adam shrugged. "We'll worry for a time and then we will find an answer."

Looking down at the other man, Zvi said, "Just like that?"

His companion shrugged.

"That Arab," Zvi told his companion. "He lived in Jerusalem before the war. And before that I'd seen him near Beersheba."

"You're certain?"

"There aren't many that large and that ugly."

Adam laughed. "I don't think he recognized you, but I wouldn't depend on it."

"Can we depend on that paper you have with the Imam's permission?"

It took the shorter man a few seconds before he answered. "I wish I could be certain."

Dropping down beside his companion, Zvi asked, "Why is the Imam letting his Jews out? It will upset his economy. They make everything his people use. They clean his chamber pots and mint his money." Zvi thought about what he had said before adding, "And I'm told every one of them pays a head tax for the right to be alive."

Adam nodded. His hands folded behind his head as he leaned back against the wall. "I think a lot of people would like the answer to that." He fell silent for a time and then he suggested, "The Imam is not friendly to the Egyptians, the Syrians and most of the other members of the Arab League. Particularly his cousin, the King of Saudi Arabia. Maybe he's spiting the lot by letting the Jews go to Israel. The Imam has heard how the Jewish hordes have swept over Palestine, defeating the Egyptian, Syrian, Iraqi, Jordanian and all the other mighty armies, and maybe—just maybe—he's buying some kind of protection, no matter how remote."

Zvi thought any of these answers might be correct. "But isn't he a bit removed to need the friendship of *our* mighty armies?"

The Agency man looked at his companion with a kind of gentle tolerance as he explained, "The Americans made big atom bombs, but the Jews taught them how, and in Israel the Jews make small atom bombs which they can ship over by airmail or camelback. Hell, everyone knows the Jews are clever and rich and they can all make atom bombs in their kitchens and workshops, and with a clever man like Weizmann at the Hebrew University actually using a real scientific lab and a mighty king like David the Ben Gurion, there isn't anything the Jews cannot do. They drive off the seven invaders. Any wise man knows that seven is an important number in astrology and a dice game." Adam was warming to his subject, and Zvi realized from the way the man was eyeing the door that he hoped someone was listening. "And if the Jews could drive off and defeat the seven armies in less than seven weeks then why, of course, the Imam knows he wants to be their friend."

Trying hard not to laugh, Zvi agreed. "It was a mighty time for mighty men." Then he dropped his voice and asked, "Where did you get seven weeks?"

Adam winked.

The cell was almost dark now. Zvi leaned against the wall and tried to decide how he could help the refugees who had been left near the city. Without looking down at Adam, he asked, "Those thalers you dropped?"

"They'll come back for more."

Still uncertain what his companion was trying to do, Zvi asked, "And then?"

"We'll see what comes next."

Neither of the Jews knew how long they had been in the cell when Zvi first remembered he had not yet eaten and asked his companion if he should raise a fuss.

Adam thought about this and shook his head. "They'll feed us when they get around to it."

Zvi felt something crawling over his leg and slapped at it. "How did you get here?" he finally asked, as much to talk as to get an answer.

"Jeep."

"Jeep? They allowed you to ride?"

"That jeep the police were driving. It was mine."

Zvi laughed softly. "Maybe that was your crime."

"My crime here is being a Jew."

"But riding . . . ?"

"No," Adam explained. "Don't think they enforce all laws equally. Some Jews ride and they say nothing. However, a few years ago a little Jewish boy accepted a ride in an American army jeep and both he and his mother went to jail in chains."

Zvi did not understand and said as much.

"It depends on which Arab you meet."

Somewhere a dog howled. Zvi slapped at his legs, wondering what was crawling over him and was pleased that he could not see it in the dark.

There was a noise outside the cell and a moment later the door swung slowly open, letting in light from a candle held by one of the two policemen who had brought them into the city.

"You," the policeman said, pointing to Adam, "you come with me."

Very slowly Adam pulled himself to his feet, placed a hand on Zvi's shoulder for an instant as though to reassure him, and then followed the policeman.

After the door closed again, Zvi considered sprawling out on the floor and sleeping, but there was something else crawling on his legs and he decided that he did not want whatever it was on his face and so he forced himself to sit upright.

The sentries started shouting from tower to tower. Looking up at the slit where a vague bit of night came through, Zvi thought about Isaac and Havah and he wondered what was happening to them and if they would be able to go on without him.

The dogs barked and again he slapped something on his leg. His hand came away sticky and he wiped it in disgust on his trousers.

Then there was a sound outside the door again and when it opened, he was partially blinded by the sudden appearance of candlelight. Adam rejoined him and the door closed once more.

"And?" Zvi asked.

"He's going to see if he can make contact with a Jew here in town."

"What good will that do us?"

"How the hell do I know?" Adam was annoyed. "Took most of the thalers I had."

They fell silent and waited. Neither one of them had any idea how long they waited, but both of them became aware that the light seeping through the slit was becoming brighter and morning was almost on them.

"Are there any Jews he could contact in this city?" Zvi asked, hoping his question did not sound too foolish.

Adam shrugged. "I gave him an alternative."

Swinging to face his companion, Zvi waited.

"The English," Adam explained.

Before either of them could say anything else, the cell door opened, and Zvi sprang away from it, startled by the sound and annoyed at himself for not having heard anyone approaching. This time, instead of the policeman, a tall, lean redheaded English officer dressed in a tan cotton uniform stood in the doorway looking at the two.

"Jews, aren't you?" he asked

Zvi decided to let Adam handle the question.

The Agency man rose to his feet, put out his hand to shake the other man's and agreed, "We're both Jews."

Ignoring Adam's hand, the English officer said simply, "A bit far north aren't you?"

Dropping his hand to his side, Adam shook his head. "I gave that Arab captain my travel permit."

As though he had not heard the answer, the Englishman looked from Adam to Zvi and then back to the Agency man again. "Which of you bloody bastards is Zvi Mazon?"

Not too surprised that his name was getting around, Zvi was relieved that Captain Layton had as yet not seemed to link it to the man he had sought a couple of years before in the column evacuating the Old City.

"I am Major Mazon," Zvi said. There was harshness in his voice as he assumed the authority his position entitled him to with this Englishman.

Very slowly Layton swung back to Zvi and with great deliberateness he looked the stocky Jewish officer over. Zvi wished his slacks and shirt were not so dirty and that he was shaven, but at this moment he did not think appearance too important.

"You were looking for me?" the Israeli asked.

Layton shoved the garrison cap he was wearing back on his head and scratched his red hair. The man's pale skin and faint blue eyes annoyed Zvi, who was waiting for an answer. Trying not to remember why he hated this particular Englishman, Zvi smiled.

From where he stood at the other side of the cell, Adam Ibn Shukr watched the two curiously. "Seeing you asked which of us is the major, I assume this is not old home week," Adam said flatly, when he feared that Zvi might lose his temper.

The Englishman forced himself to smile, but he did not take his eyes off Zvi. "A friend of mine asked me to find out if you were all right, and then I received a message that there were two Jews in jail here."

The explanation was only partially complete because everyone in Ibb must have known two Jews had been jailed. However, Zvi did not think he had to ask who the captain's friend was.

And with the man's next words, he knew he had guessed right. "Where do you know her from?" Layton snapped.

Increasingly curious as to what he had stirred up, Adam leaned against the wall, "Gentlemen, this is a hell of a place to take up the name of any woman. It isn't the gentleman's way of doing things."

The cynicism in his voice brought Layton about sharply. "You're the Jew from the Agency?"

Adam nodded.

"I've had instructions to expect you to show up here."

Puzzled, Adam ceased smiling. "Instructions?"

Layton's smile broadened. "Aden thought you would go too far north." Then as if it pleased him, he added, "And I was told not to interfere if you became involved with the Yemen government because if you reached Ibb you would have exceeded your authority or permission to travel."

That Layton liked his instructions was obvious. The Englishman asked a second time, "Where do you know her from?"

Deciding that he could lose nothing by playing ignorant, Zvi asked, "What lady?"

Something was crawling up his trouser now and he wanted to bend over and knock it off, but that would have meant taking his eyes off Layton and at this moment, he did not want to do that.

"Miss Hassani."

Zvi's head bobbed as though this was sudden recognition. "Long ago and far away."

This did not seem to satisfy the English officer, but after a moment, he said, "I'll talk to the *mudir*." The others assumed he meant the fat Arab officer. Layton started for the door and then looked back at the two Israelis. "I don't know what the messenger cost you, but my help is going to cost the two of you more than you know." Then he was gone and the cell door was closed.

Once the two were alone again, Adam asked, "Why didn't you tell me you had important friends here?"

Zvi leaned over, swatted a scorpion off his trouser leg while he shook his head. "Don't count on my influence with that bastard."

Neither Zvi nor Adam knew how long it was before the door opened again, but when it did, the two policemen who had brought them in the afternoon before beckoned for Zvi to follow them. At first both Adam and Zvi rose to their feet, but the stouter of the two Arabs shook his head at Adam, grabbed Zvi's arm and jerked him out of the cell. Without a word they led him to the front door of the small building and shoved him through it.

"You can go, Yahud," the leaner of the two snarled.

When he regained his balance, Zvi turned back toward the door, but the police were gone and the door was closed. Zvi stood looking at the concrete building. He wondered if he should go in and demand that they release Adam also. Shaking his head in bewilderment, he glanced about. There were several Arabs in the street watching the foreign Jew. One of them—an old man with a twisted leg—hobbled over to Zvi, looked up and spat in his face. Zvi's hand went back to strike the Arab, and then he remembered where he was. Wiping the spittle off his face with his sleeve, he made his way through the streets and to the main gate.

The caravan which had stopped on the sloping road that led out of Ibb had moved on. The donkeys were chewing some dried grass from a basket while an old Arab woman stood between them. There was no one else to be seen.

Trotting down the road, Zvi went looking for the refugees. Ten minutes later he found their camp, looking as it had every other time they had spent a night in an open field. As he approached, the Jews began to gather and wait for him. The mori threw his arms about the Israeli and said a *berakhah*. While over the small man's shoulder, Zvi could see Isaac, his wives, the blacksmith and his wives and beyond them Havah and all of the others whom he had come to know in the weeks they had traveled together, and to his own surprise, he felt comfortable. He put his arms about the old silversmith and embraced him before he stepped back.

"Have any of you seen the Arab?"

The others did not understand whom he meant at first. "The Arab? The man with the hunchback who's been traveling with us?"

The weaver pointed to a tree on the far side of the field. Nodding, Zvi ran toward the tree. Isaac joined him and as they ran together, the silversmith asked, "Are you all right?"

"Everything is going to be all right," Zvi shouted and, stepping up his pace, he moved far ahead of the Yemenite. At the base of the tree, he found the guide sprawled on two blankets, his horse lying at his side. Recognizing the blankets as his own, Zvi was tempted for an instant to kick the guide in the ribs. However, at this moment, he knew he needed this little man, and so instead he knelt beside the hunchback and shook him gently until he awakened.

Surprised at the sight of the Israeli, Ali pushed himself into a sitting position. Fear spelled his face as he tried to move back on the blanket.

With a gesture of affection, Zvi took the small man's arm, squeezed it and smiled broadly to indicate that he held no resentment. "I've something for you to do," he said quickly.

Ali Harja cocked his ugly face to one side while he waited to learn what the Jew was asking.

"I'm going to give you five thalers," Zvi offered, "and I want you to go into Ibb and send a message over the wireless to San'a and tell the Imam that the *mudir*—the chief of the Ibb police—is holding in his prison a Jew from the Holy Land. Tell the Imam that this Jew is important and he knows how strong the armies of the Jews are."

Zvi waited to be certain the man had understood him, but when he saw no reaction, he repeated his message. Still no reaction, except the head cocked to one side as though the guide was waiting for some kind of an explanation. Reaching out, Zvi shook the Arab by the shoulders. "You heard me, didn't you?"

After a moment Ali Harja nodded slowly. "You want me to send a message over the wire to the Imam and tell him the *mudir* is holding your friend and that your friend knows about the armies of the Jews." The voice was flat, half afraid and at the same time taunting.

Not knowing just what the Arab was thinking, Zvi shoved his hand inside his shirt, pulled out five thalers and, taking the guide's hand, dropped the heavy coins into his palm.

The Arab drew himself upright as he stared at the coins, his hunched back rising grotesquely as high as his ears. Then, Zvi watched as the guide shook his head slowly from side to side. "Me send a message to the Imam?"

The small man's obvious disbelief in the request made Zvi smile.

"You can pay for the message. I can't," admitting his rights were limited.

The Arab dropped his head back and for an instant he seemed to be looking at his swaybacked mare. Then he turned his attention once more to the foreign Jew. "I will send the message if you will give me the belt where you keep the thalers."

Zvi's first clenched, but as it did, he turned away so that his anger would not show, and even though he felt his neck muscles tighten in fury and frustration, he slowly shoved his hands inside his shirt, unfastened the money belt and drew it out. The several pouches were still heavy with coins and before Zvi could even check to see how many were left, Ali Harja grabbed it from his hand, hefted it and smiled.

"I'll send the message."

Opening and closing his fists, Zvi considered the offer. "How do I know I can trust you?"

A wry smile crossed the small Arab's ugly face. "You don't have to." And he started to hand back the money belt.

Rising, Zvi said simply, "Send the message."

Five minutes later after he had mounted his mare and slung both of Zvi's blankets across its neck, Ali Harja looked down at Zvi with a grin, "I shall not be back, Yahud."

Without realizing what he was doing, Zvi reached out to drag the guide from his saddle, but the little man, pleased with himself, began to cackle loudly while Zvi stared for a time at his own hands, dropped them to his side in frustration and nodded. "I won't expect you."

With deliberate pacing, the Arab slowly rode his horse across the field, past the Jewish camp and onto the road which led up the slope to Ibb.

Zvi watched the little man disappear, and after a time he shoved both fists in front of him as though he had never seen them before. His eyes narrowed. His head dropped back and he stared at the sky. How long he remained in the corner of the field, he did not know, but the sun was already setting when Havah brought him a small pan of beans. She squatted beside him and tried to smile.

"We did not know what we would do if you did not return," and for the second time Zvi was glad to have been missed.

Reaching out, he took the platter and set it on the ground at his side. Even though he was aware that he had not eaten for more than a day, he wanted to take the time to let her know how he felt. Both of his hands came out and his palms framed her face while he tried to smile at her. "I am glad that I am back," he said, wishing that somehow he could tell her and all the others that he had some news for them, some word that the rest of their journey would be easier. He drew her to him and gently kissed her cheek. "It ... it ... " and he was speaking haltingly because he was combing his words with care, "It will be all right now."

She nodded as she sat down, her trousered legs drawn up before her. "The hunchback has all of your thalers?"

Zvi nodded. "It had to be."

"And the other man from the Holy Land?"

Wiping his face with a dry palm, Zvi looked past her to the high walls of Ibb which on the mountainside looked even higher than they actually were.

"We will wait for him."

Havah did not understand what he was trying to tell her, but she thought she had to ask, "And the Arabs released only you?"

Taken aback that he had not even thought of Adam or Layton since he had left the jail, Zvi considered her question in the light of the Englishman's actions. "It is a long story," he finally said and that seemed to satisfy her.

She smiled, picked up the platter and offered it to him again. "It's warm."

He nodded.

Later, after darkness had covered the small camp and the shouts of the Arab sentries were heard from the distant towers, Zvi rolled over on Havah's blanket and looked at her face. As always, he was surprised how old she looked for a woman who was probably no older than he. And yet in spite of the lines of age that had gathered about her eyes and her mouth, the delicacy remained. He realized that it probably always would.

The night was chill and he wished he had another blanket with which to cover her. He came up onto his elbows and stared at the darkness and thought about Zella. Someday he would tell her about Havah, and when he did, he hoped she would understand that this woman and he had two things in common: they were lonely and they were outsiders.

He was still thinking about this when he heard the sound of a motor approaching. Springing to his bare feet, he sought his shoes, shoved his feet into them and stood with his hands on his hips as the headlights of a vehicle cut a white wedge through the night.

Dust rose in the darkness and the jeep came to a stop beside him. Blinded by the lights of the vehicle, Zvi shielded his eyes and placed a protecting arm about Havah's waist as she rose to his side.

"They said I would find you here," Adam laughed as he cut the motor and, leaning out, took Zvi's hand. "Thanks. Your little hunchbacked friend sent your wire and the Imam told them that if they had no charges other than my clothes to hold against me, they should release me." Adam was laughing as he added, "And they were so afraid of the power of my armies, they gave me back my jeep."

He was standing beside Zvi now, his hand on his companion's arm. "It cost me a lot, but I guess I'm worth that."

Zvi's head dropped to one side, "Cost you?"

"Of course," Adam explained. "You didn't think he was going to send the wire for nothing. That would be naïve."

The others were startled at Zvi's sudden burst of laughter which broke over the field. "Indeed, that would have been naïve of me."

While Havah heated up some beans for Adam, the three sat about the small fire Zvi had built and they talked. The rest of the refugees hung back, listening, and because Adam knew they were there, he made it clear to Zvi there were things he would say when they were alone.

Away from what he considered civilization for months, Zvi sought news he had not asked in the prison at Ibb where the Arabs could hear. Adam admitted he knew nothing about Zvi's wife and he knew nothing about what was happening in the army. However, he spilled out the story that the Wafdists had returned to power in the Egyptian election and that all Egyptian cabinet members dropped in 1944 were back in power, and both men admitted they did not know what difference this would really make to Israel; the British had recognized China; Persia had a new government; India, finally free of England, had opted to stay in the Commonwealth, and both men wondered what would have happened if Israel had been given that choice; there had been a purge in Poland; the Russians and Chinese had signed a thirty-year peace treaty; the Russians had announced they had created an A-bomb, and with a wry smile Adam concluded his report with the news that Britain had recognized Israel. Both men were silent for a moment as they thought what this might mean.

"Where do we go from here?" Zvi asked Adam after a time.

The Agency man was silent as he stared into the dung fire. Combing his black hair with his thin fingers, he sighed. "I am not sure." Then he shook his head, seemingly to disavow his own answer. "I know, but I wish I didn't."

Zvi leaned forward and waited for an explanation.

"It isn't all that bad. You go on."

Adam's hands came out as he picked up a small pebble and rolled it back and forth between his palms. "You aren't alone though. None of you.

The oriental Jews have been coming from the north, the highlands; from the Saudi border and beyond; they've been gathering in the lowlands, and they've been moving out from the desert; they've emerged from the rim of the Red Sea to the west and from the Hadhramaut hills; they've even been coming from the edges of India and Iran. Ever since they knew there was a State, they've been coming, and much of the time they come from villages we have never heard of before, places where no one knew a Jew lived. They've been walking though broken country with bad roads or no roads. Like yourselves."

"How many?" Zvi asked.

Smiling bitterly, Adam asked, "How many from where?"

Trying not to laugh, Zvi said, "Spoken like a true Jew, a question for a question."

Adam shook his head. "I'm not trying to fob you off it." He put his palms together in front of him and rested them on his knee. "There are going to be six hundred thousand from the Red Sea to the Atlantic. Jews who have been stripped of everything they ever owned, money, clothes, tools, dignity, and even the language they have been speaking. People weep about the Arab refugees, but they forget no one drove them out. They fled Israel when their leaders told them to get out of Palestine so the Arab armies could move in. But these people," and as he spoke he looked at the faces near the fire: the scarred face of the weaver, the sad face of the blacksmith's second wife, the wrinkled face of an aged lapidary. "The Arab refugees went on their own and mostly during the mandate period. Our people have had life made impossible for them, and even on their leaving, they have not been allowed to take anything but their books, which the Arabs feared, and their lives, which the Arabs also feared because of retribution on the Day of Resurrection." Adam shook his head. "I'm not given to speeches," and as he said it, Zvi knew this was the man's way of making his speeches.

"But," Adam continued, "it is happening. The Jews are going home. And when they arrive, there will eventually be housing for them and food and education for their children and jobs to work at and places to worship in with dignity." He smiled, knowing that the faces about the fire were all fixed on his, and he was only looking humbly at his hands, palms still together. "Refugees. The world has forgotten our refugees from the East, and there are those who say we really didn't need a country to hold the few who survived the West."

In spite of his own cynicism, Zvi admitted to himself that he was carried away by the simplicity of Adam's exhortation. Putting a hand on Havah's back so that she would not fall when he rose, Zvi came to his feet and looked down at Adam and the Yemenite woman. "How many from Yemen?" he asked.

Shrugging, Adam shook his head. "The guess runs to fifty thousand before the next few months are over."

Zvi whistled at the unexpected number. "And what's happening to them?"

Without looking up, Adam said simply, "They're reaching Aden and getting home from there."

It took Zvi a moment to realize that Adam was not telling him everything, and because he wanted to know more, he suggested, "I think it's time to go to sleep." He smiled at Havah and the faces about the fire. "We've lost time and we have to move on in the morning."

A few minutes later, Zvi was alone with Adam Ibn Shukr, who waited for the questions.

The two men were sprawled on their backs and stared at the sky while the dying fire tossed sparks at their feet.

"And what's happening to them?" Zvi asked again.

"More are dying than should. It would be nice if we could set up stations with food. We can't in this country. More are starving, dying of malnutrition and beans, of malaria and sheer fatigue than should. We are doing the best we can, but we aren't going to get them all through."

Without looking at the man, Zvi was aware of the pain that ran through his companion.

"And these people with me?"

Adam watched several leaves rubbing each other as the wind passed among them. "These people are lucky. You're with them. Most are coming on alone."

"I haven't done them much good," Zvi confessed.

"You're here and that's good."

Not satisfied with small consolations, Zvi was seeking neither pity nor praise, and so he shifted the subject. "What next for us?"

Adam twisted up on one elbow. "You'll go south and south. There are gathering points short of Aden, and you could go there and be flown in, but this is not for you."

Puzzled, Zvi rolled his head and stared at the other man.

"You're going through until you cross the border near the frontier between Yemen and the Aden Territorial Frontier—if we're lucky—we'll have rented trucks for you. Forty reals a day for a Jew, but we'll rent them and they'll bring you in the rest of the way."

Zvi nodded, not fully understanding. "And we'll be allowed to ride?"

"You'll ride so they can make money." Adam snorted and dropped back on his blanket. "And you'll get through if the British don't stop you."

"Are they likely to?"

Rolling his head from side to side even though the major was not watching him, Adam tried to think of the answer to that question. "There's talk we're bringing in some kind of plague and the British may stop us." He fell silent before he added, "That may explain Layton's having been here. But

I'm not saying they have no justice on their side." He laughed bitterly. "The British always try to have you understand why they cut your throat. Logical people."

"Justice?"

"Over one third of the population of Yemen died of typhus in 1942 and '43 so the British may have reason to be afraid."

Very slowly, Zvi lowered himself again, folded his hands behind his head and stared at the night sky. The fire was no longer throwing shadows. The only noises that could be heard were the distant shouts of the Arabs manning the sentry towers along the walls of Ibb.

In the morning, Adam went his own way, promising to see them all in Aden, and the refugees moved out of the fields of Ibb.

They moved south down the great mountain, from Mauris over the stone bridge toward the village of Zishrong. The weak grew weaker, the sick more sick, and the pace slowed with every kilometer. Four times the first day they stopped long enough to say Kaddish over a grave and pile the stones high against the evils of the countryside. Each time they moved on Zvi became aware that there was going to come a time when they might not be able to start out again.

The men and the boys clutched their holy scrolls. The women carried their children or dragged them when they no longer had the strength to carry them. For several hours Zvi cradled a child whose mother kept crumbling to the ground at his side. Each time the tanner's third wife collapsed, Zvi waved the column on and helped the woman to her feet with an arm about her waist even though she shied from his touch. The tanner stopped long enough for his wife and the foreign Jew to catch up with him, and then he trotted on to help his other two wives and the old mother of his first wife.

That was the afternoon they buried both the aged mason and his wife. The sores on the man's feet had burst into a putrid green ooze; and when Zvi saw the man an hour later, there were already worms crawling over his thighs. Try as he would, the small mason could not hobble fast enough to keep up with the column. Several hours later Zvi dropped back to see how he was faring. He need not have bothered; the man was dead. Isaac and the blacksmith left the column long enough to hold the funeral, and when they rejoined it, the mason's wife lay by the roadside.

The next morning they walked south by the stone road. The wadi disappeared and hills rose before them. Gullies cut the scarred earth. There were jasmine shrubs and jackals, mountain badgers with long teeth and blooming clematis. The tanner's third wife died before noon, and they buried her under a small, withered dun palm. Kaddish was said, and the column moved on. Zvi and Havah took turns walking with the child, a boy who could have been three or four years old with large brown eyes, a thin face and olive skin.

Outside the village of Saiyanah, they were stopped by five Arab soldiers mounted on camels. Their leader, a fat man with a gray beard and laughing eyes, explained to Zvi that it was time the Jews paid their *jizya*, and Zvi appealed to Isaac for an explanation.

"Protection money," the silversmith explained while the column settled down beside the road and waited for the business to be settled. Glancing over his shoulder, Zvi could see that most of them were too weary to rise again that day, and though it was only mid-afternoon and they had gone less than half the distance he had planned, he told Isaac, "Make camp here."

The Arab with the laughing eyes brought his head up sharply, and Zvi fell silent for a moment as he too listened to the awful voice of the muezzin singing on the distant minaret in Saiyanah.

> O thou most merciful,
> Be thou merciful to us . . .

And when Zvi looked back at the Arab leader, he asked, "Did you hear what he was saying?"

The Arab's jowls bounced as he nodded. "Yahudin pay tribute so that they will not forget they are Yahudin." The laughing eyes crinkled in the corners, "And the paying of tribute reminds them of the prophet's tolerance and benevolence."

Though he sought an answer in his mind, Zvi knew he had none he could give that would satisfy this man. There was no answer other than money. And he had no money.

It took him almost an hour to convince the Arab that the Jews were unable to pay him anything for his mercy, for the ransom of their holy scrolls, for their lives. Finally, the fat Arab agreed to accept Zvi's note for the total, pointing out that if he could not send the money from Aden, no more Jews would pass Saiyanah.

That night the women of the camp drew their water at the village well which stands under the famous tree the Arabs call *Taulagah*—the Tree of Joy. To the surprise of Zvi none of the villagers interfered with them. In fact, several veiled Arab women paused at the well to help the Jewish women with their waterbags. One elderly Arab came out of his house, watched the Jews for a time and then, approaching Zvi, suggested, "I can buy your people food if you have any money."

Unused to such consideration, Zvi hesitated.

The ancient Arab rubbed his dark cheek with one hand. "I have traveled far and have known the world. Someday my people will know that there are other ways to live."

Still fearing a trap, Zvi only nodded.

A wry smile spread over the Arab's face. "I am known as the *Aegil* here.

That means 'the Quiet One.' I don't know if I am wise, but I think I know a frightened man when I see one."

Angry with himself for showing that he was afraid for the Jewish women filling their waterbags and pots, Zvi stared at the last of the women as she nodded to him, indicating that they were done with what they had to do in the village.

Zvi watched her disappear into the field beyond before he turned once more to the *Aegil*. "Afraid? I think I've been afraid *in* my life, but not usually *for* my life."

The Arab nodded and saw that they were alone. "You use your head, young man. An Arab only uses his when he fights."

Zvi still was not convinced the old man was as open as he appeared. " 'There is no fate more ghastly than to be a stupid Jew.' "

"That offer of food," the *Aegil* repeated, "it will remain an offer."

Opening his palms wide before him, Zvi shook his head. "I would like to thank you. In fact, I would like to buy what you offer, but for my people this has been the shearing time. There is not anything left. Nothing. I'd like to buy some food. I haven't anything to buy it with."

Zvi looked out toward the field where the dung and twig fires burned in the dusk. "You have seen the world, Wise One. Have you ever made skeletons walk?"

His hand came out before him, and he himself was taken aback, not that his hand shook but that it was so thin that he could almost see the bones beneath the parchment skin.

Almost tolerantly, the old Arab nodded. "No one said that life was easy. No one promised you that. No one said that your people would go happily. All that the Imam said was that he would not prevent their going."

"Thanks," Zvi snorted.

And to his amazement, the Arab's face seemed sad.

"I am sorry for you, Yahud. I am sorry."

As the old man turned away, Zvi reached out and grabbed his robe. "Thanks," Zvi said again, sincerely this time.

Without even turning back, the old man merely nodded. "Do what you have to do to get them home," he advised, and walked on.

That night the winds were still. The moon painted the countryside a pale green. The Jews slept as though they would never rise again. And when morning came, the mori called to Zvi to join him at the edge of the road.

"There are some who will not be going with us," the mori explained. And from the rents in the old silversmith's clothes, Zvi knew that the mori had lost one of his own family. For an instant, Zvi feared it might be Isaac, but then he saw his friend coming across the field toward him. Zvi smiled with relief, and then he felt ashamed until the mori saw whom he was smiling at;

and he, too, smiled. "It is good for Isaac that you lean on him. It will help him when we get there."

Zvi wanted to say something that would comfort the mori, but the old man was already walking toward the place where Zvi saw several men digging a grave with pots. However, it was not the grave-diggers who attracted his attention. The mori seemed to sway on his feet as though he would collapse. Before Zvi could take two steps after him, Isaac grabbed his arm. "Don't. He knows how weak he is. You can't do anything about that."

Zvi nodded. "What can I do?"

"Get those of us who live to the Holy Land. That will make the deaths of those who do not get there worth their having died."

Though the statement sounded both meaningless and pompous, Zvi knew this was not Isaac's intent. Then, almost mechanically, he strode into the dirt road, raised his arm and shouted, "Let's walk."

They left Saiyanah.

The countryside was green. Scattered cactus grew wildly, throwing strange shadows in the morning light. There was a sweet odor in the air, and in the distance wheat fields grew in patterns.

Looking down the length of the column, Zvi saw that Havah was carrying the orphan boy, who had been walking with them, on her shoulders, and then he looked up at the sun. The men and women were passing him once more, meandering under the heat. Several paused to drink from the stinking goatskin bags. One of the women offered hers to Zvi, but he shook his head and waved her on.

Now as the people passed him and tried to smile, he did not return the smiles. His jaw line became hard, his face tense and set. He could not care. He could not see a face again. He could not do anything for them and for himself, and accepting Isaac's commission, he intended to get them through if he had to see half of them die getting through. *"It will make the deaths of those who do not get there worth their having died."*

The mori meandered past almost addled as the sun reeled his frail body. The sores on his legs were green. The bones of his face showed through the translucent skin. But the man's eyes were on the people in front of him as he held his hands together and prayed.

Spitting anger into the dust, Zvi glared at Havah while she passed. For a moment she seemed to hesitate, and he snapped, "Close up that line."

When her dark eyes met his, she looked as though someone had struck her. Jerking her head forward, she dropped her eyes to the heels of the man ahead of her and followed him quietly. When the last woman had passed, Zvi remained where he was and let the gap between himself and the column grow.

The sun was bright. There was no breeze. Acacias hung limp near the road. A yellow buttercup drooped. A wasp buzzed near Zvi's face. He was on the rooftop and the Arabs were shooting at him and his back was rigid and he knew he could not yield an inch more ground or they would lose the Old City, and he would not survive the loss the the Old City.

His head dropped back and for a mad moment he met the sun with equal eyes. Then he looked after the column moving slowly through the hazy heat.

Suddenly, he broke into a trot, caught up with the last woman in the line and moved on to the van. Only when he found that there was no one else in front of him did he slow down, and setting his own pace, he walked on.

For the next three days the Israeli officer drove his people pitilessly. He ate alone, slept alone, and kept his emotional distance from those dying around him. They buried twenty-four in three days. They died from malnutrition, old age and exhaustion. However, since there was no doctor, Zvi never really knew from what each died.

At the end of the third day, they approached the refugee camp on Yemen's southern border. The road led through a stretch of desert. The rising wind drove the sand into their faces, laced it through the holes in their tattered clothes, bore it into the open sores of their skin, scratched it over their cheeks, battered it into their eyes with small misery.

Leading the column, Zvi did not turn about. His shirt was buttoned to his neck. He had a blanket over his shoulders which covered the lower half of his face. Leaning against the wind, he felt the sand lash his head. The only sound he heard was that of angry wind. The refugees shuffled silently along behind him. Something rose in the brown whirl ahead and he paused to see what it was. Approaching carefully, Zvi made out the figures of several Arabs standing beside a row of large, open trucks. Taking a deep breath, he looked up into the sandstorm and smiled in spite of himself. Adam Ibn Shukr had kept his part of the bargain.

Stopping the others where they were, Zvi shouted above the sound of the wind, "The trucks to take us south. They're just ahead."

The others did not seem to understand what he had said. Annoyed, he shouted again, "The trucks, they're here," and he hoped they would feel as good about this as he.

Then the mori stepped forward and asked, "What is a truck?"

Sand blew between the two and for a moment blinded both. Zvi's hand came up to cover his eyes and in that instant he did not know if his gesture was for protection or from despair.

The wind slackened and the sand seemed to fall away.

Still shouting, Zvi explained, "They are cars, vehicles, wagons without horses." With the wind fallen, he had no need to shout and he became embarrassed. "We will ride from here," he said, his voice dropping.

The mori appealed to his son with an anguished look and Isaac stepped forward. "It would not be safe."

162

Zvi reached out and grabbed his companion's shoulders as the wind rose again, slapping sand in gusts across their faces. "It will be all right. The Arabs are going to drive us. They will be with us." He relaxed as he suddenly began to laugh. Patting Isaac on the back, he explained, "We have permission."

The mori's fear would not leave him and, starting to protest when he saw the Arabs approaching, he appealed once more to his son. Seeing the fear on the old man's face, Zvi spun about in time to watch a dozen Arabs start to separate the children from their parents. Without taking time to weigh his reaction, Zvi jumped into the group, grabbed a small boy from the hands of one Arab and shoved another away from a toddling girl.

"What is going on?"

Before the Arabs could answer, a tall man stepped out from the group. Shoving the tarboosh of his burnoose back, Layton revealed his red hair. "It is all right, Major," he reassured Zvi. "It is all right."

"What the hell is all right?" Zvi demanded over the blast of wind and the shrieking of the children. They were speaking English now and no one else about them understood. "What the hell is all right?"

An almost friendly smile covered the English officer's face as he explained so softly that Zvi had to move still closer to be certain he was hearing correctly. "The laws of Yemen are simple. The Imam has not forgotten them and we will have to live with them, old man."

Not knowing where the Englishman's humor was taking them, Zvi grabbed the man's burnoose just below his collar and shouted, "What are you getting at?"

Layton very carefully put his hands on Zvi's wrists and, stepping back, shook his head. His incredible calm and overt patience were like a slap at Zvi who had reached the end of his own endurance.

Balling one fist, the Israeli closed with the captain, "What are you trying to tell me?"

"All orphans under fourteen will be converted to Islam and sent to schools belonging to the Imam."

The words seemed to tumble in the wind as Zvi sought to grasp their meaning. Suddenly, he felt like collapsing in the sand, but the faces of the children looking up at him and the faces of the older persons standing behind Layton seemed to expect something of him.

"How much do you want now?" Zvi demanded.

Layton cocked his head to one side as he considered the question. In that moment the wind rose once more, and the sand swept over the small group on the open road. Zvi had difficulty seeing the child whose hand he was holding, and while a long gust swirled sand about his brazed face, he could not even see Layton. When the wind paused to catch its breath for another blast, the two men were facing each other again.

"I don't want anything," Layton said as calmly as before. "I am not for sale."

Zvi looked about. The dozen Arabs were watching the two officers not knowing what was being said and not seeming to care. However, the Jews were trying to hide their children in their thin cloaks, behind their thin backs and behind the small bundles they carried. Zvi saw the startled look on Isaac's face, the passive acceptance on the mori's; and then he saw Havah holding the boy whose mother they had buried days before, the little boy with the dark eyes, small features and olive skin, who held his frail arms about Havah's neck.

Blind to the wind and the sand and the Arabs about him, Zvi lashed out with his fist, striking Layton in the face and following the blow with two others. The Englishman dropped to his knees, put one hand up to protect his head and reached for a pistol in his belt. Zvi was calm now and in control of himself. He was aware of the wind washing sand over them. He heard a woman scream in the background. He saw the curious expression on the faces of the Arabs standing behind Layton. But he waited long enough for the English captain to bring his pistol from his holster before he kicked the man's hand. The gun spun off into a dune, and then Zvi battered Layton about the head with both of his fists until the Englishman lay still. Standing over his enemy, Zvi heard only the wind. He did not bother to look at the faces around him. Kneeling, he jerked the loose cloak over Layton's head so that the sand would not cover it. And then with a sigh, he rose to his feet and looked around for the Arabs, shouting over the wind, "Who is in command here?"

A young Arab stepped through the crowd of refugees. The Arab youth's heavy mustache was covered with clinging sand and a piece of his keffiyeh—headcloth—draped his chin.

"Nothing has changed, Yahud," the Arab said bluntly. "The orphans will be converted."

Zvi nodded, more to gain time to think than to agree. "And then?"

The young Arab touched the palms of his hands together. "Then you will be taken south in the trucks to the border and on to the other side if the English agree."

Squinting against the wind and the sand, Zvi considered the prospects. Finally he shook his head to clear it and turned to Isaac, "Will you have every family gather its own children to it, and then the orphans will be sent over there," and he was pointing to a small dune, "where they will be given over to the care of the Imam."

At first, Zvi did not think Isaac understood, and so he walked over to Havah, put his arm about her, took the small child she was carrying into his arms and stood facing the young Arab.

Slowly the other families began to assemble. Husbands who were widowed stood beside women who had lost their husbands, old men beside young girls, and each family had several children and each woman no less than two, and if the woman was young enough to match the ages of the

164

children, she had several about her. After a few minutes, only three men and two women stood alone. All were in their twenties or older.

"There," Zvi pointed toward the dune he had selected earlier.

The five moved to the dune and waited.

For a long time the young Arab looked at the Jews. Then he slowly moved among the families asking the children which woman was their mother and which man their father. Some pretended not to understand him. One child whose parents had died days before grabbed Isaac's hand and sobbed.

Moving along with the young Arab, Zvi explained, "He's afraid of you." Then he appealed, "You don't look like the kind of man who frightens children."

The Arab brushed the sand off his mustache as the wind blew more into his face. Drawing the robe up to cover his mouth, he shouted at Zvi, "I'm not here to frighten children."

Stomping away from the families, he crossed the open space to the dune and the five who stood there. He peered into the faces of each of the men and each of the women, and with a shrug, he said, "They are all too old."

Satisfied, he walked over and stood looking down at Layton. "You know him?" he asked Zvi in English.

The Israeli nodded and answered in the same language. "We've met. Nothing more."

The Arab nodded. "There are your trucks. You had better drive out of here."

"Thanks," Zvi said, aware all of the time that he had not fooled this young man.

"I am the Imam's man, not Britain's. But in Aden south of the border the British foot the bill. Remember that."

Believing he understood the warning, Zvi smiled, "I mean that thanks."

"I want nothing from you, Yahud. Just leave."

It took Zvi less than half an hour to get his people into the trucks. The Yemenites were small, they weighed little, they possessed almost nothing, and so they could sit thirty to a truck. Zvi watched them approach the large wheeled vehicles uncertainly. He doubted if most of them had ever seen a truck before. Surely none had ever ridden in one. Standing in the rear, he helped each family into the trucks, showed them where to tuck their possessions and how to sit with their backs against the sides when possible.

When the gate of the last truck was fastened, Zvi mounted the runningboard of the first, waited for the Arab drivers to take their places and shouted for them to drive on. Several times while he was loading the trucks, Zvi had looked about for Layton. He had every reason to expect the Englishman to appear and cause trouble, but when the last truck pulled onto the road and began to move south, Zvi relaxed. Layton, if he had recovered from his beating, had not bothered with the Jews.

There were screams of awe and surprise from the refugees as the trucks moved into the sandstorm and on down the road. Several times, Zvi heard shouts, and when he climbed out of the cab and looked back, all he could see were the huddled refugees trying to hide from the wind and the sand.

Finally, Zvi waved the driver of his truck on, crawled over the side and into the truck bed. The shouts continued, and when he could not find a reason for the confusion, he knelt beside a potter with a wen on his nose and asked, "What is wrong?"

Surprised at the naiveté of the foreign Jew, the potter explained loudly over the roar of the motor, "We are scaring off the jinns who are sure to come now that we have changed the nature of things and Jews ride."

"You do that," Zvi agreed.

The winds struck the side of the truck and shoved it half way across the road, but the Arab driver did not seem to mind. Zvi squatted behind the cab so he could see the driver through the rear window and still watch the trucks behind. They had traveled for almost an hour, when one of the trucks near the rear of the column sputtered, farted and stopped. Banging on the window of the cab, Zvi signaled for his driver to stop, and a moment later, the entire column came to a halt.

Yelling for the refugees to stay where they were, Zvi leaped over the side of the truck and trotted back to the one that had first come to a stop. Behind the truck several men were gathered around a stonecutter who lay in the road with his leg twisted cruelly beneath him.

Zvi looked about at the others for an explanation. At first no one said anything, and then a potter explained. "He thought he would step out and walk to the one behind us."

"He what?" Zvi shouted over the sound of the wind, and then he noticed people were getting off the trucks. Grabbing Isaac's arm, he ordered, "Get them back into the trucks. Don't let anyone off. Now. Move."

It was the first time he had ever spoken to the silversmith this way, and he knew he would not apologize. A moment later he was alone in the road beside the stonecutter. Everyone else was back in the trucks and watching to see what he would do. Bending down, Zvi picked the little man up in his arms, walked back down the line of trucks until he found one in which there was enough room to lay a man down, dropped the gate open with one hand and set the stonecutter on the floor of the truck. For a moment their eyes met, and Zvi could see this man was in twisting, agonizing pain.

He put out his hand and touched the other man's. "We'll get you to a doctor," he promised. As he walked back to the lead truck, he shouted for Isaac to keep the people where they were when they were moving. Five minutes later the column drove on. From where he sat, Zvi tried to understand how the accident had taken place, and the only decision he could reach was that the poor stonecutter, like all of the others, had no sense of distance or time or speed. And the last thing he could expect them to understand was how dangerous a truck could really be.

They drove through the sand country, through untilled fields and on toward the border. Once they passed a large camp in the semi-darkness of the late afternoon, and Zvi wondered who the people were standing silently by the roadside watching them pass. From the clothes they were wearing, the shapes of their heads and their quiet manner, he would have sworn he was passing a large camp of Yemenite Jews. But this did not make any sense to him, because if Yemenite Jews had arrived in the area, they would have been moved south into Aden as he was moving his people south now.

A short time later, he understood much more.

The sandstorm had fallen off and the trucks were rolling through the open country. The unpaved road did not seem to deter the drivers and at times they reached speeds of twenty miles an hour. The refugees who had never traveled so fast before were only aware that the countryside was slipping by.

Suddenly Zvi sighted something on the road ahead and, rising so that he could see more clearly over the battered green cab, he made out a sign: FRONTIER. He relaxed. His hand came up in the semi-darkness and he wished there was someone with him who could share the meaning of this sign. At the same moment he saw a strange truck roll across the highway and block their path. Zvi's driver did not slow his pace until they reached the roadblock, where he jammed on his brakes, jolting the refugees against each other. Furious, Zvi started to berate the man; and then he realized that the driver of the truck blocking the road was equally responsible. Zvi jumped to the ground and approached the other truck. As he did, two British soldiers, carrying their Tommy guns at port, trotted out to greet him.

"Something wrong?" the Israeli officer yelled in English.

The older of the two wore sergeant's stripes while the younger appeared to be a private. Zvi glanced about for an officer. There was none to be seen. However, he noticed that there were half a dozen ranks in the back of the British truck. The heavy, eight-wheeled vehicle was painted the dull browns and greens of open-country camouflage. The half-dozen men inside were all armed. The driver had already left his cab and was lighting a cigarette.

The two soldiers did not speak at first, and then the sergeant said, "The end of the line."

Drawing himself up, Zvi asked, "What's going on?"

Shaking his head, the sergeant repeated, "The end of the line, Mister. This is the Aden frontier and we've orders to keep all Hebes out."

With great restraint, Zvi asked formally, "And what is the reason, Sergeant?"

"Orders, Mister."

Very slowly, Zvi turned on his heel and looked back at the line of trucks he had brought south. Over the cabs of each he could make out the puzzled faces of the Yemenites who had risen in curiosity. His own Arab drivers were out of their seats now, squatting on the windless side of their vehicles. For a long moment, Zvi tried to understand what stopping here could mean to his people, and then he knew he could not stop. They had no food. There was no water in sight. Turning back to the sergeant, he introduced himself, "I am Major Zvi Mazon of the Israeli Defense Force."

The Sergeant cocked his head to one side, "Israeli Defense Force?"

Zvi nodded and added the indentification, "Army," hoping this would help to create a bond between two soldiers.

The sergeant looked at his companion, shrugged and asked, "Where or what is this Israel, Major?"

Taken aback at the question, Zvi wondered how long this soldier had been stationed in Aden. "Do you remember Palestine?"

"Served there once."

"Well, that's Israel now."

Sighing with relief as though somehow a problem had been solved, the sergeant asked ingenuously, "You still having trouble with those Jews there, sir?"

"No." Zvi tried hard not to laugh. Then, as though he were taking this man into his confidence, he asked, "Why's the border closed?"

Uncertain about how far his orders went, the sergeant decided to play safe, "I ain't been told, Major."

"But it's closed?"

The sergeant looked at his companion and both of them nodded at the same time as if it took a joint effort to make the point.

"And what about these people? They have to eat and sleep and have medical care and water and——"

However, before Zvi could continue, the sergeant shook his head. "The captain said it weren't none of our business what happens on the other side of the frontier. We're just to see no one goes down this road."

"Or through the fields neither, sir," the other soldier added.

"Got a cigarette, Sergeant?" Zvi asked, and when the other soldier handed him one, he said, "Thanks," lighted the Player and stood where he was, trying to decide what he could do.

"How long's the road been closed?" he asked after a time.

The sergeant, assuming this foreign major must have had his own trouble with the Jews, smiled, "About four days, sir."

"Any idea when it will open again?"

The sergeant appealed to his companion, who shook his head, and then the sergeant looked at Zvi and shook his in turn.

"Thanks. Any food around here?"

The heads shook again.

"Water?"

The sergeant started to shake his head when Zvi half shouted, "Come on, you drink."

This caught the two up and the private said there was a well on their side of the border.

Accepting this, Zvi tried to smile at the two as he sucked on the cigarette, his first in months. "Any idea when your officers will arrive?"

The sergeant looked at his watch, thought about the question and then said, "Tomorrow morning sometime, Major."

Baffled at how the man arrived at this answer, Zvi nodded. "Thanks." And then once more as if he were taking the two into his confidence, "We'll spend the night here by our trucks, and tomorrow you and I will talk to your officer."

Zvi dragged the last puff of smoke from the cigarette, looked at the small butt, dropped it and then drew himself up as the two British soldiers saluted. He was returning the salute, when the sergeant said, "I'll tell Captain Layton you will want to see him, Major."

"Thanks." Zvi tried to smile, but he had trouble as he turned and walked back to the column of trucks.

Soon Zvi had his people encamped near the side of the road. There was no water in the area, and he drove back to the nearest well to fill the goatskin bags. By the time he rejoined the refugees, it was already dark. The wind was still, but the night was cold. Dropping off the back of the truck, he waved for Isaac to join him. They stood together looking at the British lorry which blocked their passage south and the row of ancient trucks where the Arab drivers were gathered.

"We haven't any fires yet?" Zvi asked.

Isaac shook his head.

"Why not?"

"What would we use them for?"

Grabbing the young Yemenite's arm, Zvi swung the man about so that they were facing each other. "There's nothing?" Zvi demanded.

"Nothing," almost surprised that the Israeli did not know.

Without thinking, Zvi moved his hand inside his shirt, seeking the money belt that was no longer about his waist.

Sighing, he nodded. There was nothing any of them could do now, and he did not know what they could do when Layton arrived.

"I'll work something out in the morning," he promised, knowing as he spoke that he might be lying.

Isaac nodded. "That sign?" and he was pointing at the post on which was written in Arabic and English, FRONTIER.

"We have to get to the other side of that," Zvi explained. The two men stood for a time looking at the sign and the British soldiers who sat about a small fire near their lorry.

"There's nothing at all left to eat?" Zvi asked, hoping that somehow Isaac had not told him everything.

Shrugging, the silversmith smiled. "If there were, I would tell you."

Zvi went in search of Havah. The refugees were seated in family groups, their blankets pulled about them. The children who had been restless on other nights were silent now and still.

Zvi rubbed knuckles on the scalp of a small girl. The child did not respond, her thin, dark face set with a blank expression. "Tomorrow is another day," Zvi said, feeling fatuous at the sound of his own words.

On the far side of the camp he found Havah cradling the little boy she had gathered to herself. Her pantalooned legs stretched out in front of her, and even in the semi-darkness Zvi could see the sores on the soles of her bared feet. Dropping to his knees, he rubbed one foot between his hands and then another, knowing that she was cold. Neither said anything for a long time. Then Zvi asked, "What is his name?"

Somehow the little boy seemed to know they were talking about him, and he turned so that he could see the Israeli.

"Aaron," she said softly as she brushed the child's hair with her lips. "His name is Aaron and he is going to the Holy Land and he is going to grow up to be a big man like you, and he, too, is going to be a soldier." She smiled at Zvi as she added, "A Jewish soldier who walks in proud shoes."

Not feeling very proud at the moment, Zvi's thoughts drifted back to his meeting earlier in the day with Layton. Had he moved too quickly? He had seen himself readily enough as a soldier but never before as a violent man. Maybe that was where the confusion lay. Had his temper created problems which he could not cope with and in this way made things more difficult for these people whom he had come to love? Suddenly, he sat down and stared at Havah. Then, very slowly he turned his head and surveyed the field where he could make out the shadowed forms of the huddled families.

Somewhere a child was crying, and Zvi wondered why more of them were not. They had eaten nothing for a whole day. For one brief instant he wanted to blame their hunger on Isaac, who should have told him there was no food, but then he wondered what he could have done about it even if he had known. Somehow, in the corridors of his mind he had tracked the notion that once they crossed the border, they would reach Aden within hours.

He, and not Isaac, should have known better.

"I'm going to keep the boy," Havah told him, and without really hearing, he nodded and came to his feet.

Bending over, he touched her black hair with an open palm and then he brushed her cheeks with his fingertips. "Of course."

Then he wondered why his cheeks were suddenly damp, and when he touched them, he knew he was crying.

170

"Aaron is going to be all right," he assured Havah. "He is going to be all right," and Zvi was thinking of all of them and not just Aaron.

He stood where he was and watched car lights approaching fast on the road behind the British lorry.

Zvi wondered if he should have his showdown with Layton now or let it wait until morning. The lights came to a stop and he could see two figures silhouetted in the headlamps. Then the figures disappeared and the lights swung around the lorry and started toward him. Taking a deep breath, Zvi walked away from Havah, hoping that any trouble would take place beyond the small, quiet camp.

A moment later a jeep drew up beside him and Adam jumped out.

The two men shook hands while they scanned the field. When their eyes met, the slight fieldworker shook his head. "You did it. You sure did."

Zvi nodded, assuming he knew what the other man meant. "But that's not as important as the fact that we need some food."

Bellowing loudly, Adam called for the men to join him.

Slowly, the Yemenites rose to their feet and drifted toward the jeep. When the first ones reached it, Adam grabbed a large sack and handed it to them. As others gathered, he handed out more sacks.

The mori opened the first sack and stared into its darkness for a moment until he realized it was food. "Bread and sardines," Adam explained. The mori nodded, set the sack down and said a berakhah. The others joined him, and when they were done, they took the food back to their families.

Adam waited until they were gone before turning to Zvi, but when he did, the major was not there. He was walking across the field toward the woman who cuddled a child in her lap. Adam waited a moment before he joined them. When Zvi offered him a piece of bread, he shook his head.

After several bites, Zvi handed the rest of his bread to Havah and walked away so that he and Adam could talk alone.

"How did you hear about Layton?" he asked.

"Radio. His jeep sent back a message."

"How is he?" Zvi did not really care, but he felt he had to ask.

The Agency man stopped where he was and looked at the soldier. "You don't know what you did to him?"

Zvi shook his head. "He deserved it."

Adam did not agree. "Your justice is a luxury these people can't afford."

Zvi decided not to even try explaining why he had beaten the English officer, and instead, asked simply, "And now?"

"I've got to get you south before he arrives."

Zvi looked at Adam. The other man was serious. "And these people?"

Sighing, Adam explained, "You can't do them any good."

Zvi looked about the field where the refugees were now beginning to light their fires with brown grass and camel dung. "And when will they follow?"

Adam shrugged. "Tomorrow or next month."

"They can't . . . ," Zvi was angry now, " . . . they can't last that long."

"Any suggestions?" Adam, too, was angry because the officer had spoken as though somehow this injustice were his fault.

Very slowly, Zvi shook his head. "Can we get them more food?"

"I don't know if the government will let me cross back into Yemen again. There's been talk we cause too much trouble." He was trying to be reasonable where he knew he could not be. "The Imam only promised to let our people go. The British never promised we could enter their country."

Zvi slammed his fist into an open palm and then banged the side of his fist against his leg.

"We've got to get you out of here; staying would cause them more trouble," Adam warned.

Accepting the decision, Zvi went in search of Isaac, who was seated with his family. Zvi watched the young silversmith turning a sealed can over and over, unable to make up his mind what he should do with it.

Zvi smiled, took the can, ripped the key off the bottom and carefully opened it so that none of the oil spilled. Then he handed it to Isaac, who had been watching. The Yemenite sniffed the sardines and passed them to his older wife before he started to open a second can by himself. When he was done, he looked up at the two foreigners for approval.

"That's right," Zvi said. "And you'll show the others?"

There was something in the soldier's voice that brought the younger man's head up. "Something's wrong?"

"No," Adam was with them now. "We're going south now, and when they let you cross, we'll have trucks back here to take you the rest of the way."

Isaac came to his feet and stood staring at Zvi. "You are going to leave us?"

"I'll meet you in Aden," Zvi promised. He put one hand out and affectionately clasped the silversmith's arm, and then, turning, he embraced the old mori who had joined them. "You'll lead your people to the Promised Land," Zvi said softly. "You have earned that right."

The old man rocked back and forth on his heels as he tried to understand what was happening, and all Zvi could see was how much the man had aged since they had first met.

"You'll both look after Havah for me?" he asked, acknowledging for the first time that a tie existed between himself and the Yemenite woman.

"You will take her as a wife?" the mori asked flatly.

Adam glanced at the soldier to see how he would react to the question and was surprised to see Zvi appear to nod. "We'll talk about it—she and I—when we reach Jerusalem."

The mori seemed satisfied.

The four men stood awkwardly silent for a moment. Then Adam strode across the field to the jeep, leaving Zvi alone with his people.

Unsure of what was expected of him, Zvi raised his hand and his voice. "We will meet again in Aden."

Then, he was walking back to Havah. Bending down, he took the little boy from her and set him on the ground before he pulled the small woman up and into his arms. And at that moment he was as surprised as she by what he was doing.

He set his cheek against hers and promised, "We'll be together in Aden." His hands flat on her back, he realized that she was thinner than when he had known her that first night when they lay together between his blankets. "Isaac will show you how to open the cans," he told her, "and he will look after you." Even as he spoke, Zvi felt he was talking merely to stay with her that much longer.

He stepped back and looked at her. "We will be together in Aden," he promised. "You and I and Aaron." And he believed what he was saying.

Havah shook her head. "Aaron," she said.

"What about him?"

"They won't let him leave if he does not have a father."

It took Zvi a moment to understand what she was saying, "Conversion?"

She nodded and he could see the headlamps of the jeep reflecting off her hair.

For a long time he stood very still, and then he shouted, "Adam!"

The jeep lights swerved and the vehicle was at his side.

"I'm not going unless they go," Zvi declared.

"You've got to go and she can't," Adam snapped. "And you've got to go now."

"If I leave the boy without a father at his age, they'll convert him."

"Others could care for him."

Zvi shook his head stubbornly.

Adam remained silent for a long time. Then he stepped out of the jeep and stood looking down at the child who was chewing on a piece of bread almost as large as his face. "No parents?" Adam asked.

Havah nodded her head.

None of them said anything as Zvi waited for Adam to solve the problem. When he spoke, it was to Havah. "I can't take you. They," and he was pointing at the British soldiers, "they wouldn't let me." Then, as if he had to be certain she understood, "We—he and I—we're Israelis and they will let us pass." He was shaking his head, hoping she would forgive him. "Not you."

"And Aaron?" she asked.

Reaching down, Adam emptied the sack of food that lay on the ground, and without a word, he handed it to her, open at the top. Zvi did not seem to understand what was happening, but Havah obviously did as she held the sack while Adam lifted the boy and held him out to her so that she could kiss his cheeks. Then with a jerk Havah turned her head away so that she would not see Adam put the child in the sack.

Zvi started to protest, but it was Havah who told him. "Be quiet." Then softly, as she covered Aaron, "Be very quiet." After a moment she handed the sack to Adam who gently set it down in the rear of the jeep.

Looking from one to the other, Zvi wished he could say something that made sense. His hand came out to touch her face, but she suddenly whirled about with a wild cry of pain and ran off into the darkness.

"Let's go," Adam growled.

It was dawn when Adam swung the jeep off the main road to Aden and the fences of Camp Hashed—Redemption—rose before them. An Arab guard recognized Adam and passed them. As they drove through the camp, Zvi half rose in his seat, the child in his arms.

A full square mile in size, Camp Hashed was almost filled with pyramidal tents set in neat rows with clean streets running from one end of the camp to the other. There were lanterns hung in front of some of the tents, and more lights could be seen through the flaps of others. When they neared the low brick buildings at the center of the camp, Zvi saw that several temporary barracks had been raised since he had left months before.

"It's changed," he said as he settled slowly back into his seat.

Adam smiled, "Anything would be better than what we had. The straw mat huts were crawling with bugs and we burned them."

The jeep drew up in front of a long wooden barrack with a sign ADMINISTRATION above it.

"How many people here now?" Zvi asked.

Shaking his head, Adam admitted, "That's the problem. Almost thirteen thousand."

Zvi whistled softly and stepped out of the jeep, still holding Aaron in his arms. "I've got to put him to bed," he said.

Adam led the way into the Administration Building where they found two young women and a middle-aged man sitting behind desks, filling out forms.

"Shoshanna," Adam called, and one of the young women came to her feet. Zvi smiled. She looked clean and neat, and he thought she was pretty even though her nose appeared to tilt, which reminded him of his wife.

"Can you find a place for this boy for tonight? Tomorrow we'll have to make some kind of arrangements."

The young woman called Shoshanna took the child and held him as she shook her head. "He looks as if he hasn't eaten for weeks."

"Months," Zvi said and winked as she looked at him dubiously.

"I'll put him in the hospital until morning." And she left.

Zvi slowly turned around so that he could see the room better. It was large. There were half a dozen desks scattered around. "Who's responsible for all this?" he asked.

"An American. We call him the Colonel, Colonel Max. He was once in the American Air Force. He works for the Agency now."

"Quite a job."

"You'll meet him in the morning." And Adam was leading the way to the shower room in one of the nearby buildings.

The next morning, after he had shaved and showered again, Zvi put on some fresh clothes issued by the camp quartermaster and walked out through the camp. Families were lined up at a central kitchen drawing cooked food. Poking his head inside the building, he smiled to see Arab cooks working under the supervision of Yemenite women, who themselves had possibly never cooked inside a building before reaching Camp Hashed. Farther on he paused to look into the hospital. The young woman he had met briefly the night before was there, and they talked for a moment as she explained that she had placed Aaron with a family that had lost a child coming from the Hadhramaut.

"He'll be all right," she said.

Zvi nodded. "Who's in charge here?"

"Here?" she asked, and he wanted to laugh because he felt so good hearing his question answered by another one.

"Welcome home," he said, and when he saw that she missed the joke, he laughed, "The camp? Who's in charge?"

"You're Major Zvi Mazon?" she asked. "Adam didn't introduce us last night."

Zvi nodded.

"I think the colonel wants to see you. You'll find him over there," and she was pointing toward a large pen inside the camp where a tall man was inspecting a small herd of cattle.

Puzzled, Zvi walked over to the pen. Several Yemenite children ran past him and he paused for a moment to watch them play tag. A woman emerged from a tent and stood looking at him and then at the children. It took Zvi a moment to understand why she looked so grotesque. She was wearing a full-length white silk evening gown. She nodded to him and he nodded back. Then he saw the man who had been inspecting the cattle emerge from the pen.

They introduced themselves while Colonel Max stood watching the cattle. "My father was in the meat business," he explained. "We get fresh meat and kosher-kill it ourselves."

He smiled when he noticed that Zvi was staring at the woman in the evening gown. "We take whatever clothes people send us. The last shipment came from South Africa. May look foolish, but we haven't much choice, have we?"

"I guess not," Zvi agreed.

They were walking together through the camp toward the Administration Building now. "It was rough?" The Colonel asked.

Zvi wondered why he thought about the question. After a moment, he nodded. "If they get through, it was worth it."

The colonel, a gray-thatched man who stood half a head taller than Zvi, smiled. "We're living through something more romantic than anything that has happened since Moses led the Jews out of Egypt."

The Israeli did not think that the word "romantic" described the journey he had just finished, and shifted the subject. "Those people out there, the ones I left last night?"

They were standing still now as a young Yemenite wearing a pith helmet strode past them toward the gate. Zvi looked at the colonel for an explanation.

"Police. They've never worn anything that could pass as a uniform before, and I think the helmet gives them a kind of pride."

Zvi thought he was going to like this American.

"Those people," the colonel was saying, "we'll try to get them through as fast as we can. The British will do what they can to help, but there are pressures on them, and they're taking care of themselves. The Arabs resent the build-up of Jews in Aden, and there's an honest fear of a typhus epidemic." They were stopping now as the colonel checked the fuel supply of a large generator set under a canvas tent.

Arab resentments and fears did not interest Zvi. "Any idea what my next assignment is?"

They were approaching the Administration Building and the colonel stopped to scan the camp. It was neat, quiet and orderly, and from the smile on the man's ruddy face, Zvi saw that he approved.

"I heard it was coming through. You'll get it in two weeks.

"There's nothing more I can tell you about it until we know that it's been arranged between the Agency and Zahal."

"Nothing?"

The American ran his fingers through his gray hair and seemed to pat the bald spot on the back of his head as he repeated, "Nothing."

ADEN

Later in the day, after a medical check-up, Zvi drew money from the camp's bursar and hitched a ride into Aden. When the Arab driver dropped him off in front of the Crescent Hotel, Zvi stood for a moment watching the confusion of the city about him. The city appeared to spill into the sea on the far side of a mountain. Aden is actually more than one city. Built on two prongs of land which extend out of the surrounding hills, the Arab Quarter, known as the Crater, lies inside a dead volcano; Steamer Point, the main harbor, lies on one side of the same tongue of land; and on the other tongue lie several small fishing villages.

The Arabs had used it as a port, and for one brief period in the sixteenth century the Portuguese occupied it, only to be expelled by the Egyptians and then the Turks. And in the centuries that followed, Aden crumbled, a twist of rock around a bay that was silting up. Finally, the British arrived from India and captured the area, splitting it in time into the Colony of Aden, which was no more than seventy-five square miles, and the Aden Protectorate, which stretched north and east. The British changed the shipping base to the unsilted bay; and after Suez was opened, they began to use Aden as the only coaling station that lay between the canal and India. With that careless casualness with which the British ran their empire, they left Aden under the control of their Indian government. For the people of Aden this meant few schools, fewer trained administrators and almost all legal work in the hands of the better-educated Indians. However, most of the buildings around Steamer Point and the Crescent Hotel were modern.

The Aden that Zvi saw reminded him in many ways of the mandated Palestine in which he had grown up. And for a moment he felt uncomfortable as he watched two Royal Air Force officers riding in the rear of a sedan. Turning finally to the hotel, he recognized that this was again Imperial England. The massive stone building that dominated its surroundings reminded him of the King David in Jerusalem, and he recognized the colonial hand in its architecture.

Almost self-consciously, he brushed his dark hair back and mounted the steps leading into the hotel. There were people sitting in the large, marble-floored lobby. And staring at the scattered rugs, he believed he was in the King David five years before when men in British uniforms and cool British women with white, open-pored skin lounged there in the late afternoon. Throwing his shoulders back and bringing up his head, he admitted to himself that he would feel like a damned colonial unless he remembered that he was an Israeli and part of the army that forced the British retreat from Palestine. He crossed the lobby to the large hotel counter.

A clerk, wearing the familiar dark blue uniform of British hotels, waited for his question.

"Colonel Max said I should use his suite while I'm here," Zvi explained, holding his hand out.

The clerk looked the stranger over with care and then, seemingly satisfied, gave him the room key.

"The bar?" Zvi asked.

The clerk nodded in the direction of a hallway, and Zvi made his way to the bar. Only after he reached it did he remember that there was almost no reason for his having come. He rarely drank.

Embarrassed at finding himself in the small room without any purpose, he tried to ignore the several men and women who turned in their seats to see who he was. None of the faces was familiar though he recognized the types, and again he recalled Jerusalem under the mandate. Approaching the bar, he ordered a brandy.

A tall blonde standing nearby turned to look at him quizzically.

"A brandy at this hour?"

Zvi tried to smile, wishing that he had the talent for meaningless conversation. "At this hour," he confessed. He thought the young woman pretty, and then he recalled that he had thought the same thing about Shoshanna the night before. He drained the small glass and set it back on the bar. He had been away from civilization too long, he thought. However, he continued to stare at the girl's bright blonde hair until she became self-conscious and tried to brush it casually back.

"Is something wrong?" she asked

Zvi shook his head. "I'm sorry."

Puzzled, the woman ordered another Scotch, and Zvi watched her drink it. Her white cotton dress revealed everything it was intended to, and he enjoyed the woman's cool and immaculate appearance. When she turned toward him again, she said, "You don't live in Aden."

"That's right."

The woman perched herself on a tall barstool, and he knew she had drawn her skirt higher than necessary about her thighs. "And what brings you to Aden?"

She was trying to be friendly; and as much as he wanted company, he did not think he should seek it here.

"What brings me to Aden?" He smiled as he said, "Orders."

She cocked her blonde head to one side and looked at him dubiously. "That's not a uniform you're wearing."

Then he became aware of someone standing behind him, and before he could turn, he heard a woman's soft voice explaining, "Major Mazon wears all kinds of uniforms."

Zvi slowly pivoted.

Bedia Hassani.

She was wearing a bright blue sleeveless Parisian cocktail dress. Her dark hair was up and she held a cigarette from which she playfully blew the smoke into Zvi's face.

"You get around, Major."

Ignoring the strange English woman, Zvi considered the comment. "Not as much as you."

She seemed to agree. "And yet our business is not too dissimilar."

Zvi laughed, "I'm not exactly in the banking business."

Ordering a Scotch for herself and telling the waiter to fill up Zvi's glass with "whatever he's drinking," she smiled. "We're both interested in the exodus of the Jews from the Arab countries."

Puzzled, Zvi waited for an explanation.

The Arab girl sipped her Scotch slowly, looking at him over the rim of the glass. When she set it down, she said, "You've taken over our land and uprooted our people." She seemed to be jabbing at him with her cigarette as she spoke. "We aren't forgetting that. We never will."

Reaching out, Zvi shoved the filled brandy glass down the bar toward her. "You've done me some favors," he said. "Just why, I'll never really understand, and for that I owe you thanks."

He started to leave the bar when she chuckled. "Are you beating a retreat, Major? Or is it a strategic withdrawal? I saw you withdraw once."

Zvi swung back to face her, wishing as he did it that she were not so lovely and that the lines of her face were not so fine. He forced himself to remember that she was Layton's, and said, "I don't think we have anything to talk about."

She chuckled again. "We have everything to talk about, Major." And she struck the rank hard, as though somehow she were belittling it. "We share the same country, or should I say the same piece of land. What more could people have in common?" And as she spoke, she held out the brandy glass to him as an invitation to continue talking.

The English woman to whom Zvi had been talking earlier, asked, "Where the hell are you two from?"

"Palestine," the Arab girl said simply.

"Israel," Zvi explained. And they looked at each other. "You see what I mean?" he said. "We don't even speak the same language."

He started to set the brandy glass down again, but she brought up a white-gloved hand and closed it on his. "I'd like to understand you." Uncomfortable and uncertain of himself, Zvi carefully removed her hand from his and set the glass down.

"Why?"

"It's Zvi, isn't it?"

He nodded.

"And you know my name?"

He nodded, trying to decide what point she was hoping to achieve.

"And so we have a beginning." She sipped her Scotch again and patted the barstool next to hers as an invitation for him to sit down.

When he shook his head, she took his hand and led him to a table on the far side of the room where they could look out of a large window upon Aden and the port. For a moment she stood looking down and then she settled into a chair across the table so that she could face him.

Neither one said anything as she sat sipping her drink. When a waiter passed, she ordered another, looking at Zvi to see if he wanted one. He shook his head and reminded her, "Your cousin said he would kill any Moslem he found drinking alcohol."

The girl smiled at him, and he wished he was not so conscious of her face and the way her silk dress clung to her breasts.

"My cousin is a fool," she said simply.

For an instant Zvi hesitated to agree, and then he remembered that he was no longer in Yemen. "He's a damned fool." And as though his two comments were related, he added, "He's in love with you."

The Arab girl smiled. "I believe the Americans call boys like him a 'bumpkin' and the British 'callow.' "

"He's a stupid, vicious bastard."

Laughing, the girl pointed out, "You're enjoying your new-found freedom."

And he laughed with her. "I'm not exactly the humble type, and Yemen was a kind of hell."

"What do you think Palestine is for the Arabs now?" she snapped.

Pushing his chair back, Zvi was tempted to rise and walk away. Instead, he explained, "They don't have to tear a new piece of cloth and sew a patch on it, they can ride, they can build any kind of house they can afford, they don't pay special taxes just because they are Arabs, and they can vote." Then as if she were ignorant, he asked flatly, "Do you know what it means to be able to vote?"

The way she drew her arm back he thought she was going to empty her glass in his face. Instead she smiled, a smile he knew was not a smile.

"My people have lived in Palestine for generations," but what she was saying did not seem to satisfy her; and with a gloved hand, she brushed her words away. "For tens of centuries."

Zvi watched the heavy smoke rising in the wake of a small tramp steamer. He wondered if he should argue with her.

"We lived our own way," she continued. "Migrants, perhaps, but that was our right."

Almost angrily, Zvi shook his head. "Most of the Arabs who fled Palestine had not been there sixty years before. They came to the land because we had come to do something with it. And as far as being migrants, that's all they were. They never ruled it. The British did and before them the Turks, but your people . . ."

He could see that she was having difficulty remaining in her seat, but so long as it was she and not he who had started this discussion, he did not care if she left.

Bedia stubbed out her cigarette and lighted another before she answered him. "Let us even assume what you say. We lived on the land in our own way. We farmed. We kept the land as it was and that was our right. There is nothing written anywhere in any mandate of men or gods that says we had to make it modern."

Zvi smiled and he saw that this made her even more angry. "Hell," he said, "you got caught in the vise of history."

And it was her turn to smile. "Pretty phrases don't change what I've said. We got caught between the Jews."

"The Jews and the twentieth century," he said, quietly watching a cutter near the tramp steamer. "The Jews fought in the Second World War while you backed the Germans and the Italians and lacked the guts to even fight for them. You were on the losing side. Face it. You haven't the vaguest notion about history and right."

He was looking at the Arab girl as she held her cigarette almost cupped in her hand and drew on it heavily.

"What you're saying is that because the British won the war, we had to solve the Jewish problem."

Her anger seemed to be under control now, but Zvi was not ready to accept her statement. "Solve the Jewish problem?" He shook his head. "You say that as though we are foreign to that land. We aren't." And as he spoke, his voice went soft. "You were there. No one can deny that, even though one can dispute how long you were there and how many of you were there. But we were there, too. Even though we weren't always on the land, we were there." A gentle smile crossed his face, "And, as strange as it may seem, there was always our presence on the land both actually and in a way no other people in history has come to be related to a piece of land. Someday better men than I will come to an understanding of that, but for us that piece of land and the Jews were part of what someone has called a hypersensitivity to history. That's part of our claim. There never has been anything else like it in time. With us that piece of land we now call Israel became a religion, a way of life, a dream that lasted for thousands of years." A note of personal pride came into his voice. "If we weren't on the soil, we at least kept the dream about Israel alive."

"That's a damned romantic notion," she hurled at him.

And to her surprise, he nodded. Both of them were silent as he watched the cutter circle the tramp steamer. When he finally answered her thrust, he was no longer smiling. "Perhaps romantic, but the holocaust made it necessary."

"As I said, you wanted us to solve the Jewish problem." She was triumphant as though she had scored a point. However, he could tell from the tension about her eyes that she was really interested in something more than making points with him.

"And you want us to solve the Arab problem."

He watched her face cloud for a moment.

She flicked her cigarette into an ashtray and asked a waiter standing nearby for another Scotch. Seeing the dubious look on Zvi's face, she smiled. "If I didn't know better, I'd think you cared how drunk I got, Major."

When he failed to pick up her comment, she did. "Your need. The need of the Jews. Don't *we* have needs or rights?"

Closing his hands together before him on the small table that lay between them, Zvi thought about her question as though for the first time.

"There may be a case, I guess," he agreed. But as he did so, he shook his head. "Only for some of the Arabs: those who lived in Israel, on that land. There is no case for the Egyptians who never held Gaza before now, or for Jordan which is an abortion created by the British to keep from giving us what she had promised in the Balfour letter. Jordan." He snorted as he said it. "It was Trans-Jordan, the land beyond the river Jordan. Then because you got greedy, you dropped the *trans*, invaded the West Bank, and—"

"Kept the Old City and half of Jerusalem from falling to the Jews." She finished his sentence for him as the waiter brought her Scotch.

For the first time her words reached Zvi as he suddenly felt the muscles in his neck tighten and his clasped hands tremble. It seemed as though it took forever for him to exhale as he thought about the Old City. Then, trying to ignore her words, he continued, "The Syrians, Lebanese, Iraqi, Saudis, none had any rights to that land."

The Arab girl seemed to relax now as she rolled the glass between her gloved hands. A slight smile came over her face; and he thought she looked almost like a challenge—wondered, too, if the Hasidim had a special word for an enchantress.

"The Arabs came together," she said, proudly. "Came together to help their own."

Zvi snorted again. "That's crap. They came to see what they could grab. They told your people in Palestine to get out of their homes so they could drive us off the land." He was silent for a moment, and then he added, "And that's all they came for. The Arabs never fought for their land, but they were given eleven states. We want only one, and that is the one we have."

The girl's voice was tense as she said, "Are you saying there is no case for my people?"

Shoving his chair back from the table, as though by moving away he could see her better, Zvi nodded. "There may have been a human case. You don't really see it. You and people like you don't. There's the land and there were people on it. What did you ever do for most of them? Lived in London, drew out fortunes, had fun and dressed expensively. What are you doing for those people now?"

She started to answer, but his anger had grown beyond control and he slammed his fist onto an open palm, drawing the glances of others in the bar; but Zvi did not care about the others. "You weep over them; you keep them in concentration camps and weep. You don't finance them. You don't move them onto better land. You have a problem you created and you won't solve. *We* have a problem. Half a million Jews thrown out of Arab countries where they have lived for generations, Jews without money; their lands, jewels and tools confiscated. But we are spending everything we own and can borrow to bring them home. And you want me to weep for the Arabs who fled before Israel even became a state. You have no case." And he was smiling at her. "We've done something with that land, and you have other places to live out your destiny."

The Arab girl set her glass down on the table and stared at him. "I said I wanted to understand what made you people think the way you do."

"You should have spoken to someone who was better with words and ideas. I'm only a soldier."

A trace of a smile crossed her mouth. "It is usually described as a 'simple soldier,' Major."

"Touché."

Her voice dropped as she thought aloud. "A little like the Confucianists caught in China by the Marxists. The dynamism of the Jews and the static sense of time of the Arabs." She was looking around for her waiter again. Satisfied that the waiter understood her need, she turned to Zvi once more. "That's what we've been caught in."

He did not want to dispute this point. Believing she knew what he was trying to say in spite of his wandering argument, he said, "Maybe there is a case for the Palestinian Arab on the land. But there is a case for us, too." He was trying to be generous even though he knew it was not a safe position. "Two rights seem to come up as a wrong." Then as the waiter set the drink before her, Zvi added, "But don't get lost in the notion that we created Israel to solve Arab problems. We have enough of our own."

To his astonishment, she nodded. "My people are ignorant, our schools are bad, our training is as good as nothing. You are right; we don't belong in this century. But I will tell you this, and believe me—we will make it our century, and we will, as our leaders say, 'Drive the Jews into the sea.' "

Zvi's hands came up flat as he began to applaud softly, "Spoken like a true bitch." Coming to his feet, he bowed, "Now if you will excuse me?"

Bedia laughed softly, "You running, Major?"

He shook his head. "No. But in a moment I'll forget that you are dressed like a lady." Then he strode out of the bar, down the corridor and into the lobby. He stood for a moment looking at an Arab urchin polishing a man's shoes.

"Major?" and he turned to see the British woman who had spoken to him in the bar. Nodding, he waited. "That woman," and the blonde was embarrassed as she apologized, "she's an Arab and only here because her father's so wealthy."

Cocking his head to one side as though this helped him to understand her problem, Zvi nodded. "Don't worry, girl. This place has people in it worse than Arabs." A smile crossed his face as he whispered, "Hell, I'm told they even let Jews in here."

While the woman stared at him, he nodded sympathetically, turned on his heel and went in search of the colonel's suite.

Later that evening, Zvi went down to the main dining room. He was wearing his military insignias—national, branch of service and rank, and the maître d' was taken aback to find an Israeli officer among his guests. Smiling a slightly frozen smile, he led the Israeli major through the crowded dining room to a table on the far side of the room away from the pianist who was playing "Star Dust." Aware that he was being relegated to a distant corner, Zvi decided he did not mind. After the waiter handed him a menu, he scanned it quickly and then more slowly. Setting it down, he signaled for the waiter.

"Can you bring me a telephone?"

The young Arab nodded and a moment later returned with a phone he plugged in nearby, explaining as he did it that the American guests who came with the ships on their way to or from the Far East often asked for telephones. Not particularly caring why the phone was available, Zvi asked the operator to connect him with Colonel Max at Camp Hashed. Several minutes later the phone rang and he found he was talking to Shoshanna. The Colonel was out somewhere. Was there anything she could do for him?

"The group I brought in from San'a, have they crossed the frontier yet?"

She was certain they had not. There had been no one coming into the camp from Yemen all day. Others had come from the Aden Protectorate, a place called Habben, but she was sure none had come from Yemen.

"Will you call me here at the Crescent if there is any news?"

She agreed and hoped he would have a good time. In fact, she said, if she were able, she would join him.

Accepting the hint, Zvi asked, "Why don't you?"

"Duty calls," she laughed and hung up.

Zvi started to push the phone across the table when he noticed for the first time that Bedia Hassani had joined him. Looking at the phone a moment, he signaled for the waiter to take it away before he turned his attention to the Arab girl. She was wearing a white silk sheath now, and he thought she looked better than any other woman in the room, but then he admitted to himself there were probably none who could afford to dress as well as Bedia, and at the same time he agreed with himself that there were none who less needed to dress as well. Her small, round face was almost *café au lait*, and her black eyes seemed to sparkle under the crystal chandelier that hung above them. She wore a small silk scarf over her head as though somehow she were maintaining the privacy and seclusion of purdah.

Sighing, he asked, "Is there a shortage of tables or did you come to argue again?"

"Shalom," she smiled.

"Shalom," he said. When she did not say anything, he shook his head, "Look, girl, I'm weary. I've had a rough few months and I'm going on another assignment soon, and I'm worried about other things than your need for an 'understanding' of Jews."

She laughed softly. "Do I upset you, Zvi?"

He thought about this a moment and then nodded.

This time she did not laugh. Instead she asked him, "Why do you call me 'girl'?" I'm as old as you are."

He smiled slightly. "I doubt it, but I'm not here to argue even that with you."

Her hands came up, palms out. "Let's declare a truce for tonight."

"And you are willing to wait until tomorrow to drive the Jews into the sea?"

Her small head dropped to one side as she considered this. "Don't laugh at me, Major. People don't do that."

Zvi nodded. "I know. Your father owns banks and all men are afraid of you."

"They are afraid or they want something."

Smiling, he agreed. "I'm sure most men do." And he hoped his tone indicated what he had in mind.

"And so you think you're safe with an Israeli because he would not dare to want anything from you?"

To his surprise, she nodded.

It took Zvi time to understand the implications of this before he said, "But there is always the dashing Captain Layton of His Majesty's forces." Before she could comment, he added, "I saw both of you in the Quarter. Remember?"

For a long time the girl stared at him; and then, ignoring what he had said, she picked up a menu.

Zvi shoved his chair back and prepared to leave the table when she glanced up. "For heaven's sake, Zvi, are you always running away? Sit down and order dinner. I'm hungry."

Her imperious tone startled him; he laughed, and decided to stay.

After the waiter had taken their orders, Zvi asked why she was staying on in Aden.

"My father has a ship coming through. I'm going to Egypt when it arrives."

The simplicity of her answer made him believe her.

"And you?"

"I don't know." When he saw that she was skeptical, he repeated his answer.

She stared at him for a time and then glanced about the large dining room. There were almost a hundred persons eating now. Most of them were obviously English. Many of the men wore RAF uniforms. Some few wore RN formal whites. The women wore long gowns, and Zvi thought they looked almost elegant. And yet somehow the room gave the appearance of the shabby gentility which he had seen during the last days of the Palestine mandate.

"I wonder," he said, "how long before England leaves Aden."

Bedia turned her attention toward him again. "Does that make any difference to Israel?"

Seeing that she could not drop the subject, he snorted, "It might."

Very slowly she shook her head. "Forget it, Major. Suez is closed and the Gulf of Akaba is closed and there is nothing you can do about it. If you want to go to the Far East, you go around the Cape and maybe we'll find a way to close that, too."

The waiter was bringing their dinner now. After they were both served, Zvi decided to ignore the girl and enjoy his meal. He was almost done when she looked across the table and asked, "Are we going to see the turtles tonight?"

Curious, he set his knife and fork down and stared at her.

"The turtles, Major. This is the time of the year they come to spawn."

Nodding dubiously, he rejected the idea. "Go with my blessing." And he started to eat again.

"Sometimes I wonder if you are stupid or just ill-bred." She spoke just loudly enough so that those at the nearby tables could hear her.

Seeing that heads were turned toward him and that some of the British women were smiling behind their napkins, Zvi said loudly enough to be heard, "If you want to spawn, my dear, you have, as I have said, my blessing."

One English woman with a large mole on the side of her chin giggled while the portly sailor with her snorted, "That's no gentleman."

Turning to the man, Zvi nodded. Determined to finish his dinner and not be driven away, he continued to eat. After a time he became aware that Bedia was not eating and was instead merely sitting back in her chair, staring at him.

Wishing he were some place else, Zvi decided to ignore her. However, this became difficult when she signaled for the waiter to bring the maître d'. That lean and almost emaciated looking man hastened across the room, indicating he knew who his guest was.

"Something, Miss Hassani?"

The girl tried not to smile as she could see that Zvi was waiting to hear what she had to say. "Will you arrange for my car to be brought out front? Then will you give the driver a basket of cold chicken and whatever else we will want for a late dinner." Smiling disdainfully as she looked at the Israeli who was trying without success to ignore her, "The major and I are going down to Fisherman's Bay."

She thought about what she had said and then added, "Be certain there is a flashlight in the car, several blankets, and call my suite and ask my maid to bring down a coat."

The maître d' repeated her instructions to be certain he had them right before he trotted off on his mission.

Zvi was done with dinner, and shoving his chair back from the table, he excused himself. Rising, he left the girl staring after him.

In the lobby, Zvi stood for a moment looking about for a cigarette counter. He had not been able to smoke enough cigarettes since he had reached Hashed to satisfy him; and as long as he was going up to his room, he wanted to be certain he had enough. He was paying for the cigarettes when he felt someone's arm come through his and heard Bedia say, "The car's out front now."

Reaching down, he removed her hand from his arm and turned to look at her. She was wearing a fur jacket loose about her shoulders. Without any recognition of what he was doing, she said again, "The car's waiting."

Zvi tried not to smile as he put both of his hands on her shoulders. "Look, Bedia or whatever the hell your name is, I'm going up to my room and read for an hour or so and then I'm going to bed. Why don't you just bug off someplace? There are plenty of army men in Aden."

As if she had not really understood what he had said, she asked, "Would you rather have me run off to your room, or are you coming with me?"

Suddenly Zvi found himself laughing and she was laughing with him.

"If all Arabs had been as determined as you, maybe there wouldn't be a Jewish State."

She stopped laughing suddenly and thought about what he had said. "Are you afraid I'm going to seduce you, Major?"

For a long time he looked at her and wished that the swell of her breasts was not so obvious under the white silk sheath and that she would not look at him as though he were important to her.

"All right," he finally agreed.

Ten minutes later they were driving in the back of her Bentley toward Fisherman's Bay on the south side of the Gulf of Aden. The moon was full. The tide was almost at flood. Beyond the bay, Zvi could see the rugged Crater serrating the edges of the dark sky. To the east he could make out Ras Marshag and the tall, ancient lighthouse cutting bright slices into the darkness.

Bedia had said nothing since they left the hotel, and now she sat on the far side of the seat from him, watching his silhouette while he stared out the window.

Shifting in his seat, Zvi looked at the back of the driver's head. He was not certain if this Arab was wearing a family livery or a uniform he did not recognize, and at the same time he wondered how much privacy he and the girl had.

"Don't worry about Harab," she assured him as though she knew what he had been thinking. Then, changing the subject, she said, "I miss Palestine. Our part of it. We lived in Jerusalem, the New City, where your people are now. I grew up there. We had our own villa." Then, as if it would have meaning to Zvi, "My brother grew up there." To make sure the Israeli officer understood, she explained, "He was killed in the Jewish riots of 1939."

Zvi recalled the Arab terror of that year.

Lights from the Arab Quarter in the Crater brightened the sky. The girl kept talking compulsively.

"My father loved my brother." She laughed, "Don't think I'm the unloved daughter trying to play the role her father planned for his son. It isn't that way at all. My brother was a sullen cripple, but we all loved him. And as for my father, he's not a traditionalist. I think he's had a kind of pleasure out of showing me off and letting me do what I want."

Zvi said nothing, convinced nothing was expected of him, though he was wondering why she was telling him all of this. And then he thought he understood. As strange as it seemed, this girl and her thoughts were safer with him than with anyone else she knew, because he was the enemy and he would not repeat them to anyone who could make any difference to her.

"I think," she went on, "that he's unhappy with what I've done, but I'm not going to say I'm out to make him unhappy, because that wouldn't be true." For an instant she fell silent and then she continued. "I'm out to make myself happy." The lights of an oncoming car filled theirs. "He wouldn't say anything. If he did, that would mean he had been wrong." There was a surprising bitterness in her voice.

Wanting to keep himself clear of any involvement, Zvi kept his silence and his distance.

"And one thing I know he's right about," the girl said. "That's the boycott. He's going to break Israel with it. When he gets done, you won't have any economy to keep your pirate state afloat."

Zvi was surprised at her obvious slogans and even more at his own lack of anger. However, he wished he were in his room at the Crescent. Then suddenly she dropped back across the seat, placing her head in his lap, bringing her knees up so that her tight skirt slipped part way down her thighs.

Grabbing her shoulders, he flung her upright with one hand and slapped her face with the other. At the same time he kept his eyes on the driver, expecting some reaction. There was none.

For a long time the girl sat stiffly with her hand on her cheek while she stared numbly in front of her.

"You struck me once before," she reminded him.

And Zvi wondered if she was a masochist. Then he almost laughed as he knew Zella would have also laughed at his amateur psychiatry. The Arab girl was trying not to weep.

Leaning forward, Zvi tapped the driver on the shoulder: "Take us back to the Crescent."

The driver looked in the mirror for his mistress' instructions; she nodded almost imperceptibly.

Twenty minutes later the driver opened the door and both Zvi and Bedia climbed the stairs to the lobby. Zvi did not object when she followed him to his suite. At the door he paused to look at her. She suddenly seemed very small and almost frightened as she waited for him to enter. He started to put his key into the lock when he noticed a white slip of paper shoved part way under the door—an envelope. Quickly opening the door, he knelt, picked up the paper, crossed the room to a lamp and tore off the edge of the envelope. He was not even aware Bedia had followed him into the room and closed the door after them.

For a long time he read the note over and over. Then, because the message made very little sense, he picked up the phone and asked the operator to connect him with Camp Hashed.

He lighted a cigarette while he waited for his connection and for the first time seemed to notice Bedia sitting on the couch, her shoes before it, her feet drawn up under her and a cigarette already lighted between her lips. He stared, wondering what he was going to do about her, and was about to tell her he had other things on his mind when Shoshanna came on the phone.

Yes. He had read the note right. Adam had heard from one of the British frontier guards. There were deaths in the Yemenite camp. Half a dozen. They did not know what three of them had died from but the others had died from malaria.

Yes, Adam had said Zvi's friend Havah was one of those who had died of malaria.

No. They had already buried her there. The British were letting the others come through in the morning. They would arrive about noon.

No. She did not know anything about an Isaac.

Then she asked if Zvi was still there.

He nodded and looked, unseeing, at the receiver in his hand.

When she asked again, he said, "I'm still here. I'll see you in the morning unless there is anything I can do now."

There was not, and he said goodnight and hung up the phone.

Only after that did he seem to realize what she had told him and he remembered Havah's wild cry as she had run off into the darkness. Emitting a loud moan, he stalked into the bedroom and, crossing it, stood by the window, staring out into the night. They had shared the night, he and Havah. The room he was standing in was dark. Beyond in the bay there were the lights of ships bouncing with the waves. There was the bright torch of a distant lighthouse. There was silence. And he was alone in Yemen with Havah at his side. He recalled that moment when he had suddenly sat down and stared, unbelieving, at her and then about their camp, that moment when he realized he loved her people because they were dignified and courageous and somehow wonderfully beautiful and that of them all he loved Havah best because he knew her best and because she was Havah. Then he felt stupid and guilty because he had spent the evening she had died with a spoiled Arab tramp who thought she was sophisticated and lovely and instead was cheap and obvious. He rubbed the sides of his head with open palms as though to mark upon himself the night that Havah died.

He did not remember afterward how long he stood alone in the dark room thinking of Havah. His head hurt, though he could not have explained just how it hurt or what caused it to hurt. His thoughts were bleared, his feelings dulled, his ideas rejected as unbelievable. He had left her and she had cried out in pain and now she was dead and he could not tell her how much he liked her or loved her and he felt guilty, too, because he had never made up his mind what he would have done if they had reached Israel together. And as he stood in the darkness, he wondered what he would tell Zella about Havah and if he ever would, and if he did not was he a coward or kind, and which was the truth and which was the lie.

The cigarette in his hand burned down to his fingertips and he dropped it into an ashtray beside his bed. He lighted another cigarette and then another. But he was not seeing them and he was no longer even aware that he was smoking. All he knew was that Havah was dead and that somehow her dying was like the loss of the Old City, the Quarter and the Wall. Everything he came near was lost or destroyed in its own way. He felt his guilt and his shame, and he took upon himself more than he had the right to take, because he knew that somewhere, even though he could not say it, was this thing or that thing, he was guilty of some crime or some sin of omission or commission, but certainly some sin or some crime. Havah was lost as surely as the Wall was lost, as the Old City, as many of his friends of the last years and most certainly as his youth was lost. Just when he sat down on the bed, he would never recall, but it was about that time that there ran through his mind like a catalogue the things that youth's as separate from the things that are maturity's—the innocence, the gentleness, the ready acceptance, the simple love and the simple hate—the things that are youth's. The things that were apart from pain and realization and acceptance and patience and anger that has to be controlled and the long look back as well as the knowledge that the future is not indefinite, that people die, come apart, move in different directions perhaps to meet again but most likely not, that there is little to be gained by hate and not so much by love as the poets say.

He had finished the package of cigarettes and finally turned on the bed lamp when he remembered he was still wearing his uniform jacket. Slipping it off, he set it over a chair and went in search of a drink of water and the other cigarettes he had bought earlier in the evening. Only after he entered the sitting room did he realize that Bedia was still sitting on the sofa, still waiting for him.

Nodding in her direction, he crossed over to the sofa, picked up the package of American cigarettes which lay on the couch beside her, took one, pocketed the rest and asked, "Don't you think it's time you went back to your own suite?"

The Arab girl shook her head slowly. "You lost someone tonight?"

"Yes," he admitted, not wanting to talk to this girl about Havah.

"A woman?"

He nodded.

"Your wife?"

"No, she was not my wife though maybe I wish she had been."

She reached out and tried to take his hand, but he jerked it away. She ignored his gesture.

"Then you are married?"

"Why don't you buzz off? This is my problem."

But the girl did not move as she stared at his face. Not used to being ignored, Bedia was not confident for the first time in her life.

"Were you in love with this woman who died?"

Almost angrily, Zvi put his hands on her shoulders and shook his head. "I don't know." Then with a snort he asked, "Where the hell did you learn the word 'love'? I'm not even sure it exists in Arabic."

She drew away from him as though he had struck her a third time.

"Was that necessary?" she asked, knowing he would be embarrassed and even possibly feel guilty.

A wry smile flitted across his face. "I'm right? Arabs don't know the word?"

She wanted to tell him he was wrong. "Once we did not, but that was a long time ago, and besides I was educated in England."

"And that's where you learned all about love? In England with Captain Layton and a whole brigade of Captain Laytons?"

For an instant, he thought she was going to strike him, and he almost wished she would because he needed very little excuse to strike back himself. Instead, she said, "You liked this woman very much."

"Yes," he said as he crossed the room and stood looking out of the window. The ship's lights were still bobbing in the water and the lighthouse beam was still turning in circles.

"What was she like?" the Arab girl asked in a low voice and he flung himself about to face her.

"Like?" He thought about this and then tried to answer, "Everything you aren't. She was simple and unaffected. She was like every Jewish girl from the beginning. She was . . . " He was groping for words. "She was like a child and like everyone's mother, only she never had a chance in San'a to be either." Then as though it would explain both Havah and his own feelings better, he said, "She was the reason I killed those two Arabs. That knife your cousin had, it came out of the throat of one of them who had raped her while I had to watch." And he slammed his fist down on the table beside him so that his knuckles hurt.

"Are you sure it isn't guilt you are feeling?" the Arab girl asked.

Laughing loudly, Zvi snapped, "Don't try psychoanalyzing me now. Don't." Then because he could not stop himself, "Guilt? Yes, there's a kind of guilt, but it comes from being with a cheap slut when I should have been trying to get her across the frontier."

Bedia rose from the sofa and approached him. "And that's all you think I am?"

He held a hand out to keep her at a distance, touching her breast as he did. She did not shy away. Pressing herself against his hand, she did not smile as she asked again, "And that's all you think I am?"

Sighing because he did not want to get involved with answers he felt called upon to give, he said, still angry, "I've seen you with Layton. I've seen you with that bastard sayid, at the bar downstairs, and I've seen you try to crawl into my lap with your dress wrapped about your waist." He was smiling now and he could see that she was not. "Let's just say that whatever you are, I wouldn't call you a lady."

She laughed more loudly than she need have. His hand closed on her breast and he drew her to him without even thinking about the gesture. "Do you know what you want?" she asked. "I never would have thought you Jews—in Palestine—were puritans. From what I've heard about those of you they call sabras, I never heard anyone accuse you of conservative morality." His hand was about her waist now and he was looking into her face only inches from his as she said, "Your immorality is one of the things that has made our people angry."

Zvi smiled at the inadequacy of the word "angry." "I'm not sure just why we should care what the hell you people think." And as he spoke, his hands wandered over her silk sheath, closing for an instant on her breasts and then moving on down until one of them rested on her thigh while the other restlessly spread over her bosom.

In another moment, he knew he would be moved to more than caressing her, and as he thought of Havah, his hands both closed, pinching her so that she winced.

Stepping out of the circle of his arms, she looked up at him.

192

"I heard you say on the phone that you would be back in camp in the morning?"

He nodded.

"I'll drive you out there," she offered.

His hands came up to touch her cheeks lightly as he asked, "And why would you do that?"

She closed one hand on his and shook her head, "Maybe because I want to."

Thinking about this for a moment, Zvi nodded. "Friends?" he asked.

"Friends."

Then he picked her up and carried her across the room. Her arms closed about his neck while he nuzzled hers. Only after he had opened the door leading out of the suite and set her down on her feet in the hall did she realize what he was doing, and by that time, he had closed the door between them.

Dawn came abruptly to Aden. The mountain overlooking the city cast a long shadow. Then it was suddenly light. Lying on the bed where he had flung himself and spent the night staring at the ceiling, Zvi Mazon watched the first light crawl like a roach across the floor. The floral patterns on the wall brightened, and he rolled over and stared at the window. It was time he go down and arrange for a car to take him to Camp Hashed, and yet he did not want to go because somehow his going and not finding Havah there would bring to an end what he had spent the night trying to keep alive. Pulling himself off the bed, he showered, shaved and dressed once more in his light slacks, tossed his uniform jacket over his shoulder and went down to ask the desk clerk to help him find transportation.

"It needn't be anything fancy. Just a car. And I'll drive if there's no driver available."

The clerk gave him a baleful look, disappeared into a small room behind the desk and left Zvi alone. Turning slowly, Zvi took in the large lobby. The only guests were a young couple just coming in from the street. Her touseled blonde hair hung in wisps about her shoulders, and as she walked past Zvi, he noticed green stains on the back of her white cotton dress. Zvi wondered where they had found grass.

Looking around once more, he started toward the desk again to inquire about his car when Bedia entered the lobby from the elevator. She was wearing a bright green cotton dress now, green shoes and silk stockings. Her hair was up and her face smiling.

"We going?" she asked as she crossed the room to his side.

Zvi looked for the desk clerk, and when he did not see him anywhere, he wondered if British clerks showed the same kind of courage as young British soldiers.

Bedia followed his glance and explained, "I asked him to call me when you came down." To be certain Zvi appreciated her efforts, "It cost me three pounds."

Finally, Zvi shrugged, and without taking her arm, walked to the front entrance and out into the bright morning sun.

It was already hot. The streets appeared to be steaming and Zvi saw that dust was merely covering the dung of camels, donkeys and asses. That explained the odor that made him wince. Aden itself was quiet. There were some Arabs sweeping in front of the Crescent. Two doors away a large staff car pulled up and several British officers stepped out. Zvi recognized Captain Layton as the last to emerge and decided he did not want to meet the man at this moment.

Swinging back to face Bedia, who had come out of the hotel after him, he asked, "The car?"

Having seen Layton herself, she smiled and motioned for the doorman to have her car brought forward. Two minutes later, Zvi and his companion were racing out of the city toward Camp Hashed.

Driving wildly, the chauffeur approached the camp in less than fifteen minutes while Zvi wondered if all Arab drivers were mad. Suddenly, a swirl of dust, and they were in front of the gate of Camp Hashed.

Stepping out, Zvi identified himself to the Arab sentry and then to the Yemenite policeman on duty. The gates swung open and the Bentley drove slowly through the camp street toward the Administration Building. Several Yemenite families stepped out of their tents to watch the car go by. One Yemenite policeman pointed to his sunhelmet before he shook his fist at the car and the driver as though they symbolized a world to him. Zvi smiled as he watched Bedia become uncomfortable.

Several men he had met when he first arrived at the camp stepped out of the Administration Building as well as two of the doctors and a nurse from the hospital. All were curious to see who owned the Bentley and what it was doing at Hashed so early in the morning. Tapping the driver on the shoulder, Zvi gestured for him to pull up and stop.

After the driver opened the car door, Zvi stepped out, reached back and, taking Bedia's hand, helped her from the car. The colonel came forward.

"What the hell have we here?" and he was smiling as he spoke.

When Zvi introduced the Arab girl, the American smiled more broadly. "We have all kinds of guests. Most of the legations from Aden have people coming out all the time. We've had sheiks and sharifs and sayids and . . . " The torrent of words ran down as though he had come to the end. "Welcome to Camp Hashed," he said proudly.

Bedia thanked him and before she could say anything else, Zvi stomped on the beginning of her sentence, "Did that group get in yet? The group I came south with?"

The Colonel thought for a moment. "There," he said, pointing to rows of men and women lined up in front of two small buildings which Zvi recognized as the shower rooms.

"Thanks," he shouted over his shoulder as he started running toward the two lines of men and women.

He was almost among them when Isaac's younger wife recognized him and shouted his name loudly. The lines broke apart as the Yemenites ran to greet him. Several of the men threw their arms about him and a few of the women came close enough to smile at him. He was the foreign Jew whom they knew. He was their friend and he had brought them to the gates of Yemen. The aged mori embraced the stocky Israeli and for a time neither of them felt like letting go of the other. Isaac in his turn took his friend's hands, clasping them in his own. Several of the children came and shouted until he recognized them, touseled their hair or lifted them up in his arms and swung them about. The children looked smaller than he remembered them, and their parents looked thinner. But among all there was a smile and warmth for their friend.

Isaac's older wife reached out and touched Zvi's arm and to the astonishment of her husband, the Israeli bent down and kissed her cheek. Then he walked over to a cooper and tanner and, putting his arms about both men, held them close.

"It is good," he said, and the man said a *berakhah*.

Standing back and watching the group, the colonel murmered to Bedia, "They love him."

She nodded. She had never thought of Jews in this way.

Taking the mori's hand and the younger silversmith's, Zvi led the two men to the colonel. "These are men you should know," he said, introducing the two. And then remembering that Bedia was with him, he introduced her. "She helped us get through Yemen," he said. Both of the Yemenite Jews half bowed toward the Arab girl, not knowing quite what was expected of them. "She helped us," Zvi said again.

Bedia accepted their thanks. However, before anyone could say more, Zvi put his arms about the father and son and led them away from the others, down a camp street where other Yemenites had poked their heads out of pyramidal tents to see what the commotion was about.

Zvi was no longer smiling. The sun was hot on his face. Finally, the three men were alone. Dropping his arms from about their waists, Zvi said, "She's dead?"

The mori nodded. It was Isaac who explained, "Two days ago. The man called Adam says she died of a fever, but I don't think she cared what she died of."

Accepting this, Zvi asked, "And she was buried well?"

The other two men were silent as they considered the question and then the father said, "She was buried on the road to the Holy Land. I think that is being buried well."

Holding his breath for an instant, Zvi weighed this. He wanted to know if she had been buried deeply and covered well so that no tahish would dig up her grave, but he decided not to ask that question.

"We said Kaddish," the mori consoled him in the only way he knew.

"I will, also," Zvi said. And he was pleased to see the old man smile.

"Maybe in time you will learn."

Not wanting to hurt his friend's feelings, Zvi nodded. "Is there anything? Was there anything?" He knew that somehow he was not asking the right question.

Isaac seemed to understand. His lean head bobbed, "There was."

Zvi waited patiently as he knew the silversmith was trying to remember what he had been told.

"The child called Aaron," Isaac said. "She wanted to be sure you took care of the child called Aaron."

Ashamed that he had not seen the boy once since he had brought him to the camp, Zvi asked, "And that was all she said?"

Isaac started to nod, but the mori shook his head. "She became all mixed up and she thought the boy was her child and your child and she kept saying that we should be sure to tell Zvi to take care of the child you had."

The Israeli officer swung about so that his back was toward the two for a moment as he tried to realize what had happened. Without looking back at them, he asked, "Did she die easily?"

"There are no easy ways to die when you know you are going to die," Isaac said simply.

Nodding, Zvi realized that Isaac in his own way was trying to be honest, and he wished his friend had been more kind than honest.

When he turned back to the two, he wished the sun were not on his face because he was having difficulty not weeping. But Havah was dead, and weeping would not change that. Very slowly he walked back with the other two toward the shower building where their companions were disappearing one after the other to be introduced to their first showers and new clothes and modern medicine. Just as the two Yemenites were about to rejoin their families, the mori asked, "And the child?"

"I will take the child," Zvi promised.

His companions appeared pleased.

"We will see you again?" Isaac asked.

The colonel and Bedia were with them now. Zvi looked at him for an answer.

The tall American shoved his hand through his thatch of white hair, and tipping his head to one side, explained, "Those of you who can are going to be on a plane tonight."

"Now?" Zvi demanded. "Tonight?"

The colonel nodded. "We'll get some out right away even though there are others who have been here longer." Seeing that this was not really an explanation, he added, "The hospital is crowded here. The hospital in Aden, thanks to the British doctor, has as many of our people as it can hold."

Knowing that his friends would not understand all of this, Zvi assured them. "I will be with you in the Holy Land, if not before."

The Yemenites smiled. "Tomorrow in Jerusalem," the old man said.

And the three laughed, joined by the colonel.

Embracing his friends once more, Zvi said, "Soon," and then the young Israeli who was tending the showers led the two away.

Zvi watched after them for a moment and then asked the colonel, "You meant it about tonight?"

The American nodded. "We'll borrow some trucks. We have two planes ready to go. I'll probably be able to put a few dozen of this group on." Then he lost his temper as he continued. "I've got to get some of these people to a hospital. I've got to."

Both Zvi and Bedia recognized the tone of near desperation in the man's voice.

The Israeli officer asked simply, "And will there be room on the plane for a small boy about five?"

The Colonel nodded. "I'm sure he does not weigh much." Then as though he had to explain about weight. "If I send some of these people tonight, I can get about one hundred and twenty on one of these planes. If I wait a few weeks, I may be able to get a hundred on." With what sounded like an apology, he said, "They need to have something to eat for a few weeks to become what they can be." And aware that he had said this badly, "I'll do the best I can."

Zvi clasped the tall man's arm and squeezed it affectionately. "You sure don't look like any Messiah I ever imagined."

"I don't feel like one." Then, almost as if he wished to end the conversation, "That child is in the third tent on the second row of tents from the Administration Building."

Startled, Zvi stared at the man.

"Adam thought you would want to know."

Zvi said, "Thanks," and started toward the Administration Building. He had gone only a few paces when Bedia caught up with him and they walked through the sandy street together.

"This child," she asked. "Is it really yours?"

Zvi thought about the question as he watched the Yemenites standing in front of a tent admiring each other's clothes. "It is my child," he finally said.

The Arab girl looked at him dubiously. "I could take care of him for you," she offered.

Taken aback at the gesture, Zvi paused in the street to look at her, and he believed she meant what she was saying. "Thanks," he said after a time. However, as he spoke he shook his head. "She left the child to me."

They walked on a short distance before he said flatly, "And besides, he is a Jewish child. He will remain Jewish." He hoped his anger at the threat against the child only days before when he had to bring him across the frontier line in a sack did not show, but he assumed it did when she looked at him and then ran to her car. For one brief instant, Zvi though of following her. Instead, he shrugged and went down the second row of tents in search of Aaron.

Zvi did not hear about the riot until his Yemenite friends and Aaron left the Khermaksar Airport. He saw them off, promising that their holy books and scrolls would reach Israel safely. He had started back for Camp Hashed with Colonel Max when their jeep was waved to the side of the road by a British army convoy.

It was Colonel Max who asked the officer-in-charge where the convoy was going.

The young British captain, whom Zvi recognized as the one who had entered the hotel with the grass-stained companion, leaned out of his jeep and shouted, "It's all hell down in the Crater."

"What's all hell?" the American asked.

"Arabs running wild, tearing up the Jewish sector." And the British jeep spurted forward, leaving the two Jews looking after it.

"Let's go," Zvi suggested.

The camp commander nodded, gunned the motor of his jeep and sped down the dark road after the British troops. It was a cold, clear night. There was enough moon to brighten the weird tufa landscape. Broken rocks created grotesque shadows over the road.

Zvi, wearing only cotton slacks and shirt, wished he had a jacket with him.

Colonel Max caught up with the British, raced past them and on toward the Crater. Where Zvi had seen the lights of the area bright against the sky the night before, now he could make out smoke and the flickering of fire. There were few vehicles in the area as they approached it. However, there was noise. Racing past a camel caravan stopped for the night on the edge of the Crater, the jeep bearing the two Jews entered the main square. There were mobs running wild, pouring quickly and violently into the unnamed streets of the Jewish sector. Passing through A Street, Colonel Max rammed his vehicle into a mob gathered around a young Jewish boy and his girl friend.

The couple were backed up against the wall of an old synagogue while a dozen or more Arabs stood back, throwing stones, pieces of paving-block and broken glass at them. Zvi saw the boy, probably not yet twenty, trying to shield the girl with his body. A stone struck his head and he slipped to the ground, exposing the girl. One middle-aged Arab wearing a ripped gray jacket, started to throw a paving-block at the girl when Zvi leaped out of the jeep, grabbed the man from behind and hurled him against three other Arab men. Startled at the assault, the Arabs hesitated, and in that instant Colonel Max scooped the boy up from the ground, tossed him into the rear of the jeep and was about to reach for the girl when several Arab youths grabbed him.

One of the crowd recognized the American as the commander at Camp Hashed, screamed his name, and his companions started to pummel the tall colonel. An old Arab woman began to swing a jack handle at the colonel's head, when Zvi grabbed her arm, twisted the long piece of steel from it and swung it about him in a large circle, driving the mob back. Two stones struck him in the chest and shoulder and for an instant he paused in pain. However, when the Arab youths started to close in on him again, he swung wildly and blindly at no one in particular. His weapon hit something soft and then he swung again and heard the crunch of bone and the shriek which told him he had broken an arm or a leg or a skull. He did not know which and he did not care. Colonel Max was rising to his knees now and, reaching out, he thrust the young Jewish girl into the jeep, following after her. Zvi swung several more times in a wild arc and then, as the jeep started to run into the mob, he leaped back into his seat. Stones fell about them, breaking the windshield, sprinkling glass across the front of the vehicle. Angrily, the American jammed his foot down on the gas pedal, slamming the jeep through the Arabs, who fell back. Zvi could tell from the screams that they had crushed one against the wall and then another, as they backed away and sped down the street.

There were more Arabs in the streets now, and the noise of violence filled the air. Reaching the front of a home with a mezuzah on the door, Colonel Max jammed on the brake and helped Zvi carry the injured youth into the house. The girl followed.

A Jew wearing a business suit and yarmulke stood beside his door waiting for the strangers to enter. "Why aren't you out there helping?" Zvi shouted at him.

Taken aback at what seemed an absurd suggestion, the man shook his head.

For a brief moment, Zvi glared at the Jew who would not defend himself, closed his hand more tightly about the steel jack handle and jumped back into the jeep as an Arab mob approached the house. The heavy door slammed after him and Colonel Max moved the vehicle down the street once more.

A stone crashed into the dashboard and both men put their heads down.

A small crowd of Arabs had broken into a store across the street and were dragging out furniture. Half a block farther on, they could see a bonfire consuming handfuls of books as Arab after Arab approached it and threw more into the fire.

"Hold on," the colonel said softly. Both put their heads down as the jeep slammed directly into the fire, scattering both Arabs and burning manuscript and breaking up the fire. A young Arab thrust a dagger at Colonel Max as the jeep passed him, but Zvi swung about, breaking the man's arm with his jack handle.

"Get you?" he asked.

The American held up his left arm to show where the blood was flowing.

The street ahead became a haze of smoke and flames as house after house was set afire. In the headlights of the vehicle, the two could make out the figure of a Jew being kicked as he lay in the street. Before the jeep could reach him, an Arab landed on the man's head with both feet. Once more, Colonel Max slammed his jeep into the crowd, breaking it apart.

Three Arabs ran ahead of them driving two donkeys they had stolen. Zvi watched them go, certain there was nothing he could do or cared to do about the stolen property, and then he saw a large Arab holding a small boy by the arms. The child's payot swung loose about his pale cheeks as he covered his head and screamed. However, before Zvi could point the child out to Colonel Max, the Arab swung the child up and smashed his head against a wall. The screams ended with a dull thud which Zvi believed he could hear over the noise of the shouting crowd, and only afterward would he doubt that he could have heard it. The Arab tossed the dead boy aside and started out in search of another victim.

Jumping from the protection of the jeep, Zvi ran madly after the Arab. Several of the crowd saw the race begin, did not know Svi was a Jew and watched the brief chase which ended when two British soldiers emerged from a doorway and blocked Zvi's path, their rifles at port.

"Where do you think you're going?" one of them demanded.

Glancing at the soldier's sleeves, Zvi recognized him for a corporal. "After that man. He just killed a boy."

"He or someone else," the corporal snapped. "You couldn't prove anything tonight."

Zvi started to bring up his length of steel bar when the other soldier shook his head. "I don't know who you are, but I'll kill you."

By this time, the jeep had caught up with Zvi, and Colonel Max jumped out to stand beside his companion. "What's the problem, Major?" he demanded with complete authority.

Uncertain what they were coping with, the two British soldiers looked at each other. The corporal stepped back and, playing safe, saluted the two Jews. By this time Zvi could no longer see the Arab who had killed the child.

There were four British standing together now, and Zvi recognized the officer they had met on the road.

"What's wrong?" the youthful Englishman asked.

"Look around you," Zvi shouted.

Calmly, the captain glanced about. Several of the buildings near them were burning now. Most of the metal-curtained shop fronts were smashed in and Arabs were carrying out their loot—jewelry, cloth, shoes and canned food.

From a small house that faced the street, Zvi could see three Arab men dragging a woman. He started after them, but the British officer stepped in front of him. "Leave that for the police."

Zvi's hand came up, but before he could strike, two British soldiers shoved him back with their rifle butts.

The captain did not appear offended as he turned to the American, "I don't know who your friend is, mate, but you'd better cool him down or he'll be arrested."

The tall camp commander combed back his white hair with an open hand and nodded. "Easy, Major. Easy."

"Major?" the Englishman demanded.

Colonel Max nodded. "Major Zvi Mazon of the Israeli army."

For a moment the British officer stared at the younger man. Then he shook his head. "If you were in our army, you wouldn't be a first lieutenant yet."

Zvi looked at the man in disgust and started once more toward the house where he had seen the Arabs emerge with the woman. Once more the British officer blocked his path. Clenching his hands tightly, Zvi shoved his face close to the captain's. "When I was in your army eight years ago, I was a captain." Swinging away from the startled Englishman, he appealed to Colonel Max, "What the hell *can* we do?"

The screams in the street continued, only growing louder as a mob of more than a hundred streamed past.

The colonel and Zvi remained still while the British soldiers kept their rifles at the ready. Swinging about, the British officer pointed toward four Aden police making their way through the mob. "We'll have it under control soon enough," as though to console the two Jews.

The group stood watching while the Aden police in suntan shorts started blocking the path of the Arabs who shied away and then started to fall back as the police moved slowly down the street, clearing it as they went.

"What started this?" Zvi demanded.

"Your planes. Someone reported that you were flying more Jews to Israel and the Palestinians here—and there are a few hundred—spread the story."

The homes behind them were burning now, but there were fewer Arabs in the street. Shouts could be heard from distant points. Then a well-dressed Arab approached the group.

"Captain," he shouted, "my caravan, they are looting it."

The British officer nodded and then his orders flowed in short, sharp sentences. "Corporal, take five men to the caravan. Clear the area. Don't let anyone loot. Try not to kill anyone. However, if you have to, then do it."

The corporal saluted, selected five men and followed the caravan-owner down the street.

"Why protect that?" Zvi demanded.

Bewildered by the question, the Englishman explained, "It's property."

Zvi glanced at Colonel Max, who shook his head in disbelief.

"You've got to understand," the captain offered. "These people are frightened by the tens of thousands of Jews out in your camp. They are afraid for their lives and their property. They are afraid, too, because you have typhus and yellow fever and malaria there." He was trying to be reasonable. "I know, because Captain Layton's friend told us tonight at dinner."

It took a moment for Zvi to realize what he was hearing. "Captain Layton's friend?" he asked.

The young Englishman nodded patronizingly. "An Arab girl. She'd been out to the camp herself today and she saw."

"Saw what?" Zvi demanded.

"The people dying of fever and pox, the lines getting their shots and the thousands waiting to come through here to the port."

The Englishman was trying to be patient with the Israeli officer who had been a captain in the British army while he himself had still been in school.

However, it was the American who grabbed the British officer's shirtfront and spat out, "There is no fever. There is no pox. There are not tens of thousands. They do not go through the port. There are no . . ."

However, he dropped his hand and spun about when Zvi leaped into the jeep, started the motor and drove away without looking back.

"Where the hell's he going?" the Englishman asked.

The American shook his head. He did not know either.

Smoke from a burning building filled the street and they could no longer see the jeep.

Racing out of the Crater area toward Steamer Point, Zvi saw a wall collapse, the dust and stone crash into the street before him. Smoke filled the air and he was back in the Old City. There were shots in the distance and he was waiting for the next shell to fall. Then, swerving, he raced the car down a side street. Arabs still clogged it, but they jumped back as the headlights caught them. Zvi knew he struck one and then another. Shouts followed him, but he did not hear them. There was a burning building ahead and more smoke. Two Arabs shouted something as he passed, but he was confident they did not know if he were Jewish or British. Then a police van was blocking the street.

The British police officers approached and Zvi identified himself. One of the police officers, a handsome young Yorkshireman, smiled. "I'm sorry, Major. The whole thing got out of hand. I hope none of your people is hurt."

Sitting back in the jeep, Zvi started to say something in anger, changed his mind because of the youth's courtesy and said, "Thanks. There have been a lot killed, but I'm sure you didn't want that."

The police officer nodded. "The Jews here have been quiet, minding their own business." Then as though he himself were somehow responsible, "I'm sorry, sir." And with that he waved Zvi around the truck.

Fifteen minutes later Zvi jerked his jeep to a stop in front of the Crescent and raced up the steps and into the large hotel. The lobby was filled. None of the people seemed aware that anything untoward was taking place in the Crater. It was not really their concern what the Arabs and Jews did to each other. They would have all objected to seeing a child killed or a woman raped, but their business was twofold: business and the running of a colony, and none of them felt he was responsible for anything else. Certainly not a clash between Jews and Arabs. How could anyone expect them to be responsible? One dowager turned toward Zvi, startled at the blood on his slacks, and drew away, whispering to her companion, an elderly naval officer.

Zvi crossed to the clerk behind the desk. "Miss Hassani?" he asked.

The clerk looked at the Israeli, recognized him as the man who had taken Colonel Max's suite the day before and shook his head. "She's in her suite."

"And which is that?"

"Six-twenty-one." Then, not sure of himself, he said, "I'll have to ring her."

Smiling wryly, Zvi advised, "Don't bother." And he was off toward the elevators. The clerk shook his head at the unseemly way the Jew was crossing the lobby, shrugged and went back to sorting the mail.

Zvi found himself alone with the elevator operator, an Arab with a slightly crossed eye. Neither of them said anything after Zvi asked for his floor. However, the Arab kept staring at the blood on the stranger's slacks.

When they reached the sixth floor, Zvi stepped out, looked both ways, found the direction he was seeking and walked swiftly down the corridor. A British couple with a little girl passed him, the man taking the time to look back over his shoulder, puzzled. At 621, Zvi paused, started to knock, changed his mind, swung the door open and stepped into a large sitting room. Slamming the door behind him, he wondered for the first time just why he had come.

"Is that you, Maria?" Bedia's voice from the next room. Balling his fist and holding it tightly against the leg of his bloody tan slacks, Zvi called back. "It isn't Maria."

He was half way across the room when Bedia emerged. She was wearing a sheer, white lace peignoir. Pausing at the bedroom door, she looked at Zvi's angry face, started to step back, changed her mind and smiled at him.

He knew that she was lovely; and he knew, too, that at this moment it did not matter how lovely or how wealthy or how willing she was.

"You were so hard to get yesterday," she admonished him. "And now . . ." Her arms came up as though she expected to be embraced.

Almost blindly, Zvi swung his open palm, slapping the side of her head, knocking her over a chair which fell on its side. After a moment, she sat up, clenched her head with her hands and stared at him. "Have you gone crazy?" she asked in complete innocence.

Moving so that he stood over her, Zvi jerked his foot back as though to kick her. For a second she thought he really would, but, relaxing, he leaned down and picked her up with his hands under her arms. Steadying her gently, he said, "You don't know anything about it. Rumors running like rats through the Crater and people being killed and fires burning and homes puffing out and exploding from the heat and old women beaten, but you don't know anything about it." He was not asking her. In fact, he was surprised himself at the control he was able to retain as he spoke.

"Rumors?" she asked as though she actually did not know what he was talking about, and at the same time showing that the things he mentioned did not in any way relate to her. Grabbing the front of her peignoir so that the lace gave under his closed, rough hands, he drew her toward him, half lifting her from the floor. He felt her breasts under his knuckles but at that moment he was not thinking of her as a desirable woman.

"Like the Quarter," he snapped, trying to remind her of the first time they had met. "Only this time there was no fighting. There was just the killing and looting."

She was looking at him puzzled when he removed one hand from the front of her gown and slapped her.

"Don't say anything. Don't deny anything," he warned so softly that she was more frightened by his words than the blow. "Only you knew when we were flying those people out. And you talked to Layton."

She started to shake her head and he slapped her again. This time with the back of his hand so that her head jerked back; and as she stumbled away, his other hand still clutched the lace he was left holding. She wore a short silk nightgown underneath.

Zvi looked at her; and with both of his hands clenched, beat down on her until she fell to the floor, and he fell to his knees and continued to beat her about the head and breasts until he was out of breath and she was almost unconscious. Then he looked down at her frightened face marked by his blows, and at her breasts where he had struck her. Somehow he had no satisfaction from this, though he felt he had done nothing wrong. "There was a little boy," he said, almost reasonably and completely dispassionately. "A small boy. And a man picked him up and broke his head against a wall."

Bedia was up on her elbows now, glaring at him. "He was a Jew boy?" she asked.

Slamming his fist out, he struck her on the side of her head and she lay still. For a moment he thought he had killed her. When he shoved his hand down on her breast, he could feel her heart beating. Then he came to his feet and stumbled out of the room, leaving the door open behind him.

Twice he had to ring for the elevator before the cross-eyed Arab brought it to the sixth floor. Staring, baffled by the stranger, the Arab decided not to ask any questions. They had reached the ground floor when Zvi asked flatly. "Know anyone named Maria?"

The Arab shook his head at first, and then as the elevator door opened, he said, "That would be Miss Hassani's maid." Zvi nodded and was out of the hotel and sitting in his jeep when he recognized Layton climbing the broad stone steps into the building. Gripping the steering wheel, Zvi decided that they could meet another time. Maybe there was something he could do for Colonel Max and the others.

He was sitting at breakfast the next morning when Shoshanna brought in the news from the Crater. "Eighty-two dead," she told them, and the half-dozen Israelis and the American all seemed to hold their breath for a moment. Then she added what sounded like gossip. "The Aden police found some British officer lying in an alley near the Crescent."

Zvi looked at Adam, and the Agency man queried with his eyes.

"Not I," Zvi said softly.

"Do they know what happened?" Colonel Max asked.

Shoshanna half smiled even though her reaction was somehow incongruous under the circumstance. "Arab justice. The police officer I met on the road back from town said there's a rumor some lady's maid found him standing over her mistress and her without anything on and him trying to rape her." She shook her head. "From what the policeman said, no one's going to press charges because the lady was beaten up."

No one said anything for a time though the colonel sat looking at Zvi.

Finally, Zvi said, "I doubt if he tried to rape her if she was all beaten up, and besides, he probably could have gotten what he wanted without the effort."

Adam and the colonel were staring at him.

Zvi lit a cigarette, offered the pack around, but no one accepted it.

Confused, Shoshanna explained, "If he wasn't raping her, why would they have. . . ," and she faltered to a stop.

"Have what?" the colonel asked quietly.

"Cut off his . . . ." Her hands came wide. "You know . . . and put it in his mouth."

The others were silent. Zvi rose. "Maybe they thought he had raped her."

And he walked outside into the bright morning sunlight.

He was alone in front of the temporary barracks building for a moment until the colonel joined him.

"Your assignment came in last night. Let's talk about it later."

"Thanks." Then Zvi apologized. "I brought her here."

Putting one hand on the younger man's shoulder, the American said, "Don't blame yourself about what happened in the Crater. We all talked in front of her." And it was obvious that the others had guessed what had taken place.

THE RED SEA

Zvi took in the view from the dirty deck of the Italian freighter and wondered how he had got this assignment. He had had very little to do with ships in his life. He had landed in Italy in one during the war, had returned to Palestine in another. But those voyages had been under very different circumstances. He had not commanded then, and he had not been responsible.

Looking back at Aden as it faded in the distance, Zvi was happy to be leaving. The heat of the city, the dirt, the deaths—and most of all the loss of Havah—would always be linked in his mind with Aden. Looking about, he watched the Ethiopian crew lashing four cargo packing cases to the deck. The cargo was small: three hundred sefer torahs and three thousand holy books. No one could claim his cargo was military or commercial.

The little Italian captain with the neatly trimmed beard sticking out under his unwashed face grinned down at him from the poop.

Zvi had been introduced to Captain Diego Balbini the night before when Colonel Max had brought the two together for dinner at the Crescent. The Italian's English was good. He had learned it in a hundred ports. In a few minutes after they met both of them understood the importance of their mission. The *Hatikvah*, until recently the *Napoli*, was going to make the run from Aden, through the Red Sea, the Straits of Tiran and into the Gulf of Akaba. The *Hatikvah* was going to be the first ship flying an Israeli flag to reach Eilat in over two thousand years, and the voyage was going to be difficult. Both men agreed with the American that the voyage was going to be difficult.

"I want you to know," Colonel Max had said, "the Egyptians will be looking for you and if they can stop you, they will."

Captain Balbini, probably thirty years older than Zvi, had winked at the young Israeli, "I do not fear Egyptians."

Zvi smiled.

However, that had all been said in the comfort of the Colonel's suite in the Crescent Hotel when the air was light, the stars out and from the window the distant sea looked friendly. Now the sea was rolling and Zvi had had time to evaluate the *Hatikvah*. Little more than ninety tons, the tiny, coal-burning coastal freighter had thirty years of unscaled rust over decks, thirty years of battering by the seas. Salt had dried over her gear. Thick grease seemed to be all that held her warped plates together. Above hung a tattered Liberian flag.

The fifteen Ethiopians who made up the crew did not know their destination, and Captain Balbini decided that he would not upset them until he had to. Turning once more to the long poop which served the coaster as a bridge, Zvi watched the bearded Italian shaking his leg as though he had wet it. Smiling to himself at the clownish aspects of this historic voyage, Zvi tried to evaluate the ship's captain with the same detached eye he had evaluated the ship. Balbini was not a patriot of any country. He could not care less if the vessel reached Eilat. However, he was completely intrigued with the notion of ten thousand Israeli pounds as a bonus for getting the vessel through the Arab seas. When Colonel Max had laid the deal out before him, Captain Diego had accepted without hesitation. Only afterwards had the American warned Zvi, "He'll jettison you if he gets into trouble."

But as he watched the captain, Zvi was not so certain. On his deck, Balbini looked like a sailor. From what Zvi had learned of men in his twenty-six years, he decided that should the occasion arise, he would trust this man. Scanning the long foredeck, Zvi wondered if he would take the same risk with the *Hatikvah*.

A megaphone in hand, Balbini was shouting something to his crew and Zvi could not even guess what it was until two dark-skinned sailors moved away from one of the crates, and then Zvi realized the captain had seen them trying to break into it. Theft had not come to mind before. Now that it did, Zvi smiled at the lean Ethiopians. They were going to be surprised when they found out what they were carrying north.

A cool Egyptian wind rose from the west.

And Zvi turned to look at the sea. The Red Sea. The tiny sea, that narrow strip of water which lay south-southeast from the Gulf of Suez to the strait of Bab el Mandeb—the Gate of Morning. Twelve hundred miles to the north lay the *Hatikvah's* destination. Twelve hundred miles of blue-green water sliced beneath by knives of sand which reflected the sun above.

The vessel lumbered slowly northward through the still warm waters. Very slowly Zvi turned to watch a dhow pass southward toward Zanzibar or Madagascar. A wealth of carving marked her stern where ornamented lanterns hung beside a row of decorated windows. The last remnant of the Portuguese presence in the sea, the last symbol of better times. In the distance coming toward the *Hatikvah* Zvi made out the large silhouette of a buggalow, seagoing and plank-decked, bound for the Indian Ocean and the east-blowing winds of the monsoon.

Through his mind ran the catalogue of cargoes he had heard Captain Balbini talking about as they came aboard the night before. "From all over," the small Italian had said as he shoved his spade beard forward. "From all over. Dates from Oman and rice from Bombay. Timber from East Africa and sheep from Somaliland. Wheat from Karachi and silk from Japan. Machinery from America and England. And on the journey back there are shark fins for the Chinese, wild honey for Java, dried fish for Zanzibar and coffee for America and Europe."

The captain had stood looking at the dhows and buggalows in the harbor before he spat. "I've sailed all the waters and carried all cargoes, and now I'm carrying holy books and holy scrolls." And he spat again.

The sun was high, and the buggalow was coming closer now. There were no lifeboats on her and as Zvi looked about *Hatikvah*, he noticed for the first time that they, too, were without lifeboats. *Inshalla*, he smiled. They would not need them. Only he was not of Islam and would be willing to save his life if the occasion arose.

For the first time, too, he became aware of the smell from the open hold beside him and he wondered what combination of cargoes had left their mark on the morning air.

Looking up at the Captain, he saw that the older man was now wearing only his cotton shorts as he stared at the bottle of wine in his hand. Waving at his passenger, Balbini shouted, "*Hatikvah*," as though it were a joke. Then he raised the bottle toward the cargo and drank.

A moment later Zvi watched the Italian rear back and throw the empty bottle into the sea. Following its arc, Zvi saw a shark's fin cutting the clear water. Moving to the rail he stared as the shark was joined by three companions. And again, he wished he had a lifeboat. *Inshalla*, but not for him.

Bab el Mandeb lay behind them. To the east were pale rocks, sand and empty desert. How far away, Zvi could not even guess. The distance was deceptive and the sudden appearance of a sharp cliff left him wondering how high it was. There were mountains behind the desert. Several times he thought the beaches were close, but as he watched a gull sailing the sky between, he knew he was wrong.

Balbini held another bottle now as he watched his compass. The tiny man lifted his bottle, toasted the cargo once more and then pointed to the shoreline. Zvi turned to look. A straggle of camel caravan moving north. Beyond it the ruins of an ancient fort perched on the edge of a cliff.

Over the fort was a flamingo and near the beach stood a solitary crane. Waving to Balbini to indicate that he, too, saw the caravan, he wondered how many caravans had taken the route north to Egypt over how many centuries.

He looked up at the sky and then back at Balbini. Shouting from where he stood, Zvi reminded the Captain, "It's time."

The Italian nodded, disappeared into the small cabin behind him and a

moment later came out with the package in his hand. Suddenly, Zvi knew
that he himself wanted to take care of what came next, and climbing to the
poop, he took the package from Balbini, ripped it open and stood staring at
the bundle of cloth in his hand. Walking over to the single mast of the ship,
he lowered the Liberian flag, folded it with care and raised the flag marked by
the blue Mogen David. Tying the rope in place, he stepped back and saluted.
Behind him he could hear the Italian chuckle, and when he looked forward at
the deck, he could see the startled expressions on the faces of the Ethiopian
crew.

"Is there anything I can do?" Zvi asked Balbini.

Pushing his beard forward with the hand that held his bottle of wine, the
Captain shook his head. "Get drunk," he suggested.

Smiling, Zvi said, "In that case I'm going to sleep until you think I
should be doing something else."

Balbini roared at what he assumed was a Jew's joke and went back to his
wine.

For the next five days Zvi slept through the day and watched the
shoreline at night. They passed half a dozen small islands, several ruined forts,
and saw hundreds of pelicans. They passed the Island of Perim and lay off the
decaying port of Mocha at night. In the morning they edged westward to
avoid Kamaran Island with its airfield and radio station. There was no wind.
The sea remained still. Balbini remained drunk, but the crew knew its job,
and the small coaster edged the land where there were no villages and moved
into the sea where there were.

Once they passed a British destroyer moving south. Four times they
passed buggalows moving in the same direction. Once a French passenger liner
overtook them as it headed for Suez. Three cargo ships flying Liberian colors
and one Panamanian tanker passed them sailing north. The crews of the other
vessels waved. One cargo captain pointed at the blue-and-white flat and
shouted, "I wish you well."

Zvi waved back his thanks, hoping at the same time the captain did not
radio the news that they were coming. Since they had left Aden, the *Hatikvah*
had maintained radio silence. Once Balbini was asked questions by a British
motor ship, but he merely waved his greetings and sailed on.

The fifth night on board while the two of them ate dinner in the small
and dirty cabin, Zvi asked, "We're no secret any longer?"

Balbini shrugged. "I've shifted speed so often, they can't tell when we're
coming."

"But you think they know we're coming?"

Again the captain shrugged.

And Zvi knew the other man thought their secret was out. Somewhere
before they reached the Gulf of Akaba, the Egyptians would try to stop
them. As they sat eating their baked fish and beans, neither man wanted to

press the subject further. The Egyptians could merely board them and claim the vessel. Or they might try to teach the Jews a lesson, in which case they would sink the ship and the *Hatikvah* would disappear without a trace.

When they finished eating, Captain Balbini shoved his plate away and, pulling out a battered, leather-bound pipe, filled it from a can on a shelf beside him and sat smiling at his wine glass.

"We go west from here," he offered.

"West?"

"Luhaiya." As though the name had meaning. "Small port on the northern end of a narrow bay. Urmek. Mostly mud huts. About five thousand people, a mosque. And a telegraph line running south toward Hodeida and north to Meidi."

He was pulling himself from the chair and patting his small belly. "Someday I'm going to carry a cargo of meat and then I'm not even going to find the time to drink." He leaned across the table, belching as he did, "Imagine eating just meat." And there was a tone of awe in his voice. "Just meat." Picking up his bottle, he walked a wavering line out of the cabin. Zvi watched him for a moment and then followed. By the time he rejoined Balbini, the Captain was checking his compass and shifting his course westward. The Ethiopian who had been at the wheel nodded to the Israeli and clambered down the ladder, leaving the two alone in the night.

Balbini shouted something into the night and Zvi saw the ship go dark. Now for the first time as he looked eastward, he could make out lights moving slowly south somewhere between the *Hatikvah* and the shore. The more Zvi saw of the diminutive Italian the more he was impressed with the professionalism of the man.

"You've been on these waters long?" Zvi asked. He could barely make out the other man's face in the dark.

Shoving one hand under his beard, Balbini thought about this question. Minutes passed before he answered. "These waters. I came through here first when we held Eritrea. About the time *Il Duce* came to power." He sniggered as he said, "Before *your* time. I had grown up in a small village in the mountains and my brother had put on a brown shirt and marched into Rome, leaving me with all of the work on the farm." Balbini fell silent as he remembered. "Don't ever try to work a mountain farm in Italy. There's only one crop—rocks." He guffawed at his own joke. "And so when my father asked me to marry the girl on the next farm so I would have twice as much land and twice as many rocks, I ran away. Naples."

The *Hatikvah* began to roll, and Zvi grasped the rail. His back to it, he waited for Balbini to continue.

After a drink from his bottle, the Italian went on. "Cabin boy at first. Saw India that voyage out." He snorted. "All foreigners, but Indian girls have what every other girl has and I was young. Was young and impressionable in

Capetown, Madagascar, Ceylon, Hong Kong, Shanghai, Singapore, San Francisco, Panama, Buenos Aires." He guffawed once more at his own humor. "Young and eager to be impressed."

"Then I was older and *Il Duce* took us to war against the Ethiopians."

He was silent now as he seemed to be thinking about that war. "I was a first mate then. They gave me a small naval cargo vessel. I carried airplanes and bombs. One night part of the cargo broke loose in a storm." Then, as though he did not want to say anything else, he stared at the sea and the sky. Finally he warned, "Don't ever have a cargo of poison gas break loose in the hold."

Surprised at the comment and taken aback at the thought, Zvi asked, "What did you do?"

"Do?" the little Italian asked, "Took to the lifeboats after opening all the cocks. I sank the damned thing."

"Anyone hurt?" Zvi asked.

For a long time Balbini drank from his bottle of wine and then he hurled it past Zvi's head into the sea. "Just me. Just me. I never got a vessel again except this one, and I never went home again." He was changing his course now, north by northwest. "Hell, who needs a rock farm?"

Zvi wanted to say, "You do," but he did not.

That night as they talked the two became friends.

The next morning the *Hatikvah* was sighted by a low-flying Egyptian fighter plane.

TEL AVIV

As the concert ended, Fishel Warshow bowed to his audience and limped forward to accept its applause. The lights half blinded him as they always did. And in all the years he had played the violin in public he had never become used to either the lights or the applause. He bowed again, waved and stepped back so the curtain could close. He was tired. His leg hurt him as it had since it had been broken in the Old City. However, after a long concert and hours of standing, it hurt more than usual. Handing his violin to the young woman who waited for him in the darkness of the wings, he bent down and rubbed his thigh. Even through the welt of his trouser, he could feel the scars on his leg. Rising, he removed his formal coat, slung it over his shoulder and thanked the members of the symphony for their help. Then he limped off the stage and into his dressing room. The young woman followed from the darkness.

There were flowers as always, and there were the after-concert friends who wanted to congratulate him. Moshe Gilead, looking as thin as he had when they first met in the Quarter two years before, was out of uniform. There was a woman standing with him, and Fishel did not particularly pay attention to her name when Moshe introduced her. Every time he met Moshe, there was a different girl with a different name.

Then he found he was accepting congratulations from Zella Mazon who was just coming in. She looked happy and tired.

"School going well?" he asked

She nodded. "Another two years."

"Practice," he said with a gentle grin.

Both of them laughed. She did not introduce the young man with her. Like Moshe, the young man looked like a soldier, even out of uniform. Fishel wondered if he did himself, and then he smiled. He had not even looked like a soldier when he had been one. He decided to ignore Zella's companion because, like Moshe, she, too, often came with a different partner since Zvi had disppeared "on assignment." Fishel would have liked to ask her what she heard from her husband but decided that he would be more discreet.

"You're tired," Zella said, and he nodded.

He enjoyed the proprietary look she gave him. They were friends, had been friends most of their lives, and they had been in the Quarter together. No matter what happened to them in the years to come, they would always have that in common. Sadly, he wondered if she and Zvi would always have as much in common. Zella's friend was leading her to the door. She paused long enough to smile back at Fishel. Then she noticed the girl in the dark dress who was standing with the violin case and holding his suit out for him to change. Zella's face froze and for an instant Fishel believed she recognized the girl. Looking across the small dressing room, he could see that Moshe was also staring at her. Then Zella was gone and all Fishel could remember was Zella's upturned nose and the way she dropped her head back against her companion's shoulder as they departed. Turning once more to Moshe, Fishel asked, "You're still at the university?"

Moshe could not take his eyes off the girl with the violin case. Fishel had no intention of bringing them together, even though he was fully aware that Moshe recognized the girl, even though he and others who did made a point of not speaking to her.

Finally, Moshe answered, "Another three years and I'm going to be a lawyer." He smiled and added, "If I get through."

Fishel laughed. "You'll get through."

Shaking his head, Moshe said, "I can't be sure. Maybe I'm not for a classroom any more. Maybe what we did finished me for studying." Then as though he had to explain, "It's coming hard. It's coming hard."

"No," Fishel disagreed. "It may be coming slowly, but nothing is going to be as hard as the days you've lived."

Moshe was staring at the girl with the violin case again. She was still holding the suit for Fishel and at the same time seemed to be looking at the door as if she expected someone to enter. After a moment Moshe realized she was waiting for him to leave. He wanted to say something to her and decided not to. "I'll see you in two weeks," he offered, knowing that was when Fishel was due to play again.

"Thanks," Fishel said, wondering sometimes why his friends left him alone between concerts, and then he remembered that the decision was in large part his own because he never responded to their invitations. "Zvi?" he asked. "Any word of him?" And he was staring at the door.

It took Moshe a moment to understand that there were two parts to Fishel's question. "About Zvi, not a word." And he knew he was not being honest, because he had been briefed two days before about the *Hatikvah* sailing north, and he had asked then to be allowed to meet the ship when it landed at Eilat. Now all he was doing was marking time until he received word he could fly south. "Not a word," he lied again. "And about her," gesturing with his head toward the door where Zella had left, "I don't know who he is, but so long as there are so many, I feel Zvi is kind of secure."

Fishel nodded. This was not the time he wanted to talk about Zella, though he hoped he would be able to sometime when he and Moshe were alone. "Maybe he can get to the university when he returns," Fishel suggested.

"I hope so," Moshe agreed. "Maybe, if they're together." And then he said, "You'd better get some rest."

Fishel smiled and nodded. At last he was alone with his companion. He took the suit she held for him.

As Moshe walked out of the concert hall, all he could bring himself to say was, "I wonder where the hell he dug up that bitch." The girl with him was shocked.

Neither Fishel nor Dvora said anything until he had finished changing his clothes in the washroom and rejoined her.

"A bite to eat?" he asked.

She shook her head. "If I'm going back to Jerusalem tonight, I'd better catch the next *sherut*."

Fishel smiled warmly. "You sure you want to go back tonight? You could stay and have dinner with me."

He knew she would not. She never did. Ever since he had recognized the dark-eyed girl with the long black hair sitting in one of the front rows at all of his concerts and one of his friends had brought her to his dressing room, she had continued to wait for him in the wings until the concert was finished. Then she waited until he was ready to go home before she disappeared. He learned that she worked as a maid in one of the smaller hotels in Jerusalem. And after every concert, whether in Haifa, Beersheba or one of the kibbutzim, she returned to Jerusalem as soon as she could after the concert and what she seemed to think were her duties were over. He had asked her several times before to join him for dinner. Each time she had said No. Once he had put his hand on her arm to reassure her that she was safe with him, but that time she had disappeared and not attended the next three concerts until he sent a note to the hotel where she worked and told her that there was no one to put his violin away and fetch his clothes for him after a concert. The next week she had reappeared as though nothing had happened between them, as indeed, as far as he was concerned, nothing had.

Six months had passed since he had last asked her to dinner, and now after watching Moshe and Zella both walk away with friends, he did not want to eat alone. After his evacuation from the Old City and after he had finally left the hospital, he had lived alone. Days he practiced and nights he composed or performed. For two years he had had no company other than professional associates, except for the few old friends who dropped in to congratulate him, and there were times when he wished they would say more. The seven months he had toured Europe and America he had been no less lonely. It had taken him a long time to realize that persons his own age were somewhat in awe of his international success while they were just beginning their careers. And persons older than he were involved in their own lives. Several times ministers of the government and even the prime minister had invited him to meet visiting dignitaries, and though he went when asked, he always left quickly because he disliked being on show. When Israel had more concert artists, maybe they would be called on in turn, and he would be called upon less often.

As he stood looking at Dvora's face, he wished he could do something for her. People kept telling him, as though he didn't know, that she was the girl who had shot the young hero, Zvi Mazon. Fishel usually nodded, but he and Dvora never mentioned the incident. He had felt as sorry for her then as he had felt for Zvi. Now that he knew her better, he felt even more pity for the girl who was so shy of him that even now she was preparing to flee the dressing room. For an instant he wanted to take her arm and lead her to the small restaurant where he would be able to buy wiener schnitzel and drink a beer and relax until he was ready to go to sleep.

Dvora was edging toward the door now. "In two weeks," she said as she opened the door.

He started to nod, and then he surprised himself by shaking his head. "Could you do one more thing for me?" and he knew he was pleading.

She waited to hear what it was.

"I don't want to eat alone."

To his surprise she remained silent for a long time while she weighed his request as though it were very important to her. When she nodded, he noticed that she did not smile. But then he could not recall her ever having smiled except when he was playing. Sometime, he promised himself, he would pick up the violin in the middle of an afternoon and play just for Dvora Rabsky so that he could watch her smile in a way he could not in the concert hall.

He tucked his violin case under his arm and started to take hers when she drew back. Opening the door, he stood waiting for her to leave first, and then they were outside on the street. An old taxi wandered by and for a moment Fishel thought of flagging it down. Then he changed his mind and asked Dvora, "Could we walk a ways?"

She nodded and they continued on. He knew the restaurant was too far away, but he knew, too, that he did not want to rush there and finish dinner to find himself alone again.

They had gone several blocks before she stopped and said, "You've got to get off that leg." It was the first time she had ever mentioned his limp.

Fishel leaned against a building, set the violin down between his legs and stared at Dvora. She was lovely in her own dark and angry way. The light from a street lamp created strange shadows over her face and not for the first time was he aware that the swell of her black dress indicated firm breasts. He wondered how old she was, believed she was younger than he or Zvi or Zella or Moshe. She was probably even younger than Ruth. As he smiled at her, he wondered what did frighten this girl. She was too strong and too angry to flee from fear. Maybe that was why he liked her. And at that moment, Fishel knew that he liked Dvora more than he had realized.

"We can go to my apartment and have some dinner," he suggested. He saw her face cloud as she stepped back, and he was afraid he had frightened her off—she whom he had just believed could not be frightened. "Is there something wrong with me?" he asked.

Dvora shook her head hesitantly. "Just dinner and then my *sherut*?" she asked and he heard the trembling in her voice as she put the question tentatively.

"Of course," he said. "If that's what you want."

She thought and nodded. "I'd like that."

Later at his small apartment, after Dvora had cooked Fishel's late dinner, they sat at the table and talked. He told her about his concert trips to Europe, how embarrassed he was when people asked for his autograph, how he was considering continuing in the army reserves even though he was no longer called upon to serve because of his leg. They talked through two pots of coffee and several packs of cigarettes. Most of the time Dvora did little more than nod or ask a question. And then she looked at the clock on the kitchen wall and rose.

"I've got to find a *sherut*," she said. "I work in the morning."

Fishel looked at her and knew that he did not want her to leave.

"The hotel?" he asked.

She nodded, cleared the last of the cups and saucers from the table and set them in the sink. "I've got to work," and for an instant he thought she had smiled.

"What you mean," he said, "is that you have to earn a living."

She whirled to face him, her back against the sink, her hands grasping the edge of it. "That's right," and he realized he had been misunderstood. At this moment as he faced her, Fishel Warshow thought she was the loveliest girl he had ever seen. Her features were small, but they gave the impression of great strength. He was tempted to touch her but he feared she would misunderstand him once more.

"Look," he began, faltering from the first word. "If it's a living you have to earn, you can do it here." And he knew from her reaction that he had said the wrong thing again. She slipped out from between him and the sink and half ran into the sitting room where she grabbed her small purse and started for the front door. Limping as quickly as he could, he started after her.

"Dvora!" His shout brought her about so that they faced each other. He started to close his eyes while he tried to explain. "I can't take care of this place and my bookings and my transportation and collecting my fees and seeing that the concert hall is lighted the way I want it." His hands came wide in a gesture of helplessness. "I need your help. You can work for me." Then fearing she might once more misunderstand, he added, "And that's all I want from you."

Dvora looked at him dubiously as she fumbled with the black purse in her hand. After a time she asked, "That's all?"

"I want your company, too. I want someone to travel with and to eat with and to be here when I'm practicing." Then as though it were even more important, "I want someone to talk to and take a walk with."

At first he did not think she understood him as she glanced about the small apartment. It was well furnished with that Scandanavian modern that spread over Israel in trade for oranges. The carpet was a pale green, as were the walls and the draperies. Several silver cups stood on the large piano along with a picture of Fishel, Zvi, Moshe, Ruth and Avram. Crossing from the door to the piano, she stared at the picture and picked it up in her hand. "This one," she said, pointing to Zvi Mazon, standing in uniform with his arms about Avram on one side and Ruth on the other, "this one, he's all right?"

Fishel nodded. "He's all right. The woman who came in after the concert tonight, she was his wife."

Dvora looked up across the picture, "And that man she was with?"

"I don't know," Fishel admitted, wondering where this was leading them.

"You know about him and me?" she asked.

At first Fishel was hesitant to admit that he knew, and then he realized if he did not tell her, she would feel compelled to tell him. "I know. It was something that happened. That's all."

Setting the picture down on the piano, she ran her hand down the length of it, looked at the dust on her palm and, without looking at Fishel, she said, "I would do that again."

He knew that she was warning him now and he accepted it. "You haven't told me you would take the job."

The purse went under her arm as she wiped the dust from her hands. Then she looked up at him as though considering him for the first time. "How much will you pay for this work?"

Fishel had not considered the position before he blurted the description out. Shrugging, he offered, "Whatever you think it is worth." Then, as an added inducement, "If you accept, I think I shall purchase an automobile, if you will learn to drive it."

"You will pay all of my expenses?" she asked.

And he wanted to laugh because he knew she was taking the position, and from this point on details were unimportant. "I'll pay all expenses," he agreed.

"And a vacation?"

He nodded soberly.

"And a hundred pounds a month?" She seemed to think she was pressing him, but he nodded once more.

"Where will I live?" She was holding the small purse in front of her now, and he could see that she was nervous by the way she kept turning it over and over in her hand.

He glanced about the room and then toward his bedroom. He knew what he wanted to suggest. He did not. "Tonight you'll take my room and I'll sleep on the sofa. Tomorrow we'll take a larger apartment. There is one in this building."

She thought about this for a time and then shook her head. "I'll take the *sherut* and fetch my things, and after you have the apartment, I'll come back and I'll have my own room."

For the first time, Fishel was determined to disagree with her. "You aren't driving to Jerusalem tonight. You're staying here." He meant what he was saying partly because he thought her suggestion was foolish and partly because he wanted her to know that some decisions would be his.

To his surprise, she acquiesced. "I'll sleep in here," she said, keeping part of the decision to herself.

Fishel knelt and rubbed his leg as he weighed her counteroffer. He wanted to smile when she set her purse on the piano and knelt beside him. Putting both of her hands on his leg, she rubbed it gently. "You get to bed now," she ordered.

He was tempted to touch her, but more than anything, he feared he would upset the delicate balance of the relationship they had just agreed upon.

Later, when he was lying in bed, he heard her in the other room. He wanted to call out and thank her for staying. Instead, he looked up at the dark ceiling over his head and wondered what Zvi would think when he heard of the strange agreement.

JERUSALEM

Two hours later Hertzela Mazon was awakened by a knock at her door. Fumbling for the night table, she turned on the lamp and looked at the clock beside her bed. Five in the morning. The man who lay beside her flung one bare arm over his eyes to shut out the light and asked, "Who the hell is that?"

"I don't know," she snapped. Sitting up, she slipped into her slippers and, grabbing a robe, drew it on.

"Get rid of them," the man said and she nodded even though he could not see her. The knock could be heard twice more, and she yelled, "I'm coming." Switching on the light in the living room, she glanced about. He had all of his clothes in the bedroom and for this she was thankful. The only things on the table were her textbooks and the small black case which held her medical instruments.

Zella shook her head so that her blonde hair settled about her shoulders, pulled the dressing gown more tightly about herself and opened the door. A man in a strange blue uniform stood there with a young boy.

"Mrs. Mazon?"

Zella nodded.

"Your husband wrote you about the boy?"

Puzzled, Zella shook her head. "What's this all about? Don't you know it's five in the morning?"

The tall man knelt beside the boy, picked him up in his arms and held him closely for a moment. "The major told me he would write you," the man said.

"Well, he didn't," she said angrily. "And why do we have to talk about it now?"

The man introduced himself. "I'm an American pilot. Alaskan Airways. Just got here from Aden and the major asked me if I would leave the boy with you. I said I would."

Very slowly Zella shook her head in disbelief. "Leave the boy with me?"

The American nodded. "He said he was going to adopt the child."

She saw a sleepy Aaron, his small arms about the burly American's neck. "His name is Aaron," the pilot explained. "His parents died and the major said he had promised someone he would look after the boy."

The pilot's head came up as he saw a strange man wearing nothing but trousers enter from the bedroom. "If I've come to the wrong place . . . ," he started to apologize.

Zella whirled and shouted furiously at her companion, "Who needs you here?"

"I'd come another time," the American was saying, "but I've a flight in a few hours and have to get back to Lod."

Zella nodded. The airport was an hour's drive and the stranger could not be blamed. Shrugging, she asked, "And did the good major tell you what I'm

218

supposed to do with a child when I'm in school and where I'm supposed to sleep him?"

The American smiled cynically. "Maybe he thought you would be willing to work something out until he got home." Then, angrily, he held the child more tightly. "I'll take him to the airport and ask someone there to get him a home." Shaking his head in disgust, he started down the apartment hall before Zella could fully understand what was happening. She turned to her companion. "Idiot," she snapped and then ran out into the hall, calling, "You, bring that boy back here."

The American walked on toward the elevator.

Chasing after him, Zella caught up with the two just as the pilot started to open the elevator door. Pushing it closed, she apologized. "I haven't checked my mail for the last two days. Exams and then a trip to Tel Aviv. I'm sure he had something in mind about the child."

The American had difficulty not smiling. Her dressing gown was thin and she obviously was wearing nothing under it, and the dim light in the hallway was just enough to fully silhouette her figure. The word "ripe" slipped through his mind, then the word "plucked," and he did smile.

"Are you going to leave that child with me?" she demanded.

Taking Aaron's arms gently from around his neck, the pilot held the boy out at arm's length so he could see his small dark face better. "He's been a good boy," he told Zella as she took the child in her arms.

They stood looking at each other a moment, and then she asked, "Did the major say when he would be home?"

The pilot shook his head.

They continued to stare at each other; and then without another word to him, she turned and walked back to her apartment. He watched until she closed the door behind her.

Inside her apartment Zella remembered her companion. She barely knew him. They had met over coffee when she was studying with a friend. He had come home with her twice before and both times he had remained to spend the night. She knew almost nothing about him beyond the fact that he was married and his wife was expecting a child and that he worked in one of the offices of the Foreign Ministry. When she came in, he laughed loudly. "Mama!"

Zella shook her head, half in disgust with herself and half in disgust with him. "You go to hell!"

"I'll go, but that little one won't be as much fun in bed."

She wanted to ask him why he thought he was such a pleasure, but she went into the kitchen instead. There she sat Aaron down on the kitchen table, drew up a chair, settled into it and stared at the boy. She knew he was from one of the Arab countries. His eyes were bright and his skin dark. Even though he was sleepy, he tried hard to keep his eyes open while he stared back at her. A short time later she heard the living room door close and, picking Aaron up, she undressed him and carried him to bed with her. A moment and he was asleep. She switched off the light and lay with one arm about the boy, wondering why Zvi had felt called upon to adopt this child. He had not been gone that long.

THE RED SEA

And it came to pass that on the fifth day out of Aden the *Hatikvah* went into hiding.

Balbini had taken his small vessel into a sherm—one of the many bays that marked the edges of the sea—and had hidden it among the overgrowth. Pelicans topped each bush. Generations of mosquitoes bred across its deck. Twice Zvi saw Egyptian planes overhead. But Balbini and Zvi did not think the Egyptians had seen them a second time. While they remained where they were, the search for their vessel moved farther north.

On the ninth day they went on.

The shores were barren. The sky bright. They passed west of the Farasan Islands and Darb. They moved along a route followed for millennia when the products of the East moved through the Red Sea to Egypt, and from Egypt to North Africa and Europe or to Syria.

Awake in the Red Sea night, his blanket spread out on the deck, his clothes in a neatly folded pile beside him, Zvi stared first at the stars and then at the few scattered lights on shore. A caravan? A village? Merely a Bedu camp? Had the same lights been seen by the Akkadians and Sumerians as they brought copper from Oman tens of centuries before? Had they been sought by the Egyptians or someone else? Had they, too, moved only at night?

He folded his hands behind his head and thought for a moment of his wife waiting for him in Jerusalem. He smiled as he felt a slight breeze across his face. Solomon sent trading fleets from the Gulf of Akaba, and he "made a navy of ships in Ezion-Geber on the shore of the Red Sea in the land of Edom and brought gold from Ophir and a great plenty of Almug trees and precious stones." Zvi wished he were bringing her at least the precious stones.

And for a few moments his thoughts drifted to Havah, who lay buried in a grave on the far frontier between nowhere and no place, and he wondered if he would ever tell his wife about Havah. But to his surprise he saw the face of Bedia behind his eyes. And then somewhere to the west he could make out the sound of another ship's engine and it was not theirs. He hoped none of the Ethiopian crew would suddenly break radio silence. He hoped no one would light a cigarette, that the captain would not go in search of another bottle. He hoped he would sleep, and he did.

On the fourteenth day they saw dry wadis cutting into the shore. They saw a school of sharks in their wake, and they watched a small Norwegian freighter slip by.

By the fifteenth day Zvi and Captain Balbini had talked about their cousins' sisters, the women they had known and the women their cousins' friends had known. And as they squatted on the poop deck in the late evening before they put to sea from the narrow sherm the captain had found the night before, Zvi finished his last pack of cigarettes and Diego Balbini his last bottle.

"There's no more?" Zvi asked.

"No more," the Italian said, and the Israeli was surprised to find his companion was not disconsolate.

"You had some idea how long we would be at sea?" Zvi said.

Balbini nodded, lifted his seaman's cap and patted his bald pate. "I knew that soon we would have to prepare to run a blockade. I knew that one of these nights the engine would groan and poop and sigh and maybe even die on us."

"The engine would what?" Zvi was alert now and no longer staring at the sea.

The Italian nodded again, his hand still patting his pate as though this were some kind of ritual.

"It always has," he explained. "Always. Ever since the British engineer who took care of it left Suez."

Confused, Zvi asked, "And what does the engine's dying have to do with the British engineer leaving Suez?"

It took all the patience Balbini could muster to answer the Israeli's silly question. "The British run shops. A man could call in a British engineer who had worked on a ship and who knew it and you could ask him to look at an engine and he would know how to kick it and curse it and find the part that was going to give out like the valve in a man's heart and he would replace it or put it on board so that I could replace it when it finally gave out." He looked at the last bottle of wine in his hand and then at his Israeli friend. "That British engineer should never have left Suez," he said, as though this man had committed a crime against everything he stood for. His bright eyes looked sad in the dusk and he thought about the way the world was betraying an old sailor.

Zvi smiled at the man. Then his head went back and he looked at the sky. It was not quite dark enough yet to put to sea.

Both of them froze as they heard the sound of an airplane overhead. For a moment they thought it would pass on. Then they barely made it out in the dusk. It was east of them for a moment and then, moving west, it was over them and they hoped the pilot would miss the small ship in the sherm. And then they knew he had not missed them as he dropped down the sky and circled overhead. One circle, large and sweeping and then three more, smaller and farther down the sky until the plane seemed to be hanging over them. Zvi wished he had some kind of a weapon. Quickly scanning the ship, he saw that only one of the crew was above deck, leaning against a rail and staring up at the plane with the Egyptian markings on its wings. Suddenly Balbini reared back and hurled his wine bottle toward the plane. Flying in an arc, it dropped into the sea. The plane continued to hang above them, and Zvi dashed inside Balbini's cabin, switched on the radio at the same time he grabbed up the headphones. The Egyptian was broadcasting their location. Twice Zvi heard the coordinates given and once he heard the ship described. "Small. An Israeli flag on its mast. By its lines, the Italian ship. The long deck. The single poop. The cabin on the poop. One stack showing no smoke." And then the pilot was warning someone that it was almost dark and he was low on fuel.

A moment later, Zvi heard the plane move away. Then he could no longer hear it. When he looked up, he saw Balbini standing in the doorway of the cabin, his legs apart, his hands on his hips and his cap shoved back on his small head.

"It's time," he said.

Zvi stared at him, puzzled.

"That's why I ran out of wine." And then he repeated, "It's time," again. "We start running." A smile crossed his leathered face, *"Inshalla."* And both of them laughed.

"It's time," Zvi agreed.

Balbini left the dirty cabin and lumbered—a most difficult thing for a small man to do—across the deck where he started shouting for his crew and his engineer. When they were all assembled, he explained that now they would race north and east and west and if need be south. And he explained, too, that there was a bonus for everyone of them if they could bring the *Hatikvah* north without being killed. He repeated the simple fact that he did not want to get killed this voyage. Then he shouted for all of them to remember that the Jews were going to pay them well to survive and then he sent them back to work.

It was dark now. There were no lights along the shore. The Egyptian plane was long out of sight. The *Hatikvah's* engines started slowly. And Balbini took his place at the ship's wheel.

Standing beside the old seaman, Zvi was enjoying the way his companion reminded him of a buccaneer. And all the while, he was wondering how long it would take the Egyptian plane to reach its base and whether or not it made any difference if the Egyptian had taken any photographs of the *Hatikvah*.

JERUSALEM

Two days after Zvi and Balbini broke for the open sea on the fifteenth day of their voyage northward from Aden, Zella Mazon met Moshe Gilead at the small bookshop which served the university. It was almost evening. And after they bought the books they had come for, Moshe offered to drive Zella to her apartment. They had fought together in Haganah and they had both been in the battle for the Old City. To Zella, Moshe—slight and wiry—appeared so tense that he seemed to be ready to move in any direction as though he were still on a battlefield. He was driving a battered army jeep, and as she watched him climb into the driver's seat, she thought that somehow he had not yet come to terms with peace. Starting the small vehicle, Moshe suggested without looking at her, "I'd like to drive over to the YMCA building. Would you mind going? I'll get you home for dinner."

Zella thought about this, wondered what would be taking Moshe toward the YMCA and finally said, "All right, but I have a child now you know."

Five minutes later they were driving across town toward the Y. There was a flow of cars coming toward them and some few were already showing headlights. Zella leaned back on the seat of the jeep, her textbooks on the floor by her foot and the first button open on her tan blouse. She felt what breeze there was and wondered if she would ever be able to live in Tel Aviv with all its heat again.

Finally, out of courtesy more than curiosity, she asked Moshe, "What are you studying?"

The thin face bobbed forward as he acknowledged hearing her question. His deep-set eyes remained focused on the traffic. "Law. I think I would like to be a lawyer." Then he almost grinned, but Zella knew Moshe well enough to understand that he was not really grinning. It was part of his tension cracking through. "It isn't easy. In Israel there are as many kinds of law as Jews, and believe me, there are a good many different kinds of Jews."

Zella almost felt sorry for him as he tried to be humorous and failed. Zvi had always told her that Moshe was one of the best fighting soldiers he had ever known. She thought he was certainly one of the least engaging.

"Law, here," he went on as though he were delivering a lecture, "it's British law for crime and most problems, it's Hebrew law for matrimonial problems like marriage and divorce, and it's Turkish law for the land. And all of that gives us three different traditions and three courses of law and none of us really knows it well enough at first." Then the lecture ceased and he glanced in her direction, stepping up the speed of the jeep. He noticed the open button on her shirt and was tempted to smile even though he knew it had not been opened for his benefit. A large truck approached and Moshe swerved to one side, allowing it to pass and at the same time throwing Zella against himself. For an instant he was physically conscious of her, but in the next instant he was already thinking of Zvi.

The jeep was traveling faster now and Moshe almost had to shout over the noise of the motor. "When did you last hear from Zvi?"

Believing that Moshe knew more about her husband's whereabouts than she, Zella was tempted to say so. Then she wondered why he was asking the question and if there was something more involved in their driving to the Y. She turned in her seat so that she could see his face more clearly. The hawkish expression that came from his gaunt look seemed unchanged from the worst days of the war. He remained, even in his youth, a man with a fierce mien, and she thought he worked at this appearance the way some men like to be thought tough, others difficult, and still others proud or always angry. She smiled to herself at the thought of Moshe Gilead wanting to look like a hawk or an eagle. Neither image quite matched his tense personality, his drive for perfection.

And he was asking her again about Zvi.

"I heard from him in a way," she said. "He sent me a child." She hoped to watch Moshe's reactions to this but there were none. She was surprised, and then he said, "I know. I know." And he had known from the time the child had entered the country at Lod when a friend of his had called to tell him about Aaron.

And he asked, "What do you think of the boy?"

For a time she said nothing as she averted her eyes from the road ahead so that the lights of the oncoming cars would not blind her. When she finally spoke, she explained, "I don't know. He's a nice child, but primitive. Never saw a bathroom or a toilet, never ate in a kitchen or sat on a swing." Then, because she hoped Moshe would tell her, she asked, "His name is Aaron and he speaks Arabic and he did not say where he came from. Do you know that, too?"

Moshe ignored her question as he drew the jeep to the curb and helping her out, led the way to the roof of the YMCA, from where they could see Jordanian Jerusalem, Mount Scopus and the Old City laid out as though on a relief map.

Several minutes later Zella realized he was no longer thinking of her or Zvi or Aaron. Moshe was working the terrain over and over in his head. Finally, he pulled an accordion-pleated map out of his pocket and started marking it up. Twenty minutes passed before he shoved the map back into a pocket and, without a word, led her back to the jeep once more. Zella did not have to ask what he was doing: she knew. There was going to come a time — in a year or ten years — when Moshe Gilead would try to take back the Old City.

As Moshe waited for a break in the traffic so that he could turn the jeep about and drive her home, she cursed softly under her breath. She had had enough of these men. And she had had enough of war.

Almost as though she were telling Zvi, she said, "I'm studying to be a doctor. Medicine. Bringing babies into the world and trying to keep the old from leaving it." Her voice almost cracked, and Moshe glanced at her, a question in his eyes.

"What the hell was that all about?"

"You don't need to fight again," she snapped.

The side of his hard fist came down on the steering wheel. "I told you I'm going into law." He was angry at her doubting him and in that single statement, she knew he was more angry with himself and with his own doubts.

They drove for several blocks without saying anything, and then Moshe asked, "Did you notice that girl who was with Fishel after the concert, the one in Tel Aviv?"

Zella nodded. "I thought they'd lock the bitch up. She's crazy."

"Crazy? If that was a reason for locking people up, who would be free in this country?" He tried to laugh as he added, "Or any other country," but Zella knew he was not thinking of any other country or even of anyone else but himself as she watched him light a cigarette off a cigarette and close his hand over the butt of the dying stub so that it would burn his palm. She flinched at the sight and wondered when he had last relaxed and if that girl he had been with the night of the concert had done him any good.

They stopped for coffee at a small shop both of them knew. Neither one particularly wanted coffee, nor did either want to be alone. There were half a dozen people seated at the small tables around them and for a few minutes after the waiter had served, they listened to the conversation flowing unevenly.

"They're going to take jobs," a middle-aged man with a Polish accent growled to his companion.

The companion laughed. "They take jobs. Don't be a shnook. They aren't really people. The government is bringing them in to build up the head count. One Yemenite and one Egyptian and one Iraqi and all you have are three warm bodies." The accent was German, the clothes a business suit and tie.

Zella saw Moshe's hand open and close as he balled it in anger. Closing a palm over his fist, she shook her head.

The companion was talking now. "They gave one of those families from Yemen a place with a built-in bathroom and they washed clothes in the toilet and went out into the street to shit. Don't worry about their taking your job."

Moshe's glum face swung toward the man. The two at the next table saw his angry stare and shrugged. "Something bothering you?" the one with the German accent asked, offensively.

Very slowly, Moshe grinned. "I was just thinking of a story I heard today about the difference between a Yekke ..." and he could see the German lose his smile as the epithet for a German Jew was used, "... and a virgin," Moshe continued. "A Yekke remains a Yekke."

Drawing himself up in his seat, the other man looked away. Not allowing himself to be cut off, Moshe reached over and jerked the man half about so that they were facing each other again. "I don't think the same will be true of the Yemenites." Then he smiled at Zella. "I'm sorry." And in that moment he realized that she did not know where her husband had been posted or what he had been doing. The two men at the adjoining table were leaving now, and Moshe ignored them.

"What do you hear of Zvi?" and his question was only to find out if she had any idea at all of his assignment.

Zella knew Zahal well enough to believe that Moshe would know where Zvi was and how he was faring. She knew it well enough, also, to understand that he would not tell her anything. "I went to his sister's funeral last week."

Taken aback, Moshe shook his head. "I didn't know he had one."

Smiling, because she had caught him unawares while he was trying to learn something else, she enjoyed the moment. "A half-sister. His mother ran off when he was a boy." She scraped the Turkish coffee on the bottom of her cup. "Teamed up with an Irishman. Zvi never really knew either his mother or his half-sister very well. Last week I had a phone call. She was dying of cancer — the sister, that is — and wanted to see Zvi."

Moshe waited for her to continue.

"It seems there wasn't anyone else except an uncle. The mother's brother who lives in the north." Zella shook her head as she thought about her visit to the dying woman. "You know, she looked like Zvi." Then she shook her head again as she added, "I was the only one at the funeral. She worked in a hospital as a receptionist, but no one came except strangers."

Suddenly Zella thrust the notion from her as she said, "Let's get out of here."

A short time later Moshe stopped at Zella's apartment. It was already quite dark. For a time they sat in the parked jeep without talking. There were few cars in the streets. In the distance they could hear a KOL Israel Broadcast through an open window. Neither of them could make out what the announcer was saying.

Remembering their visit to the YMCA, Zella asked half in jest and half in anger, "When will you take the Old City?"

Moshe reached out and closed one hand on hers. "It isn't funny," he warned.

Zella looked down at his thin, strong hand. "That's what's so sad," she said. Then because she did not want to enter the apartment alone and spend the evening with Aaron who would already be asleep in the bed the neighbor had made up for him in the living room, she asked, "Do you want to come up?"

Moshe withdrew his hand from hers. "No," he said too loudly and quickly. "That man you were with the other night, won't he be waiting for you?"

Turning aside so that the lights of an oncoming car would not strike her half-closed lids, Zella said, "No." Then she added, "His wife's already had her baby, and he can sleep in his own bed now."

Moshe tried to smile at her candor, but he failed. "Is there something wrong with Zvi?" he asked, and for a moment she did not quite understand what he was asking.

When she realized the implications of his question, she laughed too loudly as he had spoken too loudly. "If you're asking how he performs in bed, I'm sure there are plenty of girls who could give him a testimonial. If you're asking why I'm not sleeping with him these days, it's because he isn't here."

"Just like that?"

Zella nodded. "There was a time," she said, and she knew she was only talking now to keep from going upstairs, "there was a time when I knew men other than Zvi and I slept with some of them and I didn't sleep with some of them. There were those who said that it all came about because we had women in the army, but that is a lot of crap. I slept with men because I liked them then and that is why I do it now. And it has nothing to do with being a nymphomaniac or anything else quite so exotic." She chuckled, "Maybe it's just the opposite. Me," and her hand was on her face now as she tried to avoid the lights of another car, "me, I don't like being alone. It's as simple as that. I'd have a man in my bed and just sleep, but there aren't any who will come just to lie in the dark and talk to a girl. None that is whom I'd want to lie and talk with through the dark hours until I fell asleep."

She looked at him, her hand closed on his now. "Can you understand that?"

Moshe's head fell to one side as though he could see her better that way, and she wanted to say that was the way Zvi would look at her and she wondered if he had learned that gesture from Zvi, or if Zvi had learned the gesture from him, and all the while she was hoping he understood.

Instead, Moshe removed his hand from under hers and said, "I'll see you in school one of these days. Maybe we could have lunch."

To her surprise, Zella found herself laughing hysterically while staring at him. He had understood her and he wanted her company, but he was Zvi's friend, and she was almost glad that he reminded her of that.

"Let's have lunch sometime," she said so gaily that she thought for an instant from the look on his face he would strike her. His hand came up to touch his forehead in a gesture of pain and then he let it drop and she understood he was ashamed to show that he was in some kind of pain. That was where he differed from Zvi. Zvi was not as cold and not as confident, though he could give the impression of being both. And in a gesture of forgiveness, she leaned over and kissed Moshe on the cheek. Drawing back, she smiled at him. "We understand each other?"

He hesitated a moment and then nodded.

After Moshe drove away, Zella looked after him for a time before she went upstairs, picked the sleeping Aaron off the small bed in the living room and set him under the covers in her own room.

THE RED SEA

On the twentieth day the *Hatikvah*, hugging the west coast, sailed through the shallows at Ras Benas northward toward the gulfs of Sinai and Akaba. There were few clouds during the day and fewer still at night. Heat clung to the ship like damp wool. Zvi had joined Balbini in stripping down to his shorts.

It was almost midnight. The vessel crawled slowly along the shallows. Balbini prepared to swing his vessel onto the closest beach if an Egyptian plane came strafing across his deck. However, it had been five days since they had last spotted an airplane. Twice they had seen other vessels pass them in the darkness; and both times Balbini had signaled for his engineer to stop engines. Only after the strange lights had disappeared to the north did he start the creeking engines again.

Zvi washed his face for the eighth time that night and climbed to the poop where he could sit on the deck and talk to the diminutive Italian. The captain nodded greetings.

"Did you hear it?" he asked.

Puzzled, Zvi shook his head, not quite sure what it was he was supposed to have heard.

"The engine," Balbini said. "It's changed its tune."

Zvi listened to the constant chug of the engine and could not tell that it sounded any different from the way he had heard it on other nights. Loud and uneven with a clang in the background. "How bad is whatever it is?" he asked.

Balbini shrugged. "It is old. How bad?" and he shrugged again. "How would you feel with pressure in your boilers for twenty years and no relief? Nothing but bad coal chucked in and the slamming together of cheap steel?"

Squatting on the deck, Zvi asked, "And if it stops?"

Laughing softly, Balbini said, "It stops. That's all." His head fell back as his face sought some breeze. There was none. "This ship," he said with a kind of pride. "She's been in all the seas of the world. I took her to England once during the war. There were other freighters sinking around us. Men clinging to liferafts or broken spars. This ship, she never got hit." Then he laughed again. "Maybe she was too small to waste a torpedo on, but small or large, we sailed into Portsmouth and set out our anchor beside one of the Canadian cruisers and sat proudly in that great harbor like any other ship; and when we went back again to North Africa, we brought two tanks and one hundred and fifty men sprawled out on our deck."

Zvi weighed the story and doubted it. "You sailed for the Allies?"

Balbini nodded. "I told you I never sailed for *Il Duce* after the poison gas." He was indignant, and somehow this time Zvi believed the man.

Both of them fell silent while Balbini listened to his engines. Once he shook his head, but when he remained silent, Zvi decided not to press for more vague information.

Zvi turned his head from side to side, trying to catch a breeze. Disappointed, he came to his feet, crossed the deck to the tap and washed his face once more. Shoving his hands under the tepid water, he let it run over his wrists. The damp-wool heat remained.

Dropping his head back, Zvi watched the stars for a time until he became conscious that something about him had changed. Turning off the tap, he looked about, trying to determine what it was. Though Balbini had started to yell, Zvi could not understand him. Then a crewman appeared and the captain gave him the wheel and instructions.

Ignoring the Israeli, Balbini half leapt, half climbed down the steel ladder and ran toward the engine-room hatch. Zvi followed closely. They descended in total darkness. Then a turn in a passageway and there was a light shining below.

The scrawny engineer was bending over something Zvi could not identify. As the two approached, the engineer waved them back and started tapping a piece of equipment. Balbini glanced at the gauge on the boiler and then at the wiry, thin engineer with the balding head. The Ethiopian shrugged.

"Will it get us there?" Zvi demanded.

Balbini growled. "How the hell would I know?"

"What is it?"

"Silence!" the captain ordered as though he were on the bridge of a great liner. For several minutes he conferred with the engineer while Zvi, who could not understand a word they were saying, stared at the boiler gauge even though he had no idea what he was looking for or what it should read.

When Balbini was done with the engineer, he turned to Zvi. "The boiler could blow up." The statement was flat without emotion or a suggestion of fear.

"And?"

The captain smiled at his engineer, said something else to him and started out of the engine room, back through the passageway into the darkness and then up onto the open deck. Once there, he looked back at Zvi.

"If we run, we could lose the boiler. That would scald the men below and probably sink us."

"And the alternative?" Zvi was hoping there was one.

"Stop the engine and be caught out here in the morning. Possibly be sunk."

Zvi smiled wryly. "Some choice."

The Italian drew himself up to his full height, creating an appearance of great dignity in spite of the fact that he was in his underpants. "I am captain and I have made my decision."

Waiting, Zvi knew he would be told.

"We sail on tonight. Hide before morning. Then one of us will have to go into Egypt and buy a valve for the engine."

Zvi whistled softly. "Just like that."

Balbini nodded. "I have made my decision."

"What do we use to pay for it?"

"We will sell food at the first port we find and then one of us will take the money and go as far as Port Said."

It was obvious the little man had been thinking.

But Zvi was wondering if one of them had lost his senses under the Red Sea sun. Port Said meant crossing Egypt to the north. However, he realized the Italian was right. They had no other choice. "Where do we hide while the ship's engine's broken down?"

"Let me see how far we can go tonight. Then I will know better."

Zvi cocked his head to one side. "How far tonight?"

"We might not make another mile." The captain grinned. "We could go *woosh*," his hands going up wildly, "and then go down," and he dropped almost to his knees. "We will know when it happens."

Accepting the situation, the Israeli said bluntly, "I'll make the trip across the desert. I speak Arabic. You just hide her well."

Balbini looked at his companion with great patience. "We may just hide it down there," and he was pointing toward the bottom of the sea.

The *Hatikvah*'s captain took his place behind the wheel and steered a course as close to the shoreline as he safely could while Zvi sat on the poop beside him staring into the darkness. The lumbering old tramp crawled slowly through the shallows. Zvi was aware of little more than the *thump-thump-woosh* of the engine which every few seconds sounded like a *thump-thump-clank*. Neither man spoke and their luck held for the first half hour. Then the Ethiopian cook brought them both coffee, and Zvi nodded to his friend, one thumb up but his eyes never really coming off the dark distance.

The *thump-thump-woosh* shifted slightly in tempo and Zvi came to his feet. And then there were lights off the shore and lights coming down the Red Sea southward in their direction. Balbini froze his hands on the wheel of his ship, never letting it waver on its course as he thought only of the shortest distance to his point of hiding. Zvi still did not know their destination and almost superstitiously, he was afraid to ask. As Balbini had indicated, what difference did it make where they were going if they were not going to get there anyway? Another half hour and Zvi felt more relaxed. Then he saw the engineer coming up on deck and trotting across it to join his skipper on the poop. The two jabbered for a moment before the engineer disappeared below again.

Zvi looked at Balbini for an explanation and though he never turned his head toward the Israeli, the captain said flatly, "The pressure's up and rising."

Then to Zvi's surprise, warm rain swept the deck. Neither Zvi nor his companion paid any attention to it. The few members of the crew who had been on deck disappeared below. The Italian and the Israeli were alone.

The second hour passed and the third.

Then there was a faint ray of light spreading across the sky to the east over Arabia. Zvi's head finally fell back and he stared at the fading night. Suddenly his eyes focused on the blue-and-white flag hanging on the stern. Leaping to his feet, he quickly ran down the Israeli flag and ran up the Liberian. Carefully folding his country's colors, he ducked inside Balbini's cluttered cabin. In the center of the small stateroom he slowly pivoted. The unmade bunk was an obvious place. Too obvious. Underneath a table? Under the pillow of the single chair? Under the torn carpet? The safe? His attention closed on the safe and he slipped the Israeli flag into that small crack where the safe stood away from the cabin wall. Sighing, he returned to the poop where the captain was now guiding his small ship into the narrow waters. Zvi could make out a native village ahead. There were several corrugated-sheet buildings, fifty or more thatch huts and two wooden buildings bleached almost white by the desert sun. Beyond lay the edges of the Nubian desert. He stood, his hands on his hips, his eyes on Africa, and wondered if they were going to land in Egypt or in the Anglo-Egyptian-Sudan. He did not know, and he knew even less how much difference it would make. Slowly looking about the vessel, the only thing he could see that would possibly indicate that the *Hatikvah* was in the service of Israel were the three crates of books lashed to the deck. If he were carrying any other cargo he might have considered jettisoning it. But the books . . .

"Where can we hide these?" he asked Balbini, who was watching him now.

"Below," the Italian assured him with a smile. "We'll break the crates open and carry them below." Then he added as though his friend needed assurance, "A ship like this is built to hide part of its cargo." Seeing the puzzled expression on Zvi's face, he asked, "You didn't think we make our living carrying only legitimate cargo?" Another guffaw at his own words. "Today a cargo is contraband. Tomorrow, another government, and it is legal. Tomorrow *kerplew*. Two revolutions and three officials dead and the cargo is illegal again. And so it goes. An honest man today, a dishonest one tomorrow and then back in the good graces of bad governments." He was not apologizing but, rather, explaining the facts of life along the Red Sea.

Half an hour later while the *Hatikvah* was still more than two miles offshore, the crew scurried below decks to carry the holy books into hidden compartments while Zvi supervised and Balbini listened to the *thump-thump-clank* of his engine.

An hour later the *Hatikvah* was anchored off the village. The sun was already high, and an Egyptian port official boarded to check the cargo. For ten minutes Captain Balbini berated his fate at having to travel without a cargo because his owner had failed to make proper arrangements. The Egyptian, a middle-aged clerk from Cairo who agreed that the fates were indeed not with a man who lived along the Red Sea or on it, was completely sympathetic. So sympathetic, in fact, that he agreed to help the unfortunate Italian ship's captain sell part of his provisions ashore — for a reasonable profit to himself, of course. Finally, the Egyptian left with regrets that he had no radio and no means by which he could contact Cairo so that parts could be shipped to Balbini. The Italian prepared to move what he could of his foodstores ashore.

An hour after nightfall, Major Zvi Mazon put ashore with the damaged valve and the money that had been raised from the sale of food. Neither he nor his friend knew if his journey to Port Said would take a week or a month. Neither could even be certain the Jew would ever emerge from the Nubian desert. They shook hands and parted. Ahead of Zvi lay enemy territory and certain execution if he were discovered. For a short distance, he walked along the shore, pausing once to put his hand into the warm Red Sea water. Then he turned and cut directly across country, hoping to locate the nearest road, hoping, too, that he could hitch a ride north.

BEERSHEBA

It was almost midnight when the small school building which served Beersheba as a concert hall started emptying out. In one of the classrooms, Fishel Warshow put his violin in its case and smiled at his companion. Dvora regretted that the circumstances had not allowed for Fishel to wear a swallow-tail coat or even a formal dinner jacket. However, Beersheba was too much a frontier town for anything fancy, and Fishel had explained that he was going there to entertain the people, not to frighten or embarrass them. She had understood, but she still had regrets. One of the few things she possessed was the image of herself which her employer created.

And for Dvora Rabsky, Fishel remained her employer. They had been living together in the apartment he had rented. They ate their meals together. She went to school to learn to use a typewriter so that she could answer his mail. And she had already learned to drive the small French Peugeot he had bought so that they could travel at their own convenience. "It's cheaper in the long run," he had explained, and at that time, too, she agreed, but whenever she stopped to buy petrol, she was not so certain. However, the relationship remained what they had agreed upon that first night when she had had dinner with Fishel. Others who knew Fishel Warshow found this relationship difficult to accept, not that Fishel was a rake by reputation, but because he was one of the most normal men they knew and Dvora was beautiful. She remained thin, but at Fishel's insistence — put on the basis of his own need for a proper image — she dressed with more flair.

Checking the classroom to make certain they were leaving nothing behind, Dvora picked up the leather briefcase which held Fishel's music, tossed her worn wool coat over her shoulders and waited for Fishel beside the door. He paused to rub the back of his neck, a gesture she had come to recognize as fatigue, and then he smiled at her. "I saw some people I know out there. They may want to stop for a bite before we return home." He knew Dvora well enough to avoid surprises and to know that she would not join them.

"I will wait for you in the car," she offered.

For an instant he was tempted to argue. However, changing his mind, he opened the door and limped out into the school corridor where Zella and Moshe and a dozen others were waiting for them. Fishel shook hands with the chubby mayor of Beersheba, the resident of the hospital, three schoolteachers and the wives of several engineers working on the water line. Finally, after rejecting invitations to eat here or visit there, always with a smile and the simple explanation that he was tired and he had to return to Tel Aviv, Fishel was alone with Moshe and Zella.

"It was good of you to come down," he said.

And it was Zella who laughed. "Save that for the official greeters," and Fishel laughed along with her.

"Put a face on long enough and you find you're wearing it."

"We were coming separately until we found that out." Thus Moshe explained his being with Zvi's wife and hoped that this was enough for Fishel.

"We're going to eat somewhere," Zella began, and before she could say anything, Fishel felt he had to introduce his companion. Standing several paces behind the others, Dvora clutched the briefcase in her hands, and when Fishel turned toward her, he thought for a moment she might run. Then he knew better. She was not the kind who ran. Maybe that was what was wrong with her.

"My secretary and driver," he finally said, avoiding Dvora's name.

Zella looked at the other woman. Nodding, Zella believed she had gone as far as Fishel could expect of her in greeting the woman who had shot Zvi.

Moshe, wanting nothing to do with the girl, merely smiled and turned back to Fishel. "We've found a small place. Not much in the way of good food but some humus and maybe some brandy."

Fishel half shut his eyes, though he was not thinking of the food or the brandy or even his two friends. Deciding the kindest thing he could do would be to ignore Dvora for the moment rather than press her to join them, he asked, "Where?"

And after Moshe told him, the three left.

Dvora stood in the corridor of the empty school. Near the door stood an old man, waiting for her to leave so that he could turn off the lights and lock the door. Dvora's head went up and she strode down the corridor thinking of the gay green-and-white print dress Zella Mazon was wearing. Reaching the door, she took a coin out of her small purse and gave it to the old custodian. Accepting, he thanked her, "And may you have a hundred healthy children."

Dvora wanted to shout something at him but the words never came and she turned once more toward the door, clasped the briefcase to her breast again and walked slowly into the night. The sky was clear. The air was chill. There was no breeze off the desert. The small Peugeot was parked a dozen paces down the road. She approached it and then looked off toward the desert to the south. There were the lights of a Bedouin camp beyond Beersheba. Nearby she recognized the cemetery where the British had buried their dead during the First World War. Glancing at her watch, she believed she had at least an hour before Fishel would be too weary to talk any more with his friends about their days in Haganah. She slipped the briefcase onto the seat and turned slowly toward the cemetery.

It was well maintained and there was greenery in spite of the fact that Beersheba was the northern entrance to the Negev desert. Dvora wandered among the graves reading the name plates in the dim light cast from nearby buildings. Lieutenant Mortimer Weaver: Sydney. Private James D. Herman: Eucla. Private William Pennsfield: Warrnambeel. Private Godfrey Swan: Barrow Creek. She wondered where these exotic places were and what the plaque meant which described the action of the Australian Light Cavalry. Another war, another time.

For a moment she almost smiled at herself. In all the days of all the months since she had found herself in the internment camp waiting to be evacuated and led to Palestine, she had not felt sorry for herself. She recalled almost nothing of her youth. That small part of herself as a child and then a woman had been hidden, blocked out by the faces of German soldiers appearing before her one after another. Some of them smiled. Some of them wept. Some of them tried to be gentle. A few were cruel. Most were merely indifferent. The Jewish girl was no more to them than something to satisfy a need. And in their hands she had created a world for herself which was neither warm nor cold but simply detached. When a girl she had come to know was ripped up the belly by a drunken *Wehrmacht* soldier's bayonet, Dvora had remained detached. When the girl who lay on the cot next to her was beaten to death by a rifle butt because a *Wehrmacht* physician found she was diseased, Dvora had remained detached. When three of the girls whom she lived with were taken out and shot because they had entreated two sergeants to help them escape, Dvora had remained detached. When one young soldier no older than herself had kissed her, Dvora had remained detached. When others died or were crippled for life, Dvora remained detached.

And more than anything else, as she sat on a small ledge overlooking the graveyard at Beersheba, Dvora Rabsky was aware that she had survived. In its own way that was a victory over those who had tormented her and beaten her and used and abused her. She had survived.

Now as she looked back on that night when the last Nazi fled the camp, which had been moved farther and farther west in the face of the Russian advances, she remembered having risen from her cot to sit on the edge of it and wait for whoever would come next. At first she had thought it might be the Russians. Then she had thought that no one would come and she and the girls with her would starve. And the whole night passed and no one had come. She had had a night alone, but she could not sleep. Then the morning came, and it was almost noon when she jerked a sheet from one of the cots, drew it about her and stepped outside the trailer in which she had survived for years.

There was the noonday sun. There was a slit trench near which lay the bodies of two *Wehrmacht* soldiers. One she recognized as the sergeant who commanded the camp. The other she did not know. She walked over and stood looking down at the sergeant for several minutes before she put out her foot and toppled him into the slit trench which served as a latrine. Another of the girls had come out of the trailer now and stood beside her.

"Who will come next?" the girl asked.

Shaking her head, Dvora had answered in that toneless voice she had learned helped to keep her alive, "Does it make any difference?"

The other girl thought about the question and ran back into the trailer. Later in the day when the first troops arrived, Dvora led their commanding officer inside the trailer.

Several of the girls in numbed reflex were already on their cots. However, the girl who had joined Dvora in the afternoon light was lying face down on the floor. Kneeling beside her naked body, the young Russian lieutenant turned her over to find her throat cut. In horror, he had glanced up at Dvora. She could recall the expression on the lieutenant's face in the moments which followed, and she wondered if the dead girl frightened him more than her detachment.

In the months that followed she found herself little better off in Russian hands, and so with the help of two other girls she escaped to the woods where she survived for months as a guerrilla caught between the advancing Russians and the retreating Germans. Finally, when she was the only one of her group left, she made her way through the German lines to the British and eventually through the underground to Palestine.

Now, as she sat staring at the graves of the Light Australian Cavalrymen who had died opening the flank of the Turkish army over thirty years before, she wondered why she was thinking of her own emotions and if she were beginning to feel sorry for herself, and if she did, would she be able to continue to survive.

Off somewhere on the other side of Beersheba, Fishel Warshow was eating pitah and humus with his two friends. And for the first time in all the years which had passed, Dvora Rabsky wished she, too, were sitting with other people and drinking brandy and talking about the concert and the days they had spent in the Old City.

Now as the night air seemed to turn cooler about her, she remembered the nights in the Old City. Somehow she felt better because she had fought there. Somehow she was pleased that she had learned something from the Nazis even if it was only how to kill. And she remembered, too, the arrogant young sabra commander with the stocky build, the bright eyes and the nervous habit of scratching his belly when he wanted to think. She had not killed him that day of surrender, but she knew she had tried to, had wanted to. He had touched her and she had warned him. She had warned him. She felt her cheeks grow cold; and when she touched them with her hand, she knew that she was weeping. It had been years since she had wept. And now she was crying for herself, and she felt that she was losing her strength and she became frightened because she was losing her detachment.

Glancing at her watch, she made out the time. Wiping her eyes angrily, she rose and stalked out of the cemetery, found the Peugeot and drove through the streets of Beersheba until she located the small café where Fishel was standing and waiting for her.

He was alone now. The others had apparently left. The violin case was resting on his shoe, his coat collar was pulled high against the cold. She thought he looked tired as he crossed the street and joined her.

"Do you want something to eat before we start back?" he asked.

Angrily, she shook her head.

"I could get you something," he offered a second time.

Her voice was flat and toneless as she told him, "Leave me alone." Stepping down firmly on the accelerator, she spun the car about and sought the road back to Tel Aviv. Fishel turned to stare at her profile in the darkness.

Neither Dvora nor Fishel said anything. There were no cars on the highway. The night was dark. The air was cold. The small car raced north through the empty countryside.

That night after the lights in the apartment were out, Dvora slipped into Fishel's bed, and when he embraced her, she grew rigid until she cried. But morning found her asleep in his arms.

THE NUBIAN DESERT

Heat and darkness and the bray of a jackass.
Dunes and dirty villages.
Past Aswan to Luxor and ruins. The noise of tourists and the shouts of vendors selling cold drinks, hashish and pots.

Eight days on the road now. Most of them through desert. Two nights sleeping beside the Nile. One near an Egyptian village where he bought a meal at an inn and the rest moving on foot or on the rear of passing trucks.

More desert and Luxor was behind him.

The road twisted.
Sometimes it was dirt, sometimes gravel. Near Qena it was paved, and there Zvi waited two days before he moved on.
The great wadis stretched southward to the Nile, and above it an escarpment with steep cliffs, yasar trees, and a camel caravan. To the west grew tamarisk along an old Roman road, the Via Porphyrites.

A viper on the road. A viper hiding under a dry sille bush.

North past two wells, past Akhmîm and the countryside closing in upon him with more villages, more farms, fellahin working the fields under the blanched sky.

Past El Minya. Past Beni Hasan.

The Nile muddying slowly north beside him. Tourist vessels with pretty women in white dresses, drinking cold drinks. Middle-aged men with paunches, white suits or brightly colored sports shirts, drinking cold drinks. Barefooted waiters in cotton shirts. And the river barges carrying guns and wheat and corn and tobacco. Camels in greater number on the roads now, as all roads were converging toward Cairo.
More trucks and more lorries with their black-and-tan and brown-and-dirty-green camouflage and British soldiers with suntans and rifles lining the sides of the lorries.
And Zvi remembering the frontier above Aden with a lorry blocking the road, and the bellowing voice from the lorry's loudspeaker over the Quarter telling the Jews to surrender.
Swallowing to keep down his gorge, the Israeli moved on.
Twice he hitched rides with jeep drivers who asked him where he had learned English, and both times he explained that he had worked for the British in Cairo. Once he was offered a job as a batman. Once he was told a story about how valiantly the British had fought to keep down the Jews in Palestine and how the driver had won himself a medal for turning in a cache of Jewish arms from the United States, which, of course, the driver assumed his passenger understood was run by Jews who were trying to take over the world with Palestine as their base.

And finally, passing between Cairo and Suez, Zvi reached Port Said. Here he sought out the ships store which Balbini had described. The valve was not available though the Greek owner thought he might know where Zvi could get one if he were willing to wait a couple of weeks. Zvi was not willing and so they talked about Captain Diego Balbini, and Zvi bought the fat Greek two drinks of bad brandy, and the man agreed that he had a friend who could obtain such a valve as Zvi wanted. Zvi pressed two more brandies on the man and they agreed to let the Greek try his friend who was an Armenian and would not charge his old friend Balbini more than twice its value. And as this was the price which Balbini had anticipated the valve would cost, Zvi was pleased with himself.

For two days he wandered about Port Said, feeling strangely secure. He knew of nothing that could link him up with the vessel lying to the south and did nothing that would bring him to the attention of the Egyptian authorities. He was thinking about this the afternoon of the second day when he recalled the surprise appearance of Bedia Hassani at Dhamar and Aden. He was wondering if he wanted to be surprised again. Seated in a small café with a cup of dark coffee in front of him, his thoughts drifted to Bedia as she had sprawled out on the seat of the car the night they had started out to hunt turtles, of Bedia as she had smiled at Aaron in the camp and of Bedia as he had last seen her, the negligee ripped away, her firm breasts thrust forward and the expression on her face as he struck her. He closed his eyes and continued to see the image. He was both repulsed and intrigued by it. Dropping some change on the table, he half ran out of the café before he remembered that he did not want to draw attention to himself. Three hours later with the grease-covered valve wrapped in cloth to protect it from dampness along the river, he started south again.

TEL AVIV

Moshe Gilead left the Zahal headquarters at Hakiryah in the late afternoon.

As he slipped into his jeep and slowly surveyed the collection of old houses which served as military headquarters in the center of Tel Aviv, the area seemed quiet. The situation was under control, and he almost smiled at the implications of that thought. His open palm nervously rubbed the flat of one cheek as he weighed what he had learned. Finally, starting the old jeep, he drove out of the headquarters area, down Derech Shalom to Fishel's apartment. For a moment he sat in the jeep thinking about what he had learned at headquarters. The grumblings of the Arabs did not disturb him very much, but the other news — that was unexpected. Finally, he made his way to Fishel's suite where Dvora Rabsky opened the door and called for Fishel — and was gone. Grasping Fishel's hand, Moshe explained that he had come to town to nose about headquarters and that he thought he would drop in for coffee before he returned to Jerusalem.

As the two men walked through the apartment to the dining area, Fishel called to Dvora to bring out another cup and more coffee. To Moshe's surprise, on the other side of the dining-room table, Avram Ben Ezra came to his feet. Taller than the others, Avram was wearing his uniform and the insignias of a lieutenant-colonel. At the sight of Moshe's tense face, he smiled. Friends since childhood, he could not recall when he had seen Moshe relaxed. Fishel waved them into chairs by the table.

"You were at headquarters?" Avram asked.

The lean man nodded, his chin thrust forward, his prematurely gray hair falling into place.

"You heard?" the staff officer asked. Fishel looked from one to the other.

"Zvi?" Moshe asked, nodding again.

"Zvi," Avram agreed.

And then as though neither of the two officers trusted her, they fell silent while Dvora served them coffee and they waited until she had left the room. Fishel was aware of this, and he assumed that Dvora, never insensitive, had also been aware of the silence.

When they were alone again, Avram explained to Fishel. "Zvi's lost. I can't give you any details, but we think he may be dead."

Very slowly Fishel's head dropped back as he considered what he had heard.

Finally, Moshe asked, "Has Zella been told?"

Avram shook his head.

Turning to his friends, Fishel wondered how they would react to what he was about to ask. "I want to pick up my service again," the violinist announced flatly.

"Pick it up? Meaning just what?" Avram wanted to know.

Shoving his injured thigh so that the others could see it, Fishel slapped the numbed side of his thigh. "Reserve duty once a year and the chance to be available if I'm needed."

"If you're suggesting this because Zvi Mazon might be dead, don't," Avram told him.

Fishel brushed the idea aside. "I've been thinking about it for months."

Sipping his coffee, Moshe thought about Fishel Warshow as a soldier. He had fought beside the violinist, and he was not going to push his fighting abilities aside lightly. However, as a major on detached service, he felt the least of all created persons at this moment.

Avram Ben Ezra, serving as the secretary to the general staff, was weighing the suggestion in a different context. "Look," he began, "we couldn't afford to have anything happen to you." He was smiling as he explained, "You're a national asset like oranges, a lousy border, the Negev, and . . ." As he groped for another valid asset, his friends laughed.

Almost annoyed that his approach to a serious problem had gone astray, Avram tried to be gentle in his rejection of Fishel.

"Don't humor me," Fishel said so coldly that both of the officers weighed the suggestion again.

"You're serious?" Moshe asked.

The violinist, his eyes on the woman in the other room, nodded.

Moshe appealed to Avram with his eyes.

Sighing, the staff officer offered, "I'll arrange it if the medics will approve limited reserve duty." To be certain he had not overcommitted himself, he repeated, "Limited duty." His tone was light, but the others understood what he meant.

Fishel smiled, "Thanks." He wanted to clasp Avram's hand to thank him but he knew his friend would be embarrassed. He looked instead at Dvora who stood beside the window now while she looked at him. He hoped she was pleased and proud of him.

Then Avram started asking Moshe about his classes.

An hour later the two officers left the apartment. A small staff car drew up to the curb and waited for Avram while he stood talking to Moshe.

"If you can find a way to prepare Zella . . ." he suggested.

Moshe nodded.

"I wonder if it is any easier to hear the third time," Avram mused.

"You haven't gone shy about telling a widow. You may not like it. In fact, I'm sure you don't. But there's no one in this army who can handle the human side of things better." Then, almost enviously, Moshe added, "I wish I could do half so well."

Avram shook his head. "It isn't the telling that I mind this time. It's the loss of Zvi." He did not think he had made himself understood. "I've told women before that they've lost a husband, and they've lost something. With Zella . . ." His hands came wide. "What does a man say when his friend's wife is a whore?" He was going to say more, but he noticed Moshe's reaction. For an instant Avram wanted to say he was sorry, and then he knew he was not sorry, only that he felt cold inside. Moshe and Zella. The notion had never come to him before. Shifting the subject, he glanced up at the window where Dvora Rabsky stood watching them.

"I wonder if she would shoot Fishel, too," Avram said. He scratched the palm of his hand on the corner of the jeep's windshield brace.

Sitting behind the wheel of his car now, Moshe looked up at his friend. "Take Fishel. He can fight if he has to, and he can think, which is more than I would say for most staff officers."

Understanding that this jibe was as close to affection as Moshe could achieve, Avram smiled. "Next time I'm in Jerusalem, coffee and talk?"

Moshe nodded, hesitated, and then realizing that neither he nor Avram wanted to talk about Zvi now, he quickly drove away. Avram took his time walking over to the waiting staff car.

Turning from the window as the two men drove away, Dvora stood and watched Fishel as he sat back in his chair at the table. Crossing over so that she stood in front of him, she put her hands on his shoulders. "They lied," she said. "You know that. They won't take you. And you'll feel it was something you did or did not do right or it was something the doctors said, but it won't be. They lied. That one, Avram — he's a professional liar. A staff officer who is supposed to see that no one shakes things."

Accustomed to her fears for him, Fishel smiled. "We're friends — Moshe, Avi and I. We fought together in the Old City." He wanted to add Zvi's name, but hesitated discussing him with Dvora.

"Fighting in the Old City," she mocked. "I didn't know that was how people made friends. Maybe I missed something. Tell me about it."

And for the first time since he had known her, Fishel wanted to strike out at her bitterness. Instead, he took her hands off his shoulders, held them for a moment, and then locked himself up with his violin for the rest of the day.

JERUSALEM

It was eight o'clock when Moshe Gilead jerked his jeep to a stop in front of Zella's apartment. Just why he was coming to see her now, he could not explain even to himself.

When he reached the top of the stairs, he heard talk beyond the door and for an instant was tempted to leave. Then he realized Zella was talking to Aaron. The few times Moshe had called for her, he had met the little boy. And though he did not know why Zvi had shipped the child home, Moshe envied Zvi the child the same way he envied Avi his humanity. And then he remembered the rumor about his friend's death.

Zella opened the door. "You were supposed to be in Tel Aviv." She drew him inside.

Aaron lay on the floor pushing a small plastic airplane across the carpet. The child looked up and grinned a greeting and then turned his attention once more toward the toy.

Moshe winked at Zella, his head gesturing toward Aaron, "They learn fast."

Zella laughed and waved him to a chair.

For a few minutes they watched Aaron playing. It was Zella who quoted the bigot they had met days before. "One Yemenite, one Egyptian and one Iraqi and all you have are three warm bodies."

"He's going to have his problems," Moshe admitted, and then he slammed a fist into an open palm. "Who doesn't have his problems?" It was the gesture which Zella noted, not the words, and she knew that if anything happened to Zvi, Aaron would have a friend.

It was almost dawn when Zella pulled herself off the sofa where she had sat curled listening to Moshe tell her about his boyhood and his failures at love and his interest in the army and his friendship for Avram and Fishel and Zvi and Ruth and the others whom he had fought beside, and his admiration for Kineret Heschel, who now served as a legislator in the Knesset — Israel's parliament—and who some said would make a great political leader.

Moshe had talked and Moshe had fallen in love. And he knew that if Zella Mazon had been anyone else's wife he would have picked her up and taken her to bed hours before. He knew, too, that she would not have protested.

As she stood watching his lean body, she smiled. Though none of her husbands had been old, Moshe was probably the youngest man she knew. She was aware how injured he would feel if she ever said as much, but she believed now, after a long night's talking, he would always be young in spite of the gray in his hair and the crow's-feet about his eyes.

He approached, put one hand out and touched her arm, and paused as though this was as close as he felt he could or wanted to get to her. Zella closed her hand over his, and smiling, came to her toes and kissed him. The thin cotton dress she was wearing was all there was between them, and Moshe suddenly became more aware of her body than he had ever been before and then he understood that he was actually in love for the first time. Stepping back, Zella jerked her head so that her hair fell loosely about her shoulders, and as her eyes came up to match his, his eyes fell to her breasts, held for a second at the gentle swell and returned to her face once more.

"Next Saturday, if there isn't too much homework, we could take Aaron for a ride in the jeep. Maybe Caesarea."

The effort at both domesticity and courtship brought a small laugh from Zella, who in the same instant, feared she might offend. "We'll talk on Friday," she agreed.

And then he was gone.

Standing alone in the small living room, Zella smiled to herself. She had enjoyed the quiet talk with Moshe. However, she wondered now why he came. The fact that he was in love with her was not reason enough, because she believed he had been in love with her for weeks and perhaps even longer. He had picked this night to come when he had avoided coming in the past. The swirl of possibilities chased through her weary mind. Could something have happened to Zvi which no one had told her about as yet? It was the least of paths through the maze, but it was the one she was thinking about when she went to sleep alone.

THE RED SEA

It came to pass that there was a wind on the sea the night Zvi Mazon returned to the little port where the ship had been hidden. There were no stars and it was growing cold. Approaching the single dock, he looked about for someone to take him to the *Hatikvah* when he spotted Balbini standing off in the shelter of a shed. The two threw their arms about each other while the Italian babbled his greetings. In the days that had passed since Zvi had gone north, the captain had become increasingly convinced that his friend would not return. As they rowed out to the ship, he told Zvi that all had been quiet in the village. He had had to cross a few palms with almost the last of the food they possessed, but he believed no one had alerted the Egyptian government to the possibility that they would be sailing for Eilat. He also told Zvi that he had made arrangements with the captain of a passing ship going south to send a motor launch north. It was due at any hour.

Zvi listened to the report. They had discussed the possibility of using a decoy when they passed through the Gulf, but the Israeli had not known where the money could come from.

"I used some money I had in the bank at Aden," Balbini explained.

Not quite knowing how to thank the little man, Zvi affectionately squeezed his shoulder. "We'll make it yet," he said.

Balbini was not so sanguine. "A motor vessel put into a port in the south two days ago and was asking questions about us. I suspect that it was not Egyptian, but English."

Puzzled, Zvi tried to understand what this could mean. He did not know and obviously Balbini did not.

Passing his package to the captain, Zvi waited while the captain looked it over, beamed and said, "Two days and we'll be on our way."

And two nights later, the Israeli flag flying above them and the motor launch heading north in front of them, they put to sea once more. The crew was smaller by three who had jumped ship — presumably partly because of the delay and partly because they feared the rumors they had heard about the eventual destination of the *Hatikvah*.

The night was dark, the wind up and the sea rising. For the first time since they had left Aden a storm swept the Red Sea. The tiny vessel pitched and almost broached twice in the first few hours. Standing on the poop beside Balbini, Zvi stared into the darkness. The motor seemed to be running smoothly. Its *thump-thump-woosh* had replaced the *thump-thump-clank*, and they were making better time than they had made in the days before they put into the port.

They had slipped out shortly after nightfall without letting any of the villagers know of their impending departure. Neither the Italian nor the Israeli had complete confidence in the villagers. Now that they were away and the storm was driving any planes out of the sky, both men felt more secure than at any time since Aden.

As the hours moved on, the winds grew stronger, whipping the flag on the mast. Waves broke over the deck. The crew huddled below except for a single heavy-set Ethiopian who stood watch at the prow. Under other circumstances, Balbini might have sounded his ship's whistle for fear of meeting another vessel while crossing the narrow sea, but now he moved on silently and darkly.

The next day they were off Sinai. The long, thin fingerlike peninsula of Ras Muhammad rose to their left as they edged in close to the wind. Moving north and east, they slipped as far out to sea as they could from Gebel el Safra and the large guns north of Sharm el Sheikh. Standing on the poop, Zvi watched with fieldglasses for some sign of life from the shore battery. There was none so far. Moment by moment they approached the range of the Egyptian guns. Closer and then closer. The sea was rough, the sky clouded and there was no sun.

From where he stood against the rail, Zvi made out the shape of the guns. Larger by far than anything he had ever seen before. He had no way to judge their exact range or the accuracy of the Egyptian gunners. The huge guns were set in heavy concrete bases and beyond them lay the few scattered buildings of Sharm el Sheikh. Swinging sharply, Balbini moved his vessel still farther out to sea, hoping that he had not been seen and yet certain that someone had to be on duty even in the early morning.

No sound and no sign of life ashore. Zvi swung his glasses so that he could scan the entire shoreline. He made out half a dozen camouflaged trucks and several jeeps. Near the edge of the village he saw a herd of camels. They came as no surprise because he had heard of an Egyptian camel corps in Sinai. The only real surprise was the size of the guns. He estimated the *Hatikvah* was several miles offshore now and moving farther out. He could have questioned Balbini's feint toward Sharm el Sheikh rather than a more circuitous route to the Strait, but he knew it was just possible that the captain's boldness was what was actually taking them through.

Still no sign of anyone manning the guns.

No stir ashore.

No movement of any kind.

Neither man spoke. The crew stood along the rail staring at the Egyptian guns. One Ethiopian restlessly rubbed his hand over a greasy rope, looked at it and without being aware that he was doing so, licked off the grease. Zvi smiled, but his eyes returned to the guns. Fully dressed now in tan cottons and a heavy green jacket, he still felt the cold wind blowing off the mountains.

Silence except for the wind and the high water.

Then they were past Sharm el Sheikh and moving along past the airstrip at Ras Umm Sid on the far side of the tiny bay. He could make out three planes. No one was near them. The shed which probably housed the pilots appeared empty. Perhaps the flight crews were in Sharm el Sheikh. Perhaps they were waiting for the small vessel to move into the narrow Strait to the north.

There was no way for Zvi to know.

One of the crewmen coughed and the sound seemed so loud that for an instant Zvi wanted to shout for silence. Balbini's eyes never left the sea.

The motor seemed muffled and Zvi knew the sea was drowning its constant thump. The waves rose and the vessel seemed to be moving too slowly, and yet it was driving forward with full speed.

And still no sign of life on the shore.

Past the wider bay at Marset el At and moving closer to shore now as their options narrowed with the sea.

Swinging about, Zvi could make out the island of Tiran on their starboard quarter. At its highest point it appeared to rise to about five hundred feet on the side facing him. Beyond it lay Sinafir Island, slightly smaller, flat and washed by the high seas.

Back now toward the coast which shelved low where they passed it. Moving slowly closer to the shore as they approached the Egyptian guns at Ras Nusrani. Large guns on a bare tongue of land. The shallows reduced their options as they started to move through the Strait of Tiran.

Glancing west and then east and then west again, Zvi felt as though the land were closing in on them.

Glancing into the sea, he could make out the large rocks on both sides of the ship. The sea beneath was bottle-green but he could see the shallows where the color of the sea changed to a vivid blue.

His eyes were on the few buildings at Ras Nusrani now.

No movement. No signs of life. A few parked vehicles, the guns and a trace of smoke above one of the buildings. The strong wind scattered the smoke.

The sea continued to rise. There was no reason for any Egyptian to be out in this weather. Since the truce two years before there had been no attempt to break the blockade, and there should have been no reason to expect one now. However, Zvi remembered the Egyptian planes and he looked at the guns.

If they were ever going to be fired, this should be the moment. Focusing in on them, he could make out their large, open steel mouths.

Slowly the *Hatikvah* pushed through the heavy seas past Ras Nusrani.

Behind Zvi lay the flat coast of Saudi Arabia. Before him the tongue of land.

Swinging quickly about, he scanned the island of Tiran once more. As far as he could tell it was barren. He did not know. He could not be certain.

And now the guns were falling farther to the south as Balbini pointed his vessel almost due north, ignoring the shoals behind him, ignoring the Egyptian bases he had passed.

The heavy seas rocked the craft and one of the crewmen grabbed hold of the rail. Two others went below feeling secure.

Then one of the Ethiopians came out of the cabin on the poop and handed Balbini a piece of paper. The Italian read it over quickly, never really taking his eyes off the huge waves breaking over the prow of his vessel. Zvi looked at his friend for an explanation.

With a smile, Balbini explained, "The radio operator picked up a report. They have taken the motor launch into custody."

Zvi laughed, relaxing for the first time in days. "They can't hold it," he shouted over the blasting wind. "It was flying an Italian flag."

Balbini nodded.

"Except for planes, we should be home clear," Zvi shouted.

The Italian shook his head. "Unless they have fast boats someplace."

Without a word, Zvi swept the seas about them with his glasses. Empty. Then he remembered that he had seen no Egyptian vessels of any kind in the small bays. The notion disturbed him because he could not believe there were none.

"The launch," Balbini shouted.

And it took the Israeli a moment to realize how successful their decoy had been.

The sea remained high. The wind continued to break waves over the deck and drowned the sound of their engine. Neither man left the deck through the long day. Several times the cook brought them coffee. Once Balbini explained that they were down to drinking their bilge. When dusk closed in over the Gulf of Akaba, the cook brought both men an open can of sardines. "That's all we have," Balbini explained once more.

However, Zvi was smiling now. With the darkness settling about them, he felt there was little to concern them.

Twenty minutes later the Ethiopian at the prow of the ship let out a cry and then came running back toward the poop. His head was averted and he was pointing to something. Grabbing his glasses, Zvi tried to see what the man was pointing to. Darkness and rain, and with the heel of his hand Zvi wiped his glasses. Trying once more, he made out a light. Then more lights. A few minutes later he could tell that they were coming toward him. A ship of some kind. Wheeling his vessel sharply eastward, the Italian moved aside to let the other ship pass. Their own silhouette was set against the land to the east and Zvi felt secure in the darkness. The ship grew larger. Two stacks. A freighter from Jordanian Akaba. Cursing, Zvi wondered how he had forgotten the Arab port which lay less than two miles from Eilat. He wondered if there were any naval vessels at Akaba, and then he decided that the chances were slight.

246

Mostly landbound, the Jordanians probably would not turn their one small outlet to the sea into a naval base. However, he could not be sure. And so there was one worry left.

Neither man tried to sleep that night.

In the darkness they made out the lights of the Egyptian village at Dahab.

In the morning they passed Wasit.

The only thing Zvi feared from this tiny scattering of huts was a radio which could summon a plane, but when he glanced up at the lowering sky, he smiled, happy with the overcast and cold.

Later, they made out the Arabian villages of El Himoida and El Haki to the east. Nothing more than huts. Places for fishermen and dhows. No possibility of threats from here.

On both sides of the narrow gulf, mountains edged toward the sea.

Zvi surveyed them in the subdued light of the overcast. How would a man take troops through Sinai south to Ras Nusrani and Sharm el Sheikh? How would a company or brigade traverse these rocky heights? Someday he would sit down with Moshe and a map to see if there was a way. At this moment he was looking north toward Eilat and then in the distance he could make out the far end of the gulf. To the east of the Israeli port lay Akaba. Four vessels were anchored there. Freighters as far as he could see.

And then Eilat.

Home.

Spreading back from the flat land which was the southern edge of the Negev desert lay a few modern buildings and a few older ones.

Turning his head, he smiled at the blue-and-white flag at the stern.

Eilat and the first Jewish flag to reach it by sea in two thousand years and bearing the greatest cargo in the world.

The Italian beamed, proud of what he had himself accomplished.

Laughing loudly, Zvi embraced his companion.

An hour later Zvi went ashore to be met by Moshe Gilead and Avram Ben Ezra.

Book III
WINTER, 1952 | AUTUMN, 1956

THE ISRAELI–JORDANIAN BORDER, JANUARY, 1952

It was a quiet night. The kibbutz was asleep except for two old men who sat outdoors on the porch talking about their childhood in Vilna. One of them was recalling the first time he had been to the cheder, and the other was listening as he, too, remembered the small synagogue where his father had taken him as a child. Now the synagogue and their parents were long destroyed. A small bird alighted on a nearby rock and the men turned to listen to its call. Suddenly the bird flushed, and in that instant a short burst of rifle fire destroyed the old men who had been remembering their days as children in Vilna.

The young woman was not afraid to leave the shelter of her house because her fiancé was going to join her at the crossroads. She knew it was safe because they had met there many times since she had joined the kibbutz three months before. The older men and women smiled when she left the dining room. There were young women who were envious. Her fiancé was a tall, handsome youth who had fought in Haganah and had served with the paramilitary border police. And now he was living less than a mile away, working on a small kibbutz which had just put in kilns to make dishes, and he was going to go to school to learn how to run the kilns. They met at the crossroads and walked south. They talked about his going to school and they talked about the kilns and they were talking about their marriage plans when the rifle burst from the darkness cut the young man down. For an instant the girl wanted to run toward him and then she wanted to run away. However, it did not make any difference what she wanted, because the three Arabs who emerged from the darkness raped her with cold passion before they slit her throat.

The youth from Tel Aviv was happy that he had made the decision to move out of the city to work on the farm of his former comrade-in-arms. While he might have made more money working in an office, here on the farm he was enjoying the sun, the ready companionship and the fact that the sister of his friend was watching him as he drove the heavy tractor through the small field. He felt the warmth of her eyes and the warmth of the sun and he almost forgot that he had lost part of his arm in the battle for Latrun five years before. And then in that brief flash, when the heavy tractor struck the mine, he remembered the battle of Latrun and the loss of his hand.

And then he was dead and he remembered nothing.

The small boy whose father ran the school for the kibbutz sat on the rock listening to the music from the radio in the building behind him. Tomorrow was going to be his birthday. Tomorrow his mother and his father were going to borrow a truck and drive him all the way to Jerusalem so that he could meet his two cousins who had come from South Africa and who, his father had told him, had seen honest-to-heaven lions. The boy thought about lions and wondered how he would react if he were to meet an honest-to-heaven lion as his cousins from South Africa had, and then he smiled because tomorrow he would be five and he was certain any boy five would be brave. When the rifle shots broke the night, the little boy who was going to be five lost the opportunity to learn if he would be brave, because he was dead.

The patrol was moving close to the frontier. All five men held their rifles at the ready. None of them spoke. The night was clear. Off in the distance they could hear a calf complain. The field through which they walked had been tilled only the day before and none of them believed it to be mined. The young corporal in command glanced up at the stars and started to tell the youth beside him that this was really more beautiful country than the land near Gaza where his parents lived. He never had a chance to explain why, because in that moment he spotted the six infiltrators. Four rifle shots announced that the Arabs had no intention of fleeing without a fight. Half running, half prone, the Israeli youths returned the fire. Then the corporal formed his men into a single, large arc and swung them between the infiltrators and the Jordanian border. One youth from Beersheba was shot in the leg as he ran into position. Another knew that he had killed an Arab infiltrator, because the Arab had come to his feet screaming before he dropped. The battle lasted for seven minutes, during which time three of the Arabs were killed; no one could be certain how many made their way back to the frontier by other routes. And when there was silence again, the corporal whose parents lived near Gaza lay dead beside the youth from Beersheba with the bullet in his leg who sat rocking back and forth beside the corpse.

The small detachment of Israeli soldiers moved out of their barracks, loaded up in trucks and headed for the border. There were forty of them. They were armed with a mixed bag of weapons: submachine guns, carbines, hand guns, grenades and knives. They wore baggy camouflaged uniforms.

Several had taken the time to smear shoe polish over their faces. Some calmly smoked cigarettes which they passed around the truck. The major rubbed the side of his cheek with a warm hand while he stared into the darkness ahead. Spread on his lap was the map he had marked earlier in the day. He did not really need to look at it because the red-and-green markings were etched in the back of his memory.

The truck bounced over the unpaved road and one of the soldiers quipped that next time they should take a better route because he wanted to go to his funeral in comfort.

None laughed.

They drove for almost an hour. Most of the time they were silent.

Twice men pointed out farms where their friends or family lived. Their leader, who sat beside the driver, continued to rub his cheek with the flat of his hand even when they passed the kibbutz where he had been raised as a child. Twice he glanced back in the truck to make sure his explosives were riding gently. The man who years before had been a sapper with a British unit in the Netherlands patted the sensitive cargo to reassure the major. The sapper had seen this major in combat before and he feared him almost as much as he feared the enemy. There was an angry look which never seemed to disappear from the major's eyes. There was a sudden explosion of emotions which carried all before him. But worst of all was the frantic drive which he demanded of himself and his men. Some said the major had been disappointed in love. Some said he had lost a battle once and had never recovered from that. Those who thought they knew him best said that he really resented having to leave the university and give up his future as a lawyer to return to the field. However, none ever questioned him about his ready anger or his constant demands, partly because none had the nerve and partly because all knew that it was his high level of tension which helped bring them through the months of specialized training.

The three-quarter-ton trucks moved north and east. The terrain was broken. There were few trees. The road was paved for a short distance. Most of the time they traveled on gravel. Then the major's hand came up and he waited for the truck behind him to come parallel. In a quiet voice he asked the young captain if he was ready.

The officer riding in the front seat of the second vehicle nodded, and waved for his men to detruck, before he joined the major.

The slim major held the folded map under his arm and his carbine in his hand as he stood facing the frontier. It was almost midnight. In the distance he could make out the lights of Bethlehem. Less than two weeks before, Christians from all over the world had gathered there to celebrate the birth of Jesus. Some had been allowed to cross the frontier. Others had come from the east. As he thought of this, the lean young officer wondered if any of them had been wise men and if any of them had taken the time to read of the girl who had been left dead with her throat slit, of the two old men from Vilna, of the tractor driver with the single hand who lay beside his smashed tractor, of the little boy who had never lived to be five or the corporal whose parents lived near Gaza. The major wondered if any of the Christmas visitors to Bethléhem knew what was taking place around them other than the fine music and the quaint charm of the Arabs selling cheap souvenirs of carved camels.

His head went back. The night was dark enough. He glanced at his watch. The hour was late. He had lost fifteen minutes crossing over the graveled roads. Jotting this fact in the back of his memory so that he could take it into account another time, he nodded to the captain who had waited quietly for further instructions. There were none.

"Let's go," the major said softly and started toward the frontier. Forming his men into an irregular column and making sure that the musette bags carrying the explosives were distributed, the captain followed at the tail of the column.

Forty men moving through the night. Rocks and broken walls loomed up suddenly in the darkness. There was no sound. There was no challenge.

The major moved off to one side and let the column pass him once, before he trotted to the van again. No one spoke or lighted a cigarette, though several wanted to. They had all served too long under the major to make that mistake.

They walked for an hour. One of them quietly suggested to the captain that they ought to take a break, but the captain looked up toward the head of the column where the major made his way through a rocky field, and he shook his head.

They were in Jordan now. All of them knew it. Twice they passed Arab farms. Once a dog barked at them. Once they passed near a village.

Then the major's hand went up in the dark and he waved the others on. Before them was a small knoll and beyond that their target. The lights from Bethlehem were closer now. Lying flat on his stomach, the major made out the silhouette of the Church of the Nativity against the sky. The old fortresslike holy place would be almost impossible to take, and he was pleased that this was not his target and would never be.

Rolling onto his back, he watched the captain spread his men out for the attack: groups of two, as planned. The explosives already out of their dark green bags. The primer cord wrapped from open palm to elbow, the sapper checked his charges.

Glancing down at the carbine in his hand, the major checked the safety. And then the captain was crawling toward him.

"We're ready."

Again the flat hand against the flat cheek, as Moshe Gilead thought about the possibility he might have forgotten something. Nodding slowly, he came to his feet and started toward the village that lay on the far side of the knoll. The others followed, half to his right and half to his left. The village was small. There were no lights. Somewhere a dog barked. There was a scattering of mud huts, several concrete and stone buildings, and a few dozen stone houses along a dirty, narrow street. A ram tethered to a post watched the column approach.

Half the soldiers blended into the dark, taking up defensive positions selected days before from a layout of the village. The major moved on with only the sappers and three others. One stocky soldier rested the butt of his submachine gun on his hip and slowly surveyed the street. At a gesture from Major Gilead, the sappers moved quickly now, setting their charges along the base walls of several buildings where it was known the enemy terrorists resided. Somewhere a light suddenly appeared in a glassless window. A single soldier set his rifle sights on the window while his companion selected the door of that same house for his target. The sappers were ready now.

Standing in the shadow of a building, Moshe Gilead raised his hand. The sapper who had fought with the British in the Netherlands nodded.

The major's hand dropped.

The charges rocked the night.

First, there was dust rising and then there was the sound echoing through the hills of Bethlehem.

And then there were screams of terror.

From someplace a rifle shot splashed into the darkness and the Israeli soldiers laid down a screen of fire. The Arabs of Beth Jallah remained indoors. Some of them were already dead. The major's hand rose as his closed fists circling each other ordered his men to scramble. A moment later there were no Israelis in Beth Jallah.

The dust settled with the fallen stones of the shattered houses.

The next day the Jordanian government would protest that its civilians had been violently and viciously attacked without provocation, without cause, with great inhumanity.

JERUSALEM, APRIL, 1953

Throwing his textbooks into the rear of his small Fiat, Zvi Mazon stood for a moment watching a young woman walking past. Sighing at the misfortune which had not brought them together, he looked at his watch. Time to be home. Wrenching the doorhandle of the car, he wrestled it open and slipped into the driver's seat.

There was little traffic now. It was past dinnertime. He should have been home two hours earlier, but he had had to finish some research in the library. Now he knew he had better get home before his neighbor put Aaron to bed.

The boy was about eight now. Strong. Lean. Wiry. He could move faster than Zvi and sometimes even faster than Moshe Gilead, who liked to take him for walks on those Saturdays when he was not on duty.

Driving north through the city, Zvi honked two cars out of the center of the narrow street, and then he swung the Fiat over to the curb, jumped out and entered the old apartment house. Reaching the fourth floor, he opened the door and bent over. Aaron exploded across the room, wrapped his arms about his father's neck and held on while Zvi rose, and pivoting, swung the boy around. Then he walked over to the sofa, shook his shoulders fiercely and dropped his son onto a pillow. Both of them were laughing.

Then Zvi stopped laughing.

Avram Ben Ezra stood watching him from the far corner of the room, his back against the window, his uniform collar open and one hand shoved into his trouser pocket.

Without taking his eyes off his friend, Zvi tossed his books on the sofa and asked Aaron to run next door and tell Mrs. Kaplan he would not be over for dinner tonight.

Aaron trotted out, wondering what his father had in mind.

When they were alone, Zvi asked, "Been waiting long?"

Avram nodded. His shoulders hunched slightly forward as though he were about to tackle someone. "I got into town this morning. Decided not to hunt you down at the university."

Zvi waved his friend to a chair; however Avram ignored the gesture. "But you had to see me?"

A low chuckle as Avram asked, "Are you afraid of meeting me?"

The director of the chief-of-staff's office looked slowly about the small apartment as though he had never seen it before. He knew the single bedroom beyond, which Zvi shared with Aaron; and the small kitchen, which no one used because the woman next door made meals for both of them. The sitting room was tiny but not untidy. That was partly Zvi's personality as well as the fact that Aaron played at the neighbors' when he was not in school and his father was away.

Deciding that there were questions he wanted to ask and that he had no right to ask them now, Avram approached his subject bluntly. "You've been in school over two years now."

Zvi half smiled as he said, "You've looked in my file recently."

"Twenty-seven months to be exact," Avram said.

"And if I stay another ten, I graduate with honors." Zvi did not want his friend to forget this point.

However, something about Zvi's information brought a smile to Avram's long face. "You know what's going on?"

"I think so."

"I could give you statistics," Avram offered. "The number of Arab crossings per month and per year. The number of deaths we are sustaining and the number of wounded filling the hospitals, but somehow the sum equals less than the whole."

Zvi pulled a cigarette from his shirt pocket and lighted one while he thought about this. "The numbers wouldn't include the fact that they have closed the Strait since I came through and would not include the fact that the UN has condemned them for closing the canal, and yet it remains closed, and the UN has condemned them for violations of the truce and none of it stops them." He shook his head angrily, "No, you're right. The sum is more than the total."

Sucking deeply on his cigarette, Zvi stared at the rising smoke for a moment. The room was almost dark. He had not noticed that before. Finally, he raised his head. "What brought you here?"

Avram glanced toward the window. He could make out Mount Scopus in the distance. And he started talking even before he turned back to Zvi. "The chief picked you yesterday. We talked about it for an hour, and I told him you could finish school if he let you, and then he reminded me that Moshe had not finished either."

"What about *him*?" Zvi asked, gesturing with his head toward the door through which Aaron had left.

Sighing, Avram knew he had to approach now what he had decided earlier he should not. "Can't Zella take him?"

Zvi stared at his friend for a moment and then laughed. "It might surprise you to know that she probably does love him in her own way." He was shaking his head. "I'm not giving her the boy. She's gone her way and we'll go ours."

Avram wanted to ask why, but he believed he knew the answer. From the time Zvi had returned from Yemen, the separation was inevitable. As far as he knew, it had been without overt rancor, but he admitted to himself that no one knew the gut truth of anyone else's marriage.

Suddenly Avram drew himself up and said quietly, "I'll leave that for you to work out. Let's say you come in next Sunday." And as he spoke, he pulled a folded sheet from his pocket and set it on the table beside him.

Accepting his orders, Zvi said, "Thanks for telling me yourself. What's the assignment?"

"The same as Moshe's. You're to get your own battalion. You'll have to shake it down and train it yourself."

"How much time have I got?"

"Not enough." Neither of them laughed.

"Why me?" Zvi asked, more out of curiosity than any need to know or have his selection justified.

Avram moved to the center of the room and stood looking at his friend. Taller by several inches, the lieutenant-colonel almost bent down as he said,

"We've lost something. The Chief thinks we have to get it back. You have to get it back."

Zvi's head cocked to one side as he tried to understand what the staff officer was saying.

"Maybe it was we who were in the British army. Sometimes I think it was. Maybe it was because the conflict seemed over and done with in forty-nine. In any case, we've lost it and the Chief thinks you can do as well as Moshe is doing to bring it back. We've grown formal. Paper work and parades and snap and security and maybe getting fat in the wrong places." He smiled. "We salute too damned much and too damned well."

Zvi thought he understood. "We're no longer the 'bandits of Haganah.' And I'm the cross between the British formality and Moshe's wildness."

Avram was pleased. "Lean on the last part for now." Then he was saying goodnight while Zvi walked him to the door.

"Sunday," he reminded Zvi, who repeated after him, "Sunday."

Then Zvi was alone and wondering what would happen next. He would have liked to discuss his plans with Zella, but he knew he would not.

Zvi Mazon was not the only reason why the Director of the Israeli General Staff had come to Jerusalem that day. Two of Moshe Gilead's command companies had been racing through the countryside on a set schedule to see just how long it would take to swing them from one frontier line to another. It had been fortunate that they had been near Jerusalem when the Arab Legion began a small fire fight. There were other troops stationed specifically for the protection of the Central Command; however, it was quickly agreed that the assignment should be Moshe's.

Satisfied that the entire incident along the Jordanian line of the city would not come to much more than harassment, Avram wandered over to the King David Hotel where he had agreed to meet Moshe for dinner. There was a hushed quiet about the David. The rows of tables on the stone patio were almost empty. A few American tourists sat in the early dusk listening to the rifle fire several blocks away.

There was no one on the patio whom Avram knew. He started to turn back to the lobby when he saw a young woman watching him. From the looks of her plain, light blue dress and the way she wore her hair drawn straight back, he assumed she was an Israeli. There were no lines on her face and she wore no makeup. He liked what he saw; he assumed she was about twenty-eight or possibly a little more. He drew himself erect, pleased that he wore a well-pressed uniform and hoping that it still looked neat after the drive from Tel Aviv. He found that he was continuing to stare at her. There was nothing shy about the woman: she stared back. A nervous smile spread over Avram's face and he moved toward her table. There was a small pot of coffee before her, and as he came closer, he could see a briefcase on the empty seat beside her. Suddenly the firing near the Old City rose in intensity. Halting where he was, Avram looked around. There was nothing he could do about the gunfire. Raising his hand, he gestured for a waiter, and when one came over, Avram asked, "Will you tell the desk and the telephone operator that in the event anyone is looking for Colonel Ben Ezra, I'll be out here."

The waiter, a portly, middle-aged man with balding head, smiled. "Certainly, Avi. You just sit anywhere and I'll find you."

Avram stood where he was as the man walked quickly into the hotel. The nickname he had been given as a boy had remained, and Avram liked it. Turning about, he looked once more at the young woman who now had her briefcase in hand and seemed to be fumbling through it for something. Moving rapidly, Avram approached her table and pulled out a chair. "May I?"

Her head came up and without any embarrassment, she nodded. "I'll have to be going in a few minutes," she told him.

"If you're alone . . ." And then as he sat down, his hands went wide in a gesture of futility. "I'm Avram Ben Ezra," he introduced himself.

The young woman smiled. "I know. Your picture is in the papers often enough."

Somehow she was putting him off balance, and he could not quite understand why.

A trace of a smile as she said, "People call you Avi?"

He nodded, pleased that she knew of him.

"When I was a child, I thought like a child, et cetera." Avram was trying to be friendly and at the same time retain his dignity. He waited for her to introduce herself. When she did not, he asked, "And your name?"

By this time the portly waiter had returned and waved to assure Avram that he had taken care of the details. Avram's hand went up as he pointed to the coffee already on the table.

The young woman followed his glance and his gesture. "Should I evaluate your tactics as aggressive, Colonel?"

And he knew she was laughing at him again. Once more he tried to smile and failed. His head came up: the rifle fire was supported by light machine guns now. When he looked at the woman again, he could see that she was staring at him.

"Isn't there something you should be doing?" she asked.

Avram listened to the rifle and machine-gun fire. There were Sten guns now. Very slowly, he shook his head. "Major Gilead knows what he's doing," he tried to reassure her.

However, she shook her head. "He's not all that bright, Colonel." Seeing the surprised expression on his face, she continued. "Maybe the word I want is stable. I'm not so certain he's that stable."

Sitting back in his chair, Avram stared at the young woman. Her face was full, her cheeks pale, her eyes a dark blue, but there was an almost unfeminine look about the way her jaw was set at this moment. He wanted to take his eyes off hers for an instant, but he felt challenged. "Do you know him?" and there was a snap to his voice which he had hoped he could keep out of it.

She shook her head, not averting her eyes a fraction. At that moment the waiter placed a pot of coffee between them with the question, "Anything else, Avi?"

Trying not to frown at the familiarity, the staff officer shook his head.

"Anything else, Judge?" The waiter was asking the woman now, and Avram knew she was enjoying his reaction.

With a pleasant smile, she asked the waiter, "My check please."

After he set it on the table, they were alone again.

"Judge?" Avram asked.

She nodded. "Judge Malin Talmon."

Avram's hand slapped the back of his neck in a gesture of confusion. "You don't look like a judge."

"Is there some special way a judge is supposed to look?"

And they were both laughing and Avram was pleased with her laugh and with his taste and his good fortune, and even though he could hear the firing from the Old City, he asked, "Will Your Honor have dinner with me tonight?" Then he was embarrassed. "You aren't married, are you?" The question was tentative, hesitant, as though he knew the answer would be Yes.

Shoving the pot of coffee away, she bent over the table, her hands clasped before her as she stared at him seriously. "We've only been talking for five minutes, Colonel, and we've already found grounds on which we disagree. Think of how much we might find to disagree about during a whole dinner."

"Disagree?"

"Your friend Moshe Gilead."

Relaxing, Avram said, "And to be certain you know my side of that discussion, I'm going to ask him to join us for dinner."

However, she was shaking her head. "I'd rather not." And then, as if she had to explain, "I don't like what I've heard of your friend."

Avram considered this before he answered. "I wouldn't want to argue the case before your court. However, I'd like you to remember what made him."

She did not smile when she said, "If you're reminding me of his years as a boy in Haganah, don't. I spent as many years in it as either of you. I won't accept that as a reason for liking — for enjoying what he's doing."

"What's he doing?" Avram poured more coffee, and looked closely at her. Judge Malin Talmon was probably not tall, slightly plump and full-breasted, and seemingly unconscious of his eyes evaluating her. When their eyes met again, he had the impression of a strong woman, one who was not particularly gentle. Rather, she seemed to exude competence.

Malin considered his question before she answered. "I'm not convinced these retaliation raids are getting us anywhere."

Avram had heard objections to the policy before, and even though he had answers, he did not want to reveal anything that had not yet been released to the public. Instead, he used the routine answer, "Let the Arab countries assume responsibility for what goes across their borders and we won't cross those borders."

She watched him finish his coffee, and then to his surprise, she asked, "Where did you plan to eat?"

Pleased that she was accepting his invitation, he suggested the grill in the hotel.

Later, after finishing their dinner, they sat over some native brandy. She smiled across the table and said, "You really didn't have to tell the waiter who you were and where you could be reached. I already knew who you were."

Both of them laughed as he reminded her, "And you didn't use that out you left yourself when you said you had to be leaving in a few minutes."

Then both of them fell silent and they stared at each other.

After a while, she asked, "You don't live in Jerusalem?"

Avram shook his head. "I've an apartment in Tel Aviv."

Malin thought about that as though it were important. Before she could say anything, Moshe Gilead joined them. He was in battle dress, bareheaded, and wearing a sidearm. Approaching the table, he looked from Avram to the strange woman and back to his friend again.

"The clerk said I'd find you down here."

Beaming, Avram told Malin, "You see."

And they laughed again.

She pushed back her chair and rose to leave as Avram introduced her. Shaking hands with Moshe, she said, "And I will have to be going."

"But I'll see you again?" Avram asked.

He had been right. She was shorter even than Moshe, who barely came up to Avram's shoulder. She thought about his question and nodded. "I live at number eighteen, Balfour Street."

Ignoring Moshe, Avram walked her to the door of the dining room and then to the steps. "We'll be done in an hour," he told her. "Can I call on you then?"

Her head fell back as she looked up at him. At first he thought she was going to say No, but she smiled and said, "Yes." Then she walked away, leaving him to watch her climb the steps. Slapping the back of his neck in delight, Avram grinned broadly as he turned to Moshe, who had seated himself at their empty table.

The business the two had to complete took almost two hours. Moshe agreed that the threat to the city was nil at this time and that he would move his men out by morning.

"How many were killed?" Avram asked as they walked back into the hotel lobby.

Shrugging, Moshe said, "Five as far as I know. There may have been more." Then he added, "There were eight civilians hit. One woman was killed."

"Any idea how it started?"

The two were outside the hotel now, their drivers in the circular drive before the entrance.

"I don't know," Moshe said. "If I had to take a guess, I'd say some Arab soldier was nervous." To be sure he was not being judged, he concluded, "We had no choice except to hit back hard."

Thinking of Malin's protest earlier, Avram nodded. *Ein brera,* no choice."

They were about to part when Moshe asked, "That woman — you know her well?"

Avram shook his head. "Why?"

Moshe shrugged. "I don't know. I've heard of her. Supposed to be wise or something."

Avram smiled. "I'll let you know sometime." He had no desire to discuss Malin with Moshe, but he was surprised that the two so obviously disliked each other.

Moshe stepped into his jeep. "I'm going to the hospital," he told Avram. "I've four wounded there, one seriously."

"I'll be in touch," Avram said, and the jeep drove off, leaving him standing beside his staff car.

Fifteen minutes later, Moshe entered the hospital. There was some confusion on the lower floor, and he had to push his way through the crowd to the main desk, where he introduced himself and asked where his men had been taken. After he received his directions, he started across the waiting room. There were over fifty civilians crowded in there. Several women were weeping. One old man sat on a couch and rocked back and forth, numbed by the day's happenings. Moshe was tempted to speak to him. However, at that moment Zella came into the waiting room wearing a white surgical gown and Moshe hurried over to her.

Looking up, she smiled. "A rough day?"

He nodded.

"The one who was shot in the stomach," she told him, "he died half an hour ago."

Sucking on his cheek, Moshe considered this before he said, "We weren't playing patty-cake."

They were walking down the long green corridor now. "Zvi's dropped out of school," she told him.

Nodding, Moshe said in a cold voice, "I know, but you weren't supposed to."

Zella smiled. "Someone at the university called to tell me."

They were at the end of the corridor where she opened a door that led outside. He followed her out into the night. It was cool. Scattered rifle fire could be heard faintly from the direction of the Demarcation Line. Turning to face Moshe, she asked, "What's he doing with Aaron?"

He paused to look at her before he answered. Ever since that time three years before when Zvi was believed to have been lost in the Red Sea, Moshe knew he had been in love with Zella. He had not made any move in her direction while she and Zvi had lived together, but now, as he saw her tired face, her tip-tilted nose, and the way her hair fell loose about her shoulders, he wanted to kiss her. It took all the restraint he had to bring his thoughts back to her question.

"I'd guess he'll take him to Ruth's."

Zella thought about Ruth. They had never been friends, and in the years since the siege of the Old City, their paths had not often crossed. "She has a child of her own, hasn't she?" And Moshe knew that Zella was envious.

"A girl. Someone for Aaron to play with." Then, as though he had to say more, "Aaron's a few years older."

Zella turned away and faced the lights of the city as she thought about this. "I wonder if he thought of bringing him to me."

Not knowing, Moshe remained silent. Lights from a window reflected off her hair. Very slowly, he reached out and touched her hair. Surprised, Zella did not move as he stroked it. She was aware of the thorn in his eyes as he tried to smile and failed. Then his arms came about her as he drew her close. She did not resist, nor did she encourage him.

Feeling both frustrated and angry at her indifference, he tried to kiss her, and when he did, she stepped out of the circle of his arms. Almost tauntingly, she reminded him, "I'm still married to Zvi."

For an instant Moshe was tempted to tell her that there were times when she forgot that, that she had known other men. And he wanted to ask her what was wrong with himself.

Her hand came up and touched his arm. "Maybe sometime when we have time," she said, as though she did not want to shut him out completely.

He stepped away. "Sometime when we have time," he agreed. "Meanwhile, I've men to see here."

"And after you're done here, you're going south?"

He shook his head angrily. "After I'm done here, I'm going to find some whore and get laid." Before she could react, he spun on his heel and stalked back into the hospital.

Across the city, Avram was sitting with Malin in her mother's apartment.

The sitting room was larger than most in Jerusalem, well furnished, and the walls were lined with books. However, Avram was unaware of the room. Unable to take his eyes off the woman sitting beside him, he did not notice when her mother and sister left them alone. For nearly an hour they were both conscious of the fact that they had been talking of nothing of importance and yet they were comfortable with each other and they were happy.

Malin Talmon sat back and smiled at his eager expression. "Do you have to drive back tonight?"

Wondering why she asked, he nodded. Pulling out a pack of cigarettes, he offered her one. She shook her head and lit his while he smiled at her.

Then, because it was very important at this moment, he said, "I've a leave coming."

Shaking out the match, she waited for him to explain.

"You have to live here in Jerusalem?"

Believing she understood now, she nodded. "My work's here."

Neither of them said anything for a time and then he told her, "It's going to be difficult at first because I have to live near headquarters." He fell silent once more and she could see that he was trying to cope with something.

"Look," he finally began, "neither one of us is a child. I'm thirty now and . . ." his voice trailed off as he tried to clear his thoughts once more. "Look," he started again, "is there a good reason why we shouldn't get married?"

Very slowly Malin rose from the couch and he was aware of the way she moved, the way her dress flowed over her breasts, the way she tugged at her ear while she thought about his question. Crossing the room, she stood at the far side of it and turned to face him as though for some reason she had to have perspective before she answered.

"I'm not much . . . ," he said. "I'll never make a chief of staff. I'm not Moshe or—"

"Don't," she snapped in a flat, forceful tone. "Don't." The harshness of her voice split the air between them and Avram was startled. "You're a lieutenant-colonel. You've been a kind of hero along with your friends Mazon and Gilead. You've got things they haven't got and one of them is the ability to be a staff officer, and because of that no one can tell me you haven't something, that you aren't something different and somehow better than that nervous little man who can't keep his hands off women and only seems to be happy when he's fighting." She was still angry when she demanded, "If we're going to be married, I don't want you playing games with me—overt humility, self-denigration—any kind of games. I could not live that way."

Her face relaxed and she smiled, and Avram knew he was in love. Shaking his head, he tried to comprehend exactly what this meant. "It's going to be interesting," he said simply.

And Malin knew that she, too, was in love.

For the next several months Zvi Mazon trained his battalion at Ein Hasb south of Beersheba. The Negev spring became summer. The gray earth and the red earth burned. The sun stood bright overhead through the day, and the night chilled the vast spread of broken ground. There were snakes and scorpions. There were Bedouins watching from dry wadis. There were visits from headquarters and inspections.

But most of the time there were long marches with heavy equipment, weapons training, hand-to-hand mock battles, periods without food and stretches without water. There was first-aid training and motorized movement. Map studies and compass studies. Light-tank movements and heavy-armored. Long jogs and push-ups. The training of muscles and the training of minds. The call-out in the middle of the night and the forced march. Parachute-packing and parachute-jumping. Wrestling and boxing. And there were more forced marches and the delousing of enemy mines and the specialized training in explosives. The training was as difficult as Zvi Mazon could make it and still keep his men moving. He did not care how weary they became as long as they toughened and could move on the next day and take another grueling day and night and then move on once more.

They crawled over the hot sand, climbed the broken hills, rolled through the dried wadis, moved trackless through desert, skirmished and disappeared. They hardened into troops. They followed the stocky major, and to the men who had volunteered to serve in the newly formed battalion, Zvi Mazon became a symbol.

The two women were neighbors. They had grown up together as neighbors in Morocco where the father of one had been a physician and the father of the other had been a peddler. They had both been married in Casablanca to men known to their fathers. The physician's daughter had had two children before her husband deserted her, but, as she was telling her childhood companion, "What does a woman want of a man?" And her childhood friend, whose father had been a peddler and therefore a wise man in their small community outside Casablanca, laughed. The two had gone over the story of the man who had deserted his wife so often that there was very little new in the tale for either of them. However, it remained a reason to talk when all other subjects were exhausted, and as the peddler's daughter had told her husband, "She likes to talk about him, and I like to hear her talk about him so that I can appreciate you better. Besides, how long can one talk about the inefficient government, the rising taxes, the lack of jobs and the Arabs?" And so the two women were talking as they sat outside their small concrete block houses at Bet'Arif when the grenade exploded between them.

The woman in the small farm house at Beit Nahala had just put her eldest child to bed beside her youngest. For a long moment she looked at the boy and the girl and felt proud and somehow content that this much of life had been left for her. In that brief instant, she almost blocked out the dark memories of barbed-wire camps, the lingering smell of furnaces and the cries of those about to be cremated. She was not a pretty woman, more because she had not smiled for years rather than because of any flaw in her features; and her husband, who had come from Budapest after the War of Independence, accepted them as part of a terrible tale. When he entered the bedroom and saw her looking down at the children, he almost believed she was smiling, but he had known her too well and too long really to accept that. He put his arm about her waist and drew her to him. She came readily and, dropping her head back, rested it against his shoulder. They were standing that way when the burst of gunfire splattered the room. When the world was silent again, the man from Budapest lifted his head from the floor and saw that his wife was dead. Several minutes later the sound of weeping children came through the fog of his shaken thoughts and he drew himself up long enough to see that both the girl and the boy had been wounded. Then he collapsed across the body of his wife who had survived Germany but not Jordan.

The watchman had just come off duty and he dropped his light Belgian rifle down on the cot where he knew he would have to move it again if he wanted to sleep. However, he was tired and he did not really care about much more than a cold drink of water and a chance to take off his shoes. They were new shoes. He had saved for weeks to buy a pair of shoes just like the ones he had seen on a British sentry in Cyprus when he had been interned there. Of all the things he could recall wanting in his life, he had no more eager memories than those of shoes. Maybe, he told his friends, it was because in his *shtetl* in Lithuania there had been few shoes a man could buy that were comfortable. Maybe, he told his friends, it was because a pair of shoes set a man apart from a peasant, and he was no peasant because his mother's uncle had been a famous rabbi whose opinion had been sought by men of wealth as far away from Lithuania as Estonia, and any man who has traveled must know that is a far distance. Kneeling down and unlacing his new shoes which were like the shoes of the British sentry on Cyprus, the watchman tried to ignore the blisters on his feet and the fact that he was tired, as he conjured up once more his dream of a pretty young woman who would look at his shoes and say, "That man is not a peasant." He had just reached the place in his dream where the pretty young woman was admiring his shoes when the small house imploded from dynamite set about its walls. He was still wearing his shoes when they buried him the next day. All the border police could tell his friends was that the terrorists' tracks had led straight to the Jordanian border.

It was early winter when headquarters notified Zvi that his battalion was to have two weeks' furlough and be ready thereafter for operations. Leaving his second in command at Ein Hasb, Zvi drove directly to Tel Aviv and Ruth's apartment to see his son. In the months since he had left the boy, he had seen him only three times. For the next two days they were inseparable, and he saw more of Ruth than he had in the years since the battle for the Old City. Widowed now, she ran a small dress shop on Allenby Street while her younger sister took care of the children. As an old friend, Zvi felt comfortable with Ruth. Neither one felt called upon to be aware of the other's sex. Neither one felt the need for formality. And the two days Zvi spent at her apartment he relaxed for the first time since he had left Jerusalem. She was able to tell him about Fishel, who was becoming even more famous on the concert stage, about Zella, whom she had met twice at concerts, about Kineret Heschel who was now part of Israel's UN delegation.

As he sat in Ruth's kitchen, a cup of coffee before him and a cigarette in his hand, he thought of the stories he had heard about Fishel's desire to enter the reserves, and even though Fishel limped badly, Zvi knew that should the occasion arise when he needed someone he had to depend upon, he would select Fishel.

Ruth, a worn cotton dressing gown pulled tightly about her, watched Zvi flick an ash into his saucer. The months in the desert had blackened his skin. There was a strange look about his eyes which she did not recall having seen there before. Though she was tempted to ask him about himself and Zella, she refrained. Twice she had seen Zvi's wife, each time with another man.

They talked for a time about Avram's sudden marriage. Ruth believed it odd that they lived in different cities, but she told Zvi, "Maybe that's the best way for marriages to work."

Zvi nodded slowly, committing himself to nothing as he thought about his own marriage and wondered about hers.

"Maybe I shouldn't have said that," Ruth added after a moment.

Zvi shrugged. "Mine didn't come apart because I was abroad. I don't think so, anyway." He watched his cigarette smoke for a moment and then continued, wondering why he was talking about Zella, and then realizing he never had discussed her with anyone before. "It would have happened." A strange and self-conscious grin came across his face. "One of the things a marriage needs is something in common, and by that I mean more than a bed." Sucking deeply on his cigarette, he took the time to light another off it before stubbing the butt out in the saucer.

And he closed the subject by rising from the table. He stood looking down at Ruth. The scar on her forehead was white now. She was barely thirty, but there was a touch of gray in her hair which surprised him. He wondered if he had any. Sometime he would have to look. Reaching out, he put his hand on the side of her head, tipped it up so that he could see her better and smiled. "I don't know about you, but I'm feeling older."

She laughed softly. "Maybe you're getting too old to be running around in the desert."

"I'm thirty," he reminded her.

She nodded sympathetically. "You'll live through it." And then she finished her coffee. "You'd better be going now if you want to get to Avram's yet tonight."

Zvi nodded, bent over and brushed his lips on her forehead. "Sure you don't want to come?"

"Me?" she said deprecatingly. "Me with staff officers, commanders and judges?" She rose from the table and looked at herself. "I'm a peasant and I will always be a peasant." There was a smile on her face when she looked up at him. "And if you want to know something, Major Mazon, I'm glad."

Zvi shook his head. "Don't forget that he's no less a peasant than the rest of us. He came from a kibbutz just like you and ten thousand others in spite of what the papers are saying about him and in spite of the rank he wears now."

Trying to feign surprise, she looked at him. "Whom are you talking about?"

Zvi was patient with her because he was fond of her. "All right. Forget it. But if you want to know, Lt. Colonel Moshe Gilead is to be there tonight."

Ruth shook her head. "There's more to him than what you read in the papers."

He waited for an explanation.

"You'll hear," she said. "Half the women in Tel Aviv think they have to crawl into his pants or that he should crawl into their beds."

Zvi could not bring himself to laugh because he, too, had been hearing about Moshe's escapades and because he had always thought she liked the man more than she was revealing now.

As he slipped into his jacket, they stook looking at each other, neither speaking because they did not need to.

"I'll drop in tomorrow," he finally said. "Tell your sister that I'll pick Aaron up at school."

Ruth nodded and walked him to the door. "He's a good boy."

Zvi smiled. "I'm glad about that. So damned glad no one will ever know." And he left her standing in the doorway as he went out into the night and waved his driver over. He stared at the sky. No moon. A good night for crossings and operations. He hoped the frontier would be quiet. If it was not, either he or Moshe would know about it soon enough.

Twenty minutes later at Lieutenant-Colonel Ben Ezra's house he mentioned the darkness to Moshe, who said that he, too, was aware of it. The young woman whom Moshe had brought with him for the evening commented that only lovers cared if there was a moon or not, and she added with a smile, "I'm sure you two aren't lovers," and she laughed at her own bad joke. Looking about, Zvi noted the other guests: several officers with whom he had served; the deputy chief of staff, now almost forty and old for his rank; wives whom he had met at other times, as well as his host and hostess. Pausing where he was near the doorway, he tried to evaluate Judge Ben Ezra. She was, he thought, a year or two older than Avram, plump and handsome in a dignified way. Zvi wondered if she ever laughed and if the tales he had heard about her being one of the more demanding judges on the bench were true, or if the tales came from those who liked Avram and disapproved of the fact that she spent six days a week in Jerusalem. Zvi himself had met her only once. She was coming toward him now, a drink in her hand. Tamping out his cigarette in an ashtray, he smiled at her.

Malin Ben Ezra had been watching this young major ever since he had entered the apartment. After a perfunctory *shalom,* he had started talking to Lt. Colonel Gilead and that silly young singer with whom he had come. Now she did not know where Gilead was, but the major was standing alone.

Approaching him, she tried to weigh what she saw. A mirror on the wall behind his head gave the illusion that she could see him more completely. He was taller than Gilead, considerably shorter than her Avram. His square face had been burned black in the desert sun. His eyes and hair were both brown, and she thought his hair had faded. Seemingly shy in social circumstances, he was supposed to be quite bold, a dashing man in his work or in the field, but as she asked him, "Can I fetch you a drink?" she thought the word "dashing" ludicrous, because instead, she thought he was probably more driving than driven, more firm than flighty or nervous the way Gilead was, less brilliant but probably as intelligent as Avram. When his broad smile greeted her, she wondered about the stories she kept hearing in Jerusalem of Dr. Hertzela Mazon and her many lovers.

"I don't drink," he said.

"And you don't talk much?" she asked, trying to strike up a conversation.

"There may be times when you would wish that were true."

And because she wanted to be his friend for Avi's sake, she asked, "In my house you don't feel like talking?"

To her surprise, he countered, "Now, Judge, who would want to talk when they have a lovely hostess to stare at?"

Malin considered this, and somehow she knew that even though the compliment was heavy-handed, Zvi Mazon was not a flatterer the way his friend Gilead was. "My friends call me Malin."

He thought about her name as he translated it into English to see how it tasted: "A tower of strength." And with a smile, he nodded, "I'm happy for Avram."

Then, as though it were necessary, he went to the window and glanced out. The smile left his face.

Coming to his side as he leaned toward the window with his hands on the sill, she, too, stared into the darkness, wondering what held his attention. "Is something wrong, Major?"

He did not turn toward her as his eyes sought something in the dark. "Zvi," he said before he answered her question. "It's a good night for frontier crossings."

"And if they come over, you will go back and kill more of them," she said.

She was not asking a question, but he nodded his head. "There is a great deal of talk these days about the difference between reprisal and retaliation. Most of that is legal and covers different levels of justification in trying to keep someone from killing Jews." Pushing himself away from the window, he turned to her. "I was thinking that one of these days the UN is going to give the Arabs a quota of Jews. You know: come across a Jewish border and kill so many a day and no one will vote sanctions against you and no one will vote to censure you." He was becoming quietly expansive, which did not match the image of the shy man she had heard about. "Now, as for Arabs, there is a different quota there. Kill one and we'll slap your wrist, because the limit on Arabs is zero." The smile was long gone as he added, "Next thing you know, there will be a bounty on Jews," and as he said it, she saw his face cloud over. "There is already from what I've heard. These so-called suicide attackers get paid so much per Jew."

And now he was almost relaxing again. "But," and he shifted back on his own words, "being Jews, maybe we should be happy that it isn't the United Nations as a whole who are offering the bounty but only those Arab members in good standing."

Malin was bewildered by the quick shifts in his thinking and the emotion behind his last words as he placed his hands on the sill once more and averted his head as though he had to stare into the darkness. He did not match what she had heard of him, and she wondered about the bitterness, which no one had ever mentioned.

"It's all going to take time," she said. And then thinking of the assininity of her own words, she placed one hand on his shoulder. "They're trying to take up so much at the Security Council," and this, too, she knew sounded inadequate. "They've been meeting in New York for months on three issues, and we should get some kind of a decision soon." She wished she did not sound quite so much like a judge.

Zvi did not look at her, and for a moment she stared at the glass of Scotch in her hand and wondered if she should not be taking care of her other guests. Glancing back to the sitting room, she could see them in a heated discussion, and she wondered if Jews ever held any other kind of discussion. Pieces of talk drifted toward her.

"And so they've said all they've done is close the Strait of Tiran because the Strait is in Arab waters . . ."

"The Convention of Constantinople said in 1888 that Suez would always be open to the ships of all countries . . ."

". . . and the British are defending the Syrian position that we haven't the right to drain the swamps and use the water . . ."

"And with old man Hassani running around trying to build up the Arab League boycott, we aren't going to get fat."

The banker's name struck a responsive note in Zvi's memory, and he thought of Bedia Hassani, and he wondered where she was and if she still wore silk all the time and if she were standing somewhere at a cocktail party talking about the Jews.

The conversation drifted back over Malin and Zvi as they stood, the two of them with their backs to the window.

"In a thousand apartments tonight . . .," Zvi said sadly.

She nodded, deciding that she liked this young man who was her husband's friend, liked him because of his warmth and compassion and because he really was a quiet person.

"You were studying history?" she asked to make conversation as well as to learn more about him.

He nodded, staring at the deputy chief of staff leaning forward in his chair trying to make a point by jabbing his finger toward Avram.

"I thought this would be the wonderful country to study history in," Zvi explained. "There's not only so much of it, but it's all controversial. And there's nothing a Jew likes better than an argument."

The voices in the sitting room rose and Malin smiled at him.

"Yadin," she began by referring to the former chief of staff, "were you planning to study what he did? Biblical history?"

Zvi shook his head. "I was working in the history of ideas. Take an idea and trace its twisted and curving past through history. The idea of the Jew. The idea of a nation. The idea of right."

He turned toward her and she could tell that he was embarrassed. "I'm sorry," he blurted out. "I've been keeping the hostess from her guests."

"Zvi," she assured the field officer, "please keep this hostess from her guests any time." She smiled and excused herself.

He thought that she was not as formidable as he had been led to believe. And as he watched her walk toward the bedroom, he thought she was probably good for Avram. Because he was watching her when she opened the bedroom door, he was the only one who saw her bring her hand up in front of her mouth to muffle a scream. Glancing toward the sitting room, he did not think anyone else heard her. Closing the distance between them, he took the few paces toward her down the hall. When he reached the doorway, he looked beyond. She stumbled back a step and fell against him, shocked, stunned and offended. Cursing under his breath, he grasped her shoulders to steady her.

On the Ben Ezras' bed, Moshe Gilead and his young blonde lay naked.

Turning his head toward the door, more because of the look on the girl's face than because of Malin's stifled cry, Moshe glanced over his shoulder at his hostess and friend. After a moment he pushed the girl away. She brought her hands up to cover her bared breasts and then down to cover other parts of her and then burst out laughing as she knew she could not cover everything with her hands. Moshe tried and failed to smile as he told his hostess, "We thought we would use the shower, and then we couldn't find where you'd put the towels and so we decided . . ."

Before he could finish what he was saying, Zvi carefully pushed Malin away from the door, his hands still on her shoulders and her back to him as he said softly, "Go back to your guests and I'll take care of this."

Watching her for an instant, Zvi thought she might collapse, but then her head came up. Turning once more, Zvi entered the bedroom and closed the door.

For what seemed a long time he stood looking down at Moshe who had his arms about the girl, his hands on her breasts. Flatly, because he was trying to control his temper and because he did not want his words to be heard by anyone else, most of all by the Deputy Chief of Staff in the next room, Zvi said, "Get dressed and go out the back door without a word and then get lost." He might have laughed if he had not seen Malin's reaction and known how the DC/S would react to anything which might bring the army bad publicity.

Moshe kept one arm about the girl, whose grin annoyed Zvi though he could understand its attraction for Moshe. "Look," Moshe said, "I've got to be where HQ can reach me, and I told them I'd be here."

The matter-of-factness and the complete lack of self-consciousness confused Zvi. "I'll be here," he said. "Just get out. For God's sake, get out. Think of Avram and the deputy sitting out there and then get out."

The blonde winked at him and said softly from behind Moshe, who was sitting up now with his legs over the side of the bed, "Moshe, I'll bet your friend blushes."

Gilead leaned back so that his bare body came in contact with her breasts. However, he saw that Zvi was serious. "Rest easy. We'll be out of here and into another bed in ten minutes."

Zvi nodded, walked out of the room, closed the door and stood with his back against it. Down the corridor he could see Malin pouring herself a glass of Scotch, and from the glance she gave him, he wondered if she had judged him along with his friend. He shook his head, wishing somehow that he could have remained lost in the Negev instead of becoming involved with women and parties and politics. Behind him he could hear Moshe trying to get his girl friend dressed. Closing his eyes, Zvi wished that he had someone, if only for this single night. Then he made up his mind that after he saw Aaron in the morning, he was going to Ein Hasb to wait for his orders. Glancing toward the night sky beyond the window, he knew his orders would come soon.

After their guests had left and they were getting ready for bed, Malin Ben Ezra told her husband what had happened with Moshe Gilead. Sitting on the edge of his bed, taking off his socks, Avram thought about the incident. "Maybe," he finally said, as he watched her slip her dress over her head, "just maybe it's time that Moshe be relieved for a few months."

Then, as she slipped off her bra and rubbed the skin under her breasts where the elastic had left small red welts, he saw her shake her head.

"He can live with the pressure better than the other one," she suggested.

Avram's head came up as he tried to understand what she was saying. "The other one?"

Seating herself on the small bedside chair, she slowly pulled off her stockings, knowing Avram enjoyed watching her. "I think your friend Zvi Mazon is everything you said about him, but he may be the one close to the breaking point."

Watching the stockings drop into a filmy pile beside her feet, Avram wanted to say that he really was not interested in either of his friends at this moment. However, intrigued by her suggestion, he asked, "Why?"

"He's not what he appears," she said simply as she rose, stretched, and without much success tried to touch her toes. "Zvi is so caught up in his work he isn't thinking of anything else."

"And that's bad?"

She was standing with her hands on her hips now and she nodded. "Moshe's found a way to relax. Zvi hasn't."

Avram watched her while she hunted for a nightgown in the dresser, and he thought about the time she was wasting because she would not be wearing it very long. When she finally turned toward him, she asked, "Does he ever see his wife any more?"

Shrugging, Avram said, "I doubt it." And he was already flicking off the light switch.

Later that night he lay beside his sleeping wife and weighed with care what she had said about the two commando leaders.

Zvi had guessed right. It had been a night of terror. Twenty-four hours after the report reached headquarters that two young women living near a kibbutz had been killed, Avram's Piper Cub landed at Ein Hasb. Zvi had one company ready to move. They were only waiting for their orders, and Avram's presence indicated that those orders had come.

Jeeping across the burned countryside to the small barracks that served as Zvi's headquarters, the two friends talked.

"At the same time, Moshe's going to strike at Wadi Taman, Sini and Ibad. You've got . . ." Then Avram pulled out a map from the envelope he was carrying and tapped the site.

Zvi stared at it: Nahalad. He tried to recall the village from the years when it was a part of the mandate and he had traveled the area. Small. No more than five hundred. A British battalion camp had been located there. Tucked into the hills between Hebron and Jerusalem. Just east of the road.

Ten minutes later, as they sat in his room, he pored over the intelligence reports Avram had brought with him. There were Arab Legion units in the area. The Jordanian police had two military buildings at the edge of the village and one large police station to keep watch on the Palestinian refugees, whom they never quite trusted. Taking out the map which Avram had handed him earlier, Zvi marked off the distance to the closest refugee camp. Two kilometers east of Nahalad. Looking across the table at Avram, who was sipping a cup of hot coffee, the battalion commander asked, "Know if there are any UN personnel in the immediate area?"

The staff officer shook his head. "Intelligence says it's too far removed from the frontier for the Mixed Armistice Commission. Maybe UNRRWA personnel coming through and a camp administrator." He set the cup down on the rough-hewn table and leaned forward. "You should be in and out before they can make that two kilometers."

Zvi agreed. "I just don't want to surprise some refugee camp worker sleeping in the village with the wrong man." He was smiling because he knew this was not his real problem. "When?"

"Tonight. The timing is yours. Just get rid of the Legion HQ."

Zvi whistled softly as he had been thinking about this building ever since his friend had explained the mission. With a nod, he pushed the maps and papers away from him and sat back in his chair.

Looking at the overstuffed furniture from someone's sitting room and the table from someone's kitchen, Avram wondered when this headquarters had been put together. Then he asked, "The company going out, what's its composition?"

"The usual. Less than ten per cent have ever been blooded. One officer of the company was fighting in forty-eight. Like the rest of the battalion. Probably sixty per cent from Arab countries. Thirty percent European backgrounds and the rest like thee and me. One officer from a concentration camp." He thought about this for a moment. "Many of the company commanders are." And then, as if he had to justify this decision, "They understand soldiers better than most of us." However, before Avram came to the defense of the sabras, Zvi admitted, "Of course, the sabras know the terrain and the enemy better. Maybe we even make our decisions more quickly." He was smiling now as Avram relaxed. "We take chances more often."

"That's what we need: mobility of mind. In a thing like this, you have to move fast and be bold."

Wondering when Avram had heard this line from Moshe, Zvi wished that Avram would leave, so that he could set to work. "That daring is good for the quick battle. I'm not so sure it is as good for the long campaign."

Avram smiled. "You leave tonight and you return tonight." His hands, palms together, came before him on the table as he watched Zvi's face. There was a tenseness about the stocky officer's eyes he would not have noticed if Malin had not spoken of it the night before. "Are you going to have any problems?" Avram asked, and with a shake of his head, he brushed the question away. "What I mean is, is there anything you need that you don't have now?"

Zvi wiped his hand on the side of his tan shorts. When he answered, he said merely, "Luck."

Avram smiled and playfully punched Zvi on his shoulder. "I wish I were going with you."

Accepting this as the truth, Zvi smiled and walked his friend to the jeep which would take him to the airstrip. After Avram had left, Zvi wondered what kind of a report his friend would give the Chief of Staff. He started toward company headquarters to discuss the night's work with his company commander.

Darkness had spread over the land west of Nahal Hever which lies where the Jordan frontier swings east to the Dead Sea. To the south lies that strange truncated height known as Masada. Zvi had let the other vehicles go on ahead when they had passed Masada shortly after dusk. The familiar shape of Israel's national monument stood large against the night sky. Masada, the site of the Jews' odd victory-in-defeat, when Pax Romana had been held at bay for years by fewer than a thousand men and women who had taken their own lives rather than be taken to Rome as slaves. Masada.

When the company left its vehicles at Nahal Hever and started out across the broken countryside on which someone had drawn that invisible line known as a border, Zvi scanned the sky. Dark enough for them as it had been dark enough for the Arab marauders the night before. The company commander, a young French-born soldier who had spent part of his youth in a Nazi concentration camp, led his troops forward. As they passed him, Zvi counted fifty charges. Bangalore torpedoes. Twenty automatic weapons. The rest Mausers. Old, but usable. The men moved quietly over the flat and broken stones, over the hard sand and the loose. One man stumbled under his load, recovered his balance and pushed on. Taking a deep breath, Zvi puffed on his cigarette in his cupped hand for a brief moment before he spun his heel over it and followed the others. His communications sergeant and his bodyguard were walking behind him now. Paul Marouix, the company commander, was putting out his point men.

Zvi watched several men spread wide of the column and five fall back to protect the rear. Now the captain was trotting to the van. Smiling, Zvi approved of what he saw. They were moving quickly, and after a few minutes he realized the men would be too tired to withdraw later if they continued this pace. Cursing softly, he ran to catch up with Marouix. Without comment, Zvi set the new pace.

Hours later they approached the UNRRWA camp and started to swing wide of it. Marouix was in the lead now, and Zvi had fallen back to give the youth his head. The distance between them grew longer. Zvi checked the time, waved to his communications sergeant to rest and nodded for the soldier armed with the Belgian submachine gun to take his place as watch.

Kneeling on a knoll from which he could barely make out the road that led from Jerusalem south, he wondered how Moshe was doing and if they had made the best decision when he had agreed to strike at the same time. Picking up a handful of dirt, he felt the warmth of it in his palm before he let it sift back through his fingers. The Arab Legion would be stirred up the instant both units struck. Could they have better been kept off balance if he and Moshe had struck seriatim? For the moment he was committed.

Then he heard the firing. It was louder than he had expected. He waited. His men were not firing. Then they were. Then he heard a machine gun. Then the exchange became too heavy for him to separate the weapons. He held his breath and waited for the sound of the explosions which would tell him that the charges were going off. He listened to the exchange of gunfire before he glanced at his watch.

It was all happening too soon. There were not going to be any explosions, because the company had never reached its target. For an instant he was tempted to run forward to learn what had happened. Then he changed his mind and shouted for the communications sergeant. Grabbing the radio, he called Marouix. Nothing. No contact. The firing seemed closer now. He estimated half a mile. Shaking his head in disgust with himself at being a fool because he had no way of really knowing how sound traveled in these particular hills, he called for headquarters. Nothing. The firefight sounded closer. Nothing on the radio. Then he thought he heard Moshe's voice. However, it could have been anyone's.

Slamming the field set into the sergeant's hands, Zvi came to his feet and, standing in one place, he pivoted all the way around. He made up his mind how he was going to take them out. Remembering Avram's warning: you leave tonight and you return tonight, he knew his friend had been right. He could not be caught in Arab territory.

Wishing now that he had led the company in, he recalled the very specific orders given him months before: that unless two companies went into action the battalion commander would not. Cursing himself for having obeyed orders, he felt Avram's words pounding in his head – *mobility of mind*. Waving for the two men with him to follow, he moved forward to join his men. They had to be coming this way. The firefight sounded even closer. Grabbing the soldier with him, Zvi shoved him toward a rock. "Stay there and lay down a cross fire," he ordered. And all the while he hoped Marouix would come through the way he had gone out. Trotting ahead, Zvi met the first of his platoons stumbling toward him. When the lieutenant leading it tried to pass, Zvi grabbed the man, spun him about and ordered, "Hold here with all you have and let the others pass through before you start to fire."

Stunned, the young officer looked at him and nodded. Then he tried to sort his platoon out and station the men in a semi-circle. Satisfied with what he saw, Zvi continued on. The rest of the company was coming toward him now. There were Arab troops pressing them from behind. Marouix was holding a half-dozen men at the rear of the column where they were laying down fire to cover the retreat.

Furious, Zvi shouted to the two platoons heading his way, "Turn around. Damn it, turn." Forced by his stocky figure blocking their path, the first men to reach him fell prone, facing the enemy. Marouix was falling back now and Zvi grabbed him from behind. "Move back there again and take out that machine gun."

The youth, shaken by his first firefight, nodded and tried to turn back the men with him. Twice they started forward and twice the Arab machine-gunners laid down a heavy field of fire. Angry, Zvi jerked a submachine gun from one of the soldiers lying nearby and started by himself for the enemy gun. From the sound he could tell there was only one. Scattered rifle fire from the Arabs as he spun behind a large rock and started firing at the machine gun. Arab bullets splattered on the rock, but Zvi was already gone up another to the left of the Arab position. Now he was reaching into his pocket for a grenade. Without bothering to count, he held it as long as he thought he could before he tossed it. Hurling himself flat, he heard the grenade explode as he bellied into the dirt. Now his men were returning the Arab fire, and then there was no Arab fire.

Taking a deep breath, Zvi trotted back to where the company lay scattered. "Let's go!" he shouted and started due east. Somewhere he could hear trucks, but he was not going near any roads. He was not even heading back toward Nahal Hever. Instead, he was leading his command to the oasis at 'En Gedi on the Israeli side of the border. Forming his men up as they passed him, he slapped one on the shoulder, smiled at another, spoke softly of cold water to another and asked still another if he could run as fast as his friends. The company commander tugged at Zvi's sleeve, "It's shorter if we go west."

"And right through the place where you stirred them up and where Moshe's operating." Almost losing his temper, he snapped, "Move!"

Then he went in search of his own communications sergeant and the soldier he had set out as a possible protection. Gathering the two in, he followed the retreating command.

One man stumbled and fell and Zvi saw that he was wounded. Calling for two men to help, he started the three back on the route east before he sent his guard forward to bring Marouix to him. The men flowed on as the young captain returned to join Zvi.

"Did you leave any men back there?" Zvi demanded.

The captain shook his head. "I don't know."

It took Zvi a moment to realize what he had heard. Then he half closed his eyes while he thought about the possibility of getting any dead or wounded out now that the hills were alive with Legionnaires. Nodding slowly, he ordered, "Go on ahead. Stop your men and get a count." He paused before he added, "I'll wait for you here."

Five minutes later Marouix returned. "One's missing. Five are wounded."

"And the missing man?" Zvi demanded.

"Someone says they saw him take a bullet in the head."

Knowing there was little he could do now, Zvi led his men on and east through the desert night. The sky remained dark and kind. They met no one as they passed through the scarred wasteland west of the Dead Sea. When they finally reached the roll of chunky hills that edged the sea itself, they moved south to 'En Gedi, where Zvi had already ordered the vehicles by radio an hour before.

Without disturbing the people of the kibbutz, he turned his wounded over to the battalion medical officer, whom he had left earlier with the vehicles and started directly across country toward Ein Hasb.

When they reached the road that led west toward Beersheba, Zvi halted the column and asked the medical officer which way he wanted to go. The middle-aged physician looked into the truck carrying his patients and said, "The hospital."

Waving the man on west, Zvi continued south with his command. The small column spilled into its base camp shortly after dawn. Zvi had given neither his drivers nor the company much rest, and he himself was as tired as they. However, he was also angry. Leaping out of his jeep, he strode forward to meet Avram and the tall, sunburned man who stood beside him. Zvi was aware he was going to have problems with both the Director of the General Staff Office and the Chief of Operations. About two years Zvi's junior, the Chief of Operations was known for his own quick temper, which was even worse when the icy side of his naturally cold personality was revealed. Not bothering to greet Zvi, Colonel Cohen snapped, "Let's get to your headquarters."

Nodding, Zvi led the way to the small room which served him as an office. There were already half a dozen mugs of coffee on the table. Pulling up his chair, Zvi waved the other two to the chairs opposite before he bellowed to his sergeant, "Get Captain Marouix in here."

The other two said nothing while Zvi emptied one of the mugs and then took time to light a cigarette. Finally, he looked up at the Operations Chief. "Did Moshe make it?"

"All three targets, though it wasn't made easy for him."

The implied criticism was obvious.

Zvi accepted this for the moment and waited to hear what Avram might say, as he spoke for the chief of staff, who must have expressed an opinion. However, his friend remained silent.

"Do you know what went wrong?" Colonel Cohen was asking.

Though he didn't intend it to be a joke, Zvi half smiled. "Everything. The worst part of it is——"

"You left a man," Avram cut in. Rising from his chair, his broad shoulders rolled forward as though he were going to charge, the staff officer set his clenched fist on the table as he bent down so that his eyes met Zvi's. "The worst part of it is that you left a man. He wore identification tags. They know his name. The Mixed Armistice Commission has already seen the body and they are going to scream." He came upright and seemed to be staring over Zvi's head when he added, "I can hear the UN rocking with that name for the next few years."

"And you haven't made an investigation yet?" Cohen said. He was not asking a question but, rather, was making an accusation.

Zvi snapped, "That's right. I've sent my wounded to a hospital and I'm going to make sure my men are getting some breakfast and then some rest." Without asking permission, he stalked out of the office. Standing in the warm morning sun, he watched Paul Marouix approaching.

"The men are eating?"

The young French-Israeli nodded. "I've told the platoon leaders to stand by in case you want to talk to them."

"And the others?"

"They'll probably sleep. They are tired." He thought a moment and Zvi knew it was not the troops the youth was thinking of when he added, "Damned tired."

Grabbing the man by the shoulders, Zvi half choked out his words, "Everything. I'm going to want to hear everything." Then he dropped his hands to his side and stood back. "Have you had some coffee?"

The captain nodded, but Zvi was already walking back into the headquarters.

Avram was seated now, his feet on an empty chair, his head back as though he could see better that way. Colonel Cohen sat rigidly upright, his long arms dangling at his side. Zvi wanted to tell the younger man to relax, but decided that would be unwise at the moment. Swinging his own chair about so that the seat faced him, he put one foot on it and introduced Captain Marouix to the others.

No one offered the captain a chair.

"You lead this fiasco?" Cohen asked the youth.

"No!" Zvi interrupted. "I did. And I'm going to ask my company officers the questions. If you want to have an investigation, fine. Order it and we'll have one. However, only after I've talked to my officers." As his temper after the night of tension spilled over, Avram's hand came up to placate him.

"Easy, Zvi. Eli was only . . ."

"Getting in to my business." Then, with great effort to control himself, Zvi offered, "You can relieve me or you can let me handle this my way."

Slowly, Elihu Cohen's hand came up while he scratched at his ear. "The battalion is yours, Zvi."

Turning so that he could see the young captain better, Zvi waved him to a place on the overstuffed chair near his own. "Tell me exactly what happened after you went forward from the position where we parted." As he spoke, Zvi drew a folded map from his pocket and spread it on the table, pointing to the place he had spoken of so that the staff officers could follow the discussion.

Marouix took a deep breath before he began. "We walked down the trail you and I had selected earlier," and Zvi's hand was tracing it for the others. "About five hundred yards from the UN camp we saw an Arab."

He was silent for a moment, ordering his recollections. "I think he was a shepherd." Before anyone could ask him why, he added, "Just a hunch. Could have been anything."

"What was he doing?"

A shrug. "I don't know. As far as I could tell, he was sitting on a rock. Suddenly he was there and we were there."

The others nodded.

"Lieutenant Levin went forward and grabbed him and we tried to figure out what to do with him, and while we were talking, he just up and ran. Ten paces in that darkness and he was lost."

Picking up one of the mugs of coffee, Zvi handed it to the captain, who shook his head. "We . . . no, I . . . decided to go on. We had a target. As we approached the village, the whole thing just sort of gave way and there were Arabs running and shouting and shooting. Then by the time we took cover I heard some trucks and then a light machine gun from somewhere." He thought about this for a moment and shook his head. "I think the light machine gun came into play after we had exchanged shots for a few minutes." Nodding approval of his own recollections, he said, "Right after the trucks came."

"And the man you left behind?"

The captain shook his head. "I knew someone had been hit, but they were coming at us, and I just fell back because we couldn't hold that ground against a battalion, not with our firepower and no defensive position." Then, almost defiantly, "We fell back until we made contact with you and then you took over." He was looking directly at his commander.

Zvi nodded. For a long time no one said anything. Then the youth said, "I'm sorry, Zvi."

"You're what?" And Zvi half rose from his chair.

"I'm sorry."

In a very soft voice, Avram asked, "Just what are you sorry about?"

Looking at the staff officer, whom he recognized from his pictures, the young man considered the question. "It's my men who are wounded and dead."

Zvi leaned forward and picked up a mug of coffee. Everyone was staring at him now, waiting to hear what he was going to say. Only after he had finished the coffee did he look first at the operations chief, then at Avram and finally at the young company commander.

"After you have had some sleep, I want a detailed written report on what happened." Almost cynically he explained, "Headquarters will want this one on the record. And after you've done that, pack your gear and catch the first ride back to Tel Aviv. You'll be returned to your unit."

Shaken at his dismissal, Marouix reacted sharply, "What the . . ." His voice trailed off. He fell silent for a moment and then began once more. "I'd like to stay, Zvi. I know I can do better."

Zvi shook his head sadly and there was a distant quality in his voice as he said, "You have been relieved. I don't owe you or anyone the opportunity to serve in this unit. You volunteered. You've been unvolunteered, *now*." He paused and then added, "If you've got to feel sorry about something, it should be that your mission was not completed."

Startled, Marouix started to object once more, but he saw the others were no longer looking at him and he left.

When Zvi was alone with the two staff officers, he turned on them. "It's your own damned fault and not that boy's. Get that clear."

"Easy, Zvi," Avram advised again.

"No, I'm destroying his pride and his career because he did not kill that Arab. One thrust of a knife through the guts. However, he's young and he's never been blooded before."

A dubious and almost resigned expression came over Cohen's hawklike face as he seemed to rock back and forth in his chair. "I'm sure the chief of staff will be curious. Just how is it our fault?"

"A commander commands. I should have gone forward with them the first time. I should have made the decision regarding that sentry." His voice dropped as he added, "Let's assume it was a sentry. We have to assume that, unless he was contemplating a whore in heat in the middle of no place in the middle of the night." His hand came up as though to brush the irrelevant aside. "It comes down to headquarters telling me how I should fight. That's something I have to decide. If one man goes in or five hundred, where I stand is my business." And then, as if he had to repeat it, "A commander commands." The detached expression came over his face again as he looked directly at Avram. "The spirit of the bandits of Haganah. Can you imagine the chief of staff or Yigal or even you or me standing back in forty-eight and forty-nine? I can't. And yet my orders were that company commanders command companies. That's true only to the point where their immediate superior is responsible for them. I'd have let him move until he made his error, and then I would have corrected it. I would have seen that my wounded and dead were with me."

Avram glanced at the operations officer, who nodded as though he understood what was expected of him. "You want headquarters to change its order?" Cohen asked.

Zvi shrugged. "I don't give a damn about that order any longer. I'll assume my responsibilities in my way and as I see them until I am relieved." He was not making a threat, and the other two understood that. "It's simple. Either I command my battalion or I don't."

The Colonel was tugging at his ear again, and as Avram watched, he wondered what his own nervous gesture was.

"Tell me, Zvi," and Cohen's tone was friendly and almost personal, "Tell me, how do you grow into a brigade and maybe, sometime, if we have to create them, grow into a division. Tell me how you do that and lead every company."

A trace of a smile crossed Zvi's face as he had been expecting the question. "I could say I'd worry that out then. I could say I wouldn't want a larger command, but that wouldn't be true. What I think is that by the time this kind of unit is ready to be a brigade it will have men who've seen battle, who know how to react, who don't fear killing what appear to be innocents or risk a whole company. When I've men who I know can take over smaller units, I'll give them their head the way I'm asking for mine. Until then, I'm the battalion commander here."

"Tell me, Zvi, what would you have done last night if you had had three objectives as Moshe did?"

"Taken my risks, made my judgments — successes along with failures. And if there were too many failures, you wouldn't have to be sitting there wondering if you should do to me what I just did to that captain."

It was Avram who laughed. And as he did, Cohen smiled. "We're going back and we'll talk to the chief. He may want to see you himself. Stand by for that." And the staff officers both came to their feet.

Zvi smiled because he knew very well that he was going to have a session at Hakiryah, and it would be very soon.

He won his argument at headquarters the next day; and when he left there in the late afternoon he went to visit the widow of the dead soldier. The call was brief. There was little he could say except that he had known the young soldier well, had admired him, and that the man had died bravely in a good cause. And he left feeling the inadequacy of his words.

Jeeping across town, he stopped at Ruth's apartment. He wanted to see Aaron even though the boy would already be asleep. The boy was the roots Havah had given him.

However, when he arrived at the apartment, Aaron was not asleep. He was ill. Ruth's sister led Zvi directly to the bedroom which Aaron shared with Ruth's daughter, Hannah. The girl sat in the bed with her blanket wrapped around her and watched her mother bathe Aaron's head.

Looking up, Ruth said, "Three days and none of the mighty doctors can tell me what it is."

Zvi jerked off his beret and knelt down. Aaron was awake, but the expression on his face was remote, and though he tried to smile when he saw his father, he failed.

"I hurt," the child whimpered.

Worried, Zvi looked up at Ruth; at the same time enfolding one of the boy's hands in his own. "Three days and no help from the doctors?"

The old cotton wrap Ruth wore hung half open as she kept wiping the perspiration off Aaron's face. "I called two of the yekke doctors who live on the block, and they both said it would pass. Then I called a woman who studied medicine in Switzerland," and the awe in her voice was as obvious as the contempt for the two Germans had been. "She said she did not know what it was, but she would be back tomorrow to see him again."

Listening to Aaron, Zvi could tell the boy was delirious as he heard him say over and over, "My father's gone away and he is, too, going to come back. He is, too, going to come back."

"Is it any worse than it was?" Zvi asked.

Ruth thought about this. "His temperature went higher half an hour ago."

Zvi rose and looked down at the boy. "I could take him to a hospital," he said, thinking aloud.

It was Ruth's sister who shook her head. "It's night and it's cold."

Zvi agreed. Bending down, he tousled his son's dark hair. "Where's the phone?" and with Ruth's baleful look, he understood there was none. Tousling the boy's damp hair once more, he swung about and left the apartment. Downstairs in the street, he waved his driver to the curb. Taking over the wheel, he raced through the already traffic-free city to Fishel's, hoping that Fishel would know where Zella was staying.

"Turn it around," he snapped to the driver as he jumped out and started toward the building. Fishel's was the only name on the mailboxes that meant anything to him. Taking the stairs two at a time, he climbed to the third floor, where he banged on his friend's door. A woman answered. The light from the room silhouetted her head, and all that he could see was a brightly colored dress and someone almost as tall as himself asking belligerently, "What do you want?"

The voice was familiar. Thinking that some place he must have met this woman, he barked, "Fishel!"

The woman had stepped back from the door as though she were afraid of him, and he asked her, "Where can I find Dr. Mazon?"

For an instant he thought she smiled, but the light was such he could not be sure. "I'm Major Mazon, " he explained, as though he had to tell her that he had a right to ask. Then Fishel appeared.

"Where's Zella?" Zvi snapped.

"Second floor. Right below us," and Fishel came out into the hall as Zvi strode away. "Can I help?"

"It's Aaron," Zvi called back over his shoulder. "He's ill."

Fishel limped after him, and as they reached the second floor, he explained, "She always stays at my old place when she's in town."

Arriving at the suite below the violinist's, Zvi glanced back at his friend, reached out and affectionately clasped his arm. "I'd heard that months ago." Then he knocked on the door with his fist.

"Are you sure you should?" Fishel asked quietly.

Puzzled, Zvi snapped, "She's his mother." He banged on the door again. After a moment he could see a light under it, and he heard someone inside. Once more he raised his hand and pounded with the heel of his fist.

"Who is it?" and he recognized his wife's voice.

"Zvi. Open up, goddamn it."

Through the door, he could hear her laugh, "Oh, for heaven's sake, get lost."

His fist came up and he was pounding again.

"It's Aaron," he shouted. "The boy's ill."

Other doors on the corridor were opening up now as neighbors came out to see what was going on. Fishel turned back to reassure them while Zvi continued to pound on the door.

It took a moment for Zella to respond, but when she said, "I'll be right with you," Zvi slacked off his pounding and slowly turned to see Fishel talking to the neighbors. At least half a dozen were watching him now. Hearing the door being unlocked, Zvi whirled toward it. Zella stood in the open doorway, tying the belt of a green silk negligee. Sucking his breath in at the sight of his own wife, and surprised at his reaction, Zvi stepped through the doorway and into the sitting room.

"You coming?" he snapped at Zella.

"Have you had a doctor?" She was trying to be professional.

"Three," he growled.

She stepped back and stared at him as though she needed the perspective. He remained handsome in spite of his wind-hammered face and in spite of the fact that he seemed to have lost fifteen pounds since she had last seen him. "What do they say?"

"We can talk about it on the way," he said so flatly that she knew he was losing his temper.

For a long moment she stood quietly watching him, and then he heard someone at the door to the bedroom. Whirling about, Zvi saw a tall, middle-aged stranger standing there in bare feet, zipping up his trousers.

"Look, soldier," the stranger said in a foreign accent, "find yourself another doctor." And as a grin spread over the man's face, Zvi realized the man was actually charming. "Dr. Mazon is busy and this city is full of all kinds of doctors."

Zvi pinned the man with a stare before he turned back to his wife. "Are you going to get a dress on and come or am I going to have to take you the way you are?" He saw that she was not going to argue with him. Aware that he had been shouting, he dropped his voice. "It's Aaron."

Before she could reply, the stranger took Zvi's arm. "Be a good fellow and go on now."

Frightened by what she knew was coming, Zella started to step between the two men, but she was too late. Zvi reached out, grabbed the tall stranger by the back of the head with both hands, forcing him forward and down. In the same movement, Zvi brought his knee up sharply in the man's face. As the stranger's head bounced back from the knee blow, Zvi's hands rode with it; and then a second time and more easily now, he repeated the attack. This time, he brought his hands away from behind the stranger's head and watched the man fall back across a chair. It appeared for a moment as if the chair would hold him. It did not, and he slipped unconscious to the floor.

Swinging once more toward his wife, Zvi called, "I'm waiting."

A cynical smile crossed her face, "Defending my honor or your own?" And she walked into the bedroom.

Kneeling beside the stranger to see how badly he had injured the man, Zvi heard someone behind him, and looking back saw Fishel.

"You'd better get this fool a doctor." Rising, he glanced toward the bedroom. "My guess is he has already had one tonight."

"I'm sorry," Fishel said.

"Don't be," Zvi assured him. "We'll all survive it." Then he fell silent while he waited for Zella. A few minutes later she emerged from the bedroom dressed and carrying a small bag. The man on the floor was rolling his head from side to side.

While Zella took the time to open her bag to check what she had with her, Zvi knelt once more beside the stranger. "I don't know where you are from, but tell your friends that Israeli men have natural reactions when they find strangers crawling into their wives' beds."

Raising the man's head off the floor, he saw that the nose, pushed to one side of the handsome face, was shattered. Blood was oozing in an ugly pattern down the man's cheeks. "Just say her husband came home early."

Behind him he heard Fishel gasp and Zella chuckle. Then he rose, and taking her arm, jerked her into the hall and down the stairs to the waiting jeep.

They had driven several blocks before Zella turned to look at him. His face was set, his eyes focused on the road before him, his broad hands gripped the wheel as though it might escape.

"It was anyone's guess just when you would take the other night out on someone," she said softly.

Zvi tried not to react. She obviously knew of his failure. It was not completely surprising because most of her friends were his own.

Shifting the subject, he said, "The boy's had a high fever for three days. It's been rising again this past few hours."

"And the other doctors?" Zella asked.

"They all said wait." He was swinging wide around a traffic jam and driving down the wrong side of the street.

Zella noticed this and she could see the sergeant in the back seat lean forward to grab hold of the jeep's side. She had not seen Zvi this way since they had been together in the Quarter. He was tense, alive and almost like an animal ready to spring. In fact, she admitted to herself, he had already sprung in the apartment. She wondered if she could ever love him again, and then being completely honest, she wondered if she ever had. Zvi Mazon had become a kind of hero in the last days of the War of Independence. After that he had drifted, done garrison duty, disappeared for months into the east, and when he returned, there had been Aaron. Now she was thinking of Aaron. She often did. Three times married and many times bedded, she had never had a child. Either she was lucky or she was not, and ever since Aaron had been brought to her apartment that night by the American pilot, she had not been able to make up her mind. At this moment she wished she were back in her apartment with her husband and son. The jeep swerved around a corner and approached the Mediterranean. Zella knew the neighborhood. There were better, but she was not a snob. Nor, she told herself, as she watched Zvi driving through traffic, was she sentimental. There were not many men in Tel Aviv who could make her as angry as her husband. And her thoughts drifted to Moshe. Another hero. She wished she were done with heroes.

Moshe had called her earlier in the day and had asked if she was all right. He had learned her address from Fishel, and as long as he was going to be seeing Fishel . . . She had told him then she was busy.

Watching Zvi's set face and the crow's-feet about his eyes, she wondered what would have happened if it had been Moshe whom Zvi had found her with, and who would be lying on the floor, and the idea made her laugh.

Glancing at her, Zvi shook his head. He did not understand this woman any more than he understood any other. Maybe Moshe had the right idea. And then he braked the jeep in front of Ruth's.

In the small apartment, Ruth gave way to Zella, who lifted Aaron in her arms and held him as she listened to his fevered talk. First he was asking for his father and then he was asking for his mother and he kept assuring everyone that both of them would come home to him. When she put him down on the bed again, Zella sent the others out of the room so that she could be alone with the boy.

From where she sat on the sofa, Ruth watched Zvi pace the floor, lighting one cigarette off another. Waiting for Zella to emerge from the bedroom with some prognosis, Ruth's thoughts drifted back to their days together in the war before Haganah had become the army. Most of all she recalled the months in the Old City and the last days in the Quarter when her life had been so closely entwined with the lives of the very few who had survived. And then suddenly it had been over, and she had gone to Tel Aviv to look for a job and instead had met her husband. Shmuel. He had been a good man. He had been gentle. He had been a bit of a fool. But as she watched Zvi and thought of Zella in the next room, she wondered who was not a bit of a fool. Shmuel had brought his own death with him from the concentration camp, or if he had not brought it, it came seeking him less than a year after they were married. And after his death, she had decided to remain in Tel Aviv, had borrowed the money to open the dress shop and had earned the money for this apartment. As the months passed into years, she wondered if her life was always going to be made up of, "Yes, ma'am, we will have it ready for you soon," and long nights of watching over two children. Not given to complaining, Ruth knew she was turning into something she herself did not like: a dour woman. Watching Zvi stub out a cigarette and light another, she wondered if anything was going to change for her, and why she had never thought of Zvi Mazon for herself, and why he had never thought of her.

The bedroom door opened and Zella came into the room, a stethoscope about her neck, the black tube hanging down the front of her white dress and resting between her breasts, her head high. "He's going to be all right," she said. Turning to Ruth, "I don't know what the others have given him, and rather than duplicate something, I put him to sleep. But he'll be all right." She stood where she was and thought for a moment. "I'll be by in the morning." And then, as though this were not enough, she asked Zvi, "Can you be here in the morning?"

Zvi tried to remember what commitments he had made and decided none was important. "If you think I should."

Zella nodded. "On top of everything else, he's frightened." She weighed this before she explained, "He's been moved around just too much for his own good."

Her head fell back and she seemed to be staring at the ceiling while she thought. "Eight. He should be eight now. Maybe seven." She was looking at Ruth because she believed the other woman would understand her better. "He's been in too many homes with too many parents." Then, as though it had all been her own fault, she said, "I'm sorry." Smiling at Ruth's sister, whom she did not know, she asked, "Would you fetch my bag?"

While they were waiting for the girl to bring her the bag, Zella walked up to Zvi, opened his shirt pocket, took out a cigarette and waited for him to light it before she turned once more to Ruth. "The fever isn't going to last much past tomorrow. I wouldn't feed him anything until it comes down." She thought a moment, "If you can get him to take some water, that would be good."

Zvi, who had been watching his wife's professional manner, wanted to laugh at the difference between the woman he now saw and the one he had seen earlier in the evening with the silk negligee drawn about her. "What's wrong with the boy?" he finally asked.

Swinging toward him as though she had forgotten he was in the room, Zella asked, "You want a name for it?"

He nodded, angry that she would think he did not care.

Sighing, she accepted her bag from the young girl, who said, "He's sleeping." Nodding to indicate she had heard, Zella stared at her husband. "Call it Benjamin." Then she tried to smile at Ruth, "In the morning." She was standing at the door when she looked back at Zvi. "You are taking me home, aren't you?"

With great effort he controlled his temper, nodded and then smiled at Ruth. "See you in the morning." He opened the door for his wife and followed her into the night. Helping his wife into the jeep, Zvi turned to the driver. "Your girl friend lives in town, doesn't she?"

The driver nodded.

"Enjoy yourself," Zvi offered. "I'll see you here tomorrow at nine." Then he took the keys and, seating himself next to Zella, drove off.

The night was dark, and staring into it, Zvi wondered if there would be crossings. Shrugging inwardly because he knew there was nothing he could do about that problem at this moment, he relaxed.

Zella set the medical bag down beside her heel and turned so that she could see her husband better. For the first several blocks neither of them said anything, and then she asked, "It's a bit small for the five of you in that apartment, isn't it?"

Very carefully, Zvi stubbed the brake and swerved toward the curb. Bringing the jeep to a stop, he turned in his seat and stared at her. He wished she were not so pretty and that he were not so aware of the way her body, twisted on the seat, thrust her breasts toward him. However, with effort, he kept his eyes locked with hers, "You little *kurveh*. For a hundred pounds a month she takes care of my son for me, which is more than my wife is capable of doing." His head tilted to one side as he continued to stare at her, "And other than that, there's nothing between us except some memories of the times when we were both free and young."

Zella smiled wryly at his sentiment. "What's wrong with her?"

It took Zvi a moment to cope with the question, and when he had he, too smiled. "I wouldn't know." Then he was serious, "What's wrong with you?"

Shifting in her seat so that she stared through the windshield, she said, "Will you drive me home now?"

As it had a thousand times, Zvi's hand went out and his forefinger touched her forehead and he slowly traced the lines of her face, skidding down the bridge of her nose and up the tip. It was a gesture of affection which he had never thought he would profess again. However, when she stiffened at his touch, his hand fell away and he started the jeep slowly down the street. Neither of them spoke until he drew up in front of Fishel's apartment.

Zvi stepped out and helped her down. For a moment they stood together, and then to his surprise, she asked, "Aren't you coming up?" A wry but gentle smile crossed her face. "After all, we're married."

Laughing bitterly, Zvi agreed. "After all."

Later, as they lay in bed together, he smoking and staring at the ceiling and she resting her head on his extended forearm, he asked, "When did it start happening? You, me?"

For a long time she did not answer and he thought she might not have understood his question. He finally said, "In forty-nine when it was done, and people kept saying we'd have peace for a while. I thought the only thing that mattered was you and me. And yet when I got home from Yemen, nothing seemed to fit together any longer."

Zella turned onto her side so that she could see his profile. The heavy jaw seemed to dominate it. She watched as he puffed the cigarette in the darkness. After a time she reached out and scratched that place on his stomach he was always reaching for. "It never had anything to do with you." She fell silent for a moment before she explained, "I got bored. Three husbands in four years.

"I talked it all over with a friend of mine, a psychiatrist." Then, as though she had to somehow strike at Zvi, "We spent almost a week in bed together, talking it over and over and over. He convinced me it had nothing to do with you.

"The world is full of Zvi Mazons. Every other person I meet is a man. Maybe they are not all heroes. Maybe they aren't all so completely alive, but they satisfy. Believe me, they do."

He felt her kissing his cheek and she said, "I'm leaving for Eilat as soon as Aaron's well. I've taken a job there. It isn't much of a place, but I'm going. Make a point of seeing as much of the boy as you can. You're important to him."

And before Zvi could answer, she rolled over, presenting him her back. Turning so that he could see her, he smiled. Two nights before there had been the sand and the cold and the darkness and the Arabs chasing him. Sucking deeply on the last of his cigarette, he thought for a moment that he understood what drove Moshe.

Zella, her eyes closed, kept thinking of Zvi's face as she had seen it in the jeep; the tense eyes darting, the rigid hands on the steering wheel. She hoped she had done him some good, and she wondered why she cared, and because she wondered, she knew she did.

The next morning they had breakfast and drove over to see Aaron together. As she had predicted, he was much improved.

Just before noon Zvi contacted headquarters: he was ordered back to Ein Hasb. Uncertain if he should request an extension of time, he asked Zella and Ruth what they thought.

Both women reassured him there was nothing he could do for his son, and when Zella agreed not to leave for Eilat until she was satisfied the boy was well, Zvi went into the bedroom to say goodbye. Aaron, conscious now, greeted his father with a proud smile. "I told them you would be back."

Dropping to his knees beside the bed, Zvi put his palm on the boy's warm cheek, at the same time realizing how small his son actually was. "I'm going away for a few days, but remember, that no matter what happens, I will always be back. And as soon as you get well, you just tell your Aunt Ruth you want to talk to me, and she will take you over to headquarters, and they will put you on the radio and we will talk as long as you want."

"On the radio?" Aaron was awed at the thought.

Zvi nodded. "But first you have to get well." Then he kissed the boy's cheek, patted it once more and told him, "I'll see you in a couple of weeks." Glancing about the room, Zvi saw the rumpled bed where Ruth's daughter Hannah had slept the night before, and he wondered what he would do when the two outgrew this arrangement. Squeezing his son's hand, Zvi said again, "We'll talk on the radio."

Zvi returned to the living room where the two women were waiting for him. Explaining to Ruth what he had promised the boy, he turned to Zella, "You know where I'll be if you have to contact me?"

She nodded, wondering if he was going to kiss her goodbye. Instead, he smiled at both women and left without another word.

The next time Zvi returned to Tel Aviv, Zella was living in Eilat. However, because he was busy, he got to Tel Aviv only three times in the months that followed.

The battalion which had failed on its first mission was worked over by headquarters until the chief of staff thought it was ready for another try at operations.

TIRAT YEHUDA

The old man had not been in the field for three days because the infection in his feet made walking difficult. And now as he stood in the middle of his small farm, he was glad he had come in spite of the pain in his feet. And somehow as he felt the sun strike his leathered face, he recalled the times when both the pain and the sky had somehow become confused in his brain. As a boy, he had learned to trust the sky. It brought the sun and the rain. And then there had come the time when the sky and terror and Stukas all blended into one. Looking up, he smiled. There was no barbed wire between himself and the sun. There were no Stukas. Taking a deep breath, he was about to make a *berakhah* when the lobbed hand grenade exploded. In that brief instant when he lost both his infected leg and his life, he knew that only the sky was neutral.

RAM ON

It was night and the young woman sat in the grass waiting for her husband to come home, as she had on other nights since he had met the girl from Poland the year before. At first she had thought he would lose interest or the girl would lose interest. However, a year had passed since he had first gone out, saying, "There are things I must do," and she had waited. Her friends told her she was a fool; and, waiting now, she knew she was a fool. But there were the little memories and the big ones. She was thinking of the big ones when she saw him walking down the road, his shoes in hand. And she smiled because she knew his feet hurt as they always did on a long walk. The little memories. She was about to walk back into the house, but she never had the chance. The first Arab charges exploded on the road and then she heard the hand grenades burst along with the fire of hand guns. And she saw her husband fall, his shoes slipping out of his hands as though there were something else he had to reach for as he crumpled. And running toward him, she felt the three steel slugs rip through her side and then she reached him and knew he was dead and that there would be no more memories of him to add to those she already possessed.

NE'OT HA KIKAR

It was dinner time and the men and women had come in from the fields. The sky was still bright to the west. The wind was chill, as a wind is chill in October when the season has not yet made up its mind if it is going to lean toward winter or linger to recall the summer. Thirty families were gathering to eat. The children were scattered around the open field which lay to the east of the dining hall. One of the mothers sat on a step and watched them play. Her boy was the tallest, her girl the fairest. She felt sorry for the other mothers whose children were only children. She stretched her legs and wished

290

she were not so weary. Two women drifted out of the dining room and sat looking at their children who for them were the tallest and the fairest in the group. The children were playing tag now, running about the field, shrieking each other's names as though there was a certain magic in names. *Tuvia. Tuvia. Tuvia. Gabriella. Gabriella. Gabriella.* And both of them ran toward their mother, who, as they approached, forgot that her legs were weary, and as the tallest boy and the fairest girl came into her arms, the last thing she could remember were the sudden bursts of Arab gunfire tearing through the tallest boy and the fairest girl and then her breast as she drew them to her. And somewhere in the background, bouncing against the torn fragments of her brain, she heard, *Tuvia, Tuvia, Tuvia,* mingled with *Gabriella, Gabriella, Gabriella.*

Less than twenty-four hours after the last killing, the Director to the General Staff walked out of the Prime Minister's office where he had been briefed by the Chief of Staff and the Prime Minister. Their orders were simple enough. Now all he had to do was carry them south. An hour later his Piper Cub landed at Ein Hasb where he locked up with Zvi Mazon. Less than half an hour after that, he sat back on the uncomfortable couch in battalion headquarters and waited while the major went out to discuss the night's operations with his company commanders.

Three hours before dusk, while the first two companies moved north toward the Jerusalem area, Zvi bade Avram goodbye and agreed that he would contact headquarters at Hakiryah as soon as he completed his mission. They drove together as far as the landing strip, where Avram boarded his small plane and returned to the north. While the Piper circled the field, he made out the column of vehicles moving out of Ein Hasb. Closing his eyes, he wondered how long it would be before they knew if Zvi had done the job right this time. And then he kept remembering his wife's arguments that there was no way to do it right and his own arguments that something had to be done to keep the Arabs on their side of the border.

The Mixed Armistice Commission talked in behalf of the United Nations, and in New York the United Nations talked in their own behalf and all the while the Arabs kept crossing the border from Jordan to the east and Gaza to the west. How long can a man listen to strangers talk while his own are dying? Avram's busy thoughts mingled with the sound of the small plane. The face of the Prime Minister was before him now, and he could hear him saying in that deep voice which was so familiar, "There are places I would rather be and things I would rather be doing, but we have to take action now. We have to raise the cost of killing a single Jew so high they will find it does not pay."

Seated in the lead jeep of his company, Zvi Mazon stared at the cactus lining the road. By the time he returned, it would be dark. Maybe, just perhaps, if all went well, he could take the next day off and spend it with Aaron. Now that the boy was better, he was thinking of entering him in the Canadian boarding school near Natanya. The school was small, but it was for boys and girls whose parents had to work or whose parents were gone. Gone. The jeep lurched over a bump in the road and the stocky major rocked in his seat as he thought of his wife.

For the next several hours the column drove north until it reached Ramla, where Zvi scattered his vehicles so that they were reasonably well hidden under what few trees were there. It was late. The night had spread across the countryside like a shelter. There were no stars. A few of the men who had spent the recent months in the desert felt cold. Their commander stood by his jeep and watched them detruck.

Calling for his two company commanders, the major went over the plan with them once more. And when they all agreed that they understood it the same way, he put out his cigarette and gave them his final words of caution: "Quick. Hard. And out."

Both of the young captains nodded. Both also remembered what had happened the last time a company officer had failed in his mission.

There was no smile on Zvi's face as he picked his helmet up from the floor of his jeep and shoved it on his head. "Take them out," he ordered, remaining where he was while the two columns passed him moving due east. A short time later they crossed that vague line known as no-man's land. Somewhere to the east lay Latrun. Zvi, walking near the head of the column, wished he could see the landmark now. Aware of how much Latrun meant to his friends who had fought here in 1948, he hoped he knew these folded hills as well as they. Brushing the notion aside, because it did not signify, he trotted to the head of the column. Somewhere about four kilometers to the northeast lay his objective, Abasir. Half a kilometer beyond lay Shiryan. Approaching this hamlet in the darkness, Zvi forced into the fore of his mind the two village plans he had seen. Abasir: almost a hundred buildings. The police station. The road leading in from the north. Above the town – the highway leading to Ramallah to the east. Troops of the Arab Legion, fifty or more. No more than one company. Some small arms other than those of the Legion. And at Shiryan: fifty buildings, most of them houses. The others barracks. Legion barracks. These latter worried Zvi more than anything else. These and the short half kilometer from Shiryan to Abasir. The road paved.

He glanced at his watch. Almost ten now. Moving to the side of the column, he waved for the leader of the first company to join him. "Let's make up some time. Move on out now. Cut east and make for Shiryan. Be certain you are not seen. Set up your positions, but remember the time we agreed on." As he saw the captain's face bobbing before him, he warned, "Whatever happens, don't be eager." With an affectionate slap on the back, he sent the man on his way. Standing where he was, Zvi watched the campany swing out of the line and move on at double time. Again, he glanced at his watch. The second company kept up its quick pace and he trotted to the head of it.

An hour later, moving on east, he made for the hills that lay beyond the coastal plain. Approaching them, he swung north and west in a large arc. They were deep in Arab territory. As far as Zvi could tell, they had not been seen. Twice he had sent men to reconnoiter near farmhouses they passed, but they had seen no sign of life. Once they had passed Bedouin tents scattered near the foot of the hills. Dogs had barked, but as far as he knew, he had passed through without attracting attention. However, he was aware he could never be certain of this until he was out of Jordan. Sending his guards out on both flanks, he ordered five men to drop back to make sure his rear was covered. Three more times he looked at his watch. By now the other company should have reached the hill near Shiryan. Sucking on his cheek, Zvi wondered if the young officer had enough sense not to be eager. Then, with a shrug he dismissed the notion. There was nothing he could do about that now. Hearing the clank of equipment behind him, he whirled and ran down the length of the column until he located the noise: a canteen bouncing against the butt of an automatic rifle. Grabbing the rifle from the startled soldier's hands, Zvi raised it above his own head as though he intended to bring it down on the soldier's. Then he shook his head and with what appeared to be great control, he hissed, "Keep it quiet or you will kill all of us." With that he handed the man back his weapon and trotted once more to the head of the column. Trying not to smile, he knew that his gesture would be remembered by his men and that was good, because they would tell one another how closely he had come to striking one of them down for making a sound. And that, after all, was what he wanted: a dark and silent passage. Now, Abasir lay to the west in front of him. Moving forward slowly, he gestured for his troops to remain where they were. As Zvi edged toward the village, he was joined by the company's commander.

The police station was lighted. It reminded him of all of the others which the British had built in the days of the mandate. Large blocks designed to serve as forts as well as stations. Fifty troops, Zvi had been told. He hoped so. More than that and he would be in trouble approaching the village because of the protective fire that could be laid down from the station.

There were lights in some of the other buildings. Most of them were stone. The village was ancient.

Zvi glanced at his watch. He had to allow another ten minutes for the first company to set up its mortars above Shiryan. Whispering to the young captain at his side, he ordered, "Flanks covered. Mortars in place now. Keep your cover. Return any fire wherever it comes from as long as it is not our own." He reassuringly slapped the younger officer on the arm. "We'll strike when I give the order and that should be in ten minutes. I don't want to dawdle after that. When I say we disengage, we disengage. No hesitation."

Then to be certain even at this late moment that he had not been misunderstood, Zvi sat up and warned, "We stay until we get what we came for."

The youth nodded and disappeared into the darkness. Zvi edged closer to the village. He did not know exactly why headquarters had selected this particular village. However, he could guess. Holding his breath, he watched two Arabs emerge from a building and move toward another. A house? A coffee shop? He could not tell.

Relaxing, he recalled the report of Arab terrorist activity Avram had handed him earlier in the day. The Jordanians admitted the Israeli tracker had followed his dogs to the border.

Nodding in the darkness, Zvi agreed with his enemy. It was indeed regrettable. *Gabriella and Tuvia and Aaron.* The names pounded through the back of his mind until he shook his head to disperse them. He had not come because of three names or three children or the mother. He had come as a soldier to do what had been ordered because it was decided this was the answer. And he did not question that this was the answer. In spite of the arguments that this answer was too simple and too primitive, no one had shown him any other that would stop the raids across Israel's borders. It was the 816th attack from Jordan since 1949.

Zvi watched the door of a building open. Several Legionnaires appeared in the light of the doorway. Following their course toward the police station, he wondered if there were any others in the building they had left.

Silence again, and the street was empty again. And the number banged through his head — 816 — and all the while, Jews were being killed, crops burned, homes destroyed; and all the while, the calm foreign soldiers of the United Nations forces were telling his people to be calm and that the Jordanians would see that the incursions ceased if Jordan were given time and *given time and given time and 816* mingled with the word "time" until Zvi heard the company commander coming to his side; whirling about, he brought his automatic rifle to hand in a single gesture.

"They're all in place," the captain whispered, and Zvi brushed the numbers and names from his head as he focused his attention on the village before him: Abasir.

Pointing out the building from which the Arab Legionnaires had emerged, he said that he wanted that building to be blown along with the other. The captain nodded. They looked at their watches.

It was time.

Zvi rose to his feet and saw others behind him rising to theirs. Moving slowly toward the village now, his hand went up. He could hear the first mortars *woosh* upwards; and then as they reached their apogee, he could hear the strange complaint of steel and wind and burning air as they descended. Then the explosion.

A corner of the police station disappeared in dust and smoke. Now the men with him were firing. The fire was returned. Swinging himself about where he stood, Zvi sprayed his fire toward the houses from which he could see the bursts of gunfire.

There were more Arab guns firing at him, and he was waving his sappers forward. More and more buildings alive with rifle fire.

Moving in directly ahead of his sappers, he decided that the Arab Legion had scattered its men through the village in anticipation of attack. Cursing under his breath as he felt the ground shudder, he gave the Arabs credit for planning their defense well.

The mortar fire brought down several houses. The gunfire of his own men pocked door after door. Almost pleased with the Arab reaction, Zvi felt confident that these Arabs must have evacuated their women and children before they set up a defense this strong. And he felt relieved that his task would be simpler with the women and children gone from the village.

There were screams from some of the houses as the Israeli fire found targets. Then the Arab fire became heavier, and Zvi, waving the sappers down, slammed onto his belly. The fire between the houses and the dark hill rose in tempo.

From somewhere in the distance he could make out the sound of mortar fire. The first company was keeping the Legion pinned down at Shiryan. Wishing them success, he rolled over so that he could survey his own situation better. Dark figures from another building and firing as soon as the door opened. Once more his men drove the Arabs back. For a moment Zvi wondered if there were any chance of a coordinated attack against his position. Doubting it, he waved the sappers nearest him forward. The Arab fire intensified and his own men returned it. Ten of the sappers were crawling, belly down, explosives cradled like children in their arms. Over their heads the two sides exchanged fire.

Wiping his sweaty face, Zvi wondered what was happening at Shiryan. He could not afford to face anything stronger than he faced here. He could not. All of his men were moving closer to the village to give the sappers more cover. He knew the months on the rifle ranges were paying off as the Arab fire subsided. A few moments later the Arab force dwindled to sniping. Deciding that this was not going to deter him, Zvi came to his feet, and the sappers and the forty men who were going right into the middle of the village with him were on their feet and all of them were running in a zigzag pattern toward the center of Abasir.

A few paces from Zvi, a sapper fell and, whirling, the battalion commander ordered two of the riflemen to take the man back. Picking up the sapper's load himself, he moved to the closest house from which he had noted firing earlier. Seeing a rifle emerge from a window, Zvi slammed himself to the ground with his load, rolled over empty-handed, and before the Arab could bring his rifle onto the moving target, Zvi had thrown a grenade into the house. A pause, a scream and a muffled explosion. Recovering his charges, Zvi set them at the base of the house, waved for one of the riflemen and shouted, "Take this one." The man nodded and began to place the explosives with care.

Zvi was already moving toward the sappers who were setting their bangalore torpedoes at the police station. As he raced down the street toward them, several Arabs were suddenly silhouetted in his path. Ducking behind a building, he drew his pistol from its webbed holster and fired twice. The Arabs disappeared into the closest building.

Waving for one of the sappers and his guards to take this building on, Zvi continued toward the police station. The charge was in place now. Moving several of the sappers, he concentrated his explosives near the entrance of the station, hoping that if he could weaken its arches, he would bring down the entire structure. Sniper fire from within was answered by automatic rifles. More Arabs broke from homes into the street, most of them firing as they came. Grabbing the rifle from one of his own wounded who knelt beside him, Zvi joined in the return fire. For what seemed like an hour and for what he knew was only a minute, the Arabs and the Israelis faced each other in the street, and then the Arabs broke and fell back into the houses.

To Zvi's surprise, he could still hear the mortar fire in the distance. The first company had to hold the Legion away from Abasir. Had to. Had to.

His head was clear now and he looked about the street. The charges were all in place, the sappers withdrawing, the rifle fire only a scattered noise breaking the night. Checking his watch again, Zvi surveyed the street to make certain none of his men remained. There had been wounded, but they had been removed. He did not yet know if there were any dead. Waving to the company commander, he gave the order to blow the charges. Then, taking his time as though he had all there was, he lighted a cigarette and walked out of Abasir. A rifle cracked behind him and some of his men returned the fire. At the edge of town, the night enfolded him like a familiar mistress. Very slowly he turned to look at Abasir.

A moment.

Another moment.

The number 816 mixed with the scattered rifle fire and the names of a boy, a girl and their mother, and then the village was ripped apart by a series of sharp explosions. Building after building seemed to rise from the ground and settle back as though in slow motion, one heavy stone parting from another and finding a new resting place in the twisted mass of rubble which became the center of Abasir.

The heavy block station was the last building to go, and instead of rising with dignity, it seemed to kneel to one side and then forward as the entire structure sagged wearily to the ground.

A heavy pall of dust lay over the town.

Zvi checked his watch. It was almost four in the morning. His hand went up and the company commander joined him. "The other company?"

"No sign of them yet."

Zvi started looking for his radio operator, who emerged from the darkness. "The other company?"

"They are coming now."

Reaching out, he pushed both the radio operator and the company commander forward. "Let's go," and the captain moved ahead to form his men into the long column that still had to find its way out of Jordan.

Zvi stubbed out his cigarette when he saw the second company approaching. Waving for the captain to hurry, he led the column west as the two companies joined. He snapped his orders at a sergeant who brought up the platoon behind him. "No talking."

Again, a dark and silent passage. Half an hour later they crossed the frontier line.

Only after he had seen his men onto the trucks which had been brought up to this point did he take the time to ask about his wounded.

"Five," one company commander told him.

"Three," the other said.

"Any dead?"

"One won't make it through," the first captain prognosticated.

Zvi walked over to the truck where the battalion medical officer had already gathered the wounded. "Go right on into Jerusalem," Zvi ordered. "I'll see you later."

Zvi sat in his jeep where for one brief moment he took the time to light a cigarette and drag on it a while before he turned to the signals sergeant. "Send a message directly through Army headquarters to Lieutenant-Colonel Avram Ben Ezra. 'This was not Nahalad.' " With a wry smile he started the convoy toward Moshe's headquarters where his men would sleep the day. He was tired, but he knew he had done what he had been sent to do. He did not find out about the real tragedy of Abasir until late in the afternoon.

As soon as he had made certain his men had been bedded down and he had visited the hospital, Zvi called headquarters and was told that Avram was in Jerusalem and waiting to see him. Hanging up the phone, Zvi weighed the possibility of getting some rest before he met with Avram, thought better of it and drove to Malin's apartment, where Avram was waiting.

"Malin isn't home yet," Avram explained. "We really can't afford one suite, but we are keeping house in two cities."

At this moment, Zvi could not find much sympathy for his friend. Looking about the sitting room, Zvi settled into an overstuffed chair and pulled another over so that he could rest his feet on it.

For the next hour he answered Avram's questions, wondering why they were so detailed and why the Operations Chief was not present and if he would have to go through the whole procedure once more for the staff.

Finally, Avram asked for the third time, "Did you see any women or children?"

Sitting up now and pushing the chair before him aside, Zvi leaned forward, put his palms together between his knees and asked, "Should I have?"

Avram, who sat on the edge of the sofa taking notes, looked up and nodded slowly. "The MAC is there now. The first reports we get estimate over forty dead and most of them women and children. Ruling out the fact that the Arabs are inflating the figures and no Arab soldier is ever reported killed, the MAC still claims it has seen a large number of dead women and children."

A gasp, and both looked up to see Malin standing by the door. They had been too preoccupied to hear her enter, and neither knew how much of their discussion she had heard. Standing with one hand on the back of a chair, she shook her head slowly as she told her husband, "I've heard the radio reports most of the day." Then she turned to Zvi. "Half an hour ago the MAC reported there might be as many as sixty bodies in Abasir."

Zvi nodded. He knew people had died there. This was to be expected.

Malin was in the room now, standing between the two men, but her eyes were on the major, who rose to his feet as she approached. For one fleeting instant he was aware of how bright the blue of her dress was and how angry her eyes. "The MAC claims that most of the dead are civilians," she said.

Very slowly, as though the words she had just shouted into his face were coming from a long distance away, Zvi turned from her and then back toward her. He wiped his face as he tried to comprehend what she had said, and somewhere through the fog surrounding his brain he heard Avram telling his wife in a detached, distant voice, "The MAC is anti-Israel. And the intent of the raids is to make the Arabs aware of how much it will cost them if they come across into our country and kill without discrimination." The words were too formal. At this moment they had no meaning.

Zvi's hand dropped to his side, and the Ben Ezras could see that he was shaken. His head came up and his eyes met with Malin's. "You trust the evidence that you have heard?"

She almost smiled at his effort to bring the argument into line with her position on the bench. She nodded. "I trust it." However, because she feared she might be misunderstood, she shook her head. "Look, both of you. Try to understand that no matter how much of an idiot the man is who is heading the MAC, the fact still remains that he must bring into the Security Council enough evidence to support his position. It may not all be valid, but are we standing here and arguing if ten or twenty or fifty or sixty civilians died? We are not. The point is that civilians died." Before her husband could cut her off, she snapped, "I know they have killed our people. I know it as well as you. I know that Zvi was obeying orders, but that is what every Nazi said."

For a moment she thought her husband would strike her, and then she stepped back and away from Zvi because of the strange look in his eyes. His face, taut most of the time in recent months, broke into a wry smile. "For a moment you had me believing that I was the one who had done something wrong. And mind you, I don't approve of killing women or children or anyone else, except the man who is shooting at me." His hands went wide as he tried to show her they were clean. "No building in Abasir was touched by my men without my orders, and I gave no orders to destroy any building from which the Arabs did not fire on us. And those firing on us were Arab soldiers in most cases, and Arab men in every case."

He was speaking quickly, his words coming out in defense of what he had done because he could recall the firing in the night and the dark figures coming at him. "I saw men shooting at us. And the decision to keep their women in homes from which they planned to fight was theirs, not mine. If the women died, I am sorry, profoundly sorry. But get one thing clear, there was no intention of killing any women. It is not our plan. It is not in our tradition, and the entire world knows that."

However, Malin was shaking her head. "The MAC reports that you drove the people back into the buildings before you blew them up, and they can tell because they find bullets in the doors."

And Zvi was laughing now as he appealed to Avram. "I damned well did order my men to fire back at anyone who fired on them, and if anyone thinks I was going to let them organize a counterattack against me when I'm that deep inside their country, they must be mad."

He took the time to light a cigarette, while Malin very slowly reached behind her, seeking a chair. Finally, she settled into one and sat looking up at the two men.

"You believe what you've just said?" she asked Zvi.

His head bobbed. "Nothing I've told you is other than as I have seen it."

She looked at her husband, who nodded. "Everything in his report substantiates this." Then, because he thought he should explain, Avram added, "We heard the first MAC reports hours ago, and that's why I came up alone so I could get this report for the Chief of Staff and the Prime Minister." He thought about what he had said. "This is going to hit the United Nations, the Security Council. There is going to be a great deal of talk and no one is going to listen to our argument because no one thinks in terms of a dead Jew here and a dead Jew there. So many Jews have died, no one seems to notice or mind if another goes, and so because we retaliated, we will be condemned." Appealing to his wife, he asked, "Is there anything we can do to be heard? Is there anything we can say that people will hear?"

However, Malin was not looking at Avram. Her eyes were on Zvi, whose face was almost contorted as he thought about the toll of the previous night.

"If it was as you said it was, and from what you say I believe that, there is still nothing any of us will ever be able to say." She was coming to her feet now and both of her hands came out as she placed one on her husband's cheek and the other on Zvi's. "The world's become numbed, insensitive to the death of Jews. After all, if they've killed six million, what difference does another one or twenty or five hundred make?"

Almost as though he were a child, she put one arm about Zvi's waist. "We embarrass them. It would have all been so much simpler if we had been wiped out, if the Final Solution had been, indeed, just that. There would have been no forty-eight war, there would have been no continuing argument over Suez, over water rights and lives and the establishment of a Jewish State."

She shook her head, "We embarrass them, and what Zvi did last night is in a way the final embarrassment: Jews having the effrontery to stand tall and strike back as though they were the equals of Moslems and Christians. This is something that will have to be judged, and I can assure both of you, it will be judged."

Her hands fell to her sides and she stepped back so that she could see both men better. "I've often wondered how the person on the other side of the bench felt while he waited to have sentence passed when he himself believed he was innocent, and he knew the court would find against him. Maybe a few months from now the two of you will be able to tell me."

Two days later, Zvi attended a funeral. The widow and parents of the dead soldier did not reproach him. They appeared grateful that he had taken the time to come. The aged father, who had survived Treblinka to bury his only son that day, asked Zvi to say a few words. Embarrassed, Zvi stood at the grave beside the rabbi and said softly, "Bernard Kletzky was a youth I was proud to know." His voice held firm as he added, "I, and the men who fought beside him, will always remember the way he made us laugh." The aged father nodded approval and thanked the major. The rabbi was intoning Kaddish.

In many ways the next three months were as difficult as Malin Ben Ezra had predicted. In fourteen terrorist raids, seventeen Israelis were murdered.

And in New York the United Nations Security Council voted to condemn Israel for the armed attack on Abasir.

It was at the party in late February which Avram threw in honor of Zvi's promotion to lieutenant-colonel that Zvi met Shoshanna Haim again. When Malin introduced them, Zvi thought he had seen the girl some place before, but he could not remember where. And because he was celebrating, he had already had two glasses of peach brandy and wasn't thinking clearly. In the crowded room of the Ben Ezras' Tel Aviv apartment, old friends were pressing around Zvi to congratulate him, and the tall, slim girl with the tip-tilted nose which reminded him of his wife's disappeared into the background. Zvi shook hands with each person who came in, thanked the Chief of Staff for coming, winked at Moshe in appreciation of the young

Englishwoman he had brought with him. The Operations Chief stopped in for a short time to congratulate Zvi and then disappeared after talking with the Chief of Staff.

From where she stood in the far corner of the room, Malin watched Zvi and smiled. In the months since their clash over the raid on Abasir, they had become friends. She had grown fond of Zvi, as she would have of a younger brother, and she often had difficulty remembering that he was actually her own age. Then Zvi was alone for a moment and lighting a cigarette. His eyes seemed to cloud, the smile left his face and he looked lost. Turning to Shoshanna, who stood beside her, Malin asked, "Where are you living now?"

The other woman was also watching the guest of honor, and she, too, had seen the change in him when he was alone. "Natanya. I'm teaching school there."

Malin nodded. She and the other girl had been to school together, and for a time when they were younger, they had served together in Haganah. Shortly after the war, Shoshanna had disappeared for a year or more, and Malin knew better than to ask questions which might be embarrassing.

"Have you known him long?" Shoshanna was asking, and Malin assumed she meant Zvi.

"He's an old friend of Avram's. I met him soon after we were married." However, as she spoke, she saw that Shoshanna was looking at Moshe Gilead now. Shorter than Zvi, Moshe seemed to make up in presence what he lacked in size. There was something almost elegant in the way he wore his uniform and carried himself. Those who had known him most of his life wondered when and where he had picked up this strange quality, strange at least for an Israeli. "Which were you asking about?" Malin queried and then laughed. "It doesn't make any difference because I met them both about the same time."

Shoshanna nodded, her eyes still on Moshe. "That one's Colonel Gilead?"

Malin nodded, trying not to show her distaste for her husband's friend. "I'm told he is a great soldier."

Her right hand coming up to rub her left shoulder as though it hurt her, Shoshanna nodded. "I've heard." And then with a smile, "I'll wager ten to one that the English girl is . . ."

Before she could finish her sentence, Malin was moving away.

Remaining where she was, Shoshanna watched the flow of newcomers greeting Zvi, and as she watched, she became aware that he was embarrassed, or was it that he was shy? She could not quite make up her mind. He was alone now and moving toward her end of the room. He smiled at her as though he knew her from some place, and then he stood with his hands on the windowsill staring out.

Stepping closer, she asked, "How is the little boy now?"

Puzzled, Zvi glanced over his shoulder at her. "My son?"

A smile came over his face while he scraped his memory. He was looking at her closely. Slight and yet as tall as he; her white cotton dress showed off her slim figure. Appreciating what he was seeing, and aware that she was not shying away from his stare, he asked again, "Do you mean my son, Aaron?"

She nodded, her hand still resting on her shoulder. "Camp Hashed. The middle of the night and you came in with the boy."

Standing upright, Zvi nodded. "And you were the girl who said she would care for him that night?"

She was pleased that he remembered her and she was trying to recall what she had heard about him. The vague items in the *Post* ran through her head. Soldier. One of the commando leaders. Studied history at the university. One of the men the Chief of Staff praised in his speeches. A man men talked about in a tone of awe, and yet he was uncomfortable at this party in his own honor.

"Your name is . . .?" he was asking.

And when she told him, he thought about it in silence as though it was a subject on which he should have an opinion. When he finally spoke, he said, "Aaron's fine. He's staying with a friend of mine now." He was offering her a cigarette from his shirt pocket, but she shook her head, and he continued, "I've been thinking that this school I've been hearing about near Natanya might be the place for him if I'm in the field for the next year or two."

"The Canadian one?"

He nodded.

"It's a good place. I teach not too far from there. I know the people who run it, and if he has to be away from you, you won't do much better."

The assurance with which she spoke came through to Zvi. Then Avram called him from the other side of the room, and he said, "I'll see you in a minute."

Twenty minutes later he was still in a hushed discussion with the Chief of Staff, Moshe and Avram. Word had just been received that Colonel Gamal Abdel Nasser had taken over as premier in Egypt. The Chief of Staff was giving his companions a quick evaluation of the man as he recalled meeting him on the island of Rhodes during the peace conference several years before. "Tough. Ambitious. Can be charming as a colorful snake. Nobody's fool, but I'm not sure he has the strength now to hold power."

Avram said, "I've read that book of his. A kind of *Mein Kampf.* Don't underestimate him."

Moshe reminded the others, "Right after I was exchanged from Mafrak, we had him trapped at Faluga Pocket in forty-nine, and if they had been able to keep the UN off my back for another few days . . ."

"I gather none of us is weeping for General Mohammed Naguib?" The Chief of Staff was referring to the former premier.

Zvi shrugged. "He looked handsome riding in the back of sedans. Maybe that's what I would prefer in charge over there: a man who just looks handsome."

"I've got to be doing things," the Chief of Staff told the others. Then he shook Zvi's hand and left. Moshe drifted over to his English companion, while Zvi and Avram stood alone for a moment watching Moshe. His hand was already about her waist and as he rubbed her back, she arched toward him.

Shaking his head in envy, Zvi looked about for Shoshanna. "That schoolteacher — Shoshanna — is she married?"

Avram's huge shoulders rolled forward as he glanced down at his friend. "Open country."

But Zvi could not find her anywhere in the room now. Starting in search of Malin, he saw both women emerge from the bedroom down the small corridor. Smiling, he apologized, "Something unimportant came up," and he explained, "like a change in the Egyptian government."

"We know," Malin told him. "It was on the radio," and she was gesturing with her head toward the bedroom. Then she went to join her other guests, leaving Zvi alone with Shoshanna.

"I'd like to learn more about that school," Zvi said.

The girl nodded, looking beyond him to Moshe and his English companion. They were trying to leave unnoticed.

Turning to see what held her attention, Zvi grinned. "There goes the best soldier in Israel."

Bewildered at the appreciation in his tone, she turned back toward Zvi. "Don't be a fool," she snapped. "There's more to being a soldier than fighting."

And only after he laughed, did she realize it was not Moshe Gilead's fighting prowess he had admired.

He lighted another cigarette before he offered, "Can I drive you home?"

Shoshanna had been expecting the offer from the way he had looked at her earlier. "It would be hours out of your way," she warned him. "Natanya."

Zvi tried to smile because she did not know where his men were quartered. "That much longer together." And then he laughed at himself. "I wonder how Moshe would have said that."

Reaching past her, he tamped the cigarette out in an ashtray on the windowsill, and when he withdrew his empty hand, it brushed against her side. Their eyes met, and he stepped back as though he had done something wrong. And yet she had difficulty believing that he was shy. Malin had told her about Dr. Hertzela Mazon, who now lived in Eilat. Uncertain if she was going to let herself in for more than she wanted, Shoshanna shrugged. He had only offered to drive her home.

She tried remembering that as she sat beside him in the jeep racing up the road north along the Mediterranean. The night was cool and he had draped his field jacket over her shoulders.

Sitting back in the small hard seat of his military jeep, she listened while he told her about Aaron. He was proud of the boy and, like any father, believed his son was a genius. "And he's handsome too," Zvi was saying. "Smaller than most boys his age. Some people say he's almost pretty for a boy."

"Do you see him often?" Shoshanna asked, drawing the field jacket more tightly about her shoulders.

"Once a week if I can. He has been staying with an old friend." His voice trailed off and Shoshanna turned to look at him. "She has a girl of her own who will be in school, and her sister who's been looking after both Aaron and the girl wants to go to work, and there won't be anyone at home. All kinds of domestic problems."

Shoshanna wanted to ask him about his own domestic entanglements, but she decided against it. His eyes were on the road ahead and his profile seemed large in the night. His eyes, deep set, flashed in the dark above a large, but sharply lined nose. His jaw jutted out even though it actually receded from his upper lip. There was something about the way his upper lip pressed forward which reminded her of a little boy.

They drove in silence for a time before he asked her about herself.

"There's nothing much to say," she told him. "I teach in high school. History most of the time. Sometimes English."

"And the rest?" he asked.

Shaking her head in deprecation, she said, "There isn't much 'rest.' My father was a teacher. My mother kept house. We lived on a kibbutz a while and then we moved to Haifa. There was a war and after that I went to Aden."

Knowing she was only telling him fragments, and because he wanted to hear more, Zvi waited.

However, Shoshanna added nothing to what she had already said, and now they were nearing the road which turned toward the sea and into Natanya. A few apartment buildings stood against the night sky. When they drew up before a building which she pointed out, Zvi's head fell back and he stared at the stars for a time.

"You live alone?"

At first Shoshanna shook her head, and then she remembered he was not looking at her. "I live with four other teachers. All women," and there was an element of tease in her voice.

Zvi caught it and wanted to laugh. His arm went about her shoulders and he drew her toward him. Suddenly he was looking at her, and her face was close and he kissed her. For a brief instant she seemed to be surprised, and then she was returning his kiss. His arms came about her. For a second they parted and stared at each other and then they were kissing again. His hand dropped from her shoulder and cupped one of her breasts. She clung more tightly as his hand wandered down her flat stomach and then onto her calf where it gently rose up and down, rubbing her firm thigh. She started to push him away and his hand closed about her breast again. Finally she pushed him away. For an instant he wanted to resist, and then he sat back in his seat and stared at her while she touched her hair self-consciously with one hand which came to rest on her shoulder, bringing up her breasts but covering them with her forearm at the same time.

"This is what Moshe fights for," he said softly, his words seeming to blur as though he had drunk too much.

Very slowly, Shoshanna shook her head. "Please don't play the boy with me."

His head came up and he was staring at her. Her eyes met his, and he was surprised that she was not even smiling. Pulling a cigarette from his shirt pocket, he lighted one, never taking his eyes from her face. The faint light of a distant street lamp reflected off her flat cheeks. He wondered what color her eyes really were. "Four girls in the apartment?" he asked, as though he did not really believe her.

Nodding, she smiled for the first time.

"Damn," was all he said, and then he reached out and touched her face with the flat of his hand. She did not seem to mind. And as though it were completely natural, his hand dropped down and with his forefinger he traced the shape of her breasts under the thin cotton dress. Her eyes closed and she leaned toward him in the small seat, and even though the steering wheel of the jeep pressed into his side, he leaned over and kissed her once more. When they separated, he said, "Damn," once more.

Her eyes were open now, and with a single gesture, she swept the jacket from her shoulders and held it out to him.

"We could drive into Tel Aviv," he offered. "I could find a hotel and more privacy than you would have here."

It seemed that she was considering this offer, but then she shook her head. "I've school in a few hours and you probably should be back wherever you are living." Then, as though she had to force both of their minds from the subject, she asked, "Where are you living now?"

Flicking his unfinished cigarette away into the darkness so that its arc caught their attention, he said, "In a camp."

She nodded, fully aware that he really could not tell her anything. "You were at Abasir, weren't you?"

His head bobbed in the semi-darkness, but it was obvious he was not thinking of Abasir when his hand came out to reach for her again.

However, this time she leaned away from him and backed out of the jeep. "Maybe another time, Colonel."

He leaned toward her, his forearm resting on the back of the seat she had just left, his head thrust forward. "Does the man who was at Abasir frighten you?" he asked bitterly.

She stood with her hands on the side of the jeep as though she could not take them away.

He lifted her head by the chin so that their eyes met once more. Then she took his hand off her chin and held it for a moment. "I hope to see you sometime again, Colonel."

"The day after tomorrow," he promised. She nodded, dropped his hand and fled. He sat where he was and watched her disappear into the building before he remembered he should have taken her to the door, and he wanted to kiss her again. However, she was gone.

Later, as he lay in bed with one arm under his head and a cigarette in his mouth, he kept thinking of Shoshanna Haim and the way her nose turned up like a *shikseh*'s and how much like Zella's it was, and before he put out the cigarette and fell asleep, his thoughts drifted to his wife and he was aware that she was not beside him, and he remembered the months after they were first married and how much he had liked to feel her warm beside him even on those nights when she had studied late and did not want him to touch her. However, even on these nights he had rolled over onto his side and looked at her, tempted to waken her and at the same time reluctant to face her petulance at being awakened for what they could do another time. And then he was wondering if Shoshanna would mind being wakened at night or if she, too, would be petulant. And then he wondered how she would like being a colonel's wife and what she had been doing at the Ben Ezras' and if he should call Avram in the morning and try to ask casual questions about her, and then he was asleep.

The next day when he contacted headquarters there was no report of an Arab border crossing, but Avram told him on the phone that the Egyptian government was still in an uproar and that nothing was settled. Lieutenant-Colonel Nasser was "in" and he was "not quite in" and General Naguib was making noises that sounded like a revolution, but Intelligence did not think he had the strength to stir his coffee let alone a country. And then Zvi asked, "That woman — Haim — I believe her name was, you know her well?"

"That's what she was asking Malin about you an hour or so ago," Avram said.

However, only after Zvi had hung up the phone did he realize that Avram had not answered his question. For a moment he was tempted to call his friend again, but he knew that this would be silly. For the rest of the day and the next night, Lieutenant-Colonel Mazon meshed his troops with those of Lieutenant-Colonel Gilead while they held a field exercise. The judges gave the victory to Gilead's battalion, though everyone was agreed that Mazon's men moved better and faster.

Afterward, back at Hakiryah, the Operations Chief said that something was wrong with the way Zvi kept swinging his troops around the enemy and not confronting him.

Leaning back in his chair at the conference table, the Chief of Staff chuckled. "Sometime, I'm going to find out what you have against Zvi."

However, the cold face of the operations chief did not reveal even a faint smile when he said, "We can talk about the strategy of the indirect approach, we can talk about what we learned from Wingate and Liddell-Hart, but there comes that time when you have to close with the enemy."

The Chief of Staff smiled at Avram, who sat puffing a pipe, his long hands wrapped about its bowl as though he wanted to keep them warm. The Apostles of Movement. The arguments were old and had never been resolved. It came down to a point of view which they both held: one bypasses his enemy, one cuts him off and lets him wither behind while driving on. And as Zvi Mazon had said after the exercise a few hours before when he dismissed his men, "Drive on *and on.*"

"But there comes that time they have to be destroyed," Elihu Cohen was saying.

The others with him were thinking about this, while Avram's thoughts were on Zvi's face when he had listened to the judges explain why Moshe had won the exercise. Colonel Gilead's force was still intact and he had planned with greater care. "But he isn't going anywhere. He can't go anywhere now," Zvi had half shouted as he slammed one fist into his own side.

"It would take more men than you have to maul him," Cohen had said in justification of his decision. And while the others in the conference room were listening to the Chief of Staff justify Zvi's sweeping moves, Avram wondered where Zvi was going and what had happened to the young lieutenant who had always moved with such assurance and at the same time had always planned with such care. And in that instance he realized that the assurance remained, but for reasons he could not fully explain, the care, the detail, the planning was gone and Zvi was moving more wildly these days. When he heard the Chief of Staff ask him a question, he tucked the thought of a wild Zvi into the back of his memory as something he would have to bring out again and look at later when he had leisure. And now he was expounding upon the turn-down they had received in their effort to purchase arms in Eastern Europe.

After the staff had left, Zvi dressed and drove into Tel Aviv where he spent the next several hours with Aaron. They played in a nearby playground, drove about the city looking for a toy airplane which they finally located in a shop on Allenby, and then Aaron flew it back home to Ruth's while his father followed below in the jeep. After having dinner with Ruth and the children and seeing Aaron off to bed, Zvi drove north to Natanya.

The sea lay to his left and the desert nibbled in toward the road from the east. Aware of the lay of the terrain as only a night-fighting soldier can be, Zvi's thoughts ran over the exercise he had been a part of during the day. He remained convinced he had fought the only way possible. There could be no defensive position in Israel, because Israel, unlike the Arab countries, could not afford to give up land. Not a meter. Not a single pace. No battle was going to be fought on Israeli territory. They could never allow it. Everything he believed in as a soldier determined that the war be fought on the other man's land, and because of that he himself had to attack. Always the offensive. In no retreat. This was the spirit he had been building into his men, and all of the arguments that there would come a time that he would have to meet the enemy toe-to-toe made no sense when he could cut him off and drive on.

A smile crossed his weary face as he thought about the only reason why he was not asleep. Natanya lay tucked into the dunes before him. Part resort and part factory town, Natanya had never quite made up its mind which it was going to be. Too close to the Arab triangle of Tulkarm, Nablus and Jenin to be completely safe, Natanya lay like an abatis on the Arab route to the Mediterranean.

Zvi jerked his vehicle to a stop at the crossroads as he looked over the terrain. There was almost no way of defending it. The coastal plain offered nothing in the way of cover. It was something he would have to remember.

Twenty minutes later he was driving south, Shoshanna beside him. Neither of them mentioned where they were going, and he assumed she had left the matter up to him. Once, as they drove silently, he wiped his face with an open hand and Shoshanna smiled.

"Tired?"

Nodding, Zvi admitted, "It was not an easy day. Field work. There are those who say that I did it well, and those who say that I didn't." She knew by now the nature of his work was secret and so the matter was ended.

"I looked into that school," she offered. She shifted in her seat so that she could watch his face, and she saw she had his attention. For the next half hour as they sped south along the almost empty highway, she told him about Hadassim, the school founded by Canadians where the children lived in their own buildings according to age and had their own tasks according to age. And when she told him how much it cost a year, he whistled softly and made no other comment.

Suddenly, as they neared the cut-off that enters the highway from the east below Herzliyah, they almost ran into a small military convoy. Drawing up beside the road to let the vehicles pass, Zvi counted them. A company, more or less. Moshe was not getting his night's rest, and Zvi wondered if he had been called on. Jamming his foot down, he raced the jeep around the convoy and headed for the nearest telephone. At a petrol station half a kilometer away, he stopped and phoned his headquarters. No calls. Sighing, Zvi said, "Thanks." Then, before he hung up, he snapped, even though he knew as he did it there was no one at fault, "Take this address. It's an apartment in Tel Aviv." And he gave the duty officer the address of the apartment he had sublet the day before. "If you have to reach me, send someone in fast. As soon as I get a phone, I'll post the number on the duty list." He slammed the phone down and stood for a moment staring at the wall before him. With this one call he had given up his hopes for privacy. Shaking his head in disgust with his own fears — or was it his own overblown sense of responsibility — he tried to imagine Moshe calling in a number from the bedside of every woman he had slept with over the past few years. He rejoined Shoshanna and explained his actions with "It's all right."

Not knowing what he was talking about, she decided not to press him. She was still thinking of the wild manner in which he had left the jeep and even wilder way in which he had suddenly dashed around the convoy to find a phone. He had said he was tired. She thought there was more to it than that, and she did not think she was the reason for the tense look about his eyes.

Swinging off Ibn Gabirol, Zvi entered Jabotinsky and then two blocks farther on pulled up to the curb. The street was dark except for passing cars. Glancing up, Zvi saw the slit of moon was gone now. Turning in his seat, he looked at Shoshanna. A smile spread over his face as he explained, "I sublet an apartment yesterday. It isn't large and it isn't fancy, but I thought it was time I had a place." He came around the jeep and helped her out. While they walked to the apartment, he stared at the sky. "It's going to be cold tonight," he said, referring to nothing in particular.

And then they entered the building, and he led her down a long corridor. Opening a door, he stepped aside for her to enter before he searched about the wall for a light switch. The room became bright from an overhead light, and Shoshanna slowly looked about it from where she stood. He had been right: it was small. She could make out a small kitchen and from the door leading off the living room, she assumed there was a single bedroom.

Zvi was slipping off his tunic now and draping it over a straight-backed chair. "You should have brought a coat," he said. And she realized why he had mentioned the cold: he had even then been thinking of taking it off her. A wry smile on her face, she shook her head, "It won't be cold here."

Jerking his tie off, Zvi tossed it over his tunic. "Maybe I should have filled the refrigerator," he suggested. "Maybe you're hungry."

She shook her head and, to her surprise, he lit a cigarette and stood puffing it as he stepped away from her, never taking his eyes off her face. After a moment of silence, he apologized, "Maybe I should have tried to find a better place. I didn't have time."

"It's fine," she said, wondering why she should be interested and why he was apologizing. "It's fine," she said again for want of anything else to say.

Waving his hand to take in the apartment, he said, "I'm going to try to get a telephone installed. I know that takes time, but perhaps I have enough *protectzia*," and they both laughed at his reference to influence, knowing that his position made a phone necessary.

"You think the place is all right?" he asked again.

"It's fine," she repeated.

"I could try to find another one," he offered.

"It's fine."

He swung away from her and looked toward the kitchen, which she had been facing. "There's a stove in there." Then he turned back to her. "It's not too far from here to a *sherut* stop and there's a taxi stand not too far away." Then, believing he had said the wrong thing, he rushed on. "Not that anyone will have to take a *sherut* from here. I can get transportation."

She was smiling at his efforts to impress her. "I know."

He stubbed out his cigarette in an ashtray with a picture of the Victoria Hotel, Cairo, painted on it. "I never asked if you wanted to come." He was watching her. "You did want to come, didn't you?"

For a long time Shoshanna thought about this and what any answer would commit her to. She was smiling when she nodded. Crossing the small carpet, he took her face between his hands and kissed her. Her arms went about his shoulders and she felt for a time as though she had to hold onto him. Then his hands came away from her face and were searching about her body and she clung more tightly. When they separated, she stood looking at him until he picked her up and carried her into the bedroom.

It was almost midnight when he rolled over on his side in the narrow bed and, reaching out once more, clutched one of her firm breasts in his hand and kneaded it. She lay on her side facing him. The light from the living room cast shadows on the wall, and her clothes piled on the floor looked in the dark like more than there really were.

"You're all right?" he asked after a time, and she reached up and closed her hand over his.

"I'm fine," she said and then laughed. "After all the years I've spent in school, you would think I could find another word."

"It's a word I don't mind hearing."

For almost half an hour neither one spoke.

Because of this, Zvi was surprised when she started to speak. "I knew we were going to end up like this," she said. "I knew it when I saw you in Malin's apartment. Everyone was looking at your friend, watching him and telling each other how handsome Colonel Gilead was, and even though I have to admit he is kind of handsome, there is something about him that sets my back up. And then I saw you." She smiled, "And I knew about us."

While she spoke, Zvi's hand went under her and started rubbing her bare back and she nestled more closely to him. In jest, he asked, "Do you always know about your men?"

Her reaction came swiftly as she drew away and pulled his arm out from under her. "I wondered," she said. "I wondered what you would think." There was fury in her voice as she spoke on before he could say anything. "A quick conquest. A line of men all waiting and expecting me to jump into bed with them."

She started to rise from the other side of the bed and before she could, he grabbed at her arm and jerked her back across the bed. The sheet lay between them, but he did not seem to notice that as he stopped her talking with a kiss and his hand wandered over her again, firmly and patiently while she struggled and he waited for her to relax. Finally she broke free and he grabbed her shoulders, "If we can't joke, you and I, then there's nothing." Because of the darkness, he could not quite make out the expression on her face, and so he pleaded, "Give me leave to joke a bit." And when he drew her to him again, "I need it almost as much as I need you."

Hours later they lay in bed talking. Zvi had put out the light in the sitting room and his cigarette shed the only light there was.

"And so that was what happened between Zella and me." There was no rancor in his voice. If Shoshanna had been called on to describe his tone, she would have said "flat."

"It came to nothing because we had gotten together for the wrong reason. I used to think that somehow love and sex were the same thing."

"And now?"

He was silent for a moment before he explained. "Today, when the chief of operations ruled me loser in an exercise, I kept thinking how I'd tell you about that. Yesterday, when I started to look for this apartment, I was wishing you were with me. And this evening, when Aaron and I were hunting around for a toy airplane he could fly around town in — a real honest-to-goodness airplane with two wings and four engines — I wanted to tell you about that hunt and how he offered to fly me home with him."

Shoshanna believed she understood him when he added, "And that is what I think love is."

He cupped the cigarette in his hand as he waited for a reaction. It seemed a long time coming; and when it did, it was not quite what he had expected.

"I used to think that was just about the description," she seemed to agree.

"You don't now?"

Her head rocked from side to side on the lumpy pillow. "Once . . ." and her voice trailed off before it picked up again. "Once upon a time there was a Jewish girl who thought she was in love with an ever-so-handsome young British lieutenant." She fell silent again and Zvi waited for her to continue. "He was so very handsome and all the British girls and all the Jewish girls knew it when he walked into a room or down a street. And he found this Jewish girl and they walked together and talked together and he told her all about his father's business in London where they made maps, all kinds of maps of the British Empire. Maps even for the king and queen. And he was so very quick and so very good at laughing, and at night when they lay in bed together, they would talk about what they did during the day, and he would tell her what it was like to be an artillery officer with a Colonel Blimp as a commander, and she would tell him about the things she was studying in school." Her voice trailed off once more. "It was so much like love."

"And then?" Zvi finally asked.

"One night this girl was coming out of the handsome — oh-so-handsome — lieutenant's apartment and bidding him goodbye with a kiss and arranging to meet the next morning, and he was complaining that he had to drive all the way back across Haifa to spend the evening with his Colonel Blimp. A girl friend of hers joined her and they went to a meeting of Haganah. A small meeting. Two officers and five men and three girls. They drove out into the country to where they had their buried weapons to make sure they had not been damaged by a recent rain." Before she fell silent, she added, "That was all a long time ago."

"But what did it have to do with love?"

"The next morning the two officers were arrested. We didn't know how they were known and we met again — the rest of us — and talked. Just as we had given it all up, the girl who had come past the apartment asked about the handsome lieutenant." Silence for a moment. "It was an innocent question about what I was going to do when the British gave up the mandate." Silence again. "Then someone asked what he was like, and we both described him, and someone asked if his father was a mapmaker, and I was surprised and I said he was."

"What has mapmaking to do with anything?" Zvi asked.

"The handsome, the oh-so-handsome young lieutenant was not in the artillery, but intelligence. He had found companionship and a great deal of information at the same time."

She stared at the ceiling and Zvi's hand came out and covered her hand which rested on her shoulder.

"And then?"

"The next time I left him someone — it was Malin — followed me. I went down to the beach past the Arab section of the port and near the water, and when I saw Malin ahead of me, I knew she wanted to tell me something: the handsome lieutenant was following me. And then Malin went on, and I slipped into a doorway." She was forcing herself to remember, and after a time she did. "When he passed, I came up behind him and jabbed a knife under his ribs, and he started to struggle and for some reason or other he never screamed, but when he fell, the knife was still in him and I knew I had to take it away, and when I knelt down beside him, he looked at me and in a very small voice he said, 'You Hebe bitch. I think you've killed me.' "

Zvi felt her hand come away from under his and he clutched her shoulder as her body seemed to roll from side to side, but she kept on talking.

"I told him, 'I hope so,' and then he grinned and said, 'You were fun in bed, except you talked too damned much.' " With a twitch, she pulled away from Zvi and faced the window, her back toward him.

And all Zvi could say was, "He's lucky he's dead." His voice was cold with anger and his arms went about her while he promised, "I'll always want to hear what you have to say."

They fell asleep with his arms about her, one hand clutching her breast as though he feared she might leave.

The next morning, he drove her back to Natanya and returned to his camp. They had agreed to meet for dinner or as soon as he could leave camp again. He was to call her at school even though there were rules about her taking calls there.

The next day Zvi and Moshe Gilead met to evaluate for themselves the previous day's exercise. However, instead of an exercise to evaluate they had the small operation which had taken place the night before. Moshe's two companies had been called in to patrol the border near Latrun where saboteurs had been reported. Both companies had clashed with an armed Arab band. They had killed two men and driven the rest back across the frontier. And yet, as Moshe explained, "Too damned late. An hour after we chased them off, a train struck a mine and three men were killed."

They were still discussing the frontier line with Jordan when Zvi's signals officer informed them that Colonel Nasser had been replaced by General Naguib. Sitting in the small headquarters office, the two old friends smiled at each other. "May they have confusion," Moshe laughed softly.

With the *protectzia* he could muster, Zvi arranged for a phone in Shoshanna's apartment and another in the one he had rented on Jabotinsky Street. And when she was not in school, she waited for him at his apartment. One long evening they discussed her moving into the city, but they agreed that the daily trip to her school would be too difficult and that she had to complete her contract for the year. They agreed, too, they would discuss what came next when it came.

How much the Ben Ezras, Ruth or others knew of their relationship, neither of them could be certain. As time was the one thing they could not count upon, they did not share what little they had with anyone except Aaron, who came to look upon the apartment on Jabotinsky as a place where he met his father and the pretty woman who told him what life had been like in Yemen, as she had heard about it from people who had been there. Often she would pick up the boy from Ruth's shop and take him to the apartment on Jabotinsky to wait there for Zvi. And many times they waited and Zvi never came.

The frontier was heating up, and there was no one in Israel who was not aware. During this period Arab terrorists shot up the train from Hadera to

Lod, wounding the engineer, fired on the Haifa-Tel Aviv railroad, wounding two trainmen, murdered two young men of the Israeli border patrol and kidnaped two others in the Irgun Simka area. They shot down an aged Arab farmer at Beit Safafa south of Jerusalem and kidnaped his wife, murdered a farmer near Beit Kika the same night they killed a farmer near Lifta, cut down a kibbutznik at Mahassia, a fifteen-year-old cowherd south of Tacbeith, and a policeman who came to investigate that murder.

Later that week, Zvi sat watching Shoshanna pour coffee. This was the first time she had seen him in a week, and from the way Zvi's eyes kept darting angrily about the kitchen as though he expected something to appear, she knew he had to talk.

Setting a cup before him, she leaned over and kissed him. Her robe came open and he touched the tip of her breast lightly with an open palm. After a moment she stepped back and picked up her cup. They were in no hurry now. They had the whole night before them. He stretched out his legs and rubbed his feet against hers while he told her about the need for vehicles and the problems they were having buying them on the world market. She listened, not because she cared about military trucks, but because Zvi was talking.

Later they laughed at the idea of the United States and Japan signing a mutual defense pact. They did not laugh as they talked about the tests the United States was making on Bikini Island, and they wondered if Israel would push to create an atom bomb. When she told him that she had taken the *sherut* into town two days before to hear Fishel Warshow's concert, he smiled and asked how Fishel had been accepted, and he smiled even more broadly when she told him that there had been a standing ovation.

He rose from the table and poured another cup of coffee for himself and set the pot down again after she shook her head.

"I've a letter from Zella today," he told her. "I'd written her about a divorce," he explained. "She said we can talk about it when she comes north from Eilat on the seventeenth."

Shoshanna did not react at first because neither of them had mentioned marriage, love or Dr. Hertzela Mazon since their first night in the apartment. She knew he had to make the next move, and so she merely nodded.

"When we've talked — Zella and I — then you and I can talk."

"When you've talked," she agreed.

He was about to come around the table to her when the phone rang. Swearing to himself, he strode into the living room and answered it. From where she sat in the kitchen thinking about the woman she had never met, Shoshanna suddenly realized this was the first time the phone had rung when they were together. From the other room she could hear him say, "And that's all of it?" There was a brief silence and he added, "It's a police job. I'll get the details in the morning. No, I'm glad you called." Then he came back into the kitchen, where he poured a third cup of coffee for himself and filled hers.

"Problems?" she asked.

He nodded. "Near Shuval in the northern Negev. Tracks indicate three Jordanians came along the road leading to Beersheba." He sipped his coffee, staring at her over the top of the cup. "There was an Arab there — a Bedouin — who has been cooperative. They murdered him in his tent. His wives saw it. The tracks lead back to Jordan."

"And?"

Zvi shrugged. "All I can do is wait for orders. And wait. And wait." She saw that his hand holding the cup was shaking. He was more tense than she had ever seen him before. Very carefully, she set her own cup down, and slipping off her robe, tossed it across the chair on which she had been sitting and walked from the kitchen, through the living room, and into the bedroom. Zvi joined her there.

Later, as they lay in bed together, his arm about her, his breathing deep, Shoshanna wondered if his wife understood him this well.

It was late in the afternoon of the seventeenth.

Zvi had finished his work at staff headquarters in Hakiryah, driven out to pick up Shoshanna, and they had stopped off at the apartment on Jabotinsky Street for coffee before going to Ruth's to see Aaron. On the way back from Natanya, they had visited the Canadian school, and Zvi had made the necessary arrangements for Aaron to attend for one year. He hoped by that time he would be married and that his family would be intact in Tel Aviv.

Sitting in the small living room, Shoshanna confirmed Zvi's judgment. "It's the best thing you can do for the boy."

Zvi stirred his coffee and thought about this. Havah had not given him the child to put away in some school run by strangers. He was certain that had not been her intent. However, he did not feel like discussing Havah with Shoshanna now. Sometime in the next few hours he knew he should be hearing from Zella. They would meet somewhere and discuss the divorce as two persons whose life together had come unzipped. He hoped there would be no recriminations. For his own part, he only wanted to be done with it. Shoshanna knew what he was thinking, and she wondered how she would feel if she were either of the two. She picked up her cup between her palms. The coffee remained hot. Setting it down, she glanced at her watch. If they were going to spend any time with Aaron, they should leave now. And yet Zvi made no move to go.

He lit a cigarette, dropped his head back on the chair and tried to relax. From where she sat, Shoshanna could see the crow's-feet about his eyes, the way his hand had trouble settling in any one way about the cigarette and, worst of all, the way his eyes kept staring at the ceiling.

If it had been later, if Aaron were already back from school and at Ruth's . . . Shoshanna's thoughts trailed off as a knock on the door brought Zvi to his feet.

With a single step he reached the door and, swinging it open, revealed Avram and Moshe standing in the hallway. Zvi's head cocked to one side as he stared at his friends. Neither had been to the apartment before. Neither had ever even indicated he knew it existed. And now they were standing in the hallway and Zvi noted that Moshe was wearing a sidearm.

"Well?" he asked bluntly.

Moshe looked to Avram, who nodded.

"I think," Avram began, "I think we'd better come inside."

Stepping out of the doorway, Zvi waved them into the living room where Shoshanna had already come to her feet. Zvi closed the door and stood with his back against it while he waited for an explanation. He did not bother to bring Shoshanna into the discussion and he had no intention of explaining her presence.

Avram hesitated a moment, turned to smile at Shoshanna to let her know that he was aware of her. "Zvi, there's been an incident. You're involved. We'd better get down there."

Uncertain what his friend was talking about and conscious of Avram's sense of security, he knew nothing more would be said in front of Shoshanna. He crossed the room to her side and apologized, "I guess that's it. If you can take the *sherut* back . . ."

She smiled. "Don't worry about me. Maybe I'll stop over and see Aaron."

"Thanks." He wanted to say more, but he knew the others were watching him. His hand came up and touched her cheek, he smiled, and then he started for the door. Holding it open for the others, he looked back toward Shoshanna, "If Zella calls, ask her where she's staying."

Then he closed the door, and the three descended the stairs to the street. Avram's staff car was at the curb and the driver stood beside the door. Letting the other two in first, Avram closed the door behind them and took his place beside the driver. A moment later they were racing north along Ben Yehuda toward the small airport on the other side of the Yarkon River.

Twisting about in his seat so he could see his friends, Avram explained, "There's a Dormier waiting for us. We'll fly to Ein Hasb where we'll pick up a jeep."

Zvi nodded, still uncertain what was so important it had to take the time of all three.

Looking out the window beside him, Moshe avoided the face of his friend as he said, "There was a bus coming north from Eilat. Scorpion Pass."

Zvi nodded even though Moshe was not looking at him. There was something in Moshe's voice Zvi could not quite understand. "Scorpion Pass," and he repeated the name. He knew the place well. South of Beersheba about seventeen kilometers from the frontier.

"The bus was ambushed," Moshe added.

And again it was the way he was talking rather than what he was saying that disturbed Zvi. If there was any man he knew incapable of tears, it was Moshe Gilead, and yet at this moment Zvi was confident that the averted head was hiding tears.

"How many were killed?" Zvi asked Avram.

"Only first reports now." And the staff officer was being tentative, which left Zvi confused.

"How many?" Zvi asked again.

"Eleven killed. Two wounded badly. The others we are told survived by playing dead."

Fumbling in his shirt pocket for a cigarette, Zvi kept shaking his head from side to side in disbelief. "Eleven?"

Avram nodded.

"Oh, tell him already," Moshe half shouted. "Tell him."

And then Zvi knew that there was no need for anyone to tell him.

Swinging about, Moshe saw the stunned expression on Zvi's face. "She's dead," Moshe confirmed in a flat voice. "She's dead."

And as Moshe spoke, Avram understood more than he wanted to. The extent of emotion in his toneless voice caught both of them. Avram was puzzled, but Zvi was no longer thinking of Moshe.

For a long time he sat unseeing, his eyes on the back of the driver's head. Zella's face in a hundred forms flowed through the funnel of his memory. The image blurred and cleared and blurred again. Finally, he found that he was fighting to separate a single moment which would not be flooded over by other moments. He found he was fighting to clear away the debris of past visions and past views. He wanted a single picture that was sharp and clear, and all he could find wavering through his brain were interwoven pieces of a face with an upturned nose and pieces of dialogue from good days and bad, pleasant memories and foul. His hand came up before his face and he appeared to be wiping something away.

Avram settled back on his seat, his eyes settling on the road ahead. Moshe rocked back and forth on the car seat, his head seemingly loose on his shoulders. He was the one who said again, "She's dead." Then, as though he had to strike at something, somewhere, he shouted at Zvi, "She's dead. And while she was dying, you were holed up with some *kurveh* just because she looks like your wife."

Startled by the assault, Zvi turned to Moshe. However, before he could say anything, Avram swung about in his seat and ordered coldly, "Moshe, shut up."

For a moment the others did not know how Moshe would react. Then he nodded slowly and asked, "When do we move the battalion?"

Avram shrugged. "You know the cabinet decides that."

But Moshe was not listening. "I want this one. It's mine."

Zvi settled back in the seat and stared at his friend. And a wry smile spread over his face. "I didn't know you'd been one of them," he finally said, more sadly than he had expected.

That was when Moshe struck, the back of his hand swinging wildly for Zvi's face. Zvi's wrist blocked the swing, and with great patience, he pushed Moshe away from him while Avram was asking both of them to calm down.

The driver was taking the car along the runway toward a plane which waited, propeller slowly turning.

None of them spoke during the flight to Ein Hasb. A jeep was waiting for them. Zvi, knowing the country best, took over the wheel and raced north on the road to Beersheba. Fifteen minutes later they crossed Wadi Fuqra and approached Scorpion Pass. A dozen vehicles were parked near the bus as Zvi came to a halt beside it. He sat in the jeep for a moment as Avram and Moshe left him alone and started toward the row of bodies laid out on blankets beside the battered yellow bus.

There were two ambulances parked off the road. Several medics were tending the wounded. Zvi was trying to recall how many had survived: four, two seriously wounded. Pulling himself out of the jeep, he noted the two white vehicles with the United Nations markings on their side, the United States naval officer and the other four men with UN armbands. He brushed past them to view the row of bodies: women, children, men. One woman's face was so smashed by a bullet, he could not tell her age. One child had been laid out on his stomach because the bullets had torn the back of his head away and only the front could cup what remained. Moshe was standing over a body near the end of the row. Avram stood talking to one of the trackers and a Swedish captain from the Mixed Armistice Commission.

Trying very hard not to hear the conversation, Zvi approached the body of his wife. Her head lay facing him. Her hair was shorter than he recalled it. Aware of the two red spots on the front of her dress where the bullets had entered, he half closed his eyes to keep from shrieking. Dropping to his knees so that he could better see Zella's face, Zvi reached out to straighten her arm, cruelly twisted under her. He held it for an instant and then left it where it lay. She would not feel the difference, and he did not want to look at her hand where the fingers had been cut off so that her wedding ring could be removed. Glancing up, he saw Moshe kneeling on the other side of the blanket. Zella lay between them.

There was pain on his companion's face and Zvi could only recall the last time he had called on his wife and the stranger he had found with her. He had never before thought of Moshe as one of his wife's lovers. Glancing angrily at his friend, he said bitterly, "Don't fret. Don't worry. I'll get married again." And then, as he saw the expression on Moshe's face, he wished he had not said anything.

With great deliberateness, Moshe rose and stood looking down at Zvi. Very slowly he swung his arms back and forth as though he had to move to keep from breaking apart. "I never touched her," Moshe said. "I loved her, but I never touched her." And he walked away before Zvi could apologize.

The medical officers were passing down the row of bodies now, taking notes while the MAC officers took pictures. Stepping back to give them room, Zvi stood alone. He finally turned and stared into the desert where the trackers were already following their dogs north toward the Jordanian border.

He knelt beside her and without thinking traced the tip of her nose with his finger. It had been an old joke between them.

Rising, he strode off toward the jeep. Avram left orders with one of the soldiers standing by to tell Colonel Gilead that transportation would be sent back for him. Then he joined Zvi just as the battalion commander was turning the jeep about to return to Ein Hasb. Neither looked back. Both knew the incident at Scorpion Pass was not yet settled, but there was nothing more they could do here. A few minutes later, Zvi slowed the jeep, put one knuckle between his teeth and upon it marked his anguish. Then, as though he had to get away from the Negev, he raced the rest of the way to the waiting Dormier.

It took Zvi's friends some months to realize something had happened to him with the death of his wife. It took them even longer to understand it.

Zvi did not marry Shoshanna that spring or summer, though the two continued to see each other. Zvi did not bring up the subject, and Shoshanna refrained from mentioning it.

In the months that followed Zella's funeral, he never missed a conference at General Headquarters. He was the first to arrive at each meeting and the last to leave. He knew what was expected of him as well as of the other officers present. He knew the details of every operation that was planned. He kept abreast of all the newest equipment that was purchased as well as the latest being used in other countries. He was aware of all the changing nuances in the Arab political world, and he read all the Arab papers he could find. When any unit was out on an exercise and he was not otherwise occupied, Zvi drove his jeep to the area and, sitting by, made his own evaluations of what was taking place. There were no junior officers who did not come to know him in time, and few senior officers who were not aware that something had changed in Zvi Mazon.

If he was not in headquarters or in the field, he was sitting in on the class lectures of the various staff schools, watching the education program set up for the senior officers and the foreign ministry staffs, watching the training programs for the junior officers and the classes for the foreign-born students newly drafted into the army. If he had spare hours, he spent them with the flying officers of the air force. Though he never planned to fly himself, he wanted to know the implications of ground and air integration and the best ways in which coordination could be achieved.

When Avram mentioned this excessive drive, Zvi merely said, "If I'm responsible, I have to know." Beyond this he would not discuss his activities. He saw Avram professionally, but the time they spent together was perfunctory. He saw Shoshanna as much as he could at first, and then he saw her less, even though he needed her more.

The first person to break through his working pattern was Isaac Ben Aaron, the Yemenite silversmith. It was midsummer when headquarters informed Zvi that Isaac was trying to contact him, and, taking the address left at Hakiryah, Zvi went in search of his friend. The address turned out to be nothing more than the shambles of an old stone building in the slum of ancient Jaffa to the south of Tel Aviv. Stumbling through the maze of windowless rooms, Zvi finally located Isaac and his older wife, seated on the floor, a small iron stove between them, their two children lying on a mat in a corner. The stench of the airless room and the midsummer heat brought Zvi's head up sharply when he saw his friend. Taking Isaac's hand, he led him outside into the narrow street where the dust was thrown up by each passing car.

"What in the hell has happened?" Zvi demanded with his first words.

The mori's son tried to smile, his payot shaking as his lean face bobbed back and forth. "We came and there was nothing for us to do. For months they let us live in a camp, and then I decided that we did not belong in a camp." It was obvious the Yemenite was not complaining. "I went as far as Jerusalem, but I could not see the Wall. There was no work in Jerusalem, so we came to Jaffa."

Uncertain just what he was being told, Zvi asked, "And your other wife?"

A sad smile from Isaac as he explained, "The old ways don't belong here. She married someone else a year ago. I think they are happy."

"And what do you do now?" Zvi demanded almost harshly because he felt guilty for not having looked up Isaac before.

"I try to find work. Sometimes I find some silver and I make a trinket." He shook his head. "None of it is very good now. My hands are not what they were." He held them out and Zvi could see that they were even thinner than when the two had traveled the road south from Sa'na.

Putting one arm about his friend's shoulders, Zvi drew Isaac over to the jeep, recalling as he did, the first time Isaac had ever ridden in a vehicle. "Let's go someplace for coffee," he suggested.

Isaac looked at his tattered shoes, his patched shirt and started to shake his head. Then almost proudly, "You are a lieutenant-colonel now."

Zvi nodded and ordered quietly, "In!" pointing at the jeep. Fifteen minutes later they entered the apartment on Jabotinsky Street. Isaac stood for a moment in the doorway and scanned the room. His small head bobbed approval.

"It is good, my friend." And Zvi could see that the Yemenite was happy for him.

In the kitchen while Zvi waited for the coffee to heat, he put out a plate of fruit and some cold meats. To his surprise, Isaac stared at the meat for a moment and then shook his head. *"Treif?"*

Zvi apologized. "I forget." Then, "We'll get something else after the coffee."

Pulling up a chair, he waved Isaac to the other side of the table, and the Yemenite sat down hesitantly.

For a time they stared at each other.

It was Zvi who eventually asked, "And your father?"

"Of blessed memory," Isaac explained.

"I'm sorry." And Zvi was.

A smile came to the dark face opposite him. "He came to the Holy Land before he died. And as he told me, that was more than his father's father had ever been able to do."

"And the land has not been good to you," Zvi said.

The silversmith was silent for a long time before he shook his head. "It has nothing to do with the land. I have no skill a man would want." To make certain Zvi did not think he was complaining, "The fault is no one's. There is little need for silver right now. Maybe another time."

Rising, Zvi poured coffee for both of them, never taking his eyes off Isaac as he thought about the problems of a silversmith.

"How old are you?" Zvi asked after a time.

Isaac grinned. "Too old." Then he added, "Thirty-two."

Zvi nodded. "I have two suggestions." Then, he in his turn smiled. "Let me say they are supported by *protectzia*." Tapping the insignias of his rank with a forefinger. "You are a craftsman. You know metals. You could work in ordnance." Seeing the blank expression on Isaac's face, he explained, "Weapons."

The other man nodded, sipped his coffee and remained silent.

"Or you could join the army and be my driver." Spilling his words quickly before he could be misunderstood, "There is nothing I need more than someone I know and can trust." He thought about this. "The work will not be easy, but I could use you. I really could."

This seemed to satisfy Isaac. "And my wife and the children?"

Zvi weighed this. "You would have an apartment for them and a salary. Small at first, but it will go up. There will be weeks and sometimes months when they will not see you."

"But there will be enough food for them?"

Nodding, Zvi waited to hear the decision.

"And school for the boy and the girl?"

Again, Zvi nodded.

"And I can remain a good Jew?"

Zvi wanted to smile. "I'll be the bad one." However, as he joked, he saw Isaac's face cloud and so he laughed loudly. "I'm not offended, old friend." Setting down his cup, Zvi shoved his chair back so that he could better see the silversmith from San'a. "I'm sorry. I should have done this a long time ago," and he was thinking of Havah. "I'm very sorry."

But Isaac was shaking his head. "You make me ashamed that I sought you."

Puzzled, Zvi cocked his head to one side and waited for an explanation.

"I was hoping you would help me get the boy into school. He needs clothes, books. I was not looking for anything else. Believe me."

Trying not to become embarrassed, Zvi nodded. "I believe you. And the boy will go to school."

And two weeks later the boy did. During those two weeks, Zvi helped move Isaac's family into a small apartment in one of the sections of Tel Aviv where the landlords would rent to oriental Jews, promising that he would help him find a better place soon, and then he arranged with Avram for Isaac to start his military training.

Though Isaac was able to reach Zvi that summer, none of his other friends really could.

Shoshanna became increasingly aware of the changes in him. She was aware he was seen wherever the army was operating, but that she saw less and less of him. It was not, she believed, that he loved her any less but, rather, that he was caught up in the web of work into which he had thrust himself and had no desire to shake free, partly because he sincerely believed he had responsibilities beyond any man's, and partly because he did not want to think about himself and what he was doing or where he was personally going. And strangely, though Shoshanna knew he was in some way trapped by his belief in his responsibilities, she knew that she was not one of them.

The Arab raids continued. It was late in the year that Zvi led one of his last retaliation raids against Jordan. Moving out with two of his companies, he slashed at the Jordanian police headquarters at Karem Saih, killing eight Arab terrorists and wounding three others. But the cost was too high. Zvi returned to his base camp near Tel Aviv with four wounded men. He arranged that they be sent directly to a hospital and then he sat back and waited for further orders. He was tired, more tired than he could recall since the battle for the Old City seven years before. At times, as he wandered about his small headquarters, he wondered if his age was not already beginning to show. The weight he had put on since the war remained, and even though he felt stronger and more agile than ever before, the overwhelming fatigue continued to linger. The only way in which he could count results for the costs to himself and his men was in the dropping figures of Jordanian incursions into Israel. Knowing better than most the impossibility of bringing statistics into focus in terms of individuals killed and wounded, he still was able to take into account the fact that in 1950 the Jordanians had killed 57; in 1953, 34; 44 in 1951; 46 in 1952; and in 1955, 11. If Avram and his staff were keeping an accurate count and the records he received regularly were correct, he was convinced the policy was paying off.

Twice in recent months he had been offered leave from duty for a matter of weeks or even months if he wished it, and both times he had refused. Now, as he threw himself onto his bunk in the early hours of the morning and stared at the light just beginning to come through the window, he wondered if he had been wrong. With a leave there would be more things that he could look into without the immediate demands of his battalion. However, he did not think that he could depart now. There was already talk of turning the battalion into a brigade, and he was not going to trust anyone else to take on the job that had to be his.

Yelling from where he lay on his bed, he asked his sergeant to send in Isaac. The Yemenite had been in service for months now, had undergone the basic training required of any soldier, and then had been short-cut into Zvi's unit at the commander's request. Looking up from where he lay, Zvi smiled at his old friend. No amount of training and no amount of repeating would ever make Isaac Ben Aaron look like a soldier. He could be neat. He could go through the motions of saluting when called upon. He could even hold his own position on a firing line, but one look at his thin ascetic face, and no professional would ever accept him as a soldier. Aware that there were those who believed he had erred in his choice of a personal driver, Zvi knew that he had something other than a soldier, and that difference was what he personally wanted of Isaac. Swinging his feet over the side of the bed, Zvi picked up a clip-board and jotted down Shoshanna's address. "If you will pick her up as soon as school is over in Natanya, I'll meet you at the apartment later this afternoon."

When he was alone again, Zvi slipped once more onto his back and stared at the light from the window until he finally threw one arm over his eyes and tried to fall asleep.

Isaac remained outside the commander's door until he was sure that Zvi was asleep before he left the camp for Natanya. He would have hours to wait, but he had nothing else to do. The life into which Zvi had taken him was strange. His duties were light, as Zvi himself drove except when they were in action or meeting with other commanders. Almost every night he was able to get into Tel Aviv where his family now lived. Pleased that the two children were in school, and not quite certain if he approved of the fact that his daughter was going to study the same subjects as his son, Isaac was, however, satisfied that he had made a good choice.

It was after four when Shoshanna turned onto the street and recognized Zvi's jeep in front of the apartment. For a moment she thought that something had happened to Zvi. It had to have, because though she had not seen much of him in recent weeks, he had always come for her himself. Dropping her bookbag, she ran to the jeep and waited for an explanation. Isaac's dark face worried her until she saw the smile that spread across it as he proudly announced in that gentle voice she had come to recognize as Yemenite, "The Colonel has asked me to bring Miss Haim to Tel Aviv."

Shoshanna nodded. "He is all right?"

Isaac's head bobbed. "He worked last night," as though Zvi held a job in a factory or shop and was making overtime pay.

Shoshanna thought about being sent for, decided that she would settle for what she could get of Zvi and said, "I'll be down soon."

Ten minutes later she had changed her dress and returned and Isaac was driving wildly down the coast road toward Tel Aviv. Holding onto the side of the jeep, Shoshanna asked, "How long have you been driving for the Colonel?"

"Six months." Then, as though this needed explanation, Issac added, "I knew him in Yemen."

Swinging about so that she could see him better, Shoshanna wondered why Zvi had taken the man onto his own staff. There was such an obvious gentleness about Isaac Ben Aaron that it contrasted sharply with the image she had of Zvi and the army.

"You came with him from San'a?"

Shoshanna was trying to sort out Isaac's face from the more than forty thousand who had passed through Camp Hashed; she came to focus on none.

"I am the one who told him Havah gave him the boy."

Very slowly Shoshanna turned back in her seat so that she was facing the oncoming traffic. "Did you know the boy's mother?"

"I knew her in San'a." Then he added, "She and her husband died on the road coming south."

Shoshanna nodded, knowing she had not learned what she had expected. "And they gave the boy to Zvi?"

A truck slowed ahead of them and Isaac remained silent as he swung the jeep onto the shoulder and around the truck. He was racing again. "It was Havah sent him the boy."

"Havah?"

"Havah. She was a good woman in her own way." Then, because he thought he might be misunderstood, "She did things that helped keep the rest of us alive, and I think there were times when she helped keep Zvi alive."

"Keep Zvi alive?"

Again, Isaac nodded to himself as his thoughts drifted back and sifted through the terrible months of the evacuation from Yemen. "The way a woman keeps a man wanting to wake up the next morning when he is too tired to open his eyes, the way she makes him see how things grow and the color of the stones along the side of the road."

However, Shoshanna was not thinking of the color of stones, but of a woman she had never heard of before who had kept Zvi Mazon going when he may have wanted to keep his eyes closed in the morning. "What happened to Havah?" she finally asked.

"She died," Isaac said, as though death was something one took for granted.

It was Shoshanna's turn to nod; it seemed curious to her that the women who had been closest to Zvi Mazon died.

The jeep burst out of the traffic and drew up in front of the apartment on Jabotinsky Street. When Shoshanna opened the door, she expected to find Zvi waiting for her. He was not there. Wandering through the three small rooms, she saw that they had not been cleaned since she had been there almost two weeks before. Moving through the apartment, she set the coffee pot on to heat.

Two hours after the coffee had percolated she was still alone. The small alarm clock in the bedroom matched the time on her own watch: seven-thirty. Uncertain what she was going to do about dinner, she stood for a moment before the pantry. Sardines and tuna fish. Annoyed, she slammed the pantry door closed as the phone rang. In anticipation she ran out of the kitchen until she gathered her poise and took the last few steps to the instrument with a measured pace, wanting to laugh at herself as she did so.

Malin. Zvi was not coming. He had asked Avram, who was calling his wife, to have her call Shoshanna. He would have called himself. There was a meeting both men had to attend. It was important. He was sorry. He hoped he could see her later.

Listening to the explanation which had been passed on through two others, Shoshanna kept nodding at the telephone. She had been disappointed before. She had spent nights in the apartment waiting for him in recent months, nights when she would rather have been in her own bed in Natanya than wondering if he were going to return alive; and if he did, would he be able to call her.

And now he was having Malin call. This was the only thing that was new.

"Can you meet me for Fishel Warshow's concert?" Malin was asking, and Shoshanna forced herself to think of more than Zvi.

And Shoshanna was agreeing when Malin informed her, "Zvi said that you should use his driver." Then she knew that he had been more thoughtful than she had been willing to credit him, and in the same moment when she was cradling the phone, she smiled to herself. Thoughtful, or was he deciding how someone should do something? Of all the qualities which were becoming distinct as she came to know him better, his compulsive need to settle details for other people became one of the more omnipresent. She was not certain she disliked it.

When she arrived at the theater, Malin was waiting for her, and Shoshanna realized she had not seen her friend more than twice in the year since she had met Zvi at the Ben Ezras' apartment. Malin appeared at least five months pregnant. "Do judicial robes cover that?" Shoshanna asked.

Malin said she hoped so. They were moving through the crowd into the theater, and Malin was explaining that the program was Mendelssohn and Beethoven and that Fishel had announced he was taking the next four months off the concert stage.

After they had found their seats, Malin relaxed and closed her eyes. "I drove down from Jerusalem expecting to be able to spend the evening with Avram." Sighing, she explained, "I have not seen him for more than two hours in the past month." Then she smiled and, without thinking, added, "Don't marry a military man. You can never depend on him." Her eyes came open and she was staring at her friend.

Shoshanna's head was raised as though she were watching something on the far wall of the auditorium.

Fishel appeared on stage. "We've been invited to his apartment for coffee after the concert," Malin whispered as the house lights dimmed.

When Fishel began to play, Shoshanna leaned forward in her seat, her hands clenched tightly in her lap, her eyes never leaving his bow.

Beethoven. And more Beethoven.

Somewhere someone was whispering too loudly, "Why do we always have to hear those damned Germans."

Malin's head came up, fearing an outburst.

Shoshanna never heard the whispers. As she had once told Zvi, there was something about a violin which enchanted her in the oldest sense of that word. Her head swayed to the music. She was hearing things in it she had never heard before. She always did, or at least she thought so. And then for the first time since she had attended her first concert as a child with her father, she knew that she herself had changed between concerts. The music meant more to her than it had before. Instead of being something she was able to relax and enjoy, the music had become a kind of exquisite pain, and she moaned softly.

The small, muffled sound from Shoshanna brought Malin's head up. Something was wrong. She did not know what it was. She remembered

Shoshanna as a beautiful girl, at least by the standards of most of the girls with whom she had grown up, and at this moment Shoshanna was anything but beautiful. Her hair, piled high on her head, lacked any luster. Her eyes were bright, but it was from tension rather than pleasure. Looking more closely, Malin noticed the clenched hands writhing as though they had a life in themselves. Whatever was driving Zvi Mazon was also reaching into Shoshanna.

And now Bach, and someone else whispering, "More of the damned Germans."

A hiss from the back of the hall.

The sound broke like a wave bearing scum.

And suddenly the enchantment was gone for Shoshanna, who sat rigidly upright; and then as Malin watched, she appeared to settle limp into the back of the seat. Around them people were saying, "Hush."

But the hiss was there again.

Then it was joined by other hisses.

Malin leaned forward now as Fishel, standing small on the stage, lowered his violin from under his chin and very carefully set it down on the piano. He gestured to someone by raising both hands, palms up. The lights came on in the hall and everyone fell silent.

"Friends," he said, "let us talk a moment."

Surprised that anyone could be heard in this large hall and yet have so gentle a voice, Malin clasped the seat in front of her.

"There is none here who has not reason to hate, who is not justified in his hatred, if hatred is justified. I will deny none the right to hate. All I ask is that I be left the right to love." His voice rose in emphasis now, "And I do love that which is beautiful. Because the men who came after these artists were ugly does not mean that these artists were not beautiful."

A hiss from the back of the hall.

Fishel's hands came up as though to block the sound from reaching him.

"It is a strange thing," he continued. "We Jews have seen the glory of the Lord, known the greatness of our tradition, chased what is right like a nation of hunters. Ah, but the search for beauty for the sake of beauty, that is a chase we entered late. Let us not be thrown off the scent by the garbage history has thrown over the trail."

His voice broke as he pleaded, "We Jews are too experienced, too much a part of history to be led down false avenues. Perhaps I do not play these artists' works as well as others might, but while you are with me, please do not confuse history with beauty and beauty with history. You are too experienced for that."

He half bowed, nodded to someone offstage; and as the lights dimmed once more, he picked up his violin from the piano, and after an unexpected burst of applause, he started to play once more.

For Shoshanna the concert was ended, the enchantment fled. For the next forty-five minutes she sat back in her seat with her eyes closed and tried to relax by thinking of Aaron as she had seen him on the Sabbath the week before when his father had disappointed both of them by remaining in the Negev. She was still thinking about the boy when the lights went up once more, and Malin pulled herself with difficulty from her seat.

Half an hour later, after arranging with Isaac to wait for her at Fishel's apartment, Shoshanna sat down at the large table with the others. She was aware that Dvora Rabsky was obviously her hostess. For a few minutes the talk drifted about the concert and the incident that had taken place.

"We Jews are funny," Fishel said without animosity. "We are really more different from other people than they know." He shook his head as he explained, "The Hebrew University is a great school, but there is no decision as yet whether or not art should be taught there and whether music would be appropriate." Afraid he had slighted the school, he added, "Given time, they will learn. I suggested music courses once," he chuckled. "And an elderly professor shook his head angrily and told me, 'That's not what was taught in Vilna.' " The others were laughing.

"And you know, he was probably right."

Dvora gestured for the Moroccan maid to bring the coffee after asking if anyone wanted brandy. Seated across the table from Fishel, she could see him rubbing the side of his leg. The pregnant woman was wholesome looking. She spoke with a quiet authority, and Dvora wondered where Fishel had met her. The other one was nervous, the napkin in her hand revolved slowly in her tight grip. She was thin, and Dvora wondered if she were well. A friend of Zvi Mazon, the other woman had said. The others were talking of Moshe Gilead now.

"He will be promoted in the next few months," Judge Ben Ezra was informing the others.

"And Zvi?" Shoshanna asked, defensively.

A trace of a smile crossed Fishel's lips as he felt happy for Zvi.

Malin shook her head. "Moshe made it first and he will make the next one first." Then, because she felt Shoshanna might blame Avram, "Zvi is scheduled. I'm sure of that."

However, Fishel was not satisfied. "Avram really got to lieutenant-colonel before either of the others."

"Thanks for remembering that," Malin said. "He's a staff officer, and he says they go up more slowly. It's a matter of so many open ranks, the way he explained it to me. Most of them go to the field officers."

Fishel nodded. "As Zvi explained it to me some years ago, 'We aren't going to become a Latin American army with a lot of generals and no privates.' There is going to be a sharp limitation on the number of high ranks. One goes so far, and if he thinks he isn't going to the top, he gets out in time to start another career."

Malin nodded. "Or the Chief of Staff lets him in on the secret by not renewing his contract."

"Maybe," Shoshanna ventured, "there is an advantage in being a staff officer."

Fishel laughed. "Maybe. I think staff men will be allowed to stay in until their mid-forties. For the others — out and into another career while they are young enough to start it."

Shoshanna was startled. "Out before their mid-forties?"

Both Malin and Fishel nodded. "Out at forty if possible. No more than a year or two beyond that."

"If they live that long," Shoshanna said cynically.

It was Fishel who pushed back his chair to see her better. "The chance of being killed is what a soldier gets paid for."

"It isn't his dying I fear," Shoshanna said softly, remembering the way Zvi's eyes seemed lost in his skull and the way his hands shook now. "It isn't the dying," she repeated. "For over two years he's been taking his men out and coming back with fewer after each raid." Then, as if her appeal for understanding could make any difference, "He's had young men he's trained and lived with and slept beside and watched grow up and get killed beside him or because of orders he's given them." She was trying to explain to Malin now. "He's been their father, stood up for them when they married, listened to their stories about their children, watched their girl friends collapse when he appeared at the door with the news people know he brings with him." And turning to Fishel, "What kind of man would he be if it didn't get to him?"

"Moshe Gilead," Malin said flatly.

The others looked at her and only Dvora seemed to be amused. Fishel disagreed. "The other night I was having coffee with one of Moshe's officers who knew I was an old friend. He told me he overheard Moshe returning from a raid one night talking to two lieutenants who were killed almost three years ago. Moshe was telling them that he had seen their families and that everything was well and that he hoped they would do as well in the next raid as they had done in the last. And them almost three dead."

"Shouldn't he be relieved?" Dvora asked, showing some interest for the first time.

Fishel sighed. "Why? Because he feels? What kind of officers would we have if they didn't feel?" He was trying to explain to Shoshanna now. "Moshe and Zvi have lived with death as a companion for years. Someone else would have to make his acquaintance, and who knows — maybe that someone else would not be as companionable."

Shoshanna wanted to argue, but instead all she could bring herself to do was ask, "How long do they expect him to go on?"

Fishel was rubbing his leg again and Dvora could not take her eyes from his hand. "I don't know," he finally said. "Until they get killed or go mad or fail to do the job they set out to do."

"That could give them three honest ways out," Dvora said.

"God help them," Malin added.

Shaking his head, Fishel smiled, "Peace could be a fourth way out."

Shoshanna asked hopefully, "Is it likely?"

Dvora laughed cynically.

Frowning at his mistress, Fishel tried to reassure Shoshanna. "Don't worry. They'll survive." Then, to show Dvora that he had forgiven her laugh, "I'm sure even Dvora will admit that they are both good fighters."

All three were looking at Dvora now and she brushed her hair back with a self-conscious gesture and then her head came up and she met the eyes first of Malin and then of Shoshanna. Neither had paid enough attention to her before to realize that she was the only really beautiful woman in the room. Her dark eyes seemed remote and at the same time completely focused on this moment. Her skin was a transparent white, while the black hair which hung about her shoulders sparkled with light cast from the chandelier. She did not take her eyes off Shoshanna while she tried to decide what she could say to this stranger who was obviously in love with the young man she remembered. "He has courage," she said after a time. "He isn't always wise, but he has courage." Then, because she wanted to be understood, she added, "I hope he is more . . ." And she groped for a word, straining her vocabulary for the right one. "More . . ." She smiled as though she had caught something in a net. "More of a *mensch*."

Before Shoshanna could dispute the point, Malin caught Fishel's eye and he changed the subject. "And what do you think of Moshe as a soldier?"

"He's like a tank. He'll plow through anything, believing it will yield because Moshe Gilead is coming. I imagine women are like any other objective for him: to be taken."

Turning to Shoshanna, Dvora said, "I think Mazon is the one who will look like a tank but act like a racehorse when it comes to a battle."

Shoshanna asked, "Do you know him well?"

Dvora shook her head. "I'm sure he does not remember me," and only Fishel realized she was trying to turn the conversation aside.

"Dvora fought with us in the Old City," he explained.

The other women nodded, wondering if that was where Fishel had met her and what she meant to him.

Later, as they were leaving, Malin asked bluntly, "The four months without a concert, where are you going?"

He started to say something, but Dvora spoke first, "He's going to be away." Then, with surprising consideration, "I'll let you know when he comes back."

After the two women left, Fishel settled into an easy chair, stretched out his leg, which obviously hurt, and drew Dvora to him. As she settled into his lap and he started to unzip the back of her dress, he asked, "Did you like them?"

"I feel sorry for the one who is in love with Mazon," she said.

He was slipping her dress off her shoulders now and trying to unhook her brassiere. His nimble fingers became still as he held her away from him. "Why?"

"He's the kind of fool who gets himself killed in the headlines. And in a country that has to survive by fighting all of the time, maybe that is not a bad thing."

Seeing that she was serious and knowing there were things about which one did not argue with Dvora, he finished what he was doing before he kissed her.

Even afterward he was trying to decide if she meant Zvi's being killed was a good thing or if heroes were a good thing. Neither of them talked that night about Fishel's removing himself for four months from the concert stage. However, he asked her to marry him as he had every night since she had slipped into bed years before and she still said the same thing, "I have to feel free to leave. I have to belong to me."

Isaac first drove Malin to her apartment on the east side of the city and then swung back to the apartment on Jabotinsky Street where a staff jeep was parked in front of the building. Shoshanna thanked Isaac and, entering the apartment, found a light on in the sitting room. Zvi had actually arrived. She found him in the bedroom, lying fully dressed on the bedspread. It appeared as though he had waited for her until he fell asleep. Pulling two blankets and a sheet from the closet, she threw one blanket over Zvi, made a bed for herself on the couch and wished that Israel had not bought so much Danish furniture with wooden-armed sofas. She pulled her dress over her head, laid it across a chair and her shoes beside it. For a moment she stood thinking of Zvi in the next room, and then with a smile, she grabbed the blanket from the sofa and walked back into the bedroom. Stretching out beside Zvi, she drew the blanket over her and snuggled up next to him. It was almost dawn when he awakened to find her there.

It was noon when he drove her back to Natanya and then headed once more for his headquarters, feeling better than he had in weeks.

The months that followed were among the worst in the brief history of Israel. The saboteurs and terrorists shifted their activities from the Jordanian border on the east to the Gaza border on the southwest. Colonel Gamal Abdel Nasser, who was both premier and military governor of Egypt, intended to show his people that he was as tough a dictator as any in the world and that it was he who would "drive the Jews into the sea."

The incursions from Gaza were insignificant at first. Small pinpricks. A drop of blood here and a drop of blood there. Pipelines destroyed. Orchards stripped. Cattle and sheep stolen. Farm tools and equipment stolen. Israeli crops destroyed. Roads mined. An Egyptian army unit fired on an Israeli frontier patrol, killing one and wounding two. A tractor driver

killed, another wounded. Fedayeen killed three men on the Gaza border
patrol and the same night they shot down two farmers at Ein Hashelosha six
kilometers from the Demarcation Line. Near Zeilim they murdered a farmer
patrolling a water line. They struck down a student near Beit Hanun and an
old watchman at Rishon le Zion. Thirty miles north of Gaza, near the
Weizmann Institute at Rehovot they ambushed and murdered a young
physicist. And in Cairo the Egyptian government held a national celebration
to hang two Jews from whom they had forced a confession of espionage after
six months of torture.

Two days after the hangings in Cairo, Zvi Mazon was out with
Shoshanna. It had been weeks since they had seen each other, and now they
had just come from a visit to Aaron and had heard the reports from the boy's
teachers that he was doing well and that his chickens had laid more eggs than
any other in the henhouse. They were laughing with pleasure at Aaron's
achievements and the pride in which he held them.

"He's a lot like you," Shoshanna said.

"Me?" and Zvi turned so that he could see her better. A car was bearing
down on them on his side of the road, and he swung wide to avoid it.

She nodded. "He thinks there isn't anything he can't do better than
anyone else."

Zvi considered this. Then he, too, nodded. "Is there anything anyone
can do better than I?"

Believing he was serious, she swung her hand playfully at his cheek.
Accepting the blow, he asked, "Is there anyone you know who does some of
the things I do better?"

They continued to exchange meaningless jokes all the way to the
apartment on Jabotinsky Street. Later in the afternoon when they lay in bed
watching the shadows crawl across the wall, Zvi reached out and touched her
bare flat stomach. "Do you envy Malin?"

She was silent for a long time and then she shook her head. "I'm
happy," she said without conviction. "Other things can come later."

His hand passed up her body and cupped her breast. "Thanks," he said.

He was embracing her again when the telephone rang. Trying to ignore
it, he held her closer and kissed her neck. He would have continued if she had
not pushed him away.

"You have a command," she reminded him, and in that instant she
realized that this was probably the first time since Zella's death that anyone
had had to remind Zvi of anything.

He was out of bed and striding into the living room with the comment,
"I'll have the phone either taken out or put in the bedroom."

Shoshanna puffed his pillow and lay back to listen as he picked up the
phone.

"Me. Yes, of course. Set assembly for . . ." and he cursed under his breath. "What time is it?" A pause and he ordered, "Set assembly for ten tonight. Have Isaac report here. I'll be at Hakiryah in twenty minutes." Then she could hear him coming back to the bedroom, and even though her eyes were closed, she knew he was standing at the edge of the bed looking at her. She never bothered to draw up the sheet which had slipped down to her thighs.

"Isaac will take you home," he told her. The play was gone from his voice, and he started to dress as quickly as he could.

Opening her eyes, Shoshanna watched him pull on his trousers; and when he sat down on the edge of the bed to draw up his socks and slip into his shoes, she ran a finger down his bare back.

After he finished dressing, he leaned over, ran one hand over her breasts and then kissed her.

"Take care," she said as though he were going out to fight the traffic on Allenby Street.

Smiling at her, he nodded. "I'll call you as soon as I can."

Then she was alone, pleased that she had not told Zvi what she had heard about Ruth.

It was almost dawn. Zvi listened to his platoon leaders brief their men. Three kilometers to the west lay the Gaza Demarcation Line. Kneeling in the open field, he shoved his beret back on his head while he drew hard on the last cigarette he had brought with him. This was the fifth raid against the Gaza area in as many months. Five retaliations to more than a hundred terrorist incursions, more than a hundred Israeli dead. Ever since April of 1955, when the Egyptian high command had formally organized their "self-sacrificers" — the Fedayeen — the level of terror against Israel had been raised.

Since that first failure, he had always brought back his dead from every retaliation raid. And his men had sat in the trucks with their dead companions silent on the floor between them. The next day they had buried their dead and prepared for the next retaliation. Now he wondered how many more raids they could make. His head went back and he saw what he thought was light to the east. How much more could he himself take? He picked up a clod of earth. The dirt broke dry between his fingers. Tossing it away, he rose and moved closer to the first half-track.

"Limited," he heard the platoon leader telling his men. Zvi shook his head as though to brush the word out of it. His hand sought the worn tracks of the vehicle. They would make it over this dry ground. He doubted if they would make it twice more. Someone started to approach him and, turning, Zvi walked away from the unit. Not now. Not at this moment. He had to think. Days could pass and he could not bring himself to think, but now, before he led another group across the Demarcation Line and brought home what remained of it, he had to think.

His staff, knowing him well enough to fear his sudden temper, left him alone as he walked toward the Gaza line. Out of sight of the others, he knelt once more. He wished he had another cigarette. Only a fool goes out on operations without a cigarette. The sun was rising now. Limited, perhaps. But he was playing it bold this morning. If the Egyptians were sleeping after their night's raids, they were going to be hit in the early morning. He had his plans and he knew he was right. Every other time he or Moshe struck, they had come in darkness. Now he was going to throw the enemy off balance. He knew it might cost him dearly. He did not want to count his costs now. The word "costs" hung on the fringes of his brain, and he thought of the cost to the Egyptians: a flat salary for each terrorist, a bonus for each crossing of the line, and another bonus for every Israeli killed. The high cost of living and dying. And it was his job this morning to raise the ante in this game.

His broad palm washed his face while he continued to stare toward the Gaza frontier. Beyond it lay three terrorist camps financed by the Egyptians for the sole purpose of killing Jews. He had no intention of leading his men back to their base as long as one of these Arab camps was intact.

A young platoon leader was approaching and Zvi forced a smile. "Yes?"

"It's almost eight."

Glancing at his watch, Zvi asked, "Any problems with the time?"

Surprised, the lieutenant shook his head. "No, only we . . . ."

Zvi put his arm about the young man's shoulder and led him back to the field where the half-tracks and tanks were lined up. He wanted this young man to relax. With a gesture of affection, he shoved the youth toward his own platoon. "Find me a cigarette."

While the lieutenant went in search of cigarettes, Zvi checked with the three company commanders. They were ready. They were not eager, but they were ready. One kept opening and closing the web-holster at his hip. This gesture was new. This captain had never shown his tension before. The second kept toeing the dirt in front of him as though it were alive, while the third could not bring himself to look away from the Gaza line just three kilometers distant.

Glancing once more at his watch, Zvi calculated the time again for the distance and finally said, "If you're ready, let's go." His voice was low but firm. Only the three heard him. Sighing as though relieved of pain, they trotted toward their own units. One hundred twenty men. Zvi had brought more than enough captains. What he needed was coordination this morning, and that would not be gained with only three company commanders. He heard the truck engines start. The motors of the heavier half-tracks warmed quickly. The tanks rumbled where they stood like armored oxen in an unplanted field. He watched the guns swing slowly about and then back again as men checked out their equipment a final time before battle. From where he stood, Zvi could hear the bolts of the machine guns slammed into place and the tanks being buttoned up. The half-tracks were loaded. Trucks with machine-gun mounts were moved into place behind the heavier transport. Raising his hand, he gestured for Isaac to join him. The wiry Yemenite gunned the jeep motor and swirled about the field to come to a halt beside his commander.

Zvi was looking off toward the Gaza line three kilometers distant beyond a small roll of earth. There was every chance the Fedayeen knew he was here. He no longer depended on his approach being a secret. As far as the Egyptians were concerned, he could be leading another patrol along the border, another worried body of Jews trying to evaluate the damage of the night before. He did not care. They could be certain only the moment he crossed that line and headed directly toward them, and only he could declare that moment.

Standing in the jeep beside Isaac, he glanced back at his signals sergeant, trying to make sense of the confused sputter on the radio.

Zvi's eyes half closed as he recalled the reports of casualties he had read at Hakiryah: three young men from Toronto, two tractor drivers near Ein Hashelosha, the two innocents hanged in Cairo, the attack on the line near Zeilim, the boy who had been coming home from the university, the old watchman at Rishon le Zion, the young physicist near Rehovot, and the others: the two men killed outside Tel Aviv, the woman whose wedding had been turned into her funeral when a grenade burst in the middle of the ceremony, the small boy who had chased one of his sheep and been found beside it, the blood of his slit throat mixing with the blood of his sheep. Zvi tried not to think of the distorted look on Zella's face.

Isaac, watching, wondered if there was something wrong. The company commanders kept their eyes on the jeep waiting for instructions. The tank drivers relaxed because they trusted Colonel Mazon.

The radio behind Zvi sputtered. The vague images fled his mind. Now he was able to bring his thoughts to the task in front of him. Standing rigidly in his jeep, he waved the first company on, their target: Camp 9. Then the second company, their target: Camp 10, and then the men moving toward Camp 11.

Pleased that he had stripped his command back for this operation, Zvi watched the three units move out. He was bound for Camp 9 himself. The others knew where he would be. He would meet them as he fell back from the farthest penetration. Tapping Isaac on the shoulder, he dropped into his seat and waited until his own jeep led the column.

They were topping a roll of hill now. The Gaza Strip lay before them.

On now.

Faster.

He had given up all pretense at an indirect approach. He was not planning to hold a piece of ground, just maul it and pull back.

The columns moved as one until they approached the Demarcation Line and then, swinging his head from right to left, Zvi approved of the way the two rear units swung off in their separate directions. They were almost at the Demarcation Line. Barbed wire stretched before them.

Isaac slowed the pace and one of the tanks moved across the wire, flattening the concertinas while three men dropped off a half-track and pulled what remained aside. They moved on.

Off to his left, Zvi could see the white of a UN jeep. His hand went up and one of the trucks peeled off the column as a lieutenant moved toward the UN jeep. The truck and the UN jeep would come to a shouting impasse for no less than an hour, and then the lieutenant would apologize to the UN officer.

Somewhere ahead of them a rifle opened fire. Isaac, once more in the lead, ignored the single shot. Reaching down at his feet, Zvi scooped up the helmet lying there and jammed it onto the Yemenite's head.

Neither of them spoke. The radio behind Zvi fell silent. There was more firing off to the south. Somewhere, Zvi heard the sucking *woosh* of a mortar. Camp 10 was under attack.

The column moving toward Camp 9 rolled on. They were not racing. There was something deliberate about the way in which Zvi was setting the pace. To the north he could hear firing. Almost eight-thirty. Camp 11 was engaged.

The radio sputtered, and then the operator was shouting in his ear. "The UN jeep is trying to alert the Egyptians."

Zvi shrugged. There was nothing he could do and the terrorists in camps 10 and 11 were already engaged.

Now the buildings of Camp 9 were in front of them. The tank moved forward while the half-tracks took their positions and started to shell the buildings. The barbed wire about the camp gave way before the tank and Zvi followed. Someone was returning rifle fire.

The half-tracks leveled their guns and fired point blank into the wooden barracks.

Zvi waved Isaac to one side, and then with his hand gestured for him to stop. Scanning the camp, he found it was what he had expected. Ten wooden barracks. Fenced. A dirty gray which might have passed for white. There was the smoke of a stove above one. The tank was already shelling a barrack.

Arabs were spilling out of the others and trying to make their way to the fields beyond.

Zvi came to his feet as he watched one lead half-track move slowly after the escaping terrorists. The half-track swung up onto a knoll and sprayed machine-gun fire over the fleeing Arabs. Some screamed. One man stood his ground and tried to pump a shell into the breach of his weapon. Two machine-gun slugs struck the rifle, which bounced against his chest and then to the ground as he toppled across his weapon.

From one of the buildings, a machine gun opened up at one of Zvi's trucks. He saw two of his men fall. Cursing, he watched as four sappers dropped off the back of a truck and moved toward the wooden barracks. A bangalore torpedo struck the lower part of the building, but the machine gun kept firing and two of the sappers dropped, their charges exploding as slugs reached them.

Pointing directly toward the barrack where the machine gun was located, Zvi jammed his elbow into Isaac's side. The jeep jumped forward. Two more Arab machine-gun bursts brought down sappers who were laying their charges beside other barracks.

As he approached the building, Zvi realized the gun was located on the second floor, and leaping out of the jeep, he grabbed up his own submachine gun, jammed his hand into his pocket and threw himself into the dirt as a burst from the enemy gun splashed the ground about his jeep. Isaac was already taking the command jeep around the side of another building. Inching forward, Zvi could see from the corner of his eye the first charges bring down a barrack to his left. Another explosion and another building collapsed into a twist of broken lumber. A fire burned to his right. The machine gun above him tried to depress, but it only kicked up dirt ten feet from his heel. Feeling secure, he came to his feet and raced toward the door of the building. One of his platoon leaders was already there. Zvi started to set his shoulder against the door. In that same instant, the young lieutenant thrust out his hip, blocked his commander and hurled himself against the door. A burst of submachine gun fire from inside as the door split open and the youth fell before it. Jerking a grenade from his pocket, Zvi pulled the pin, waited a beat, and then lobbed it through the open door. Two beats, and a scream mixed with an explosion.

Jumping over the body of his platoon leader, Zvi emptied his submachine gun into the room, and then without pausing, dropped the clip, jammed another in its place and started for the staircase on his left. Someone standing there fired a rifle, but Zvi dropped him with a controlled burst.

He knew the rifle had been fired at him, but he was not certain he had heard it, and as he leapt over the limp body of the Arab terrorist at the base of the stairs, he wondered how he had known. Up half a flight and all the while he could hear a machine gun shaking the building. Pressing flat against the wall at the top of the stairs, he lobbed the second grenade. Two beats and he felt the barracks rock. The machine gun was silent. Without bothering to look at what he had done, Zvi walked back down the stairs, picked up the lieutenant lying across the front door and stepped outside. Two sappers had set their charges near the entrance.

"Blow it," he ordered.

And when Isaac rejoined him, he dumped the body of the lieutenant into the back of his own jeep across the radio.

A moment later the barrack blew high and a fire started. Swinging about in his seat, Zvi saw that four of the ten buildings were burning. Static over the radio behind him and he glanced back for information.

"The UN," the sergeant said.

Zvi nodded. Then he pulled himself to his feet with difficulty. Very slowly, he evaluated the damage. No fewer than twenty dead Fedayeen. He hoped there were more. Next time he would block the fields behind the camp before he attacked, but he could only do that at night. His hand went up and the column began to reform once more. Off to the south there was silence. Firing continued toward the north. Waving the tank and half-track on, Zvi paused to scan the camp, and as each of his platoon leaders and company commanders passed, he asked if they had all the wounded and dead.

Finally, satisfied, he started to sit down once more in the jeep. However, as he jammed his hand inside his battle jacket he was not certain if the warm stickiness he felt there was the lieutenant's blood or his own. His eyes began to cloud over and twice he had to shake his head before he realized that he had been hit. He could keep this problem to himself until they reached base camp. Waving his unit on, he saw that the column which had struck at Camp 10 was already withdrawing down the same path. The third column was silent now and he assumed they, too, were following. Five minutes later he saw them coming toward him. The company commander could account for his men. There had been losses. The camp was battered. He believed more than twenty dead. Zvi saw the blood on the man's arm and told him to move directly to the hospital.

All of his men were accounted for and back in Israeli territory, and he nodded to the sergeant seated behind him. A signal and the truck which had blocked the UN jeep gave way with profound apologies and headed home.

Once more Zvi told his signals sergeant, "Tell the medics to take the ones they must, and the others are to head back to camp without speaking to anyone." And as he said it, he wished he would be moving in darkness instead of the bright light of midday.

That was the last thing he thought about as he slumped forward in his seat.

Isaac and two of the captains helped Zvi into his quarters at their camp near Tel Aviv. It was midafternoon and their colonel had been either asleep or unconscious for more than three hours. Now that he was stretched out on his bed and his shirt was being cut away, he opened his eyes. The middle-aged battalion medical officer, who had been with Zvi from his first withdrawal at 'En Gedi, years before, was bending over him. They were old friends. Though their respect for each other was complete, neither trusted nor believed anything the other said.

"You're fine, aren't you?" the physician asked.

Zvi nodded. "I'm going to take a shower and get dressed and drive into town in an hour."

The other man nodded vaguely and probed the wound.

"An hour's all the time I'm going to give you," Zvi assured him.

"Uh-uh." And the doctor was not arguing. He had seen worse wounds. He had also buried men with wounds not as bad. Placement, he had been saying for years. *Placement. Give me the wound in the right place, and a man does not die. It all depends on the place a man is shot.* Zvi had heard all of this before, so he asked, "Placed just right, wasn't it?"

The doctor laid one palm over the wound to see how large it was. There were threads from the battle jacket in the opening. There was even dye from the camouflage staining the skin. But most important of all, he measured with his fingers the distance from Zvi's heart. Then he stepped back and smiled.

"Zvi, you are as lucky as you are ugly."

The Colonel's head rolled to one side so that he could see the medical officer more clearly. "For an old futz, you aren't so bad."

Then his eyes closed and he shouted for his company commanders. A moment later all three of them were in his room. While the physician continued to work over his wound, Zvi snapped his questions. "Camp 9, how many did we lose there?"

"Four, Zvi. Two sappers, one gunner and the lieutenant." There was no apology in the captain's voice, and Zvi expected none. There was a silence and then Zvi asked, "And how many did we kill?"

"I think about twenty-four."

"It cost too much," Zvi growled. Then, without opening his eyes, "And Camp 10?"

"Two dead, one seriously wounded, and thirty-three Arabs killed."

A trace of a smile crossed Zvi's face, but the sound from his throat belied it. "Camp 11?"

"Three dead, and as far as I can tell, about twenty terrorists killed."

For a long time the three captains doubted he had heard the last report. Finally, the medical officer waved them from the room. Zvi lay with his eyes closed, thinking of his dead. When he was alone with the older man, he said very softly, "Four and two and three. Nine. Nine. Nine." Then, as though oblivious of the medical officer trying to clean the wound in the flesh below his armpit, Zvi asked in a strong voice, "Well, Zella, was it worth it?"

The doctor glanced up and then continued with his work as the one-sided conversation continued.

"It cost me more than the whole fight cost me in the Quarter, and all we got for it was a bunch of dead terrorists and not an inch of ground and not a single person returned from the dead. Tell me, Zella," and his voice trailed off as he asked, "How much is a dead Jew worth? A live one?"

The doctor was surprised to see a flicker of a smile cross the colonel's face as he asked, "Havah, you remember: It was somewhere near Ibb when that old bastard wanted to buy some Jewish girls, and I wouldn't set a price, but that damned sayid did." His voice dropped for a moment and then with a grimace of pain as the physician stretched a piece of tape across the bandage, "She was there that night. I don't think either one of you would have liked her." The smile returned for an instant and then he began to rise from his pillow while his voice rose to a shout, "That stupid Arab bitch."

Placing both hands on his commander's shoulders, the doctor gently forced him back onto the pillow. He was not surprised at what he was hearing. In his several years with the commando battalion he had heard other men talking to themselves. He had heard other men talking to their dead. The one Zvi had called Zella, he himself had known. The one called Havah was a stranger.

The doctor cut the last strip of tape and set it in place.

The Colonel was mumbling something to someone. Stepping away, the doctor considered giving Zvi a shot of morphine, decided against it and left the room, closing the door behind him. Outside, he waved for Isaac to join him. He had known this Yemenite for over a year now, and he respected the man and his open affection for his commander. "If he sleeps, fine. If he wants to go into town, don't fight him. Just see that he doesn't try doing too much."

By the time Isaac entered Zvi's room the commander was out of bed and looking for a clean shirt. "Let's get the hell out of here," he said sharply.

Before Isaac could protest, Zvi added, "Call Shoshanna and ask her if she can meet me at the apartment on Jabotinsky Street."

Half an hour later, Isaac helped Zvi into the apartment and out of his shirt. For a moment the two old friends stood looking at each other. In a very soft voice, Zvi said, "If you see Havah, tell her I'll be all right." And with that, Isaac knew he had been dismissed. He wanted to wait for Shoshanna to arrive, but Zvi was waving him toward the door.

Alone, Zvi slumped into a chair and his hands came up to hold his head. His legs spread out before him and his head fell back against the bolster of the chair. After a moment he no longer recalled where he was and the sound of Isaac's voice blended with the sound of Fishel's in the old synagogue as they fought the Arabs hand to hand and there was a thin, dark face breaching his consciouness and he could not make it out. It was not Ruth and it was not Zella and it was not Shoshanna because she had not been there, and it was not Kineret because she had not been in the synagogue, and there was a dour look on the dark face and a black dress seemed to flow about the edges of his mind and then in an instant he saw the face beneath him and he heard a gunshot and he knew he had been wounded.

Then there was another sound, and it took him a moment to understand that the door of the apartment had opened and Shoshanna had arrived.

His eyes came open and he stared at her as she stood by the door. The last light of the afternoon struck the planes of her face and extenuated the tilt of her nose and the brown of her hair. He forced his eyes open as he stared at her face and then at the swell of her breasts and then once more at her face.

"You?" The bitterness in his voice struck her like a slap across the face. "Who the hell needs you? I didn't marry you. And I won't marry you. You or anyone else. I don't want any more women dying."

As she moved almost numbly into the room, Shoshanna could see the bandage on his chest and she could hear both his resentment and his guilt. His voice fell even lower now, but the bitter anger remained while he chanted over and over again, "Not any more. I won't marry any more. Not you or anyone else."

He stared beyond her and he almost wept as he said, "I'm sorry."

And suddenly Shoshanna realized he was not talking to her. Then he was rising from his chair and moving toward her, and she thought he was going to take her in his arms. However, he slapped her as hard as he could and she stumbled back. Before she could steady herself, he moved forward once more and struck her cheek twice with the back of his hand as he shouted, "*Kurveh*! Arab bitch."

Horrified, Shoshanna fumbled for the door behind her and fled. Downstairs in the street, she saw the Yemenite driver waiting. Approaching the jeep with one hand on her bruised cheek, she said, "You had better call Colonel Ben Ezra at once." Then before he could say anything, she ran down the street and away from the apartment, the word *kurveh* battering the corners of her bewildered brain, all mixed up with "Arab bitch," which made no sense.

Half an hour later, summoned by Isaac, Lieutenant-Colonel Avram Ben Ezra drew up in front of the apartment on Jabotinsky Street. The Yemenite driver came over from where he had been sitting in the jeep to explain that he had twice tried to enter the apartment but had been ordered away both times. Avram listened, nodded and walked into the building alone.

Three times he banged on the door of the apartment before Zvi Mazon told him to come in.

Closing the door behind him, Avram stared at his friend. Zvi, his shirt off revealing his bandaged shoulder, sat back in an easy chair.

"What brings you here on a sunny day?" he asked flatly.

It took Avram a moment to react because he did not really know why Isaac had called him. "I was told you weren't feeling well."

A wry smile crossed Zvi's face. He closed his eyes and when he opened them again, he tried to grin but failed. "I never thought you listened to old wives' tales."

Avram also tried to grin and failed as he crossed the room, pulled out a pack of cigarettes and, handing Zvi one, lit it for him. "Rough morning?"

Zvi tried to understand the question, and when he thought he had it in focus, he nodded slowly. "Actually, we've had rougher ones." He fell silent for a time and then continued, "I don't think any of my men are complaining. They talk about it at night when they sleep. I've heard them scream out at night. I saw one of them get drunk the other day." He leaned forward as he thought about this. "I've been in this man's army since the day it became an army, and that was one of the few times I've seen an Israeli soldier drunk." His head fell back and Avram thought he had finished speaking, but he started again. "Rough? I don't know. Good men die, but that's how you know you've been in battle. And then I remember that innocents die, too. Women minding their children, old men minding a warehouse, a boy driving a tractor. What's rough, Avi?" He snorted, "Whoever said everything's relative might have been right." His hand sought the inside of his shirt, but he was not wearing one. He laughed mockingly at himself. "That was not very profound."

Slipping into a chair opposite his friend's, the staff officer nodded. "I think I know what you mean." He watched Zvi scratch his bare belly for a moment before he suggested, "It's been a long time since you've taken any leave. Maybe a week. Two weeks. Six or more, if you want it. I'm certain it would be approved."

Zvi shook his head. "There's a whole battalion over at my base camp that needs a leave." Then he looked at his hand out before him and, embarrassed, let it fall into his lap. "You know, Avi, I had the radio on a few minutes ago and I heard the Czechs are going to arm the Arabs." A wry smile now as he asked, "What does that do to the odds?"

The staff officer combed his mind for the figures he had heard earlier in the day and decided to see just how rational Zvi was. "They are getting two hundred more tanks, two hundred armored troop carriers, and one hundred self-propelled guns." He could see Zvi calculating the totals before he shook his head.

"And?"

"Five hundred artillery pieces, almost two hundred fighter aircraft, as well as some naval vessels."

"Poof," Zvi said flatly. "Just like that. And we can't buy a damned truck on the open market." His head tilted to one side, and he laughed bitterly. "It's going to come as soon as they've been delivered." While he spoke, Zvi heard the noises battering in his head subside. The sobbing and the singing still mingled with gunfire and the smell of smoke, but all were fainter now. He almost wanted to thank his friend, but to do that he would have to tell Avram what was wrong, and Zvi sensed that he could not do that and retain his command. Brushing his hand in front of his face as though pushing something away, he asked again, "What actually brought you here?"

Avram tried to laugh. "I guess it was some old wives' tale." Then, because he felt for the sake of so many others he had to know, "If you need me or need a leave, you'll ask?"

Zvi nodded.

Coming to his feet, Avram said, "I feel foolish, but . . ."

"Don't," Zvi reassured him. "Don't. You heard a friend was ill and you came. That's not foolish."

There was nothing else to be said, and after Avram was gone, Zvi pulled himself to his feet, put on his shirt and left the apartment, wondering as he did so when he would return. That night he slept in his own bed at camp. The next morning he saw the doctor, had his bandage changed and returned to duty.

Two nights later the Fedayeen machine-gunned an Israeli border patrol, killing three men.

The next day a mine planted by the Fedayeen destroyed a truck returning from Jerusalem to a kibbutz. Two women and three men died.

The Arab officer was pleased with the accounts he read of the night's activities. It would cost money, but Colonel Nasser had told him that every piaster was well spent. Two radio messages had arrived from Cairo congratulating the general on his good work. One of them hinted at a medal. Only the day before he had been told that a precious copy of the Koran was being sent to him as a gift. And now the package lay on his desk. Picking up the phone, he asked his deputy if the two fedayeen who had been arrested for murder by the civilian authorities had been released as yet. They had been. Setting down the phone, he leaned back in his chair, more pleased with his power than ever. It was not important that the fedayeen were killers, so long as they tried to confine their killing to the other side of the border; and when they did not, there were few who would complain.

He leaned forward and started to unwrap the Koran. A rare copy. When the wrapper dropped away, he pressed the leather cover with his thin hands. It was well-tooled and he could feel the Moroccan work. Taking a deep breath in anticipation, he opened the book. The explosion which followed left one of his hands lying on the desk and the other in a corner on the far side of the room. When they assembled the pieces to bury him, they could not find a face.

And the tempo of the propaganda offensive rose.

> Only wantonness, hatred and barbarism are the means of exterminating Israel from Palestine and in every other place.
> *Voice of the Arabs,* Cairo

> Our war against the Jews is an old struggle that began with Mohammed and in which he achieved many great victories. ... It is our duty to fight the Jews for the sake of God and religion, and it is our duty to end the war which Mohammed began.
> *Al-Ahram,* Cairo

The curse of Heaven is upon Israel — from the time of Moses until Judgment Day.

Al-Gomhouriya, Cairo

God has gathered the Zionists together from all corners of the world so that the Arabs can kill them all at one stroke. Before, this was impossible because of their dispersion.

Al-Ahram, Cairo

Journalists are mistaken if they think that by calling Nasser Hitler they are hurting us. On the contrary, his name is proud among us. Long live Hitler, the Nazi who struck at the heart of our enemies! Long live the Hitler of the Arab world!

Al-Manar, Damascus

And with the rising tempo of terror, retaliation and propaganda came changes in the Israeli government.

The old man walked out of his small wooden house, looked south toward the Negev, kissed his wife and waved to his friends. He was not smiling. His strong but aged hand ran through his wild hair while he nodded. The young pilot from the air force who had been sent to fetch him waited patiently. For a moment those assembled thought the old man would say something. Instead, he seemed to shrug. Then he turned to the pilot and nodded. Five minutes later the small plane left Sede Boqer, and David Ben Gurion left his retirement to pick up the chores of government he had laid aside to spend his last years thinking and writing. There was not time now. He had been called upon to act.

Two hours after Ben Gurion arrived in Jerusalem everyone in Israel knew it. Zvi Mazon listened to the report in his headquarters in the heart of Tel Aviv and scratched his shoulder where the bandage had been removed the week before. The itch and the scar remained. He sat back in his chair and thought about the phone call he had received only that morning. One more retaliation raid.

Five hours later he led his troops south toward the Gaza Strip. When he returned to his camp the next morning, Zvi felt very little different from the way he had when his other raids were done. He was tired. His body hurt from fatigue. He wanted to sleep. He knew he had to report on the success of his mission and it had been a success. He had left many more fedayeen dead than he had expected to. What he did not know now was how many more terrorists he would have to kill before either they stopped their incursions or Israel would have to face the real enemy, the men who sent them out and paid them whatever they thought a dead Jew was worth.

Without stopping to rest, he drove directly to the home of one of the sergeants who had been killed that night. He had known Ruven Blatoff for over five years. They had been friends. Ruven had named his youngest after

Zvi. And Zvi did not want his wife to hear of Ruven's death from strangers. Drawing his jeep to a stop near the field where Tamar Blatoff was hoeing, Zvi made his way slowly through the crop of lettuce. He was less than twenty yards from her when she turned and saw him and screamed. Only after he picked her up to carry her to the house did he realize she was several months pregnant. He sat with her for almost an hour. There was nothing he could say, and finally one of the neighbors told him that maybe if he left, Tamar would feel better. Coming to his feet beside the small bed, Zvi stared down at the tear-streaked face of his friend's wife and considered what had just been said of him.

"I'm sorry," he said. "Tell little Zvi I'm sorry."

Then he fled into the sunlight. Neighbors who had heard the news were gathered about. Some of them recognized the officer. Staring at them for a moment, Zvi blurted out, "Tell Tamar I'll be at the funeral." Then he slipped into his jeep and was about to drive away when he looked back and said to no one in particular, "I'm sorry." Then he raced out onto the highway and north toward Natanya.

He had not eaten yet. He did not want to eat alone. Shoshanna would be teaching. He hoped he could talk to her superior, and maybe he and Shoshanna could drive into town to eat and talk and relax. He had to talk to someone. He had to relax. Weeks now and all he knew were the sounds which kept rising and falling like a fragmented symphony in the recesses of his brain.

Jamming the brakes, he brought the jeep to a stop in front of the school. There were some children in the playground. He sat and watched them for a moment. His lower lip came in as he sucked on it. *Aaron.* He had only seen the boy twice in the past two months. He had to see him again as soon as he felt he would not frighten the boy, and at this moment Zvi believed, himself, that he was frightening. He knew his own men shied away from him in fear of his temper and the way he ripped into a man's pride. Ashamed, he had said more often than he wanted to that he was sorry. But he was having trouble keeping himself under control. *Under control.*

Leaving the jeep, he entered the schoolhouse. There were children calling to each other in the corridor. A small girl bumped into him, looked up startled and laughing, said, "I'm sorry." Then he was in the office asking a woman about Shoshanna. "I'd like to see her if I may."

"She's gone. She resigned some weeks ago and left town. No, I don't know where she went. No. The others don't know because she said she would send an address, and when I asked the women she lived with if she ever had, they said she hadn't." The words were coming quickly to questions he was having difficulty framing.

"Thanks," he finally said before he turned away and walked out into the afternoon sun. Behind him he could hear the voices of children reciting.

Very slowly he drove south to Tel Aviv. Stopping at the first place where he found a telephone, he called Judge Malin Ben Ezra in Jerusalem. She knew no more than the woman at the school. Twice she asked if Zvi was "all right," and both times he said, "Fine." She promised to let him know when she heard anything about Shoshanna.

Half an hour later as he sat alone in a restaurant he decided to call Fishel Warshow. The woman answering the phone said that Fishel would be with him in a moment.

Only after the violinist gave his name did Zvi realize he did not know what he wanted to talk to his friend about.

"It's Zvi Mazon," he said, embarrassed.

"I know," Fishel assured him. "How are you?"

"Fine."

A long pause.

"Was there something you wanted, Zvi?"

Another pause.

"I just wanted to know if you were all right."

"I'm all right. The operation was a complete success."

Puzzled, Zvi did not know what he had heard. "Operation?"

"The one on my leg. It was perfect. I don't feel it when I walk now."

Cursing himself for not having known what had happened to his friend, Zvi said, "I'm glad. I'm happy for you."

"Zvi?"

"Yes?"

"You'll call me up when you need me."

"Call you?" A long pause. "I'm glad to know you're well, Fishel. It's important. And believe me, I'll remember. Shalom."

The phone settled back in its cradle and the soldier did not hear the anguished, "Zvi!"

For another hour Zvi sat alone at the table. There was no one who needed him or wanted him except his son. And he did not feel he could call upon the boy now. The only thing he really did feel was sorrow for himself. Rumor had Moshe Gilead going with Malin Ben Ezra's younger sister. Rumor had Fishel living with a beautiful young woman who spent her every hour taking care of him. Rumor had . . . Lieutenant-Colonel Zvi Mazon sitting alone in an empty restaurant.

Laughing at his own sentiments and at his image of himself, he rose and walked out of the restaurant. Outside in his jeep he sat thinking of Shoshanna, and he wondered where she was and then wished that Fishel and he had been able to see more of each other.

He started the motor and drove slowly toward Hakiryah before he realized the one thing he did not want to do was stop in at headquarters and talk to Avram. The staff officer had probably heard enough stories about Zvi in recent months, and the way Zvi was feeling right now, he did not want to add reality to those tales. Wandering through the city, he ignored the cars honking behind his aimless driving.

Turning down Ben Yehuda Street, he recalled that Ruth had her shop somewhere nearby. Nodding to himself, he admitted that he had neglected her for too many months. He would surprise her now. Maybe she would eat with him and talk with him. After all, he told himself, we're friends.

Parking his jeep, he entered the small dress shop where a woman he had never seen before asked,

"Can I help you, Colonel?"

Zvi felt embarrassed inside a dress shop, and to be certain his presence would not be misunderstood, he said, "I'm looking for Ruth. Is she around anywhere?"

The woman looked puzzled. Her hand went to her gray hair as though somehow it was important that it be in place. "I'm afraid you must have the wrong shop."

Zvi shook his head. "Ruth." Then he snorted at his own ignorance. "I don't remember her married name, but she owns this place."

The woman slowly shook her head. "I'm sorry, Colonel. I own this shop. I bought it at a bankruptcy auction more than four months ago."

Rocking back and forth on the balls of his feet, Zvi wanted to protest, and all he was able to say was, "You're sure?"

Angrily, the woman ran behind a table and pulled out a file. "I don't know what you're trying to do, but here are the papers." Watching him while he continued to stare at her, she demanded, "Do you want to discuss the matter with the police?"

A bitter smile crossed Zvi's face. "No thanks." And then, as he had so often of late, he added, "I'm sorry. You see, she and I are old friends."

Without waiting to hear what the woman had to say, he left. Driving toward the sea, he reached Ruth's apartment fifteen minutes later.

Taking the steps two at a time, Zvi was surprised at his own agility in spite of his fatigue. Then he knew that he was eager to see Ruth. Knocking on the door of her suite, he stood looking down at his combat boots. He should have changed before he left camp. A moment later the door opened and he recognized Ruth's younger sister.

"She's home?" he asked as he entered.

The apartment looked much the same. The sofa bed was closed and in the room beyond where he had last seen Zella with Aaron, he assumed Ruth's daughter was asleep. Looking about, he asked again, "She home?"

Ruth's sister, several years younger than Zvi, shook her head. "She's due soon." Then, as though it were important, "She's got a job now."

Seeing the girl was impressed with his rank and uniform, Zvi wanted to put her at her ease. After a moment the girl smiled.

"Where's she working?" Zvi asked.

"A factory. It isn't much, but she sews buttons and . . ." A shrug, "She gets paid for it."

Zvi nodded as he dropped into a chair, "Do you mind if I wait for her?"

The young woman shook her head. "I was going out when she came, but if you'll stay with Hannah, then I can go now."

"A date?" Zvi asked, knowing it was none of his business, but wondering what other conversation he could have with this girl whom he barely knew.

As she slipped on a sweater, she smiled. "He's in one of Moshe Gilead's companies." Then proudly, "He's a sergeant."

She was standing by the door now and to Zvi's surprise, he found himself envying a sergeant; not the girl as much as the interest. "Stick with sergeants," he said almost seriously. Then she left him alone in the apartment.

Five cigarettes later Ruth arrived. When she opened the door and found Zvi, she did not appear surprised. "It's been a long time," but there was no accusation in her voice.

"I thought maybe dinner," he suggested.

Ruth slipped off her sweater and without being self-conscious picked up a comb and ran it through her hair, while she stood looking in a mirror at him standing behind her.

"I've eaten," she explained.

Uncertain exactly why he had come, Zvi said, "I'm sorry."

"What's with your Shoshanna?" Ruth asked bluntly, turning about so that she stood almost face to face with him.

"I don't know where she is."

Ruth's head came back as she jerked her skirt straight and tucked her white blouse in at the waist. Her breasts filled the looseness of the blouse and both of them were aware that he was staring at her.

"You don't know where she is this minute, or you don't know where she is tomorrow and the next day?"

Zvi stepped back, pulled a cigarette out of his shirt pocket and handed Ruth one. Accepting, she lit her own while she waited for an answer.

"She's just gone some place. I don't know." His voice was flat and Ruth almost wanted to laugh at the little-boy tone in it.

Moving past him, she kicked off her shoes and sat down on the sofa, pulling her feet under her and letting her skirt fall in a circle about her folded legs. Zvi stood looking at her shoes.

"How is Aaron?" she asked.

He tried to grin, "Fine."

"When did you see him last?" She was watching the smoke curling upward from the tip of the cigarette.

"A week, two weeks ago." He stumbled over the words and Ruth tried not to smile.

348

"And Shoshanna?"

He sat on the arm of an easy chair and sucked in the smoke of his cigarette. From where she sat, Ruth could see his hand shaking and she knew her question had not caused that.

"Three, maybe four weeks ago."

She nodded as though this explained something to her. "You seen Moshe lately?"

He did not know if she was trying to make conversation with him, and even though he had come because he wanted someone to talk to, he did not want to discuss Moshe Gilead. "Twice this past few months. Conferences." Then because he thought she ought to know, "We — Moshe and I — "

"I know," she cut him off. "I know. Avram told me." Then, she reached over and knocked the ash from her cigarette into a tray, and he could see the swell of her breasts and the way her body curved, and he thought of her in her old cotton robe which usually hung loose, and he found himself wondering if she still owned it.

"You're a damned fool," she said, and he did not know if she knew what he was thinking, but he understood what she meant when she added, "Moshe was about the only man who never slept with Zella. He was too much in love with her." She laughed so coarsely that Zvi's head came up, and he knew that what he was seeing now was not the girl who had fought beside him in the Quarter nor the woman he had left Aaron with when he had first returned into the service. Something was not ringing right and he could not comprehend the differences, and at the same time he knew he was tired and some place in the back of his mind he thought he heard sobbing and gunfire and the smoke from his cigarette became mixed with the smell of smoke he had known some place else. His hand holding the cigarette shook and he tried not to see it.

"Moshe's the kind of man who can lay any woman in town and most of them come to him looking for it, but he wouldn't lay a woman he loved because that is his kind of *meshugas*."

Zvi nodded, not quite believing, and at the same moment wondering if he had actually done Moshe an injustice. Then he recalled that Ruth had always been fond of Moshe.

"Has he laid you?" he asked, uncertain why he was angry and knowing at the same time that it involved the possible injustice.

"That's none of your damned business," Ruth said, but he could see that she was smiling, which did not tell him anything.

Zvi laughed, and after a moment she laughed, too.

"You used to do that more," she reminded him.

He fell silent and he could see that she was still watching the smoke rising from her cigarette, and a second time she stretched out to knock off the ash, and he was even more aware of her.

"I'd forgotten," he said. "Laughing. I'd forgotten that."

She looked at him dubiously. "Poor boy," and the taunting made him laugh again.

Then he stopped laughing and said, "Your sister — I never remember her name — told me you work in a shop sewing buttons."

Nodding, Ruth asked, "So?"

He did not know if she was making a pun or asking a question.

"Yes," she said. "I work on buttons. I'm paid so many agorot for so many buttons." She leaned back against the sofa arm, her head up and her breasts thrust forward as she smiled. "I wonder how sewing buttons compares to sewing zippers."

He couldn't follow what she was saying and he did not know if it was his own fatigue or if she was taunting him again. "Does it make any difference?" he asked.

Ruth smiled and he was aware for the first time in years of the scar on her head and for reasons he could not explain to himself he could smell smoke that was not from his cigarette and the sobbing was gone and instead of silence in the far reaches of his head, he could hear twenty-five-pounders slamming into stone.

Ruth watched his face carefully. She had known Zvi most of her life. She had seen him under stress and she had seen him happy in those first few months after he had married Zella and those first few times he had brought Shoshanna to the house. Right now he was not happy, and he was not under any kind of stress she understood.

Rising from the couch, she placed both her hands on his cheeks and when his hands came up to close on hers, she drew his head between her breasts and she could feel his body quiver. She had taunted him before as a boy, and at this moment she knew he was not a boy but something very different.

He did not draw his head away as he placed his arms about her waist and held her tight. Ruth's head fell back. In all the years they had known each other, she did not believe they had ever touched before. And she knew she did not want to hold him now. She was not his mother and she was not his mistress. But she did not draw away.

Without looking down at him, she asked, "You came because you did not want to be alone?"

She felt his head brush up and down between her breasts and then she felt his hands rubbing her thighs. She flinched, and then her head slowly rocked from side to side. His hands wandered over her thighs and one of them settled on her buttock.

"*Gevalt,*" she finally snapped, breaking away. Her breath came short and she felt herself shaking. Zvi's head rose and he stared at her.

Almost as though she had no choice, she began to unbutton her blouse, counting each button as she did. "One and two and three and four and that's five agorot." She fell silent, her eyes on his tense face as she shoved the blouse off her shoulders and let it drop to the floor. Reaching back, she twisted her bra and, unhooking it, let it fall in a small pink pile beside the blouse. Her forearm came under her full breasts now as she shoved them up and forward. However, in the same gesture, her head fell back and the light of the overhead bulb revealed the tears on her face.

"Oh, my God," Zvi half shouted. "Stop it. God damn it. Stop." Coming to his feet, he reached out and took her by the arms and held her at a distance. Her own arms dropped numbly to her side and her head rocked from side to side in anguish.

After a moment she stiffened. "I can't," she said. "I tried, but I can't."

Zvi drew her to him, holding her closely about the waist while he put one hand behind her head and forced it down on his shoulder. "I'm sorry," he told her. "I'm sorry."

Her head came away and her eyes matched his. "That's what you came for wasn't it?"

Shrugging, he admitted, "I don't know. I guess I was alone."

To his surprise, she laughed. "Join the human race, Zvi." She broke the circle of his arms and sat down on the sofa once more, ignoring the fact that she was half undressed. "Join the human race."

He could see she was trying not to sob even though there were tears on her face. Before he could bring himself to say anything, he lit another cigarette without offering her one. After two puffs, he asked, "Why did you even bother to try? It's never been that way with us."

Her voice came as though from a distant place as she explained, "It wouldn't have been for nothing. I can assure you, you would have had to pay."

"Pay?" He did not understand.

She went on talking as though he had said nothing. "Five agorot for four buttons doesn't pay the rent or buy food or pay doctor's bills, and I have a child." Then she tried to laugh. "I wasn't offering you anything, Zvi. I was trying to sell you something." Her voice dropped as she offered, "You can still have it for whatever they're paying on the open market."

Reaching out, Zvi slapped her face as hard as he could, knocking her head back against the sofa.

When she straightened up again, her hand on her cheek, she looked at him bitterly. "If you didn't want it, you could have just left it alone."

"You damned bitch," he said softly. "You aren't Zella Mazon. Forget it." Then he turned away, trying to think and finding it almost impossible. Without looking back at her, he asked, "Does anyone else know you're not making a living?"

"My creditors," she said with a chuckle.

He was looking out the window now, his back to her as he snapped, "Stop playing games with me, damn it." Then with a sigh he pleaded, "Stop."

His head went back as he tried to measure the darkness of the sky and then he knew he was not doing that for any reason other than to escape from thinking. With great effort, he turned where he stood and faced her. Ruth's hands were covering her breasts now and she seemed to shrink back on the sofa as though she wanted to avoid the light of the lamp on the table beside her.

Pulling out his wallet, he started to go through it to see how much money he had with him when she rose and tried to flee into the bedroom. Stepping into her path, he let her bump into him and then watched as she shied away, embarrassed. "No, Zvi," she pleaded.

"I'm not giving you anything," he said. "Tomorrow you find another location and open another dress shop." Then he asked, "Why did the last one fail?"

"When I sold dresses, I should have bought other ones, but I needed the money for the house," she explained. "Then there wasn't anything left to sell." She was making an effort to be businesslike as she bent over and picked her clothes off the floor. He saw her full breasts which she tried covering with the blouse.

"Don't run my business that way," he ordered. "Tomorrow you get papers drawn up. Half the business is mine. I'm furnishing the money," he snorted. "In a way I'm buying more than you planned to sell." There was a flat bitterness in his voice and her head came up. "I'm angry," he explained. "You shouldn't have done this to either one of us." His voice became more gentle. "All you needed to do was ask." Dropping his folded pounds on the table beside her, he touched her bare shoulder. "All you needed to do was ask."

She nodded without looking at him and he could see that she was ashamed and wishing he were gone. His hand came up and gently touched her cheek. "I'll see you get what you need tomorrow." They were both silent for a moment and then he added, "I wish you would move into the apartment I leased on Jabotinsky Street. I'd like to know you were there."

Her hand closed on his and she nodded.

"I'm sorry," he said. "It's my fault. I don't know where Shoshanna is, I didn't know Fishel had been operated on, I didn't know you were in trouble. I'm sorry," he said again.

Leaning forward, Zvi brushed her hair with his lips. "Take care," he said and then he left the apartment, and as he descended the stairs, he did not know if the sobbing he heard was coming from the recesses of his mind or from the room he had just left.

Out on the street Zvi felt the heat of a *hamseen* brush his face, and for a moment he was bewildered. Behind Ruth's apartment he could hear the

Mediterranean roll along the rocks; and without thinking, he moved toward the sea. It was night. There were few lights other than those cast from the apartment windows. He stood on the edge of the sea, his hands on his hips and his chin thrust forward and the sound of the sea mingled with the sound of a machine gun shaking the barracks, and somewhere he could hear mortar fire and beyond that the sound of twenty-five-pounders and over it all the soft voice of a rabbi intoning Kaddish. And then from somewhere he heard a sound he could not identify, and he whirled about to see a young woman standing a few yards away. There was only the figure — no face in the darkness, no sound other than a low chant and he tried to find the source and he made out another figure on the sand by her feet and the chant broke through the pattern of machine-gun fire and mortars and the ground shaking under his feet and he closed the distance between himself and the woman and he tried to make out her face in the darkness and all he could be certain of was that she was Bedia and he shouted, "You crazy Arab bitch," and his hands came together in one large fist as he swung them up and then down across the strange girl's head and shoulders. "You crazy bitch. He was only a small boy and a man picked him up and broke his head against a wall." And Zvi was shouting more loudly and the woman screamed and her screams mixed with the sounds in his head, and as she stumbled away, he followed shouting, "I won't marry you or anyone else." And then she fell to her knees and his hands came up once more to strike her and he was no longer shouting as he said flatly, "Who the hell needs you or anyone else?" The man who had been chanting was on his feet now and throwing himself at Zvi, who shrugged him off while he grabbed the back of the intruder's head and forced it down toward his knee. And Zvi shouted again, "Tell you friends Israeli men have natural reactions when they find strangers crawling into their wives' beds."

Then there were men emerging from the darkness and as the girl came to her feet to scramble away from him, he raised his fists once more and started to shout, "*Kurveh.* You aren't Zella Mazon. Forget it." His fists started to come down, and the men from the darkness dived at him, and Zvi whirled about to face them, his fists up, his shoulders braced. And over the sound of the mortars and the machine gun shuddering the ground, he could hear someone say, "He's gone crazy." And someone else shouted, "For God's sake, get the police," and Zvi was battering at strange faces until he knocked four of them away from him and the others swarmed over him, taking him down onto the sand with them. And then he was very still.

Three hours later, Avram found him lying on a cot in a cell at the police station. With great effort Zvi pulled himself to his feet and, looking beyond Avram, he made out the face of his battalion medical officer. Embarrassed, he looked from one to the other, finally settling on Avram. "You still chasing down old wives' tales?"

The staff officer nodded. "I guess so. Someone told me that something had happened to you."

Zvi's hands came wide as though he wanted to show they were empty. "As you can see, there's nothing wrong." Then he slowly sank back onto the cot. His body trembled and his face went into his hands as he said, "They gave me some kind of a shot and I'm dizzy."

Avram looked to the medical officer for an explanation.

"A sedative. He'll be all right."

Almost brightly, Zvi looked up at Avram. "See. That's what I told you."

Squatting, Avram placed both of his hands on Zvi's arms and gently raised him to his feet. "I've taken care of everything. Relax." And he was leading Zvi out of the cell. Two police officers watched them go, the physician following after.

They were seated in the back of Avram's staff car when Zvi turned to explain, "I only wanted someone to talk to."

Closing his eyes as if this would block out what he was hearing, Avram nodded. When he opened his eyes again, he looked beyond Zvi's head to the medical officer who smiled and nodded.

Suddenly and without warning, Zvi collapsed in his seat.

Then for the first time since he had received the phone call about his friend, Avram relaxed. "Now we know how far they can go," he said to no one in particular.

Two weeks later after he was discharged from the hospital Lieutenant-Colonel Zvi Mazon was ordered on leave. Taking his son out of school, he arranged for Ruth's younger sister to care for the boy and that same day the papers were signed between himself and his partner.

There were only two things more Zvi felt he had to do before he took his leave. The first of these was to talk with Malin Ben Ezra. Driving to Jerusalem, he met her as she came out of court and drove her home. Surprised to see that she was pregnant again, and only eight months since her first was born, he was happy for Avram. Neither of them said very much as they crossed the city to her apartment. It was the same one she had been living in when Avram had met her. She explained that her mother was dead now, but her younger sister kept house for the two of them and when she was in Tel Aviv on weekends, her sister had the place to herself. Zvi was tempted to ask questions about Moshe, but decided that could wait. What he had to settle with Moshe, he would settle himself.

Inside the apartment, over coffee, Malin sat back and waited for him to ask what she knew he was going to ask.

"Shoshanna," he began, "have you seen her or heard from her?"

Malin started to shake her head and then, changing her mind, decided to tell him what little she knew. "She's left the country. I think the United States or Canada."

Zvi slowly turned the cup between his palms. "Did she tell you anything about what happened?"

"Should she have?"

He shrugged. "I don't know." Then he wondered how much of what had happened he should never mention. "Just let it go that I acted like a bastard."

"And you're sorry?"

Trying to decide if the word were adequate, he nodded. "I may have loved her. I don't know." Then he admitted again, "I treated her pretty badly." Setting the cup down on the small table he rose to his feet, his eyes never leaving Malin's face. "If you ever get the chance, tell her I'm sorry."

Malin nodded. "And that's all?"

Zvi weighed the possibility of there being more and then shook his head. "If she will understand that, it will be enough." He tried to smile. "Just tell her what I said." His head came up and he started for the door where he paused and turning, smiled at Malin, "Tell Avi I'll see him before I go."

She said she would.

"And tell him, too, that he's the lucky one of the lot of us."

After he had gone, Malin sat for a long time thinking about her husband and how much of what had just been said she was going to tell him. She had never learned what had taken place between Zvi and Shoshanna before her friend left, but she knew it had been enough for Shoshanna to warn Avram that Zvi could be dangerous to himself and others. She had been right. Relaxing in her chair, Malin did not think he was dangerous now.

Later that evening, Zvi drove into the base camp which housed Moshe's battalion. The sentry at the gate slouched against a post and waved him on. Pulling up in front of the barrack which he recognized as Moshe's headquarters, he entered the building and asked the duty officer where he would find Colonel Gilead. It took the young lieutenant a moment to locate his commander on the phone, and five minutes later Moshe entered his headquarters. He stood at the door looking at Zvi.

"You wanted to see me?"

"Can we talk some place?"

Moshe led the way into his own office. The small room was sparsely decorated. Two chairs, a wooden bench, a conference table and a desk. There were maps on the wall, but Zvi recognized the information was innocent. Walking to the far side of the conference table so that it lay between them, Moshe waited.

"I'm going on leave," Zvi said.

"I've heard."

Groping for a place to begin, Zvi asked, "You know Fishel was operated on?"

"I've heard that, too." Moshe's arms were folded before him, his head was rigid on his shoulders and his eyes were almost glazed.

"Ruth's fine," Zvi continued.

Half squinting as though something were annoying him, Moshe said wryly, "I didn't know this was old home week."

Pulling a cigarette from his shirt pocket, Zvi lighted it and stared at Moshe. It was difficult and it always would be to remember that Moshe outranked him now.

Finally, Moshe said, "It's late, Colonel. Is there something you wanted?"

Taking a deep breath, Zvi watched the smoke from his cigarette before he said, "I owe you an apology. I drove over a hundred kilometers today to deliver it. I'm sorry about what I said at Scorpion Pass. I was wrong." Then, stubbing out the cigarette in an ashtray on the table between them, he spun on his heel and walked out of the room, down the small corridor and out into the night. The sky was dark. His day of atonement was ended.

The next morning he flew to Paris.

PARIS, SPRING, 1956

Paris is a city in which to play. However, Zvi Mazon did not know how to play. He had never had time to learn.

For three days he wandered bored through the Louvre, the Tuileries, down the Champs Élysées. And, like any other tourist, he bought and mailed gifts to his friends and family. On his fourth day in Paris, he stopped in at the Israeli embassy on Avenue de Wagram for want of someone to talk to and to read the latest reports. The middle-aged colonel, who was serving as military attaché, greeted Zvi warmly. Yes, he had known Zvi was due in the city. No, there was no mail for him. Yes, he had the latest reports on activities. Glancing about the plushly furnished room and wondering what wealthy Frenchman had once lived there, Zvi waited for a clerk to fetch the latest report which had been submitted to the United Nations. The attaché tried to be friendly, but though he and Zvi had many friends in common, they barely knew each other. The clerk returned with a copy of the letter for Zvi. Then Zvi was alone. Walking over to the window, he scanned his correspondence. Signature: Arthur Liveran, the permanent representative from Israel to the United Nations. To the president of the Security Council. Ignoring the formalities which began the letter, Zvi read the details with care. Three days before at 1655 hours an Israeli military command car struck a mine near Kissufim. Three soldiers were wounded; at 1730 two workers were attacked with hand grenades in an orange grove between Hatsor and Gan Yavne. At the same hour an Israel patrol spotted a group of fifteen Egyptian soldiers who had crossed into Israel west of Erez. They exchanged fire for half an hour. At 1900 a crowded bus and truck were fired upon while traveling between Bet Dagan and Tserifin. Six of the bus passengers were wounded. At 2030 an Egyptian murder gang entered the agricultural boarding school for boys at Shafir. They fired on twelve boys in the synagogue saying evening prayers with their teacher. Three killed, four wounded. Only seven kilometers from Tel Aviv.

For a moment Zvi closed his eyes, remembering his son and wondering if he had done the right thing taking Aaron out of school. It was something he could decide later. He read on.

At 2130 a policeman was shot and killed near Lod.

At 2135 hand grenades were thrown into two buildings in Ahi'ezer about nine kilometers south of Tel Aviv. A man, a woman and an eighteen-month-old baby wounded.

The next day at 1215 rifle fire was opened by an Egyptian outpost. The exchange lasted twenty-five minutes.

At 1216 Israeli planes intercepted four Egyptian planes over the Negev. One Egyptian plane went down in flames near Sede Boqer.

Quickly glancing down the rest of the letter, Zvi saw that the Canadian general representing the UN was talking to the Egyptians. Zvi turned back to see that the attaché was with him again.

"I see the UN is going to talk about it," Zvi said bitterly.

The attaché nodded. And then to Zvi's surprise, he said, "I've some news for you, Zvi."

"For me?"

They were standing in the middle of the luxurious room and Zvi wondered how a man could do business in such a background.

The attaché, who had once served as a field officer with the British, nodded again. "A letter from Avi."

Zvi's face brightened.

"It was to me. It made a single point. When you came in to read the reports, you were to be told you should not cut your leave short to return home. If you planned such a thing, you would be assigned to the embassy until released from embassy duty." The portly officer brushed his mustache with the back of his hand as though to signify he had completed his duty.

Dropping his head to one side, Zvi looked at the man, "Was that all?"

The older man thought for a moment. "There was something about the Chief of Staff wanting you in the best possible condition when you returned." There was a smile on the florid face now.

Extending his hand to shake the other man's, Zvi said, "Thanks."

When he returned to his hotel, The St. James and Albany near the Tuileries, the young desk clerk handed him a note with his key. Curious that anyone should know where he was, Zvi read the single piece of information on the slip: a telephone number. He called from his room. It took sometime for the operator to understand him. Then he heard the phone ringing and someone answering in French. However, even though he did not know French, he was almost certain whom he had reached.

"Someone left a message for Colonel Mazon to call."

There was silence for a moment and while he waited, he fished a cigarette out of his pocket and lit it.

"Zvi!"

He recognized the voice. For a long moment he let it flow over him while his thoughts drifted back to the last time he had seen Bedia Hassani in Aden, crumpled on the floor of her suite, her gown ripped away.

"Yes," he said flatly. "It's Zvi Mazon. I found your number here when I returned." He knew that the Israeli embassy must be under surveillance. Though he should have taken that for granted, it certainly made no difference to him.

"Zvi," she was saying, "can we have dinner tonight?"

"Just like that?"

She was laughing, and he wondered where she was and what she looked like now. But most of all he wondered why she wanted to see him and how safe it would be, because he had not forgotten Captain Layton.

"I've invited you to dinner," she repeated. Then she asked, "You haven't a better invitation, have you?" Zvi started to shake his head, looked about the dingy hotel room which was costing him so much, and conceded, "No better invitation but I keep remembering your friend Layton."

A silence on the other end of the phone. "Did you mourn him deeply?"

Chuckling, Zvi said, "May I suggest we have dinner together?"

"I'd be delighted," and she sounded as though she actually would be.

"I'll meet you at eight at Ledoyen," he said.

Her voice dropped a note as she asked, "You won't call for me?"

"I'll explain later," he said. And after she agreed to his arrangements, he dialed the number of the embassy and asked for the attaché.

"Mazon," he introduced himself. "I thought you might like to know — ought to know — I'm having dinner tonight with," he shifted his ground, "at the invitation of Miss Bedia Hassani. We've met in the past."

There was a long silence. "Enjoy, Zvi," the deep-voiced Colonel encouraged before he warned, "Don't play spy. It isn't your game. You're a soldier. If you learn anything, fine. Just don't go looking for it."

Zvi agreed.

"And, Zvi?"

"Yes?"

"Don't feel important. You're not that valuable to them. The Hassanis throw their money wherever they think it will do them any good — long-term or short. But remember, they never just throw it. The father's the toughest banker in the Arab world, and if he withdrew his cash from Lebanon or Egypt, either country would panic."

Zvi tried to understand what all of this meant in his terms and then he understood: nothing, and that was the point. It was not his game. "I'll remember," he agreed.

"Enjoy," the attaché suggested with a leer in his voice.

Before Zvi could protest, he was alone on the line.

That night at eight he was seated at the table he had reserved. Wearing his best dress uniform, he did not feel too conspicuous as he looked at the several NATO officers who were filling the room with their wives and women who were not their wives. He had just lit a cigarette when Bedia Hassani was led to the table by the maître d'hôtel. Rising, Zvi stared at her. Wearing a white silk Parisian gown, a diamond tiara set in her hair piled high on her head and a regal look about her as she slipped into her chair, she was beautiful. Zvi was almost tempted to say that he was pleased that she was not running to fat as most Arab women her age began to, thought better of it and asked, "A drink?"

She smiled at him warmly and shook her head.

Sitting down once more, he continued to stare at her across the table.

"You've gone up in the world," she observed, looking at the insignias on his shoulders.

He nodded.

"You've been busy, too," she said, smiling.

He wondered how much she knew about his work. There were attempts to keep the commando leaders' names secret for the sake of their families, but it was what the papers called a "well-known" secret. "Busy?" he asked, fencing.

"You've been traveling outside Palestine again. Jordan. Gaza." There was a twinkle in her eyes, but he realized she was still referring to Palestine.

Cocking his head to one side, he admitted, "One tends to get around in my business."

She laughed.

"You know what I do?" he decided to ask.

Bedia nodded. "You invade and terrorize and kill civilians." For a moment she fell silent, and then she added, "Somehow I never would have thought of you doing anything like that." Neither of them said anything for a time and finally, she was the one who broke the silence. "The young man I met that night in the Quarter, he did not impress me that way."

Sighing, Zvi watched the smoke curl upward from the tip of his cigarette. "Did you want to see me just to talk business?" He knew he was being difficult.

"I'll have that drink," she said and after he ordered a Scotch for her, she sat back in her chair. "I never thought we'd meet again."

Not knowing what she was leading up to, Zvi said nothing.

"And then you showed up here."

"How did you know?"

"Know?"

And he knew she was being coy. "Know I was here."

A soft laugh and she said what he had already guessed. "There's a curious thing that happens when people go into embassies."

Her Scotch served, she remained silent while the waiter added the soda. When they were alone again, she smiled. "You wonder why I asked you to have dinner with me?"

Zvi felt relieved.

"I've been here for two months. I've been reading about how the British are about to walk out of Egypt and leave the canal. I've been reading about your invasions, I've been reading about the people you've killed, and I've been wondering how much you've changed since you became a terrorist." Before he could say anything, her hand went up. "I've not forgotten your comments that night that there were two peoples destined to live in the same land which couldn't hold them both." She stirred her drink with the swizzle stick and looked up at him. "You almost seemed human that night. It was as though you could be made to see the justice of our position."

Trying not to smile, Zvi wondered if she thought she could recruit an Israeli officer. "Almost?"

She nodded and he saw once more that she was beautiful. "Zvi," she began, pushing the drink aside and leaning toward him, "Zvi, could we be friends?"

The strangeness of the question bounced through the maze of memories as he considered the notion. He, too, leaned forward, his arms on the table and his hands only inches from hers. "Miss Bedia Hassani is one of the wealthiest young ladies of the world. She is lovely, and I am certain there are newspapers who follow her every movement." Almost as an apology, he added, "I'm sorry I don't get a chance to read those papers." He smiled cynically. "Miss Bedia Hassani can be friends with any Arab in the Middle East or out of it, with any man she wants or at least any man whom money can buy — and I'm not belittling the value of money."

He paused to wait for her reaction, and when there was none, he picked up the thread of his own conversation, "In view of all the things Miss Bedia Hassani is and can have, why does she want to be friends with a man she has just called a terrorist and a killer of civilians?" A bitterness came into his voice as he added, "*Al-Ahram* in Cairo describes me in even more vivid terms. Assassin. Defiler of women. Destroyer of children. They have some very fancy names for the commando leaders. And why would a loyal Palestinian woman who can have anyone else, want to be friends with such a person?"

Before she could answer, the waiter came for their order. For the next five minutes, to Zvi's annoyance, they discussed menus and wines. Not caring much about either, and with the lack of interest in fine food shared by most of his compatriots, he asked Bedia to select for both of them. When they were alone once more, he settled back in his chair and waited for her answer to his question.

Before she said anything, she finished her Scotch, and he could tell from the way she was slowly rotating the empty glass between her palms that she was having difficulty answering. Then she looked up with a bright smile. "Who wants anything they can *obviously* buy?"

Snorting, Zvi evaluated her question, which was not really a question, "And so an Israeli colonel is a kind of unobtainable sport." His eyes half closed as he tried to remember something, "There was a story I read in school years ago. Had something to do with the most dangerous game — man-hunting." He was leaning forward again as he asked, "Is that what you're playing?"

To his surprise, she shook her head and, setting the glass aside, closed her small hands over his. Zvi was embarrassed at the thought of anyone who might know either of them seeing him in a Paris restaurant holding hands with a beautiful Arab girl. "Maybe," she countered, "just maybe a Palestinian and a Jew could be friends." There was a twinkle in her eyes as she taunted him. "I'm not so sure it's against nature."

He was aware of the way her breasts swelled the front of her gown and the way in which she was looking at him in spite of the fact that his head was lowered. And he was aware that her hands were warm on his. For one brief instant he wanted to withdraw his hands and then he changed his mind, set one of his on top of hers and, holding her hands between his own, he smiled. "It may not be against nature, but it certainly would be against the politics of our time and even, perhaps, against good sense." He had never been seduced before, but he could not decide whether he should really object.

Then she pulled her hands away and laughed tauntingly, "You see the possibilities."

For the first time he had the impression she had been laughing at him all along. He had to find out if he was correct. "Layton, he saw all," and Zvi emphasized the word so that it contained every possible implication, "all the possibilities. And where did it get him?"

For a long time she said nothing, and then she smiled, but he knew she was no longer laughing at him. "Maybe, just maybe," she said once more, "you are afraid of the possibilities." And before he could answer, she added, "And just maybe, Lieutenant-Colonel Zvi Mazon is not as stupid as he would have people think."

Puzzled that anyone would think he tried to give the impression of stupidity, he cocked his head to one side and waited for an explanation.

"The big rough soldier gambit. The burly colonel who is all muscle, who looks like a tank." She nodded and smiled once more. "It is all part of an act except to those who know him better." Then she said warmly, "He plays the part so well he fools even himself."

"I don't understand what you are trying to say."

She laughed softly. "You are making my point. You know damned well what I want. I'm going to be in Paris for another few months, and so long as we are both here and you haven't anything to do but sight-see, I thought we might try some of this 'talking' you Jews keep saying you want to do with the Arabs." A look of anger and pain came into her eyes as she clenched her empty glass once more. "If I hear one more damned Yahud say all he wants is the chance to sit down with the Arabs and talk . . ." She punctuated her anger by slamming the glass down on the table so that it shattered. Ignoring it, she looked at her hand. There was no cut. With a curse, she came to her feet and stood looking down at him. "You know damned well why we met tonight." Then as he rose, she said, "I'm going for a drive. A long one. I want to see what Paris looks like tonight and tomorrow night."

Puzzled, Zvi cocked his head to one side, "And you're panting for my company?" He had no illusions about himself and he kept recalling the attaché's comments: *Don't feel important. You're not that valuable to them.* And then the final comment: *Enjoy.*

Shoving back his chair, Zvi walked around the table, took her arm and held it while he dropped franc notes on the table. Then he led her out of the restaurant past the bewildered maître d'hôtel and the waiters. Outside in the night air, Zvi glanced about continuing to hold her arm firmly.

"My car is over there," she pointed.

He nodded, then waved for the car. The large Rolls came to a stop in front of them. Without comment, Zvi flung the front door of the car open and, reaching in, jerked the chauffeur out onto the street. "My sympathies," he snapped as he took Bedia by the arms and half lifted her across the driver's seat to the far side of the car. Looking to make certain the keys were in the ignition, he started to reach for his wallet. As he did so, out of the corner of his eye he caught a glimpse of the driver coming at him. Zvi kept his head down, and when the man raised his arm, Zvi drove his elbow into the man's belly, doubling him up. Hearing a gasp from Bedia, he slipped into the driver's seat and slowly drove away from the curb.

"I was going to give him cab fare home," Zvi explained.

She twisted in her seat so that she could see him better. "Why didn't you let him drive?"

They were turning a corner now onto Avenue George V, heading toward the Seine.

"Why didn't you let him drive?" she asked again.

Zvi's head rocked back and forth as he weighed the question.

She was about to ask it again when he said softly, "I heard you." They crossed the Seine onto Avenue Bosque.

"Well?" she demanded.

A wry grin came across his face. "I don't trust you, my dear. It's just that simple." He wished he could see the look on her face, but the traffic was heavy and he could not take his eyes off the street as he approached Avenue

de Lowendal. He slowed the large sedan near the United Nations headquarters, swung east on Avenue de Suffren and then left on Rue de
Vaugirard toward Montparnasse, hoping all the while he had studied the
tourist map with sufficient care.

At Montparnasse, he drew the car over to the curb, turned off the motor
and, shifting in his seat, looked at her for the first time since they had left the
restaurant. She was leaning toward him, her feet tucked under the white ends
of her gown, her hands clasped tightly in her lap.

Very slowly, he shook his head. "You are frightened."

"Frightened?" she picked up the word as though it were something she
could look at. "I think I am," she admitted.

Zvi reached out and, placing his hands on her bare arms, he held her at a
distance. "You wanted company, you said. If you still want it, fine. I'm not
particularly enjoying Paris." He shook his head slowly as he remembered
something. "Earlier today I received orders to enjoy myself."

He could see that she was beginning to relax now as she smiled weakly.
"In fact, the secretary of our general staff said that I had to stay in Paris and
enjoy myself. Then the attaché said, 'Enjoy.' " Zvi's large head rolled from
side to side while he smiled cynically. "And then you said you wanted to
have company, and with all that influence coming to bear by people who
possess *protectzia*, I say, 'Yea and amen.' I'll enjoy." He was no longer
smiling.

"However," he continued, "I don't think I'd enjoy getting killed and so
we go where I say and when I say and how I say, if only because I think it
prudent." His hand came up and touched her cheek as he waited for a
reaction.

"You damned Jew," she said softly. "Always on your terms."

Zvi roared loudly.

"You expect us to just give up and die, don't you?" And he continued
to laugh.

After a moment, she joined in the laughter.

Then he drew her to him and kissed her.

At first she did not resist and then she placed her hands on his chest and
pushed him away.

Puzzled, Zvi waited for an explanation.

"You still think I would let someone kill you?"

He sucked in his cheeks and thought about this, but not for long. "The
first opportunity." Then he explained, "I'm probably more important dead
and propaganda than just one more live Israeli lieutenant-colonel. And so I
believe it's dead that you would like me." His hand came up to brush off
anything that she might say as he continued. "I don't think you'd *let*
someone kill me, Bedia love. I think you'd arrange for it."

He was disappointed because she was no longer protesting, and then he suddenly realized she had never protested the issue. His humor ended, he fell very still and felt suddenly emptied. He half closed his eyes and, looking beyond her head, saw the tower of St. Suplice Church. And then he did not see the church because he was remembering his sordid moment less than a week before with Ruth, the loss of Shoshanna and the bitterness which had remained in Moshe's face as the apology lay in the air between them.

And he asked of no one in particular, "What in the hell am I doing here?"

Something touched his hand and he was alert. Reaching out from the corner of the seat to which she had withdrawn, Bedia had placed her hand on his.

He stared at it and then snorted, " 'Enjoy,' the man said."

He touched the place below her neck where her dress lay in an open oval. She did not object and then he drew her to him again. However, before he kissed her he said, "I think we both know where we stand."

She nodded.

After he kissed her, his hand wandered down the front of her dress. She was soft and the silk smooth. Turning away, he started the car and drove back toward the Seine. Fifteen minutes later, he parked in the entrance of the St. James and Albany and, leaving the keys in the ignition, said flatly without looking at her, "I'm going in for dinner. Then I'm going to take a walk, stop for coffee and then to bed. You can have any one, all or nothing." With that, he stepped out of the car and walked slowly toward the door of the hotel. He was climbing the four short steps when she took his arm and matched her pace to his.

While he waited for the doorman to swing the door, Zvi relaxed for the first time since he had arrived in Paris.

It was almost an hour past midnight when Zvi put Bedia in her car and went up to his room. They had spent almost five hours together. They had quarreled and they had talked. For over an hour after dinner they had walked through the Tuileries and neither of them had brought up the problems which lay between them. She was good company. Just before he turned the light off to sleep, the phone rang.

Bedia. Could they spend tomorrow together?

Zvi stared at the glowing tip of his cigarette and weighed the dangers. Then he agreed that he would call her in the morning.

And they spent the next day together and the next. The third night she didn't leave the hotel, and in the weeks that followed she usually remained for breakfast. Week followed week. Bedia knew well enough what security measures he was taking for his own safety, but she never commented on them. He knew, too, that she could break through the small barriers of inconvenience he was setting up, but each barrier stood as a symbol of his lack of trust and kept him aware of how dangerous their relationship was.

It was late in the third week that they were walking along the Seine on the Ile de la Cité when they unexpectedly came upon France's memorial to her Jewish dead. The low, flat building surprised Zvi, who had not known that it existed. Taking Bedia's arm, he started down the flight of stairs which led to the underground structure. However, he had only taken two steps when he felt her draw back. Looking up, he saw that she wanted to flee.

A bitter smile crossed his face. "Do the dead haunt you?"

She shook her head, drew her hand out of his and straightened her skirt, nervously, as though she had to divert her attention. "No," she said after a moment. "Your dead don't haunt me." When she started to walk back up the steps, he grabbed her from behind and swung her about.

"What the hell is your problem then? Did your noble Daddy support the Grand Mufti? Did your family wind up publishing the Arab edition of *Mein Kampf*? What's your commitment to our dead that you want to run away from them?"

She shook her head from side to side as she tried to reject his words. "I thought we were friends," she said and he, too, was shaking his head.

"Friends?" he laughed. "Lovers I can understand — but friends?" He was no longer laughing.

Bedia nodded, bringing one hand up tentatively to his sleeve. "Did you have to throw this down between us?"

Very slowly, he nodded. "All I did was ask you to come with me." Then, with an angry and flamboyant flourish which was so completely out or character that he was himself surprised: "What have we here? The names of Jews. Who remembers the names of Jews killed, Jews burned? Who recalls one name from another when the names are on lists so long no man could record them all in a single lifetime? What have we here that frightens you?"

Her hand fell away and she cringed, clearly afraid. He was different at this moment from when he had struck her down in Aden almost six years before. Then, he had only been angry. Now, he had a look about his eyes which spelled something remote and almost mad.

Trying hard to defend her own distaste for the memorial, she countered simply, "Have you ever seen the list of names of the Arab refugees? Have you even seen the Arab dead after one of your terrorist raids? Have you ever seen the starved and hungry faces of the Arabs you drove out of Palestine?"

The two stood facing each other on the narrow staricase, open to the late afternoon sky. The walls about them were painted white. The river muddying past was silent. Only the odd hum of the city could be heard and at this moment it sounded both dim and distant.

"Your damned refugees," he snapped.

For an instant she thought he was going to strike her for having made the comparison. "This is ground we have plowed before, you and I."

"Your poor refugees," he snorted. "Fifty million dollars flowing in from their families living and working elsewhere and money from the UN and the U.S. Babies passed from family to family to increase the numbers for the accounting. Your poor refugees. Syria could hold forty million people and has four. Iraq could hold fifty million and has five."

He shook his head as he spat out the words. "Was it your cousin who proclaimed in the Jordanian parliament this year, 'The existence of the refugee problem is an important harassing factor vis-à-vis the Jews and the West. As long as it remains unsolved, Israel's political and economic existences are actually endangered'?" The words flowed easily after his lectures to his men on the Arab attitude toward the refugees.

Pulling a cigarette from his pocket, he stepped back to allow a French couple to pass them on the stairs, and for a brief moment he though Bedia would take the opportunity to flee. However, she remained. Lighting his cigarette, he stared at her over the match before he flicked it away. When he finally spoke again, all he could say was, "You stupid bitch. Compare our six million with what you did to your own people." Shaking his head in disgust and frustration at his inability to reach her, he took several drags and then turning his heel on the stub, walked slowly into the memorial.

When he came out half an hour later, he had trouble holding back his tears. Emerging once more into the afternoon sun, he slowly climbed the stairs and faced the river. To his surprise, Bedia was waiting there.

A silence hung between them as he started down the walk which led to the Quai des Fleurs. The sun was warm. The day was clear. There were pleasure boats on the Seine. A child offered to sell them a tourist's map. They walked on. The Quai de la Corse. Boulevard de Palais. Through the steel gates of the Palais de Justice and into the Sainte Chapelle.

It was late in the afternoon. They were alone. Bedia did not know why he had come to this place where the shrine of the crown of thorns and other Christian holy relics had once been housed. The last bright light came through the vividly colored windows. She watched Zvi settle down on the long stone bench; his eyes rose and he seemed to be reading the Holy Scriptures laid out in primitive leaded figures set in the glass. In a voice so soft Bedia had to approach him to hear, Zvi said, "She will not be comforted for her children, because they are not."

His eyes half closed as though he were squinting to see the figures in the glass more clearly. There was Moses climbing a hill and Abraham sacrificing Isaac. There was Ruth going into the land of her husband's people. His eyes came open once more and he looked at this woman who had come with him. He glanced back at Ruth.

"I envy the French," he said. And when he saw that she did not understand what he meant even though she was trying, he explained. "They have their holy places and their monuments in their own country." As he spoke, anger settled into his voice. "I remember when my friends came back from Rhodes and the writing of the truce in fifty, there were those innocent enough to believe that an Arab had honor and integrity and that we would be allowed to visit the tombs of Rachel and the Cave of Machpelah, that we would be allowed to pray at the Wall."

He came to his feet and stared up toward the finely wrought windows of stained glass. "You and I will see the Jews at the Wall again."

His eyes met hers. "Tell me, what do you think you're going to learn from me? You're lovely. Dainty, too. But I can recall Aden and other times when the dainty lady was a cast-iron bitch, so if you think you are going to learn anything of value watching a Jew, forget it. We really aren't any more mad than other people. The difference is that we have our own brand of madness, and that is the thing that sets us apart. Our own special brand of madness brought about by our own enemies." He almost smiled as he added, "Our enemies made us, and maybe we're in their debt."

Somehow, Bedia found herself curiously pleased with his reactions to both the memorial and the church. She was seeing something about this Jew she had never seen before, and she wondered how universal this was — this attempt to explain the Jew to himself. She was thinking of this when he started to tell her a story:

"A long time ago when the world was young and the mountains stood proudly, there were two whores in Askelon. They had a fight and one of the whores told the other, 'Go away. You look like a Jewess.' And later when they patched up their quarrel, the second whore said, 'I'll forgive you everything but saying I look like a Jewess.' " His head bobbed in mock respect, "There, my dear Bedia, go you and all of your kind."

Trying to make her way through his insult, she stood where she was while he walked out of the chapel. When she finally looked about it for the last time, she saw the sun was almost gone and the windows high above her dark. Chasing after Zvi, she did not find him in the street beyond the gate. Shrugging, she waved for a taxi. As she drove back to her apartment, she wondered about his comment, "We aren't really any more mad than other people." She was not so certain.

Stopping at the Israeli Embassy, Zvi made his way to the attaché's office. The middle-aged colonel greeted him with a smile and handed over the most recent reports. Settling down in a chair, Zvi scanned them slowly.

The Egyptian forces were compelled to penetrate into the territory of occupied Palestine. Radio Cairo

Egypt has decided to dispatch her heroes, the disciples of Pharaoh and the sons of Islam, and they will cleanse the land of Palestine. Therefore, ready yourselves; shed tears; cry out and weep, O Israel, because near is your day of liquidation. Thus have we decided and thus is our belief. There will be no more complaints and protests, neither to the Security Council, nor the United Nations, nor to the Armistice Commission. Nor will there be peace on the border because we demand vengeance and the vengeance is Israel's death.

Radio Cairo

Zvi looked up and stared across the room at the attaché. "They talk a good game."

The older man nodded.

And then Zvi glanced quickly through the activities report:

On 20 April 1956 fedayeen from Syria exploded the water installations in the village of Gonen in western Galilee.

On 29 April a soldier was killed and two wounded in an Israeli command car which hit a mine laid by fedayeen units nine kilometers south of Nir Yits'haq.

On 6 May fedayeen operating from Jordan blew up a two-story house and on the same day attacked a police car.

On 9 May a civilian vehicle traveling along the Ramat Hakovesh-Kefar Sava road was attacked by fedayeen.

On 15 May two motorcyclists were wounded by fedayeen near the Megiddo police station.

On 21 May fedayeen penetrated into Israeli territory in the vicinity of Nirim and one of them was captured by Israeli security forces.

For a long time Zvi held the reports in his hand. When he finally looked, he informed the attaché, "I'm going home."

The attaché understood. "When?"

"Tomorrow night. Will your secretary arrange it?"

Nodding, the older man said, "I wish I were going with you."

And Zvi picked up the phone and called Bedia to suggest they have dinner together. He would let her know the details later.

After Zvi cradled the phone, the attaché smiled. "I'm told she's beautiful."

Winking, Zvi said, "Love thy enemy."

It was late that evening when Zvi and Bedia finished dinner at the small restaurant on Rue de Rivoli and wandered over as they had so many times to the Tuileries. He had not mentioned his leaving, and they had not discussed the incident of the afternoon. They had talked instead about life as he had known it as a boy north of Beersheba, and she had told him what it had been like to grow up in a household where her father dominated, not only their home, but the countryside about Jerusalem and Ramallah. Zvi was fascinated by his first view of the Arabs as they had seen their lives in Palestine. She said nothing of the Grand Mufti of Jerusalem other than that he had visited their home often and had at one time been a friend of her father. She told Zvi of her trip during the war as a young girl to visit Hitler and the months her family had spent in Iraq when it was thought the Arabs would successfully defeat England.

And then he told her of his service in the British army; the years in North Africa and in Europe.

They walked hand in hand while he told her of the time he had been able to spend in school after the war and how he wished he had been able to continue his education, and she told him what life had been like as a student in England.

They had stopped for a cold drink at a stand served by an aged Frenchman when she asked him about his wife.

Zvi paused, and looking at her over the top of the bottle which he was clutching, asked, "What do you know about her?"

"Only that she was killed at Scorpion Pass," Bedia admitted.

Nodding, he said, "Butchered or murdered would be a better word."

"And you blame the Jordanians?"

Again he nodded. He saw her shaking her head in disagreement and said nothing while he finished his drink and set the bottle on the counter, which the aged Frenchman kept wiping as though it had grown dirty by itself. "You doubt it?" he asked without any bitterness.

"I talked to the American who commanded the search," she said.

Zvi snorted. "That is not an unbiased opinion."

"He did not say there was no massacre at the Pass," she said. The drink she was holding no longer interested her, and setting it on the counter beside his, she took his hand and they continued walking. "He told me that there were no tracks that led all the way to Jordan, but that he had taken the time to go into Sinai where he heard the killers were passing Bedouin."

Trying not to argue with her, Zvi said simply, "That's a tale only an outsider would believe." Then he repeated what he had told someone else a long time ago: "Christians don't understand Jewish problems."

Bedia held his hand more firmly. "Being killed is not only a Jewish problem."

Zvi considered her comment, "At this point in history being killed by an Arab is."

They were approaching the small museum at the edge of the park. It was closed. In the entrance-way they could make out the dark figures of a young man and a girl kissing. Zvi smiled. "I'd rather not talk politics tonight." Then lightly added, "I've reason to believe that the two of us have different opinions on the subject."

Laughing softly, Bedia agreed. Then to his surprise, she said, "You don't trust me, but you should."

They were walking back toward Rue St. Honoré now. Though the shops were closed, there were lights in some of the windows.

"Why should I trust you after Aden?"

They paused to look in a jewelry-store window, and he admired a watch. She pointed out a diamond pin and said she had been planning to buy one just like it. Zvi's hand went into his pocket as he counted with his fingertip the last of his folded notes and remembered the differences in their fortunes.

They walked on a block before she said, "You should trust me because you're alive, Zvi."

Puzzled, he waited for an explanation. They were in front of a bookshop now, reading the English titles among the books displayed: *Bonjour Tristesse, Peyton Place, The Mandarins* and *The Search for Bridey Murphy*.

"Don't you think you could have been killed anytime you were with me?" Seeing the dubious expression on his face, she glanced back and he noticed a car stopped some distance away. There were two men in it. There were no lights.

Nodding to show that he understood, Zvi asked, "Why haven't they?"

"It may hurt your ego, my Jewish colonel," she said, "but you aren't so important that we're going to get involved in assassination in France. Kill you and then a Jew would kill one of our ambassadors or officers abroad and there would be no end to it."

"I'm glad I'm not that important," Zvi grinned as they walked on. The car followed at a distance. Neither of them said anything until they reached the St. James and Albany.

"You could offer me a drink," she suggested.

"But I haven't any," he explained.

"Then maybe I could help you pack," she offered.

Very slowly, Zvi turned toward her. "You know?"

"Someone ordered a ticket for you on BOAC this afternoon."

Taking her arm, he led the way into the hotel. The clerk at the desk did not look up as the colonel and his girl friend walked through the lobby. The tourists from Memphis noticed the officer and tried to figure out what country he came from. Reaching the door to his room, Zvi looked down at her. Bedia's eyes met his, and he thought she was beautiful. Drawing her to him, he kissed her. She returned the kiss and her arms went about his neck. They embraced until they heard someone in the corridor, and then, embarrassed, he opened the door and switched on the light in the small sitting room. She followed him in and waited to hear what he was going to say.

Glancing about, Zvi wished his dirty shirt was not lying on the red-tapestried spread which covered the Napoleon bed, the only furniture other than a table in the room. After a moment, he shook his head. "No one would believe me."

He had difficulty taking his eyes off her bosom which filled the tight green sheath she was wearing.

"Aren't Jews always spreading tales?" She was laughing at him.

She was in his arms now and his hand caressed her breast. Zvi was serious when he said simply, "Jews aren't always doing anything because no two Jews are alike. Now my friend Moshe . . ."

"Colonel Gilead?" she asked.

He nodded and his hand wandered down the flat of her stomach. "You know him?"

"He commands the other terrorist battalion," she said, and he realized she was serious.

A dubious look came into his eyes. "No one who knows Moshe would call him a terrorist." Neither said anything as he turned her about so that her back was facing him and his hands came about her, cupping her breasts. "Moshe is a man who knows women," he said. "Maybe that way he is different from me."

She smiled as she felt him upzip her dress and thought about his words. Then she felt him pulling the shoulders of the dress down and, stepping away, turned to face him. "I'm not so certain any longer," she commented coldly.

"Certain?" and Zvi did not really know what she was trying to say.

"You said something about the most dangerous game, and I thought I had found it: lying down with a Jewish murderer. Now I'm not so sure." And reaching behind her, she zipped the back of her dress up and started toward the door.

It took Zvi a moment to realize she had been playing with him to show she was the one leaving and not he. And when he understood, he stepped in her way, grabbed her arm and twisting it behind her, swung her about so that her back was toward him once more.

"Don't," she snapped angrily. Then, as though she thought she knew how to reach him, she added, "You wouldn't want to prove the claims of the Egyptians that you are a 'defiler of women.' " He could not tell if she was laughing at him now or not. He did not think she was.

"Are you appealing to a Jew's honor?" He did not release his grip on her wrist. "You? Remember, there isn't anything I don't know about you now. Between us there aren't really any secrets left."

Zvi stood very still for a long time while he considered how she wanted to save not her honor but her dignity, wanted to believe she was rejecting him rather than he her by his decision to go to Israel where she couldn't go.

He shook his head in disgust with both of them, released her wrist, pulled two cigarettes from his tunic, offered her one and lit them both.

She puffed on the cigarette, her back against the wall, the door beside her. When she spoke, her voice was so soft he could barely make out her words. "There are times, Colonel Mazon, when I think I could love you, and then there are times when I remember you're a Jew . . ." She repeated "a Jew" so firmly that she appeared to be reassuring herself.

Accepting her evaluation of the situation, Zvi held up his cigarette and stared at it. When he lowered his hand, his eyes met hers. "There's a military phrase that encompasses the two of us and at the same time draws the line which separates us: *terrain and circumstance.* They determine the conditions under which a soldier fights. For us the terrain has never been right, and until there is peace between our people, the circumstances will always be wrong." Then, almost brightly, he added, "I do not believe I love you, Bedia Hassani. I think, however, had the terrain and circumstances been right, I might have."

He knew now that she was smiling.

"We're a very silly pair," she said.

Grinning almost stupidly, he agreed. "Silly. Two people should not talk this way." Then his voice hardened. "If we hadn't been idiots, we would have known you and I weren't going any place together that really mattered."

Then to his own surprise, he said, "I'm sorry. I wish you happiness."

Flicking the ash off his cigarette, he dropped the butt into an ash tray and opened the door for her. He was holding the door when she reached out and put her hand on his arm.

"I should not say this, but I wish you luck, Zvi Mazon." She was on her toes now, her lips brushing his cheeks. Before he could take hold of her, she slipped past him and half ran down the corridor.

The after-image of her remained with him for a long time. As he packed his bags, he looked about the room and suddenly felt lonely.

ISRAEL, SUMMER, 1956

The first days after Zvi returned home were the happiest he had spent in years. It was summer. Aaron had no school; and so Zvi borrowed a battered Fiat and drove north with his son. They spent an evening in Haifa. They slept one night in a kibbutz. The father and son wandered about Galilee, watched the farmers and fishermen, watched the Arabs and Druse, slept in the open one night where Zvi told Aaron what it had been like sleeping in the desert when he was a boy. He recalled for the boy the last time he had seen a desert elk and the last time he had tried to swim in the Dead Sea. They laughed that night until they fell asleep.

The next day while they drove on southward, Zvi listened to Aaron's problems with the girl who sat beside him in school, the girl whose mother did not like Yemenite Jews. Zvi's hands clenched on the steering wheel, but he merely nodded. He listened while Aaron told him how much he liked watching the soccer games in the park and how, when he grew up, he, too, would play soccer.

The most important thing that happened the week Zvi came home was that he and his son became friends. The commando leader did not know when, if ever, they would be able to spend a week together again, and so when he reported to Hakiryah, he was pleased that he had taken this one.

The chief of staff was away when Lieutenant-Colonel Mazon reported back for duty, but it was clear that arrangements had already been made for him. Meeting in that small upper-story room which served as the director of the chief of staff's office, Zvi and Avram discussed Zvi's leave briefly. Intelligence had already reported the meetings with Bedia Hassani. Zvi could add little to their reports, and he was glad about that.

Avram confessed that he had learned nothing more about Shoshanna. "Just dropped out of sight."

Accepting this, Zvi asked simply, "What next?" Avram leaned back on the rear two legs of his desk chair, set his hands behind his head and smiled. "Where you came from."

Zvi waited for details.

"Moshe's going on leave soon, and you have to take over your battalion as soon as possible."

"As soon as possible, but you didn't call me back?"

Avram shook his head. "You have about half a year of accumulated leave coming. The Chief thought you could have six or ten weeks without stretching his generosity."

"The situation?"

Shrugging, Avram rocked back and forth in his chair. "Nothing has changed. Nothing." Then before Zvi could comment, Avram shook his head, "Just say that the balance of power has shifted." A snort, and he concluded, "If you ever thought there was a balance of power."

For the next month Zvi did what he had done ever since he had left school almost five years before. He kept his men in fighting condition, made a retaliation raid, buried four dead, sent his wounded to the closest hospital and selected his replacements.

Less than four weeks after he was back from Paris, Zvi felt as if he had never gone away. On lonely nights in his quarters, he sprawled on his bunk and stared at the ceiling and tried to recall what Bedia had looked like and what Bedia had worn when they had stood at the entrance of the Opera House, when they had walked through the Tuileries, when they had . . . His thoughts wandered back beyond Bedia to Shoshanna and he wondered if he would see her again and how he would feel if he did.

He was lying on his bunk trying to work up the energy to drag himself into mess, when he flicked on the radio. Music. A news report. Static. Then a voice he recognized: Nasser. The Egyptian dictator was shouting.

Only the week before Nasser had been the Hero of the Arabs — the New Saladin. His friends Nehru and Tito had sung his praises. And together they had signed papers of enduring friendship. Nasser's star had never been higher.

Then on July 20 he had flown home from Tito's conference center on the lovely island of Brieni.

And when his plane had arrived at Cairo airport at three in the morning, the multitudes were out to meet him. So was the news that the Americans were not going to loan him the money to build his monument, the Aswan Dam, which he hoped would stand with the Pyramids.

The Arabs reacted to this new blow to their pride and their pocketbooks. For a week Nasser had been weeping over the insult which he read into the fact that the Americans and British would not loan him almost a billion dollars. "We are sensitive. We like nice words," the Egyptian dictator shouted.

Zvi listened while he shaved. He had heard much of this before. Now the attack was turned on Washington again. Nasser accused the United States of "disregard for the principles of international relations."

And now Nasser's hysteria was rising: "I look to the Americans and say, 'May you choke to death on your fury.'"

The voice shouted on wildly, ecstatically: "Today, O citizens, the Suez Canal has been nationalized, and this decree has in fact been published in the *Official Gazette* and become law."

During the next two hours Zvi heard that the General Staff was meeting, and that the United States Secretary of State was "shocked." The officer who phoned Zvi this comment laughed at the American's reaction to the trouble he had triggered. Finally, Zvi received the call from Avram telling him he could relax. They expected no additional trouble because Egypt had just taken on England.

Both men agreed: the days to come would be interesting.

After Colonel Nasser's confiscation of the Suez Canal, he did not relax his campaign of terror against Israel's civilians. With the cooperation of Jordan's leaders, he shuffled his fedayeen raiders from border to border in an attempt to keep the Israeli Defense Force off balance, and August was a terrible month for Israel.

On August 15 the terrorists planted a mine near the home of the Prime Minister at Sede Boqer.

On August 17 terrorists machine-gunned the school bus to Eilat as it pulled through the Negev. Two children and three adults were killed. Nine children were wounded.

I consider that if Egypt has ordered these fedayeen raids it has now put itself in the position of an aggressor.

General Burns, Canadian Army Chief, UNTSO

I believe in the strength, the ability, the loyalty and the courage of the fedayeen.

Nasser

The forces of Islam are sent to terrorize God's enemy and ours.

Voice of the Arabs

Israel must be wiped off the map.

Nasser

Israel must be annihilated.

Radio Cairo

It was the first day of September when Zvi Mazon received word that he was expected at Hakiryah as quickly as possible. Glancing at his watch, he saw that it was almost noon. Without changing from his field uniform, he drove alone into Tel Aviv. There was traffic on the road. In the heat of the day the sun and dust created strange images ahead.

Uncertain what was behind his orders, Zvi ran the current problems through his mind. The United States had taken a position on the nationalization of the Canal which was making the British and French squirm. For weeks the Security Council had been haggling over a strange projection created by the United States Secretary of State which would bring into being a financial monster to be called a Users Organization. Zvi did not know the details, but he believed that nothing would work except force. For weeks he himself had been looking for some kind of Anglo-French force to be applied. It had not been.

A truck swerved into his path and he slowed the jeep. Israeli intelligence estimated that the British could not place an intact division into the field. The disarmament of the British had been too complete for their own good. And now when they needed to act, they lacked the capacity.

The traffic was funneling into the city now and he slowed down. A honk from the jeep behind, and glancing over his shoulder, Zvi recognized Moshe Gilead seated beside his driver. To Zvi's confusion, Moshe waved. And fifteen minutes later, they drove past the sentry station at Hakiryah. Parking his jeep, Zvi was about to walk into the house where Avram was quartered when Moshe trotted over to him. "I guess the same thing brings us here."

The two had not met since Zvi had walked out of Moshe's headquarters the night before he had flown to Paris. And now Moshe slapped him on the back. "Did you get some rest?"

Puzzled, Zvi said, "It seems like something that happened a long time ago." Then, curious, "Weren't you supposed to be going on leave?" They were entering the building now and making their way to the second floor.

Moshe laughed. "At the moment what I want is in Israel, and I suspect something's up. You don't think I'd miss it, do you?"

Neither one was talking about their last meeting or the afternoon at

Scorpion Pass. When they entered Avram's office, they were personally where they had been years before – friends.

The Director of the General Staff Office was pleased to see the two together.

Avram shoved a file across the table to Moshe, who was the senior. Flipping it open, Moshe read quickly. At first he did not react. Then his browned hand clutched the back of his neck while he turned his head from side to side. His eyes finally came to rest on Avram's face. "Is it true?"

Avram nodded while Moshe pushed the open file to the other commando leader. It took Zvi a moment or two fully to realize what he was reading. The British and French were staging a build-up on Cyprus and Malta. Paratroopers. Planes. Ships. The report described the activity as *Operation Musketeer*. When he closed the file, Zvi looked at the other two with the comment, "That makes life viable."

Avram nodded. Moshe, however, only asked, "Can we get help from them?"

"Help?" Avram did not understand the question.

"Supplies," Zvi explained for his friend.

Silent for a moment, Avram seemed to be weighing his answer. When he spoke it was almost as though he feared to believe what he was saying, "The Chief is flying to Paris."

Both battalion commanders were satisfied. They had waited a long time for an ally.

"And England?" Moshe asked.

Avram shrugged. "She has a mutual defense pact with Jordan."

Trying to unscramble the threads of this, Zvi asked, "But this is Egypt."

"England loves the Arabs," Avram explained sarcastically. "She may chastise Egypt in a parental way, but she isn't about to throw her hand in with us. Jews aren't colorful."

Avram reached over, pulled two files from his desk and handed one to each. The battalion commanders silently read their orders. Each was being given a brigade with his present battalion as core cadre. They were to be prepared to assume their new commands at once.

Closing the file before him, Moshe handed it back. "And equipment?"

"I think we can manage it," Avram said. "But it won't be as good as what the Czechs have given Egypt."

Satisfied, Moshe asked, "And that's it?"

Coming to his feet, Avram held out his hand for Zvi's file, and after he had set the papers on his desk, he held his hand out once more. "Congratulations, Colonel Mazon."

Clasping his friend's hand, Zvi asked, "Congratulations?"

"Your promotion will be official tomorrow. The chief of staff wanted to tell you himself, but he's gone now."

Moshe shook Zvi's hand. Then almost accusingly, he turned to Avram, "That took too long."

Zvi felt embarrassed because Avram had been in rank longer than either of them, and he was obviously not going to be promoted now.

"I'll expect both of you at the house on Friday," Avram said. "We'll celebrate this one, too."

Remembering it was at the celebration of his last promotion that he had met Shoshanna, Zvi said, "Thanks."

And then he and Moshe were walking out of the office and down the stairs together. Though other things were to come between them in the future, each knew that he would never mention Zella to the other again.

The party which Avram had suggested had to be postponed for three days because the guest of honor was not available. Two days after Zvi had left Moshe at Hakiryah, he received orders to move once more against the Arab terrorists. Shortly after dark, he drove out of his base with two companies. Rolling east, they left the highway several kilometers beyond Ramla and moved directly across country. Seated in the lead jeep, Zvi decided he wanted Isaac with him again. The young reservist who was driving for him had courage but lacked the instant response Zvi demanded. It was almost midnight when the trucks rolled up to the Jordanian border and across. Waving his recce unit ahead, Zvi kept pace with other jeeps as the trucks fell behind. Twice they passed Arab villages. Once, when they knew an Arab Legionnaire posted on a small dirt crossroads spotted them, one of Zvi's men leaped from his truck and brought the Arab down with the butt of his rifle. Satisfied the man could not sound an alarm, Zvi waved the other vehicles on while he returned to pick up the soldier. Then he watched two truckloads peel off and set their trap on the road closest to a Legion camp. He stopped his driver so that he could watch as the commandos set long ropes across the road and attached explosive charges to the ends strung along the roadside ditch. After cans of fuel had been attached to the explosives, the men took cover. In the distance, Zvi could hear the firing which told him that the rest of the two companies was now engaged.

Deciding to watch the ambush, a new tactic he had conceived, he waved his driver to the shelter of a cluster of twisted olive trees and sat back to wait. The firing in the distance rose in tempo. Grenades now. Now mortars. Then the explosion he had been waiting for. Another Arab police station demolished. Suddenly there were lights on the side road as the Legionnaires were coming to block the escape route of the Jews.

Very carefully checking the ground, Zvi could not see one of his men. The others should be on their way back. He hoped they would not meet the Arabs at the crossroads.

Then the Legion trucks were passing him. One and then two more.

Suddenly the ropes stretched across the road were caught up by the front of the trucks, dragging the explosives to the sides. With a white flash, the lead truck exploded, splashing fuel over the other two. They started to burn. There were screams from the trapped Arabs.

Then the Israeli commandos laid down their fire.

It was all over by the time the rest of Zvi's men came racing back down the highway. The crossroads was as bright as noon. The ambushers entrucked and joined the tail of the column.

Pleased the Arabs would remember he had been there, Zvi signaled for his driver to follow the others. Only when they had crossed the border into Israel, did Zvi check out with his company commanders. One man killed and two wounded. No one left behind.

Sending his wounded back, Zvi left his men parked in an empty field for twenty minutes. He knew they were tired. He knew, too, that there were some who had made their last trip into enemy country. While he walked silently among the scattered groups of men who stood near their trucks smoking and talking or just staring into the darkness, he saw which were too wounded inside to make even one more run against the Arabs. Given time, these wounds, like other wounds, would heal. Reaching the edge of the field, he turned back to look at his men. A few months before he had been as ill as any of them, as tense as any. He had no difficulty recalling the night he had gone berserk.

His hand slipped inside his shirt. Taking the last puff on his cigarette, he waved to the company commanders. They started back for their base camp. It was almost dawn when they reached it. Half an hour later, Zvi flopped down on his bunk and fell asleep.

The party which the Ben Ezras held to honor Zvi's promotion brought out all of his friends. And even some he had not expected. Arriving late in the evening because of his duties, Zvi brought Ruth with him. Most of the others were already there. The small apartment was filled with people. The Chief of Operations was the first to congratulate Zvi, and he also told him how pleased headquarters was with his most recent retaliation raid. For a moment the two stood almost alone near the door while Zvi asked, "Aren't we coming near the end of this as a policy?"

Joining the two, Avram heard the question, and he waited to learn what the others thought.

"Why do you ask?" The Operations Officer wanted to know.

"They're waiting for us every time out now. It is beginning to cost more than it should."

Avram looked at the other staff officer for a reaction and seeing that there was going to be none, said, "I can assure you that it's being weighed."

Realizing that he was probably not going to receive an answer, Zvi smiled. Turning where he was, he scanned the room. Malin and Ruth were already talking about children. The Operations Chief and the Director of the General Staff Office were off in a corner now talking about something. On the far side of the room near the corridor which led to the bedrooms, Zvi could see Moshe, in his best dress uniform, talking to a young woman. They did not seem to notice the people milling about them. Zvi thought the girl was probably ten years younger than Moshe. She stood about as tall. When she turned so that he could see her face, he thought she was plain, and then he remembered she was Malin's younger sister. Quickly, he tried to calculate Moshe's age. Two years younger than he. Twenty-four in the War of Independence. Eight years. Thirty-two, give or take a year. Zvi felt old. But the girl he was looking at was very young. A smile came over his face as he remembered that with only one exception, which he knew, Moshe was rumored to like them young. Continuing to stare at the two, Zvi tried to remember the name of Malin's sister. Zippy. And he was pleased with himself.

Fishel was approaching him now. The limp was almost gone. The friends shook hands, and Fishel congratulated him. Zvi was watching Moshe, who was holding both of Zipporah's hands. Fishel followed his glance and said, "I like him. I imagine I will always remember him as the youngest of us on that rooftop in the Quarter."

Zvi did not quite understand. "That rooftop?" There had been so many.

"The one you brought Dvora to." And because he thought he had to explain: "That was the first time all of us were together." After a second he sighed. "And the last. We got mauled on that roof."

Zvi nodded. He could not tell Fishel that he had fought so many battles since that day that though he recalled it clearly, he would rather not. He was not ready for nostalgia yet. However, he saw in the back of his head the dark face of the girl from Poland. "A crazy bitch," Zvi finally said, unconsciously moving his hand over the place on his chest where she had shot him. Then to Fishel's embarrassment, Zvi shook his head, "Maybe not a bitch, maybe just crazy."

Fishel was tempted to tell Zvi they were talking about his mistress, but he decided not to, not at this time.

They stood listening to the conversation wash over them from the clusters of twos and more.

"*The French have to move against Egypt as long as Egypt's keeping the pot bubbling in Algeria with all those arms shipments. And now France has Suez for an excuse.*"

"*If they keep the Strait of Tiran closed, Eilat will die. It's dying along with our trade to Africa and the Far East.*"

"*Do the Americans know the British and French are consorting?*"

"*Sounds like a dirty word, but I doubt it.*"

Laughter.

"What's wrong?"
"Just thinking of Mollet and Eden consorting."
More laughter.

Fishel smiled at Zvi. "One nice thing about Jews, they never discuss politics or anything important."

They stood staring out the window, and then Zvi said, "I hear you have a lady friend." His hand came up, "I envy you that." He paused for a second and then plunged on, "Marry her. Don't discuss the matter, just marry her."

From habit the violinist rubbed the side of his leg. Zvi obviously did not know whom he was talking about, and at the same time Fishel wished he had been able to make Dvora come with him. "I will tell you something no one else knows," the artist offered. "I have asked her every day for years, and she keeps saying No." There was a kind of pride in his voice, pride at having been so faithful and pride in Dvora's stubbornness.

Zvi sucked on his cheek for a moment as he thought about this. He looked about. "Is she here now? I'll tell her to marry you myself."

Fishel shook his head, "She's not here."

Then suddenly, Zvi shifted his tone. "If you don't mind, I'm going to ask that they call you up and assign you to me."

"Delighted," the violinist was clearly pleased. "In what capacity?"

Zvi hesitated to answer. "I'm getting a brigade," he finally said. "I want you as a captain and as a recce commander."

The shocked expression on Fishel's face pleased the commando leader. "Don't you want a reconnaissance unit?"

Reaching out, Fishel pumped Zvi's hand. "Thanks," he said. "Thanks." He fell silent and was embarrassed at his own show of emotion. "I don't know what else to say."

"Next week?" Zvi asked. And before Fishel could answer, he offered, "I'll keep it open if you want longer."

"Next week," Fishel assured him.

Zvi's head went back and he half closed his eyes as he listened to the voices ebbing over the room. Looking around a few seconds later, he saw Moshe and Zipporah slip out the front door. He glanced toward his hostess. Malin's eyes were narrowed and she, too, was staring at the door. Zvi hoped the judge was not thinking of Moshe as she had found him in her bedroom several years before. He was about to move toward her when Fishel took his hand again. "Thanks, Zvi. I'm going home to tell her now."

"Tell her?" Zvi countered. "The only thing you should tell her is that she should marry you before you put on that uniform again."

Then he saw Kineret Heschel coming toward him and he was alone with her. The Deputy Foreign Minister was dressed more formally than the other women, and Zvi thought she looked more impressive than any of them even though her hair was almost white, the lines on her face were strange to him and the sparkle in her eyes had disappeared.

She congratulated him and he thanked her for coming.

Kineret was looking at Fishel as he said goodbye to Malin. "He's walking better now."

Zvi agreed. "An operation. I gather it was more than one, but it must have helped. I've asked him to join my brigade."

For a time Kineret acted as though she had not heard, and then she said, "He's important." Her eyes met Zvi's. "How does one say it? In a democracy every man is equally important. In a small country or a large one, every life is important. In a civilized society an artist is more important." She paused a moment. "Please, Zvi, see that he isn't killed." A wry smile as she added, "I know you don't guarantee that you can bring every man back, but Fishel, well, he's more than others."

"No," Zvi snapped. "You underestimate him."

Puzzled, she waited for an explanation.

"He's as good a soldier as most. More courage. More sense of responsibility. At least that is the way he was in forty-eight. And I'm sure he hasn't changed. But more . . ." He shook his head. "The thing that none of you seem to realize is that Fishel hates being thought of as special or important. And to think of him that way belittles what he believes about himself."

Kineret nodded. "Our squad commander of the roofs has grown up." Her hand touched his sleeve. "Of all the things they say about Colonel Zvi Mazon, none had mentioned that to me."

Flushing, Zvi shook his head, trying in the gesture to deny her words.

Now she was smiling at his confusion. "And he remains a boy."

Now it was Zvi's turn to smile as he realized no one else would have dared call him one. A deputy cabinet minister, Kineret Heschel was almost old enough to be his mother, but no one ever thought of her as anyone's mother. Leaning over, he kissed her cheek.

Malin came by with a tray of coffee cups and they each took one.

Kineret stirred her Turkish coffee and, staring at it, commented, "The Egyptians are now calling it Arabic coffee." Her head came up and she smiled at Zvi. "You and Moshe fight them more than anyone else. I hope you don't hate them."

Zvi's mind drifted back to a conversation he had heard earlier in the evening. "We all talk about not hating them. I guess we don't, maybe we feel sorry for them." His fist clenched as he almost bent the spoon in his hand. "I don't know. I'll tell you this: there are nights coming back from raids when I don't feel sorry for them. When I read the reports of Fedayeen actions, I'm not so certain." He relaxed. "What the hell can I say? They're sick in a way almost no people in history has been sick."

Shaking his head, he started to talk again. "Do you remember in thirty-nine, right after the British issued the White Paper. A hundred and twenty young people went down to the Dead Sea to build a kibbutz. You remember?"

Kineret nodded. "They washed out the salt."

Zvi's head bobbed. "They labored in the potash works digging out chemicals until the land was usable."

She was puzzled, wondering why he was telling her this now.

"They raised and sold flowers and vegetables. The land was good. Nothing had ever grown in it before, but they made it sweet and it was as rich as earth could get."

"Then in forty-eight," he said. "In forty-eight they were told to get out because we could not protect them against the Arab armies."

"I remember," she told him.

"Well," and Zvi bent the spoon in his hand almost double. "A few weeks ago, coming through that area after a raid, I saw that land." He leaned forward, "Do you know what the Arabs did with it?"

Kineret's hand closed tightly about the cup. She braced herself.

"They bulldozed salt back into it." The horror stilled him for a moment. "Good farm land. The single most important shortage in the Middle East, and in their hands. And instead of planting it, planting food they need so badly, they hate us so much they bulldozed salt into the earth so that it would never grow again."

"Oh, my God, that is pathological."

Zvi nodded. "You ask if I hate them. I guess I don't because I can't see how a man can hate anyone so damned sick."

Kineret nodded. "Once I thought the British were sick that way. I don't now."

He nodded. "I fought in their army. There were decent and brave men fighting then." And he agreed with Kineret, "I guess I don't hate them either."

She smiled at him. "And that girl, the one who shot you as the Quarter fell? Do you hate her?"

Zvi's head fell to one side as he stared at her. "You won't believe this, but until Fishel reminded me of her earlier tonight, I don't think I have thought about her in eight years." He snorted, "I'm not even certain I would have remembered her name until he said it."

Kineret watched him light a cigarette. Finally she decided it was time that someone made it clear to Zvi. "You don't know that she is the girl Fishel wants to marry?" She received her answer in the startled expression on his face.

"Fishel and her?" He waved his hand as though to brush the notion away. "She's——"

382

"The woman who's lived with him for years, saw him through his operations, helped him in a way no one else probably ever did."

"*Gevalt*," Zvi said. "Only tonight I told him I was giving him my recce command, and I told him she was crazy."

"Does it make a difference?"

He thought about this for a time before he shook his head. "I guess it shouldn't." However, he frowned when he added, "And now if anything happens to him, people will say that I was getting my revenge."

Kineret's eyes flashed angrily. "Don't be stupid, Zvi. People know you too well."

"Thanks," he said. Then he smiled at her. "You know, it's been good meeting you again."

She returned his compliment. "It's been too long, Zvi. Friends should see more of each other. Joseph Ben Dur thought of you as a friend."

Zvi's memory crashed against the name Joseph Ben Dur. The portly judge who had come to see the Wall and had died in the attempt. Joseph Ben Dur. Zvi wondered how many people knew Kineret Heschel had loved that man.

"I hope he saw the Wall," Zvi said to let her know he had not forgotten.

The look in her eyes softened before she shifted the subject. "I'm going to be working closely with Avi these next few months."

Puzzled, Zvi nodded.

And she rose from her chair with the comment, "It's time I get home."

It was only later, after he had taken Kineret to her apartment and was alone, that he wondered why she and Avram were working together.

That night when he returned home from the Ben Ezras, Fishel told Dvora everything that had happened. This had become their way of life and both of them looked forward to the long hours after the affairs which Fishel attended without her. Their coffee sat on the table before the sofa, and Fishel lay with his head on her lap, his nimble fingers toying with the white silk of the robe he had bought her on his last trip to Paris.

"And so you're going?" she asked, not as a question so much as a way of giving herself time to understand what was happening to them.

"I'm going. I have to." Then he looked up into her face as she smiled.

"And you want to."

"I want to," he admitted. Both of them knew that it was more than joining an army; it was proof to himself that he was as able as he had been before he had been wounded. "There was one other thing," he said.

She ran her hands playfully through his hair while she waited to be told.

"I have orders from Colonel Zvi Mazon himself." He smiled as he said, "I think I can quote them verbatim. 'Tell the girl to marry you or I'll come over and convince her.'"

Both of them smiled.

"And so I'm telling you."

Dvora bent over and kissed him lightly. Then she leaned her head back against the sofa and was very still for a long time. "Because your colonel ordered you to?"

He knew she was laughing. "If that's the only way I can get you to say you will."

"There could be another way."

And as he started to sit up, she pressed his shoulders down so that his head remained in her lap. He tried to meet her eyes, but she was not looking at him. "What way?"

"Ask me."

Fishel's hand closed on hers. Then he realized what she had said. "Will you marry me?"

He could see her head bob as she agreed. "When you come out of service."

And when he kissed her, he knew that she was frightened and that she was crying.

About midnight on 11 September, in reaction to increased terrorist activity, a battalion of Colonel Gilead's brigade crossed the Demarcation Line and blew up the Khirbat ar Rahwah police post and an empty school building in the same area, killing five Jordanian policemen and five Jordanian soldiers. Moving with the cold detachment which had made him famous, Moshe also laid an ambush approximately six kilometers inside Jordan along the Beersheba-Hebron road where he killed five Jordanian soldiers and wounded three more.

At an emergency meeting the next day the Mixed Armistice Commission held Israel responsible.

On the evening of 12 September Jordanian terrorists killed three Israeli guards at an oil drilling camp near Ein Ofarim.

At 2100 hours on 13 September, Colonel Mazon led an attack on a Jordanian police post and school at Gharandal in Jordan, destroying both. Nine Jordanian policemen and two Jordanian civilians were killed. Six other Jordanian soldiers were wounded.

Four days later both Colonels Mazon and Gilead were called to headquarters where they were presented with specific military problems. In the event of war, what would Colonel Mazon require to take Sinai and how would he go about it? In the event of war, what would Colonel Gilead require to capture the Gaza Strip and how would he do it?

In the weeks that followed each man worked out his plans and at the same time met the Arab terrorist threats on Israel's borders with damaging retaliation raids. The tension along the Jordanian-Israeli border grew with every action and reaction.

On 23 September Jordanian machine-gunners opened fire on the members of the Israel Archeological Congress inspecting ruins at Ramat Rahel in the Jerusalem area of Israel. Three were killed and seventeen wounded.

The next night the Jordanians killed a woman picking olives in a grove near the Ora settlement in the Jerusalem area.

Later that same day they killed two tractor drivers in the Ma'oz Haiyam area.

On the night of 25/26 September Colonel Gilead's men attacked Sharafi police post near Husan village. The post was completely demolished. Thirty-seven Jordanian soldiers were killed and eleven others wounded.

During the second week of October, England warned Israel that she would be obliged to assist Jordan under their joint 1948 treaty.

That week Avram and the Operations Chief met again with both Moshe and Zvi at Hakiryah. The Chief of Staff had already been to France seeking equipment and supplies and the details were being laid out for an operation not against Jordan, but Egypt, the strongest of Israel's enemies and the one that was supplying and financing the terrorist operations from Jordan, Syria and Gaza.

The four officers went over the operational plans as they had already been presented. When they were done, Avram ordered coffee. For a long time none of them said anything. They all knew the retaliation raids were costing too much, and they all feared a last-minute mobilization and flow of new equipment which would create confusion when fed into the army.

"It's got to come to an end," Zvi said flatly, assuming the others were thinking about the same thing.

The thin face of Eli Cohen, the Operations Chief, bobbed back and forth and waited for Moshe's reaction.

"Time's the whole problem," Moshe explained. "There isn't enough time. We've only a few hours of complete darkness. In that time I've got to cross hills with boulders and brush spread over them, and before I can get to my objective I have to take dug-in emplacements along the border. Have to take them head on."

Zvi agreed. "Before we move against one of these damned Tegart police posts we have to clear a path for trucks to bring in enough explosives to do the job right. You know a Tegart." And the others nodded, all aware of the fortresslike structures named after Sir Charles Tegart, the British designer.

"And then we have to bring everyone back," Moshe added.

"The dead and the wounded," Zvi concluded.

"We can keep going," Moshe said, "But the PM has to realize the cost is getting high. And while he can give us everything else, he can't give us what we need to cut that cost — time."

The next night because of a lack of time Moshe Gilead's men sustained their highest losses in a retaliation raid.

Two weeks later word reached them that Iraqi advance troops were ready to cross the border into Jordan and take up positions on the Israeli border. No one at the United Nations seemed to think that such action by a state not on Israel's borders and not having any cause for belligerency was a cause for alarm.

However, this action caused a most important trip: Avram flew to Paris with Kineret and the prime minister to go over the joint plans for what the Israeli were to call *Operation Kadesh* — named for that biblical place where the Jews stayed before preparing to enter the Holy Land — and the English and French, *Operation Musketeer*.

The agreements among the three countries were simple: The Jews would invade Sinai and approach the Canal as quickly as possible.

The RAF would take out the Egyptian air force on the ground and keep up the bombing both to nullify Egyptian air power and warn the other Arab countries against attack.

The French would base twenty fighters on Israeli territory to help protect Tel Aviv and Jerusalem from bombers.

The Anglo-French landings would be shaped on the excuse of keeping both the Jews and Egyptians away from the Canal and would follow an Anglo-French ultimatum to cease fire. The Jews would accept when they were within ten miles east of the Canal.

The ultimatum would be issued twelve hours before the Israelis reached the ten-mile zone.

The French agreed to naval and air support for Israel and a written document was drafted agreeing to these terms, committing France and a reluctant England to war.

The other action which took place that October was the mobilization of the Israeli army.

A young linotypist listening to his radio heard, *Is it any pleasure to the Almighty?* And he turned off his machine and started for a rendezvous with his company.

A middle-aged waiter from Glasgow, serving some American tourists from Tucson, had paused in the hotel kitchen in Tel Aviv to pick up the orange sherbet when the cook told him the radio had just broadcast a funny line from the Bible: *And they continued three years without war between Syria and Israel* — and the waiter smiled and walked out the back door of the hotel, leaving the tourists waiting for their dessert.

The taxi driver drew up to the curb in Herzliyah and waited for a passenger. The first man who climbed into the taxi said, "Joseph is waiting for us two blocks down." And they picked up Joseph and drove in the taxi to their assembly point.

A young woman in the office of the port clerk in Haifa was about to go home to cook dinner for her lover when someone walking past whispered into her ear, *And the Lord delivered the Canaanites*, and the young woman left to join her unit.

Half an hour later the lover of the young girl who worked in the office of the port clerk was about to bid his wife goodbye when a neighbor told him someone had been looking for him with the strange message: *And it came to pass.* Neither of the lovers kept their tryst that night.

A plumber fixing a broken sewer pipe set his tools aside when someone called down to him that *This people go up to do sacrifice* and went to join his tank unit.

A handsome young pilot on the El Al airline had just stepped off his plane, newly arrived from Athens, when he received a phone call from a friend telling him *On the wings of eagles* and he drove directly to his fighter base with the driver of a milk truck who was his commander, both changing uniforms as they went.

The forty men seated at dinner in the kibbutz in western Galilee listened to the dinner music on the radio and were arguing about whether or not they should open a set of tourist cabins on the kibbutz and how much work and money this would entail when the announcer said, *I delivered you out of the hands of the Egyptians.* Fifteen minutes later the only man left at the table was an aged widower from Ramla who had lost both his wife and his leg in the War of Independence.

And so it went from one end of the country to the other until the tourists became aware that there were few Israeli men in the streets of the cities and fewer still on the farms. Where a young man had greeted them at their hotel desk, a middle-aged woman now passed on their messages. Where a burly bus driver with an Irish brogue crinkling the edges of his Hebrew had taken them out earlier in the day, a young woman with her two children in the seats behind her was driving them back to their hotel.

Among the first to be aware of the changes taking place was the American ambassador, who notified his government. Less than ten hours later a lengthy and unhappy message came from the President of the United States to the Prime Minister of Israel warning against acting on the assumption that the United States would be divided or immobilized by the Zionist vote in the forthcoming American elections.

Israeli intelligence immediately began to spread the rumor through the coffee shops of the Middle East that the war was scheduled to begin against Jordan.

Panicked by the Israeli mobilization, Jordan formed a unified military command with Egypt and Syria.

On 25 October, Zvi was visiting the Southern Command headquarters where he had just completed an inspection of his brigade. The three battalions — almost 1,500 men in total — his supply and service companies, his heavy mortar battalion and his air recce units were in as good a condition as he knew he would ever be able to get them. Almost all of the men were young. His battalion commanders were no more than twenty-five, his company commanders were several years younger than that. Their morale was high, their equipment as good as any Israel could scrounge. He wished he had more four-by-four and six-by-six trucks, but what he had would do for the short run. His main concern in the event of a war was petrol. In a defensive operation it would have been ammunition, but Zvi did not expect to fight defensively, and therefore, should he have to move, it would be fast and far.

He was about to go inside when a communications sergeant trotted over from a weapons carrier.

"They want you in Tel Aviv."

Zvi shoved the beret back on his head and weighed the order. "Tell them I'm on my way."

Ten minutes later he and Fishel drove north in Zvi's jeep. "You can see your fiancé " Zvi had suggested when he invited Fishel along.

When they reached headquarters, Fishel agreed to return in an hour for his commander and sped off toward his apartment and Dvora.

Inside the headquarters building, Zvi found Moshe had already arrived. His friend knew no more than he why they had been summoned.

A short time later they both knew. Contacting his staff officers by radio, Zvi arranged to meet them at his own headquarters as quickly as he could obtain the added information that he would need. Moshe listened to Zvi's arrangements, wished him luck and left to meet with his own staff. Sitting at the table in front of Avram's desk, Zvi made a list of what he thought he required; and by the time he was done, Avram joined him.

"Dinner?"

Zvi nodded. "A good trip wherever it was you went?"

The staff officer smiled. "Interesting. Someday when you've a lot of time, I'll tell you."

Downstairs they found Fishel and walked over to the mess. None of them mentioned the problems just presented Zvi, and after a few minutes, he knew he was not going to be able to eat. Shoving his plate aside, he smiled. "I wish I had Moshe's calm."

Fishel laughed. Avram did not. "He's heading for trouble and he doesn't know it."

Puzzled, Zvi waited for an explanation.

"My sister-in-law. I think she's fallen in love with him, and you know Moshe."

Fishel tried to smile. "Am I to gather that the two of you could clash over that?"

Avram shrugged. "It's Malin. She doesn't like Moshe. Never has."

But Zvi could not think of Moshe's love life or even Avram's concern. Rising from the table, he excused himself and returned to the maze of rooms which surrounded Avram's office. He wished he had more tanks. The dozen he had were too light for what he would be doing, but he also knew that the Chief of Staff was giving him everything that could be shaken loose. The

French AMX tanks were undergunned and even though Israeli ordnance had changed over to heavier guns only a few weeks before, they remained inadequate. Still, Zvi knew he would have to live with what he had.

At eight o'clock he met once more with the operations staff. When he finally left Hakiryah, he had only one question in his mind. Was this really it?

Sitting in the back of the jeep as they raced to join his own staff, Fishel saw Zvi close his eyes. This was not the kind of fatigue that came from a day or a night without sleep. It was cumulative.

Forty-five minutes later they reached their own base headquarters which had recently been moved south of Tel Aviv. It was almost two in the morning when Zvi opened his eyes. For the next two hours he, his staff officers and battalion commanders went over the plans he had presented earlier in the evening at Hakiryah. Together, they refined them in detail. They computed their needs for five days of continuous operations. They selected the units which would move first and those which would move last. They estimated their timing on a move across open country and their timing in battle. "Count on bypassing anything that causes trouble," Zvi kept pounding at the others. "I want a race. I want to make contact as quickly as possible." The others understood what he had in mind. Most of them were eager. None was afraid. The order which Zvi had brought back came almost as a relief. They hoped, as he hoped, that this was the end of waiting.

Ten times they evaluated their transportation, and ten times Zvi had to explain that the Chief of Staff would give them better if he had it.

By four in the morning they had the detailed outline of their plan in their minds and their problems on paper. Satisfied there was nothing more they could do, Zvi urged them all to get some rest. There would be little in the days to come. At noon, he drove to Beersheba with Fishel and his operations officer, a young major. The major, now a professional soldier, had once planned on being a lawyer. It was something they joked about when they were weary and anything seemed funny.

At Beersheba, Zvi and his companions laid out their plans before the Southern Commander. The General, stockier even than Zvi and shorter, sat back in his chair and listened.

"It makes sense," he said. Then, he quickly altered some of the details to match what he knew about the terrain they would have to cross.

Rising from behind his desk, he smiled. "I've seen the Chief's operational orders for the other commands," and he laughed. "He doesn't like to write very much."

Zvi smiled. His own orders had been concise.

Create a military threat to the Suez Canal by seizing objectives in its proximity.

Confound the organization of the Egyptian forces in Sinai and bring about their collapse.

And then the list of objectives to be captured. The most important was Mitla Pass, the entrance from Egypt to Sinai.

The General was speaking again, and Zvi's head came up as he smiled.

"Up at headquarters I saw the orders of the Central Command. They were simple: 'The Central Command will defend its own area!' "

Watching Zvi smile, the general knew he had achieved his own objective and it had not been humor. "Remember one thing," he said, "we have no interest in destroying the enemy's forces. We don't want any excess of bloodshed."

Zvi had reservations. A battle plan which allowed the enemy merely to withdraw did not please him. "But if we have to . . ."

"Then do what you must. This is not going to be simple. You know that. But I want you to make the best time you can." The General thought for a moment. "Of the three area commands, we may not be the only one fighting. The Northern Command is going to be stripped and if the Syrians or Jordanians move," he shrugged. "That's the gamble." A slight smile came over his florid face. "Like Gaul, we, too, are divided into three parts. Let's just hope *we* keep all three of them by the time you're done."

Zvi rose along with his Operations Officer and Fishel. "The maps and air photos?"

"Avram sent them down two hours ago." The General thought a moment, "That fourth battalion of yours, I think you're right about holding it in reserve. Stick with your regulars now."

Shaking hands with the three, the General left them alone in his office with the new maps and air photos.

For four hours Zvi remained close to headquarters at Beersheba. At three in the afternoon of the twenty-seventh he received his official orders and arranged for his brigade to move to its concentration areas southeast near the small village of Hatseva on the Jordanian border.

TEL AVIV

On Saturday, 27 October, Moshe Gilead sat with his unit north of the city waiting for his orders to move. He knew that Zvi would start his brigade southward that day, and reading his orders over in the small barracks which served him as headquarters, he knew that he would have to start for the Gaza Strip and the battle to be fought there. It was almost noon and he still had no orders to take to the road.

The night before he had spent in Jerusalem with Zipporah and he had almost clashed with Malin when he brought her sister home. None of them had seen Avram for several days and Malin was distraught. It had been an effort to withdraw without a fight, and as he sat back at his desk, he wondered how long he could avoid clashing with Malin. He was thinking about Zipporah when his second-in-command entered with the radio message.

Reading it over twice, Moshe could not understand what was taking place. For months he had planned his move against Gaza, and now he had orders telling him to send his brigade to Beersheba and report directly to headquarters.

Fifteen minutes later, he was on his way, having left orders to shift the brigade to Beersheba. As he flew south to Tel Aviv in the small Piper Cub, he kept thinking of the map which he knew so well he did not have to bother taking it out of his case. From Beersheba where . . . He could not decide.

Landing at the small airstrip, he drove straight to Hakiryah, where he was closeted with the Chief of Staff for an hour. When he left, he had difficulty understanding why he had been selected for this assignment and Zvi for his. Believing his own unit better suited to the drop at Mitla, he resented the difference.

He moved on to wait for his brigade at Beersheba. Arriving in the late afternoon, he started to work on his plans. The brigade knew nothing yet about the task assigned to it, and he wondered how his officers would react. It was early evening when he reported into Southern Command Headquarters. The portly General listened to the plans Moshe had laid out, and then he sat back and waited.

"I am going to need air photos," Moshe pointed out.

The General nodded and waited.

"And I'm going to need vehicles. More and better ones than I have now."

The General nodded again.

"I have to switch over to six-by-six trucks. Nothing else is going to get through."

Rubbing his forearm, the General agreed. "I'll get what I can. And if I can scrounge any extra half-tracks, they're yours."

Neither of them spoke of the drain Zvi Mazon's operations had already made on the Southern Command. This was not Moshe Gilead's problem, and the General had known Moshe long enough to understand that the cold look about the young Colonel's eyes came from years of exertion. Thinking how unlike Zvi Moshe was, the General decided that there was no time now to see if he could help this young man relax. He knew Moshe had his own ways of doing that.

"You're going to get sea support."

"I know," Moshe snapped. "I know. And a hell of a lot of good that's going to be. They have to drag those damned landing craft overland from Haifa to Eilat. I can't wait for them."

"They'll do the best they can," the General assured him.

Snorting, Moshe said, "Just help me get the six-by-six trucks. I need every bit of mobile power I can get."

Both men fell silent as the General's Operations Officer entered with the air photos and maps. He spread them out on the table in the office and the three gathered about.

Tracing his proposed line of march with a pencil, Moshe moved from Beersheba to Kuntilla, from Kuntilla to a crossroads village in Egyptian territory west of Eilat. From there he ran the pencil almost due south to Sharm el Sheikh. When he was done, he slammed the pencil down and said, "If they'd only let me make a reconnaissance. If I had the time to . . ." Shrugging, he gathered up the maps and air photos. "I've got less than forty-eight hours to make my plans, get new equipment, set up a supply system and organize a new desert marching order."

The General almost smiled at his Operations Officer. Moshe did not notice the glance that passed between the two as he started for the door. "I'll be back," he warned.

And after he had left, the two officers of the Southern Command agreed. "He's enjoying every moment of it."

Back at the barracks, Moshe spread out the maps once more. Four hours later the brigade arrived from the north. In a meeting with his deputy, Lieutenant-Colonel Leon Sharlin, Moshe explained: "Our problems are clear enough. The solutions are not. The central one is how to organize the column. Then, how do we build it to function on the march? There are three things against us all the way: the time factor, because we have a deadline." He did not want to tell Leon what it was as yet. "Then there are the roads, or should I say there are no roads?" He was at the air photos again. "Not a damned thing all the way." He grinned wryly as he added, "And, of course, there is the enemy."

Both men knew this was not the central problem, though under almost any other circumstance it would have been.

"What's the time factor?" Leon asked.

"No one's sure just how long we are going to have."

"That doesn't make sense."

"Wait until you've been around a while longer. Half the problems are political. Who knows how long before the UN shuts us down?"

Shaking his head, Leon asked, "Then the only answer is the quickest way possible."

"With that bit of wisdom," Moshe said curtly, "we can proceed. We have to plan for minimum logistics." His hand was on the lower part of Sinai as shown on the map. "No one's taken vehicles into these mountains before. We don't even really know how wide these canyons are." And he was pointing. "We could dead-end in any one of them."

Leon was already marking off the distance, and when he was done, he looked across the table. "Three hundred kilometers in how many days?"

Moshe's head bobbed back and forth as he weighed the problem. "I'm going to try for three days. We'll take supplies for two more in case we bog down, and in any event we have to fight when we get there."

The Deputy Commander had forgotten about the enemy for a moment. "How many Egyptian troops?" His finger was on Sharm el Sheikh and the surrounding complex.

Moshe shrugged. "Intelligence is to let us know." Both men fell silent and Moshe looked up. "We will count on emergency supply by sea." He was looking at the map once more. "We'll be close enough for that." He was thinking quickly now and Leon took notes as he listened.

"Each vehicle will have its own food, water, ammunition and fuel except the jeeps. Each vehicle will be self-sustaining. Compact and intact. No outside support and no resupply if we can avoid it."

Leon nodded.

"After we've prepared the trucks as their own base, we will add the men." Moshe fell silent again. "The space that is left, and not the enemy, will determine how many we take."

The round-faced kibbutznik was happy that he was with Moshe, because in spite of anything else people might call him, Moshe Gilead was a soldier.

"There will be no issue on the march," Moshe repeated. Then he started calculating the dimensions of his column. Finished, he looked up. "It will run twenty miles more or less and that means there can be no movement of supply from tail to head." He dragged a chair over with his feet, swung it about and planted a boot on the seat. "Weight," he said. "There's the rub. A history of warfare could be written about weight. Too much and you stop cold. Too little and you haven't enough supply. Weight." And he wiped his hand on his slacks.

"Zvi planned to carry ten tons on his two-and-a-half-ton trucks. That's stupid." Before Leon could comment, Moshe shifted the subject. "I want this thing designed so that we can build up strength from behind if the head of the column gets stopped. Each unit should be designed to complement the one in front of it."

"And maintenance?"

Moshe almost smiled and for a moment Leon thought the commander would. "We can't spend time solving that problem." And while he talked, Moshe ticked off his thinking with his fingertip tapping the back of the chair. "If there is a problem with a vehicle, maintain it on the spot. If that is going to take time, move on. The unit behind has more time than the head of the column. If they can't move it, they will either drag it or leave it. The main body following as the third element will have whatever equipment we need. If it looks like a vehicle will take too long to repair, we'll cannibalize it and keep on moving." He thought a moment and added, "When we strip a vehicle, strip it of everything that can be carried — wheels, tires, spare parts, and most of all, supply riding on it."

Leon was still taking notes because he knew he would have to brief the battalion commanders.

Moshe was shaking his head now and Leon wondered what was wrong.

"Let's count on some extra water and petrol in the rear of the column in case we have to use it."

"How much?"

"Work it out," Moshe cut him off abruptly. "I'm not worrying about that now." And he was already reaching for the phone. "Get me Southern Command." Leon sat back to listen. "Gilead here. Can you shake loose a surgical unit for me?" A pause. "And I want my own air liaison unit traveling with me. Direct communications with air and the ability to move in and build an airstrip." Another pause. "Thanks." Hanging up the phone, he turned once more to Leon. "I want air liaison beside me all the time. All of it," and he was moving across the room to the map hanging on the wall. The Gulf of Tiran spread blue on the pasted sheets. "Ship our tanks to Eilat," he ordered. "They can come down by boat." He fell silent again.

Calculating how long it would take to put the plans into being, Leon studied his notes.

Moshe was moving back to the phone again. "Get me Southern Command."

When he had the General on the phone a second time, he asked, "Can you move out from Eilat and take Ras el Nakib? I'd just as soon have it sitting for me when I need it." Leon was reaching for the air photo once more. Ras el Nakib lay just across the border into Sinai from Eilat. From the information he could gather from the photo, it was small.

"I want to cut west and approach it from that direction," Moshe explained on the phone. "If I come into Eilat, the British will know damned well what is going on."

Leon recalled the British were still using Akaba as a base, within fieldglass range of Eilat.

"I don't know whose side they are on," he heard Moshe growl. Then Moshe's voice dropped. "I've got to arrive in condition to fight." Then he hung up the phone again. Swinging toward Leon, he picked up an air photo of Sharm el Sheikh. "It looks as though they have built a small Tobruk there."

Leon, who had been in the desert with the British when younger, wondered just how much Moshe knew about that battle.

"We'll make no specific plans for taking it," Moshe said in a soft voice. "We'll decide on the spot." Seeing the puzzled look on the kibbutznik's face, Moshe shrugged. "I don't know much about it."

Both men were silent as they stared at the obvious fortresslike structures about Sharm el Sheikh as revealed in the photos. Finally, Moshe's head came up. "Let's move. You start shaking down the column, and I'll go to headquarters with the plans we have."

After a brief stay at headquarters, Moshe returned to Beersheba. He was both angry and pleased with the results of his mission. Headquarters was too busy with the operations in the north of Sinai and with Zvi Mazon's problems to pay much attention to his plans, which left him all the freedom he wanted.

IN THE NEGEV

On Sunday the twenty-eighth, at four in the afternoon, Zvi Mazon received his first operational orders from Hakiryah.

Sometime that day he knew the PM would place *Operation Kadesh* before the entire cabinet. Zvi wished he could see the reactions. He wished, too, that he could find the time to keep up with Moshe's movements. But like so many other things, the larger picture and perspective were slipping away from him as he became completely involved with his own problems.

It was almost dark when he received word from Hakiryah that two hundred French six-by-six trucks had just come off a boat. A hundred had been allotted to him.

Then he called in his battalion commanders who were still in the concentration area and explained that he was leaving them: his deputy was in command. They would move on orders and he would rejoin them at Wadi Faran or Kuntilla on the twenty-ninth. He shoved the operations maps across the table to his recce commander.

"Remember that when you start to move, don't hide from the Jordanians. Let them think we're moving right at them. The feint will do them good."

Shaking hands with the group, he walked across the field to his own jeep. Isaac was waiting for him. Looking back at his men bivouacked in the fields about the villages, Zvi waved and was pleased that they waved back. They knew nothing of what lay ahead. He hoped they would understand why he had kept his secret as the Chief of Staff had kept his. Slipping back into the jeep beside Isaac, Zvi said "Let's get back to Beersheba."

While they drove north, the signals sergeant in the back of the jeep turned on the radio. President Eisenhower was once more protesting the Israeli mobilization and he was even planning to take the matter up with his British and French allies. Zvi grinned to himself.

The announcer reported that this second American note attempted to reassure the prime minister that no Iraqi troops had been moved into Jordan. Then the report that the American ambassador had ordered arrangements to withdraw United States nationals from the area.

Zvi asked Isaac, "Your son?"

"He's in school. And Aaron?"

Surprised that he had not thought of the boy since that moment when he had been called to Hakiryah four days before, Zvi felt ashamed. "Doing well," he said. "He wants to be a flyer." Both men laughed at the ambitions of an eleven-year-old.

"I'm glad you're with me," Zvi said, turning so that he could see Isaac better.

The Yemenite smiled at the compliment. They had both come a long way since San'a.

When they arrived at Beersheba, Zvi met with his paratroop battalion commander, a tall, lean young man from Haifa who had been with him from the beginning. They were friends now. Zvi knew the man's wife and both of his children. As they stood alone in the small headquarters building near the airport, Zvi slapped the man on the back, "I wish I were going with you."

The young man smiled, "Zvi, I'll be looking forward to meeting you."

Zvi smiled. His paratroopers were going to be dropped far into Sinai, and his job would be to take the rest of the brigade across enemy territory, fighting as he moved, and finally bring his men together against Mitla Pass.

They discussed how long it would take Zvi to come over land and how much they could count on the Egyptians being tricked into thinking the first moves of the game were only a large retaliation raid. Then Avram joined them.

The cabinet had approved the operation. The PM was in bed with a high fever. The old Dakota transports were ready to fly when Zvi gave the orders.

Listening to his friend, Zvi realized that Avram was envious. For the first time he understood how much the tall, bull-shouldered staff officer wanted a field command and how little chance there was of his getting one because he was too valuable to the General Staff. Excusing himself from the paratroop commander, Zvi walked with Avram into the small operations room of the airport and closed the door.

"Anything else I have to know?" he asked.

Avram thought a moment and shook his head. "The Americans are raising hell about the mobilization, but the PM says he can live with it for the present. There's a weird complication which might just help."

Zvi waited.

"Hungary. There's some kind of an uprising there. I don't know what it's all about yet. Started a couple of days ago. It just might take some of the heat off our actions in the press and at the UN."

Lighting a cigarette, Zvi shrugged. "Doesn't mean very much to me."

"If there's anything to be afraid of at this moment," said Avram, "it is how the Americans are going to react. All we would need is for them to interject their ships between the Canal and the Anglo-French forces sailing from Malta." He was about to say more when the paratroop commander flung the door open.

"Zvi, take a look at this." Shoving a set of aerial photographs at his colonel, the young man stood with his hands on his hips.

Quickly scanning the photos, Zvi shook his head, passed them on to Avram and turned once more to the map before him.

His finger came to rest on the spot marked Mitla Pass, deep into Sinai, within striking distance of the Canal and the port city of Suez at its southern end. This was his objective, the gate he was ordered to close to keep the Egyptians from pouring reinforcements and supplies into Sinai, and at the same time confuse them by blocking their own exit from the peninsula. Mitla Pass. Looking back at the photos, Zvi saw some buildings on the west side of the Pass. These had been in the earlier set of pictures he had seen. The tents and vehicles he now saw had not been. The others waited for his reactions.

"If we drop on the west side," he said, "we may just be coming down on a new troop concentration. Twenty-three tents. That could headquarter a large outfit."

The others nodded.

"Is there a reason why you can't close the Pass just as well from the east?" Avram asked.

Zvi considered this. The decision was obviously his to make. He wished he knew more. Glancing at his watch, he knew he did not have time to ask for more photos. It was past noon. His men would be jumping in a few hours. Turning to the battalion commander, he swung the map about so they could both look at it.

"You will drop on the east side. However, dig in and don't move. If they start to come through, do what you've already planned: stop them until we reach you with reinforcements." He thought for a moment and then explained to Avram, "We had counted on having more time. Not more travel time, but time before the Egyptians could react. However, if that is a unit located there, they could close with the men we drop, spread the word we've arrived and kill off much of the surprise we've been counting on."

Avram understood the problems.

"Do you want me to contact headquarters?"

Zvi shook his head. "I'm responsible. I've made the decision."

The other two understood.

Taking a deep breath, Zvi addressed the battalion commander, "Better get your men fed; and if they can, see that they sleep. There's still a long day ahead." Once he was alone again with Avram, he pointed out, "This race could take twenty-four hours if I'm lucky. More, if I've any additional problems."

He was looking at the photographs. Twenty-three tents which had suddenly appeared at the Pass.

"You know that if they move south across your axis, they can cut the paratroop battalion off," Avram warned.

Nodding, Zvi remained silent. He, too, had been thinking of this. "I'm going to see the General," and they both knew he meant the Southern Commander.

Twenty minutes later, Zvi had agreement on his decision and had left it to the General to contact the Chief of Staff in Tel Aviv. Looking once more at his watch, he excused himself and walked out into the corridor of the headquarters building. He was tired.

It was almost 1500 hours. His main force should have made their pass at the Jordanian border and be approaching the Sinai border now. Piling into his jeep, he led the way to the airfield while Avram followed in his staff car. The aged Dakotas were lined up on the field, their propellers slowly turning. Sixteen transports with twenty-eight men to a plane in four formations — a paratroop company to each formation.

Zvi moved among his men, checking a strap of one, smiling at another, promising a third he would see him soon. In ten minutes he had met them all. And it was driven home to him again how few they were to be taken so far into enemy country and out of contact until he reached them. Twenty-four hours, he had said. Unless . . .

The men were boarding their planes now. They were calm and quiet. Turning to look for the battalion commander, Zvi was surprised to see the Chief of Staff. They nodded to each other. There was nothing to be said. Both men knew the gamble they were taking. Both knew it had to be taken.

While Avram talked to his chief, Zvi told the battalion commander, "I promise you we'll get there."

And then the plane door was closed and Zvi stood looking up at it. Mitla Pass was forty flying minutes west and a day or more overland. It had to be closed.

Then the planes were taking off, and for the first time he really believed it was happening.

Avram and the Chief of Staff joined him while he stood watching the planes move down the runway, become airborne and form above.

"If the Egyptians get their wind up . . ." And then he saw the ten escort planes join the formation.

"We'll have a dozen Mysteres over the Canal," Avram reminded him.

Zvi nodded. His men would still be an easy target for an Egyptian MIG. The Dakotas were flying low now to avoid the Egyptian radar. When they reached their target, they would rise to fifteen hundred and the men would jump.

Then the planes were out of sight and Zvi swung toward the others. "Unless there's something more, I've things to do."

The Chief of Staff smiled. "Easy, Zvi." And then he was walking back toward his car.

Avram said, "I can assure you, he wishes he were with them."

Nodding, Zvi said, "So do I." He slowly walked back to the small base office and started checking on the supplies which were to be dropped when the planes returned. He was still at work when the first of the returning Dakotas was sighted in the sky. Racing out, Zvi met the pilot as he brought his plane to a stop.

"Three hundred and fifty-nine men dropped at sixteen fifty-nine hours, Colonel. All safe."

Lighting a cigarette, Zvi ordered the loading of the eight jeeps which were to be dropped, the recoilless guns and the large mortars. The rest of the Dakotas were coming back now.

Satisfied that everything that could be done to support his men had been, Zvi left to join his main force moving overland toward Kuntilla.

OVER SINAI

The Israeli pilot saw the telephone wires below and, dipping his Thunderbird, matched the level of the wires and flew slowly over them. The hook dragging from the rear of his plane failed to catch the wire, and he tried once more. Again, the hook slipped off the wire. Aware that the lines led from the Egyptian airfield to the Egyptian brigade less than forty miles from Mitla Pass, the pilot knew he had to take the phone wires out.

He dove a third time and a third time the hook slipped.

Swinging his plane about, he flew parallel to the wires, trying to catch them with the edge of his wing, but the plane bounced and almost flipped over. Looking back, the pilot saw the wires remained intact.

Turning about, the youth who only the week before had been driving a delivery truck in Tel Aviv approached the wires head on until his plane seemed to be racing into them. Then he pulled back the stick slightly, raising the nose so that only the tip of the propeller struck the wire. For a moment the entire plane shivered and there were sparks. The plane wobbled unsteadily as he made another turn. Nothing hung between the telephone poles. Now that he knew how to do it, he smiled. There were more wires to be cut.

Colonel Zvi Mazon flew south from Beersheba to join his brigade which had started southwest from Hatseva, skirting the Jordanian border in a feint and then moving on past Wadi Faran toward Kuntilla. When the commando leader reached his main force the new trucks had not yet caught up with the brigade. As soon as he waved the Piper pilot away, Zvi checked the organization of his column. The advance guard had one infantry battalion, two platoons of light French AMX tanks and two batteries of artillery. He called to Fishel in the van: "They look familiar?"

The captain turned to look at the guns. Twenty-five-pounders. No different essentially from those the Legionnaires had used to batter them in the Quarter. Fishel grinned.

Satisfied that the main body of his men was also organized as an intact combat unit, Zvi thought he might try to throw it around the Egyptian locations where he knew he would have to do battle and rush the vanguard on toward Mitla by itself. He did not know, but it seemed reasonable. Checking his time, Zvi realized the column was already more than four hours behind schedule, and as much as he wanted the rest of the trucks promised him, he could not stop to wait for them. The only substitutes were the few civilian trucks which had been pressed into service: two milk trucks, a bakery truck and one panel truck with a dry-cleaner's sign on the side. Most of the others were farm trucks brought in from kibbutzim.

It was already 2100 hours. Overhead Zvi could hear a formation of planes, and as he sat back in his seat beside Isaac, he shook his head in disbelief: it was really happening.

There were no roads ahead, and he knew he still had about one hundred and thirty-five miles to drive before he caught up with his dropped battalion. One hundred and thirty-five miles and the only paved road on the southern axis of Sinai lay between Mitla Pass and Suez itself.

Between the eastern and western borders of Sinai there was nothing a man would want. Twenty-four-thousand square miles of emptiness, of sand seas and rocks; grassless, a wandering hyena or a raven and nothing else. Scattered among the sand seas and the short shrubs were a few Bedouin tribes feeding off starving sheep. Sinai. A straight line from Eilat to Mitla Pass and north of it nothing but rolling, empty space. And south of that line nothing but sand and seas and craggy mountains. Roadless. Dry.

Sinai.

A place for battles to be fought but not a place for men to live. The cruelly created waste thrust between Egypt and Israel could be a barrier set up to keep two enemies apart. But in the hands of the enemy, it brought the Egyptians less than a hundred miles from Israel's large cities and kept Israel five hundred miles from Cairo. The striking distance favored the keeper of Sinai.

Ahead lay his first target: Kuntilla. A village on a plateau, eight miles from Israel's western border. Intelligence had reported that an infantry platoon held this crossroads. However, Zvi knew the distance was greater because his column was not moving as the crow flies, and he had left the closest road with thirty-six more miles to travel.

There was no trail.

The sand was deep.

Whatever remained of the ancient caravan route that led to Kuntilla would be broken down by the first trucks over it. And looking back, Zvi could see his vehicles were moving gingerly. The vanguard had broken the trail and beneath it lay sand. However, the column was moving. The point continued on ahead and staying close to it, he suddenly saw Kuntilla before him. A mesa rising from the sand about it. Four hundred yards or more of scattered clay buildings.

Pulling his fieldglasses from the bag at his feet, Zvi motioned to Isaac to pull their jeep to one side so that the other vehicles could pass. A watch tower overlooked the village. Slotted sides for gun emplacements. To the north a wall. And a road leading up.

The Egyptians were in confusion on the mesa. There was firing now as his advance unit climbed the rise, spilled into the village and poured fire into the tower. Two explosions and silence. Waving Isaac forward and up the mount, Zvi returned his glasses to their case and, leaping out, approached Fishel, who had drawn his own jeep over to the side of the road.

"They've started running," Fishel reported.

"And the explosions?" But Zvi did not need to ask the question as he could see the wreckage of one of his jeeps, thrown onto its side and two of his men standing nearby. Beyond the jeep he could make out a half-track with one side blown out. Without waiting for Fishel's answer, he moved toward the half-track. A driver lay beside the vehicle and a medical-aid man was bending over his wounded companion.

"Bad?" Zvi asked.

The aid man looked up and shrugged. "He isn't walking anywhere."

Nodding, Zvi smiled at the driver. "Short war, son."

"Very, Zvi."

Nothing more needed to be said between them, and Zvi turned his attention to the remainder of his column. It had approached with the falling light. It was dusk now. And as far as he could tell, the rest of his trailing column was not in sight. Puzzled, he tried to figure out how they had become separated.

Pivoting on his heel, he started looking for Fishel.

He was standing on the side of the mesa looking toward the east, and when Zvi approached him, he commented: "The sand's got us, Zvi."

The desert air was cooling fast. Looking back toward the village, Zvi saw no prisoners. The Egyptian soldiers had fled and the natives had gone into hiding. A few of the men in the advance column were already breaking out rations and Zvi wished he were hungry himself. Walking back to his jeep, he accepted a canteen from Isaac. Drinking slowly, he looked over the top of it at the front of the column, which was drawn up waiting for his orders.

The battalion commander crossed over and reported that he could move on.

Zvi held the canteen between his hands and smiled. "And what would you use for petrol if we started out on a straight line for Themed now?"

The young lieutenant-colonel grinned. "I'd ask for a drop."

"In the darkness? Or do you want to get stuck and strung out more than we are now?"

The younger officer continued to grin. "We don't get rich standing here."

A wry smile crossed Zvi's face. Gesturing for his signals officer to join him, he ordered, "Get HQ to prepare a petrol drop. I'll let them know later where we want it."

Then he turned to the eager young commander, "Get your men rested and I'll tell you when we pull out." Swinging into his jeep, he started back toward the Israeli border. However, he no sooner dropped down from the mesa than he saw the first of the laggard trucks. There were more behind.

Waving down the driver, Zvi asked, "What the hell happened?"

"They're bogged down. Hundreds of trucks churning in the sand."

"It's a mess," the driver's companion shouted.

Zvi asked for details.

"It's the sand, Zvi." The driver was nervous and Zvi thought for a moment the youth was afraid.

"Easy, son. Just tell me what's happening."

The youth wiped his face with his hand. "The civilian trucks can't make it. Most of them have blocked the way and are holding up others. The petrol trucks are stuck, but someone is trying to get them out with the bulldozers. The tanks, well, some of them will get through but I wouldn't count on the others."

While they talked, more trucks were coming up the road. Three and then a half dozen. Zvi wondered how many of his original two hundred and fifty would get by the first dunes. Standing on the road, Zvi thanked the young driver and then asked, "What got you through?"

The youth shook his head. "I guess I was afraid of being left there."

Zvi laughed, "Find something to eat and get some rest."

Fishel and he sat down near the side of the road and waited to see what else was coming. By 2230 that night Zvi knew he could not wait any longer. He had most of his advance guard and part of another battalion. One of the two petrol trucks had been hauled in and that was all he could afford to wait for. Twenty-four hours he had promised the paratrooper, and time was running out.

Rising from where he had been sitting and listening to the reports of the incoming troops, he reached down and helped Fishel to his feet.

"Let's go."

And the column headed west once more.

Ahead lay Themed.

Above, on chalk and stone cliffs, the enemy was reported to have two infantry companies dug in. The air photos had revealed that the day before there were thirty vehicles parked in the area.

Eight miles west of Themed lay the problem: concrete bunkers and trenches, mines and barbed wire strung along a defile. However, Themed still lay about forty miles to the west.

Moving up behind the van of his column so that he could have its protection and still be close enough to the action to control it, Zvi Mazon followed Fishel's half-tracks and jeeps. The night was dark. There was no wind. The only sound that could be heard was the clatter of their own half-tracks and the sound of heavy motors. The stone desert and the sand sea all spread through rolling, uncertain country.

He assumed that he no longer had any advantage of surprise. The initial attack on Kuntilla had given the Egyptians time enough to get off a radio message.

However, the Egyptians might still think he was only going after Themed in a deep retaliation raid. He hoped they were thinking that way, but he could not be certain.

Midnight and on to 30 October. The road lay open ahead. And then almost four hours after midnight, Themed rose before them.

They saw no lights. They met no opposition. Zvi and Isaac raced through the wadi into the village of Themed. The Arabs, secure in their trenches, started to fire on the van of the column. However, Zvi's battalion commanders, knowing he was anxious to close with the main fortification which lay on the heights west of Themed, pressed on past the village. When Zvi joined his forward battalion, the vehicles were already positioned for an assault on the cliffs.

Fishel and his men were sweeping wide to make certain that they would not move into a trap when they attacked.

Leaping out of his jeep, Zvi glanced up at the heights and then beyond them to the sky. Slowly pivoting where he stood, he evaluated the sky, and as the battalion commander approached, he nodded.

"Let your men get some rest," Zvi ordered. "An hour, maybe two. Let's wait till they . . ." And his hand went up to indicate the Arabs on the heights, "get the sun in their eyes." He was lighting a cigarette and looking back down the road he had come. "I wish I had artillery to give you. I haven't. The sun will have to do."

Knowing that there was nothing more he could expect from Zvi, the young lieutenant-colonel trotted off to rejoin his battalion while Zvi went in search of Fishel. The recce officer had completed his sweep, set his own men out against any possible surprise and was standing beside his jeep rubbing the side of his leg.

"Race a jeep back down the road to see what's coming," Zvi ordered. Then he shook his head and waved a signals officer over. "There should be a

Piper up there some place. See what he can find out about the rest of the column." And before the signals officer could leave, Zvi added, "Tell him to fly over Kuntilla to make certain that one reserve company remains there." When he was alone with Fishel again, Zvi explained. "I need everything I've got, but we can't let them break up the line between Kuntilla and Mitla. We'll drop off troops as we go, and they might as well be the reserves."

Fishel knew that Zvi was talking as much to form his own thinking as to let him know what was happening. Then they heard the radio in Zvi's jeep crackling and turned toward it.

Listening quietly for a few words to identify the source, Zvi suddenly trotted over to the radio.

The men at Mitla.

"We've had some injured, Zvi. Thirteen. Dropped a few miles from where we should have come down but have moved to the Pass already."

Grabbing the instrument, Zvi snapped a question, "Did you get your supplies?"

"All of them. Almost hit us on the head."

Both of them laughed.

"The situation?" Zvi demanded.

"Targets in the moonlight. Trucks coming east from Suez. Got us a water wagon among other things."

"The other things?" Zvi demanded, almost angry that the man was being flippant at this moment when he himself could see activity on top of the cliff beyond Themed.

"Trucks. Half a dozen. They burned."

Zvi thought about this. "Don't let anything through. I'll get there." He had repeated his promise and the commander of the small paratroop battalion consoled him.

"We'll wait."

And then Zvi handed the instrument over to the signals officer. "Stay in touch if you can, but don't tell them everything you know."

Taken aback that his commander thought he needed the instructions, the signals officer looked closely at Zvi. The crow's-feet about the colonel's eyes were marked. His graying hair was covered with the dust of hours of open driving and his hand was once again inside his shirt as he scratched his stomach and stared at the cliff above them.

The Egyptians started firing their heavy machine guns and mortars from their forward positions, seemingly ignorant of the range, and Zvi could not understand what they were doing, expending their ammunition on the two thousand yards of open ground that lay between them.

"It doesn't make sense." Then he knew he was not going to have serious trouble at Themed. "Only an Arab or a damned fool would fire now," he said to no one in particular. Then he started giving orders.

Once more Zvi checked his watch. 0545 hours.

The Israeli tankers closed with the enemy and the battle was furious, explosive and brief.

By 0600 there was no Egyptian defense.

Zvi tapped Isaac on the shoulder and moved forward directly to the top of the cliff. On his way he passed a half-track which had struck a mine, and he wondered how he had missed that and then, smelling the acrid smoke, he knew it had been covered by his own smokescreen.

Fishel reached the enemy position first and had the report when Zvi arrived.

"Three dead and six wounded."

For a moment he did not think Zvi had heard him, and then Zvi nodded, looked at his watch and shook his head. "There's no more time." Off in the distance he could see some Egyptians in full flight. "Let them go," he ordered.

Zvi was no longer thinking of Themed.

Stepping out of his jeep, Zvi walked among his men. Some were kneeling beside their vehicles. One platoon was trying to feed itself, but he could see the men were too tired to eat. One soldier lay on the ground, looking up at the sky, and when his commander came between him and his view, he closed his eyes. Looking back at the half-tracks scattered over the area, Zvi could see that many of the men were asleep in their vehicles. One lay on a tank, eyes closed and knees drawn up before him as though cradled.

Returning to his jeep, Zvi sent for the battalion commander. "Piper the wounded out." He thought a moment. "Make arrangements for the dead to be flown home later." He waited for the battalion commander to react and saw that the man was tired, his tense face lined with fatigue. Swinging about toward Fishel, Zvi saw that the violinist was no more useful. Angry, because he himself felt elated and too keyed up to rest, Zvi waited for Fishel to join him.

"The Arabs we bypassed back there?"

Fishel shrugged. "Took off like scalded mules."

With a sigh, Zvi looked at his friend. "Go get some sleep."

A sound overhead and he saw a Piper Cub coming in for a landing to the east. His eyes closed and his head fell back. For an instant Isaac thought Zvi had fallen asleep, and then he saw him pull out a cigarette, light it and draw deeply. Zvi never had a chance to finish that cigarette.

There was no warning.

The Egyptian MIGs came in low over the desert, firing as they approached. Throwing themselves flat on the ground, the men of the brigade sought what little cover there was. Shoving Isaac under the jeep, Zvi counted the enemy planes. Six and swinging high for another pass. One truck in flames. A man screaming. The whine of the jets broke over Zvi again and he threw himself to the ground, wishing he had a helmet and wondering why they did not drop any bombs. The dust petaled near his feet. A soldier rose, started to run and collapsed. Crawling toward him, Zvi heard the jets swinging about for their third pass. Nearby a truck caught fire. A moment later, it exploded, throwing flames and debris across the scattered brigade. Cursing himself for not having taken precautions against an air attack, Zvi thought about the men at the Mitla forty miles from an Egyptian airbase. The MIGs were coming over for a fourth pass when he reached the fallen soldier. The youth lay still, blood flowing from a hole in his chest. Feeling the soldier's neck with his fingertips, Zvi discovered the man was alive. Coming to his feet, he shouted for a medic. One more sweep and four trucks burst into flames. Then the MIGs whirled and disappeared to the west.

Zvi had six more wounded. He turned and saw in the distance that the Piper Cub was burning. Shaking his head in disgust, he shouted for a signals officer.

"Contact headquarters and ask for more Pipers. Tell them we've been hit." He thought a moment and added, "Tell them, also, they can drop the petrol now. We'll stay here long enough to pick it up."

Once he was alone, he took a deep breath and looked at his watch. Time. The only thing headquarters could not give him. He saw a group of men gathering about the signals truck and ran over. They separated to let him through. Fishel was already there.

"Mitla," the recce officer reported. "They've taken two air strikes and are being hit with heavy mortars."

Zvi nodded to indicate that he understood. The men around him were waiting for orders. Pulling a cigarette from his pocket, Zvi lighted it and passed it to his friend. "It'll help," he said. Then he stared at the bright sky. After a moment he looked about for the battalion commander, told him: "We'll rest here," and started to walk away. However, he had not taken ten steps from the signals trucks when he heard the radio again. A Piper above, and Zvi looked up.

Returning to the truck, he asked the signals officer for a report.

"It looks like there's movement east from Suez."

Zvi clutched the back of his neck, tried to think what this could mean, and all he could think of was the men at Mitla who stood against the Egyptian forces moving east from Suez. His hand trembled and he reached for another cigarette.

Closing his eyes, he weighed the choice of moving on with a column so weary his men could no longer stand or staying where he was and risking the men at Mitla. Then he realized he was looking at his watch. It was noon now.

"Shape up the column," he shouted. "Let's get out of here."

They rolled out of Themed heading west. The sand rose in a white cloud around them, billowing outward and then settling as they passed on. Two hyenas watched the strange movement and slunk behind a knoll. Overhead several birds flew high on the horizon. There was no sound except that of racing trucks. Motioning for Isaac to draw up beside the parked half-track which carried the headquarters radio, Zvi pulled himself over the side of the vehicle. Most of the men were asleep. The signals officer waited for instructions.

"Ask headquarters for an air strike on Nakhal. Tell them we are not going to bypass it." He thought a moment. "We're going to move right through." The men in the bed of the half-track looked at him in surprise. Zvi smiled. "I don't want any Egyptians lying across our trail. It would make me nervous."

Suddenly there was firing from the head of the column and Zvi jumped back into his jeep. Racing past the other vehicles, he reached the van. An Egyptian half-track was burning beside the road and in the distance he could make out two running figures.

"Keep on going," he shouted to the lead jeep. Then he waved Isaac to the side of the road to let the signals vehicle catch up with them.

The signals officer shouted, "There are jets up there."

Zvi's head went up, but it took him a moment to make out the spots climbing the sky. Nodding to the signals officer, he waited for a message.

"They're ours. Say they can't see Nakhal and can barely make us out."

For a long minute Zvi thought about reaching Nakhal without air support, and then he knew there was nothing he could do about it.

Waving the signals vehicle to the side of the road, he joined it. The column raced on.

Zvi stared at the circling dots in the sun.

Nakhal could not be the target now.

Mud huts against the sand and an overcast sky.

"Tell them to interdict between Mitla and Suez."

Satisfied that the land beyond the Pass was a slot which the jets could not miss, he waved the signals half-track on and smiled at Isaac. "Let's go."

It was 1630 hours when he saw Nakhal. A scattering of mud huts and some tin barracks. Intelligence had told him to expect a battalion headquarters here and at least two infantry companies. If the Egyptians could be counted upon—and he believed they always could be—he was going against mines and emplacements.

Looking up, he scanned the sky for jets.

None.

The column was slowing to a halt and he raced down the length. "Fifteen minues and we attack," he ordered his company commanders. When he reached the end of the column, he was about to turn around when he noticed a sand cloud at the end of his column to the east. It was moving toward him. Scooping his glasses from the case at his feet, Zvi measured the distance and then came to focus on the cloud.

A smile spread over his face. His eyes closed and he tried to ignore the numbed feeling in his legs. Forty hours. Fifty. He had no idea how long he had been awake and he did not want to think about that now. *Time. Time.* Behind his eyes he could see the face of a clock and the face of the paratroop commander to whom he had given his promise. His eyes hurt in his head and then he could hear a sound and he tried not to hear it. A clock? His watch? It grew louder and he opened his eyes. Behind the column and closing fast were his guns. Twenty-five-pounders. Somehow between Kuntilla and Nakhal they had caught up with him. As the first of the battery trucks approached, he shouted, "Into position. We're attacking." The platoon leader smiled and raced by. Standing in his jeep, Zvi waved the other trucks on. In five minutes the first gun was in place.

Eight minutes later the attack began.

Zvi remained where he was and listened to the sound of the guns bracketing Nakhal. The sound of twenty-five-pounders battered his weary brain.

A sound behind him and he looked around as another battery came barreling down the road from Themed. Zvi never even bothered to give them their orders as he waved to the lead truck and stood smiling at the others as they passed.

Winking at Isaac, he gestured for the Yemenite sergeant to swing the jeep about and move. A few minutes later he was standing beside the battalion commander and listening to the plan of attack. What was left of two companies would go forward on half-tracks and trucks. Three AMXs would move forward with a rifle company to the far side of the village.

Zvi nodded his approval.

The battle, which began at 1700 hours, ended at 1720.

When Zvi entered Nakhal, the small mud village was empty. There were bodies sprawled in the open street. Several buildings had collapsed. One wall of another fell as he passed. Ordering his men to search the houses for Fedayeen, he waited in the middle of the street. A moment later someone shouted for him and he walked over to one of the larger buildings. One of his men stood, submachine gun on his hip, beside the door.

"You ought to see this, Zvi."

Uncertain what he was supposed to be looking for, Zvi entered the building. A make-shift hospital. Three rows of men on the floor looking up at him. Then he saw there were several who lay still, eyes open and seeing nothing. Walking past the Egyptian soldiers, he went into the room beyond. A pool of blood on the floor beneath an operating table. Zvi gasped. A man lay on the table. A part of a man. One leg removed and nothing to staunch the blood. Left to die in the middle of an operation. Swinging about, Zvi stalked back into the ward and asked the first Egyptian he came to, "What happened?"

The Arab soldier stared at the Israeli officer for a moment and then shook his head. Kneeling beside the man, Zvi saw that someone had wrapped a cloth about the soldier's throat and blood was oozing from under it. Rising to his feet, Zvi shouted for his own medics and then walked out into the dark street. As the brigade medical officer passed him, Zvi said, "Take care of the poor bastards and then evacuate them." The medic started to move on when Zvi added, "I want to know exactly what happened."

"Of course." And the doctor looked at the commander for a moment. It seemed as if he were about to say something. Then he changed his mind and disappeared into the building.

After shouting for one of the trucks to pull over to the hospital to throw some light in it, Zvi walked back to the middle of the street where Fishel was waiting for him, a map spread over the hood of his jeep. Zvi saw that his brigade was strung out from the Israeli border to Mitla, forty miles west. If the Egyptians to the north moved down, they could cut him into pieces at any point. If the Egyptians to the north moved down . . . He snorted. He had other things to think about.

His head fell to one side while he waited to hear from the signals sergeant in the jeep.

"They've lost their medical officer at Mitla. Wounded."

Zvi nodded.

"And they say the Egyptians have stopped attacking. The jets you sent ahead must have hit them hard."

Sucking in his breath, Zvi looked at his watch once more. It was 1730 hours. Shaking his head to clear it, Zvi calculated quickly before he ordered, "Tell them we'll be there in four hours." He was looking at his officers when he snapped, "Let's go."

TEL AVIV

In her small office, Kineret Heschel sat with Avram Ben Ezra reading the cables from the United Nations. The Americans and Russians demanded an end to the invasion of Sinai. The French were prepared to veto any negative resolution. The Israeli ambassador did not know how long the British would hold up under American pressure. Ambassador Lodge of the United States had turned his back on his British and French colleagues. So far, the French appeared unperturbed. The debate could be strung out for another two days. The Israeli ambassador did not know if he could string it out a third day. The Egyptians were demanding action, and much of the world was lined up with them. No one wished to talk about Hungary.

Avram shoved the cables back across the desk and stared at Kineret. She slipped them into the manila file and asked, "What can we do for the army?"

"Buy time."

SINAI

Zvi Mazon's column moved out of Nakhal westward toward the vanguard at Mitla. The way was smooth. There were no Egyptians to be seen. There was only the cold and the darkness. Overhead a Piper kept watch. There was nothing to report. The radios fell silent. The night sounds were few. Nobody noticed the sand and the dust they raised.

And then, almost at midnight, Zvi saw something suddenly appear in the headlights of his jeep. He waved Isaac to a halt and read a sign in Hebrew posted there: FRONTIER. SHOW YOUR PASSPORT. Wishing he had the energy to laugh at the paratrooper's humor, Zvi met with the men who had dropped. The rest of his column rolled in, and after embracing several of his officers and men, Zvi said, "Let's sit down and see where the hell we are now."

Five minutes later, he sat with his officers in a circle around him. They were telling him what had happened since they saw him last, and then he started to explain that they would have to enlarge the camp and take up better positions and . . . He saw he was the only one in the circle who was awake. Dropping back onto his elbows, he stared for a moment at the dark sky which closed comfortably about him. A face came between him and the sky and he tried to understand what the signals officer was saying and what the report meant which involved an Egyptian armored brigade that had been seen moving south toward Mitla Pass from Bir Gifgafa to the north. He tried to shake his head to clear it and his elbows gave way and he was lying flat. His eyes closed and he was asleep.

NEW YORK

The Israeli ambassador to the United Nations read the cable with care before he dropped it on his desk and stared out of his office window at the East River. He wondered if his reservations about the city would always be mingled with the fact that he never spent time here without having to fight the kind of fight he was in now.

Picking up the cable once more, he thought about Kineret Heschel and Avram Ben Ezra, who he knew had sent it. It was their cable, and they were asking him to find a way to buy them time.

Time. He did not know how he could manufacture time.

The Americans were screaming for the war to be shut down as though it were a factory, the product of which did not meet their standards. And the Russians were screaming to keep the war in front of people so that no one would notice what they were doing in Hungary.

How does a man make time?

He picked up the American resolution which the General Assembly had adopted and read it once more. It was simple enough: a cease fire now.

It was all so clear. And so was the cable.

Flipping the intercom on his desk, the ambassador sent for his secretary. Then very slowly he began to dictate a note to the Secretary-General.

"I have at hand your correspondence of 2 November. There are a number of questions about which I would appreciate clarification before I dispatch the resolution and your cover letter to my government . . ."

IN THE NEGEV

For three days Moshe Gilead and his battalion commanders worked over the column bound for Sharm el Sheikh. When the others were satisfied that they had done the best they could with it, Moshe climbed into each vehicle and threw out anything he thought was excess baggage. An extra blanket, shaving gear, mess kit with the explanation, "We'll eat out of cans," extra shoes, bottles of water, personal belongings. Twice he shouted down objections when a company commander said he thought he might need an extra set of tools or extra clothing for his men. "Get them there bare-assed, but get them there."

Tuesday night after three days of preparation, Moshe started the column toward Ras el Nakib in Egyptian Sinai. The column strung out twenty miles, as long as he thought it would, but not as long as he had hoped. Many of the trucks he wanted never arrived, and he made the decision that if they had not reached Eilat near Ras el Nakib when he had to move, he would abandon the extra men.

Each time he had a spare moment, he looked at the blank spots on the map that stretched south from Eilat and Ras el Nakib to Sharm el Sheikh at the tip of Sinai. Blank. Nothing. Mountains and canyons and nothing to sustain a man. And worse than anything else he did not know how much time he had or what he would find when he got there.

Before he swung south, Moshe saw the remains of Zvi's column which had been left behind. Thirty or more trucks. Shouting for his supply officer to cannibalize any parts he thought he might need, Moshe swung the rest of his column south and headed for Ras el Nakib. He was on a macadam road now, the Pilgrimage Road to Gaza built by the British in 1941. Stepping up his speed, Moshe dashed into Ras el Nakib a few hours later, satisfied with the organization of his column.

Dropping off the half-track, he walked the length of the column as the trucks closed together. The men were waiting for information he was not going to give them yet. Most of the faces he had seen before. Some were new to him. The twenty-three women in the column had almost all served for more than a year. Satisfied that he could depend on them, he smiled at Mitra Glasner who headed the signals detachment.

"Tell your women they can go into Eilat for a shower if they want to."

And then remembering something, he shouted for Leon. "Tell the men there will be no washing and no shaving until we get there." Certain the men did not yet know where "there" was, he wandered over to the communications half-track. The air-force captain who had been assigned as his liaison officer briefed him on what she had been hearing: "Zvi's men have dropped and he's there. The radio says the British are screaming about the invasion. The French are playing it quiet. Some of their fleet is off Haifa."

Moshe nodded, and as though he had not heard, he told Leon, who had joined him: "We're going to leave all of our twenty-five-pounders except four. I'll want extra ammunition." He was already recalculating the number of mortars, anti-tank guns and bazookas he would jettison and how many he would take.

For a moment he stood staring at a telephone pole before he turned to his Signals Officer and pointed to it. "See if you can run a line to Eilat and patch on that Egyptian telephone line." He considered what he had said and added, "If the other end of the line goes on to Cairo, call Nasser and explain that we're just borrowing the facility."

Walking back to his headquarters half-track where he could be alone, he spread out a map.

His eyes traced the route that lay ahead of him and found nothing that looked like a trail or a road. Three hundred miles to Sharm el Sheikh. Three days. Twenty miles of convoy. He wished now he had taken a leave when it had been offered to him months before. And then he wondered if Zvi Mazon felt any more rested because he had taken one. His thoughts drifted from his friend to the stories about Zvi and an Arab woman and then to Zipporah. Turning away from the map, he settled down on a bench and swung his feet up on the table while he thought of Zippy. She was young and she was lovely and, in spite of the innocence her sister believed she retained, Moshe had never met a girl less innocent. He smiled inwardly as he thought about their first night together in his bunk at headquarters and how he had awakened in the middle of the night wondering who had seduced whom.

His eyes fell on the wall map once more. The Middle East, he realized, was a very small place and Israel almost the smallest part of it.

Someday he was going to ask an Arab leader why he begrudged Israel the small sliver on which the Jews lived. He wiped his palm on the side of his trouser leg. Maybe he would be able to ask an Arab soon. That would depend on when he reached Sharm el Sheikh and what happened when he did. He tried to keep his thoughts on Sharm el Sheikh, but they kept drifting back to Zipporah. Somewhere he had read Aristotle's comment that some persons are by nature slaves. He wondered if some women were by nature whores. And then he knew that he was not being honest with himself or Zippy. She never took anything from him or wanted anything from him. It was more in the way she looked at him when they were in a crowded room and the way she acted when they were in bed. His hand sought his trouser leg again as he wondered how he was going to cope with Malin Ben Ezra.

Moshe Gilead laughed out loud. Ahead of him lay three hundred uncharted miles and a race into battle against a fortified complex held by an enemy of unknown size and he was worrying about facing a *kurveh*'s sister.

Three hours later, Moshe slipped into his sleeping bag and fell asleep. No one had yet given him orders to move, and he knew they would not until the rest of Sinai was secure and air support available when he had to call on it.

No one from headquarters came to see him that night or the next day. Even though he knew headquarters had all of its attention elsewhere and did not really give a damn about him, he never moved without having his signals sergeant at his side; and when he went to relieve himself, he arranged for one of the men to keep the telephone at hand.

When Thursday night came, he had the phone line checked out once more. Deciding that his troops and equipment were in order and that there was nothing more he could do, Moshe crawled into his sleeping bag, tucked the telephone receiver under his ear and fell asleep. It was almost midnight.

The first sound he heard was a familiar voice. "Avram here."

Shaking himself awake, Moshe looked at his watch—0400: "Moshe here."

"Move!"

SINAI

At 0400 hours Zvi Mazon was awakened with a second report that the Egyptian armored brigade south of Bir Gifgafa was on the move. Contacting headquarters, he asked permission to establish himself on the west side of the Mitla. As far as he knew, there was nothing to keep him from moving into the Pass, and while he spoke to Operations, he could see that of his three battalions only one was in any kind of defensive position; the other two were completely exposed on the open plain which surrounded the eastern entrance of the Pass.

He was waiting for answers when a Dakota flew low overhead and dropped supplies almost on top of him. Pleased to get the supplies, he cursed the accuracy of the pilot. There was a moment for consultation on the other end of the radio, and then he had permission to move. Quickly barking his orders, Zvi formed up a single battalion to make the first excursion through the worn hills which comprised the two sides of Mitla. While the battalion was shaping up, he looked at his watch. It was almost 0500 hours. Grabbing the radio once again, he asked headquarters for air support to come over the west side of the Pass at 0600 hours. The support was granted though Zvi was told that there were already too many requests for air. Knowing that he had been informed because someone was letting off his own reactions to the pressures on him, Zvi ignored the comment and gave his battalion commander orders to start moving through the Pass, and he described the defensive positions he wanted the column to take when it reached the west side. As far as Zvi could tell, the Egyptians might still try to come through from Suez, and he did not want to be caught with his brigade spread any thinner than it was.

He was watching the battalion move out when the brigade Signals Officer ran across the open field shouting.

"Order from headquarters. We are *not* and they repeated *not* to enter the Pass now."

Yelling for Isaac to bring the battalion back, Zvi stalked angrily across the field toward the communications truck. However, he had not reached it when the Egyptian jets swept over the scattered brigade. He paused to watch his men run for cover, diving under trucks, half-tracks and tanks or seeking shelter against the few rock spurs in the open fields. Looking up, he recognized the silhouette of the Egyptian Vampires. Five of them sweeping over his three battalions now, and he was thankful that on their first pass they only observed his location because the returning battalion had time to disperse. Then the Vampires were coming over again, and now he could see the ground scarred by small mushrooms of bombed dirt and stitched by heavy machine-gun fire. Wishing that he had been able to bring more of his anti-aircraft, Zvi saw his heavy machine guns firing upward. A few tracers revealed the directions of the bursts, and he knew that they were not hitting anything. However, whatever fire there was seemed to be enough to discourage the Egyptians who disappeared into the west.

Then the battalion commander he had ordered forward ran over to protest the conflicting orders. Zvi shrugged. He had enough problems without having to worry about the sensitivities of his juniors.

While he listened to the young major, he was on the radio again asking for permission to move into the Pass. Furious because he didn't even receive an answer to his request, he listened while the Signals Officer explained that the British and French had delivered an ultimatum. All Israeli troops and all Egyptian troops were to withdraw ten miles from the Suez Canal. Quickly estimating his own distance, Zvi knew he had to move forward to approach his ten-mile limit if the Prime Minister accepted the ultimatum.

Then he heard sudden and unexpected bursts of mortar fire over his position. Scanning the field, he could not quite make up his mind where it was coming from. One of the passing officers, who was on his way to rejoin his unit, yelled that it could be an isolated Egyptian patrol, but Zvi was not satisfied. Shouting for his battalion commanders to station more troops on the perimeters, he asked headquarters for more air support. This time he was told there was none. Swearing at no one in particular, he accepted the open can of rations Isaac brought him and asked if the Yemenite could scrounge a cup of coffee.

It was morning now. A fog had developed and for the moment Zvi felt that he would have no more trouble with the Egyptian jets. However, he knew that the fog would burn off in a few hours, and he was not pleased with his position. When he slowly walked over the field where his men were dispersed, he realized he had no protection from a land attack and even less from an air attack. Two of his battalions remained exposed while, as he told Fishel who was walking with him, "The third has its ass showing and it can be kicked by anything that comes past."

The recce officer did not argue. "What the hell is headquarters afraid of?"

"I wish I knew," Zvi admitted. "I wish the hell I knew."

Both of them scanned the sky at the sound of a plane overhead. One of the brigade's Pipers. "Tell that man to check out the west side of the Pass." Zvi ordered. Fishel nodded and started once more for the signals truck.

Without waiting for the recce officer's report, Zvi walked among his men. Their spirit was high. They had already done their share of fighting. And they had moved across Sinai as fast as any force had ever moved in enemy territory before. However, most of the men were anxious to do more. Passing one captain from Memara, Zvi paused to listen to his complaints. "What are we doing sitting here on our duffs? I'm sure that's not why we were sent here."

Zvi tried to be patient, but it was difficult because right now he himself had little patience with the situation. Then he saw Fishel coming back. Spilling the grounds of his coffee into the desert, Zvi watched while the dry sand absorbed them in a single dark brown spot.

Looking up, he waited for Fishel's answers.

The recce captain shook his head. "It beats the bloody hell out of me. The Piper reports that there is nothing in sight on the far side of the Pass." He thought a moment and added, "Some burned-out vehicles which were struck by our planes yesterday, but no sign of movement."

Zvi waited to hear if there was anything more. His hand nervously slipped into his shirt and he scratched his stomach.

"Those Egyptian tanks south of Bir Gifgafa are moving south," Fishel reported what the Piper pilot had passed on.

The map of his own position passed quickly through Zvi's mind. Before he could comment, Fishel evaluated the situation, "They don't have to risk coming at us. All they have to do is sweep south across our path and we're cut off."

Knowing this judgment was too simple, Zvi shook his head. "There's no reason why an armored brigade should not hit us. We're exposed. We have three light tanks and four recoilless 106s. We can't take on a brigade." He looked at the can of rations in his hand and even though he had not yet had time to eat any of it, he gave it to the nearest soldier and walked angrily across the field. Fishel followed. "If I were that Egyptian commander, I'd hit this place and hit it hard," Zvi said softly.

Fishel agreed, but added, "I'm not too sure we're any better off on the other side of the Pass. What we need is the cover of those mountains," and he was looking at the heights that overlooked the Pass.

Zvi thought about this, yelled for his fieldglasses and scanned the heights. They were more rugged than he had thought. "You may be right." Handing the glasses to Isaac, he started back to the communications center. "You know," he told Fishel, "we have our own column of tanks moving somewhere across the north of us now."

"A hell of a lot of good that will do."

Shrugging, Zvi thought of the one hundred and fifty kilometers that lay between himself and the northern Israeli column. He had no idea as yet how far it had penetrated Sinai, but he believed it would reach Suez soon if it was not held back by the ultimatum.

Wishing he knew more about the British and French plans and what was behind the confusing ultimatum which in essence allowed him to move farther west than he had yet, he contacted headquarters once more.

This time he asked to speak directly to the chief of operations. Without bothering to weigh the diplomacy of the situation, he requested permission to move "and move now into the Pass so that I can establish myself among the heights."

The Chief of Operations listened patiently before he firmly said, "You have your orders. Stay where you are." And then he was no longer on the radio.

Furious, Zvi looked at the radiophone he was holding and then slammed it back into the hand of the Signals Officer. "Get me Southern Command," he ordered, "and tell them I want someone out here as quickly as possible."

And for the next four hours he waited for some change in his situation.

Then at 1100 hours he saw a small Piper approach from the open country southeast of him and come into a landing. Grabbing the closest jeep, he shouted for Fishel to join him and the two raced to the plane. They reached it just as it rolled to a stop and both officers were standing beside the Piper when the Chief of Staff of the Southern Command emerged.

Without waiting for formalities and ignoring the General's attempts to congratulate him on his move across Sinai, Zvi pleaded his case, pointing as he talked to the exposed position of his men.

"I have to get the hell under some kind of cover," he concluded.

"Anything further about that Egyptian armor south of Bir Gifgafa?"

Zvi shook his head. "But I've no intention of waiting for it."

The C/S Southern Command nodded. "I don't know a damned thing about the situation," he confessed. Then a smile crossed his pudgy face. "I think the Army Spokesman is calling it 'fluid.' "

Zvi did not find the comment funny. "I could protect these three battalions," he said flatly. "I could just draw back."

The other officer looked at him tolerantly. "Headquarters doesn't threaten easily. Just calm down." And with that, he disappeared into his Piper. Zvi was tempted to follow, but he knew there was no room for him inside the small plane and that he was not wanted. A few minutes later, the Officer of Southern Command rejoined him.

"You have my permission to send only a recce unit into the Pass. You have specific orders to avoid any major battle." He thought a moment, wiped his cheek with an open palm, and added, "To be precise, you are ordered to 'take on' no major battles."

Zvi could hear Fishel's sigh of relief.

During the next two hours, Zvi organized his reconnaissance party. A battalion major in command, Fishel and the battalion recce company at the head of the column, followed by one infantry company, supplied with three-inch mortars, machine guns, three tanks and a battery of heavy mortars. Zvi and Fishel agreed that a detachment of Fishel's men would move out in two half-tracks five hundred yards ahead of the others.

Kneeling near the entrance of the Pass, Zvi sketched out his plans in the sand for the battalion commander while Fishel stood looking down at the pair. "You will go through and not tangle with any Egyptians on the other side," Zvi repeated for the third time. "The only intelligence I have is what the air force has passed on; the Egyptians have either fled the other side or they are there in very small numbers."

"And if I meet them?" the battalion commander asked.

"It's your battalion."

Shortly after noon the recce party prepared to move into the Pass. Zvi held the men back for several minutes while he tried to get additional information from headquarters. They could tell him nothing that he did not already know.

Looking over the exposed positions of his three battalions, Zvi made his decision, signaled for Isaac to join him, climbed into the command jeep and swung into the column between Fishel's half-tracks and the infantry. The battalion major who had been placed in command cursed softly under his breath.

Rising in his jeep, Zvi waved Fishel on. The recce captain nodded and slowly started his two half-tracks forward. Their machine guns were trained on the high sides of the Pass. They moved in slowly. Zvi waited where he was until he was satisfied with the distance between himself and Fishel before he tapped Isaac on the shoulder. The Yemenite sergeant started the jeep rolling west. A moment later the trucks carrying the infantry followed their commander into the Pass.

Sitting with the brazen sun directly overhead, Zvi relaxed. His men were trained. They knew what they were about. In fifteen minutes he would be on the far end of the Pass, and from there he would send for the rest of the brigade. He scanned the hills with his glasses. Nothing but rocks and the darkening shadows cast by overhang.

From where he sat, he could see Fishel standing in the lead half-track. The violinist was also looking at the rock walls of the Pass. They were undulating, rugged and high. The land between the heights was wider than Zvi had expected. Somehow Zvi was happy that Fishel was with him. His fondness for the artist had grown over the years, and he was remembering the time Fishel had sat down to a piano in that abandoned house in the Quarter, the piano under which someone should have placed a bucket of water to keep it from warping in the heat.

Zvi was thinking of Fishel when the first machine gun shattered the desert silence. Astonishingly loud and surprisingly close.

Then there was more gunfire. Half rising in his seat, Zvi tried to locate the enemy guns. Nothing. Then he saw that one of the half-tracks was trying to turn around. He saw, too, that the land between himself and the recce unit was under heavy fire. Then all he could see now was that the two half-tracks were cut off and the one in which Fishel had been standing was burning. Zvi moved instinctively, waving the infantry company forward.

The tempo of fire increased as the Israelis tried to reach their companions. From some place which Zvi could not find, the Egyptians were bracketing his men. Swinging the jeep about, Isaac drove back behind the infantry trucks from which the men were already pouring into the Pass.

Zvi quickly calculated he had twenty men cut off almost half a mile ahead of him. Then the enemy fire reached across his jeep, striking the hood and one tire, and he piled out, hitting the ground. Without a pause, he crawled behind some weeds. When he looked back for Isaac, he saw the Yemenite slumped across the steering wheel. A corporal crawling up to Zvi held out a radio.

"The major thought you would want this."

Zvi nodded, and while he grabbed for the small hand pack, his eyes never stopped searching the sides of the Pass, and now he believed that the Egyptians were firing from caves hidden by shadows under the overhang. Scanning both sides of the Pass, he realized he was trapped in a crossfire. He began spilling orders to the battalion commanders he had left behind. They had heard the gunfire and were moving into the Pass. Quickly countermanding their plans, Zvi explained that they would have to scale the heights overlooking the Pass. "Both sides. Climb on down from above. They have to be located in the caves under the top." He was shouting to be heard over the gunfire. The company trapped in the Pass was firing to keep the enemy back from the mouths of their caves.

"Move," Zvi shouted over the radio.

Then he handed the instrument to the communications corporal. He was about to leave the shelter of the rocks when a machine gun splashed stone and loose sand in his face. Wiping his eyes, Zvi tried to make out his position. Both of the advance half-tracks were still now. There was smoke over Fishel's. The other one was on its side. There were men scattered over the ground between. From where he lay, Zvi could make out at least ten bodies and then he saw someone crawling toward him. The infantry company commander. A leg dangled as the man sought shelter. Moving out, Zvi scooped the youth up in his arms and shoved him into the hole he had just left. Then without taking the time to see how badly the officer was hit, Zvi moved toward his battalion commander who was lying under the truck. The dirt between them pocked as Egyptian machine-gun fire worked it over. Half rising, Zvi dived to the side of the truck. He and the enemy fire reached the truck at the same time and a moment later the vehicle burst into flames. Grabbing the battalion commander, Zvi staggered over the open ground to a small depression. The petrol tank exploded and covered both of them with debris.

From where he lay, Zvi could see the infantry company trying to return the enemy fire and in that same instant he knew he had lost control of the situation. His men were trying to climb the heights from which the enemy was pouring down fire. And Zvi could see that the Israelis were not going to make it. Leaping to his feet, he waved some of them forward and others back to lay down protective fire for the men who were farthest up the steep slopes. Now Zvi was moving toward the north side of the Pass. Bending over, he grabbed an Uzi submachine gun lying beside a fallen soldier and emptied it at an Egyptian gun just above him. Even as he fired, he knew the gesture was meaningless because he was exposed to fire from the opposite wall of the Pass. The enemy had a planned crossfire, and he had no plan.

None.

Tossing the empty weapon aside, he took a deep breath and then rejoined his battalion commander who was talking over his radio to the battalions about to enter the fight. Bellied down on the hot ground, Zvi tried to see the enemy. A sudden lull in the fighting brought Zvi's attention back to the sides of the Pass. There was nothing in sight, and the only evidence that there was an enemy were burning vehicles, the half-track now on its side and a scattering of his own dead. Hearing nothing more from the battalion major behind him, Zvi turned to see the youth lying on his face, his arms outstretched as though he were trying to reach his men. None of them was climbing the slopes now. They had been repelled and the enemy was saving his ammunition for a better target. Crawling along the face of the slope, Zvi saw his troops pinned down, their officers lying either dead or wounded on the open ground.

Shouting for his men to keep what cover they had, Zvi made his way back to the communications corporal who was holding his radio in one hand and trying to stanch the blood flowing from a hole in his calf with the other. Smiling grimly at the boy, Zvi took over the radio. The paratroop battalion was moving out now and on its way to the height above the Pass on his left, crawling along the top while another unit was taking positions on the height which rose to his right. Zvi could hear firing once more as the Egyptians broke the momentary silence. Lying flat on the open ground, he tried to figure out what they were shooting at. Then he saw his own relief columns moving over the encircling heights above the enemy positions. Watching his men above as they dropped and then started to return the fire, Zvi was startled to see they were not firing at the caves. It took him a moment to realize his relief columns were firing at their own companions in the Pass below. He tried to contact the forward units by radio, but he could not make himself heard over the gunfire. Somehow his men above had become confused, and he could not understand what was taking place. Then he saw that the Egyptians in the caves were firing on the men on the opposite heights so that his Israelis thought the firing came from below.

Once more he tried to make himself understood over the radio and once more he failed. He could see that there were wounded above now and that there were wounded below and that so far none had reached the enemy positions. Handing the radio to the corporal, Zvi ran across the open ground. The land pocked about him as he waved a soldier to his side. For an instant both of them were exposed and the enemy was firing at them, but there were better targets above. Zvi and the soldier jumped into a jeep and raced back from the cauldron between the heights.

Once he reached the open land beyond the Pass, he sought out his battalion commanders. One had already started along the top of the height. The other was moving his troops into a more protected position in case they were attacked from outside the Pass. Zvi approved the notion though he had little respect for the position and did not have time to discuss it. Calling for two runners and the communications half-track, he contacted the paratroopers on the top of the heights. It took a moment for him to explain that they had to stop firing on their comrades trapped below, and then he explained where the Egyptians were holed up. The commanders on the heights finally understood and said they would swing down into the caves.

Zvi glanced at his watch. For six hours he had been pinned down and losing men. For six hours there had been almost no control over the recce unit and the men above. Speaking quickly into the radio, he ordered the commanders above to wait until darkness before making their move,

"Otherwise, they can see you from the opposite side and there's nothing you can do about it."

He turned to the battalion commander beside him. "Have you called for air support?"

The officer nodded. "It's coming up."

Zvi sought his pocket and a cigarette. There was nothing he could do now but wait. He looked over the defensive positions outside the Pass. They were as good as could be expected. He could still hear firing from inside the Pass, but there was nothing he could do there. Those of the recce unit who were still alive had found some kind of cover. Those who were going to their aid were waiting for darkness.

Then he heard planes overhead and watched as five Mysteres appeared. His own. The jets swept low over Mitla and then returned. He could hear the radio behind him and asked the Signals Officer what the hell the pilots were waiting for.

The Signals Officer brushed his damp mustache with the back of his hand as he stared at Zvi. "They can't tell our men from the enemy."

Zvi's hand clasped the back of his neck as he thought about this. His own men were really the only ones exposed. "Send them home," he snapped. A moment later he watched as the planes swept away. Once more he looked at the battalion on the open plateau east of the Pass. Waving for the commander to join him, he said, "Wait until dark and then take two companies in. See if you can clear a way out for those who've been caught and if you can go beyond that to the other end of the Pass. . . "

The battalion commander nodded.

The firing in the Pass increased now. Puzzled, Zvi asked for information. The paratroopers over the Pass were trying to make their way down, but the enemy fire was too heavy. He wanted to curse out the paratroop commander for his eagerness, but Zvi knew that only eagerness was going to get them out of this trap.

He was listening to the firing from the heights when the first Egyptian plane came over the plateau, strafing the men who had been left there. Then the second came and Zvi could see his men seeking cover where there was none. And now there were five enemy jets overhead and they were strafing the heights and the inside of the Pass. And now they were wheeling about in the sky and coming at him once more. His men stood their ground, returning the fire, but in an instant the jets swept the area and were small in the distance.

Zvi called to the company commanders who were preparing to enter the Pass, "Let's go."

And they moved out into the dusk.

From the gunfire about him, when he entered the cauldron again, Zvi could tell that his men were still on the heights above the caves and on the road below, while the Egyptians continued to hold the caves on the slopes between. He paused for a moment at the sight of a burning vehicle farther inside the Pass. It was not one of his own, and the company commander at his side commented, "They must have tried coming through with a half-track."

Zvi nodded. Though the Pass was bright with fire, there was no longer any smoke above Fishel's half-track. Taking a position deeper inside the Pass, a radio at his side, Zvi commanded the battle on the heights. For almost two hours Mitla Pass rocked with gunfire, grenades and mortars while the Jewish soldiers swung themselves down from above, blowing their way into the caves or taking the enemy hand to hand and bayonet to bayonet. For two hours the middle of the Pass was confusion while Zvi tried to keep up with the action which had now become too personal for any commander to control. Some of the troops he had brought in with him the second time made their way past the burning Russian half-track as far as the west end of the Pass and once there, started back while others moved toward them. For two hours there was a flow of Israelis in both directions as they sought to sweep the enemy from the narrow confines between the heights on which their companions were fighting.

And by 2000 hours the firing dwindled to scattered fire.

Fifteen minutes later there was silence in Mitla Pass. The narrow strip of land belonged to Israel. Coming to his feet, Zvi ordered his commanders to count their dead. Then he started walking through the silent Pass.

He could see his dead among the burned trucks which lay like the skeletons of strange animals. Approaching his own jeep, he reached out and raised Isaac's head. The Yemenite sergeant had two machine-gun slugs in his chest. Closing his friend's eyes with a damp palm, Zvi wished he knew the right prayer. And then he wondered if there was anything that he could say which would adequately recall the moment Isaac had brought him Aaron and told him Havah was dead. He shouted for a soldier to take care of his friend's body and moved on. A dead radio operator lay with his hands between his legs as though he were asleep. There were other dead on the field. And then Zvi reached the recce half-track. Fishel's burned body lay on the ground where it had been thrown when the vehicle's fuel tank exploded. And standing there in the semi-darkness, Zvi could not recall hearing the tank explode. Then he wondered why he was thinking of gas tanks instead of Fishel and he knew he did not want to think of Fishel as he lay on the ground before him. His mind whirled back to the Quarter, the sound of a piano, and then to a concert stage and the piano music was mingled with a violin and the face of Kineret telling him that he should be certain no harm came to Fishel. Kneeling beside his friend's twisted body, Zvi saw where the fire had burned away the tan slacks and exposed the scars of old wounds. Without thinking, he reached out and opened Fishel's shirt. The scar of an old bullet hole was white on his shoulder and Zvi was thinking of Fishel on the roofs over the Quarter when Dov Tervisky died. Rising, Zvi walked on. Now he wished he had refused to take Fishel with him.

A sound behind and he spun about. One bloodied battalion officer with an Uzi in one hand and his other shoved into his belt. Zvi looked beyond the man to the soldiers in the Pass. Many were just lying on the ground trying to catch their breath. Others were moving among the dead and the wounded. There were fires in the Pass and Zvi wondered how the face of hell differed.

"There are thirty-four all told, Zvi," the battalion officer reported.

"Thirty-four," Zvi repeated.

The battalion officer nodded.

"The wounded?"

"A hundred and twenty tonight and twenty yesterday on the plateau and then the thirteen who were hurt in the drop."

Numbly, Zvi nodded. "Take care of your men."

The battalion officer half nodded as he watched the stocky colonel walk slowly away in the dark. Half an hour later Zvi reported the details of the battle to the headquarters now located secretly outside Tel Aviv, ordered in light planes with the dawn, and then he slowly walked once more down that part of the Pass where his men had fought. There was a wounded man he knelt beside and talked to; a dead one whom others told him had been a hero, entering a cave alone. There was a dead youth who had swung into a cave with a bayonet between his teeth. There were so many heroes and so many dead. Zvi's pride mixed with the sick feeling he had in the middle of his stomach. He found one of the battalion commanders and told him to locate his men in the Pass while the others were sent back to the open plateau where the wounded and dead would have to be moved so that they could be flown home. It was almost dawn when a sergeant handed Zvi a cup of coffee. Holding it in one hand, Zvi looked at the sergeant, an older soldier who had once fought in the British army in Italy.

"It was bad," the sergeant said.

Zvi nodded.

"Most battles are bad," the old sergeant said.

And Zvi drank the dark coffee without comment.

"They only make sense if they are part of something," the sergeant added.

The brigade commander's head came up and he realized for the first time that he knew nothing about the war, whether they were winning or losing. Nothing. He was alone on an alien peninsula. He was cut off from his friends and the world. Just the remains of a bruised brigade. Would he ever be able to forget how lonely and isolated he felt at Mitla Pass?

There was a sound overhead and he looked up.

A Dakota coming down on the strip which the engineers were trying to clear on the plateau. Zvi stood where he was and drank his coffee. The world was coming to him now, and he knew the next few hours would not be easy. Then he handed the old sergeant the cup and thanked him.

"Tell them the men fought well, Zvi," the sergeant said.

"They already know that," Zvi said. "That much they take for granted."

And he could see the side door of the Dakota coming open. Avram emerged and then Elihu Cohen, the Chief of Operations. They looked fresher than Zvi and for a fleeting instant he felt sorry for Avram Ben Ezra who had not been part of the battle of Mitla Pass.

Someone was moving a truckload of wounded toward the Dakota and Zvi stood where he was to watch it. Then his eyes were on Avram as the tall staff officer tried to evaluate what he could from his position beside the plane. The Operations Chief shoved his beret back on his head and stared at the sky for an instant before he took in the field.

Then both men approached Zvi.

Taking the time to brush some dirt off his slacks and wiping the palms of his hands down his side, Zvi moved forward to join them.

The three met near the mouth of the Pass and stood for a moment in silence.

"Was it worth it, Zvi?" the Operations Chief asked.

Zvi looked at Avram for support, but his friend's eyes were distant.

"I didn't want the fight," Zvi said. "It happened."

They were walking into the Pass now. Troops lying about looked up as they recognized the outsiders and wondered if anyone who had not been there could understand what had taken place at Mitla Pass.

Trying not to make excuses for what had happened, Zvi decided he had to explain his own feelings. "It was simple in its own way. Should a commander, seeing twenty of his men cut off, pay any attention to his orders not to fight? I made the decision to get my men out. They were what mattered."

Trying not to notice the dark lines about Zvi's face, the Operations Chief said softly, "You did not have to go into this Pass. We asked you not to. We told you not to."

"And the tank brigade coming down from Bir Gifgafa," Zvi asked, trying to keep his temper.

Avram said, "There isn't any tank brigade coming down from Bir Gifgafa. The Egyptians have withdrawn to the other side of the Canal." And Zvi felt he had just been betrayed by a friend.

He stood where he was and stared down the Pass, trying hard not to see the debris of battle.

"I had two hundred men caught between those cliffs," Zvi explained.

The Operations Officer turned to look at him. "Southern Command authorized a reconnaissance. Two hundred men don't make up a recce unit."

They stood watching a truck remove some dead from the Pass.

"Two hundred men," the Operations Chief said again. "You were not really making a recon. You were moving in, in strength and that was what you had been told to avoid."

"You don't understand," Zvi was saying. And as he spoke, he wished he were not so weary and that he could marshal his thoughts the way the other man could. "It was the opening situation. They . . ." and his hand went up to point at the cliffs, "were up there and we were caught between. The half-track . . ." and he was pointing at it as his voice trailed off.

Avram slowly turned toward his friend. "If I were the chief of staff, I'd court martial you, Zvi. You didn't have to fight this fight. You were ordered not to fight this fight."

Sucking in his breath, Zvi fumbled for a cigarette, found none and accepted the one Elihu Cohen offered him. When he had it lit, Zvi said once more, "It was not a planned attack. It happened." Then stubbornly, "I would do it again." The others waited for his explanation, and Zvi could see they were looking at him. However, beyond them he could see the burned-out half-track where Fishel's body had lain only an hour before.

"There," he said, pointing. "There and twenty men cut off. Remember once in forty-eight I could have left some men behind and I didn't?" His head came up and he stared at the other two. He dragged on the cigarette a moment and then reminded them, "Remember what we did to that boy who left a man behind on a retaliation raid? We just don't do it."

"And we don't fight battles we're told not to fight," Avram countered.

But Zvi was shaking his head. "That's a battle you're talking about. This is more. The morale of the army, men who have to know their friends will take care of them." He fell silent as another Dakota slid down the sky toward the landing strip outside the Pass. More dead and wounded would be removed, and he wished he were with his men.

"Hell," he snorted. "You can destroy a tradition in a minute. It takes years to build one; I wasn't letting this one go." The others looked at him dubiously. "I have the record of fifty retaliation raids and I'll live with that. We did here what we would have done then."

"Zvi," Avram said coldly, "this could have cost less. You did not have to commit more than the twenty who were cut off," and he, too, was gesturing toward the distant half-tracks.

Shoving his shoulders back and rolling his muscles, Zvi listened for a moment before he said, "The situation did not lend itself to decision once we went after the twenty. And I had to make the decision to go after them." His face looked grim when he said flatly, "There comes a time when a commander may have to disobey orders."

The others were shaking their heads.

Angrily, Zvi growled, "Am I responsible for less than all of my men?"

Then as though it were an afterthought, he added, "We destroyed one enemy battalion and part of another."

But his companions were not thinking of the enemy.

"The cost was too high." And Elihu Cohen had judged him.

Zvi turned to Avram for his evaluation.

His friend shook his head slowly from side to side as he watched a truck of wounded roll past. "I'm not judging the battle you fought." He fell silent and then disagreed with himself. "Maybe I am. First, you should have saved the most men you could by withdrawing once you saw you were trapped."

"And second?"

"You should never have been in the Pass in the first place. Recce, you were told. Take a look and instead you piled on an infantry company in addition to Fishel's, then you added support troops for all of them." He shook his head in anger, "Damn it, Zvi, you should have trusted us when we said stay out. You not only fought this battle wrong, but it is a battle which should never have been fought. What the hell is there about the other side of this Pass that is worth any more than this side?"

Zvi was not looking at Avram now as he watched two men lifting Isaac's body from the jeep. The dead from the half-track beyond had already been collected.

He did not want to argue now. He did not want to defend himself for his decisions. He, not these two, had made the race to the Pass. He, not these two, had fought the battle here. Very slowly he walked away from the others and started once more toward the place where his brigade headquarters was being established.

A moment later, Avram caught up with him and they walked side by side for a time without speaking.

"Are we winning?" Zvi finally asked, trying to remember that the war was more than Mitla Pass.

"We're winning," Avram assured him. "The last phase has begun. Moshe's on his way to Sharm el Sheikh."

Zvi nodded, wondering why this did not make any difference to him now, and if he would ever stop feeling so tired and lonely as he did at this moment.

SOUTHERN SINAI

Colonel Moshe Gilead's brigade had started its race for Sharm el Sheikh and the Strait of Tiran as dawn came over Sinai. They had been traveling southwest for three hours, and sitting in his jeep twenty miles behind his recce unit, Moshe already felt the heat of the autumn sun.

Looking back, he could see vehicles in the long column behind him as they mixed with the hazy images created over the desert. Picking up the clipboard at his feet, he scanned the list once more: fourteen half-tracks, thirty-two weapons carriers, one hundred and eleven new GMC six-by-six trucks. Looking farther down the list, he smiled at the figures of twenty-seven jeeps and seven pick-up trucks. The jeeps would hold up. They always did. The pick-ups had been ingathered from merchants and he had his doubts about those. The only vehicles he believed had to keep up with the others and which he could never abandon were the eighteen water tankers. Everything else was expendable.

The sky was clear, the countryside dry. There were a few burned shrubs along his trail, a few cacti defying the heat. The countryside itself was broken rocks and black stone. There were some heights to his left and some heights before him. At the sound of a plane overhead, he glanced up. A Piper. The radio behind him crackled and he listened while Mitra Glasner, his Signals Officer, reported, "The recce unit is moving through broken ground." Then the girl added, "They are making good time." Moshe nodded without turning around.

He was not anticipating bad news, but he was not interested in good. Sixty kilometers to go before he reached the oasis at el Fatuga. Unfolding the map that he had shoved between his seat and the driver's, he checked it again. A red line alongside a broken blue line. He was supposed to be traveling on a trail but there was no sign that anyone had driven over it before his recce unit. He was supposed to be driving south in a wadi, but there was no sign of water anywhere and he did not expect to see water until he reached el Fatuga. And then there would be no more until he came out at the sea.

Waving his driver to the side of the road, they stopped to watch the column pass. The drivers shouted as they recognized him. They all seemed happy enough. None of them had shaved in days and he wondered what they would look like when they met the Egyptians at Ras Nusrani, the first and most heavily fortified position at the Strait. Maybe they could scare the Egyptians, and if they could he would accept any help he could get.

His head came up as he saw a truck trailing its winch rope. Pointing it out to his driver, he sat back while they caught up with the truck and shouted for the lieutenant driving there to tighten the winch. Then Moshe dropped off to the side of the column once again. Every other truck had a power winch, and Moshe believed they would be used before he reached the Strait.

As one of the trucks passed, he could see the men in the back eating their cold breakfast from cans. He motioned for his driver to take his place at the head of the main body again. There were going to be no stops. He planned none and he wanted none. The men in the cabs of the trucks would take their turns at the wheel regardless of rank.

The jeep bounced on at the head of the column. White cloth tied on a bush and a sign indicating his recce unit had passed this way. His driver swung close, read the instructions and started veering southeast.

Moshe wondered why he was thinking of the Signals Officer behind him, and his thoughts drifted to Zipporah and the last night he had spent with her. Had it been a week before? He was not even certain now. All he was certain of was the way she had held him in her arms and traced the wound on his chest with her lips before he pressed her back on the bed and overwhelmed her to the delight of both of them. He was still thinking of Zipporah when he saw one of the half-tracks of the recce unit waiting for him. Gesturing for his driver to close the gap between, Moshe leapt out of the jeep as he reached the half-track.

"Grease, Colonel," the lieutenant said. "We didn't bring any extra."

Moshe looked at the man as though one of them had lost his reason. Then he shouted for Mitra Glasner to contact the Piper above and have it check with the battalion commander. "Find out if they brought grease."

A moment later the Piper was overhead and the girl was telling him, "They haven't any."

Very slowly, Moshe shook his head. "Tell the pilot to pick up all he can carry at Eilat and drop it to each of the units." Ignoring the lieutenant, he climbed back into his jeep and started after the column that had already passed him. The failure to bring grease for the half-tracks did not bother him as much as the gnawing fear that they might have forgotten something else. He did not know what it could be; he did not want to know now. There was nothing he could do about that.

His eyes held on the broken ground of the wadi, and he was glad he had decided not to take his tanks with him. All he had were French AMXs which were too dainty for this country.

There were heights rising now over thirty-five hundred meters to his right and his left. And then he saw a sand sea ahead. Motioning for his driver to stop, he told the girl behind him, "Tell the trucks to pull up and let the air out of their tires. About two thirds of it." The second Piper was overhead now, picking up the instructions and passing them on down the twenty-mile length of the column.

Soon Moshe saw the trail come to an end and one of the recce vehicles waiting for him. Reaching it, he waited for the captain's report. "This, Moshe, is the end of the easy going."

Moshe nodded. He had expected as much. He could continue to follow the wadi, but it would bring him to a small village, and the one thing he did not want was to approach the Egyptians this soon. As far as he knew, they were not aware that he was coming, and he had no intention of telling them.

"Move out as we planned," he ordered.

The captain nodded. Their route now was going to be longer and there was not even the vaguest trail nor the broken bed of a wadi. Moshe watched the recce officer race away to join his men, and then he pulled out the air photos he had in his bag. Nothing he could read was helpful. He stood for a moment looking toward el Fatuga and then he waved down a passing truck.

The lieutenant climbed out and waited for his orders. The desert dust had already caked on the officer's face and he squinted against the sun.

"Take your platoon and remain here for the next three hours," Moshe ordered. "If the Egyptians have any inkling we're coming, they may have sense enough to blow our approach by moving up the wadi."

The lieutenant nodded and started waving down his trucks.

Moshe started after the main column.

Several hours later he pulled up where two of his jeeps had paused beside an Egyptian truck.

"No one here," a corporal told him.

"Anything there?"

The corporal trotted over and handed Moshe a package of papers. Reading through them quickly, he saw that he had a map. Primitive and of no real use to him. He smiled as he realized the Israeli maps of Egyptian Sinai were better. The rest of the papers seemed to be nothing more than personnel supply lists.

Waving the other two jeeps on, Moshe told his driver to follow. Sitting back and trying to rest, he wondered where the Egyptians had gone and why they had left their truck. And he wondered, too, what they might know about his penetration southward.

Brushing the thoughts aside, he listened to the radio behind him.

The girl leaned forward, "There's been fighting at Mitla Pass."

Assuming that Zvi knew what he was doing, Moshe decided not to worry about the things he could do nothing about.

Then he saw the Piper overhead. The radio again and the girl leaning forward once more: "The road ahead is bad."

Moshe nodded. There was nothing he could do about this either. For an instant he was tempted to tell her that no one had promised her anything better, and then he shrugged.

The Piper radioing again and he leaned back without turning around.

"Tracks of Land Rovers ahead," the girl was half shouting now to be heard over the roar of the trucks about them.

Moshe nodded. He tried to figure out where the tracks had come from and whose they were.

The radio once more. "The recce commander is at the oasis," the girl shouted.

Again Moshe nodded to let her know he had heard her. Nothing more, and so he assumed that the approach to the oasis had been made safely.

Twenty minutes later he entered the area. A few of his men were washing and they waved to him as he drove up. The others had obviously been posted as sentries. Moshe waited in his jeep beside the water hole, a few palms throwing shadows over him. A moment later Leon appeared.

"Two Arab civilians here," the kibbutznik reported. "They say there were some Egyptians through last night."

"What brought them this way now?" Moshe asked.

Leon rubbed the back of his neck with a browned hand. "Seems there are some reports that the Jews took Ras el Nakib by force the other day. These Egyptians have been running ever since."

Moshe saw the twinkle in his deputy's eyes and almost smiled himself. "Trouble with those damned Jews," he said. "Just can't trust them. Hit them and they hit back."

Leon smiled, though he knew the joke was not very funny. "There's more."

Moshe waited.

"There was a radio."

"And?"

"I found the thing. They left it behind before they went into the desert."

For several minutes Moshe remained still while he thought about the implications. "How many men were there?" he finally asked.

"Ten."

"And the radio?"

"They may have sent off some kind of message."

The column was passing through the oasis now and Moshe waved a driver on who had come to a halt. "Any idea what they sent?"

Leon nodded. "As far as I can tell from the two civilians we have, it had something to do with Ras el Nakib."

Moshe grinned. "It's a good thing they were in such a hurry." He watched Mitra approach the water hole and cup a handful of the warm water over her face. Leon's eyes followed Moshe's and they grinned at each other.

"It's a hell of a place to take a girl," Leon said softly.

Moshe nodded and then ordered his driver, "Go over and tell her she's not to leave the radio."

Leon cocked his head to one side, aware of Moshe's unconscious thoughtlessness. "You getting tired?"

Very slowly Moshe shook his head. "Just out of touch, and when I can't be reached, I get frightened." He almost smiled as he explained. "It would be nice to know if there was something going on ahead of me or behind me."

"It would help," Leon agreed. "Any idea who's winning this war?"

"We won't if we keep hanging around here."

Half an hour later he was driving over broken country again.

Then the column reached Wadi Gozala. The great watershed ran across their route and they moved slowly toward it. Then less than ten kilometers from the wadi they approached a vast sand sea. The first vehicles started through, bogged down and the ones falling behind also bogged down. The heavy motors of the six-by-six roared in the early dusk. The six large wheels spun and mired. The jeeps spread wide of the tracks of the others and reached the far side of the sand sea.

In an hour the whole brigade was bogged down except for the lighter vehicles and half-tracks. Moshe stood in his jeep and watched the drivers roll their trucks one behind the other, forming a chain of trucks four and five long, bumper to bumper four and five motors struggling to break the trucks loose from the sand. The men climbed down into the soft sand and looked at it for a moment before they started to shove and lift and haul their vehicles across.

Moshe gestured for his deputy to join him.

"There's a full ten kilometers of it," Leon told him. "Ten."

Moshe glanced up at the sky. In another half hour it would be dark. He looked at his watch. For an instant he almost smiled as he wished the sand would run out. Time. He had no time. The truck wheels spun, throwing loose sand into the faces of his men. He saw one man slip when his truck moved a few feet. Looking across the open desert, Moshe saw all of his hundred and eleven trucks mired and with them the water tankers. When a man paused to take a drink from his canteen, Moshe was tempted to warn him to save his water. Instead, he shrugged. The night was going to be cool. Most of the men would not need to drink.

He saw the four girls from Signals pushing trucks along with the men. "Go tell them," Moshe ordered his driver, pointing, "tell them to get into the weapons carriers and go to the far side." Then he turned to Leon. "Keep the men at it." His voice dropped as he added, "We haven't any choice."

The radio behind him crackled and he answered it himself.

A Piper above.

"You wanted grease, Moshe."

"Drop it."

A moment later the plane rode down the sky and the pilot dumped his cargo.

Several soldiers ran over to retrieve it, and Moshe watched as they shoved it into the closest truck and returned to their work. He waited where he was until dark; then he joined Leon. "We've got to risk a bombing. Turn on the headlights." A few minutes later the truck lights cut white wedges in the night revealing the trains of trucks, bumper to bumper, being hauled and pushed and even lifted over the loose sand only to bog down once more and again have to be pushed and hauled and lifted.

Moshe told his deputy, "Take over. I'm going on ahead." The jeep made its way through the sand sea and finally touched solid ground ten kilometers to the south.

Climbing out in the dark, Moshe drew his map from between the seats and told Mitra, "Stay right on that radio. If you hear anything, I'll be sleeping over there," and he pointed to a small patch of loose sand. Picking up his flashlight and a blanket, he squatted, spread his map and tried to decide what he would do next. A day gone and the Strait still far away. He tried to keep his mind on the future because there was little he could do about the present. His finger moved over the route several times before he flicked off the flashlight and stalked back to the jeep.

"Tell the next Piper you reach to contact Eilat. We'll need petrol when we get to Dahab." And without waiting for the girl to acknowledge his order, he returned to his blanket and fell instantly asleep.

MITLA PASS

Zvi Mazon sat on the blanket spread out on the ground east of Mitla Pass. Though it was dark, he could make out the silhouettes of Avram and Elihu Cohen. They had been talking through most of the day. So far there had been no order from Tel Aviv, though the Chief of Operations had twice spoken to the Chief of Staff.

"He told me that when we passed Themed the decisions would have to be mine," Zvi said, referring to the battle he had fought the night before.

"You admit you didn't know what was going on anywhere else," his friend reminded him. "And if you didn't, why take the chance?"

Zvi looked at Avram and shook his head. "I could ask where the hell you were yesterday." He shook his head. "I won't. The decisions had to be made here. Not back there."

"Yesterday," Avram said softly. "Yesterday we fought another battle in the north. One that had to be fought." He picked up some loose dirt and let it sift back through his fingers. "I wish I'd been with you. When the battles were being fought, we had to wait to hear how they were coming out ... Well, it was a dull feeling. A dull day. We talked to BG a couple of times and that was it." He snorted. "Hell, there weren't even any phone calls." Avram leaned forward and rested his palms on his boots. "We did get into the field during El 'Arish."

Zvi waited a moment before he asked, "How did that go?"

"They fought. We took the place."

None spoke for a time and then Avram said, "At night the Chief of Staff came back, and the first thing he asked was what would we do when the Americans attacked."

Picking up the canteen cup which held his coffee, Zvi wondered, "Is there a chance they will?"

"He thinks so."

"Has it gone according to plan?"

"We changed the plans," Cohen said. "Moved through the Deika Defile to Abu Agilla."

"That was the tough battle," Avram said. "They fought better than usual."

"The casualties?" Zvi asked.

The others were looking at him. "They don't match yours," Avram told him.

Silence again and then Avram said, "I just don't see it, Zvi. There was nothing to be gained strategically by going through that Pass. Nothing. Tactically it might have helped. But . . ." And his voice trailed off in disappointment.

Zvi was having trouble keeping his temper and now he decided to lose it. "Look, we had communications. We have the best there are. I could get through to you and I could find out anything, but no one can ever get on a radio and ask how he should fight a battle. No one ever. You have the larger picture where you sit and I don't even have time to ask what is happening anywhere else. All right, I'll accept that as being the nature of war and command. But you two had better accept as the nature of command that a commander commands."

Avram put his hand on his friend's knee and pushed himself off the ground where he stood looking down at Zvi. "Spending so many to save so few had no rational basis. However, morally and sentimentally . . ." He shrugged. "Maybe it's clever to do the unclever thing sometimes. On a tactical level, let's just say it was courageous."

And Zvi knew his friend was trying to paper over the battle that lay between them. Looking up, he saw his Signals Officer at his side. "Orders from the Chief of Staff, Zvi."

"And?" Avram asked as the others came to their feet.

"I'll talk to him" the chief of operations said as he walked over to the communications half-track. Avram and Zvi stood looking after him. Then they both turned to look at the scattered troops spread out on the plain.

"You got here in good time," Avram said.

Deciding that his friend was continuing to avoid the real issue of Mitla, Zvi accepted the compliment.

Elihu Cohen rejoined them. "Two of your companies have been dropped at Tor."

At first the brigade commander thought he might lose his temper, and then he knew that there had been no way to contact him to discuss the drop. "How did they fare?"

"A couple hurt, but they took the port."

Zvi was already on his knees looking at a map. Tor was a small port on the west side of the Sinai peninsula and far to the south.

The Operations Chief was pointing at Ras Sudar, which lay on a paved road more than a hundred kilometers to the north of Tor. "You'd better send out some recce units and find a route. You've orders to move out from Mitla directly to Ras Sudar and then take the road south to join the men at Tor. Once you have regrouped, you will move as rapidly as you can to Sharm el

Sheikh." His hand swept down the west side of the peninsula. "Moshe is going through here," and he indicated the route of the other brigade, on the east side of Sinai. "He doesn't have a road. He has the hills and the desert. You are to see if you can beat him there and take the Strait before he can." Zvi glanced up at Avram for any explanation he might have.

"Makes sense, Zvi. There's pressure building up at the UN for us to stop, and we'll have lost the damned war if it doesn't end with the opening of the Strait." He thought for a moment and added, "This is what it's all about."

"And Mitla?" Zvi asked.

"We're moving another unit in to hold it," Cohen assured him.

Coming to his feet once more, Zvi turned to the west, trying to hold the details of the map in his head. From Mitla to Ras Sudar and south to Tor and south to Sharm el Sheikh. He wanted to say he was tired, but he knew everyone else was also.

"We're going back," Elihu informed Avram. "They want you in Tel Aviv as soon as possible."

Nodding, Avram clasped Zvi's shoulder. "I'll meet you at Sharm el Sheikh." Then with a smile he added, "Let us know when you get there."

The three laughed as Zvi agreed. "I won't keep it a secret."

SOUTHERN SINAI

When Moshe awakened on Saturday morning, he could see most of his vehicles around him. Coming to his feet, he listened to Leon's report.

"No problem. We just picked them up and carried them."

Moshe grunted, "In that case, we don't need to spend any time resting." He looked about at his troops. Many of them lay sprawled on the ground. A few were still asleep. One of the girls from the air liaison team was sitting on the ground with her knees drawn up before her staring at a mirror and laughing at what she saw.

"How many still to come?" Moshe demanded.

"Just some of the support units. Water tanks. Engineer equipment."

Moshe made his decision. "We'll finish breakfast, refuel and then move on. You wait for the rest and bring them up."

The tall deputy nodded as he watched Moshe drink the coffee his driver had brought.

Fifteen minutes later, Moshe led the main body south toward Dahab on the coast. The brigade recce unit sped ahead while the rest of the column strung out behind.

As his jeep bounced the twenty odd kilometers through the broken countryside, Moshe confirmed his request for fuel to meet him at the small port. Knowing how difficult it had been to bring the LCTs—Landing Craft,

Tanks—overland all the way from Haifa to Eilat, he was somehow pleased they were at least going to be used. This was what he was thinking about when he heard Mitra Glasner talking on the radio behind him. Leaning back, he waited for her report.

"There's fighting in Dahab," she told him.

Moshe slapped his driver on the back, "Let's get there."

Half an hour later he approached the small port on the Gulf of Akaba which consisted of little more than some date palms and shacks. Three of his recce vehicles remained north of the town and he could hear the firing at the edge of the port. Leaping from his jeep, Moshe ran over to the closest recce half-track. "What the hell's going on?"

An embarrassed lieutenant shook his head.

Both of them turned to listen to a machine gun.

Turning back to the young officer, Moshe waited impatiently for his explanation.

"We raced into the town and they started firing."

Moshe almost lost his temper. Then as he could hear the firing fall off, he climbed back into his jeep and started into Dahab. At one end of the town near the port he could see two of his half-tracks pouring fire into a small building. Stopping where he was, he realized that this was the extent of battle. A few minutes later there was silence. Approaching his half-tracks, he saw two of his men lying on their faces in the dirt. He did not need to be told they were dead. Nearby, under the shade of a date palm, he saw three others stretched out with a sergeant bending over them. Wounded. As he moved toward the half-tracks, he knew he was having trouble controlling his anger and that there was nothing to be gained by giving vent to it.

Then he saw the tall, mustached lieutenant-colonel who commanded the recce unit coming toward him. The officer had the butt of his Uzi resting on his hip while he reported.

"Came in too fast. There were ten of them." He turned to indicate a body being carried out of a corrugated steel shed. "That Egyptian corporal fought well." As an afterthought he added, "Damned well."

Moshe glared at the recce officer. "Who the hell told you to spill into town without checking it out first? Or don't you know what a recce commander's job is?"

"We didn't see any sign of them and we moved in." The lanky officer was not apologizing.

Moshe stared at him for a moment and then both watched as the Israeli soldiers lined up the Egyptian bodies in the shade of a nearby tree.

"They had a radio."

"And?"

"They got off a message. We heard it. They reported having sighted the full column."

Sucking in his breath, Moshe tried to understand just what this would mean. If the Egyptian high command was functioning, it could block his way to Sharm el Sheikh at a hundred places. Shaking off the idea, he knew there was nothing he could do about that. The recce commander was walking toward a grove of date palms while Moshe followed. There were ten camels there. Approaching one of the light brown beasts which was lying down and staring off at the Gulf, he saw the radio strapped on its back. An instrument large enough to reach Sharm el Sheikh.

There was nothing he could do about this. Striding angrily back to the center of the small town, he watched his trucks enter. Waving for his jeep, he asked the girl in the back of it, "Any report on the petrol?"

"They're coming."

Leon was running toward him now and Moshe stood watching the trucks come in. When his second in command joined him, Moshe walked to the small port. A single crude dock bleached white in the sun.

"I'm going to take the reserve fuel," he told Leon.

The deputy nodded. "There's no sense in all of us waiting here."

"I'm moving out as soon as it's dark," Moshe decided. "Fly the wounded out and wait for the LCTs."

Leon nodded again. "Don't be too hard on the recce boys. From what I can figure out, they just came in too cocksure of themselves."

"They should know better."

Shortly after dark, seeing the first of the LCTs approach the dock, Moshe waved his driver on. The recce unit had left Dahab several hours earlier and had already reported that they had problems ahead. Convinced he was done with Dahab, Moshe led his engineers and two infantry companies south. The main body would refuel from the LCTs and follow. It was the middle of the night when he reached Sharhai Pass where the recce unit was waiting for him. The half-tracks were parked near the entrance of the Pass and as Moshe drove up, the recce commander walked over to the command jeep.

"That's it. I can take a jeep through there and not another goddamned thing."

Switching on his lights, Moshe told him, "Lead the way."

Very slowly the two jeeps made their way into Sharhai. Sheer stone walls higher than a tall building. Stopping for a moment in the middle of the Pass, Moshe rose in his jeep and slowly turned around. He could see the surprised look on Mitra's face. "Let's go on," he told his driver and they followed the lead jeep for another two hundred yards until they emptied out into rolling country. "All right. Take it back."

When he reached his engineers on the north side of the Pass, he explained. "We're going to blow the whole damned thing. Set your charges to bring down the walls, and then we'll have to go through and clear a road down the center of it."

Moshe turned toward the recce officer. "Get your jeeps rolling out ahead. We'll send your half-tracks on as soon as we're clear." Then, taking the man's arm, he led him away from the others. "Be careful," he warned for the first time that he could recall ever having given that order in his life. "Just don't get ambushed ahead there. They know we're coming."

The tall recce officer nodded. "I'm not anxious to get killed. If they're going to meet us, they'll meet us at Wadi Kid."

The brigade commander agreed.

Both turned to watch as the engineers jeeped a load of explosives into the Pass. "Get going."

The lieutenant-colonel nodded. "We'll be waiting for you on the road."

Five minutes later, the recce jeeps disappeared into the Pass. Climbing back into his own jeep, Moshe entered the Pass. He stood by and watched the first two charges fail to bring down enough wall to clear any distance. As the engineer officer began to place the third charge, Moshe took over with the comment, "I haven't time to tickle it." Under his direction, the charges were enlarged and quickly placed. Four hours later, he and his engineers had blown down the walls of Sharhai. It took another hour to clear the debris and then the column started through. By this time, Leon and the rest of the trucks had caught up with them. Moshe led the way through, headlights on, sitting in his jeep and watching the sides of the larger trucks scraping the walls as they traversed the four hundred yards of narrows.

No sooner had he reached the far side of the Pass than he heard the radio behind him. The recce detachment had stopped just north of Ras Nusrani. The route was good. It had been marked with care.

Snorting, he told her to get back to the radio and then he started the column moving again. They had not been on the road for an hour when he spotted the Dakota flying low overhead. Glancing over his shoulder, he waited for the girl's report.

"He says he is the husband of the judge."

Moshe shook his head. "Tell him I said, 'Good for him.' " And he waited for the exchange to end.

"He told me to tell you they're going to close down the war while you're still on the road. And the Chief of Staff wants to know why you're sitting on your hands."

Moshe thought about the comment, and then told the girl, "Tell him we didn't know there was a war on."

A moment later the girl reported, "Zvi Mazon is coming down the east side of the peninsula. Avi wants to know which one of you is going to get to Sharm el Sheikh first."

"Tell him that if he knows a better war, he can go to it." He thought a moment and added, "I'll give him Sharm el Sheikh as a present tomorrow and I'll bring back some Egyptian souvenirs for his sister-in-law."

Puzzled, the girl transmitted the message.

Looking up, Moshe watched the Dakota slowly rise and head north again. Under his breath he cursed the notion of a race between himself and Zvi. He almost told the girl to get Avram back and tell him that he did not think this was the moment to play games, changed his mind and looked about.

The long column was moving rapidly over the broken country. There were heights to his right now and the sea to his left. He wished the Egyptians had had enough initiative to build a road, but then he was pleased with their lack of initiative. For the next hour while they raced south, he wondered why there had been only one attempt at an ambush and why the Egyptians had fled so quickly.

Suddenly, they flowed into the flat land which surrounded Ras Nusrani.

Ahead and along the coast he could see the Arab position. Several well-constructed and well-fortified buildings. Off to the west he could make out his recce vehicles, and then he saw Leon coming toward him.

Waving down the convoy, Moshe pressed on to join his C/S.

"I've been looking at the place," Leon volunteered.

"And?"

"It's what we thought. A perfect fortress."

"So?"

Leon shrugged. "It's going to be hell to take."

Moshe nodded, accepting the evaluation. His head dropped back and he looked at the sun, almost directly overhead. The sky was clear. There were no clouds. Off to the east he could hear the sound of waves on the shore. A look at his watch and he made up his mind. Twisting about in his seat, he told the girl, "Contact the Piper and have them tell headquarters I want an air strike on Ras Nusrani at 1200 hours." Leon agreed.

"Want me to go in?"

Moshe shook his head. "We'll tell them we're going to bomb and then we'll see what happens."

Running back to his jeep, Leon sped off toward the enemy fort. For the next ten minutes he broadcast the warning to the Arabs, and then he returned.

"They won't answer."

Stepping out of his jeep, Moshe glanced upward once more. They sky was suddenly clouding over. Pointing to the clouds, he said, "That may not be too bad. If headquarters was right when we left, we could get bombed by the Saudis," and he gestured to the land mass on the far side of the Gulf of Tiran. "Those clouds might just help us."

Surprised, Leon asked, "You've been expecting a bombing?"

"No. But HQ was."

After telling Mitra what he wanted her to relay to Tel Aviv, he and Leon walked down to the water. It was a brighter blue than either of them had expected. The shoreline was rocky and, scrambling up to a height, Moshe pointed out some fish in the clear water below. "If we had time, we could get some fresh food."

At the sound of a plane overhead, both men looked up. Moshe shrugged and made his way back to his jeep.

"The Piper says that Zvi Mazon might beat us in."

Moshe shrugged. "I'll take bets on that."

Leon shook his head. He had known both brigade commanders for longer than a decade and he was not going to pick one over the other.

Then they heard the sound of planes. Looking up, neither of them could see anything but dark clouds. Even the sun was gone now. Looking eastward, Moshe noticed that the sea suddenly seemed black. Then he heard the whine of falling bombs, thought for a moment to alert his troops and then stopped where he was. Unseen planes were striking at the fortress. A collapsing wall shuddered the earth. Another bomb and then another. The fortress was stronger than Moshe had expected, but he recalled Leon's description. "Perfect." For the next fifteen minutes the bombers struck at their target and then they were gone.

Shaking his head to clear it, Moshe snapped, "Send a platoon in there and let's bypass it. I'll meet you at Sharm el Sheikh."

Five minutes later he had the convoy on the road again. It was paved now and they were moving rapidly. He saw the platoon peel off and head toward Ras Nusrani and then Leon's jeep passed his and headed for the van to rejoin the recce unit.

Leaning back, Moshe told the girl behind him, "Contact the Piper. Tell them to get the landingcraft moving. I want all four tanks at Sharm el Sheikh."

A short time later he heard firing and ordered, "Get going."

Once more Leon was coming toward him and as he looked beyond the jeep, Moshe could see a black hill. Glancing at his map, he saw that it rose a hundred and five meters. Beyond it was Sharm el Sheikh and the large guns which had blocked the Strait.

Leon's jeep swirled about in the dust and kept pace with his. "There are troops this side of the hill," he shouted.

Moshe nodded, leaned back and told the girl, "Contact headquarters and tell them I want air support now."

Five minutes later, he pulled up next to the half-tracks of the recce detachment. Pointing out the areas he wanted covered, he instructed his battalion commanders where they were to take their men. Kneeling on the ground, he read his map with care. He was standing about three kilometers from Safra el At. There was a roll of low hills between him and the black hill. Assuming the Arabs were going to make a stand on these hills, he told his men they were to move in and take the hills when the air support arrived.

At 1400 hours the Mustangs came over, strafing the hills. They made several passes before they rose high, rocked their wings and disappeared northward. Puzzled at the absence of clouds now, Moshe paused to think about this, and then he forgot the problem and shouted for his battalion commanders to get moving. For the next five minutes the Egyptians acted as though they planned to hold the ground. Their machine guns were well placed and they stood firmly.

Suddenly the land ahead became silent.

The enemy was gone.

Pleased that they had no desire to fight, Moshe started through the hills. As he passed down the macadam road, he saw several dead and dying Egyptian soldiers. "Tell the medics to see what they can do for them," he instructed the girl behind him and his attention was drawn to the black hill which rose above the others.

Moshe met part of his recce unit coming back toward him.

Leon leaped out of the first half-track. "They've got a defense line set up around the town. Not much of one, but there are trenches, emplacements, wire and mine fields." He nodded toward several Egyptians being hauled out of one of the recce half-tracks. "Picked these up on our way back from the town."

"Anything?" Moshe asked.

"As far as I can tell, they gave up Ras Nusrani the night before last. They're just arriving here."

Moshe walked to the top of the black hill, and looking down toward Sharm el Sheikh and its cluster of huts, barracks and scattered sheds, he wondered where Leon had got the notion there was a city. A moment later he was evaluating the defensive position of the Arabs.

Their lines were not well drawn. Their defenses looked impressive, but he could see that they were not prepared to defend from the direction he was approaching. He suddenly realized that they had never expected an army to come through the terrain he had crossed. He remembered what he had read of Singapore when the Japanese had taken that bastion by coming in the wrong way. When Leon joined him, he indicated where he wanted his battalions. "One from the sea to the road, and the other from the road to the hills," he explained.

"When do we move?"

Moshe knelt on the hilltop and weighed the dying sunlight. "We'll never get planes here in time to count on air support tonight. And if we wait, then the troops which they withdrew from Ras Nusrani will be dug in." He looked up at his C/S for comment.

Leon smiled, "I sometimes think we've forgotten how to fight in the daytime."

"It takes getting used to," Moshe agreed. "Get the artillery in place and we'll move out when they're set to fire."

Leon trotted off the hill, leaving Moshe alone.

Rising to his feet, Moshe saw a wire running past him. Bending down, he picked it up. His eyes followed its line from some place to the north and then in the other direction toward the town.

Shouting for his driver and Mitra Glasner, he watched while his men below moved into position to attack. A few minutes later the signals lieutenant joined him.

Kicking the wire at his feet, Moshe asked, "Can you tie into that?"

The young woman knelt, lifted the wire and nodded.

"Do it," Moshe ordered. "And when you're getting your equipment, find out if there is anyone who knows Arabic well."

Ten minutes later a telephone was patched into the Arab line and an Israeli who had spent much of his life in Cairo was talking to the Egyptian commander of Sharm el Sheikh.

"Tell him that we have him surrounded, outnumbered and outfought," Moshe ordered. "Suggest that he quit now and save his men."

It was already so dark that Moshe could no longer see his own men below. Then the Egyptian Jew was telling him, "The Egyptian was indignant."

Moshe cocked his head to one side. "So?"

"Says he will fight and save the honor of the Egyptian army." Silence as the man listened once more to the phone. "He says that Nasser has given him permission to remain."

"Tell him . . ."

But the other man was shaking his head. "He hung up."

"So be it," Moshe agreed. He looked toward the sea and then he tried to recall the landscape as he had seen it just before darkness settled in. The Signals Officer and the interpreter were both surprised to hear him snarl grimly. "The bastard got permission all right. There weren't any ships or trucks to haul his ass out of here."

Looking about, Moshe saw his bodyguard standing a few paces away, an Uzi resting on his hip. Then one of the girls from the signals unit came up the hill with a pot of coffee and behind her Moshe's driver was carrying a small radio. Accepting a cup of coffee, the brigade commander slipped his fieldglasses off his neck and covered the terrain as well as he could in the semi-darkness. The hills were against his men, and he had fears about starting this attack without air cover.

A moment later he heard the first of his artillery pieces fire. The attack began. The artillery picked up its pace and then Moshe heard the mortars exploding over the enemy positions. In the darkness he could make out a line of his men moving in from the western direction toward what was obviously an Egyptian mine field. One mine exploded. Then another. The Arab machine-gun fire was heavy now, and the Arabs were returning the mortar fire. Moshe watched while his men recoiled and then moved forward again. The line of barbed-wire fence was in front of them now and they could not breach it. Heavy machine guns bracketed the Jews between their objective and a supporting position nearby. From the top of the black hill, Moshe could see his men fall, and without turning toward the girl at his side, he ordered, "Tell them to withdraw now."

Watching his men fall back, he was satisfied he was doing the right thing at this moment. He looked at his watch. 0420 hours.

"Contact headquarters and tell them I want air support at dawn." He thought a moment and added, "They can come in from any direction, but they have to keep clear of my men moving in."

Machine-gun fire again, and he could see the half-tracks collecting the wounded and dead below.

Leon joined him.

"I briefed each of the units as they arrived," the deputy commander reported. "If anyone gives a damn about the record, we started at 0300."

Moshe knew that Leon was not thinking about the time the attack had begun, but of the losses.

"All told, nineteen casualties."

Taking a deep breath, Moshe nodded. He could hear the girl talking to someone over her radio, and he picked up his coffee again as he thought about his plans.

"We can't dig in here," he decided. "Tell the battalion commanders to withdraw out of range until morning."

The girl passed his orders on.

Turning to Leon, Moshe explained his thinking. "They've concentrated on the line between the road and the hills. We'll move in from there, but have our main strike from the other side of the road." He thought about what he had said. "Just be sure the two battalions don't start shooting at each other as they come together in the town."

Leon nodded.

"We'll lay down fire, use the air support and then cover the recce jeeps with the half-tracks and break in."

Again Leon nodded. "I'd better get the men in position to move."

Moshe thought about this. "Let the battalion that just got hit rest until the last minute." He was looking at his watch and then at the girl on the ground. "Tell them we want the air strike at O-five-thirty hours." Then he looked at Leon, who understood that was as much for his information as the air support's.

And Moshe was alone now with his bodyguard and radio operator. Dropping to one knee, he finished his coffee and set down the canteen cup. His fieldglasses swung across his chest as he rocked back and forth. Less than an hour to battle and he had to take the town this time. For a long time,

442

Moshe tried not to think of the battle ahead and he had no difficulty bringing his thoughts to focus on Zipporah. He had promised her a souvenir. He would have to remember that. Sighing, he wished he was with her now and she was in her bed.

His eyes closed again. He would like to sleep. He knew he could not. Then the face of Zippy disappeared from behind his eyes and he held the terrain of Sharm el Sheikh before him. The hills were not too high. Nor were they well defended. The emplacements could be cracked. Without opening his eyes, he said loud enough for the girl to hear, "Tell Leon to be sure we have enough bazooka shells available to the western assault."

When he opened his eyes, he could see the first streaks of lights in the sky. Then he came to his feet as he heard the Mustangs approaching. For the next hour he stood on the hill watching the battle he had set in motion. The planes rocketed the enemy positions and followed up with machine-gun fire. He watched the jeeps and half-tracks moving out along the western line of the road, taking enemy positions as they pushed toward the town. And turning, he could see the second battalion moving on the other side of the road advancing parallel to the east. The firing off toward the small harbor was heavy, and Moshe scanned the location with his glasses. One emplacement holding out. The firing along the rest of the line continued, but he kept his eye on the harbor. In his glasses, he picked up a jeep racing toward the emplacement and held his breath as one of his men fired a bazooka. An instant later the Egyptian gun fell silent.

Looking up, he saw the planes diving toward the town once more, strafing the positions between the Egyptian line and the buildings. Now he was watching his recce jeeps moving down the road and into the center of the town. Off to the east he could still hear enemy guns and, turning toward them, he saw that some of his men were pinned down in a crossfire. The girl behind him was talking to someone, and he wished he could think, and then she was telling him the tanks had arrived and their commander wanted to know what he should do.

Moshe said softly, "Tell him to silence the last emplacement there to the east."

And he watched as the four tanks off the landing craft rolled toward the last of the enemy pillboxes. Four cannon shots and the emplacement fell silent. Taking a deep breath, Moshe strode from the hill, stepped into his jeep waiting below and started toward the town. The planes were already on their way home. His men were rounding up the prisoners. He passed both his own and the enemy dead on the road.

Leon emerged from an enemy emplacement. Slowing the jeep, Moshe picked up his deputy and entered the town, where the Israeli soldiers were trying to sort out the Egyptians who had already surrendered their weapons from those who had not. A strange sound and Moshe looked around. Sheep. He turned to Leon for an explanation.

"I guess they like fresh meat."

Shaking his head at the thought of an army keeping its own herds in the field, Moshe said, "Give the prisoners our rations and let's have some fresh lamb tonight."

He paused and, turning to Leon, ordered: "The recce commander who spilled stupidly into Dahab, the supply officer who forgot the grease and the engineer who can't blow a wall—I want all three of them out on the first plane that puts down."

Startled, Leon wanted to protest, but when he saw the cold glare in Moshe's eyes, he merely said, "All right, but I think you're wrong."

"Men like that get people killed," Moshe growled as they drove on.

He saw a clearing in front of what he assumed was the Egyptian headquarters building because his men were already striking the black, red and green flag. Watching a moment, he told his driver, "Pick up that Egyptian flag. I promised it to someone."

Turning, he noticed a trimly uniformed Egyptian officer standing beside half a dozen pieces of luggage. Leaving his jeep, Moshe approached the man.

"You commanded here?"

The Egyptian Colonel drew himself up to full height and glared at the lean Jew with the several days' growth of beard and dirty uniform.

"I commanded here."

"Good," Moshe said in the best Arabic he could muster. "I've accepted your surrender." There was a trace of a grin on his face as he walked past the Egyptian officer and started toward the building. However, he had gone no more than a few paces when he swung back.

"When did you pack those?" he asked, pointing to the luggage.

"Why, last night, of course," the Arab explained, baffled that there should be any question.

Looking askance at Leon, Moshe entered the concrete block headquarters. His Signals Officer was already waiting for him there. "Get a message off to the Chief of Staff." He looked at his watch and then at Leon and the Signals Officer. "At O-nine-thirty hours, 5 November, Sharm el Sheikh is in my hands. It is closed and finished with the help of the Creator."

He saw the dubious expression on Leon's face and asked simply, "If I can't quote the Bible now, when can I?"

Half an hour later he walked back into the street to meet the first of Zvi Mazon's men entering the town from the west. Five minutes later the two brigade commanders embraced in the middle of Sharm el Sheikh.

"I think we've won a war," Zvi said.

Looking up at a Dakota approaching from the north, Moshe nodded. "I know it's done now. Headquarters is about to arrive."

Both of them laughed.

NEW YORK

The war in the Middle East was over for more than a week and the Secretary-General of the United Nations was weary. Days and nights of debate had taken their toll and the mystical-minded Scandinavian wanted a vacation. However, the letter just handed him by the Israeli ambassador was one of many items he had to read before he returned to his apartment and his own private thoughts. Glancing out the window, he stared for a moment at a tourist boat, took a deep breath and started to read: Letter dated 13 November 1956, from the representative of Israel to the President of the Security Council. It reported in detail twenty-six raids by Arab terrorists into Israel, from Jordan, Syria, Lebanon and Egypt between November 6 and November 13.

SHARM EL SHEIKH

On the morning of 16 March 1957 a young Israeli colonel turned over Sharm el Sheikh to four members of the United Nations Emergency Force. Standing near the Strait of Tiran, the sun bright on his face, the young officer informed the Danish commander who was replacing him, "If you are not able to hold the Strait open, we will have to return." He saluted, about-faced and walked directly to his waiting plane. That same day the Israelis turned over the Gaza Strip and other occupied territories to the United Nations on the pledge that UN forces would maintain the peace.

Book IV
SPRING, 1960 | SPRING, 1963

JERUSALEM, 1960

The diploma read: ZVI MAZON, MASTER OF ARTS IN HISTORY, and as he stared at it, Zvi smiled to himself. There had been times these past few years when he thought he would never graduate. He was thirty-five now, and if the army had not been cooperative, he knew he would not have been able to spend the time since the Sinai war at the university. Stepping back from the wall where he had just hung the diploma, he continued to smile. Only the sound of Aaron talking to one of his friends in the other room brought Zvi back to the present. By the clock on the dresser, he knew he had to get ready if he was going to join Moshe and Zipporah who had come to Jerusalem to help him celebrate. His eyes wandered from the clock back to the diploma: MASTER OF ARTS IN HISTORY. Zvi was proud of the degree, but now he had some doubts. He had four or five more years in the army, if he were lucky, and after that he would have to make a new career for himself. And just how much use would this degree be? He shook his head. He had gone after the knowledge he wanted, and he was not going to denigrate it. A sound at the door and he turned. Aaron. The boy laughed at his father's obvious enjoyment with himself.

"Oh, Learned One, can I go out to the movie with Carmi tonight? We'll go over to his house for something to eat afterward, and I won't be late. May I?"

The boy winked at his father, and Zvi nodded. Aaron was not going to be as tall as most of his own friends. At fifteen he stood only five feet, and Zvi did not think he weighed much more than one hundred pounds. His thin face and dark eyes reminded Zvi of Havah. And he always had trouble remembering that Aaron was not really her child. He was thinking about Havah when the boy asked again, "Well, can I go?" Then because he was not certain his father wanted him out at night, he said again, "Won't be late."

"And what's all this going to cost me?"

The boy cocked his head to one side and Zvi wanted to laugh at the unconscious use of one of his own habits. "Four pounds?"

"Two pounds?" his father countered.

447

448

"Three pounds," the boy bargained.

"When I was your age . . ." Zvi started to say, and then they laughed at what had become an old joke.

Taking the three pound-notes from his pocket, Zvi said, "Enjoy yourself but be home early."

Aaron held the three notes in his hand for a moment, and then he looked up at his father. "We're going to stay here now that you have it?" and he was pointing to the diploma.

"Would it make any difference?"

The boy considered the question, then he shrugged, "I don't know. I like Jerusalem, but if we were to go back to Tel Aviv, there's Ruth . . ." His voice trailed off.

Zvi knew Aaron was not thinking of Ruth as much as he was thinking of her daughter, Hannah, and at fifteen maybe the boy was as precocious as his teachers kept saying. However, it had been Ruth with whom Aaron had lived most of the time during the years before the war, and it was to Ruth he still turned when he wanted a woman's view of something. "We'll see where I'm posted," Zvi said. "It's kind of out of my hands."

"But you're a colonel and a master of arts," Aaron reminded him.

It was difficult for Zvi to keep from smiling. "Well, there are a few men in the army with higher ranks." He was tempted to add that the others had not fought Mitla, but Aaron had heard enough about Mitla, which was still remembered as a disaster. One classmate or another would mention it or an angry adult would ask if Aaron Mazon was the son of Zvi Mazon. It had not happened often lately, and there was no reason to bring the matter up now.

"I'll see you later," and then Aaron ran out as his father shouted after him, "Early."

An hour later Zvi met Moshe and Zipporah at a restaurant on King George Street. In the four years since the end of the Sinai campaign, Moshe had aged more than anyone else Zvi knew. His friend's face had taken on lines which appeared as crags, his eyes seemed to set more deeply in his browned face and his hair was almost all white now. And yet in spite of his appearance, Moshe Gilead was as active and well as he had ever been in his life. For the past two years he had served as chief of staff of the Southern Command and had spent as much time in the field as he had before. Zvi noticed that as Moshe held Zipporah's chair, he could not refrain from touching her. Zipporah's reaction was a soft smile when Moshe settled in the seat beside her at the table. Her hand came out and covered her companion's. Zvi was aware that he had never met a pair with such complete sexual involvement. Not shy of women himself, he was nevertheless always conscious how much Moshe and Zipporah seemed to need to touch each other, to make contact physically as though they were not certain there was any other bond between them. And yet he believed that Moshe in his own way loved her. Ever since

Zipporah had moved out of her sister's house and into her own apartment, Moshe had paid the expenses and none could understand why they did not marry. Zvi had once broached the subject to Moshe, who had shaken his head in astonishment because, as he said at the time, "We never thought about it." And now as he watched Moshe's strong fingers lock with Zipporah's, Zvi did not believe either of them had really thought about marriage yet.

After the waiter had taken their order, Zipporah asked Zvi what he was going to do next.

Picking up the spoon beside his hand, Zvi slowly turned it around and around. After a long time, he said, "I don't know. I imagine your brother-in-law will find something for me or already has."

"Avi?" Zipporah asked.

Zvi smiled, "Do you have another one?"

The girl laughed and, shaking her head, settled her long brown hair about her shoulders. "You know I never really think of Avram in that way."

"How do you think of him?" Moshe was curious.

Zipporah tamped a cigarette on her thumb and then let Moshe light it before she answered. "Avram keeps my sister pregnant and happy. How the hell can I think of him as Director of the Chief of Staff's office?"

"Pregnant and happy," Moshe repeated the description with a smile. "Maybe that's what you want?"

Her hand was closed on his again, and Zvi was lighting a cigarette so that he did not have to watch them. "What's your love life these days?" Zipporah asked, and he almost dropped his lighter.

"My love life?"

Zipporah grinned at his startled expression. "From what I've heard of Colonel Zvi Mazon over the years, I have trouble envisioning him a celibate."

Zvi looked at Moshe and shook his head in mock sadness. "The very young are very brash. Can you imagine asking someone your father's age about his sex life?"

Moshe seemed to ponder the notion before he shook his head. "But then you're not really her father's age."

Zipporah laughed, "No one's answered my question."

Relaxing, Zvi said, "I'll let Moshe tell you about his."

"I think I know about his."

"You aren't sure?" Moshe asked.

She smiled at him. "Any woman who trusts you completely is a fool."

Moshe shook his head. "They all think they know all there is to know about men."

"Even the very young," Zvi agreed.

"Drop the 'young' bit," she snapped. Then, as though she were curious, "Do you like your women 'very young'?"

Zvi could see that Moshe was considering answering the question and was puzzled. There was no doubt Moshe Gilead was thinking seriously about the age of the women he liked.

Zipporah noticed this, also, and for a moment she, too, fell silent. Then she nervously brushed her hand over the hair on her shoulders. She was bright-eyed, petite, and yet not small. There was a quickness about her as well as a vitality which fascinated Zvi. Shifting the subject from youth, she asked, "Is there anything to the delightful rumor, Zvi, that you have a beautiful and wealthy Arab mistress?"

Embarrassed, Moshe tried to brush her question aside, "Why can't you think of anything else?"

Very slowly Zipporah tapped the ash from her cigarette into a tray before she smiled at him. "I'll think of something else when you do."

Feeling uncomfortable, Zvi tried to ignore her interest in sex. Since the war he had met a few women at the university. He had slept with several of them. He had lived with one for two weeks before she let her grades slip and was forced to leave school. Another was from France, and though they had difficulty talking, it was not conversation that interested them, and so they had got along wonderfully until she learned that he had a son, and then somehow, she lost interest in him. If he were going to be honest with Zipporah, he would have to admit he had had no love life at all in recent years, and for reasons he would have had difficulty explaining, he was not certain he wanted to be involved with anyone.

Gesturing for the waiter, Moshe ordered champagne. "We're celebrating," he reminded the others.

But Zipporah was not to be put off. "About that beautiful Arab girl, Zvi?"

Picking up her words, he mused aloud, "Beautiful Arab girl? Yes, I knew one once." Then with a sad smile he mocked, "But that was long ago and far away."

"You've traveled?" Zipporah asked, and for the first time Zvi realized she probably had not, and that Moshe had not either as far as he could recall. In fact, it struck him that many of his friends had spent most of their lives in Israel.

And to his surprise, he was saying, "Traveled? The only person I ever knew who really traveled widely was Fishel." His hand came out on the table before him as he fell silent and watched the smoke rise from his cigarette without seeing either the cigarette or the smoke. The name meant nothing to Zipporah, and it took Moshe a moment to realize that this was the first time in four years he had heard Zvi mention the violinist who had died at the Mitla.

Quickly moving the conversation past this point, Moshe said, "Zvi's traveled. He's been through Yemen. He's been to France."

"And Moshe's traveled," Zvi said picking up the conversation. "He's made a round-trip to Sharm el Sheikh."

They all laughed and then fell silent while the waiter poured champagne.

When they were alone again, Zipporah softly began to sing as she turned the stem of the glass between her fingers:

Beyond the Edom Hills and far away,
A rock, a red, red rock is said to lie;
So beautiful, and yet the legends say
That anyone who looks at it will die.
Oh, rock of evil fame, red as flame.

One morning three young men, so bold and brave,
Went walking out into the desert dawn;
They knew the shifting sand could be their grave
And yet the rock, the red rock drew them on.

The two men listened to her for a moment before Zvi warned almost coldly, "One doesn't sing that."

She leaned forward as though she were reaching for another cigarette. However, instead she looked upward into his eyes as she stretched half across the table.

"Why not?"

Zvi appealed to his friend for support. Moshe's jaw set stubbornly and the creases on his face seemed to grow deeper.

"Why not?" Moshe also asked.

Looking from one to the other, Zvi said simply, "It's not a joke. I can't think of any way in which it's funny."

"That's no answer," Zipporah told him.

Taking a deep breath, Zvi decided he had to find out if Moshe was serious, because if he was, both of them could be in danger. "The minister of defense has asked that the song be forgotten. They have said that it can only cause trouble." And now Zvi was staring at Moshe while the girl sang a few lines softly in defiance.

They walked until the desert moon was high,
And then into a valley dark they came;
And there across the border they could spy
The rock, the rock as red as leaping flame.
Oh, rock of evil fame, red as flame.

When Moshe did not respond, Zvi reminded him, "That was an order from on top."

Moshe's hand closed over Zipporah's as he leaned forward pushing his glass aside for the moment. "You're right, Zvi. You're right. Petra isn't in Israel, and for us it's like something the military police put a sign on which reads 'Off Limits.' I'll agree with you there. But just because it is in Jordan and just because the Arabs will kill anyone who tried to go there . . ."

"Have killed . . . ," Zvi reminded him.

"All right, 'have killed.' Is that a reason why we should be afraid even to sing a song?"

Having learned what he wanted to know, Zvi wanted to end the conversation, but Zipporah asked, "You studied history. What is the Red City?"

Zvi considered not answering, and then he decided the question was an honest one. "Sometime, probably a hundred years or more before the Common Era the Nabateans built it." He shook his head. "I guess I shouldn't say 'built.' Carved it out of red rock at the end of a mile-long pass through the mountains. There are those who think that Petra was the center of a world trading operation. There are some who say the Nabateans kept pirated treasure there. There are some who say they made a holy city of it." He shrugged. "Maybe all of that is true. The Greeks were there, and the Romans knew Petra. And then somehow it got lost."

"Imagine a city getting lost," Zipporah said softly, but Zvi did not want to hear the fascination in her voice.

"In the early nineteenth century, about 1812, a Swiss traveler found it. There were others a few years earlier who had heard tales about it from the Arabs, but they hadn't tried to find it. This Burckhardt came onto it and wrote about it. Said it was carved out of solid rock. A whole red city carved out of red rock, and only about forty miles south of Jerusalem. But there weren't many rushing to get there because it took government permissions and all kinds of transportation and the Arabs were marauders, and so those who did get there had to pack in and move with guards."

As much as he tried to keep the awe out of his own voice, he was surprised that it kept slipping in. "Pliny, Strabo and other Roman writers described life in the Red City after the Romans had entered." He closed his eyes and quoted, "It is situated in a spot that is surrounded and fortified by a smooth and level rock, which externally is abrupt and precipitous, but within there are abundant springs of water both for domestic purposes and for watering gardens. Beyond the enclosure the country is for the most part a desert, particularly toward Judea."

He was brought up sharply by Zipporah's angry snort. "You studied it and you tell me not to talk about it."

Zvi smiled at her tolerantly. "When I took my exams last month, I was warned there would be a question on the subject, and I thought I should be able to answer it." Reaching out, he picked up the champagne bottle and was filling her glass again when the waiter brought their dinner.

The three were silent while they watched the old man in the dinner jacket serve, and after he left them alone once more, Zipporah picked up her glass and toasted, "Zvi Mazon, Master of Arts."

Moshe joined in the toast, and as Zvi was about to pick up his glass, he heard Zipporah reciting in a soft voice.

Beside the rock a silent sniper lay,
His flashing gun lit up the desert skies;
And three still figures at the break of day
Lay staring at the rock with sightless eyes.
Oh, three so cold and dead, cold and dead.

His eyes met Moshe's as he suddenly remembered that Moshe was stationed in the Southern Command — the only Israeli approach to Petra — and that Zipporah was living there with him. "Don't," he warned. "Just don't either one of you try it."

Three days after he had celebrated his graduation, Zvi received his assignment. It was not what he expected. But then, as he was later to say, it was not an assignment anyone would have expected.

After calling Avram Ben Ezra at Hakiryah, he was told to remain in Jerusalem until he was ordered in. When the call finally came through, he arranged for Aaron to spend the night at a friend's and drove directly to headquarters.

TEL AVIV, 22 MAY

The sentry at the gate stopped him to check his identification, and Zvi wondered if he should have come in uniform. However, when Avram's secretary led him into his old friend's office, the uniform seemed unimportant.

After the friends shook hands and exchanged pleasantries, Zvi pulled out a cigarette and lighted it while he waited for Avram to move the conversation in a serious direction.

"Zvi, Moshe and Zippy," Avram began. "How much do you know about what's been happening there?" The staff officer's right hand closed on his left shoulder as he sat back, rocking the small chair on its hind legs, waiting for a reaction.

Zvi watched the smoke from his cigarette before he asked, "Why?"

The question to answer a question brought a smile to Avram's face. "There have been more crossings into Jordan in the past few months, and we're afraid it could build into trouble." He shook his head and continued. "That's not all of it." He fell silent as he considered with care what he had to say. Finally, "It's Malin. She was told that Zippy was interested, has been talking about Petra." He brought his chair back on its four legs. "You know one of her girl friends was killed going in there?"

"I didn't know." Zvi continued to watch the smoke rise. "You knew I was with Moshe and Zipporah the other night?"

"Aaron told me when I called to ask you over." His head came up and his palms closed together on the table. "How can I tell you the way Malin feels about her sister living with Moshe?"

"Don't try," and Zvi was thinking of that time so many years before when Malin had come upon Moshe in her own bedroom on her bed with a woman he had brought there. "Don't try," he repeated.

Avram accepted this. "This Petra business. How do you explain it?"

It took Zvi a moment to weigh an answer. "How do you explain a mystique to yourself or anyone else? Petra has taken on some kind of aura, some mystique. I've a notion, but certainly no answers."

Avram waited to be told the notion.

"We had the Haganah. We had the war in North Africa and Europe. We came home to Haganah again and the war in forty-eight. The war in fifty-six. These young people were in their middle or early teens then."

The staff officer seemed to understand. "You mean we've been challenged?"

Zvi nodded. "In one way or another, you and I and their parents have had a chance to prove ourselves if only to ourselves."

The idea seemed to satisfy Avram as a direction. "What you're saying is that they have nothing that can match our generation or even their fathers'."

Zvi nodded. "The Zippys never knew the camps and they never knew the wars. Somehow, in a way, we've made these young people feel inadequate." Zvi was not being modest when he added, "Not that we've done anything they wouldn't have if put to the test, but we've had the opportunity to do it."

"And so to prove themselves they're trying to get through the enemy to Petra." Avram accepted this, but Zvi himself was ready to shed some doubts on his own notion.

"I'm certain it's not all as neat as that, but I'm also certain that's part of it. If you could explain a mystique, it would not be a mystique."

Avram agreed, "But the journey to Petra, it isn't very wise."

Surprised at finding himself explaining anything to Avram, Zvi smiled, "We weren't talking about wisdom. We were talking about the nature of a mystique. Today Petra."

"And Zippy is thinking about it?"

"I didn't say that, Avi. I'm not going to breach her confidence or Moshe's. Don't ask me anything about their thinking." Then because he thought he had to explain, "I owe Moshe his confidence."

Avram looked quietly at his friend before shaking his head sadly. "That's a dubious kind of loyalty, but I think loyalty's a subject you will get deeply involved in for the next year or so."

Zvi's head cocked to one side as he tried to understand. "For the next year or so?"

A smile crossed Avram's face. "Eichmann's been found." And he enjoyed the startled expression on the field commander's face.

"Found? Alive or dead?"

"He's been found and identified in Argentina. You'll get the details later. Right now he is on his way here."

Trying to clear his head, Zvi closed his eyes long enough to consider the implications of Eichmann in Israel. Eichmann the director of the Final Solution. Eichmann whose name kept finding its way into the trials at Nuremberg. Eichmann who had not allowed a photograph of himself to be taken in the years between 1940 and the end of the war. Eichmann who had disappeared by the war's end. Eichmann of the six million dead. *Eichmann.* The name slammed its way about Zvi's mind. When he opened his eyes again, he asked, "It's true?"

"Caught five days ago. BG will announce it to the Knesset soon."

Taking another cigarette from his shirt pocket, Zvi paused before lighting it.

"Nuremberg. I didn't follow the trials closely. A word in the papers here or there. Something on the radio. Things people have said over the years. Just where he really fitted isn't too clear." Then, by way of apology, "I only know people think he was responsible."

"Responsible? That's a good word. Your job won't include that decision."

Zvi's head came up quickly. "My job? Where do I fit into this?"

Avram was enjoying himself and Zvi knew it. "There will be a trial. In the past the preparations for the trials have been done by historians and lawyers. It's been decided that the army's going to furnish some of the help for the prosecution. At first there was talk of our having an observer present, but the Chief of Staff decided the only way we would get a real answer — and the problem of loyalties and responsibilities will be involved — is to have someone deeply committed to the work itself and not just a bystander." He smiled again, "You're available, and so your services have been offered to the Ministry of Justice and have been accepted. You will help the prosecutor direct the documentation research."

Zvi shook his head slowly. "That could take years."

Avram nodded.

"This has got to be a joke," Zvi growled. "I'm a field commander. I've . . ." His hands came wide before him. "You know."

"I'm not going to brief you on your duties. In a few days the Chief of

Staff will, and if I had to guess, I would say the PM will want to talk to you himself." He fell silent. When he spoke again, he explained, "It's good, Zvi. Believe me. You're a kind of hero. The retaliation raids. And Sharm el Sheikh. And now as scholar. People will believe in you. They will trust it."

Pulling himself to his feet, Zvi stood looking down at his friend. "If I said I thought I was being used . . ."

"You would be right. That's what soldiers are for."

Zvi considered this. "That would be a good defense for Eichmann."

"No," Avram snapped. "Do you think our end is the same?"

"No," and Zvi shook his head. "No." Then he grinned crookedly. "People will trust me, you say. What about Mitla?"

"You were a soldier at Mitla. You had the right to err."

The crooked grin broadened. "And you still think I erred?"

Avram's large head bobbed back and forth. "But I, too, think you had the right to." He was on his feet now and, coming around the table, he placed one hand on Zvi's arm. "It's a good assignment and it's an important one." He dropped his hand and said, "The chief of staff is very happy you are the one able to take this on. It's a soldier's point of view he wants."

Zvi nodded slowly. "And this marks the end of my career?"

It took Avram a moment to realize what had been asked. "I wouldn't know," he finally admitted. "I don't think anyone can promise you anything until this is done, and then it will have to be weighed."

"I understand," Zvi admitted. "However, there are better-trained historians."

"But you're the one he picked and the PM approved." Avram grinned, "And besides there's an expediency. You're available."

After they settled the details as to whom Zvi would report and when, Avram said, "I'll be in Jerusalem next week. I wish you'd come over to the apartment so we can talk."

After he had accepted the invitation, Zvi walked down the stairs of the small house and stepped once more into the afternoon sun.

Leaving headquarters, Zvi drove his Peugeot to the dress shop. He found Ruth in her office checking over some papers. She let Zvi kiss her on the cheek and then she stared at him. "You don't look any different," she said before she embraced him and whispered, "Congratulations." She stepped back and added, "I'm proud of you. A historian."

Zvi smiled. "I'm not too sure it hasn't done me in."

Puzzled, she waited for him to explain.

"My new assignment isn't in the field."

"And you regret that?"

He nodded. "I think it's time I get back to the field. I've been a soldier longer than I've been a historian."

Both of them laughed.

"And Aaron?"

"He wants to see you. Said so the other day."

Ruth thought about this while she accepted a cigarette and let him light it. As she bent over toward the match, Zvi was aware of the swell of her dress and the soft sheen of her brown hair. Ruth had picked up a stylish manner and a trimness far beyond that of the girl he had known in the Old City. When she straightened up again, he reached out and touched the scar on her forehead. "It's almost gone."

She smiled. "People ask me about it and I tell them all kinds of wonderful lies. The lover who tried to kill me before he committed suicide. The Arab who tried to keep me in his harem and said I would die before I left it."

She was sitting on the edge of her desk now, her nylon-stockinged leg swinging back and forth.

Looking about the office, Zvi was aware that the furnishings had been changed since he had last visited it.

"Things are going well?"

Ruth smiled wryly. "Your investment is making a good profit."

Almost angrily, he snapped, "You know damned well that was not what I meant."

She saw that he was looking at her ankle and smiled gently. "Things are going well no matter how you want to look at them." Then almost brightly, "I'm going to the States in a couple of weeks. Taking over a new line of dresses to show buyers." Before Zvi could say anything, she asked, "How about Aaron's going with us? He'll only be gone a few months."

She watched as he slipped his hand inside his shirt. She could see the lines on his face now and the gray at his temples. Somehow, he looked stockier and larger than she recalled his being. Zvi knew she was looking at him, and he wondered how he felt about Ruth now and if he could ever forget the night he almost spent with her before he took his leave in Paris. She was closer to him than any other woman he knew. He had spent more time with her than any other woman. And they had so much in common — their children had grown up together and they had both been fond of Fishel. He was thinking of Fishel when she said, "You can afford to send him with the money we've made." And it took Zvi a moment to recall her offer to take Aaron abroad.

"I'll think about it," and his eyes were on her leg and he knew he was not in love with her and, as he had so many times before, he wondered why not.

"Zvi," she said softly, and his eyes came up and met hers. "You were lost somewhere back there."

He grinned. "Just looking," and he pointed at her ankle. Then as if the idea had just come to him, "We could have dinner before I start back."

She shook her head. "I've got a date tonight. Dinner and a concert and then . . ."

The last words were obviously intended to catch his attention, and he decided to ignore them.

"Another time," he said, smiling ingenuously. "I hope your date is serious."

Brushing back a lock that had fallen over her eye, Ruth looked at him dubiously. "You want to see me married off?"

Reaching out, Zvi touched her hair with an open palm and for an instant she rested her head against his outstretched hand.

"Just take care," he said affectionately.

She looked at him and then laughed more loudly than the occasion called for. "I'm a big girl now."

Zvi watched as she came to her feet and walked behind her desk. He thought she had become better looking as she had grown older.

"I meant that offer to take Aaron with me."

He nodded.

"And now . . ." He watched as she closed the books she had been checking and picked a gown from the rack behind her and stood holding it. "I've got to get dressed," she said, excusing him.

Embarrassed, he said, "I understand." But he did not move.

For a long time Ruth stood silently watching him, and she wondered if there were something wrong.

"Your friend Moshe was in town yesterday," she said, but he did not understand the non sequitur.

"He came in with that girl and bought her several dresses."

Zvi assumed she was talking about Zipporah.

"She's pretty and young." There was a touch of bitterness in her voice which brought his head up. "She hasn't got much here," she said, touching her own bosom. "But she may be fun in bed."

"I wouldn't know," he told her. "I just wouldn't know."

"I'm sorry," Ruth said drily, "I thought you two shared things like that."

Zvi's hands came up for a second as though he were going to do something with them. Then he let them fall. Half closing his eyes, he wondered if Ruth had always been envious of Zella. And then he wondered if she had been jealous of Moshe or himself.

"I'm glad things are going well," he said, and started out of the office. He had the door open when he heard her call.

"Zvi!"

He slowly swung about.

"Take care," she said softly. "You're not the one I'm angry at."

He nodded, tempted to ask why she was angry at Moshe and saw that she was getting ready to take off the dress she was wearing. "I'll let you know about Aaron," he promised, and closed the door.

JERUSALEM

The drive back to Jerusalem was not really as long as it seemed to Zvi. When he reached the outskirts of the city, he thought about going home, remembered that Aaron was sleeping at a friend's and tried to decide what he would do with himself. He had not eaten yet, but he was not hungry. Fifteen minutes later he parked near the YMCA Tower; and after slipping the guard at the door two pounds, he took the elevator to the roof.

He was alone. Below lay Jerusalem. He did not need to look at the map of the city spread out for tourists. The silhouettes of Mount Scopus and the Mount of Olives lay before him. Even in the semi-darkness he could make out the Mosque of el Aksa and the Dome of the Rock. And when he closed his eyes, he could see beyond within the Old City, the Wall itself as he had last seen it from a rooftop more than a decade ago. He took out a cigarette and lit it. He wondered when a Jew had prayed last at the Wall. From intelligence reports he had seen over the years, he knew the Jordanians kept a soldier on guard there as though they expected someone to intrude on its lonely silence. He wondered if the Arab sentry impressed the Christian tourists who came to view what the Jews held dear, and if those same tourists realized how much the Wall meant to the people who could not visit it even though treaties assured them the right.

Grinding out his cigarette on the stone before him, he stared into the darkness. Once he had promised he would go back to the Old City. Now he was being spun off his route, taken away from the field and made into something other than a soldier. Avram had said there would be no promises.

Flipping his cigarette over the edge of the roof, he continued to stare at the Old City. If Moshe, Zipporah and their friends wanted a challenge, let them try to reach something that mattered to them. And it was not Petra. He half smiled. Fishel would have understood that. And he knew that Ruth would. They had never discussed the Old City. They had not needed to. And yet only a few nights before when he had talked about Petra, others had listened as though it were important. He shook his head. The next time he met Zipporah, he would tell her about the Old City.

And when he got home, he wished Aaron were there, and then he thought about Ruth's offer to take the boy to the United States and he knew that if he said No it would be only because he himself was lonely and wanted Aaron's company. And so the next day, he called and told Ruth he was accepting her offer.

That same day the Prime Minister informed the Knesset that the

German, Adolf Eichmann, had been captured and was being brought to Israel. Before the day ended, Zvi received his order to report to the Ministry of Justice where he was to work as an assistant to the deputy prosecutor.

It was the last week in May when Colonel Mazon began his research at Yad Vashem — the Martyrs and Heroes Memorial Authority — in Jerusalem. While the Israeli police had established Special Bureau 06 for the purpose of ingathering and selecting the documents which would be used at the trial, his own work, as it had been explained to him, was to locate and isolate those documents which would be of value to the prosecution and to prepare a report for Zahal on a soldier's responsibility to superior orders.

Sitting in the small office which had been assigned to him, Zvi wondered where he was going to begin. It sounded simple: all he had to do was find basic information which would link Eichmann to his crimes, and after the trial write a report.

Zvi picked up the document describing information sources available and started to read it as he paced the room. A cigarette in one hand, the document in the other, he paused to stare out of the window.

Yad Vashem held mimeograph copies of all the documents from the German Foreign Office which in any way related to Jewish Affairs. Four hundred and eighty-five tons of paper. Closing his eyes for a moment, Zvi tried to imagine just how large that would bulk. Failing, he continued to read the history of the find. Many of the papers were going to be excluded from his research because they dated back to 1870. He considered this and found it interesting that the Germans had set up a Jewish Affairs office so long before Hitler's rise.

Tracing the history of the records, he learned that in 1956 microfilm copies of thousands of documents dealing with Jewish Affairs had been released to Yad Vashem. Zvi hoped that this included the copies of the Final Solution dossier. Flipping the page, he realized that though all of these papers had an identifiable source, they were going to be valuable only if they could be sorted and screened. Tossing the report on his desk, he stood wondering how he would ever be able to cope — there were thousands of them.

He left the building and slowly walked to the memorial and Avenue of the Righteous Gentiles.

There were few trees planted along the path leading up the Mount of Memory. Few, but important. He paused to read a name set in bronze at the base of a tree. A Polish name he did not recognize. The next tree was Dutch. Then a German. A French. Four Danish names. Men and women who had risked their lives to help Jews. Another Polish name. A Hungarian. Zvi paused on the path and looked back over the plaques he had read.

Then he looked up. The sky was bright. Overhead, a small white cloud scudded by. *Hungarian. Polish. Rrench.* He was positive the best way they could approach the task was by breaking it down into national areas. Some had suggested the project was going to be like a great jigsaw puzzle. And he knew that the only person who knew enough now to relate the pieces of the puzzle was not going to help them because that person was Adolf Eichmann.

And the next day Zvi had his specific assignment: Eichmann and the *Einsatzgruppen* — the murder battalions. Four days later he was still trying to frame the subject and find enough about its background so that he could even begin his research into the documents. At the end of his first week at Yad Vashem, he drove home convinced that the army had made a serious mistake assigning him to the Eichmann trial.

Parking his car in front of the apartment, he sat in it for a moment, watching Aaron playing soccer in the street with several of his friends. Aaron was the smallest of the group, but he was also the fastest. Feeling proud at the way the boy outplayed and outran the others, Zvi wished there was someone else to enjoy his son as much as he did.

Zvi believed the boy did not remember his actual parents, who had died on the road south from San'a. And if he did not remember them, he would not remember Havah. Zella? Zvi was not sure. He had his doubts. That left only Ruth and Shoshanna. He smiled at the thought of how many women there had been in Aaron's life already. His thoughts drifted back to Shoshanna. He had not heard her name in several years. After the Sinai Campaign, she had dropped him a note. He had wondered at the time if he was supposed to be pleased with her congratulations on his victory or the news that she was married and had a daughter.

Then Aaron came running up to the car, and Zvi was no longer thinking of Shoshanna.

That night, after he had made dinner for the two of them and Aaron had cleared the table, Zvi told the boy he was going to the United States for a few months with Ruth and Hannah. They were in the kitchen doing the dishes together, and when Aaron did not respond, Zvi looked to see the boy was wiping the same dish over and over.

"Something wrong with the United States?" Zvi finally asked.

"No, but . . ."

"But . . .?"

"Gee, traveling with two women. You know."

Trying not to laugh, he assured his son that there were other boys in America, and that he would not be alone with Ruth and her daughter all of the time. It took almost an hour to convince Aaron and after he had, Zvi asked, "Why were you so all fired up last week about going to Tel Aviv so we could be near them?"

The boy looked at his father curiously. "You know that being near them in Tel Aviv isn't the same as living with a woman."

Zvi agreed. The matter settled, they arranged to let Ruth shop for the clothes Aaron would need and buy the tickets for his passage.

In the days that followed, Zvi began his research. He started with *Trials of the War Criminals* which had been published after Nuremberg. Here he found the detailed transcript of the trial described as the *Einsatzgruppen* Case. All told, the International Military Tribunal had sat for over 1,200 days and the final transcript without the documents came to 330,000 pages. Day after day he read of the horror of the first Nazi execution battalions which had been set up in 1938, initially to function in the Sudetenland, then given the task of destroying the Jews of Europe. He found that to retain any sensitivity to the subject, he could only read for a few hours at a time. To break up his work, he would take a long walk out into the suburbs. During the fourth day of his reading, Zvi drove Aaron to the airport at Lod where they met Ruth and Hannah. For about half an hour the four of them stood by waiting for the plane. Finally when it was time to go, Zvi almost changed his mind, wanting to keep his son with him, until Ruth pointed out, "This job you've got, Zvi. It isn't one you should be discussing with a young man."

He walked the others to the plane, embraced his son, kissed Hannah on the cheek and then kissed Ruth goodbye.

Only after the plane left and he was driving home did he realize he had not seriously kissed Ruth in years. And as he passed through Ramla, he wondered once more if he had not made a mistake when he decided that he did not love her. He knew that not loving her was not what he was thinking about as much as not marrying her. Then he remembered her reactions to Moshe. He suspected that she was in love with his friend. And he felt sorry for her because he knew that she would never marry Moshe Gilead.

The next week he began to scan the microfilms of the archives in his search for material that related to the *Einsatzgruppen*. A week later, he knew that his primary sources were going to be few, because it appeared that *Einsatzgruppen* reports were not available after February, 1942. However, Himmler's "progress" reports to Hitler probably included this information. It was during this week that Zvi began to call on the services of the archivist and her staff, and he asked that an assistant be assigned to work closely with him. The next week Libby Rosen appeared in his office, explaining that she was supposed to help him. Shoving back his chair from the microfilm reader set up on his desk, he asked, "Know much about all of this?"

The young woman pulled up a chair and lighted a cigarette. "I've been here for five years. But about the *Einsatzgruppen*, the answer is practically nothing." She smiled, and for the first time he thought that she was not an ordinary-looking woman. Her face was thin and her hair, brushed back, looked as though she had not spent much time in a beauty shop. Zvi found himself staring at her and enjoying it.

"It was suggested that we could cover twice as much if we worked together," she told him.

"It's a dirty assignment," he warned. Then to make his point clearly, he explained, "The amount of work isn't the problem. It's what you find yourself reading. The other day I was going over an account by an American interviewer. He was talking to a German — a Dr. Ohlendorff — at Nuremberg, and the Nazi was giving his record. It all looked neat and clean. A year here and a year there, and all of it seemed innocent enough. Most of the work bulked in the Ministry of Economics. But the American officer spotted the fact that one year wasn't accounted for, and he asked the good German Herr Professor where he had spent that year." Zvi watched the woman knock the ash off her cigarette without taking her eyes off him. "The year had been spent commanding *Einsatzgruppen*. The American casually asks, 'How many did you kill that year?' and Ohlendorff states just as casually, 'Ninety thousand.' Just like that," Zvi concluded.

He was watching for a reaction and was almost pleased that he did not get one.

The young woman rose to her feet and walked over to the window where she stood thinking. When she finally turned back to look at Zvi, she said, "You must remember that the figures you will find with the *Einsatzgruppen*'s work will all be smaller than those found by the persons studying the camps."

Nodding, Zvi said, "I know that. The camps were only built when the murder battalions could not really do the job, or at least they could not do it as fast as the Germans wanted." He thought a moment and added, "There will be a chronology of actual orders which can be checked against operations."

A bitter expression came over the young woman's face for the first time. "Efficiency. They shifted the emphasis from guns to gas simply because they couldn't get it all done on schedule."

Zvi wondered if there was any civilized way of discussing the subject that did not somehow keep it at an intellectual distance. He voiced this after a moment.

"A distance," she repeated. "We have to keep it at some kind of distance or we would get so emotionally involved we could not work."

Zvi nodded. "What's your name?" he asked, knowing it was almost insulting not to have paid attention when she first introduced herself.

"I gather you have accepted me as your assistant."

"We'll try it for a time," Zvi agreed, aware that she had seen his oversight and knew he had not taken her seriously when she first came in.

"Libby," she said after a moment. "Libby Rosen."

"Where did you study?"

"In the States. Took both of my degrees there. I am half way through my doctorate, but I had to put it off for a time."

Deciding the reasons were none of his business, Zvi suggested, "You arrange to have another desk put in here tomorrow and another microfilm reader, and we'll see how fast we can get this job done."

He looked at his watch, "And in the meantime, can I take you to lunch? There are some things we might as well go over before you begin."

"I'll meet you out front in fifteen minutes," she offered.

As she started to leave the office, he said, "People call me Zvi."

Pausing, she smiled. "I've heard of you, Colonel Mazon." Then with an overt innocence, "You fought at Mitla, didn't you?"

He wondered if she was trying to put him in his place. But before he could answer, she was already out of the office. He thought about her comment and decided he was not going to get involved with Libby Rosen. Picking up the phone, he dialed Judge Ben Ezra's office, and after apologizing to Malin for not being able to see her and Avram the previous weekend, he proposed to see them the next time Avram came to Jerusalem.

"He's not due in until Saturday," she explained. "There's some kind of a conference going on over the water problems of the Jordan and there's a meeting taking place in the north." Then she told him, "Moshe Gilead's going to be there." At first Zvi did not know why she had bothered to tell him this. And then she asked, "If Zippy comes north with him, will you let me know how she is? She doesn't call me herself. She's embarrassed."

For a long moment, Zvi held the phone away from his ear and stared at it. When he answered, he said simply, "I've the uncomfortable feeling of being caught between friends."

" I understand. I just want to be sure she is all right and that she is not hurt too badly."

"Are you sure she is going to be hurt?"

"I'm sure," she said flatly. "He isn't going to change from the man we found in my bedroom that night."

"I'll let you know if anything seems wrong," he said. "That's all I can do."

"Thanks," and then before she hung up, she told him she would call him the next time she heard from Avi.

Half an hour later, Zvi took Libby into a small restaurant. As he held her chair for her, he was surprised to see that she was almost as tall as he, and as he walked around the table, he was thinking her figure was better than he had the right to expect from a historian. Lighting a cigarette, he decided that she was not as pretty as either Zella or Shoshanna.

When Zvi began to brief her on what he had already learned about the *Einsatzgruppen*, she interrupted.

"As far as I can make out from a good translation," she told him, "It means *operational*, not organizational, units as you have in your notes."

Realizing that she had spent part of the fifteen minutes before lunch checking up on him, Zvi smiled. "You keep right after me. If there is one thing we can't afford now, it is mistakes."

Then for the next hour, he explained the relationship of the *Einsatz-*

gruppen to the main office of Reich Security. "All of this was under Himmler, who held rank in both the army and the police." The waiter came over; and when Zvi had given their order, he continued his explanation. "Under Security was the Secret Police, then the Gestapo, and then the Criminal Police which they shortened to Kripo and finally the Security Service, or AD." He smiled. "One thing can be said, as it is always said about the Germans. They were well organized."

Realizing that he had failed to offer her a cigarette, Zvi fished into his shirt pocket for another. Accepting it, she leaned forward so that he could light it for her. He was conscious of the way her breasts were thrust forward under the clinging sweater she was wearing, and he tried to keep his attention on his lighter.

"Where does Eichmann fit into all of this?" she asked.

"Eichmann as chief of Amt IV B4, a part of Security, reported directly to its head."

"And the *Einsatzgruppen*?" she asked.

"Was under Security, under the same blanket that warmed Eichmann and was available for his uses."

She nodded and was about to ask another question when the waiter brought their lunch. While he waited to be served, Zvi looked about the small restaurant. There was no one he knew. Most of the people looked like government clerks. Jerusalem had become a seat of government and so, of course, there would be clerks. For a moment he almost resented finding himself in this milieu.

And as though she knew what he was thinking, Libby asked, "You would have preferred a field assignment?"

He nodded.

After lunch they returned to the archives and began screening everything that could possibly throw light on the history of the *Einsatzgruppen* and Eichmann.

Two days later Zvi received the call he had been expecting. Could he join Moshe and Zippy for dinner?

They met in the early evening at the King David Hotel. At Zipporah's insistence they sat for a time out on the open patio off the main lobby.

"I like to watch the tourists," she said. "They make me feel better."

Zvi knew she was being superior and decided to be tolerant. "Explain that."

"Most of them go around with a look of awe and wonder as though they had just discovered Israel and as if we hadn't been here all our lives." She smiled and added, "We've got the thing they've been searching for—a home."

Looking from one to the other, Zvi watched Moshe close his hand over hers. "A home? You sure as hell don't look matriarchal," Zvi chuckled.

Zipporah laughed with him.

466

After a time the three went into the dining room and while they ate, they discussed Zvi's work.

"How bad is it?" Moshe asked.

"We'll get it done," Zvi said. "And I'm sure we'll get him hanged."

"No!" Zipporah cut in.

"No what?" Zvi asked.

"You're setting out to hang him?"

Nodding, he explained, "I'm doing research for the prosecution. Let the German lawyers who have offered to defend him find their own information proving his innocence, if they can." He fell silent a moment. "It's not my job to be impartial."

Moshe toyed with the glass in front of him, "Just what the hell are you doing in all of this?"

Zvi noticed that Zipporah had moved her chair closer to Moshe's; and from the way she was looking at his friend, he assumed Moshe's other hand was on her leg.

"I asked what your job was," Moshe repeated.

Trying not to show that he was disconcerted, Zvi looked down. "The discussion I had with the Chief of Staff was brief. But I think I understand what he wants. It's this whole matter related to duty and orders." He fell silent for a time as he watched Zipporah's face. The girl enjoyed being with Moshe, and she had no desire to hide the fact.

"Duty and orders?" Moshe pressed.

Zvi nodded. "You recall Kfar Kassem?"

"I do," Moshe said. His hand had come off the glass and was closed on Zipporah's.

"What was Kfar Kassem?" she asked.

"A mistake," Moshe snapped.

"Possibly," Zvi agreed.

Impatiently, the girl asked, "What was it?"

Both men started to answer and Moshe fell silent, allowing Zvi to explain.

"At the beginning of Kadesh—the Sinai War—we set a curfew for the Arab villages in our area. Nothing they couldn't live with, and it was a way of being sure we were safe from domestic Arab problems during the war. However, right after the order went out, some Arabs who had probably never heard the word were returning to Kfar Kassem from their farms after the curfew. A detachment of our soldiers fired on them. In the years since then we've heard Arab propaganda calling Kfar Kassem a planned massacre."

"That's a lot of . . . " Moshe cut in.

"I agree," Zvi said, "but just the same some Arabs died. Now the question is, Were the men wrong firing on the Arabs who had remained out after curfew? They must have known these Arabs could not have been aware of the curfew to come out into the open and risk being killed. One argument is that they were obeying orders. Another argument is that the soldiers had to make their own decision and be responsible for their own act because they knew the moral implications of this one moment whereas the officer passing down a curfew order could not have foreseen this moment, and even if he had foreseen it, the deaths at Kfar Kassem were the responsibility of the soldiers there who carried out what might have been a bad—and by that I mean a morally bad—order."

Zipporah smiled. "Are you trying to say that what those men who fired on some Arabs one night in the dark, and maybe in panic, did, was the same thing Eichmann did?"

Zvi shook his head. "I'm just saying that we, as any other army, must try to define the responsibility of the man taking orders. In the case of Eichmann's orders—hell, they were part of a plan which he knew was going to kill millions. The intent and spirit were different as well as the circumstances."

"What happened to the soldiers at Kfar Kassem?" Zipporah asked.

"Court martialed and convicted." Moshe said flatly.

Zipporah looked from her lover to his friend. "And you," she asked Zvi, "have to see how all of this may or may not apply to the Israeli army?"

Zvi agreed. "Oversimplified, but that's part of the job."

Moshe laughed softly. "Maybe the chief of chaplains should be working on this instead of you."

For a long time Zvi was silent and then he admitted, "I've thought of talking to him about the subject."

"Oh, *gevalt!*" Moshe snapped. "You're a soldier. A dirt soldier." He fell silent as he thought about what he had said, "I'll admit you lost too damned many trucks getting to Mitla, but you did get there."

Zvi winked at Zipporah. "When does he have to go north to his conference?"

Moshe's head snapped up quickly. Then, realizing that he was being taunted, he looked at his watch. Bending over, he kissed Zipporah on the cheek, "I've got to be gone in ten minutes if I'm going to make it to Safed. I'll leave you to this . . . " and he took Zvi in with a broad gesture. "He'll see that you get a *sherut* back to Beersheba tonight." He looked to Zvi for agreement and his friend nodded.

"The pleasure will be all mine."

For the second time, Moshe hesitated, not quite certain how serious Zvi was until both Zipporah and Zvi started to laugh.

And ten minutes later, after Moshe was gone, Zvi took Zipporah outside onto the hotel patio again. They were alone. The air was cool; she drew a sweater about her shoulders while they both stood looking at the lights of Jerusalem.

468

"You grew up in the south, didn't you?" she asked.

Zvi nodded.

"And you've lived there since?"

He nodded again. "When I set up my battalion and when we built it into a brigade. I know Beersheba, and there are times when I think I've slept on every rock in the Negev."

She was not looking at him when she asked, "And you never wanted to go to Petra?"

He watched as she brought her hand up to her cheek as though it were warm.

"Petra?" He fell silent while he thought about the Red City.

"Did you?" she asked again.

Cocking his head to one side, Zvi looked at the girl. She came almost up to his shoulder. He guessed she was at least ten years younger than Moshe. In the light cast from the hotel windows, her skin seemed translucent and he knew that her eyes were a pale blue. She was small-boned, and he could tell from the way she moved she was conscious of her sex. The light brown linen dress she wore was cut to show off her figure, and even in the semi-darkness of the patio, he was aware of the shape of her breasts.

"Petra," she said impatiently. "Haven't you wanted to go there and see it?"

Moving back a step, Zvi perched on the edge of one of the patio tables. "Petra." He repeated the name. "Yes, I think there was a time when I was young that I thought it might be fun to see it."

"And now?"

He shrugged. "If I want to get killed, there are things I can do which would be of more use to myself and Israel. Most of all I want to go back to the Old City. But Petra—no."

Her head came up and she moved toward him, standing almost between his knees. "Are you afraid, Colonel Mazon?"

Zvi nodded. "There are things I'm afraid of. Dying isn't one of them. Being a damned fool is. Someone said there may be as many as fifteen thousand sites in this country to be excavated. For myself, I would say that figure was high. However, have you seen five thousand of them or ten thousand?"

She shook her head in disgust. "They aren't Petra," she argued.

"I know," he agreed, and as he spoke, he wished she would not stand so close to him and that he could back away still farther. He reached for a cigarette and brushed her breast with the back of his hand. She did not seem to notice. And then as she spoke, he understood why.

"Petra's not a place," she explained. "It's . . ." And her hands came wide.

Deciding he could not avoid touching her, he placed his hands on her shoulders and held her at arm's length. "You're supposed to be a bright young woman. I've heard people say that you may be the best thing that ever happened to Moshe. Don't," he warned. "Just don't. Not only could you get killed, but you know what he would do if you did."

To Zvi's astonishment, she smiled, brushed his hands off her shoulders by raising her elbows, and moving closer to him, wrapped her hands loosely about his waist. "I know what Moshe would do," she said proudly. "In his own way, he loves me."

With great difficulty, Zvi tried to ignore her presence, knowing all the while she was teasing him. "If he tried revenge, it could ruin him. We all have orders about Petra."

Zippy smiled enigmatically. "As you were saying before, orders require some kind of interpretation." Then she leaned over and kissed his cheek. When she stepped back, she smiled. "Don't be frightened, Zvi. I'm Moshe's, and I don't want anyone else."

She walked away. Zvi, moving quickly across the patio, took her arm and led her through the hotel and into the street beyond. "If you'll wait a moment," he asked. Then he returned to the hotel lobby, from where he phoned Libby Rosen, "It's Zvi. Zvi Mazon. I've got to drive a friend down to Beersheba and wondered if you would come with me. We'll come right back."

While he waited for her to make up her mind, he wondered why he had called. Then he heard her saying she would enjoy the drive and he could pick her up in ten minutes.

As he drove to Libby's apartment, Zvi explained to Zipporah that he and Libby would drive her to Beersheba. Sitting beside him, her legs drawn up under her, she watched his silhouette in the light of passing cars and street lamps. "Do you know her well?"

Uncertain just how he could explain that he had never been out with Libby before and why he was asking her now, Zvi avoided an answer by shrugging.

Zipporah grinned. Then she was suddenly serious. "You're going to tell Malin everything's fine, aren't you?"

Zvi tried not to smile. "Is that what you want me to tell her?"

"It is fine." Then, because she thought he might doubt her, she said again, "It is fine, and he is wonderful."

"And you are in love and there will be children when you want them and they and all of your other problems and joys will come and go when you want them to."

"Damn you, Zvi Mazon," she said angrily. Then, almost as though she were much older and wiser, she asked, "You really are envious?"

He blinked as a headlight came at him and then shook his head. "I've been in love. I don't think I want to go there again. Like Petra, it's a place where people can get killed, and after you're dead, you're in no position to decide if it was worth it or not."

"Then you are afraid to find out?"

"I told you I've been there," he repeated. "I've been there, and believe me, it's an empty place."

Stopping in front of Libby's apartment, he was about to step out of the car when Libby threw open the door and slipped in beside Zipporah.

"What's an empty place?" she asked before Zvi could even introduce her.

Laughing softly, Zipporah said, "He's got love and Petra all mixed up."

Libby glanced past the girl sitting between herself and Zvi, but all she could make out was a silhouette in the darkness.

He introduced the two women and for the next several hours as they drove south Zvi and Libby talked about their work while Zipporah asked questions. It was well past midnight when they dropped her at the small house in Beersheba. She asked them in for coffee and they both said No. Standing at her door with Zvi, she glanced at Libby in the car and whispered, "You two have a lot in common. All those dead people and all those romantic documents." Then she came to her toes and kissed his cheek.

Reaching out, he touched her arm. "I'll see you soon."

She nodded and disappeared inside the house.

Rejoining Libby, Zvi sat silently behind the wheel.

Turning toward him, she asked, "Is something wrong?"

"Once I thought my friend was bad for her, and now I'm not sure he isn't the one in dangerous company."

Libby laughed hoarsely. "I don't know your friend, but I assume he's a big boy."

Heading the car north toward Jerusalem, Zvi thought about Libby's assumption. They had traveled some distance before he answered. "A big boy? I don't know."

She looked at him, surprised that he had held the idea so long. "Do I know him?"

"Moshe Gilead."

At first he did not think she had heard him, and then she said. "I met him once. It was at a concert." She fell silent for a time and then she added, "I got the impression he was a killer. Maybe, as the Americans say, 'That comes with the territory.' "

Stiffening, Zvi raced the car through the darkness.

It was almost morning when they reached Jerusalem. He brought the car to a stop in front of Libby's apartment and was about to step out to open the door for her when she put her hand on his arm. He looked at her for a moment before he leaned over and kissed her. Her arms came about his neck and she drew him closer. Then he sat back and silently stared at her. He drew her to him and kissed her again. This time, as he held her, his hand wandered down the flat of her stomach and came to rest on her breast. She moved even closer; and when he dropped his hand, she closed hers on it and returned it to her breast. Sometime later, he asked, "Your apartment or mine?"

"I room with two girls."

Zvi nodded and drove slowly to his own apartment on the far side of the city. She followed him up the stairs and into his dark sitting room. Before he flicked on the light, he kissed her once more. She melded into his arms and hugged him. Stepping back, he looked at her in the darkness, and then without turning on the light, he swung her about so that she stood with her back to him while he wrapped his arms about her, closing both hands on her breasts. Her head fell back on his shoulder and they remained very still; and then Zvi half lifted her from the floor and carried her into the bedroom where he slowly undressed her. Only after they were both naked did he turn on the light. She stood beside the bed enjoying his careful evaluation, as though she knew she was something he wanted badly. Finally, he grabbed her arm, drew her down beside him and covered her breasts with his hands, "I'd like to walk over an acre of them barefooted." Then he had her without even bothering to throw back the bedspread.

Later, when the morning light threw vague shadows over the room, she rose and romped playfully through the small apartment. Gazing at her from the bed, Zvi enjoyed the way her breasts jounced as she moved. Her rump was larger than he had thought it would be.

When she returned to the bedroom, she walked over to the window and stared out for a moment before turning to him.

"I could save money if I moved in," she offered.

He nodded. And because she seemed to be waiting for an answer, he asked, "When did you decide that?"

"The first afternoon we went to lunch and you told me your son was going to the States."

Her arms were folded under her breasts, pressing them forward as an obvious invitation.

Zvi liked what he saw, but he did not know if he liked what he was hearing.

"And if I hadn't asked you tonight?"

"I think I would have waited another day or two and then come over."

He thought about this before deciding there was something cynically humorous about her candor.

"Well?" she asked.

"Well, what?"

"Am I moving in?"

"If you want to."

She came over to the bed, and sitting on the edge of it, she leaned over and kissed his bare chest. When she sat back, she touched a twisted scar left by a rifle bullet. "You won't regret it," she said.

He grinned, and drawing her to him once more, took her again.

Afterwards, when they were lying in the morning light and he could see her clothes across the foot of the bed, he asked, "What brought you to the archives?"

She rolled over and placed a hand on his chest, touching another old scar. "There was only money enough for one of us to study in England, and so my husband went." She fell silent as she kissed the scar; and when she sat up, she said, "After he gets home and makes some money, I'll go."

Zvi laughed softly. "It's the first I knew about a husband."

Turning so that she half lay across him, her breasts dangling on his chest, she looked down into his face and said sharply, "He's none of your business."

Reaching up, he pinched one nipple between his thumb and forefinger so hard she shrieked, while he tried to decide if she was right. "I'm not going to worry about him. He's your problem." He could not bring himself to worry about the moral implications now.

"It's all settled then."

After breakfast, he drove her to her apartment, where she picked up her clothes, and then they drove to the Archives.

For the next two days they totaled the statistics they had gathered about the *Einsatzgruppen*. And for the next two nights, they did not leave the apartment.

It was on the third morning after Libby had moved in with Zvi that they began to review what they had. Zvi sat with his feet on his desk, his notes in front of him, while Libby leaned over her work table and listened.

"As far as I can make it out, the largest single murder assignment came when the Germans invaded Russia. There were two *Einsatzgruppen* there."

"C and D."

"In the area they first captured—the Russian Ukraine and Eastern Galicia—were the Jews who in many cases had already fled before the Nazis."

Libby's hand closed on the pencil she was holding and she picked up some notes. "Some of that territory the Russians got in 1939. And don't forget the Poles from whom they got it were as anti-Semitic as the Germans."

Zvi accepted this. "The only reason the Poles didn't go as far as the Final Solution was they lacked the nerve."

"Nerve?" she asked.

"It takes a kind of madness, but with it the belief that the world will stand still and let you practice genocide. The Poles didn't think they could get away with it."

"But they could have," she snapped. "No one would have moved to stop them."

"But they didn't know that. They couldn't have been sure."

Libby disagreed. "Can you remember a moment in history when any nation moved in to stop a Polish pogrom? You can't. And if you want to look at it honestly, all the Germans did was carry the Polish pogrom one step further."

"But there is a difference," Zvi insisted.

"Only in degree. Only in degree."

Zvi did not argue with her and continued through his notes. "From the figures we have here, between one hundred fifty thousand and two hundred thousand were murdered in the Ukraine by the end of 1941."

Libby snorted. "We can blame the Germans for getting it started, and . . ."

"For carrying it out."

"But I haven't read anything about a single Ukrainian protesting."

"Gentiles don't fight for Jews," he reminded her. "And though they don't, that doesn't mean they all believe in genocide."

"You would have trouble proving that," she said.

"That's not what we're out to prove."

Both of them considered the point before he asked, "Do you have that list of communities?"

Glancing at her notes, Libby read off the names of Jewish communities now vanished. "Zbarazh, Lvov, Tarnopol, Drogobych." She fell silent and then added. "The Jewish communities there disappeared in Group C's first advance. More than seven thousand killed in Lvov alone."

Zvi tried to put the date into a context. "The invasion of Russia was only a few weeks old by that time."

They continued on through the morning, adding the Jews of Vinnitsa, Kovno, Vilna, Baranovichi, Biala, Losice, Chortkoc, Minsk and hundreds of other communities to their list. They had before them the daily reports which the various *Einsatzgruppen* had transmitted. Small villages and large cities. Draymen and dairymen, pantsmakers, lawyers and teachers. Old people, young people, the ill and the strong, those in love and those in labor. And with every statistic, Zvi tried to imagine the *shtetl* as the killers swept in with their trucks, their burial detachments, their machine guns and their insanity. Picking up the transcript of the *Einsatzgruppen* trial at Nuremberg, Zvi read once more the horror story as Major General Herr Doctor Ohlendorff had explained it.

"In the implementation of this extermination program, the men, women and children were led to a place of execution which in most cases was located next to a deeply excavated antitank ditch. Then they were shot, kneeling or standing, and the corpses were thrown into the ditch. I never permitted the shooting by individuals of Group D, but ordered that several men should shoot at the same time in order to avoid direct personal responsibility. The leaders of the unit or specially designated persons, however, had to fire the last bullet against those victims who were not dead immediately. I learned from other group leaders that some of them demanded that the victims lie

474

down flat on the ground to be shot through the nape of the neck. I did not approve of these methods."

"I'm glad there was something he disapproved of," Libby said softly.

Zvi's finger traced down the transcript. "He says 'both for the victims and those who carried out the executions, it was, psychologically, an immense burden to bear.' "

Zvi slowly lowered the book and stared at Libby. The pencil in her hand was broken now and he could see her shaking her head from side to side in complete disbelief even though they had been over this testimony before.

Shoving the volume aside, Zvi went back to the notes with the statistics. As he looked at them, he tried without success to realize he was counting human beings. He read almost numbly, "Group A reported on October 15, 1941 a total of 18,430 Jews 'resettled.' Group B reported on November 3 that it had 'so far liquidated about 80,000 people.' "

They totaled on and on through lunch and into the evening without pause.

Finally, when Zvi had difficulty reading his notes, he noticed that darkness had settled over Jerusalem and they had not even turned on the office lights. Setting his notes down, he rose from behind his desk. "We haven't even begun yet."

Libby watched him light a cigarette and realized it was the first he had smoked since breakfast.

"Let's get out of here," he shouted in a hoarse voice. And he walked out of the office, down the corridor and into the night.

Five minutes later, after securing their papers in the file, Libby joined him as he stood beside his car. His arms were outstretched, his hands flat on the cold roof. He wanted to retch. He had never felt so dirty before. Closing his eyes, he wondered if the obscenity lay in his relationship to Libby or in what he had been working on or in both. All he knew was that he was repulsed by himself, by this girl who stood at his side waiting for him to take her home, feed her and lay her, and by the millions of Christians who had stood by in remote silence while the *Einsatzgruppen* moved through Europe. He felt dirty because he was alive.

And when Libby said quietly, "Let's go," he swung about, flailing his arms, striking her about the head until she screamed; and then he reached out and folded her in his arms and held her for a long time. When at last he let her go, he said, "I'm sorry."

She looked at him and nodded. "I understand. This morning I hurt and then I was numb and now I'm beginning to feel again. I understand," she repeated.

Helping her into the car, Zvi drove to the apartment and as he opened the door, the phone rang. It took him some time to make contact with the world around him, and after the phone rang for the fifth time, Libby answered it. Handing it to him, she said, "A woman wants Colonel Mazon."

Taking the phone, he identified himself. "Zvi here." He listened and Libby, watching him, could see him beginning to relax. "I'll come over now," he said. "No. No problem." After he hung up, he explained to Libby. "Malin." Remembering she might not know Malin, he said, "Judge Malin Ben Ezra. She wants to see me." He thought for a moment. "I'll be back in an hour. I'll eat then." And he was gone. Only after he stood solitary in the night was he aware that his going had less to do with Malin than his need to be alone for a while.

Twenty minutes later he was telling Malin how well Zipporah had looked the night he had driven her to Beersheba. He had just finished saying he thought Zipporah was happy when Moshe called.

And Malin was saying, "Yes, he's here," and handing the phone to Zvi.

Zvi listened without interrupting, and then he said, "I took her back myself that night." He listened again before he said, "I'll find out." Then he cradled the phone and looked at Malin.

"She's gone?"

Zvi shrugged. "I'm sure she's all right. He asked the neighbors and they said they saw her driving away from the house in his jeep the night before last."

Malin looked at him dubiously before she dialed Avram's apartment in Tel Aviv. When there was no answer, she dialed his office. A few minutes later, Avram's sergeant located him. After Malin explained that Zippy was missing, she told him Zvi was with her and Avram asked to speak to him. Malin watched Zvi nod in response to whatever Avram was saying, and finally he agreed, "I'll meet you there."

Setting the phone down, Zvi tried to smile reassuringly. "We've got some work to do at the Ministry. I'll bring him back when we're done." He kissed her cheek and then left before she could ask him which ministry they would be working at in Jerusalem when their own was located in Tel Aviv.

Driving through the city to the Orthodox community, Zvi parked near the Mandelbaum Gate, lighted a cigarette and waited. When a staff car finally arrived and parked behind his own, Zvi stepped out into the night, paused to look at the lights of the city, the lights on the distant hills, and then he was joined by Avram.

"I don't know if it's her," Avram said.

Zvi nodded. "But you think . . .?"

Avram did not answer. They turned to watch as a police van came to a stop beside the pair and two police officers stepped out. There was a civilian with them.

The man introduced himself: "Foreign Ministry." The five walked to the Mandelbaum Gate together.

For all its reputation and all that it symbolized, there was nothing impressive about the gate which opened between Jordan and Israel. Set in a low stone wall, it was little more than two sheds and a barrier between, fronted by some concertina wire. Standing on the Israeli side, Zvi saw that the Arabs had never removed the skeleton of the old building which towered above the low wall at this point. A single light hanging on one of the sheds cast shadows over two Israeli sentries. From the other shed a Swedish soldier wearing the United Nations armband stepped forward.

"Colonel Ben Ezra?"

Avram nodded, introduced those with him and asked, "When are they coming over?"

"I've already called," the UNTSA officer told him.

Five minutes later Zvi saw a truck approaching on the Jordan side. Swinging around, the truck backed up to the gate. Two Jordanian sentries with cloth-covered helmets from which ornate spikes rose swung the gate open and, lifting a blanket-wrapped figure from the back of the truck, dumped it unceremoniously on the ground on the Israeli side. Avram started to move forward in anger, but Zvi caught his arm and held it firmly, cautioning, "Easy."

After the man from the Foreign Ministry signed a receipt, the Arabs swung the barrier closed again. The Israeli police picked up the blanket-wrapped body and started toward their car. Catching up with them, Zvi flipped the top of the blanket open and stared at what lay inside. Nodding, he said, "The family will make arrangements in the morning."

He watched the police officers and the man from the Foreign Ministry drive off before he walked over to Avram's car where the staff officer was leaning with his back against the front fender, his right hand clenched over the rolling muscles of his left shoulder. He looked at Zvi expectantly and his friend confirmed his fears with a nod.

"How did you know it would be her?" Zvi asked, as he lit a cigarette.

"A couple found a jeep near Har Hemda. Southern Command identified it as one of theirs. The tracks led to the border."

Zvi said, *"The Great Red Rock, the red one."*

Avi nodded. "How did you know?"

"She's been talking about it for weeks. I don't think there was any stopping her." He fell silent and then added, "Tell Malin no one could have stopped her."

His companion nodded again. "I'll have to tell her more than that."

Zvi agreed. "Do you want me with you?"

Opening the car door, Avram considered the offer. "No," he finally said. "But if you'll tell Moshe . . ."

Zvi took a deep breath, "I'll go down tonight." He watched Avram settle into his staff car; and then before he closed the door, Zvi suggested, "If you'll just tell Moshe I'm coming down to Beersheba, maybe he'll sit still until I get there."

Three hours later he told Moshe. Zvi stood in the living room of his friend's house and waited for a reaction.

The lean-faced man clenched his hands before him on the wide coffee table, and then lifted them and with measured restraint lowered them to the table without saying anything.

After a long silence he looked up at Zvi. "We have lousy luck with our women, you and I."

Surprised at the comment, Zvi tried to understand why Moshe was not reacting more violently to the fact that Zipporah had been murdered.

Moshe came to his feet, "Coffee?"

"I think I'd better get back."

Moshe nodded. "I'll go with you." He looked around the room, noticed a bobby pin in an ashtray, picked it up and then shook his head dubiously. "Will Malin mind my being there? The funeral, I mean."

Zvi shrugged. "I don't think so."

A short time later they were speeding north toward Jerusalem. For the first hour neither of them spoke, and then Moshe said in a remote voice, "It's difficult to describe, whatever it was we had, but there was something. I guess in my own way, I loved her. Different from . . ." His voice trailed off.

Zvi remained silent. He had heard the same words recently from Zippy.

Then there was nothing more said between them until they reached the outskirts of Jerusalem. And all the time he was driving, Zvi tried to find an explanation for Moshe's almost casual reaction to Zipporah's death.

They were entering the city when Moshe said, "I'll stay with you, if you don't mind."

"Of course."

Fifteen minutes later, Zvi fished Moshe's bag from the back of the car and led the way up to his apartment. It was almost morning. Taking the bag into Aaron's room, Zvi snapped on the lamp. "You know where the bathroom is."

Moshe nodded and was about to say something when Libby appeared in the bedroom doorway. She was wearing a sheer, short gown that barely covered her behind and hid nothing in front.

"We've got company," she said drily.

Looking her over carefully from breasts to feet, Moshe waited for an introduction.

"Libby, Moshe," Zvi said. Then, as though she were not standing there, he asked, "Coffee? Talk?" His hands came wide to indicate he was prepared for anything Moshe wanted.

His friend shrugged. "If you'd go over to see Malin with me in the morning . . ."

"Of course."

Then Zvi edged Libby out of the doorway, leaving Moshe alone.

In their own room, Libby jumped up on the bed, puffed a pillow behind her back, drew her knees up in front of her and watched him undress. "What's that all about?" she asked.

"It's a long story." He switched off the light and crawled under the covers.

"I didn't hold dinner for you," she told him.

He tried to smile and failed. Drawing her to him, he stared at the ceiling for a long time, and all he could think of was Moshe's comment: "We have lousy luck with our women, you and I." Even before he became aware that Libby had fallen asleep at his side, Zvi knew his friend was more right than he realized.

Though the newspapers carried the story of Zipporah's death, there was very little public reaction. Others had died going to Petra, and the government had already taken its stand against both the mystique of the place and the foolish bravery of the journey.

Two days after the Jordanians returned the body, Zipporah was buried. The funeral entourage was small. And an hour after he had paid his respects to Malin, Moshe started back to Beersheba.

Standing at the window of his apartment, Avram watched the staff car disappear down the street. Speaking low so that only Zvi at his side could hear, he said, "If he does what I think he is going to do, he'll have to be arrested. The Chief of Staff told him as much personally."

Zvi shook his head. "He won't try for Petra. Doesn't mean a thing to him."

Looking at his friend out of the corner of his eye, Avram wondered if Zvi was serious, decided to wait until he had to act, and, turning away from the window, watched the room fill up with friends who had come to express their condolences.

LOD–TEL AVIV, SUMMER, 1960

A few weeks later Zvi met Ruth, Hannah and Aaron at Lod airport. During the long drive to Tel Aviv and Ruth's home, he listened to Aaron's chatter about the United States. It was a big place. The buildings were tall. Most of the people did not speak Hebrew. There were too many automobiles. The ice cream was good. Everything was expensive. The hotels were fun because you could call up and get things delivered to the rooms. The drugstores were not *drug* stores. The telephone service was better than Israel's. Baseball did not make much sense. There were all kinds of good programs on television. Israel should have television. And on and on. Zvi looked over his shoulder, winked at Ruth, who nodded and smiled.

It was already late when they unloaded Ruth and Hannah's luggage at Jabotinsky Street, and Aaron asked his father if he could spend the night in

Tel Aviv. Zvi agreed and they all went out for dinner. Later, after Hannah and Aaron were in bed, Zvi sat in the living room of the apartment, trying not to remember what it had been like in the years he had lived here. Ruth had redecorated, but there was still much which reminded Zvi of things he would just as soon forget. Ruth had already changed into a robe and he smiled, recalling the old one she had worn so long ago when the shop was failing.

Pouring herself a fruit brandy, she did not bother to offer Zvi anything as she watched him light another cigarette.

"I'm not keeping you from seeing anyone?" he asked.

She shook her head as she settled down on the sofa, spreading her robe in a semi-circle about her.

"Something happened in New York you ought to know about," she said.

"Know about?"

And she laughed at his question. "The last week we were in the States. I was holding a showing at a restaurant." She smiled. "I crossed that country for seven weeks from Los Angeles to New York and I don't think I ever saw so many restaurants or so many women with so much time on their hands." She half snorted. "I feel sorry for them. They have nothing to do, and they work so hard at it. And they haven't the . . ." Her hands came open before her as she groped for the words, ". . . don't have the soul to live here."

Zvi smiled. "Soul? I'd never have used that word." Then he waited for her to tell him what she thought he ought to know, hoping that Aaron had not done anything seriously wrong.

"Well, it was the last week. The show was almost done. The dress orders came in. Not as many as I would have liked, but the women did buy. Enough anyway that I had to hire some assistants from one of the American dress houses, as they call them. I was standing in the back of the restaurant when this woman who had been sitting alone at one of the tables came up to me." Ruth closed her eyes as she tried to remember what the woman looked like. "She was shorter than I. Her eyes, they looked weary somehow. Her figure — slim and not too much here." She was touching her bosom. "But her dress," and there was awe in Ruth's voice. "Paris, and must have cost ten times what I was charging so I knew that she hadn't come to see my line. So I figured I would get the usual questions: Did I know her cousin who lived somewhere in the Galilee? How did we get such nice cloth? Did I think Israel would survive?" Ruth laughed as she slipped one hand inside her robe and straightened her gown.

Zvi was lighting another cigarette now, and she paused to watch. "Well, she started the usual way. 'Your gowns are lovely.' And I thanked her, and she asked if I'd been in the States long."

"I told her I'd been in the States only a couple of months and that I loved her country." She paused to shake her head. "All Americans want you to tell them how much you love their country. However, this one started to laugh, and then she explained that she had said the same thing herself when she first came to the States."

"She wasn't an American?"

Ruth shook her head. "Said she was from Jerusalem."

Zvi shrugged. He knew a great many people in Jerusalem.

"Then I asked her in Hebrew where she lived and how long she had been gone and she got angry. Said 'I'm from the other side of the Gate.' "

"Then she said she once knew someone in 'your country' — couldn't bring herself to say Israel. After telling me she had not heard about her friend for a long time because his name wasn't in the papers any more, and after I had pointed out that there are two million Jews in Israel now, she said his name was Colonel Zvi Mazon.

"She said she met you in 1948 in the Old City." Ruth sipped her brandy as she thought about the Old City in forty-eight. Her finger went to her forehead and came to rest on the white scar there.

"I thought you were too busy in those days for Arab women," she said in a soft voice.

Zvi smiled. "I almost killed her that night, if she's who I think you mean."

"Mrs. Bedia Hassani Asarmi."

"Mrs.?"

Puzzled, Ruth asked, "Does it make any difference?"

Zvi shook his head.

"When I finished at the restaurant, she was waiting to drive me back to the hotel. Big car and driver and all that."

"Her father's the banker," Zvi explained.

"I know, and her husband's Iranian. With the UN." Then Ruth fell silent while she finished her brandy. "She told me she had also known you in Aden and Paris." And there was a question in Ruth's voice.

Zvi agreed. "And we met one night in Yemen." He was looking at the tip of his cigarette when he asked, "What did she want to know?"

"What had happened to you."

"And what did you tell her?"

Ruth wanted to laugh at his serious and anxious expression. "That you were fine." She fell silent, and then, "She told me she had met Aaron once."

"That's true. In the camp in Aden."

Laughing softly at herself, Ruth said, "For a moment I thought she might be his mother."

And Zvi laughed with her. "He was about five at the time."

"That's what she said. Then I told her he was with me, and she asked if I was your wife."

Neither of them laughed.

"What did you say to that?"

Ruth shrugged. "I disabused her of the idea." She was leaning forward, and Zvi was conscious of the way she filled the front of her gown. "I had a funny notion as she talked," Ruth said.

"Funny notion?"

"When we reached the hotel, I asked if she was in love with you."

To Ruth's surprise, Zvi did not laugh as he asked seriously, "And what did she say?"

"It took her a long time to answer, but when she did, all she said was, 'He's a Jew.' "

Settling back she waited for Zvi's reaction and all she got was a gentle smile.

"That's Bedia." He leaned back in the overstuffed chair and thought about the Arab girl. The smile remained on his face when he said, "In a way we're kind of friendly enemies."

The next day, while driving home with Aaron, Zvi thought about Bedia more than he had expected to. If someone had asked if he were in love with her, he decided that his answer might have been the same as hers: "She's an Arab."

JERUSALEM

For the next several months Zvi and Libby continued their research. When Zvi introduced Aaron to his mistress, the boy greeted her as a friend, and they got along better than he had expected. Aaron was old enough to understand his father's relationship to Libby, who lived with them. The boy was also aware that his father and Libby never went out together among his father's old friends.

If there was one way in which Zvi's life changed during the months he worked on the trial, it was the manner in which he removed himself from those who had been close to him in the past. He might have missed them more if he had not been so fully committed to his work and if he had not found Libby's company so satisfying. Both met his needs at this moment.

In late February he and Libby began the last review of their findings, most of which had been already passed on to Bureau 06 and the prosecutor in Haifa. Their secretary had typed up their evaluations and they were working on a summary.

Zvi had one copy before him while Libby sat back in her chair reading another. Looking over the papers in his hand, he tried to make up his mind how he felt about this woman who had shared this nightmare. She was warm in bed, detached in the office, quiet at home and completely undemanding. She was also a bright and cheap slut.

As time had passed, he had become used to the way she moved, her gestures, the way she dressed, the shape of her head and the way her breasts jutted forward when she leaned over to let him light her cigarette. There was very little he did not know about Libby.

She looked up, saw him staring, and shook her head. "Is something wrong?"

"No," Zvi lied. "There's just so much of this that I can read at a time."

She understood. "Where did you find this item about the milk?"

Scanning his notes, Zvi located the information. "One of the reports to Eichmann."

Making a note, Zvi nodded. "There's this item you mention a few pages farther on," he pointed out. "The one in which Eichmann admits that he was present in a movie house when the final orders were given to the *Einsatzgruppen*."

"Found that in one of the interviews he has given here."

"This material about him supplying Heydrich at that time with the information about the Jewish communities in the east, their local customs, the names of the persons who would be most likely to help and the best way to handle the subject, will that hold up?"

Libby thought about this. "In his official capacity, he admits that he was his government's supreme authority on Jewish subjects. That admission covers his relationship to the material because he himself would not let anyone think his superiors had to look elsewhere for his material."

Zvi smiled. "Better add that."

They read on, checking the details they had selected from thousands. Zvi finally set the first part of the summary down and, lighting a cigarette, said, "One of the most damning things as far as Eichmann is concerned is his close relationship to their day-to-day work. At the end of each day the subcommanders reported their killings to their chief, who sent by courier or by telegraphy the daily totals to his office."

Libby smiled bitterly. "No matter how he squirms, he cannot deny that they reported to him and directly to him, and with the copies of the reports we have which he has initialed or signed before they were duplicated and sent on by his office, he cannot deny having known what was taking place."

Half closing his eyes, Zvi rose from behind his desk and walked over to the window where he stood looking out for a few minutes. "His argument is going to be obvious. His function was clerical. You can't hold him responsible for merely initialing and duplicating and sending reports on."

Flipping back pages until she found what she wanted, Libby read from the American report at Nuremberg, "These small forces, totaling not more than three thousand men, killed at least one million human begins in approximately two years' time. These figures enable us to make estimates which help considerably in understanding this case. They show that the four *Einsatzgruppen* averaged some 1,350 murders per day during a two-year period; 1,350 human beings slaughtered on the average day, seven days a week, for more than one hundred weeks. . . . All these thousands of men and women and children had first to be selected, brought together, held in restraint and transported to places of death. They had to be counted, stripped of possessions, shot and buried. And burial did not end the job, for all the pitiful possessions taken from the dead had to be salvaged, crated and shipped to the Reich. Finally, books were kept to cover these transactions. Details of all these things had to be recorded and reported." Setting the file on her knee, Libby asked, "What were you looking for?"

"That set of phrases: 'brought together' and 'transported to places of death' and 'shipped to the Reich.' " He fell silent for a moment before he added, "The one thing Eichmann shouts is that he handled the transportation. If that is so—and who will argue with him on this?—then he had to be involved in the scheduling of the murders. Transport had to be made available according to capacity to handle, and that took planning."

Libby nodded, made a note of the context and sat back watching him.

"That section where Eichmann admits he shipped Jews east from Germany?" he asked.

Libby sought it out. "He admits he sent Jews to Riga and Minsk."

Zvi nodded. "Did you check the dates of those shipments with the schedule of the *Einsatzgruppen*?"

She nodded. "They were present in both cities when the German Jews arrived."

"And he knew what the *Einsatzgruppen* were doing."

"He has to admit that," she agreed, "because of his signature or initials on the reports."

"And he admits," Zvi said, "that he did not send any Jews into the area until he knew the area could 'absorb' them?"

Zvi was quiet for a long time as he stared out the window, seeing nothing but faces of people he had never known and who were now dead.

"I think we have everything we need about the plundering," Libby said after reading on.

Whirling toward her, Zvi said, "That's not as important as . . . " His hands came wide before him. Reaching over his desk, he pulled out a note and read it aloud without even looking in Libby's direction. "I found this the other afternoon." His voice dropped to a rough whisper as he leaned over her desk, his palms flat upon it as he said, "Blobel. Eichmann's drinking partner. The man Eichmann brought back to headquarters to help him hide the evidence. In two days, Blobel killed 33,771 people in Kiev. And he, who was Eichmann's friend, admitted before he died that he worked under Eichmann's orders. And there's Eichmann's own admission about the five thousand Jews murdered in Minsk." Zvi's eyes closed as he tried to recall the words Eichmann had said of his visit to Minsk. " 'They had already started when I arrived so I could only see the finish. Although I was wearing a leather coat which reached down to my ankles, it was very cold. I watched the last group of Jews undress down to their shirts. They walked the last two hundred yards. They were not driven. Then they jumped into the pit. Then the men of the squad banged away into the pit with their rifles and machine guns.' " Zvi's dark eyes opened angrily as he said once more, "It's the deaths I want him for. The deaths."

Libby drew back in her chair. She had heard tales of Zvi's intense emotions during the years he was leading the retaliation raids, and she had been with him long enough to understand to what he was reacting now. However, she did not approve of what she saw. "Zvi," she admonished. "Detachment. You aren't here for revenge. You're here to study and evaluate. Revenge isn't yours."

His hand came up and he almost struck her as he shouted, "Detachment. For God's sake—detachment?" Then he spun back to his desk.

Taking a deep breath, she said again, "All you have to do is research. Don't try to make the judgments."

Coldly, seeking the detachment she was recommending, Zvi read, " ' . . . 1,350 human beings slaughtered on the average day seven days a week for more than one hundred weeks.' " The effort to achieve detachment failed, and he said, "Anyone who does not judge now is no better than those who stood by and watched and would not judge, isn't any better than the nation which stood by and did not judge." He snorted in undisguised fury. "Detachment from horror leads to *Einsatzgruppen*. Detachment leads to 1,350 murders a day."

Taking a deep breath, he stared at her and then, spinning about on his heel, stalked from the room.

The next day Zvi returned to the archives at Yad Vashem and his work. He and Libby agreed that the War Crimes Trials volume which covered the case of the *Einsatzgruppen* had been too extensively abridged for their needs and they were waiting for the intact original to be shipped in from England. While they waited, they continued through the microfilm records already in the archives. Two days later, they were working on the orders which had been issued to the *Einsatzgruppen* commanders when Zvi received a call from Avram.

"You will go down to Beersheba and on to Ein Hasb where his jeep has been found. When he returns, you have orders to place him under arrest and take him to Beersheba. When you arrive there, contact me, and I will join you."

Zvi did not need to be told whom they were talking about. "Why me?" he asked.

"He'll take it better from you than from anyone else. There's a chance he'll even talk to you. There are four military police and an MP lieutenant there. Let them go through the formalities, and you just stand by in the event you are needed."

"Avram," Zvi asked after a long silence, "whose idea was this?"

"The Chief of Staff's. He does not want to lose Moshe, and it could happen." Neither spoke for a time, and then Avram added, "We need him."

Zvi nodded, then remembered he was talking on a phone, "I'll contact you when we get back to Beersheba unless he gets there before I do and in that event . . . "

"The MPs have orders to do nothing until you arrive. Do you want a plane?"

"Set one up. I'll take it down to Ein Hasb."

Avram agreed.

Before he hung up, Zvi asked, "Are you sure he's crossed?"

"I'm sure." And then Avram said, "I'm sorry it's you, Zvi."

IN THE NEGEV

An hour and a half after Avram's call, Zvi Mazon sat in the Southern Command jeep which had been found abandoned near Ein Hasb. He could see the military police vehicle parked in front of him and the jeep which had brought him disappearing northward.

The sun was high. A military policeman came over from the quarter-ton truck which passed as a command car and offered the Colonel a canteen. Zvi shook his head, "Thanks." Then a smile crossed his face as he explained, "I've been in the desert before."

"I was in the battalion that replaced your men at Mitla, Sir."

Zvi nodded.

"We going to be here long?" the MP asked.

Zvi shrugged. "I don't think anything will happen before dark. No one would stir until then. If we are really waiting for the man I've been told we are, then he's holed up some place now. He'll move as soon as it is dark enough. Depending on where he is, it could take him one hour or six to get here."

The MP accepted the evaluation. "If you want to join us for dinner . . . "

Zvi assured the soldier he would. Then he leaned back, slipped his red beret over his face and closed his eyes. He had not realized before how much he had missed the desert sun.

JORDAN

And the sun above was hot. Moshe Gilead, lying in the shelter of a high rock formation, could see the burning sands and the brazed flat stones below. In the distance he could make out the movement of a small flock of sheep. Wiping the sweat from his face, he reached out and checked the Uzi beside his heel. Satisfied that it was still there, he drank lightly from the canteen on his

486

hip, set it back in its web case and wiped his damp palm down the side of his slacks. There was a bird coasting the sky above, and he turned to watch it.

The night before he had reached Petra. There had been very little there he wished to see; and because this had not been the reason for his crossing the border, he felt a bit foolish having gone the full distance. However, he had checked the route Zippy had taken from notes she had left in the house, and he had made his mind up to follow that route. Petra was not a disappointment in part because he had not expected very much of it. The colors were startling, the formations of ancient stone surprising. And yet, for Moshe Gilead, there was very little which held mystique any longer. Having left the Red City behind, he had moved to his present position.

From the moment Zvi Mazon had told him that Zippy was dead, he knew he was going to come to this point. Below lay the main trail that led from Petra to the Israeli border. It was less a trail today than the bottom of a wadi which in season flowed wildly into an empty desert. Now it was dry. But Moshe knew it was not abandoned. In the early morning, before he had climbed to the height where he now lay watching the distant flock, he had seen footprints and in one place even the tracks of a truck.

The flock of sheep was coming closer, and behind them he could see several shepherds. Wishing he had been able to find his fieldglasses before starting out, Moshe tried to make out the ages of the men moving slowly toward the wadi. He could tell by the way they walked they were not children. As they closed the distance, he saw that two of them were carrying something. He could not make out what because of the heavy folds of their robes. Looking down the length of his own prone body nestled in the crags, he made certain once again that he had nothing on him and wore nothing that could indicate he was an Israeli soldier. This was not an official mission. This was . . . and his mind groped to find the word that described what he was about to do. This was personal, he finally decided. Now the flock was crossing the wadi below. The three men were reading the footprints in the sand which edged the wadi. One of them let out a shout and waited for his companions to gather about him.

Moshe smiled. He knew they had found the point where he had crossed eastward the night before. One man trotted down the length of Moshe's tracks until they disappeared across some rocks. All three men were drawing rifles out of their robes now, and one sat down on the edge of the wadi, sheltered by an overhanging rock, his rifle across his lap while he stared to the east from where the Israeli would apparently have to return. The second Arab climbed up the slope toward the place where Moshe lay hidden. The third took a position off to one side of the wadi, setting his rifle on a rock. The Arab approaching Moshe slowed his pace and settled down on a rock several paces below the Israeli. Looking up, Moshe watched the bird for a few minutes. When he turned his attention to the Arabs once more, he saw the one directly below him was waving a white cloth to someone in the distance. His companions did not bother to watch. Wishing once more that he had his fieldglasses, Moshe decided to wait to see what was now going to be revealed.

The waving stopped, and the Arab sat down again, his rifle across his knee. Ten minutes passed and the Arabs did not move. And then five minutes later, Moshe saw two more Arabs emerge from the distance, making their way among some rocks on the far side of the wadi. It took him a while to figure out why they had fallen so far behind their companions: they were waiting wide of the crossing route to make certain no one tried to bypass the point of ambush. When he saw the two newcomers settle down behind some rocks, Moshe drew his Uzi into his hand, checked the clip, and then the second clip he had shoved into his pocket. It would take only seconds to drop one and change to the other. Edging on his belly, he moved toward the Arab whose back was toward him. The man was older than he. His white robe was a dirty gray; his feet were shoved into sandals, and about his neck Moshe thought he saw something, and then he recognized the leather thong which held fieldglasses. The Arab picked them up and surveyed the approach from the east. Now Moshe was only a few paces behind the man. Grabbing his Uzi, the Israeli rose and deliberately kicked some rocks loose at his feet. The Arab whirled, still holding his glasses instead of his rifle. Squeezing off two shots, Moshe dropped the man from the height, did not bother to watch him fall with the loose rocks as he himself spun and cut off a short burst at the man in the wadi. Then as the third Arab, who was settled behind the rocks on the other side of the wadi raised his rifle, Moshe fired three shots at his head. The man came to his feet, took two steps forward before he suddenly reached out for something to hold, and not finding anything but air, toppled onto his face.

The two who had settled farther away fired. The first bullet ricocheted off a rock beside Moshe, who dropped his Uzi for the rifle of the man who lay at his feet. Then, kneeling, he took careful aim and killed the first Arab to raise his head. Shifting his position, he half ran, half stumbled down the rise to the bottom of the wadi, where the dry river's sides hid him. Only now did he look at the second man he had shot. Lying twisted to one side with his eyes blankly watching the bird above, the man seemed to be holding his stomach. A rifle shot passed over Moshe's head, and forgetting his victim and bending low, he moved swiftly eastward down the wadi's rock base. Another bullet flattened on a rock where he had been and assured Moshe that the last Arab did not know where he was now. Smiling to himself, he continued moving eastward and away from the frontier. The wadi was shallower now. A third rifle shot went blindly against some rocks far behind him. Remembering where the Arab lay, Moshe moved across the wadi and onto open ground. In the instant in which he revealed himself, he could see the Arab edging toward the spot where he had last seen the Jew. Taking his time, Moshe fired the rifle from his hip, slammed the bolt back and fired again. The Arab whirled about to face his enemy, and now Moshe took the time to raise his rifle and slam the bolt once more before he fired. The face before him blurred as the bullet struck it; the man spun back from the impact. Satisfied that he had done what he had come to do, Moshe returned to the place where he had dropped his Uzi, picked it up and was about to make his way toward the frontier when the bright sun reflected off the fieldglasses slung about the dead Arab's neck. Kneeling, Moshe picked up the glasses. Very slowly he turned them over in his hand. From the numbers on the side he knew they were his and could only assume Zippy had taken them on her journey to Petra. Jerking them angrily over the head of the corpse, he came once more to his feet. As he left the place where he was supposed to have died, he felt only a slight satisfaction in knowing the men he had killed had been Zippy's murderers.

IN THE NEGEV

Shortly before dark, Zvi joined the military police for dinner and together they listened to the evening news. There was a rebellion in the Congo, de Gaulle was still offering peace terms to the Algerians, and Cyprus had just come to another agreement with Britain.

The young officer tried to make conversation, but Zvi did not feel like talking. One of the men asked whom they were waiting for, and Zvi shrugged off the question.

"He must be important," the lieutenant said.

"Why?" Zvi snapped.

"You would not have spent the day in that jeep for just any soldier, Sir."

Winking, Zvi leaned back against the wheel of the small truck and finished his can of rations. Half an hour later he returned to the abandoned jeep to continue his wait. It was close to midnight when he heard someone coming, slipped out of the vehicle and stood a short distance behind it, blending into the shadows so that whoever was approaching could not see him.

From where he had placed himself, Zvi made out the figure of a man moving toward the road from behind a crag of rocks. The man was not making a sound now, but Zvi recognized Moshe from his silhouette and the way he moved. Then he saw where Moshe was going, and he smiled to himself. Five minutes passed and still not a sound. It took all of Zvi's years of training to follow the slow movement of his friend across the broken ground. Once, for an instant, he thought he saw the shape of Moshe's weapon, but he could not be certain. The field officer was closer now and moving skillfully over the loose stone. Then, suddenly, Moshe shouted, "Spill out of that truck and don't move for a weapon."

Trying not to laugh, Zvi watched the four military police leap from where they had been sitting, their officer sprawling on the ground as he jumped.

"In front of the truck now," Moshe's voice was crisp, and when one of the soldiers hesitated, Moshe fired a short burst over the man's head. Reaching into the truck, Moshe exposed the five to the sudden glare of their own headlights.

Knowing that the military police could not see Moshe, and that his friend was having fun with them, Zvi took four quick steps, flicked the lights of Moshe's own jeep on, and then shouted, "All right, Moshe. We're done playing."

The startled field officer started to raise his weapon, looked at it a moment, and then setting its butt on his hip, called laughingly, "Zvi?"

"It's Zvi."

The lieutenant came around the truck and held out his hand for Moshe's Uzi. "Colonel Moshe Gilead, I have orders from the Chief of Staff to place you under arrest."

The lean white-haired officer looked at the youth and laughed. "Zvi," he called, "is he serious?"

"He's serious," Zvi said as he stepped into the jeep's light.

For a long time Moshe Gilead looked from the lieutenant to his friend and then back again to the lieutenant. With an almost imperceptible shrug, he handed the submachine gun to the military police officer. "Here. You might as well carry it." Then, ignoring the youth, he walked over to Zvi.

"What the hell is this all about?" He could not hide the hard-bitten tone in his voice.

Zvi wanted to chuckle. "You don't know?"

Moshe thought before he shook his head.

Taking two cigarettes from his shirt pocket, Zvi handed Moshe one and lit the other for himself. "Let's save a lot of time and get where we have to go." With an almost formal bow and sweep of his hand, he waved Moshe to the jeep. A moment later he was driving north, Moshe beside him. The desert night was cold. The sky was black. Only the dimmed headlights of the truck behind them revealed any sign of life. Moshe sucked deeply on the cigarette in his hand and then stared at it.

"I've been wanting one all day," he said. Casually, Zvi asked, "And where were you that you couldn't light a cigarette?"

Moshe laughed softly. "I took a walk."

"You waited a long time to take that walk."

"No reason to rush, was there?"

Zvi could not think of any. Swerving to miss a rock, he asked, "Didn't see any frontier signs, did you?"

"Where would I see a frontier?"

Slowing down, Zvi stuck one hand out so that it was shoved right under his friend's nose. "Over there," he pointed. "Right over there."

Very slowly, Moshe shook his head. "Sorry, old friend. You must be disoriented." He fell silent and then asked, "Isn't this a bit far south for you? Yad Vashem and all that."

Trying not to show his own enjoyment in what was happening, Zvi decided to ignore the question. A short time later they were passing through Scorpion Pass—the historic Ascent of Akkrabbim. Neither of them said anything. They had traveled half way through the pass when Moshe touched Zvi's arm.

"Remember what I said months ago—'We have lousy luck with our women, you and I?'"

Uncertain where this was leading and not wanting to talk about Zella here in this place with Moshe, Zvi remained silent as he pressed his foot down on the pedal, jerking the jeep forward.

Once more they were on the open desert and Moshe asked Zvi for another cigarette. After lighting it, he asked, "What's Libby?"

"What kind of an answer do you want?" Zvi asked, slowing down to let the command car make up some of the distance between them.

"If I knew, I'm not sure I'd have asked." He chuckled. "If you had one word to describe her, what would it be?"

Without hesitation, Zvi snapped, "Available."

They traveled several kilometers before Moshe said, "I'm sorry."

"Don't be. Maybe that's the only thing you and I should look for in a woman." Zvi was driving with one hand on the wheel now and scratching his stomach with the other. "Moshe?" he said tentatively.

"Yes?"

"What happened to Zippy, is it likely to happen again?"

The lights of the quarter-ton seemed closer than Zvi wanted, and he spread the gap.

"Whom am I talking to?" Moshe asked. "An arresting officer or the not-so-bright young squad commander who almost got us killed a dozen times in the Quarter?"

The headlights revealed a desert fox. Then the road was empty again. "Both," Zvi finally said.

"Then I don't understand your question."

They were nearing the airstrip now and Zvi, slowing the jeep, twisted in his seat so that he could see Moshe better. He could not make anything out other than the shape of his friend's head. Then the lights of the military police vehicle splashed over them and he could see Moshe's eyes, tense and almost hidden in his cragged face.

"Thanks for answering my question," Zvi said softly. "By not knowing what I was talking about, you answered it."

Moshe said coldly, "Clever boy."

"Were there many of them?"

"Don't try to get too clever."

And then they drove onto the airstrip where the small plane was waiting for them. Relieving the military police officer of his responsibility for the prisoner, Zvi asked the Dormier pilot to wait for him. A few minutes later inside the radio shack he had told Avram what had happened. "He caught your MP lieutenant with his bare face exposed."

"And Moshe admits nothing?"

"Just going for a walk." Through the window Zvi was watching Moshe pay the pilot for a pack of cigarettes.

For a long time all Zvi heard was a crackling silence on the radio, and then he knew he was talking to the Chief of Staff. "Do you think we could prove anything, Zvi?"

"No." He thought a moment and then added, "Could get some trackers and dogs in the morning and try to trace his route back to wherever he came from."

"We wouldn't have any success, would we?"

Knowing the answer had already been given, Zvi agreed, "No success, but what do I do with one MP officer who feels silly and his four men who look foolish?"

Now Zvi could see Moshe beside the wing of the plane, talking to the young lieutenant.

"We could just tell them we want to be sure no one knows about a special recce operation," Avram suggested.

"That's the way I was thinking," Zvi agreed. "I'll drop Moshe at Beersheba and return to Jerusalem."

"Right, Zvi," the Chief of Staff approved. "Just tell him that Jordan is claiming an Israeli unit in company strength crossed the border last night and massacred all the men of two villages."

Satisfied that the details were settled, Zvi walked over to the plane, took Moshe's arm and helped him in. Then he took the time to thank the military police for their help and to make certain they understood this operation would have to remain secret. Joining Moshe inside the plane, he gestured for the pilot to take them up.

The plane was coming in to the small field beside the road several kilometers north of Beersheba, when Zvi told Moshe about the Jordanian complaint.

"They always exaggerate. Just one village, and it lay across the route she wanted to try."

Zvi considered the implications. There was no doubt in his mind that Moshe had taken the time to learn exactly where the Arabs had struck and who had murdered Zippy. And yet . . .

Shoving his head forward as they sat facing each other, Moshe said, "I wouldn't have done anything different if I had caught them at Scorpion Pass eight years ago."

Very slowly, Zvi shook his head. His hand came up and closed on the back of his neck. He thought about the knife slashes he had seen on Zipporah's face when he had flipped the blanket open at Mandelbaum Gate, and once again Zippy's face blended with Zella's and all he could think about were the dead and the enemy. And there had been so many enemies. The Arabs Moshe had sought were the enemy. They had murdered, and this was not Kiev, Kovno, Vilna or Minsk.

His hand came away from his neck, and he smiled wryly. "You know there are times when it is difficult to be a Jew."

Moshe nodded.

JERUSALEM, WINTER, 1960-61

For months, Zvi and Libby continued to review the material they were submitting. From the thousands of documents they had screened and the thousands others had screened, they knew over fifteen hundred would eventually be submitted as valid and usable as evidence. They knew, also, that while they were working on documentation, the prosecution was contacting and listening to the report of survivors of the holocaust. Both Zvi and Libby had long ago come to the conclusion that while there would be many who remembered the terrible days of the death camps, there would be few who survived to remember the *Einsatzgruppen*.

As he worked, Zvi's thoughts drifted to the dark face of the mad girl who had shot him as the Old City fell. The Poles, she had said, her neighbors, she had said, those with whom her family had worked, she had said—these were the people who had named her family and the other Jews of the *shtetl*, these were the ones who had pointed out the place where the Jews had hidden. And this girl had survived. Zvi thought about her and then his mind wandered on past her to the Poles who would not be tried because the Polish government was no different today in its hatred of the Jews than the Polish government and people had been during the holocaust.

His thoughts kept wandering back to the non-Jews as he picked up a paragraph he had extracted from an article about a Polish officer, a certain Prince Christopher Radziwill: "I shall never forget the day the Nazis killed 17,000 Jews at Madjanek while I was in another part of the concentration camp. That evening many of my Polish fellow prisoners got drunk to celebrate. The next day more Jews were transferred in."

"Transferred," and Zvi looked at the word and thought of the man who claimed he was only responsible for the transportation of Jews. And there was an irony about the definition of that word. *Transferred. Transported*. He opened his desk drawer for the list of words he had been collecting and read over it.

executed
exterminated
liquidation
put to death
liquidation number
liquidation of Jewry
action
finished
special actions
specially treated
subject to special treatment
cleansing
major cleansing actions
elimination
resettlement
treated appropriately
executive measure

And he added to the end, *protective corps.*

The reports followed one on the other and on and on.

And all the reports marked "Secret" and reprinted in forty copies or more and sent to Eichmann so that he could schedule more Jews into the area or ship his battalions where the Jews had already been collected. The reports carefully initialed or signed and passed on.

Zvi found himself shaking all over as he had for so many days, and he knew that he was ill and that he had been losing weight and that he could not bring himself to go home to dinner with his son to talk about soccer, and he knew it was not the boy's fault. Picking up the phone, he called the mother of one of Aaron's friends and asked if the boy could stay with her because he had to go south on duty. And when that was settled, he turned to Libby. "Come on. We're getting out of here."

When he started for the door, she walked behind his desk to see what he had been reading and understood.

ASHKELON

Two hours later Zvi signed them both into the Dagon Hotel on the beach at Ashkelon and led the way to the small cottage he had taken for two days. Once inside, he looked around and said, "I don't want to spend the night in here," and opening the door, stalked out into the darkness.

Libby watched him from the small porch for a moment before she closed the door and trotted after him. Zvi was already walking down the paved road that led to the beach. It was empty now. There was no one in sight. A car passed on the road behind them, lighting their passage for a moment and then all was dark again. Zvi could see the water and soft rolling waves. When Libby slipped her arm under his, he closed a hand on hers and continued walking.

They reached the beach and, finding a rock which he would be able to locate again in the darkness, he took off his shoes and then, drawing her to him, he took off hers, taking the time to stroke her thighs and legs before he pulled her legs out from under her so that she toppled backwards onto the sand, skirt flying.

Zvi did not laugh as he watched her and then, coming to his feet, helped her to hers with a slap on her sandy rump. Pulling up the cuffs of his trousers, he walked down to the water's edge and slowly strode along the beach, letting the gentle waves splash over his bare feet and his ankles, and every few minutes a wave reached more boldly to his calf and he felt his trousers getting wet and he walked on trying not to think of the figures, the wild numbers and the faceless people of *shtetls* he had never seen and would never see. He tried not to think of the loud words which he had listed like shouts heard on a dark night. *Cleansing. Subjected to special treatment.* The words which were lies and truths all twisted with the numbers which no reasonable mind could absorb, mingled with the names tasting strange on the tongue: *Vitebsk. Nevel. Yanovichi. Salispils.* Odd names of dead places and faces buried under dirt, buried alive or buried dead. Buried young or buried old. Buried of a bullet or buried of gas. Buried, with a German soldier, cigarette hanging from his thick lips, watching. Buried without clothes. Buried cold and buried warm. Buried from fear of epidemic. Buried from fear. Buried because they were different. Do not love thy neighbor but kill him because he is not like thee. He is a Jew. He is a Gypsy. He is not Aryan. His blood will stain your blood. Do not go in unto her because she will defile your Aryanism for generation unto generation. Do be sure you kill, make special arrangement, liquidate, treat, resettle. Do thou unto the Jew. Unto the Jew. By tens and hundreds and thousands. And millions. Do thou unto the Jew. And Zvi could not live alone with the faces and images banging through his brain and he turned to Libby and grabbing her to his chest, slipped down in the sand, trying to see her face as a single face, as the face of a Jew, a person alive and warm and, rejecting that which he had been trying to chase from his battered brain, he was ripping off her clothes and running his hand down the slopes of her stomach and over her breasts and up her thighs until, naked, he blindly started to strike her and she closed her arms about him and they lay still and quiet on the beach with the water splashing gently beside them. After a long while Zvi could make out the stars above and then Libby's face with her eyes closed and her jaw slack. And as he held her closely, he was not even certain if he had taken her, and then he did not believe he had.

He gently set her sleeping body aside and came to his feet. His shirt lay beside her foot. His trouser cuffs were wet. Kneeling, he rolled his shirt into a ball and set it under her head. Then he sat down beside her naked body and, trembling, rested his elbows on his knees before he buried his face in his hands. Later, when he could see the first bright edges of the sky, he picked up Libby's dress and covered her with it, and then he took her torn underclothes and shoved them into a hole and covered them with sand.

When she awakened, she sat up, the torn dress barely covering her, and she asked, "Do you feel any better?"

Zvi shrugged. "I think I can go back to work tomorrow."

Libby nodded. He had not answered her question, but she was not going to demand an answer.

"My husband is coming home Monday."

"You're going back to him?" And even though Zvi was certain she was not telling the truth, he did not blame her.

"I never said I wouldn't."

JERUSALEM

When they reached their apartment Libby told Zvi, "I'm not going to be working with you any more."

Zvi accepted this, and to his surprise, he did not really care. That night he slept alone for the first time in almost a year.

Zvi completed his portion of the research by the end of March, and a short time later was informed by headquarters that he was expected to attend the trial, scheduled to begin on 11 April. For the first time in years he found himself free. He spent his mornings about the apartment, his afternoons with Aaron.

The only news he had of friends was about the transfer of Moshe Gilead from Southern Command to the office of the Chief of Staff. And two weeks after that, when he heard that Moshe had been promoted to brigadier-general, he dropped him a note which brought in the return mail the suggestion that they celebrate the next time Moshe was in Jerusalem.

Finally, the trial began.

The place—a community hall of white stone from the Judean hills. Blue upholstered seats against an austere background.

And present—the reporters from Japan and Germany and England and New Zealand; from almost anywhere a man could read.

And the prosecutor—bald, slight, sad, of German birth.

And the defense—portly, a good German come to defend his countryman.

And then the accused—Eichmann in a gray suit, wearing an ashen look. Eichmann with the nervous fingers touching colored pencils. Eichmann behind the bullet-proof glass, ignoring the spectators.

And the reporters reviewing the details they knew of him—born in 1906, completed high school, worked in a mine, worked as a clerk, worked as a traveling salesman, worked for the Austrian SS, worked for the German SS as a "Specialist in Jewish Affairs," worked upon the Final Solution.

And Zvi watching as the small man, the ordinary-looking man, the man with the ashen expression on the rail-thin face, moved his fingers nervously as though they were no part of him. The small man with the averted eyes and the edge of his mouth twitching.

The whispered comment by a reporter, "That man hates."

And the three judges.

And then the quibbles over validity, over proceedings, over the capture, over the judges' right to judge.

And the prosecutor: "As I stand before you, Judges of Israel, to lead the prosecution, I do not stand alone. With me in this place and at this hour stand six million accusers. . . . Their ashes were piled up in the hills of Auschwitz and in the fields of Treblinka or washed away by the rivers of Poland; their graves are scattered over the length and breadth of Europe. Their blood cries out but their voices are not heard."

And then the names and the places, the dates the crimes were committed.

"And Eichmann will enjoy a privilege he did not accord a single one of his victims. He will be allowed to defend himself according to law."

And the reporters from almost anywhere a man could read nodded their heads.

And the observers who had come to see justice done by the Jews nodded their heads.

And day passed onto day as those in the building of white stone from the Judean hills beheld the trial.

One evening in the middle of the third week, Zvi was sitting in his shirtsleeves, his shoes off and his feet on the sofa when Aaron opened the door to Moshe and a young woman Zvi had never met before.

The General crossed the room before Zvi could rise and shook his friend's hand. "I've heard you've done a wonderful job for the trial."

Pulling himself up from the sofa, Zvi embraced Moshe.

The young General grinned proudly. "I never thought I'd beat you to brigadier and that's been part of the fun."

The girl with Moshe looked from one to the other, surprised that they would be willing to speak so openly about their competition. Zvi only winked at his friend. "I'm willing to wager you don't make it all the way up the ladder."

Grasping Zvi's forearm affectionately, Moshe said, "And you think you will?"

Shrugging, the colonel turned to his other guest and introduced himself. "I'm Zvi Mazon. My son, Aaron, too."

The young woman nodded. "I'm Tamar Doron."

Zvi stared at her, suddenly aware that she was not much older than Aaron. Embarrassed at his own rudeness, he smiled. "I'm happy to meet you." Moshe was laughing as he caught Zvi's reaction.

"Lovely as a bug's ear," he said, putting his arm about the young girl and leading her to a chair while he explained, "I'm going to be in town a few days to talk to some Knesset committee about the budget. And I thought it was time we were met."

Zvi nodded. "I'm not too free these days. The trial."

Watching Zvi automatically draw a cigarette from his pocket, Moshe smiled before he asked, "Is there any question that he's guilty?"

"We're not the judges," Zvi said softly.

Then, to Zvi's surprise, the young girl Tamar shook her head. "Guilty, innocent. Who cares? What matters is the way they let themselves be killed. Sheep!"

Raising his hand as if to strike out, Zvi wanted to dispute the point with fury and then as suddenly, he changed his mind. Controlling himself, he asked Aaron to get them all something to drink; and before he spoke again, he lit his cigarette. He knew the girl was waiting for his reaction, and he decided not to get caught up in either temper or detachment.

Settling down on the sofa, he looked at Tamar closely. Her eyes were a pale blue; her hair a deep red. She was slighter than most Israeli girls and she held her small head high in an almost arrogant manner. "What kind of a Jew are you?" he asked.

The girl tried not to snicker, "I'm an Israeli."

Zvi looked over her head at Moshe, who was standing behind her chair, his hands on her shoulders.

Aaron was passing glasses of something.

"And you think you'd have fought?" he asked.

She nodded. "I've been in the army." The arrogance and assurance again. "Why didn't they fight?"

Moshe started to say something but changed his mind to let Zvi answer.

Very slowly, Zvi nodded his head, almost bobbing his full body. "You are alone. It is night. You see that there is a hole in the German line surrounding your *shtetl*, your own ghetto. And you want to rise and walk through the line across that field and into that forest, and if the Germans learn that you did, none of your neighbors will live. Those few who still might be siphoned off into a labor camp or find that miracle in which we Jews believe—they'll be killed more quickly and more horribly."

"They died anyway."

"But there was always that chance that they might not. Would you have taken that chance away from them?"

Shaking her head in annoyance, the girl said, "That sounds like some Talmudist quibbling about a period being in the right place when one life could have been saved."

Moshe burst out laughing, "Zvi Mazon, Talmudist."

Clasping his large hands into one gigantic fist before him, Zvi asked Tamar, "What the hell do you know about anti-Semitism?"

Puzzled, she looked up at Moshe and then back to Zvi. "Why should I know anything about it? There are always some people who don't like other people. Some of the people they don't like are Jews. Some of the people they don't like could be Catholics or Moslems or . . . " Her voice trailed off as she shrugged. "What has anti-Semitism to do with me?"

Zvi shut his eyes and wished at the same moment that he was, indeed, as capable of prayer as his friend Isaac had been. When he opened his eyes, he said softly, "What kind of Jews are we raising that they don't even know about it?"

Moshe opened his hands to indicate his ignorance.

However, it was Aaron who entered the conversation now; and to Zvi's surprise, what the youth said was not what he expected to hear.

"Stop playing games." And he crossed the room and stood addressing his father. "Games, Abba. So you fought for a State. Well, so will I. And so will Miss Doron, if she has to. Don't impugn our patriotism and don't play on our ignorance and try to tell us that the holy dream you fought for has to be kept alive. Zionism is no longer a dream. It is a fact. Haganah fought to establish a State. . . . " And he stood, hands on hips, looking defiantly at his father. "We are all proud you fought, but we don't have to thank you and always remember that you fought, because we're ready to fight, too."

Before Zvi or Moshe could say anything, Tamar spoke out. "You are both sabras. But you grew up with all the complexes and twists that people say came from the Diaspora, and for some silly reason you expect us to have the same neurotic approach to life. We don't. Believe me, we don't. Maybe because of you, we don't, but we don't. We're something new. We understand that."

For the first time, Moshe Gilead entered the discussion; and when he did, he admitted his confusion. "I'm not a thinker or a scholar and no one could call me Talmudic. But this thing—this whole . . . " and he tried to find the word and, failing, settled for several. "This whole thing about the morality of the Jews, the concept of justice, the belief in the good and the belief that there is a good. In the way our fathers told stories of the past and the way our mothers told stories of the past and the things they believed in which came from the ghettos. . . . Don't either of you believe in that?" And he was appealing to both Tamar and Aaron.

It was his mistress who laughed, "I agree with you, Moshe," Tamar said. "A thinker you're not." She laughed almost cruelly when she added in flat disdain, "*Bubba meisses*. Old women's tales about the Old Country. The things Jews believed in. The twisting words of the Talmud. Are these the reasons you and Zvi fought in the Old City?"

She was going to say more, but Zvi drowned her words with a shout. "Yes. If you want to know, the answer is *yes*. That is what we fought for. There were other reasons. The plain pragmatic one that there had to be a place to live for those who did not die in Europe and those who would have been killed in the Arab countries. But, yes, there the old wives' tales—the *bubba meisses* as you call them, and there were the entwined thoughts of the Talmud. They are all a part of what a Jew is and I don't want to see any part of that lost. With me it isn't religion or honor or tradition. It is all of it. The Jewish civilization." He fell silent for a moment, and then, appealing to Moshe, who he was certain felt as he, "We've lost too much already."

The other soldier nodded. "I didn't think we had lost quite so much." A feeble gesture indicated the others and what they stood for.

Again, it was Tamar who started the laughing. "Two mighty soldiers," she said with disgust. "Sentimental and stupid." Before Zvi or Moshe could cut her short, she said, "You lost the other half of Jerusalem, and we want to get it back as much as you." Aaron was nodding his head in agreement. "But," Tamar continued, "we think we need it. It fits into our country and is a part of it. For that we will fight."

It took Zvi a moment to understand what she was trying to say. "And what wouldn't you fight for?"

Shaking her head at the innocence he was showing and the startled look on Moshe's face, she said bluntly, "I don't give a damn about the Wall, and I would be just as happy if the things you all think it stands for were forgotten along with it. The Gentiles call it the Wailing Wall. Believe me, I won't wail."

"Amen," Aaron said. Zvi stared at his son. . . .

Zvi came to his feet. Aaron, about sixteen or more now, barely came up to his father's shoulders. And yet there was a strength about the way he carried himself and an assurance about the way he walked which pleased his father.

Zvi asked gently, "Why did you say 'Amen' to the end of the Wall?"

The boy shrugged off the question, "I don't want the end of it except that you and everyone your age seems to think it stands for something. It doesn't mean anything to me and my friends. We weren't a part of that world. And as far as I am concerned, the old men with long *payot* and caftans don't represent me or the Israel I'm willing to fight for." And in the same moment that Zvi was disappointed with his son, he was thrilled that the boy saw himself as a sabra even though he was the only one present who had not been born in the Holy Land.

Placing one arm around Aaron's shoulder, Zvi drew him to his side and said in an almost inaudible voice, "Moshe, what did we do it all for?"

This time it was Aaron who laughed at his father, "You aren't that old, Abba."

And Tamar laughed with him. "The problem with the two of you," and they knew she meant Zvi and Moshe, "is that you are caught between the old men who came first carrying the Zionist dream in their heads and those of us who grew up after the State. You are both sabras, and probably history will say that the two of you were among the best of the sabras." And then she grinned, "But I don't see either one of you living on a kibbutz in the old way. You are either confused or dishonest. You're both working and living and thinking about today, but there's that clouded halo hanging over the 'Old Dream.'"

Finally, looking once more at his son and ignoring the others, Zvi started to pace the room angrily. "No. There's no clouded halo over anything. It came true and there is a Jewish State. I agree. I will live with that. But don't try to tell me that the civilization of the Jews—of the millions who have died—is without any meaning for you. Don't try. I won't believe you. I'm no Talmudist," and he was bowing his head toward Tamar. "I'm a dirt soldier. But I believe there will be a new Jewish civilization, and it must include everything that came from the two thousand years of the Diaspora and what came even before that tragedy, for if not, what comes next will be built on nothing. *On nothing.*" His voice fell off, stressing the words more loudly than any shout.

"Amen," Moshe agreed. He was beaming at his friend. "Zvi, I . . . I," he was embarrassed as he saw Zvi was embarrassed.

"Too damned many words," Zvi snapped, angry at himself and angrier yet at Tamar and his son who had prodded him into an argument.

The others fell silent, not because they agreed with Zvi, but because they were aware of his embarrassment.

"Were you really in the army?" Aaron asked the petite young woman sitting before him.

"Why not?" Tamar asked, winking at Moshe.

Aaron shook his head, annoyed at being treated as a child. "Why does a Jew always answer a question with a question?" he demanded of his father.

Zvi looked at the boy, knowing how eager Aaron was to serve in the army. "Why does a Jew answer a question with a question?" He smiled. "Why not?"

Later, however, when he and Aaron were alone, Zvi asked, "If not the State and what it stands for, what?"

"I don't know, Abba. Something to live by, and that's not making more money or making life easy."

Neither of them said anything for a long time; and then Aaron said, "Maybe the thing that we want is somewhere in this State you and General Gilead and others made. Maybe it's more than going on from day to day; maybe it's the fact that every so often we have to be pioneers all over again. Maybe when I go into the army, it will be easier. There will be a purpose."

Zvi sighed, not wanting to accept a future which required the challenge of an enemy to survive. Recalling the old saw that if there had been no Israel, the Arab leaders would have had to create one to survive, he rejected the notion that Israel had to have Arab hostility to survive.

In the days that followed the discussion, Zvi listened to the trial testimony from a new point of view. Now he wanted to know just how much of what was happening in the trial had meaning for the generation which had come to adulthood after the State had been born. He wanted to know how much of the testimony at the Eichmann trial explained why there had to be a State and how much his son and Tamar had to be prepared to ensure its survival, ensure that never again would anyone attempt a Final Solution. He did not question their patriotism: he questioned their purpose, their goals, the direction they would take the country.

As for the trial, the case for the prosecution moved on inexorably.

There were the tapes of the accused explaining away six million deaths, himself always in the background, removed, distant.

And the spectators fascinated, the reporters from almost everywhere stunned.

And the survivors, those who had seen, those with the twisted memories which led down dark corridors toward the open pit dug for the six million known to those who had been there and seen and who could tell the court what it had been like:

". . . a boy bent down to pick up a piece of bread and he was shot."

". . . I was a dentist in Treblinka, till the day I recognized the body of my sister."

". . . Another improvement was the building of a gas chamber that would hold two thousand people at one time, whereas at Treblinka their ten gas chambers only held two hundred people."

". . . the bodies had to be taken from the gas chambers and after the teeth were extracted and the hair cut off, they had to be dragged to the pits

or the crematoria and the fire in the pits had to be stoked, the surplus fat drained off, and the mountains of burning bodies constantly turned over so that the draught might fan the flames."

" . . . In January, 1943, Eichmann ordered the 50,000 Jews of Salonika evacuated to Auschwitz, arranging the transportation.

" . . . Sometime between 5 and 8 June, Eichmann said to me: 'We accept the obligation toward the Hungarians that not a single deported Jew remain alive.' And up to 27 June, 475,000 Jews were deported."

" . . . I remember the girl, slim and with black hair, who as she passed me, pointed to herself and said: 'Twenty-three years old.' I then walked around the mound and saw a tremendous grave. People were closely wedged together. Nearly all had blood running over their shoulders from their heads. Some lifted their arms and turned their heads to show that they were still alive. A thousand people, and the SS man who did the shooting sat on the edge of the pit, a Tommy gun on his knees and a cigarette dangling from his mouth."

And the reporters from almost everywhere and the observers who had come to see justice done.

And all the while the man in the gray suit with the ashen look took notes with colored pencils.

And all the while he listened he did not deny the murders, the furnaces, the graves dug up and the bones scattered, and all the while he took notes with the colored pencils he did not deny anything but his relationship to the six million murders.

He was only an underling.

He was only taking orders.

He was faithful. He believed the words of his superiors.

He had only done what he was told. After all, he was a soldier.

And for those watching, statistics became faces and the faces shouted silently to those who would hear that the first beating of a single innocent man by the brown-shirted bully boys was the first step to the open pit.

And with the first perversion of science and truth—one single cohabitation of a Jew with an Aryan woman is sufficient to spoil her blood forever. Togehter with the alien albumen, she has absorbed the alien soul—Treblinka and Auschwitz could only follow through the dark corridor where the traffic had been directed by the man wearing the gray suit and the ashen look, who toyed with colored pencils.

And those watching him could hear the phantom whistles of trains passing lonely through bare countryside, past hidden and known graves, under a sky darkened by the smoke of furnaces. The pall of smoke and the odor of gas seemed to linger in the court. The man behind the bullet-proof glass moved the colored pencils nervously, the edge of his mouth twitching.

And for Zvi Mazon, the trial became life itself. Nothing else meant much. For fifty-six days Zvi had listened, and now as he walked out of the courtroom into the late afternoon's sunlight, he wondered if he had just returned from the underworld. He stood for a time letting the crowd flow by. Lighting a cigarette, he tried to decide what he would do in the week between the prosecution's case and that of the defense.

TEL AVIV, JUNE, 1961

When Zvi arrived in the city, he did not know what to do with himself and regretted not bringing Aaron along.

He dropped into the dress shop, which had grown into a large establishment where more than ten salesgirls and models presented the dresses which Ruth manufactured in another part of Tel Aviv. She greeted him in her office with a kiss on his cheek and stood back to look at him. Zvi Mazon had put on weight over the years. Though only in his late thirties, he had begun to show age. There were the same kinds of lines across his face that Moshe had developed years earlier. The long months spent in the Negev had left their mark as leathery skin, and his hair was beginning to thin. However, Ruth saw that he still stood rigidly as though at attention and that his stocky frame hid much of his weight.

"You came down alone?" she asked. "Where's Libby?"

"She went back to her husband weeks ago, if that's what you want to know."

Ruth laughed softly, "Then I gather you're alone again."

Zvi grinned wryly. "Maybe I could get visiting privileges." And they both laughed.

"How's Aaron?"

"Fine. And you?"

Ruth shrugged. "I thought I was doing well."

"But?" Zvi's hand was inside his shirt now, and Ruth smiled.

"But he's going away. Canada."

Cocking his head to one side, Zvi said, "Why Canada and, if Canada, why aren't you going with him?"

Setting some sketches down facing Zvi, Ruth said flatly, "Canada because he's an automobile salesman and there's a depression here, and people don't buy many cars anyway, what with the taxes."

Accepting this as part of the answer, Zvi waited for the rest.

"And as for me and Canada, I'm an Israeli." Zvi enjoyed the pride in her voice.

"And your automobile salesman isn't?"

Again Ruth sighed. "He is. But he doesn't see anything for himself here." And as she spoke, she pointed to the sketches of a woman's blouse.

"Another couple of years and you will be thinking the same thing, unless, of course, you want to get into the dress business."

Picking up the sketches, Zvi stared at them and then, looking over the top of the pad, asked, "Do you think I should go into women's blouses?"

Reaching across the desk, Ruth pulled the pad from his hand. "I don't know where you're going. That's your problem," she snapped, "I'll buy you out anytime you want to invest in something else."

Slowly pulling up the chair behind him, Zvi settled into it without taking his eyes off Ruth. "You want me out?"

She shook her head. "I leave the decision to you. I'm just suggesting you might want to go abroad. Canada, maybe." Smiling bitterly, she added, "New York. When the trial is over, there will be a woman in New York who would also give you visiting privileges, even though you are a Jew."

Clasping his hands behind his head, Zvi leaned back and stared at her. "Why are you trying to start a fight?"

Taking a deep breath, Ruth countered with another question. "Did you send Moshe Gilead in here?"

"No."

"Then why does he pick my shop to dress his doxies?"

Zvi laughed. "Maybe he has better taste than you credit him with."

However, Ruth was not laughing. "Every time he finds a girl who will sleep with him, he brings her here to dress her, as though she were some kind of doll and he was playing house."

Trying without much success not to smile, Zvi asked, "Do you mind his playing house with little girls?"

Rising quickly to stand looking down at him, she put her hands on her hips and said coldly, "I don't want him playing house with Hannah. He can't keep his eyes off her if she's here when he is."

Nodding slowly, Zvi understood more than she knew. "You tell him," he said. "Don't be shy about it." Reaching out, he took both her hands in his. "Look, I'm not his keeper."

Jerking back, she bumped her desk and then sat down on the edge of it. "I don't care whose wife you sleep with and what kind of privileges you have. I don't care if he lays all of the young girls in Israel—and sometimes I think he does—but both of you have lost any sense you ever had about women."

Laughing loudly, Zvi rose and placed his hands on her cheeks, kissed her gently on the lips and stepped back. "Don't worry," he assured her. "Hannah and Moshe aren't climbing into bed together, and if either of them starts to, call on me." He laughed at the notion. "Hell, she's going to be Aaron's." Suddenly serious, he asked, "Would you mind that, too?"

Ruth slowly smiled and shook her head. "I sound awful, don't I?"

"You do."

Touching her cheek with an open palm, Ruth stood looking at him. "And you? What happens to you now?"

"Me? I finish with the trial for whatever I'm supposed to be doing there, write my final report as to its implications for Zahal and then I go where they send me." He picked up the sketches once more. "Maybe I ought to look into women's blouses."

And she was laughing when he left.

Zvi went to the theater alone that evening because Ruth was seeing her salesman off the next day. Afterward, he drove over to Avram's apartment and sat in front of it for half an hour before he decided he might as well go home.

JERUSALEM, JUNE-JULY, 1961

The next week the trial continued.

The defense began its arguments. The portly man with the smile and the white hair. The good German who had come in behalf of his countryman. The questions were his, the answers his client's.

And no one denying genocide.

And no one denying six million dead.

And no one denying the murders by the Einsatzgruppen, the gas vans, the camps, the furnaces.

In all honesty, who could deny . . . ?

But there is a point. A single point. A simple point that must be denied: that the head of the Bureau of Jewish Affairs in the Nazi hierarchy had anything to do with genocide or death or the Einsatzgruppen or gas vans, camps, furnaces.

The head of the Bureau of Jewish Affairs did nothing but schedule trains—a functionary obeying orders—a mere dispatcher of railroad cars—a considerate little man who moved trains efficiently so that the Jews reached their destinations on time.

"And all of the other details? Do you expect a man to remember?"

"It was all so long ago."

"It never came to my attention."

"It was handled by someone else."

"Someone else put my name on that document."

"I only kept records. I saved Jewish lives by forcing Jews to leave Austria before the war."

"Anything else is a lie, a forgery, a mistake."

"I was only obeying orders. That was the state of affairs."

And on from one day to the next.

By the end of the week, Zvi was numbed again. Leaving the courtroom, he felt someone touch his sleeve and, turning, found that he was standing beside Kineret Heschel. She looked much older than the last time he had seen her. Her once bright hair was now almost stark white; the once smooth skin was wrinkled. Her eyes remained sharp and she smiled at his ill-concealed reaction to her appearance.

"You don't look so good yourself, young man," she taunted him.

Taking her arm, Zvi offered to buy her coffee.

As they drove to the King David, she sat back and stared at him. "You know, Zvi, you never did go as far as I thought you would."

"I'm sorry I disappointed you."

She snorted, "It's yourself you disappointed."

Laughing, he asked, "Is this the new approach to life that you learned as an ambassador?"

She laughed with him. "People expect Israelis to be blunt. When we are really rude, they call it 'Israeli courtesy'; but they don't take offense, because they think we are an underdeveloped country without the British dignity or the American clout."

They were at the hotel now and she led him onto the terrace, where they took a table and ordered coffee. The foreign newsmen who had come to cover the trial nodded to Kineret and Zvi, whom they recognized.

Returning to Kineret's earlier comment, Zvi shrugged. "Maybe you're right. I could consider myself a disappointment."

Her hand came across the table and covered his. "Since the fifty-six war, you've gone to school and you still don't have a doctorate. You are in the army, and you still have not made general. You've had a wife and a lot of mistresses, but you aren't married and you live alone." She shook her head in mock disappointment. "You've let me down, Zvi."

Almost angry with the image of himself which she had painted, he asked, "Know anyone who needs a soldier?"

"Israel. Nasser and Hussein aren't done with us yet." She was waving to the waiter to bring her another cup of coffee as she said, casually, "There was a word that the Greeks used—*hubris*. I wonder sometimes whether we are the ones who suffer from it or the Arabs."

"*Hubris?*"

Again she revealed the tired patience which Zvi felt too many were showing him in recent months, " 'Wanton insolence or arrogance, excessive pride or passion.' "

Thinking about her definition, Zvi was sure it was applicable to the Arabs.

The edges of her eyes crinkled as she advised, "One of these days you should find a mistress who is intelligent enough to teach you something." Before he could comment, she said sadly, "I'm sure you think you've better things to do with them."

Not knowing what he was expected to say, Zvi winked.

Sighing, Kineret snapped, "Like your friend, General Gilead, Moshe, the Lion of Judea and the bedroom, you've reduced your vocabulary to a wink."

Shoving back his chair, Zvi pulled a cigarette from his shirt pocket and lighted it without taking his eyes off her face. "Why is it that everyone I meet of late thinks I'm a damned fool?"

A touch of a smile, "There could be on obvious answer to that, but I'm sure it's not the one you want."

"I'd rather not hear it," he admitted.

Enjoying his discomfort, Kineret said warmly, "You've undersold yourself. You've never gone after responsibility even though you've enjoyed it and have handled it well."

The trial moved on to the defense witnesses. The audience remained large, though the press coverage had begun to dwindle. There were those who said the trial had run too long. There were those who praised the Israelis for their slow and steady pains to allow the accused justice. Zvi listened to the sixteen depositions which were read or played from tapes. None of them helped the accused very much because most of the defense witnesses were in one way or another pleading their own cases. And then the time came for the live witnesses, and they did not help the accused as much as he might have hoped. And one of the last explained that there had been no difficulty removing himself from an awful assignment, and the word "awful" took on its original meaning for Zvi and the others listening.

Zvi watched the taut muscles on Eichmann's face while his own witnesses testified, and the accused could not hide his sense of frustration.

He had no friends who would appear in his behalf, even though some had been called to speak for the defense and some few had even made the journey to Israel.

And then in late July the last witness had spoken and the court adjourned for twelve days to allow the prosecution and the defense time to prepare their summations.

Zvi went back to his apartment and began to write his report. The findings of the judges were not his concern. He had been asked to deal with the subject of superior orders. He was no lawyer, but he had a copy of the transcript and he had the notes he had taken while reading documents and the transcripts for eight months. During the next several days he worked at home, spending his late afternoons and early evenings with his son.

They talked about Aaron's desire to become a pilot, about Zvi's feelings concerning the army and a military career, about the trial and what it meant to the Jews. Zvi explained to the boy the importance of never forgetting they were Jews, because even though a Jew tried to forget, there were others who would remember. They talked about Judaism as a religion and as a civilization and what the differences were. Zvi apologized because he had never sent

508

Aaron to a synagogue for training, but then, he said, he had never had any religious training himself. And the boy asked if Zvi wished he had had some and Zvi shrugged. "How can you tell if you miss what you have never had?"

And Aaron told Zvi about Hannah and how pretty he thought she was and how she had invited him to spend a few weeks with her and Ruth. And Zvi said he would think about it, and both of them knew that the answer was going to be Yes.

The first week of Zvi's work went well, but he was not satisfied. Something was gnawing at him and it was not the subject of his report. It had to do with Kineret's comments about his failures and Ruth's warning that he ought to look into women's blouses. He did not know what he wanted now that this part of his life was coming to an end, and he knew that he had to make up his mind. At the beginning of the second week, he suggested that so long as Aaron had a vacation they would drive down to Eilat and spend some time on the beach, and later that same day they drove south from Jerusalem.

NEGEV-EILAT

Passing through the Negev, Zvi felt more at home than he had at any time since leaving it. Somehow the desert suited him better than anyplace else. The barren land spreading wide and multicolored reminded him of Yemen and the journey he had made there and he reached out and affectionately placed one hand on his son's shoulder, and told the boy about Yemen and the people who had traveled with them from San'a.

The boy listened, always fascinated by the story, and when Zvi finished telling about the drive to the airplane and how Aaron had been flown into Israel by an American pilot, the boy asked, "And when did you decide you wanted me to be your son?"

They were south of Wadi Faran now and the countryside was burned black. Zvi felt the heat of the sun on his face and wiped away the sweat crawling into his eyes. "When they brought you into Camp Hashed and told me that Havah had died. I knew then that we were going to be together a long time."

The boy braced his back against the door of the car so that he could face his father. "This Havah, did you love her?"

Zvi wanted to smile because he did not know just what Aaron would describe as love. "I'm not sure," he finally admitted. "I'm just not sure."

"And that Arab woman, were you in love with her?"

"What gives you so many ideas about love?"

The boy was silent at first, then he admitted, "I've been thinking about it a lot lately. Some of the boys at school say it is going to bed with a girl, and some of them say it is living with one, and some of them say it is liking one around when you want to be alone."

Carefully trying to sort out what the boys at school had defined as love, Zvi believed he preferred the last definition. "Liking one around when you want to be alone. Maybe that's it," he agreed.

"Did you like that Arab woman that way?"

Seeing that the question was going to need some kind of an answer, Zvi shook his head. "I don't know. I never had a chance to find out." He glanced at Aaron's serious face and explained, "I have never been with her long enough to learn if she would wear well."

"Is wearing well part of being in love?"

Again, Zvi wished they were talking about something else, "I think so. If not, maybe all one has is a passion, and that's something easily satisfied by being in bed."

"Did you and Libby have a passion?"

Raising one hand, Zvi pointed out a small doe in the desert.

Aaron watched until it fled behind some rocks.

"There actually is some game in Israel," Zvi said.

The boy looked at his father for a long time before he asked if there were any airplanes in Eilat and if maybe he could go for a short flight.

Zvi said he would find out if there was a plane that would take the boy up, and then Aaron started talking about his flight to the United States and how much food they had served on the El Al plane, and he wanted to know if he flew out of Eilat if they would serve food.

The next morning Zvi found a friend, whom he had known years before, who was now an Arkia Airlines pilot. He agreed to take Aaron with him on his day's flight to show the boy what an airplane was from the co-pilot's seat. Watching the eagerness with which Aaron was willing to leave him, Zvi felt alone in Eilat.

In another few years the boy would be in service. After that the chances of his returning to his father's home would be slight.

Driving from the airfield to the beach, Zvi wondered what this loss would mean to him. In the years since Zella's death he had filled up his time with one woman or another, but Aaron had always been the anchor about which he swung. And now he knew Aaron would soon be gone.

Parking in front of his hotel, Zvi walked along the rocky beach. Unbuttoning his shirt, he let the sun burn his skin.

He had driven out of Jerusalem because he had to think about something other than the trial and the significance of "superior orders." He had to think about Zvi Mazon.

And yet he did not even know where to begin.

A young girl raced past him followed by a boy. A moment later Zvi watched the boy catch her arm, swing her about and roll her into the water. Diving after her, the boy started to tug at the slight bra of her bikini. Zvi walked on, but he could not forget the picture of the two. And as he thought about them, he recalled the strange conversation he had had with the girl Tamar and with Aaron. Somehow the faces of the boy and the girl in the water blended with the other faces and Zvi knew he was looking at something new. Maybe this was where his problem lay.

These young people were all living normal lives. They could have bedded down with each other in any city of the west; they could have played on any beach. They were living normal lives. He had not. Moshe had not. Avram had not. Was this the difference? He was not certain, and also he was not sure what normal was.

He was a Jew. He had always thought of himself as a Jew. These young people were thinking of themselves as Israelis, and then he remembered Ruth's answer when he had asked why she did not join her lover in Canada: *I am an Israeli.* There was a transition taking place.

A plane passed overhead. Zvi squinted into the sun. How could Aaron know what it was to be a Jew in a Jewish world when he had never been a Jew in any other kind of world? Was comparison the element that was gone? Zvi did not believe it was.

And yet as his mind drifted back to the trial, he thought he saw that there was new meaning. There was more than just the need to educate the young to what had taken place, there was the need to stamp the past upon the minds of the Jews who were forgetting it because they were not really any longer a part of it. What did the past mean to Moshe's little Tamar, to Hannah, to Aaron? Something their parents talked about, something they could read about in the newspapers.

The trial had meaning for this moment. Would it have any tomorrow? Would there have to be an endless series of trials? None could concede that that made any sense. And he least of all. And if the trial meant so little to his son and the others, what would it mean to the Jew in the Diaspora, the Jew in exile? The papers said that no one was listening, no one was hearing, no one cared. Probably they were right.

Zvi flicked the cigarette away and watched as a small wave carried it out.

Striding almost angrily down to the water's edge, Zvi kicked off his sandals and moved slowly into the water, ignoring the fact that his trousers were getting wet. He felt the cool waters on his legs and stared south toward the mouth of the strait which lay beyond the horizon. Almost twelve years before, he and the old Italian had sailed into Eilat. They had brought home the scrolls and the books. And now, who was reading them and who except a very few cared if they were read or gathering dust? Certainly not Isaac's children, now being educated in the schools of the State.

Moving along the beach, Zvi wondered what was happening and what was not happening and where he fitted into this changing people. The Jews of Yemen had remained Jews in spite of the Arabs who had made their life a misery. His ancestors, too, had remained Jews in spite of terror and want.

Zvi's own grandparents had remained Jews even though they had had to walk close to the walls when they moved out of the ghetto; they had had to yield the sidewalk to any passing *goy*, they had lived without land and they had lived as chattel, and yet they had thought enough about their being Jewish to cling to that very thing—the fact that they were Jewish. And now Zvi and his son were no longer clinging to the traditions of the Book. They no longer even looked like the generations of inbred Jews who matched the caricatures of the anti-Semites, they no longer spoke with the time-created gestures which none would deny they had known. He knew that none who hated Jews and said he could smell Jews could tell Moshe or himself from any other man walking any street in the Western world. He almost laughed as he thought of his meaningless achievement—he could pass for a Christian.

Was this why he had fought, why Fishel and so many others had died? So that they would not be taken for Jews? He wondered if the Diaspora Jew in Argentina or the United States felt he had accomplished something when he was no longer taken for a Jew. Snorting, Zvi thought for a moment that maybe what the American Jews needed was a pogrom. Then they would remember they were Jewish. Then maybe they would turn from the Diaspora and come home where their numbers and skills were needed for survival.

The girl in the bikini was splashing near him and the boy was after her again and both of them were laughing.

Zvi thought of normalcy again. These two could have been any two Gentiles on any beach. He did not want to decide if this were good or bad. He did not want to make up his mind. If anti-Semitism had helped form the Jews maybe he should be cheering Nasser on. Maybe the hatred preached by Radio Cairo and the Voice of the Arabs was making good Jews while it was making bad Arabs.

Zvi strode back to the shore and sat down on the stony beach to let the sun dry his trousers.

Closing his eyes, he remembered the Wall as he had last seen it on a dark night with rifle fire flashing across the roof tops and the sound of an Arab machine gun striving to reach him.

The Wall was the symbol of the Orthodox Jews. He wondered if it would be the symbol of the Israelis, and he could still hear Tamar saying it meant nothing to her and he could still see Aaron nodding.

Opening his eyes, he looked at the horizon where the bright sky blended with the bright water.

The Wall. Was it now only a part of ghetto memory, or was it a part of the Jewish past which had to be kept alive?

The Hasidim and the *Neturei Karta*— the Guardians of the City—would care, but would his son?

Was it only the symbol of years of wandering and years of degradation? Was it necessary now?

Someone had said the Israelis were losing the defects of their fathers. And someone had asked if they were keeping their qualities.

What, Zvi asked himself, were those qualities? Fearfulness, closeness, interdependence, a seeking after knowledge and righteousness as though they were indeed the only things a man needed other than God. In a way they were God.

He shrugged at his own inadequacy, his own inability to understand. He was aware that somehow fear had got lost, and in its place was a cockiness, a self-assurance which was in its own way beautiful and without doubt strange among Jews, and being strange appeared almost awesome to those who had never known self-assurance. Kineret had spoken of *hubris*, but she had said it meant pride and passion without justification. Maybe it was justified. A miracle had taken place. The Jews had come together on the land. And who could say that there should be no pride in a miracle?

And yet, Zvi knew that something was wrong.

He came to his feet and started back up the beach to find his sandals. The two thousand years and the six million dead and the Arabs had all led to anxiety, and was there any need to keep it alive? However, with the dream achieved, what was going to make a Jew of his son? There had to be something more to being a Jew than merely being like a Gentile living a normal life without the unique pressures and purposes.

Something more had to come of the two thousand years of suffering than just being like everyone else. For sixty generations Jews had striven to be Jews, had striven to be different in some way that was worth the effort when all they would have had to do was convert to be like any Gentile living a normal life.

Something had to come of the exile years and the dead.

It had to signify. There had to be a purpose.

His head went up, and he stared at the sky with equal eyes and he knew that if he did nothing else with the rest of his life, the search for a purpose would be enough. It was not important whether or not he became a general, though it was good to be a leader of his people; it was not important if he became a scholar, though it was good to know and to teach; however, it was important to find out where he and Aaron fitted into the scheme of things which were going to have meaning for those who had come together to achieve a miracle for their children.

He laughed at his own *hubris* and walked back to the hotel, feeling no less restless, but thinking that in some way he had found a direction, no matter how vague the trail.

JERUSALEM, AUGUST - DECEMBER, 1961

And the trial continued, the prosecutor summarizing:

—the acts of cruelty and lust for evil, degradation, oppression of body and soul, the likes of which have never been known in the annals of mankind;
—the murders, the torture, the bestiality. And all linked to the man in the gray suit with the nervous fingers lining up the colored pencils; his part in the holocaust, his part in terror, and his admission: "I implemented it with the fanaticism a man would expect of himself as a veteran National Socialist."

And the prosecutor summarizing:
—to describe it all a new writer of Lamentations *must arise;*
—for the blood of the righteous that was spilled, render a just and truthful verdict.
And the trial continued, the defense summarizing:
—a man was only obeying superior orders;
—there should be no revenge;
—punishment will not expiate;
—the passing of time must bring peace.
Let there be judgment transcending, a judgment of Solomon which will show the wisdom of the Jewish people.

And court was adjourned until November.

Zvi strode from the court into the light of the late afternoon, thinking of the plea for the Jews to be Jews, when the crime being judged was the murder of Jews for being no more than what they were—Jews.

For the next few days Zvi worked on his own report, and after he had a first draft completed he made a date with Kineret Heschel, who had offered to go over it with him.

When he arrived at her house, she kissed him affectionately on the cheek and stepped back to look at him. A smile crossed her face. "I understand why there are so many women in your life," she said as she held her hand out for the report.

Feeling both inadequate and young, he gave her the report and walked outside into her garden while she settled down to read it.

The lights of the city seemed bright. Off to the east he could make out Mount Scopus, Israel's enclave in Arab territory, and he wondered when the explosion would take place. In the past thirteen years the Arabs had tried many times to get the Jews off Mount Scopus. And with the help of some of the UN staff, they had almost succeeded a number of times. The great hospital now lay empty and unused. The university which shared the top of Scopus was now a shell which gathered dust. The immorality disturbed him as much as did the argument between himself and Avram which continued to plague their relationship—the difference of opinion concerning his right to have moved the way he had at Mitla. The issues were moral ones: What had

Zvi owed to his men and to tradition, and what had he owed to his orders? The moral aspects of war. Smiling to himself, he was almost pleased to have fought a battle with moral implications. And he was thinking of this when he remembered that Kineret did not know where he was. Glancing once more at Mount Scopus, he half saluted the small detachment which he knew was stationed there to hold the mountaintop against the Arabs. Theirs was a long and lonely vigil even though they were rotated fortnightly.

Walking back into the house, he made his way to the living room where Kineret glanced at him over the last page of the report.

"Restless, or uncertain about how good this is?"

Shrugging, Zvi explained, "I'm not exactly given to this kind of thing. A better historian or a lawyer should have done it. The more I think about it, the more I wonder why I got the assignment."

He lit a cigarette while he thought about what appeared clear to her. Finally, he shook his head.

Impatiently Kineret said, "Let's get into this report."

And for the next two hours she challenged almost every point Zvi had made.

They were on their third cup of coffee when she asked, "How much do you think this information is worth where you point out that both the British and the Americans had in their own Manuals of Military Law the statement from 1914 to 1941 that, 'Members of the Armed Forces who commit such violations of the recognized rules of warfare as are ordered by their government or their commander are not war criminals and cannot therefore be punished by the enemy. He may punish such officials or commanders responsible for such orders if they fall into his hands, but otherwise he may only resort to other means of obtaining redress.' "

Smiling, Zvi pointed out that though the manuals read that way, they were not in very good legal standing, judging by what he had been listening to the past several months.

Kineret snorted. "Think, Zvi. Think. The German higher courts have pointed out that the subordinate was obliged to assume that the superior orders were legal."

"No." he snapped back almost angrily. "Don't you see that if one does know better, he does not have the right to assume an order is legal." He thought for a moment and repeated, "If he knows better. Knows better."

Kineret smiled gently, "And you still don't know why you are on this trial?"

For a very long time Zvi stared at her almost stupidly, and then he burst out laughing. "But I did know better. I was at Mitla. The people giving me the orders not to enter the Pass weren't."

"And you did what you thought was right?"

"I damned well did."

"And you were never called to trial for disobeying orders," she reminded him.

Wiping his face with his broad palm, he agreed. "But, what I did was not against any law other than the military law of my own country."

"You're right. But you thought about your order and you made a decision. For that, there are those who respected you."

Growling softly, he shook his head. "No. No one's respected me for Mitla."

"I didn't say they respected you for Mitla and the men you lost or your damned-fool eagerness. For those things I'd have courtmartialed you myself. But you are respected for having thought and followed the course of action which you believed was correct."

Picking up his cup again, he looked at her dubiously, "That's a funny word—*correct.*"

"But you were to that extent." Then her face lost its smile and she was the woman who had soldiered and served, "Beyond that you can be judged."

Smiling wryly, he said, "I have been. Believe me, Kineret, I have been."

Moving back on the sofa, she shook her head. "If anyone had asked me, I would have said Colonel Zvi Mazon was one of the few men I have known who wasn't given to self-pity."

He wanted to slam the cup down, but she reached over and, taking it from him, set it on the coffee table.

"What about this report as a whole?" he finally pressed.

"Patience," she said. "Why didn't the US and British Manuals of War get changed from 1914 to 1944 if the weight of the law was against the position the manuals took?"

Zvi smiled. "Because like so many other things, no one gave a damn." He watched the smoke of his cigarette and then asked, "Who cares about things like that in peacetime? Who's going to sit around and change manuals on such issues when the issues are not coming up?"

"We are," she reminded him.

Nodding, he accepted the correction.

She read on, finding the points which she had marked on her first reading. "This opinion you quote from Nuremberg, was that written by the American judge who testified against Eichmann?"

"Musmano," Zvi confirmed.

"The obedience of a soldier," she read aloud, "is not the obedience of an automaton. A soldier is a reasoning agent." She paused and smiling wryly, asked, "Is General Moshe Gilead a reasoning agent?"

Zvi nodded. "Just because he likes women doesn't mean he's not a reasoning man when duty is concerned."

Laughing, she said, "There are still times when you sound like a Boy Scout." And she read on, "It is a fallacy of widespread consumption that a soldier is required to do everything his superior officers order him to do. The subordinate is bound only to obey the lawful orders of his superior."

Zvi said, "That's it on the head."

"That's in a legal document, you mean. It isn't in the rule as laid out by all countries."

"The intent," he explained. "The intent is."

Satisfied that he was not going to yield the point, she turned to another page and, picking it up, said, "I like this one. You quote no one less authoritative than Goebbels himself, and as you would say, 'That's a hell of a source.' " Zvi started to defend himself, but she began to read. "From the German Press May 28, 1944. 'No international law of warfare is in existence which provides that the soldier who has committed a mean crime can escape punishment by pleading as his defense that he followed the commands of his superiors. This holds particularly true if those commands are contrary to all human ethics and opposed to the well-established international usage of warfare.' " Looking up, she grinned. "I like that."

"He was warning the Allied bomber crews," Zvi explained.

Rising from the sofa, Kineret led him out to the garden where they stood looking at the silhouetted hills of Jerusalem and talked about the Old City.

Three weeks after his meeting with Kineret, Zvi was assigned as Chief of Staff to the Commanding Officer, Southern Command.

Arranging for Aaron to change schools, he and the boy moved into the small house in Beersheba which Moshe and Zipporah had occupied. There Zvi prepared the final version of his report and started out to learn his new duties. The southern front had been quiet since the end of the 1956 war. There had been a few periodic incursions into Israel by both terrorists and Arab military units. However, these were small-scale, and for nearly a year there had been almost no activity on the long borders.

Once they were settled in, Zvi inspected each of the units which fell under the Command.

In the several years since Zvi had been on field duty, very little had changed in the Israeli army, with the exception of an increased emphasis on tank operations.

Phantom headquarters for divisional-size units were being created. But the army itself still functioned at brigade size, and almost all the work in the Southern Command, other than training, consisted of constant patrols. In earlier years the Egyptians had tried to shift the frontier by moving the concrete-filled oil drums which marked the line farther into Israeli territory at night, a short distance at a time. Finally, the Israelis, with the cooperation of the United Nations, planted tall black-and-white steel border posts in concrete. Most of the time the Israeli patrols never saw an Egyptian soldier, though in the distance they could often see Bedouin tents or flocks on the move.

It was obvious that the Arab leaders could control the terrorists when they wished. Even though a few fedayeen laid mines along the Gaza frontier, there was an unsettled peace. The frontier to the east was equally quiet, though the Jordanians were protesting Israel's constructions along the Jordan River and the Dead Sea.

Life for Zvi was routine now, and he felt good being back at work which he knew, and for which he had spent most of his life preparing. Months passed and he heard nothing about the report he had submitted on the problem of Superior Orders; and while he had not forgotten the horrors of the Eichmann trial, it slipped into the recesses of his mind. And so when he received the call from headquarters that he was expected to be in Jerusalem for the judgment on 11 December, it came almost as a surprise. He drove to Jerusalem, which he had not visited since he had left in late September.

When Zvi arrived at the court, he found that Malin was already there and seated among the spectators. Edging into the seat beside her, he asked, "Have you any idea what will happen?"

She looked at him, smiled, and said nothing.

Court again and the spectators gathered to watch the small man behind glass, face twitching, fingers nervous, colored pencils at hand.

And silence, breath held, the accused rising.

And the verdict: guilty of crimes against the Jewish People, of crimes against humanity, of war crimes and of membership in criminal associations.

And court was adjourned pending the passing of sentence.

Zvi walked out with Malin and for a few minutes neither of them said anything. Then Zvi asked, "There will be an appeal?"

She nodded as she watched the crowd flow past.

A newspaperman tried to get an opinion of the verdict from Malin, who smiled and shook her head. Then he asked, "Have you any opinions, Colonel?"

"Would I dare, if Judge Ben Ezra has none?"

And the reporter moved on, leaving them standing alone together.

"It's been good," Zvi said. "There were times when I was not certain about that. But now I think it has been good."

She was not as certain. "Let us not credit the trial with too much. There will still be injustices, but I think I know what you mean. We stand higher because the trial was fair."

Zvi nodded. They were walking to her car now, and when he opened the

518

door for her, Malin held it for a moment as she appeared to be thinking of something. Finally, as though she was forced to say it, "I read your report."

Puzzled at what he thought was a negative reaction, he waited.

When she said nothing, he asked, "Something in it bothered you?"

She nodded, opened the door all the way, slipped in and gestured for him to join her. Uncertain what was coming, Zvi settled down in the car beside his friend's wife, offered her a cigarette, lighted one for himself and waited.

"Zvi." she said at last, "there are parts of the problem you never covered."

"Such as?"

Malin brushed her hair back and staring straight ahead as though she were looking at something other than the back of the car parked in front of hers. "You were right to bring in all of the aspects—the moral, the legal, the immoral and the illegal. They fuse in different ways."

He still did not know what she was moving toward and so he said nothing.

Carefully threading her way, Malin explained, "Let us take four cases we know well. Kfar Kassem. An order was obeyed, there was an immorality in the obedience, but certainly not in the intent of the order. And men who committed the immorality were punished."

Zvi thought about his own explanation of that case to Zippy that night at dinner so long ago. He nodded to indicate he was following.

"Mitla. Legal orders. Disobeyed. No immorality because the man who disobeyed—or, shall I say, stretched his orders in the interpretation—did not do it for immoral or illegal reasons. No one was punished even though men died."

She waited for him to comment, but he merely watched the smoke rising from his cigarette.

Taking a deep breath, Malin pursued her course, "Eichmann. Illegal and immoral orders obeyed even though the man obeying knew the orders to be illegal and immoral. The perpetrator guilty."

Zvi sucked deeply on his cigarette before he pointed out, "You said let us take four cases."

She seemed to hesitate and then plunged on: "Petra. Legal orders not to pursue the subject, not to cross the border. Legal orders disobeyed. Illegality followed and immorality at its core. Men died. No one was punished."

And now it had been said, and Zvi sat very still for a long time as he held the case up and slowly turned it around so that he could see it better. And all the while that he looked, he saw Malin's hatred of Moshe, and yet he hoped there was more than simple hatred. He liked this woman who had made Avram happy, who was the only woman he knew who had made a marriage work. There had to be more than hatred.

Very slowly, he began to talk, "The day of Zippy's funeral Avi told me that the Chief of Staff had warned Moshe. Avi believed he would disobey orders."

"Where does he fit into this?" Malin demanded, surprised to find herself on the defensive.

"When Avi called me to tell me that Moshe was believed to have crossed the border, he said, 'We need him.' He told me that others believed we need him."

Malin wanted to brush the involvement of her husband aside, but she was too honest to do that. "Hitler may have said the same thing about Eichmann. He needed Eichmann to kill."

Zvi looked at her, but she did not turn to face him. A trace of appreciation for her own integrity came through as he heard her say, "What Moshe did was wrong. But, no one approved and no one ordered."

Neither of them said anything for a time and then she continued, "What you are telling me is that Moshe's crime was condoned."

Very slowly, Zvi nodded and then he changed his mind. "No. Not condoned. Understood. He avenged your sister. Believe it or not—and I doubt if you will—in his own way he loved her. She told me as much herself."

Malin weighed this defense and shook her head. "I know that there are those who condone and understand revenge as motive. I am not one of them."

Accepting this, Zvi pressed another course, "No one ordered Moshe to do what he did."

"And no one punished him for doing it." She was angry and it was beginning to show.

With deliberate care, Zvi put one hand on hers, "We couldn't punish him. We knew that, Avi and I. And we were both happy because we could not act. I am not saying we were right. We are neither of us judges and neither of us rabbis. We know right from wrong, but we could not act and we did not bewail that fact."

He thought a moment before he ventured out. "Moshe and the trial. Aren't you reaching out for an excuse to attack a man you don't like?"

She paused before she nodded. "I never said he was Eichmann. That would be far-fetched. I only suggest his was an illegal act performed *against* orders and in some ways condoned by an army whose 'needing him' is as lame as 'I was only obeying orders.'"

Almost relieved, Malin seemed to relax as she nodded.

"And with the evidence at hand," Zvi moved on, "would Judge Ben Ezra convict him?"

She shook her head.

"But, though you deny it, you *have* convicted him."

Again she shook her head. "I'm only pointing out what I believe is a crime and one which a soldier who is neither judge nor rabbi must be sensitive to. Your report ignored that aspect of the soldier and the moral law. Because something cannot be proved does not mean it is right."

Zvi stepped out of the car and stood beside it. Before he closed the door, he leaned over so that he could see Malin clearly: "If you're telling me I don't know all there is about the subject, you're right. If you're telling me that you dislike Moshe, you may have reason. But if you're telling me that Avi and I should not be happy because we could not prove a friend guilty, you are wrong. We could not and so we shed no tears. We're happy we couldn't. For two good reasons: he's our friend and Israel needs him."

She stared at him before she asked, "Accepting the obvious fact that Moshe is not Eichmann, if you could have proved him guilty, would you have?"

Zvi smiled wryly, "Doubt me if you want, but don't doubt Avi."

She thought about this and then smiled, "What you said about the trial—you're right. It was good."

He nodded, wondering what this was leading toward.

"And, Zvi, I won't doubt Avi or you." She started her car and he closed the door. When she drove away, he stood staring after her long after the car was out of sight, but he was not thinking of Malin or her husband, rather of Moshe and the extent of her dislike of his friend as well as the crime he had not evaluated before.

And the court convened for the last time. Its business, the sentencing of the accused.

And the prosecutor demanding death—for a man who has sinned against humanity, who has denied himself the right to walk among human beings, whom society is enjoined to spew out.

And the prosecutor stating the account will never be balanced:

"So long as one Jew is alive in the world, he will carry in his heart the memory of the great catastrophe and the agony inflicted on his people by that bloodstained regime. It will not be wiped out from our hearts and the hearts of our children and our children's children forever."

And the defense stating that it is fitting that the judge who strives for the highest justice should, in his own judgment, let mercy dominate.

And the accused rising to speak, fingers straightening the colored pencils into rows, all neat, all controlled:

"This mass slaughter is solely the responsibility of the political leaders. My guiding principle in life, from my earliest days, has been the desire to strive for the realization of ethical values."

And the judges concluding: "This court sentences Adolf Eichmann to death. . . . "

It was all over.

Zvi came to his feet and stood for a long time with his hands clutching the back of the seat in front of him. The soft blue cloth shadowed as his fingers dug into it. The judges were gone. Eichmann was gone. Zvi had given almost nineteen months of his own life, as researcher and observer, to this trial. He knew he had experienced more than he had expected. He knew that he would never forget the gray man with the black crimes. His head fell forward and he paid his own silent tribute to those who had been lost and whose story had been unfolded in this large room.

The Menorah behind the judges' bench caught Zvi's eye as his head came up. This was his country, these his people. The horror had been their horror. The justice just found had been their justice. And as he turned to Malin, who was waiting for him in the aisle, he thought of his afternoon on the beach at Eilat and the questions he had faced then about whether or not there would be Jews, because at this moment he knew there were Jews, Jews in spite of Eichmann and the other men who took part in the Final Solution. He cocked his head to one side and smiled sadly at Malin. "You know the horror of it is that if it had not been that man named Adolf Eichmann, it would have been another man named something else."

"If Eichmann had not been zealous, his getting a transfer wouldn't have saved a single life," Malin agreed.

"That's the horror of it," Zvi agreed.

TEL AVIV, 1962

It was during the first week in March at Southern Command in Beersheba that Zvi received a phone call to report to Hakiryah for reassignment. Taking leave of his commander, he took Aaron with him. He flew to Tel Aviv where a driver took the boy to Ruth's to wait for his father.

"I'll go meet Hannah as she comes out of school," Aaron explained as he left. Zvi winked at his driver and waved him on.

Over the years Zvi had observed the unwritten rule of the old soldier: Stay away from headquarters. Reporting to Avram, he was taken directly into the Chief of Operations' office. Moshe looked strange behind a large desk in an office with two secretaries. Excusing both women, Moshe sent for Lev Hershel, the Intelligence Officer. While they waited, the three talked. Malin was pregnant again, and Zvi congratulated Avram on the fact that he was going to become a father for the fifth time. It was Moshe who had heard from a friend that Libby had had a child, a boy. Her husband had given up his post at the new university in Tel Aviv and the Rosens were moving to New York.

Zvi smiled wryly. "There are those who have a real talent for survival."

"Moshe almost got engaged recently," Avram taunted. "But the rabbi thought the girl was too young."

"Whatever happened to that one. . ." and Zvi tried to recall the name, ". . . Tamar?"

Laughing, Moshe said he had lived with five girls since that one. "I've a new one now. Just out of service. I think you'd like her—tits as large as watermelons."

Avram shook his head with puritan disapproval. "One thing about you, Moshe, you don't mince words describing a woman."

"Comes from knowing what's important," the General explained.

Lev Hershel joined them, and Zvi asked, "What is it this time?"

The Intelligence Officer shoved a file toward him. "Syria, and possibly war."

Zvi was dubious. "Are they up to it?"

"Extremists in power and all for a new order."

"I've heard that phrase before," and Zvi remained dubious.

"As close to Communist as an Arab state can get. It will mean nationalizations and . . ."

"Nationalism," Zvi added.

The other three nodded. "Better look at it," Lev suggested, pointing to the file.

Opening the manila folder, Zvi took his time reading the single sheet inside. A protest to the United Nations. The Syrians were objecting to the President of the Security Council that the Jews were preparing the long-planned water works on the Sea of Galilee.

Smiling to himself, Zvi read: "As soon as the project is completed, Israel will be in a position to settle several million people in the Negev, who will constitute a new force threatening the whole Arab world."

Zvi read on until he came to the third paragraph and then he shook his head in disbelief. "In any case, the Government of the Syrian Arab Republic does not consider that Israel can be regarded as a party in matters involving the Jordan River." Grinning, Zvi commented, "That river is a large part of our frontier."

Avram laughed with him. "That's not the real joker. They're leaning on the UN Supervisory Group decision made in 1953 that we shouldn't work on the river without Syrian approval."

Lev suggested, "Note the second to the last paragraph."

Zvi read with care. "The Arab States consider the activities of the Israeli authorities—they made a mistake and named us there—as serious a matter as the establishment of Israel in 1948, which violated the lawful rights of the inhabitants of the country and gave rise to a series of international crises which threatened the peace."

Zvi looked up and asked, "Where do I fit in?"

The others looked to Moshe to explain. The General clasped his hands on the back of his head. "We may be going back to fifty-four and after. This is the opening wedge for them to start trouble, if Lev is right. We think he is."

Zvi looked to the Intelligence Officer.

"They've been moving military equipment in northeast of the lake. I think they might just start some kind of action as an excuse to make the UN stop our working on the water lines."

Taking a cigarette from his shirt pocket, Zvi lighted it and sat back in his chair while he tried to understand what this could mean.

However, Moshe was too impatient to let him think about this. "You're going to take over Northern Command temporarily."

"And that means the Syrian front now?" Zvi questioned, surprised by the assignment.

"Of course," Moshe said impatiently.

"And authority?"

"You won't move until you have Cabinet approval." Moshe was giving the orders now.

Dragging deeply on his cigarette, Zvi weighed what he was being given. After a time, he nodded. "There isn't much of a Syrian army to fight."

"I'd rather not fight even what they have, if we can avoid it," Lev said. "If anything started, Nasser would have to play important and get into it to keep his leadership and Pan-Arabism alive. I suggest just enough strength to do the job and make your point. We don't want war."

Accepting the logic of this, Zvi asked, "How much action has there been to date?"

The others looked to Lev to brief him. Ticking off the points on his fingers, the Intelligence Chief listed the actions: "From 1 February, machine-gun fire on Dardara; 7 February, rifle fire on Dardara; 10 February, machine-gun fire on civilians south of Mishmar HaYarden; 15 February, machine-gun fire on vehicular traffic on the road to 'En Gev; 25 February, machine-gun fire on fishermen, 27 February, machine-gun fire on police south of Dardara. In short, Zvi, we're hanging on the edge of a war right now."

Zvi tamped out his cigarette and looked at the others. "Our response?"

"Patience," Avram said with overt sanctimony.

"Slop!" Zvi snorted. "If I'm going in there, I want it known that I have personal reactions to being shot at: I don't like it."

"You'll obey orders, Zvi," Moshe reminded him.

Taken aback at the bluntness of his friend's comment, Zvi nodded before adding, "To a point."

Reminding Moshe, Avram said, "His report."

Almost angrily, the General came to his feet, "I don't give illegal orders."

Then the others were laughing at Moshe.

"When do I report in?" Zvi asked.

Avram explained. "The day after tomorrow. The Cabinet has agreed to the appointment, and so the Chief of Staff thinks there isn't much sense in playing games. In two days you go north."

Zvi had difficulty following the logic of what had just been said, and then he realized that in his own way Avram had just told him he was being promoted. Looking to Moshe for confirmation, he saw his friend's hand extended.

"Congratulations, General."

Walking back to Avram's office, Zvi accepted his friend's congratulations and discussed moving Aaron to Nazareth, where he would be stationed.

Enjoying his friend's domesticity, Avram said, "Malin's looking for an apartment here in Tel Aviv, moving down with the children."

Surprised, Zvi asked, "Is she giving up the bench?"

Avram shook his head. "She's been promoted to a higher court and will only have to be in Jerusalem a few days a week, and so we thought that having five children and being married, it would be all right if we lived together."

Both laughed and Zvi slapped the back of his neck with an open palm.

Avram appreciated his pleasure. "You're happy being a general?"

"I hope, well . . . when are *you* getting it?"

Slowly, Avram rose from behind his desk. "It will be a long wait. No field experience since forty-eight and no one could justify a general without it." Zvi started to say something, but Avram cut him off. "You almost didn't make it, my friend. If you'd failed to get a strong recommendation from everyone involved, I think you would have been retired."

"Everyone?" Zvi was taken aback.

"There were those who thought you might protest about the Eichmann assignment. There were others who thought you might hold out for a field assignment and not let yourself grow up. There were those who thought you would try to assume too much authority in Southern Command."

Puzzled, Zvi pressed, "And?"

"It was Eli Cohen· who made the rounds and checked you out in Southern Command and reported you had done a first-class job there." Avram grinned, "Moshe didn't know if he should be happy or sad about that. He decided to be happy."

"I don't understand," Zvi admitted. "It was a routine staff job. Any colonel could have done it."

Avram agreed. "And you did it without complaining about that fact, and having had your head for years, people expected the complaints. They remember you taking your head at Mitla. It was Eli who fought for you. Because he thought you knew when to fight for yourself."

Shaking his head in disbelief, Zvi asked, "And on that a man makes general?"

"That and everything from Haganah on. Count twenty-six years toward it," Avram suggested. "Count the letters from the Ministry of Justice which praised your work there as well as your report and recommendations. Count the fact that Kineret Heschel wanted you for ambassador somewhere if we weren't going to use you."

Zvi understood now what Kineret's interest had been in him during the trial.

"And now, General, if you'll get the hell out of here and let me get some work done . . ."

Coming to his feet, Zvi winked, "Insolence."

"Go celebrate."

And Zvi walked out of Hakiryah as happy as he had ever been in his life. He had come closer to the top of the ladder than he had ever hoped to come, and now he knew the one person who would enjoy his new rank as much as he. And so he dashed to Ruth's apartment to tell Aaron. However, when he arrived, it was Ruth who met him at the door.

"I've heard," she said.

Taken aback, Zvi cocked his head to one side awaiting an answer.

"Avi," she explained. "He wanted to take you out to celebrate tonight, but Malin's moving, and . . ." her hands came wide. Watching Zvi look about for Aaron, she told him, "Your son took my daughter to the movies."

Somehow, Zvi felt as though he were alone; and though he tried to keep it to himself as he nodded, Ruth said, "We're going out to dinner tonight. You and I. I've arranged for Aaron to stay over." Uncertain just how he was taking her offer, she asked, "It's all right, isn't it?"

He tried to smile as he nodded. "Yeah. As Avi said, 'Celebrate.' " Then his head came up sharply, "The dinner. The 'you and I,' that was Avi's idea?"

For a moment Ruth thought he resented the notion, and then she relaxed. "He called to apologize for not being with you, and I told him we were going." She could see that something was bothering him, and though she thought she knew what it was, somehow she did not want to point out to Zvi what he obviously already knew: Aaron was outgrowing him and he was alone, more alone than he wanted to be.

"If you'll pick me up in two hours, General, I'll be dressed and waiting for you."

They ate at a small restaurant he knew on Yehuda Halevi. KOL Israel had already broadcast the story of Zvi's promotion, and several persons whom they did not know came up to their table to congratulate him, and Ruth enjoyed his embarrassment as well as his pleasure. They talked about very little more than his desire to buy a house in Tel Aviv and the many neighborhoods where he might look and the high cost of housing. After a time, Ruth told him that she was moving to a new apartment in a few weeks and offered to give him back the one on Jabotinsky Street as a base until he found something he liked. There was no rush, because his new assignment took him north.

Considering the suggestion, Zvi thought about the apartment and all that had happened to him while he had lived there. Finally, he shook his head. "First I leased, then I bought, now you'll sell," he suggested, "and put the money into the business."

Ruth understood his reasons for hesitating and did not argue. Then, to Zvi's chagrin, he found that he had very little to say to Ruth, and he felt uncomfortable as their conversation revolved around the things which had happened to them years before. They mentioned Fishel and moved on to the girl he had planned to marry. Neither one of them knew what had become of Dvora. And it was Zvi who said he had often felt that he should have understood her better and that since his work on the trial, he thought he did. Then they talked about the Ben Ezras and Bedia and finally came to the subject of Moshe Gilead.

Then they were reduced to talking about their children, and by that time they were through with dinner. Neither one felt as though they had celebrated, and neither one felt that they had done justice to Zvi's promotion. Several times Ruth was tempted to say as much, and then she backed off the subject. Zvi paid the waiter and turned to her, uncertain what to suggest. Both realized that not only did they have very little in common any longer, but there were very few persons whom Zvi was close enough to for Ruth to suggest they call on. Sitting in the semi-darkness of the restaurant, Ruth watched while he lit a cigarette and nervously started to shove his hand into his shirt, caught himself doing that and dropped his hand to his side. She thought he looked tense. His hair looked very little grayer than when she had last seen him, but there were more lines about his eyes. His face seemed heavy, and his eyes seemed to squint permanently when he was thinking. She wondered if she looked as old to him.

And Zvi, staring at her sitting across the table, thought she looked more sophisticated than he had ever known her to be. It had something to do with the décolleté gown she was wearing, and he wondered if it was one she had designed or if she had bought it in Paris. He was tempted to ask, but thought the idea foolish because it would reveal how little they had to say. Her hand came up to touch her bosom as though she were brushing something away, and he smiled to himself. Ruth had always been full-bosomed.

Coming to his feet, he suggested, "There's a place I'd like to go. I wish you'd come along, even though it will make a late night of it."

Curious, she let him pull her chair back while she waited to hear what he had to suggest. When he told her, she nodded and let him lead the way out of the crowded restaurant. A short time later he was driving south toward Jerusalem. Neither of them said anything for a long time, and then Ruth asked casually, "Who's going to take care of the house for you when you buy it?"

"I don't know," he admitted. "Haven't thought about that yet."

She believed him because there was no reason why he should not tell her if he was planning to get married again.

"Any men in your future?" he asked her just as bluntly.

"None that I know of."

He started to say something, but she cut him off. "Don't start asking what I do for a sex life. It isn't any of your business."

Zvi chuckled, "I was only going to ask if you were cold."

Ruth looked at him dubiously and then laughed, "And now you know all about my sex life."

They rode for another hour without talking, as both of them appeared to be content to look at the scenery revealed by the moonlight. The broken hills, the tortuous road, the fields of rock.

JERUSALEM

Making his way through the light traffic of the evening, Zvi drove directly to the King David Hotel and parked the car.

Helping Ruth out, he offered, "A drink or something?"

She looked at him, "When did you start drinking?"

"I don't," he confessed, "but if you want one . . ."

Taking his arm, she walked with him toward the YMCA building across the street. "Are you trying to ply me with liquor, General?"

Zvi closed his hand over hers, "I hadn't thought of it that way before."

She hesitated in the street and then somewhat nervously, she picked up her pace as she said flatly, "Maybe that's the trouble."

Paying the attendant at the door, Zvi led the way to the roof. He had not been there for a long time, and as he stood looking down at Jerusalem, he was aware for almost the first time how much the city had grown to both the east and the west.

"They're building, too," he commented.

Ruth nodded. Walking to the edge of the roof, she laid her hands flat on the edge of the stone wall. "Do you come here often?"

Zvi shook his head. "It's not exactly a sentimental journey," he reminded her.

Ruth was staring at the Old City in the distance, and then she turned to him in the moonlight. "You know, General," and he could tell she was taunting him pleasantly with his new rank, "you were younger then."

Slapping her rump with an open palm, he snapped, "I'm the *only* one who's aged. All of my friends forgot to."

When Ruth moved closer to him, he put one arm about her waist, spreading his fingers flat on her hip. Both of them were staring at the Old City. The walls and the Dome could be seen in the moonlight. The stones of the outer walls looked almost pink. "I remember when I came up to the roof of that house and told you there was a State," he said after a long silence.

"And then Dov Tervisky was killed."

Her lack of sentiment did not surprise him, because it was one of the things he had always admired about her.

"Did you know," she asked, "that Fishel wanted to have someone compose a symphony about the fight for the Old City?"

Zvi shook his head. "That wasn't the kind of thing he talked about to me."

Ruth tipped her head so she could see his face. His eyes seemed more deeply set and the vague light of the moon cast shadows over them.

She started to draw away from him, but he held his arm about her waist and after a moment she relaxed.

"One time when I was at the university, I looked up the details. It is forty-eight meters long and eighteen meters high. There are twenty-four rows of stones above the ground and nineteen below."

Ruth knew he was talking about the Wall.

"According to the people who are supposed to know such things, it rests on the rocky bottom of the Tyropoean valley . . ."

"Whatever the hell that is," she said.

Ignoring her, Zvi continued what he had obviously memorized. ". . . which separated the valley from the Upper City."

Ruth wanted to laugh, but she knew he would be offended.

His hand on her hip relaxed, but he continued to hold her. Glancing up at him, she saw that he was smiling, perhaps at himself.

"There are all kinds of stories," he continued. "All kinds, about how the Wall was built, about how it came to stand so long, and how it was discovered. There's one tale about how Solomon got all the people together to draw lots to decide who was going to build the walls, and the poor people won the Western Wall and they built it themselves, while the rich paid other people to build their walls. The story is told that when the Western Wall was almost finished the Divine Presence descended and rested on the Western Wall and said, 'The work of the poor is precious in My eyes and My blessing is on it.' Then a heavenly voice added, 'The Divine Presence will never be removed from the Western Wall.' "

Ruth snorted. "*Bubba meisses*. I can remember when there wasn't any Divine Presence. Believe me, I can remember."

Zvi looked down at her tolerantly. "Sometimes I think you're a skeptic."

Both laughed, and then Zvi realized she was shivering, and turning her about, he folded her in his arms.

Ruth was not laughing now, but she wanted to. "This is tactics, General?"

And to the surprise of both of them, he put one hand under her chin and kissed her. At first she started to back away, and then she stood very still, and then she put her arms about his neck. When he finally dropped his hand from her chin, she stared at him. "Either we're too old for this or too young. I'm not sure which."

He did not understand whether she meant him to laugh or say something, so he kissed her again. When they separated, she shook her head. "Let's get off this roof."

Agreeing, Zvi took a slow walk about the roof and then, taking her hand, led her to the elevator. When they reached the street, he put his arm about her and they walked to the car.

"It didn't mean anything, what happened up there," she said.

Zvi did not answer as he opened the car door for her and then slipped in on the driver's side. He was about to start the car when she said, "You can ply me with drinks now if you want to."

Laughing softly, he asked, "Do you want a drink?"

She half closed her eyes while she thought, and then she said, "No."

"Would Hannah care what time you got home?"

She thought about this, too, before she said, "No."

"Then," he said, "you and I are going to do something we should have done a long time ago."

"I told you it didn't mean anything, what happened up there."

"If that is the way you want to think about it, agreed." Then he smiled wryly, "For that reason, is there any reason why we shouldn't?"

Ruth looked at him dubiously. "Maybe you are growing up, Zvi. You couldn't have said anything less romantic." But she did not resist when he kissed her again, and finally, moving back behind the wheel, he started the car and drove to a small hotel south of the city. When he got out and opened the door, he did not know if she was going to come with him or not. And when she hesitated, he went to close the door again, but her hand came out and held it.

Fifteen minutes later they were standing in the middle of a room and looking around.

"It's small," she said.

He nodded. "We're not planning to spend our lives here."

Ruth laughed, but when he started to take her in his arms, she pushed him away and began to slip off her dress with the comment, "I'm old enough to make love in bed."

Zvi watched her undress, and then, slipping off his tunic, started to unbutton his shirt.

It was morning when he rolled over, reached out for her to find she was not in the bed with him. Her clothes were gone and tucked into the shoulder strap beneath his new insignias, he saw a note. Standing buff in the middle of the small room, he read what she had written on the back of the hotel receipt: I hope you enjoyed your celebration. Consider it a present from me. I do not want to see you again.

Tossing the note in the basket, he remembered what she had said about it meaning nothing. He was not so sure. After he was dressed, he drove back to Tel Aviv.

THE GALILEE-TEL AVIV

The next day, Zvi assumed his new command in Nazareth. All of Lev Hershel's fears seemed justified. During the first few weeks after Zvi took over in the north, the Syrians harassed the farmers and fishermen of the Galilee, shelling the Israeli villages and attacking the small boats on the lake. Three times Zvi called Moshe, who, as Chief of Operations, would have to give his approval for a retaliation raid, and three times Zvi's plan was rejected with the single comment—patience.

Then, in late March, the Syrians raised the tempo of their harassment, trying to influence world opinion against the Jews and force the Israelis to cease their construction of a water system which lay entirely within Israel. When Zvi called Moshe the fourth time, he was told to lay out his plans with care and stand by.

Selecting two companies, which he had been observing for weeks, Zvi positioned them for a raid. He planned to move on several fronts at the same time, confusing the Syrians, who must be aware that they would not go unpunished indefinitely and would be on a maximum alert.

Then Zvi got his orders and drove directly to the kibbutz from which he intended actually to make his strike. An area commander now, he knew his perspective of command had to change, and so after listening to, modifying and approving the retaliation plans, he sat back and waited through the long and shattering night while his men attacked the fortifications from which the Syrians had been shelling. By morning he knew the young major in the field had done as good a job as he himself would have done, and he went back to his headquarters to wait for the next reactions.

They came faster than he had expected, and all of them were different from what he had expected. The Syrian government fell to a military coup and everyone knew that there would be no further action until the new government got itself sorted out.

However, the UN received a complaint that same day that the Israeli army had ruthlessly entered Syria without provocation. And Zvi was ordered to Tel Aviv.

Leaving his headquarters at Nazareth, Zvi headed south. When he arrived at Hakiryah, Avram was waiting for him. "The UN is going to talk your action to death," Avram guessed.

Moshe had joined them and he stood back, looking at his friend. "General Mazon, the tales I hear about you . . ."

Puzzled, Zvi waited.

"The Syrians claim you killed only civilians and thirty at that."

"Thirty?"

Avram nodded. "They say you struck at two places and killed a child in each."

It was Moshe who broke the tension with a chuckle. "They've declared talk on you."

Zvi snorted. "Soldiers get paid to die." He fell silent and then, cocking his head to one side, said, "You two didn't bring me down here to discuss the UN, the Syrian complaints or the weather."

Again, it was Moshe who chuckled. "For years, I've planned it. All the way back when you were my senior in the Old City, I swore to myself that I would get even. Now I've done it."

Taking a deep breath and having difficulty being patient with Moshe's clumsy humor, Zvi looked to Avram for the answer.

"Moshe gets a field assignment and you wind up here as of next month."

Seeing the startled expression on Zvi's face, the others grinned. "People have been telling you to grow up for years," Avram reminded him. "Now as Chief of Operations . . ."

At the end of his tour of duty as Chief of Operations, Brigadier-General Zvi Mazon retired into the reserves. The reasons were simple: he was over forty, Israel was at peace, there was no immediate assignment for a fighting general, and he agreed the army had to have room to promote younger men.

And when he left Hakiryah for what he thought was the last time, Zvi, who had committed his life to the creation and defense of Israel, knew he was lonely and lost.

Book V
MAY-JUNE 1967

MAY, 1967—SOMEWHERE SOUTH OF BEERSHEBA

It was almost noon. The brazen sky was so bright that the soldiers sought shade. Both officers and enlisted men had been drifting into the assembly area for hours. Most of them were already in uniform. Others slipped into theirs as soon as they arrived. They came singly in taxis or trucks. They came in small groups in Volkswagens and Peugeots. They came in buses. Some few had hitchhiked to the mobilization area. Some had come a hundred kilometers, some more. The few kibbutzniks who worked near the area had arrived first and started issuing the uniforms, weapons and jerry cans at dawn. As their numbers swelled, others began to roll out the tanks, check their camouflage and line them up for movement. The truck drivers started the engines of their four-by-fours and six-by-sixes. The young major in charge of supply was a Regular. He followed a long-worked-out plan for issuing rifles, Uzis and ammunition. Most of the men off the kibbutzim were browned by the desert sun. Most of those from Tel Aviv and Beersheba were not. When the two medical officers from Beersheba arrived in a Studebaker Lark, they were already in uniform. The half-dozen women who arrived during the morning were checking out their radio equipment or going over their maps to be certain they had the ones which they hoped were the right ones. Two waiters who had worked late at a café in Tel Aviv arrived about noon. A garage mechanic who had been out on a call trying to start a tourist's Ford did not receive word until almost ten. When he did, he commandeered the tourist's Ford and drove directly to the assembly point. The young singer from the Hebrew University had missed the first call because he had had his radio off while rehearsing, and he arrived shortly before noon in a car driven by his girl friend and borrowed from a professor of mathematics. Even though most of the men were present by noon, Brigadier-General Zvi Mazon was not pleased. The entire mobilization had taken longer than he had planned. And he did not know what to do with forty-three men not in his command who had reported.

535

His Personnel Officer had assembled them in the vague shade cast by the farmhouse which served as a headquarters, and was waiting for his orders. General Mazon knew the extra volunteers were waiting for him to make a decision. He knew, too, that most of them had come a long way to join his division. Sitting inside the house, he poured over the roster which had just been handed to him. It was half an hour old and was no longer up-to-date, but almost every man in the division had already reported. There were notes about four. One had sent on the message that he would try to steal out of the hospital where he was bedded down with a broken ankle. Another would be an hour late because his wife should have the baby before noon. A third would attend his father's funeral and arrive by one. The fourth man was waiting at the optometrist's for a new set of glasses. He did not really need them, except to see, but he would arrive as soon after the noon hour as possible. Zvi looked at the roster. His officers were all present except for the captain who was reported to be flying in from Paris where he had been negotiating the sale of oranges and the major who was reported to be flying from Tanzania where he had been heading an anthropological research project. Headquarters in Tel Aviv was confident both men would arrive in the early afternoon.

Tossing down the roster in disgust, Zvi yelled for his clerk. A corporal, a slim young woman about twenty-four, came into the kitchen, which passed for his office. "Send a jeep to Lod to pick up these two." And he shoved the note from Headquarters across the kitchen table to her. "I want them both on their way here as soon as they land."

Taking the note, she left him alone. General Mazon was not an easy man to get along with at any time. His temper was short. He knew what he wanted and he expected others to know. Outside, the corporal passed the note and the message to the General's adjutant. The young major smiled. "He's going to be hell to get along with this week."

Knowing that he should not be talking about his superior in this manner to a corporal, he smiled and added, "Thank the Lord."

The Corporal from Haifa shook her head in disapproval and disappeared inside the farmhouse once more. The General was shouting for her again, and she paused only long enough to ask which of the waiting colonels had to see him first, the G-1 or the Ordnance Officer. They both had to see him first. Shrugging, she returned to the kitchen.

This time the General shoved his chair back from the table and glared at her. The Corporal stood very quietly. She had served under Mazon before. When he was not fighting, he was comfortable and at ease. Then his men could talk to him and joke with him. Though none of them called him by his first name any longer, not even his officers, they all respected him. However, when they were fighting, when they were in the field, or getting ready to enter the field, he was almost impossible. Then nothing satisfied him. The Corporal understood this, and as he continued to glare at her, she relaxed because she knew he would be himself in time. Finally, he said very softly, "Get me the Signals Officer."

She started to leave when she remembered the two colonels. "Colonels Aroti and Barshfield are waiting to see you, sir."

He sighed. "Send them both in."

The Corporal left; and, rising from his chair behind the kitchen table, the General crossed over to the small window. For a moment he watched two soldiers opening the jerry cans to make sure they were still filled with water. One soldier tossed a can aside and the other failed to tighten the top of one he replaced on a truck. Shouting through the open window, Zvi called both to the side of the farmhouse and explained that he could not spare cans any more than he could spare the water that would spill from an open can. The soldiers, properly chastised, returned to their tasks and Zvi turned around to face his waiting staff officers. "Well?"

"There are now fifty-three extra men, sir," the G-1 reported.

Zvi tugged at his lower lip while he weighed the problem. Every time there was an emergency and the mobilization call went out, extra men appeared. Some of them had fought with him before and wanted to serve under him again. Some had been dropped from the reserves for reasons of age or health. Some belonged to units which had not yet been mobilized or were in other areas. All were eager to join the army and fight.

"Have a medical officer separate those who can go with us from those who can't. Send the men who belong to other units home to wait for their own call-up."

"And the rest?"

"Keep them around until we see how many we come up short and then fill out your units."

"And what about those who are well, but overage?" The G-1 knew he would have to account to someone sometime for having brought nonreserves into the unit.

"They aren't horses. Don't look at their teeth. If they can do us any good, we'll find a place for them."

The G-1 nodded and left. A lawyer from Natanya, he had been finding ways to circumvent regulations ever since he had joined the army in 1959. He would find a way. The General expected him to.

The Ordnance Officer had a problem. "I don't know how much petrol they are going to allot us."

Zvi grinned. "That depends on two things: if we are going anywhere and how long we will have to sit where we go." He thought a moment and then added, "Remember, if we go into a defensive position—and we had damned well better not—we will need a greater quantity of ammunition. If we go on the offensive—and we had damned well better—that means we will need a greater quantity of petrol."

Both men were smiling now.

The Ordnance Officer asked simply, "Do we have a mission yet?"

Zvi looked at him blankly. He was not saying if he did or did not; and after a moment, the young lieutenant-colonel, an insurance salesman from Tel Aviv, shrugged and left the kitchen, knowing no more than he had when he came in.

The General shook his head. He could understand a man going on a fishing trip, but to accept no answer annoyed him. Glancing at the papers on the kitchen table, he was satisfied there was nothing more he could do here. He shoved his beret on his head and strode into the small sitting room.

There were a half-dozen clerks making rosters, lists of supplies and filling out forms. Snorting, Zvi Mazon walked outside where he found his Signals Officer, Mitra Glasner. She had been with him briefly in the past when he had been a Regular instead of a Reserve Officer. She had been with Moshe Gilead in the drive to Sharm el Sheikh. They knew each other well. There were those who claimed she was one of the few persons who could argue with General Mazon. There were others who claimed he merely refused to argue with her.

"You were looking for me?"

Mazon nodded and continued walking, expecting her to keep step with him. His heavy figure rolled from side to side as he walked over toward the extra volunteers. "Are you all set up?"

Knowing his distaste for imprecision, she asked bluntly, "What do you mean?"

Pausing to look at her, he nodded. Lieutenant Glasner unsettled him at times. She was more exacting than a woman should be. She was also given to challenging his statements. "Are we in direct contact with Headquarters?"

Taken aback at what she considered a criticism, she snapped, "Of course."

"Are the radios in all of the vehicles working?"

They were standing a few yards away from the extra volunteers now, and Zvi came to a halt as he waited for an answer.

"Only in those vehicles which have radios."

And he could see that she was angry. "Tanks?" Not being put off by her manner.

"And tanks."

He nodded. "Good. Then I understand there is nothing you need to do?"

For a moment Mitra Glasner did not know if he was making fun of her or if he was serious. "Is there something you want me to do?"

"Yes," he said, no longer looking at her as he eyed the more than fifty men talking to one of the medical officers. "I'm going out on a reconnaissance in half an hour, and I want to be certain I am always in direct touch with Tel Aviv and the four other half-tracks going with me."

And he was walking away from her to the line of volunteers. One of them, a middle-aged man who wore his payot long and a yarmulke on his head, smiled at Mazon. The General recognized the shochet—ritual slaughterer—from Herzliyah who had been with him in '56 and again in Syria in '62. Avram Shaki had been a good paratrooper once.

Before the General passed him, Shaki stepped into his path. "I want to go with you, sir."

Zvi nodded. "Aren't you getting old, too old for this kind of business?" His hand came up and he put it on the other man's thin shoulder. "Let's bypass this one," he suggested warmly.

Avram Shaki shook his head as he said so softly that even those standing close to them could not hear, "I'm not older than you are, Zvi. We probably became *bar mitzvah* the same spring."

Zvi's hand came away and he looked about for another medical officer. Seeing a second one not far away, he yelled for the man to join him. Meanwhile, he watched Lieutenant Glasner climb into the command half-track to inspect the radio. When the doctor from Beersheba joined him, Zvi pushed Avram Shaki toward him. "Give this old futz an examination. If he passes it, see that the supply officer gives him a uniform."

The shochet started to thank the General, but Zvi shook his head. "Don't get yourself killed. I haven't time to write your wife any nice letters or make visits to the next of kin."

And he was watching the rest of the men being checked by the medical officers. Several had already been weeded out as unfit; and though they started to approach him, the G-1 led them toward the road, where he explained they could get a ride home in the next truck going north. Satisfied that the job was being done properly and that no one was being unduly offended, Zvi walked over to his Intelligence Officer.

Colonel Dov Bar-Ilan was a regular army officer, newly returned from the American Command and Staff School at Fort Leavenworth, Kansas. Zvi Mazon had not yet had time to discover what Bar-Ilan had learned in that citadel of military wisdom, but he knew that over the next few weeks he would be told, whether or not he wanted to hear.

"We're going out. Five half-tracks down the Negev. About eight hours. I plan to leave four of the half-tracks there on regular patrol and then replace them with another four tonight. I'd like to go over your maps with you to decide the most obvious enemy approaches west of Wadi Faran. We'll cover these."

Bar-Ilan, a tall, lean man in his late thirties, nodded. He had been on tours of duty with Mazon twice before in his career, and the unorthodox commander disturbed him more by what he failed to say than what he did. After his first tour of duty with the then Colonel Mazon, he knew the stocky officer did not say many things because he took for granted his officers knew them. As time went on, he began to think that Mazon himself had not thought of the things he did not mention. However, every time he came to this conclusion he was abruptly surprised, as he was now when he suggested, "Won't that depend on what the aerial recon photos show of their dispositions?"

"The dispositions are already on my maps. Go see Mitra Glasner if you have any questions about them." And Zvi was walking away.

Half an hour later, leaving his division to the care of his Chief of Staff, General Mazon led a column of five half-tracks out of the assembly area west across country. They passed two small Bedouin camps, marked them on their maps and rolled on. At Wadi Faran, they crossed the road leading south toward Eilat and west into the large dried bed of the transient river. Smooth stones were crushed under the weight of their tracks, and they rolled on toward the Sinai border. When dust rode in their wake, Zvi and the others pulled down their heavy goggles. Twice he nodded for his gunners to test their machine guns. Once he reached down and squeezed off four test shots from his Uzi. Without pause, they continued south, swinging along the border and keeping the row of black-and-white poles which marked the frontier line to their right. Once they cut into the bed of a wadi, and when they looked up, the frontier markers were on their left. Shaking his head, Zvi gestured for his driver to cross back into his own territory. Zvi Mazon had no desire to be the first to violate the frontier line.

They swung back to their right and toward a dirt road. One of the half-tracks slowed in some sand and bogged for a moment. The drivers began to slow down until Zvi saw what they were doing, and with a wave of his arms he kept them moving. The one which had slowed broke through the crust of the hardened sand and broken shale. Keeping the other vehicles moving, he turned his own half-track in a large circle and, coming up from behind, pushed the flagging half-track onto firmer ground and then jerked sharply to one side to avoid the already churned sand.

Taking the lead of the column again, he started to cross a rock-bed road when he heard the explosion. It was loud, and for a moment, he thought it was his own vehicle. There was dirt in the air and sand over everything. Bailing out, he jumped clear with his Uzi in hand. The half-track behind his continued on and the one after that. Then, as he ran down the column, he saw the fourth half-track lying on its side, the treads like dead alligators in the open desert. The rear gearing was a jumble of broken and scattered metal which Zvi pushed aside as he reached in a pulled out the first two men he found. There were others around now, and he reached down to pull a third man clear when he saw the burst of flame as a shattered jerry can caught fire. Grabbing a limp figure by the collar, Zvi jumped backward. Others about him were doing the same. Now they were all clear of the vehicle as it became enveloped in flames.

Ordering the closest lieutenant to pull every man clear, he ran to the front of the column, shouting for his signals sergeant. "Contact Tel Aviv. I want air cover here. Tell them we have wounded. Dead. I'll let you know how many." Then he whirled about to the sergeant closest to him. "Swing those other vehicles out, checking the ground as you go. I want guards posted." And without waiting to determine if he had been understood, he ran back to the burning half-track. The flames were less fierce now, and a small group of men were standing over the limp bodies on the ground.

"Are any of them alive?" he asked the Operations Officer who was kneeling beside the bodies.

"Three, sir."

Zvi shook his head in anger at his situation. "The dead?"

"Seven."

The others in the group watched while Zvi knelt beside one of the wounded. He recognized the corporal, a middle-aged plumber. Blood flowed freely from the man's shoulder and his left cheek had been sheared off. Zvi smiled at the man, who seemed to be grinning back. "We've already sent for a 'copter. I'm sorry you're going to miss out on the ride west."

The corporal continued to grin, and only after Zvi came to his feet did he realize the man was unconscious. Looking about, he waved the soldiers back to their half-tracks. "I want all but five of you in your vehicles ready to move." Then selecting five at random, he explained, "Probe the ground around here and see if this is the pattern of a mine field or only a single sabotage job."

And then he was walking back to his own half-track. The sergeant there was talking on the radio as Zvi pulled himself in.

"I have Tel Aviv, sir."

"I would assume so." And he did not bother to take the instrument from her as he talked into it. "How long before I get air cover?" He shook his head as he heard a roar above him. "It's here. Keep it over me until the chopper gets here. I have three wounded. Seven dead."

He listened to the confirmation of his information and then said, "We'll leave as soon as they pick up the wounded. We'll bring back our own dead." And his head went up as a Mirage whined above. Cursing the noise and feeling secure in the comfort of the umbrella, he jumped out of his half-track and made his way back to the wounded. The Operations Officer and two sergeants were standing beside him. "Put the dead in one of the half-tracks," he ordered a lieutenant. Then he turned his attention to the still burning vehicle. "Better see if there is anything that can be salvaged. If there isn't, make certain no one else can salvage it." Another Mirage whirled over him, lower, as though the pilot was curious. Looking up, Zvi shook his head and yelled to his Signals Sergeant, "I don't need any sightseeing. Keep those jets upstairs where they can see if anything is coming."

Swearing softly under his breath, he slowly walked back to his command vehicle. When he reached it, he turned around so that he could survey the horizon. Men were posted on every rise. Two of the half-tracks had been moved into position west of him facing the frontier line. Satisfied that there was nothing else he could do, he turned to the Signals Sergeant. The young woman smiled sadly at him. "How are the wounded, sir?"

He half closed his eyes as he said angrily, "Wounded?" Then, he looked at her shocked face and said more gently, "I don't know. Anything from headquarters?"

The sergeant, a schoolteacher from Sede Boqer, handed him a slip of paper. He read the message twice and then glanced at his watch. A jet flew over him and he looked upward. The sun was still high. One of the men was shouting and pointing to the northeast, and Zvi assumed the helicopter was coming.

Walking back to the Operations Officer, he assured himself the dead had been placed on one of the half-tracks. The bodies were all in a neat row. The three wounded were sheltered from the sun by a shadow of a vehicle. None of them was conscious. The Operations Officer and one of the Signals Corporals were in attendance.

Looking northeast now, Zvi saw the helicopter was almost overhead and coming down. Five minutes later the wounded were aboard. Keeping the chopper waiting, Zvi Mazon called his Operations Officer and the two lieutenants together, "Take charge, Major. Follow the recce route we planned. Headquarters wants me in Tel Aviv tonight. I'll stop at the assembly area and leave orders there." He waited for any questions, and when there were none, he pulled himself into the chopper and signaled for the pilot to take it up.

CAIRO

Colonel Yusef el Sindi rose from the bed and stared down for a moment at the girl lying there. Though Bedia's eyes were closed he was sure she was only feigning sleep. Her loose hair made a dark frame for her pale olive face set against the contrast of the white pillow. Sometimes Yusef believed he loved this woman. However, she was different from others he had known in his youth back in the village of Assiut on the upper Nile where he had been born. He had been in other beds over the years. There had even been an English girl when he was attached to the embassy in Karachi, and a French girl when he had been assigned to Algiers. There had been Arab girls other than Bedia, but none of them opened so many vistas for advancement.

Crossing over to the window so that he could look down on the Azbakiya Garden across the street, Yusef thought about advancement. Ever since his brigade had been alerted a week before and marched east through the city into Sinai, he had been thinking of advancement. Now with a war so obviously only a matter of days away, he felt assured of promotion. A generalship. If he were to go to the very highest levels, he would need success in combat, and that would certainly be simple enough to achieve against the Jews. He clenched one fist and set it against the windowsill as he thought about the Jews. He had fought them twice before in his life, and both times they had beaten him. Now there was going to be a third try, and this time there would be no excuse, no British or French behind them. He had supplies, equipment and men in such numbers that nothing would withstand his brigade. And from the position they were taking up in El 'Arish, he intended to avoid all of the usual pitfalls of caution and bureaucracy and strike for Tel Aviv itself. With the capture of the main enemy stronghold, he would do what had to be done to clear the land for the unfortunate Palestinians who had been brutally forced from their homes.

Yusef thought about that first war when he had been a lieutenant under Lieutenant-Colonel Gamal Abdelnasser Hussein. They had fought well only to be betrayed by their king. The one thing he knew he could count upon now was that Gamal would not betray the army because he was both the Arab world and the army.

Advancement. The word raced through Yusef's head again. He could reach the highest of the high with Bedia's father's support, and there was no reason why the old banker would not help his son-in-law-to-be, a man willing to marry a divorced woman. Though Yusef had never discussed marriage with Bedia, he was certain she wanted it. She had been in Cairo ever since her return from New York three years before. Though probably only in her early forties, there was a weary look about her. He thought of a word he had once heard an Englishman use—jaded. Maybe that was the word to describe this woman who had seen too much of the world. However, Yusef did not care. In addition to whatever else Bedia was, when dressed and fully prepared to meet others, she was still beautiful even though there was a cynical look in her eyes no matter whom she faced. He turned to look at her, and as he did, he wondered from whom she had learned so much. His fist remained clenched as he thought of this. His father would never approve his marrying a girl like Bedia, one out of purdah, one who looked a man in the face and laughed at or with him, one who dressed in a silken gown that revealed her figure as much as the thin sheet revealed it now, but Yusef el Sindi was not going to ask his father's permission to marry. When the war with Israel was over, he would marry Bedia. Then he could take another wife by whom he would have his children. Bedia would protest at first, but would accept the Moslem facts of life.

There was a stirring in the bed behind him, and he turned toward Bedia. She was sitting up in bed now. The white sheet dropped into her lap and her delicate breasts hung forward as she reached out to scratch the bottom of her feet. Her small head cocked to one side as she smiled up at Yusef, standing in his trousers, the window behind him silhouetting his large figure. Finished with her scratching, Bedia leaned back, put one forearm under her breasts as though to push them up and asked, "You were going to El 'Arish today?"

Yusef had difficulty focusing on her question. A moment passed before he nodded.

"I think I will go to Jerusalem," she said. "I'll meet you there after you've cut Palestine in two."

He was not certain from her expression if she was laughing at him or merely pleased at the expectation of seeing him again soon.

Bedia smiled and leaned back on her elbows. "Our main bank is in Jerusalem. My father will be pleased if I assure his managers that the family is interested in their welfare." She was not asking Yusef's permission, and it took him a moment to understand this. As he did, he understood, too, that being married to Bedia Hassani would have its problems in the first days until she learned what he expected of a wife. Until then, there was nothing he could do about it.

"I'm flying out in an hour," he informed her.

Bedia considered this. "I'll leave tonight or tomorrow morning." She smiled as she added, "I'll want to learn the name of the bank manager about whom I should be concerned."

Satisfied that there was nothing he could say to dissuade her and not at all sure that he wanted to, Yusef crossed over to the bed, cupped one of her small breasts in his hand and kissed her fervently on the mouth. When they separated, she said, "I'll expect to see you a hero."

Yusef smiled, and to his own surprise, he found himself asking, "And when I am, you will marry me."

Bedia shook her head. "When you are, we will think about it." Angry at the manner in which she turned his proposal away, he rose from the bed and started to dress. If she had been anyone else's daughter, he might have struck her, degraded her, told her he had only been toying with her, but she was the daughter of Mohammed Hassani and that meant almost as much as—if not more than—being one of the many protégés of Colonel Nasser.

Bedia rose from the bed, the sheet about her, and crossed to the window. Below she could see the crowd gathering about the Russian anti-aircraft guns being dug into the park. "They aren't worth what they cost," she said simply.

Yusef, his tunic buttoned now, stared at the back of her slim figure. She was going to require all the patience he could gather until she learned that there were things which he did not expect his wife to bother her head with. And the things he did expect her to bother her head with were simple enough for her to learn. He looked at the bed and then back at her. There was much she already understood. Now, as he thought about it, there would be advantages to having her in Jerusalem. Perhaps she would be able to watch him march into Tel Aviv.

ON THE SYRIAN FRONTIER

The regular soldiers of General Moshe Gilead's division were stretched thinly along the seventy-four-mile Syrian frontier. In the large kibbutz where he had located his headquarters, Moshe Gilead reviewed the past ten days with his staff officers. The General sat with his back against a tree where he could see the Syrian heights beyond the kibbutz. Two of his officers had their shirts off, letting the sun brown their backs. One young captain from Jerusalem sat cross-legged watching his commander. He knew the legends about Gilead. There were few in Israel who did not remember the retaliation raids and the dash for Sharm el Sheikh. The General was a professional soldier, and the young captain, who had been educated as a botanist, could not imagine thin-faced, tense Moshe Gilead as anything but a soldier, and yet he knew, as did all the others seated together, that only two weeks before their general had informed the Chief of Staff that he would retire on June 10, at the age of forty-two. Some who knew the General better than others had expressed their regrets. But Moshe himself had not spoken to any of his staff about the subject, had not discussed his replacement, and he had not even gone to Tel Aviv to discuss the matter with his young wife.

Now as he reviewed the political situation so that none would fail to understand just how serious it was, Moshe appeared to be completely relaxed. His Operations Officer, a radio announcer from Tel Aviv, knew that Moshe could not be as relaxed as he appeared.

"On the fourteenth and fifteenth the UAR and Syrian military chiefs met. That day Nasser marched his troops through Cairo in daylight to let the world know he was occupying Sinai." He turned to his Intelligence Officer, a professor of contemporary history at Tel Aviv, for an evaluation.

"As far as we can tell, there are supposed to be fifty-eight thousand Egyptian troops along the Sinai frontier."

Gilead nodded and continued. "On the seventeenth, Damascus Radio proclaimed Syria had completed a general mobilization." He smiled as he added, "They described it as 'maximum preparedness.' "

The IO said softly, "The reports I have make it twelve thousand troops along the frontier line."

For a moment, Gilead computed the figures. "About one hundred sixty men to the mile if they had no tail," referring to the number of men needed to supply the actual fighting force. "And they have a very large tail."

"On the eighteenth the UAR asked U Thant to remove the UNEF troops from Sinai and Sharm El Sheikh and the good Secretary General of the UN rushed to do it." He looked at the IO for any information that officer might have.

"There seems to be some confusion here, General. There is talk the Egyptians have moved in. There are also indications that Kuwait and Iraq might be holding down Sharm el Sheikh for them."

"Ras Nasrani?"

"Occupied and re-established."

Moshe nodded. He had expected as much.

"By the twentieth, there were twelve Arab countries clamoring for war and unification. The next day Nasser claimed he had one hundred thousand men under arms."

"Would that include the men in Yemen?" the divisional supply officer asked.

Gilead looked to the Intelligence Officer for an answer and received only a shrug.

Wrapping the review up in a hurry because the details were not terribly important to him at this moment, Moshe continued, "On the twenty-second Nasser closed the Strait. On the twenty-fourth he announced that he had mined the Strait. In between U Thant rushed to Cairo and back to New York again." He thought a moment. "I think we ought to see that every man and every woman in the kibbutzim in our divisional area be kept apprised of this situation." As he spoke, he laughed, "As if there were even a child who does not know it now."

He rose to his feet and looked around him. The kibbutz seemed empty except for a few children and old men. His eyes came to rest on the Syrian heights above him. Then he looked at his staff again and chuckled. "Three years ago at an American staff school I heard lectures on how it is best to keep your troops politically informed so that they know what they are fighting for." The other laughed with him because they all knew that there was probably no army in history better informed than the Israeli.

As he finished talking, Moshe watched his Signals Officer, Captain Miriam Balosh, approach across a field.

"This just came in," handing Moshe Gilead a note.

He glanced at it, at his watch, and then he nodded. "I've got to be in Tel Aviv at ten."

Colonel Leon Sharlin, the General's Chief of Staff, grinned. "Orders at last?"

Moshe shrugged. He was about to say something when their attention was sharply drawn to the Syrian heights. Heavy artillery. Two shells landed within ten meters of where they were gathered. A third struck a building fifty meters away. Then as the staff officers came to their feet, the pace of the Syrian firing picked up. Shell after shell striking into the wheat fields and among the buildings of the kibbutz. But Moshe Gilead was no longer paying any attention to the firing as he grabbed Captain Balosh's arm and trotted with her to the embankment behind which was hidden the signals truck. Inside the truck three young women were monitoring Radio Damascus, Radio Cairo and the KOL Israel. Accustomed to the Syrian artillery, they were paying little attention to it until they saw the tense face of the General.

Moshe spilled his orders. "Check with each company down the line. Is there firing in any other area?"

Captain Balosh was already in the truck operating a radio and asking the company on their left. Nothing. A young corporal turned to Moshe. "Firing in Company B area." The other two women received negative responses. Meanwhile the heavy explosions continued to tear up the ground not far from where they were parked.

Looking around, Moshe saw that his deputy was standing beside him. "Find out how much damage they're doing to B," he ordered and then ran back across the field to the kibbutz buildings which were under direct fire. Most of the women, children and old men had already left for their shelters underground. One middle-aged man slowly walked across a field under fire and took up a position in a trench facing the Syrian heights. Smiling to himself, Moshe returned to the tree where he had been sitting a few minutes earlier. His staff had dispersed to their vehicles and the building which they had taken over for a headquarters. Only the Intelligence Officer had not bothered to move.

"Routine," he said, giving his evaluation to his commander.

Watching a small concrete blockhouse collapse, Moshe added, "So far." They stood together watching the dirt thrown up as Syrian artillery found no targets other than the crops and open fields.

"They aren't very good at it," the Intelligence Officer commented.

Gilead nodded. "There must be twenty 105s up there."

A shell whined and both men flattened as dirt splashed over them.

Captain Balosh was running toward them now. They turned from the heights to the Signals Officer. Suddenly, she dropped. A shell struck a few meters from her head. Now she was on her feet and coming toward them once more.

Neither man said anything as she reported, "Leon," she said, referring to Moshe's deputy, "wants you to know that Company B reports they lost two half-tracks and a tank."

A shell broke the ground near them. Moshe considered the information. "Anyone hurt?"

"Two men slightly wounded."

The others saw his face cloud as he nodded. "Let's go." And he was walking across a field to the place where his jeep was parked behind a stone wall. His driver, a young machinist from Tel Aviv, was watching the Syrian shells tear up two of the buildings of the kibbutz. A shell exploded in front of Moshe and he paused long enough to brush the dirt off his trousers and face. He glanced at his watch, thought a moment and then turned to his Intelligence and Signals Officers. "Jump in." Settling into the front seat of the jeep, he waited until the others were seated, before he instructed his driver. "Over to the signals truck." The wall behind which the jeep was parked shook so violently they thought it would fall. The jeep jerked forward and an instant later several of the concrete blocks toppled. Without looking back at either the wall or the two with him, Moshe explained, "I've got to go south. I could fly in, but I won't. I want every bit of damage reported to me as I travel."

The Chief of Staff still stood beside the vehicle listening to the reports the three women inside were gathering.

"Anything other than Company B?" Gilead asked.

Shaking his head, the C/S brushed the matter aside as being of little importance.

"Get over there and see where those vehicles and men were when they were hit. If they were not under good enough cover, well enough camouflaged and the men not in secure positions, you have authority to relieve the company commander." He thought a moment, "Who's the second in command over there?"

"Lieutenant Abraham Yona," Leon told him.

Moshe smiled. "Druse, isn't he?"

"Yes."

"If you think anything was not as it should have been, give him the company and send the captain back to Tel Aviv today." And he was already thinking of something else as he turned to Miriam. "I want a signals sergeant for my command car now." As he spoke, his driver was already racing toward another embankment where a three-quarter-ton truck, radio equipped, was parked. Leaving the jeep for the command car driver, the young corporal from Tel Aviv took over the wheel of the command car and started back toward the General. Moshe winked at those with him. "He wouldn't miss the chance to get home for anything. She's from Algiers and as beautiful as a Chagall window."

Miriam Balosh was giving instructions to one of the signals sergeants in the truck, and the young woman climbed out to wait for Moshe.

Looking up at the sun which stood almost directly overhead, Moshe said, "I'll make it by ten with ease and be back as soon as I can. It's all yours until then; but keep me informed."

He thought a moment and then added, "Better let me know how badly wounded the two are over in Company B." Then, to Miriam, "Keep in constant touch."

And to his Intelligence Officer, "Tell Ordnance to scream until he gets those vehicles replaced." As he spoke, he could see the others smiling because they knew as well as he that there were no replacements. But Moshe Gilead had been a soldier too long to let up where supplies or men were concerned. "Leon, get me replacements if you have to go to Haifa yourself. I don't want to start fighting with less than I am allotted."

He was in the seat beside his driver now and the Signals Sergeant was climbing into the back of the command car where she took a seat on the bench which ran the length of the truck bed. Her radio was already turned on, and Moshe could hear her talking to one of the girls in the signals truck beside them. Twice they had to be silent as Syrian shells interrupted their conversation. Waving to his staff, Moshe nodded to his driver, "Tel Aviv, and let's make it in time for dinner." The command car pulled out from behind the embankment toward the road leading south. Two shells bracketed the road in front of them and as the driver did not slow down, Moshe reached over and, grabbing the wheel, swerved the command car to the left. Unsettled, the driver suddenly braked the car, throwing the Signals Sergeant off her seat and Moshe forward. In that instant a shell burst on the road where they had been heading. With a wry smile, Moshe told the driver, "Let's go now."

NABLUS

The small detachment of the Arab Legion was dug into a hill near Nablus. Its heavy guns were ready to be moved forward. The middle-aged lieutenant sat on the hood of his U.S. jeep and scanned the road leading toward Israel with his fieldglasses. Without looking at his driver, he said, "It was like this when I served under the Englishman, Glubb Pasha. We were ready and eager to move and the politicians sat back on their asses and waited for the Jews to panic and shit in their pants." He thought about what he had said, rubbed the back of his neck and snorted, "They didn't."

"Maybe they will this time," the driver suggested.

The lieutenant—Diyar al Ilm—smiled to himself. What could a soldier expect from a farmer? A Palestinian farmer at that.

"The Jews will fight because they have no choice." The dozen men standing about the heavy guns were listening to their officer because they knew that he had fought the Jews in 1948. In fact he had won three medals for his bravery then, and the king had even mentioned this the last time he had reviewed the company.

Diyar knew his men were listening, and so he spoke to the driver for their benefit. "The Jews will fight, but they cannot win. We have tanks and the planes and we have a just cause." He continued to scan the road ahead. There was a woman coming toward them driving a small herd of goats. She was young, and from where he sat, she looked better than most of the women he had seen in the past few days. "Our cause," Diyar was saying. "The imperialists have placed the Jews here and they are trying to build themselves another empire. But history is against them. History is with us. Empires are past, dead, dung in the mouth of Allah." He was able to spit over the side of the jeep without taking his fieldglasses off the approaching girl.

As he tried to decide how he would open the conversation with her, another jeep pulled up beside him. Amazed to see who had brought the swirl of dust into his face, he noticed his captain waiting impatiently.

"Lieutenant, you'll move your men into Jerusalem at once."

Puzzled, because this was not the way they had discussed their strategy only the night before, Diyar al Ilm very slowly lowered the fieldglasses and waited for an explanation.

The youthful captain, a heavily mustached distant relative of the king's, considered whether or not he owed the old lieutenant an explanation. After a moment he decided that he would have to continue to work with Diyar al Ilm until he was transferred to the Royal Guard, and so he said, "We have a new commander. He was trained in America."

The lieutenant still did not understand why he was supposed to move his men to Jerusalem when he had been given the task of cutting Israel in half with his guns.

"We are going to attack west through the Negev. Maybe we'll join up with the Egyptians moving east. They have more armor than we and they have the air force."

The girl was passing them now and Diyar enjoyed the way the front of her dress bounded as she swatted the behind of an old goat.

"But you said I'm to go to Jerusalem," he pointed out to his captain.

"I'm moving some men out of there now. You'll replace them. Set your guns so that you can keep the Jew city under fire. The Jews'll hesitate to attack until we have beaten them in the south."

Diyar's broad face brightened. "I'll be given permission to shell the city?"

The captain's eyes were following the girl, and he wondered if he would have time to spend with her before he returned to Amman.

"You'll be given your orders when you are dug in." And he wondered why he had been so patient with the old officer who had not done anything of note since 1948 except father thirteen children among the Palestinian refugees and raid Israel twice in 1955. "Move, Lieutenant," he snapped angrily.

And Diyar al Ilm realized that he was not going to be the one to enjoy the girl.

THE NEGEV

Driving northeast toward Tel Aviv, Zvi Mazon sat back in the front of his jeep and surveyed the terrain. Behind him he could hear the Signals Sergeant listening to a broadcast from Kol Israel. The land they were racing through was barren. They were crossing the floor of Makhtesh Ramon. The great depression was dark brown and gray. Nothing green could be seen in any direction. Off to the left Zvi could make out blotches of dark red clay. Turning his head the other way he could see the soft black shale of worn mountains. They bumped their way over the empty wadi which drained the depression and headed up the twisted tortured road along Maale Haazmut to the small collection of buildings at Mizpe Ramon.

Stepping out in front of the small café, Zvi told his driver to fill the tank with petrol, and turning to the young sergeant crouched over the radio, he said, "Don't leave that. Not for one minute." Then he went inside the café for a drink of cold lemonade.

Standing on the terrace looking down from the height of Makhtesh Ramon, he sought out the site of Mezad Mohila, that ancient fort from which caravans were checked or assaulted thousands of years ago. Half closing his eyes, he pictured the slowly moving camel caravans driven by Egyptians, Assyrians and hundreds of nameless people hauling frankincense and myrrh, slaves and gold between Egypt and Babylon.

A move behind him, and he spun to see a young Arab woman washing the window of the café. Smiling at her, he finished his drink, picked up the two bottles he had bought for his companions and looked back once more at the vast empty waste which was the heart of the Negev. Why, he asked himself, why did anyone want to take this useless terrain from Israel? In anger, he shook his head and strode to the highway to join his driver and radio operator.

Handing each of them a bottle of lemonade, which he hoped they liked better than he, he climbed into the jeep. He noticed the girl had soaked her cap to keep her head cool. It would only be an illusion. "Anything on the radio?" he asked.

"Syrian artillery. Two men wounded, sir."

Zvi nodded and waited to hear more. For the first time he noticed that the girl's right eye was slightly cast. In fact, as he turned back to look at her, he realized it was the first time he had actually noticed her. He smiled inwardly at the thought that he must be getting older than he wanted to admit. But then, he never had admitted he was old in his early forties when he had retired two years before.

"I monitored the broadcast from Moshe Gilead," she was saying. "That was all there was."

Zvi nodded and waved the driver on as he noted the sergeant had referred to Moshe by his first name. She had probably never even met Moshe, and he wondered what there was about his friend which brought forth such familiarity. They were driving through the desert now. There were shelves of flat rock and the remains of a sand sea. As they passed Sede Boqer, Zvi wondered if BG were at home or in Jerusalem, waiting to tell people what they should be doing. Zvi had no doubts that the old prime minister had an opinion. Everyone in Israel had an opinion on what should be done.

As the dust rose about them and the sun bore down, he wondered if he had not made a mistake driving north instead of flying. He had his Piper Cubs and a Ðormier; Southern Command would have given him a Dakota if he had asked for it.

The land slowly turned green as they approached Beersheba, and he knew why he had driven north. This was his country, this the bleak city which had been his base for years. His father lived here after '48 until he died. When he had been retired, Zvi thought of coming back to Beersheba, but when the new university at Tel Aviv hired him he and Aaron had stayed on in the house he had bought when he became Operations Officer.

Driving by the Bedouin camp on the edge of the city, they continued on past fields stacked with empty oil drums, porcelain sinks and toilets, and then the cemetery where General Allenby had buried his Australian dead of another war half a century earlier.

The driver kept looking at the General as though he expected orders, but Zvi kept his eyes on the road ahead. They passed through Beersheba in the late afternoon. The streets were almost empty. A few children were playing with a ball on a street corner. An old Arab woman, carrying a load of dried grass on her head, watched the jeep as it left the city for the empty road.

They had gone only a half kilometer when the driver slowed the car and stared at the General. Zvi, who had been lost in thoughts of Beersheba, looked up in surprise. Beside the road stood a woman, a suitcase beside her. She was wearing khaki shorts, a white blouse and a cotton Dosh hat. Zvi noticed that she made no gesture to ask for a ride. Instead she merely stared at them as they approached. Nodding, he told his driver, "All right, if there's room back there."

He turned to see if the Signals Sergeant approved.

"There's room, sir."

And when the jeep came to a stop beside the road, Mazon stepped out. "How far are you going?"

The woman looked at him a moment and seemed to swear as she said, "To Tel Aviv, General Mazon."

And he looked more closely at her. She was probably in her mid-thirties. Her eyes were dark and he thought for a moment she was Oriental. But the pale skin edging her thin white blouse and tan shorts seemed to belie this. He did not think he had ever seen her before. But it was obvious that she knew who he was.

"We can take you that far if you want to squeeze in back there."

"But will you get me there safely, General?" There was mockery in her voice.

Startled, he shook his head. "If you don't think so . . ."

"You've been known to blunder."

He moved closer to her, peering into her face, trying to determine if he actually did know her.

She smiled enigmatically at him. "It's been a long time since we met."

Though there was something familiar about her, he could not remember where they had met.

He was not smiling as he asked, "What blunders have I made that would trouble you?" He wondered why he was taking the time.

"You fought in the Old City and at Mitla," she spoke so angrily he cocked his head to one side to be certain he understood what she was trying to tell him.

He walked half way around her so that she was forced to turn to look at him, and now the sun was in her eyes, and she was squinting. Annoyed that he was losing time, he said softly to hide his anger, "And you lost someone near and dear to you at Mitla and you blame me?"

She nodded.

"Well, I'll tell you, young lady . . ."

Cutting him short, she snapped, "Don't patronize me, Zvi."

"I'm too old to play games," he growled. "What is your name?" And he wanted to tell her that it did not matter because he had to be moving on. And yet there was every chance that she had a right to ask him about Mitla.

She hesitated as though she were debating whether or not to tell him her name. Finally, she said, "Dvora Kidron."

"Is that supposed to mean anything to me?"

Very slowly she shook her head. "I think you would remember me under another one. Does Fishel Warshow mean anything to you?"

His large hand wiped his balding head as he recalled the violinist who had died eleven years before. "And what was Fishel to you?"

It was clear that the conversation was not going in the direction she had expected it to take; and bending over, she picked up her suitcase and started to walk down the road. Zvi's hand came up and grasped her bare arm as he turned her back toward him. "You began this. Let's finish it."

She glanced down at his hand on her arm and then at his ruddy face. He did not drop his hand. Instead, with his other he took her bag and tossed it at his driver. Aware that both the driver and radio operator had been watching them, he was angry with himself for having stopped in the first place even though it was the custom in Israel to take hitchhikers when possible. He had more to do than argue with a woman about a battle she knew nothing about and which had been fought eleven years before. However, as he led her by the arm to the jeep and half lifted her into the rear seat, he knew that he was only fooling himself.

Once he was settled in his own seat, he did not look back to see if Dvora Kidron and her bags were settled. "Let's make up time," he snapped at his driver.

They had gone two kilometers when he heard the radio operator talking to someone and he looked back.

"Headquarters wanted to know where you were, sir."

He nodded, assuming she had told them. Then for the first time he looked to see if his passenger was comfortable. Perched on the edge of the small seat with her bag under her feet, she glared back at him. He wanted to smile. "I asked you what Fishel was to you."

Her hand came up to keep her hat from blowing away, and he noticed the tattoo on her wrist. "We were engaged," she said after a moment.

Zvi nodded. Then he felt the shock of recognition and his hand slipped inside his shirt where a finger touched an old wound. He remembered this woman. She had left her scar on him. He stared at her a moment. The drab young girl of the rooftops had changed, but then so many things had in nineteen years.

Angrily he turned away to the Signals Sergeant. "Tell HQ I will be there in plenty of time."

The radio crackled. Then the sergeant sent his message on. He did not hear the answer and waited. The earphones were still on her head when she told him, "General Gilead's coming south."

Trying to decide if this had any particular meaning, Zvi shrugged. He would know in time. His attention was on the long tanned legs of his passenger. His eyes came up and matched Dvora's. "Rabsky, wasn't it?"

She nodded.

Nineteen years. After a time, he said, "If you want, sometime I'll tell you about Mitla." He thought of what he had suggested and looked at his watch. He would be hard pressed for time once he reached Tel Aviv. And after the meeting he did not know what he would be expected to do. To his own surprise, he looked at Dvora Rabsky and suggested, "I've a meeting at ten tonight. I'll pick you up and take you to dinner after that. We can talk about Fishel then." He was silent for a moment and then explained, "I don't know when I'll have another chance."

Dvora dropped her head to one side as though to see him better and she started to shake her head. Then her face tightened in anger and to his surprise, she nodded. "When you're done with your meeting."

Somehow he knew that she had challenged him, though he could not understand why. Then he remembered what little he could of her—an unpleasant, dour little witch who had shot him and he remembered the story about the young Polish girl the Germans had turned into a field whore.

TEL AVIV

When Colonel Avram Ben Ezra left the office of the Chief of Staff, it was almost eight o'clock. He had not yet had dinner, and he had at least another hour of work before he was due back for the night meeting of the field commanders. Avram was angry at no one in particular, but he knew he should be. He had just asked the Chief of Staff for a field assignment and had been turned down. The Chief of Staff had said he understood. He had even been sympathetic. But he had made it clear that he expected Colonel Ben Ezra to function as operations deputy in the weeks to come. "After all," he said, "someone has to mind the store."

Walking back through the old house which served as a headquarters, Avram returned to his own office, which had probably once been someone's sitting room. It was larger than most of the offices of the headquarters. And as he thought of this, he snorted. It had to be because so much paper went through it.

As soon as he seated himself behind his desk, his sergeant brought him a handful of notes. He smiled at the young woman. "Will you call my wife and tell her I'll have a bite with her if she comes down now?"

The sergeant nodded and left him alone with the notes and the sheaf of papers stacked in the center of the desk. He shuffled through the messages quickly. All of the commanders would arrive on time. He paused as he looked at the report from Zvi Mazon. Zvi should have taken a plane. He would have to remember to talk to him about that. On through three others and then he read the note from Moshe Gilead who had sent word that they would have to talk before the meeting. Avram knew without asking what they were going to talk about, and even though he knew it would not be a pleasant encounter, he knew there was nothing he could do that would change Moshe's retirement date. Moshe had picked it. He would have to live with it. Avram tossed the note on the desk and lit a cigarette. Zvi had taken his retirement well enough. Moshe probably would not. The problems were different. And Avram knew what Moshe's problem was, Hannah Gilead.

He thought for a moment about Ruth's daughter, who had married the general twice her age. Hannah had married a hero. Would she like him as much when he was doing something else? And what would Moshe Gilead do? It sounded like melodrama. However, it was not humorous. Moshe had just returned from an assignment as a military attaché where he had not performed particularly well. He was better designed for desert warfare than for cocktails and tea. He did not understand when which fork should be used as well as he knew when to call upon his mortars and when to bypass an enemy position.

Tossing Moshe's note on the desk with the others, Avram quickly ruffled through the stack of papers his secretary had left for him. Reports. Evaluations. Intelligence. Supply. Shoving the stack to the far corner of his desk, he walked to the window and stood looking out on the city. Here lay his fear. He had faith in Israel's people, in her army, in men like Zvi and Moshe. But what he did not know was how anyone could protect the people from mass air raids, from the enemy artillery located within firing range of the big cities. He had faith and he had fears, and he knew he could not talk of either. He had not been in Tel Aviv in '48, but the accounts he had heard of the air raids lingered with him every time he looked out of the window.

From where he stood, Avram could see a few high buildings and the fact that no one was yet observing blackout, and he knew he would have to remember to bring this up at the staff meeting even though the responsibility did not lie with his office.

There was a noise behind him and he turned to see his sergeant standing by the door.

"Judge Ben Ezra said she was sorry. She had to leave in half an hour for Jerusalem. Court meets tomorrow and she is sitting."

Avram nodded, "Thanks." And he was looking out of the window again. If court was going to sit through the emergency, he did not doubt that Malin had to be there. He smiled to himself as he thought that was what he deserved for having married a judge. Then he thought of all of the jokes their marriage had begot and walked back to stand for a moment looking down at his desk.

There was nothing he had to do before nine, and so he still had about forty-five minutes. Deciding he needed some fresh air, he strode out of the office, down the steps and out into the night. It was a clear night, a full moon. The thought that this was what in other wars had been called a bomber's moon crossed his mind, but he brushed it aside. Perhaps. Maybe tomorrow. Maybe the day after.

Striding toward the gate of the compound, he realized he was playing hookey. He had gone several blocks when he noticed the young couple walking toward him. At first he did not recognize her and then he wished he had not. Hannah Gilead. Avram did not mind meeting up with Hannah, but he had not expected to see her with a young lieutenant's arm about her waist. Air force. Aaron Mazon. As they approached, he thought that that was where she really belonged, and only Moshe did not realize it.

They came together and Hannah greeted him, "Avram."

The older man nodded and shook hands with his friend's son. Before they could say anything, Hannah suggested, "You'd better hurry, Aaron, if you are going to make that bus." Aaron smiled at her, said, "Excuse me, sir. If you talk to my father, tell him I'm fine." And he started running toward the headquarters compound.

Avram wondered if he had precipitated the sudden flight, but Hannah explained. "The bus for his area leaves in ten minutes."

They stood looking after Aaron until he disappeared. Then they turned and looked at each other. Avram admitted to himself that whatever expression he found on Hannah's face, guilt was not the way to describe it. She slipped her hand under his arm and said, "You were walking someplace?"

And they started walking together. Ten minutes later they had ordered their coffee and were sitting at a bare table in an almost deserted café.

"They're posting him in Jerusalem," Hannah said, her thoughts still on Aaron.

Avram nodded. He appreciated the fine lines on her face, the delicacy of her high cheekbones and the way she exuded both confidence and dignity. She looked like many things, but none of them was the wife of a national hero who was about to be retired. He wondered if he should mention the fact that Moshe was on his way into town or had probably arrived already and might be at their apartment in Ramat Gan.

"We are going to fight?" she was asking him, and he shoved aside the image of Moshe in an empty apartment.

"Fight?"

She smiled at him. "Moshe said you never answer a question, even if asked the time of day." Her smile delighted him and he wished he were not so conscious of her leg touching his under the table. He glanced at his watch.

"Time is eight-forty and that means in twenty minutes I have three meetings. After that a session with a certain general who is going to tell me he does not want to retire in less than three weeks now that there may be a war and after that . . ." his voice trailed off as he saw her head come up.

"Retire?" she asked. "Who's going to retire?"

And he realized that Moshe had not said anything to Hannah as yet. Trying to decide if there was anything he should say himself, he shoved his cup aside and leaned across the table so that he was looking directly at her. "A long time ago we agreed in the Defense Force. There would be no old soldiers. 'Up and out' we said. There would not be too many generals."

She looked at him silently for a few minutes and he wondered if she was going to say something.

When she did not, he added, "It's the way we think. I'm sure you do not want the standard lecture on strategy. Not from me, when Moshe is the man who helped create the strategy. But we long ago decided that we would never let the fight come into our country. We have no space to give up for time. We have no space that can sustain damage without destroying us, and so we have to move out."

She was nodding now, and he could tell that she was not really listening to what he was saying, but suddenly he felt secure discussing this with her because it meant he was not talking about her or Aaron Mazon.

"To fight the way we plan means mobility. Speed. We have to keep moving. Like soccer, it is not for the old," he was smiling now. "Anyone over forty is getting old for us, but not for anyone else."

She sipped her coffee as though she still had not heard him, but when she set her cup down, she said, "Don't tell him you told me."

Avram emptied his cup and closed one hand over hers. "A trade, Hannah, a trade."

She waited to see what he was offering.

"I won't tell him we had this talk, if you will tell me where Aaron Mazon fits in."

She stared at him for a moment, and then she laughed softly. "We grew up together." The laughter ceased and she said, "No one will be casting stones."

Rising from the table, Avram paid for the coffee and then turned back to her. "And if I said your husband is both a friend and a man I admire?"

She was standing at his side as he opened the door for her and they stepped out into the night. She started walking back toward the compound with him though he had not asked her to. "First, I would say that you are getting very stuffy. Very stuffy and too noble."

"And then?"

"I would tell you that there is no man in Israel this night who is better equipped to take care of himself and what he has than Moshe Gilead, and he would not appreciate your discussing this with me or anyone else."

Avram came to a stop and turned directly toward her. "I almost think you're threatening me."

When she shook her head, he realized that instead she was alerting him to the fact that Moshe would deeply resent knowing that they had even discussed him. To his own amusement, Avram said, "Thanks." Then they hurried back to the compound gate where he waved for a staff car. While the driver brought the car out of the pool, Avram looked up at the sky once more. Puzzled, Hannah followed his glance. Without looking at her, he said softly, "Look, Aaron's a fine boy. I've known him since . . ." His hands went wide. "But . . ." Again his voice trailed off.

Coming up to tiptoes, she kissed him on the cheek. "I've always thought you were cute, Avi." And he knew she was laughing at him.

He helped her into the staff car, closed the door and told the driver to take General Gilead's wife home. After the car drove away, he started walking through the gate toward his office when he noticed the command car in front of it and Moshe Gilead staring at him.

Neither spoke as Moshe stepped out of the command car and matched steps with Avram until they entered Avram's office and the door was closed behind them.

"That was Hannah, wasn't it?" Moshe finally asked.

Avram nodded, wondered if Moshe had seen her kiss him on the cheek and then he knew he had. Smiling, he said, "We had coffee together down the street."

Moshe nodded.

The staff officer sat down behind his desk and Moshe dropped into an armchair, swung another about with his foot and put his heavily shod feet up on it. Offering his friend a cigarette, Avram lighted one for himself. "You sent a message that we had to talk before the meeting."

Moshe nodded. He had, but now it seemed less important, as his thought kept swinging back to Hannah as she stood on tiptoes kissing the cheek of his friend. To Avram's surprise, Moshe started talking softly. "I got home and she wasn't there. I thought she could be at Ruth's, but I couldn't call and ask where my wife was." He looked at Avram as if he expected his friend to understand. "She never approved of Hannah marrying me. Even when the *Jerusalem Post* carried our picture with the caption 'A Hero Takes a Bride.' She told Hannah, 'There are other generals.' " Moshe sighed. Before Avram could say anything, he continued. "The only thing I ever did that pleased either of them was when I got the appointment to London." Almost ingenuously, he added, "Hannah liked London. She said it was historic, and even after I pointed out that Jerusalem was also historic, she did not change her mind." He smiled appreciatively, "They liked her in London. It's her candor. The way she looks at people. They seemed to sense what one dowager told me was 'a colonial quaintness.' " He was proud as he said, "I think I did better there because people liked her than I did because of my own reputation." And he fell silent.

Embarrassed, Avram could not decide what he was supposed to say about Hannah, if anything, and so he said, "Your reputation as a soldier is the best there is," and even as he spoke he knew he sounded fatuous. And he knew, too, Moshe Gilead had not done well in London and part of the reason had been Hannah.

Suddenly, Moshe's head came up. "Those papers I received the other day, the ones with your signature on the bottom?"

Avram waited.

"They will go into effect as scheduled?"

"You agreed, and it has to be. You will retire into the reserves on June tenth. You set that date."

Very slowly, Moshe Gilead pulled himself out of his chair and stood looking down. "You know what this is going to do to me?" And then, "It will be even worse for her."

Avram nodded. "If you were sitting here, what would you say?"

The field officer's leathered face seemed to grow even more taut as he stared at his old friend. His hand opened and closed several times before he finally brought it, clenched, to rest on the desk. Then he chuckled softly, "That's why you're a staff officer and I'm a field soldier. I wouldn't have thought to ask that question."

For the first time since they had come into his office, Avram relaxed.

"Is Zvi here yet?" Gilead asked, as though the rest of the conversation had not taken place.

Avram shrugged. "I haven't checked."

"I'll look for him," Moshe said, and then he asked, "You wouldn't want to tell me what this meeting is all about?" Even before Avram could finish shaking his head, Moshe laughed, "I thought not."

Then he was walking toward the door where he stood for a moment before he looked back. "When I was twenty-two, forty-two looked so far away." The door closed behind him. Avram did not smile.

Five minutes later Moshe located Zvi in a secretary's office. The reserve brigadier, his beret shoved back on his head, was banging away on an old typewriter while a nervous sergeant stood in the back of the room watching. The woman shook her head in disapproval when Moshe glanced her way. Moshe laughed softly as he watched Zvi's stubby fingers race over the keys.

"Keep it up and you'll make corporal one of these days," he suggested.

Zvi nodded seriously. "Reports." Then, uncertain if Moshe knew what had happened, "We struck a mine today."

"I heard."

Zvi was no longer typing. "And you got battered by artillery."

"Yes," and Moshe brushed the incident aside. "What is this all about tonight?"

Shoving back the secretary's chair, Zvi shrugged. "My guess would be the same as yours."

He swung away from the typing table, jerking his report out as he did so and tossed it on the desk. "Sergeant, will you see that that gets into channels. Colonel Ben Ezra." And he strode out of the office, Moshe at his side. But he was not thinking of Moshe Gilead but, rather, of Dvora Kidron.

"Remember that Dvora Rabsky who was with us in the Old City?" He tried to be casual.

Moshe started to shake his head and then stopped. "The *meshugenah* who shot you?"

Zvi nodded. "I met her today. First time we've talked since forty-eight." Moshe looked at his friend. "You didn't hit her?"

Shaking his head, Zvi said simply, "No."

Only when they were outside and alone among the headquarters buildings did Zvi say, "Something's bothering you."

Moshe shook his head. He was fond of Zvi the way men can become fond of other men who have shared the same experiences and some of the same women most of their lives.

"How old do you have to be to be an old fool?" Moshe asked too casually.

"I've never been sure it was a matter of age."

Both men laughed as Moshe looked at his watch. "It's that time."

They settled down around the long table in the Chief of Staff's office. There were a half a dozen of them. They all knew each other. They had fought in the same wars, and they had all climbed to the rank of brigadier except the Chief of Staff, who was a major general, and there was Avram, still a colonel. The Chief of Staff waited until they were all present. Then he nodded to Lev Hershel, who came to his feet in an almost halting manner. "Political intelligence first. Nasser has placed the UAR on an economic war footing. I'm not too sure just what that is actually going to mean except that he can raid his own treasury without any legal devices. He will tell his National Assembly that the Soviet—and he will mean Kosygin, the prime minister—has promised to support Egypt in its blockade of the Strait of Tiran." His eyes almost closed, his head back as though he needed to see the others at the table from a distance, Lev Hershel continued, "Nasser isn't going to say if that means with vessels to assist against the blockade or if they are going to declare more talk on us at the United Nations. I'm sorry, but it remains fuzzy at this moment. Nasser will make an announcement that there is no chance for peace. No negotiation." He smiled wryly. "There has been little reason to believe he would negotiate now if he has not been willing to negotiate for nineteen years." He looked at the Chief of Staff. "Military?"

The Chief of Staff nodded.

Rubbing the bridge of his nose with a thumb and forefinger as he weighed what he was going to say, Lev Hershel began: "This will be general information. It is hard information. Information concerning your own tactical necessities has been prepared and will be given to you individually as you receive your missions." He smiled again wryly. "I wish I had the time, money and staff to make a fancy presentation with lights and projections and slides and color film. I don't. And so if you will bear with me," and he noticed the others at the table smiling.

In a very flat monotone, he went on, "Man power: Egypt military total 310,000; Syria 115,000; Iraq 82,000; Jordan 70,000; Lebanon 11,000; Saudi Arabia 55,000 for a total of men under arms of 643,000." Then as though it were not important, he said, "The only numbers that will matter are effectives." Then he added bluntly, "Egypt has had as many as seventy-five thousand men blooded in Yemen. As many as fifteen thousand of those are supposed to be available in Sinai. A blooded officer and corps must have some value beyond that of green troops. It is hoped that we will be able to bring Hussein and Jordan to the point where they will hold still as they did in fifty-six." He sighed and when the Chief of Staff nodded, he said, "Try to think in terms of effectives and that is only about five hundred thousand men against our three hundred thousand. Their effective air force is probably around forty thousand men, but that figure is deceptive. Let us say they can put a thousand planes in the air. Eight hundred of those will be fighters of all classes and ages." He smiled, "But they will be flown by Arabs and you have to make your own allowance for that factor." The others at the table were jotting down notes or doodling while they listened.

"We overflew the Egyptians yesterday to see what reaction we would discover. There were two. I shall tell you only one. It took their pilots twenty-five minutes to scramble. Our men can do it in three."

He squinted again as he recalled figures. "Tanks over all. They have twenty-seven hundred. We have eight hundred. Theirs are in all instances as good or better than ours." He thought a moment as though there were something more he wanted to say and then without another word sat down.

There was a long silence as the men at the table digested the odds against them. None of this information was new, but now they were viewing it in a context, and that context was the possibility of war within the hour or the week. Though Lev Hershel's presentation had left much to be desired, his information did not, and the men seated around the table knew that when they asked for the specific information they would need, he would have it to the enemy man and machine as well as to the plot of ground both were standing on. This was Lev's genius.

The Chief of Staff's head came up from the pad in front of him. In a measured manner he began to explain why they had been brought together. "I do not believe in pep talks. I do not believe I need to tell any man sitting at this table or anywhere else in Israel what is at stake at this moment. Therefore, I shall dispense with generalities. Avram has laid out the objectives of each of your units. By tomorrow night I shall want to see your plans for completing your mission. If there are any specific problems of supply, include them in your plans." He thought a moment and then added, "Lev Hershel will have detailed intelligence concerning any special problems dealing with enemy strength and dispositions which each of you might face." Then he turned to Moshe Gilead. "I am turning your division to the southwest. I shall want you to take up a position along the Gaza Strip ready to swing both north and west." He explained, "You've a difficult assignment and I want a regular unit on that axis." A pause, and he asked if there were any questions. Then he was gone and Avram came to his feet.

"If you'll all meet with me in my office one at a time, I'll go over the missions with you."

Where another army might have spent time detailing the mission of each division and put it into writing, the Israeli Defense Force worked with a minimum of paper; each commander would be given his specific objective as well as the responsibility of assuming it without any interference on details. Each commander knew his own unit, its capacity and its needs. And so the time that Moshe, Zvi and the other field commanders spent with Avram was brief. They knew that within twenty-four hours they were expected to present their operational plans for approval along with their lists of specific needs.

Half an hour after the meeting broke up in the office of the Chief of Staff, Moshe and Zvi walked out of the headquarters. They paused for a moment and looked at the sky. The night was warm. There was a slight breeze off the Mediterranean. There were no lights in the city. Zvi walked Moshe to his command car where they found the young Signals Sergeant asleep on the floor of the vehicle. Her earphones remained on her head. The two brigadiers smiled at each other.

"I'll see you here tomorrow night," Moshe said.

Zvi nodded. "I'll fly back to the Negev later tonight and back again tomorrow. And you?"

Moshe shrugged. "I've got to start moving the division. I'll let them come on through without me." He thought a moment, "I might as well rejoin them near Gaza." And he was looking at his watch. "If the replacement unit is all ready to move in as Avram said, I'll get my men on the road tonight."

"And then?" Avi asked.

"And then I'm going home." But the way in which he said it raised Zvi's eyes from the ground where he was toeing a loose pebble. Hesitant and uncertain as to what he should make of Moshe's bitter tone, Zvi decided that this was not his business, not now, not until his friend wanted to talk about it. And if it had to do with Hannah, he did not want to listen. Neither he nor Aaron had attended the wedding. They had not been invited. Instead, Zvi had taken his son to Cyprus just to get away.

His jeep was beside the command car now, and Zvi swung himself into the seat. "The center axis," he said, almost in disbelief. "I didn't think I would get it."

"Avram," Moshe suggested.

"I'll have to thank him for that." His hand came up and he half saluted Moshe as his driver started the jeep. Seated in the rear, a blanket around her, his own Signals Sergeant held one half a headset pressed tightly against one ear. The streets were dark. There were few cars. Lights could be seen in the windows of few apartments as they passed. It was well after eleven now. When they turned down Dizengoff Street, which was almost deserted, and passed the long row of stores on Ben Yehuda Street, Zvi Mazon noticed that for the first time the window lights were turned off. Ten minutes later the jeep came to a stop in front of the apartment house in which Fishel had lived and where he had last seen Zella. Zvi had dropped Dvora Kidron here earlier in the evening. As he stepped out of the jeep, he was surprised to find that he was actually looking forward to seeing her. He started to walk away from the jeep and then swung back toward his driver. "Why don't you go find a café where you can spend the next two hours. I'll pick you up here at . . .," he glanced at his watch, ". . . one." With a smile he looked at the sleepy Signals Sergeant. "You, young lady, are a necessary evil this evening. You'll stay with me."

Inside the apartment house, Zvi stopped to look at the mail boxes. "Apartment 3A," she had said, and as he approached the door, it opened, and she was standing there. His beret came off his head and when she closed the door behind her and came into the dim light of the hall, he saw that she was almost as tall as he.

Zvi stared at her. She was as pretty in a dress as she was in shorts. The summer cotton she wore covered her legs better, but it really hid little.

"I wasn't sure you would come," she said.

"I wasn't sure you would be waiting, and so that makes us even." He had his hand on her arm now and they were walking down the stairs. Only when they were half way down did he realize she had not flinched. When they reached the bottom, he said, "I guess I had all kinds of plans in my head. Dinner and a long talk."

Puzzled, she looked at him.

"Sorry," he apologized. "Coffee and a quick bite. Then I'll have to bring you back." They were standing beside the jeep now.

Indicating the Signals Sergeant, she said, "You still so afraid of me you need a chaperon?"

"Not afraid. On duty." He helped her into the jeep. "If I'd been thinking, I'd have taken a staff car," and he was looking at the Signals Sergeant. "Will you contact Colonel Ben Ezra and arrange a plane for me. I'll want it by one-thirty. Let them pick out the field. I'll want to go back to division and land at night so the air liaison at division had better be alerted." He was behind the wheel of the jeep now and still talking. "Tell them I'll want the plane to come back tomorrow night." Then he looked at Dvora. "Now, if you've no objections, there's the Hilton."

She hesitated a moment. "We never agreed to a party. You were going to tell me about Mitla." There was an edge to her voice and he answered in kind.

"There are fifty things I should be doing. However, I am going to have to eat dinner, and I don't want to drive to my house in Ramat Gan." Then with impatience, "Do you object to the Hilton?"

She shook her head, and ten minutes later they were being seated in the main dining room. Dinner was no longer being served, but the waitress said that she would be happy to see that General Mazon had something. The large room was empty except for the middle-aged woman who was serving as a waitress while the regular waiters were on military duty. Zvi felt self-conscious in the large, well-appointed room. His face had a day's growth of beard, his uniform was spotted with dirt from the day's recce, and as he sat looking down at his trouser leg, he noticed for the first time that he had bloodstains from the wounded and dead he had pulled out of the burning half-track. Dvora sat back in her chair looking at him. She was not in the least self-conscious, nor was there any expression of warmth on her face.

Zvi shook his head at his own thoughts. There was no reason why he should be sitting with someone who so obviously disliked him. He was not that lonely. Though in the years since he had left the army, he had had very little social life. For a short time he had lived with an American girl who was trying to finish her degree at the university. She had found someone younger and moved on. Twice he had slept with a young dancer from the Imbal troup, but then she had gone on tour. He had known other women since then. There was a dentist he went out to dinner with when he wanted company. There was a schoolteacher who lectured at Tel Aviv University he went swimming with when he could no longer stand his own company. And now as he knew what his nights and days were going to be for the foreseeable future, he did not want to sit here talking about an old battle with a woman who had once shot him. And he certainly did not want to talk to this Dvora about her dead fiancé, even though Fishel had been his friend.

His head came up and he smiled at Dvora. She did not return the smile, obviously impatient at finding herself sitting with Zvi Mazon. "I'd heard before that you were engaged to Fishel," he told her.

It took her a moment to realize that he was taking the conversation back to where they had dropped it in the afternoon. She nodded.

"And you met him before that in the Old City," knowing that she must have, but not knowing what else to say.

Again she nodded.

Without thinking, Zvi reached for the scar inside his shirt.

"Fishel and I were in Haganah together before the Old City," he said and then fell silent before he continued. "We were pinned down under British fire one night trying to get some illegals off a boat." His finger lingered on the scar. "I got hit that night." Almost smiling, "You weren't the first to get a shot at me. Others have since."

"You're lucky you've never met a good marksman," she commented, half smiling.

Uncertain how to answer this, he continued, "That night on the beach a shell fragment knocked me out. Fishel pulled me behind a dune and covered me with sand before he ran. Later, after the British left, he dragged me out."

The girl waited as she tried to understand why he was telling her all of this.

A wry smile came over his face. "Fishel may have been a great violinist. I wouldn't know. He was a good soldier. He understood what happened at Mitla and why we did what we did." The smile disappeared. Suddenly, he wished they were talking about something else, but now he wanted her to understand. "Mitla—it was a complex thing." He shook his head as though to brush aside his own evaluation. "No. In some ways it was simple."

Dvora remained silent, her eyes unfriendly. She had waited a long time to meet Zvi Mazon again, and now that she had she was not sure why, other than an old dislike changed over the years to embarrassment.

The waiter brought their chopped-liver appetizer, and Zvi noticed that she did not look at it. He was hungry himself, but for some reason he did not feel like eating.

"There have been others wanting to know about Mitla," he said. "I met an old woman once when I was shopping in a market. That time it was a son. Another time I was visiting a kibbutz and there were two men. With them it was a brother. Another time . . ." his voice trailed off as his Signals Sergeant entered the large dining room. Rising to his feet, he waited for her.

She seemed sad about something. "Colonel Ben Ezra, sir."

"Yes?"

"He thought you would want to know your son's unit has been moved from the Jerusalem area."

For a long time Zvi was silent. Then he nodded slowly while he tried to realize what this meant. Though barely twenty-two, Aaron already had several years in the air force. He was supposed to be a good pilot. Zvi was proud and frightened in a way he had never been before. And then he was wondering if Havah would have approved. His head came up and he thanked the sergeant. "And thank Colonel Ben Ezra for me."

He sat down at the table again and stared for a moment at Dvora, who had listened quietly through the interruption.

"Is one supposed to tell a general he is sorry his son is fighting?"

He could not tell if she were offering sympathies or was taunting him. He shook his head. "I wouldn't know. He's just a boy."

"Is that what you say when your own men are killed?"

He looked at her, irritated at what was obviously an evening gone wrong. Satisfied now that the entire notion of talking to this woman had been a mistake, he was prepared to admit it.

"You brought me here to tell me about Mitla." Her voice was firm.

Finishing his appetizer, he shoved the plate away. A glance at his watch informed him that the driver would not be back for some time. The whole affair had gone wrong because it should never have started.

"Mitla," he said. Then he flipped over the large menu, pulled out a pencil and started to draw two lines parallel and close together. "I'll explain it to you." He looked at her, her head came forward, and she moved the plate before her aside, giving her complete attention to his meager sketch.

He was still describing the battle when the waitress brought their dinner and stood for a moment to see if there was anything else. Zvi looked at the intense expression on Dvora's face and then told the waitress, "Coffee. Turkish for me and . . ." Dvora shook her head, annoyed at the interruption.

He grinned dubiously and talked on. Twenty minutes later he was still describing what had happened. Very slowly he brought his head up. "I had two choices. I could leave Fishel cut off or I could commit myself to rescuing him and the others." A touch of pride came into his voice. "The men with me understood."

And he shook his head in appreciation of these men.

He sighed and for the first time noticed his dinner. Pushing it aside, he asked, "Would you have destroyed that tradition in one minute or gone after those men who were cut off to help them? Years to build and one minute to destroy. What would you decide now? Fast! Fast! There is gunfire all around you. Your men are tired. You are tired. The enemy has twenty good Israelis cut off and will murder them. The enemy will not let them surrender. Will you risk to help them or will you play it safe and flee?" He was talking rapidly, not giving her time to think, applying the pressure he so obviously recalled from that moment eleven years before. "Decide! Men are getting killed while you think. Do you abandon a single man? Do you destroy a tradition? Do you give the enemy a Mitla and flee? They are firing on you. You have a brigade not fully committed. What do you do?"

She looked at him uncertainly.

"Fishel knew. I had to come for him. By the time I got to him, he was dead."

He pulled his plate before him and began to eat. Dvora sat looking at him. She had never known what he would tell her, and now she had heard his side of the story. Very slowly she started to push her chair away from the table and rise. His head came up. He reached out across the table and took her hand. "Sit down. I'll take you back as soon as I finish my coffee." He was pushing the plate away, the dinner unfinished.

Dvora shook her head. After a moment, she said, "I didn't know what it was like." She slumped into her chair again and he gestured to the waitress for another cup of coffee.

He sat back and watched Dvora's face as it slowly tensed and then strangely her eyes seemed to be unaware of anything around her. She was lovely and distant. She was prettier than the dentist and the schoolteacher. She was not so much younger than Zvi himself and he was surprised that he was thinking about that.

"You haven't been mourning for eleven years," he said, more angry with himself than her. "You may have grieved. You may have wept. You may have felt lonely. But you have not mourned Fishel all these years."

She looked at him as though he had accused her of something.

"You are not only too pretty, but it would not have been anything but sick to mourn that long for a man. I don't believe you're sick. Not that way."

A strange expression of fear crossed her face as she tipped her head. "Not that way?"

He nodded. "I don't know if I'm supposed to say I'm sorry, but I heard your story. People thought I should know why I was shot. The girl who shot me I can understand now. But to mourn a decade . . . ," he shrugged.

Aware that he had broached an intensely personal matter, Zvi stirred his coffee and looked about impatiently for the waitress who was coming with Dvora's.

"Fishel knew the story, too." She fell silent for a time and then said, "You won't understand this, but he saved my life." Then, belligerently, "He was a good man, no matter how naïve that sounds."

"A lot of good men get killed in a war. Believe me. I know because I have buried my share." He tried again. "There is nothing naïve in thinking he was good." Then, because he wanted to make conversation, "Do you live in Tel Aviv or Beersheba?"

Distracted for a moment, she said, "I was teaching in Beersheba. Nursery school."

Surprised at the simplicity of her story, he concluded it, "And I drove you to your apartment."

She nodded.

"A nursery school?" He looked at her dubiously.

Her head came forward, and he was again aware that he had never thought of her before as pretty. "Fishel left me some money. I went to school. I wanted to be near children."

Zvi smiled, trying to indicate that he understood, though he would have been the first to admit that he could not have known less about nursery schools. She was drinking her coffee now.

"And what comes next?" he asked.

A questioning smile crossed her face. "That depends on you."

Taken back, he stared at her.

"You and all of the other generals."

"And you have doubts about the future?"

She nodded. "I heard that you went to the university. Some kind of administration and teaching. Would you recommend my going back to school? What's the need going to be for nursery schools?"

Trying not to laugh at what was obviously a ghoulish joke, he shook his head. "Ask me two weeks from now. And if you can't ask me, ask Nasser, Hussein and anyone else who will be here."

"We're going to fight?" she asked so simply he almost gave her an honest answer.

"Cabinets decide if soldiers fight."

"Except at Mitla," she reminded him.

Shaking his head, he explained, "Soldiers decide how they fight, not when."

"*Mea culpa*," she said so softly he barely heard her, and for an instant he was not certain that he had understood her correctly. But there was a smile in her eyes that assured him that he had.

She looked at her watch. "You have a plane to catch."

Puzzled, he looked at her. "How do you know?"

"You went through all that business of arranging it when I was there to impress me." She was smiling as she added, "I was impressed."

They rose from the table together. She stood looking down at the penciled menu. After a time, she sighed. "As simple as that?"

He nodded.

After he paid the bill, he asked, "Would you drive to the airport with me? Either you or the sergeant can take the jeep back to your apartment." She nodded without hesitation.

When they reached the small airport north of Tel Aviv, an officer pointed out the Dakota waiting to fly General Mazon south. Driving over to the large plane, Zvi told the Signals Sergeant, "Have the driver pick me up here tomorrow night. You'd better be with him. Make it six-thirty." Then he turned to Dvora. "I should be done about midnight tomorrow. Can we have the dinner we didn't have tonight?"

"I don't know." Then she suggested, "You can phone me. The name's Hebrew now—Kidron."

Five minutes later the Dakota was airborne. Settling back in a bucket seat in the rear of the plane, Zvi tried to think about the work ahead, the days ahead, but as he fell asleep, his thoughts drifted back to Dvora Kidron.

Moshe Gilead arrived home after one-thirty. He told his driver and Signals Sergeant they were free until seven in the morning. If headquarters had to reach him, they would phone. He watched the command car drive away and stood thinking about the meeting he had just left. It reminded him of another, eleven years before. The only one who had changed was the Chief of Staff. And Moshe had known the one who had chaired tonight's meeting most of his life.

Finally he shrugged, said, "Oh, well," to himself, and started for the door of the new apartment house. A shriek of brakes and he paused to watch a heavy truck careen around a corner. Some kibbutznik. And he smiled to himself because he was certain there had been a time when people had referred to him in the same way.

Entering the apartment, he climbed the stairs two at a time. Approaching the door, he wondered if he should tell Hannah that he had seen her with Avram. When he opened the door, he found no lights inside. She was probably asleep. He crossed to the hall, turned on the night light and looked inside the bedroom. Hannah was not there. Puzzled, he flicked on the light. She had not been there since he had arrived from the north because his dirty shirt still lay on the chair where he had left it. Annoyed, he walked about the apartment looking for a note. There was none in the kitchen or in the living room. He recalled that she left him messages in lipstick on the bathroom mirror and he went looking for one. Nothing. Leaving all of the lights on behind him, he returned to the living room. He had too much to do and was too restless to sleep. Scanning the well-furnished living room, he crossed over to the framed painting of Hannah which hung on the wall above the desk. She was lovely. She would always be lovely. There was something about her eyes and the way she carried her head. There was something . . .

He slammed out of the apartment, leaving the lights on behind him and descended the steps as rapidly as he had climbed them. Out in the street he stood for a moment and looked at the sky. Bright. He was pleased that he was not fighting tonight. Much too bright. A man could see a kilometer or more in open country. Shoving his hands into his pockets, he walked rapidly down the empty street. Ten minutes later he stopped in front of a new apartment house. There were no lights on in any of the suites. But he needed none to make his way to the top floor and knock on the first door he came to on his left. He knocked several times before he saw a light go on under the door. A moment later a woman asked, "Who is it?"

"Moshe," he snapped, surprised at the tone of his own voice and the uncontrolled anger in it.

Several minutes more and the door opened, revealing Ruth, clutching a light blue robe about her as she waited for Moshe to explain himself.

"I came home," he said. "Hannah wasn't there."

"She's your wife."

"And she's your daughter." Then he pushed open the door and entered the apartment. Ruth turned on a lamp and, closing the door behind Moshe, she stood with her hands on her hips waiting for him to turn around to look at her. When he did, she was surprised at the confusion on his face.

"Where the hell did she go?"

"Don't curse," she admonished him.

Moshe wanted to laugh because this was exactly the answer he might have predicted. He stood looking at his mother-in-law. She was as tall as he. Her face looked not unlike her daughter's, only her hair was darker and her cheeks were less full. In fact, he could still recognize the girl on the rooftop in the Old City. Ruth had not only not gone out of her way to make an impression on her famous son-in-law, but it had been obvious from the first time he dated Hannah, she was opposed. In the years since 1948, she had become wealthy, but she had never married again.

As Ruth stood looking at Moshe Gilead's tense face and deepset eyes, she wondered what Hannah had seen in this man who was old enough to be her father. She knew she resented Moshe. Some of her reasons were personal. Some were not. There was nothing gentle about him, nothing warm or even friendly that she had ever seen. She knew her own emotions were never really clear where he was concerned.

"I asked you where she is," he reminded her.

Ruth shrugged. "Malin Ben Ezra was driving to Jerusalem. I think she went with her. Something about a job."

Unable to make sense of what he was hearing, Moshe crossed the living room to the small table where the telephone rested. Picking it up, he dialed quickly and stared at Ruth while he waited for an answer. Then he slowly shook his head. "Why in the hell would she go looking for a job in Jerusalem now?"

Ruth shrugged. "When you see her, ask her."

His attention was on the phone. "Gilead. I am at . . ." He looked at the number on the instrument he was holding and gave it to the person on the other end of the line. "Anything for me? Good. Send a staff car with a radio over for me now." A pause and he waited. "I'll expect it in half an hour." He stared at Ruth and then said, "I'll meet it in front of my apartment."

She shook her head. "You can wait for it here."

He hesitated and then gave the operator Ruth's address. "Tell the driver top floor. First door to the left." and he cradled the instrument.

They stood looking at each other. Finally he asked, "Why Jerusalem in the middle of the night and why a job?"

Brushing back her hair, Ruth said again, "Ask her when you see her."

His hand came up in a clenched fist and he caught himself looking at it, embarrassed. With a sigh, he let it drop to his side. "Do you know?"

"I think so."

"Goddamnit, woman, will you tell me?"

Then as though she knew it would annoy him, she repeated, "I've asked you not to curse, Moshe." And before he could say anything, she added, "I'll make some coffee."

Leaving him standing looking after her, she disappeared into the kitchen.

Five minutes later she emerged with a tray to find Moshe standing beside a small bookcase with an open book in his hand. He looked up at her and nodded. "I hadn't seen this in a long time." He closed the book and held the spine up so that she could identify it.

She smiled wryly. "The Midrash is not what I would call your style." Setting the tray down on a coffee table in front of the sofa, she poured coffee for both of them. "You like it strong," she said, not really asking a question.

He slipped into an easy chair across the table from her. "You never did like me, did you?"

Her head came up as she paused, and she seemed to be evaluating him.

"Tell me, Moshe Gilead, Mister General Moshe Gilead, why does a man like you marry a seventeen-year-old girl?"

"I wasn't as 'old as me,' " he began, "when I married a seventeen-year-old. I was younger then."

"You're quibbling."

To his surprise, he found himself nodding. "Maybe I married Hannah because I loved her." He shook his head. "I'll bet you never thought of that as a possible reason."

Ruth shook her head. "Love? Moshe, you've been in love with half the young women in Israel. And for twenty years just sleeping with them was enough."

Moshe laughed softly. "Maybe I wanted to—what's the phrase—settle down."

"A domesticated Moshe Gilead sounds ludicrous."

"Hannah was the prettiest girl I had ever seen." He smiled warmly. "She is the kind of girl who could win beauty contests."

Snorting, Hannah's mother put the notion into what was for her the proper perspective. "She's the sort of girl a man takes the back of his hand to when he comes home and she's gone out. She's the sort of a girl who should have two babies by now." Then she looked curiously at Moshe, "You can have babies, can't you?"

Shaking his head in amusement, he asked, "What in the hell am I supposed to say to that?"

"Don't curse," she reminded him.

He glanced at his watch.

"You've time," she told him. "Your driver will get lost and take fifteen minutes longer than you think."

"You should be scheduling attacks," he said with a grudging admiration for her no-nonsense approach to everything.

"If I had scheduled the last one, we wouldn't be waiting for the Arabs to attack."

Moshe tried to change the subject. "Why does she think she has to find a job in Jerusalem?"

"It all has something to do with her husband retiring and their not having more than three hundred pounds in the bank."

Doubling forward as if he had been struck, Moshe carefully set his cup down on the table in front of him. "Oh, my God," he gasped.

Before he could say anything else, there was a knock on the door. Both of them looked toward it.

"Shall I tell him to wait?" Ruth offered.

Moshe shook his head. He had opened the door and was about to say something to the driver when he felt Ruth's hand on his arm. Trying not to reveal his emotions, he told the driver, "I'll be down in a few minutes." Then as if he had to show he was in control of himself, "Is there a radio operator with you?"

"Your own, sir."

Trying to smile approval, Moshe repeated, "In a few minutes," and closed the door on the soldier. When he turned back, Ruth stood in front of him. "She really thinks I'm going to need her to take care of me?"

"I don't know what she thinks. She married a hero. Maybe she thinks she has to be another Kineret Heschel." Then she asked simply, "It's true, the retirement and no money?"

"June tenth. And as for money, I'm sure I can get a job. The government takes care of the aged."

She looked at him as though he were a prospective employee. "I dislike asking it, Moshe, but what can you do?"

He laughed bitterly. "There are those who say I can command a division better than any man in this Israeli Defense Force."

Ruth shrugged. "Even if it were true, and knowing Zvi Mazon, I doubt it, as the Americans would say, 'That and ten agorot will buy you a cup of coffee.'"

His hand came up and rested on her cheek in mock affection, "One thing I've always liked about you is the way you instill confidence in people, the way you display your profound faith in them." He laughed. "I can recall when you were a good soldier. I think we all had confidence then."

To his surprise, her hand came up and closed gently on his. "What kind of confidence should I have in a man who has been a fool from the time he left the Old City?" And she drew his hand away from her cheek and let it drop.

"We only met a few times after then." He was puzzled.

She nodded. "You always came to my shop to dress your *kurveh*. Then you came in to tell me you were going to marry Hannah. But then you always liked little girls, children. And Hannah. What else could I think except that you were a fool?"

Moshe stared at her, trying to recall the young girl with the scar on her forehead and tennis shoes on her feet. His hands came up and touched the white scar. He could feel her stiffen. Very slowly he shook his head. Then embarrassed, he looked at his hands and clasped them in front of him. "I've got things I should be doing." He thought a moment. "If you hear from Hannah, tell her I will be at headquarters all night tonight and all day tomorrow." Then as if the idea had just struck him. "You wouldn't have an address for her or a phone number?"

Ruth shook her head. "Avram might know. She will stay with Malin." Then, as if she had been withholding information: "They are holding court tomorrow. If they finish the case, Hannah will drive back with the judge. If not tomorrow, the next day."

Moshe nodded and, opening the door, prepared to leave. He paused for a moment and looked at his mother-in-law again. She reminded him more of Hannah than she ever had before. Moshe met her eyes and both of them said nothing. Then he almost smiled, "If I have time tomorrow, I'll call," and as if it were necessary, "about Hannah."

"Do that."

Then he was out in the hall and walking down the steps wondering why he had Hannah and Ruth all mixed up in his mind.

THE SINAI LINE

Brigadier General Zvi Mazon's division moved to the front they were to protect on the Sinai border the next day. There they dug in for defense. Many of the soldiers who had fought with their commander in the past were resentful that they were building a defense line. Zvi's Chief of Staff was one of the first to protest and as Zvi sat back in his command half-track and listened, he nodded complete agreement. "But we are going to dig in anyway. I want everything covered, hidden, camouflaged. I want our guns in a position to cover us against an attack." He was talking now to his artillery officer, who kept shaking his head at the notion, but both he and Zvi knew that he would do as he had been ordered.

They had moved in darkness and were hidden before morning. The division stretched for miles down a thin line, but every effort was made to be certain the enemy did not know their exact locations. Shortly before dawn, Zvi checked his locations, ordering a gun dug in more deeply at one place, a tank covered better in another, a company commander to shift his men to the top of a hill but to remain off the horizon, a small detachment to cover their jeeps. When they returned to the small wadi which sheltered them on two sides, they found their headquarters had already been set up. Two half-tracks and two trucks had been dug in, and the area between was covered with netting and tarps.

Zvi's staff had been going over the operation plans he had sketched out and each of the staff had his own solutions for the problems he would face.

By noon Zvi had met with all of them, and he was sleepy. The sun shimmered off the desert sands, dried the cacti and burned the skins of the men on patrol. Sitting back in his command half-track, Zvi made notes of what he thought he would need if they had to go into action. He also made detailed notes on the problems they would face trying to coordinate their movements with Moshe's division which lay to the north. The radio chattered all through the morning. There was noise at the United Nations building in New York. The Foreign Minister was meeting with the President of the United States in Washington. Nasser was threatening war to the end and stating bluntly that there could be no negotiated peace with Israel. His armies were strong. His men were ready. He predicted an even larger defeat than the one Israel had sustained in 1956, because this time he would destroy the country and annihilate the Jews. Finally, desiring silence, Zvi walked out of the shelter of his command post and into the field where his men were working over their equipment. The drivers were inspecting their tank and truck engines as though they had not done so the night before. The machine-gunners were polishing their weapons as though they had not done so only hours before. Some of the men lay in the shade and stared at each other while they listened to music on transistor radios. Making his way slowly through the length of the wadi, Zvi knew that his men were bored and restless. He knew that they resented sitting for hours on end. They had been called to duty, they were ready to fight. The Strait was closed. The Prime Minister himself had declared the closing was an act of war, the Egyptians had boasted that it was an act of war, Nasser said he had "thrown down the gauntlet" and was waiting for the "Jews to pick it up."

And the division was merely sitting.

Zvi glanced about him. The men in the wadi were watching him now. He strode back to the command post, where he found his adjutant listening to the radio.

"Will you tell the brigade commanders I want all men bathed and shaved by nightfall and they're to do it every day from now on until...," he thought for a moment, "... until, well, they'll know when that no longer applies."

Then he sat down at the improvised table and made notes for himself. Headquarters had to send down some entertainment. He had to check out the medical evacuation plan in the event he moved forward and in the event he had to fight where he was. Then he made a note to remind Avram that there were men in the unit who were due for promotions and this would be a better time than most to raise morale. A noise beside him and he turned to see his Chief of Staff, Gabriel Natan, who had already met with the brigade commanders and listened to their problems. And when he finished passing on what he thought Zvi ought to know, he stretched his feet out on the bench that ran the length of the half-track and leaned back.

"It's the waiting, you know."

Half closing his eyes, Zvi wondered if Gabe needed a pep talk and decided against it. The large kibbutznik with the handlebar mustache was not going to be impressed with talk.

"You have better things to do?" Zvi asked facetiously.

"There's a small lemon grove I've been working on. It's a new plant from California. I don't think it's better than anything we've had, but it's growing pretty fast and I think it may be able to get along with less water."

"I'd have been writing my final exams," Zvi said.

The Divisional Chief of Staff nodded. "There's so much unfinished business."

Slapping a fly that had landed on his bare arm, Zvi said quietly, "Most aggressive damned thing in the area."

Gabe grinned. "You haven't been listening to the good colonel lately."

The reference to Nasser's speeches brought a doubtful look to Zvi's eyes. "I tried to follow his logic a few times, but I'll admit he loses me. Yesterday he explained for an hour why the Strait of Tiran was legally his and only his and how he wasn't going to let any Jews foul his water, and though I'm no lawyer, I didn't flunk out of law school as he did, and by the time he was done talking, he convinced me that his professors were right in flunking him."

The Chief of Staff smiled. "This time he wants to grade the papers."

Coming to his feet, Zvi moved to the edge of the half-track so that the radio operator in the next vehicle beside his could hear him. "I want a copter. Have them put it down behind the dunes about a quarter mile south of here."

Gabe pulled himself up to his full height. "Tel Aviv or Southern Command?"

"Tel Aviv. I'll be back in a few hours unless you call for me." He was picking up the notes he had made through the day and Gabe Natan passed on those he had made.

They walked out into the afternoon sun to meet the helicopter. As he strode for a short distance down the wadi, Zvi could see that some of the men were shaving and that others were trying to create a shower out of a battered jerry can.

"If we're going to wait much longer, we'll have to keep them busy," Gabe suggested.

"I don't like make-work. There's enough to do just digging in what we have more securely. Get air liaison to take some pictures of our positions and we'll see where our asses are sticking out of the sand."

The C/S nodded. "And if they fire tonight?"

Zvi paused where he was. "Don't make a big thing of a few nervous shots. Anything more than that, kick them in the shins and let me know at once." They continued on over the dunes. They could see the helicopter settling down and hurried to meet it.

"If I'm going to be delayed, you'll know. But most of all, hold the fire down. We don't want to start it by accident." Zvi shook his head as he admitted, "That possibility scares the hell out of me more than a planned battle ever will."

Natan laughed. "Weren't you the Operations Officer who said no battle ever went according to plan?"

Putting one hand up on the side of the helicopter so that he could pull himself in, Zvi glanced over his shoulder. "Knowing that, you make it part of the plan."

In a moment the helicopter was leaning toward the north.

TEL AVIV

Two hours later Zvi was sitting in a general staff meeting. The Chief of Staff and his officers each in turn explained the situation as it involved himself and his support forces. And each listened to the division commanders and the three area commanders explain the situation as they envisioned it, depending on the terrain and circumstances in relationship to the objectives they had been given.

The Chief of Operations pointed out that the objectives differed with the phases of the over-all plan. In the event the enemy attacked first, then what were his likely objectives in each command and in each divisional area? This obviously was going to be dictated by what the enemy had learned from the Russians, but there was always the remote possibility that an Arab would think for himself.

When the enemy's attack had been halted, the commanders had to throw him back and break through his lines.

And this second phase of the operation had to take into account the third, which was the destruction of the Egyptian and any other participating Arab armies.

The men sitting in the large conference room all knew that in some way they had made a mistake in not building phase three into the plan eleven years before. The decision not to destroy Egypt's army then could cost them heavily now.

After each area and divisional commander had made his presentation and listened to the amendments and suggestions, Moshe pointed out, "I made a trip south in fifty-six. Who makes it this time?"

The Operations Chief smiled. "You said then that no one would take Sharm el Sheikh the same way twice. This time we're going to leave the job to the navy and give them some support troops."

Satisfied, Moshe sat back and stared at the map on the wall of the almost bare war room. He had been given the northern axis across Sinai, from which he would turn south to join up with Zvi coming through the Central axis. He hoped they did not trip over each other. He had to work this out with Zvi.

The Chief of Staff was explaining now that he was counting on the Central Command to live with what the Jordanians threw at them. He hoped that Hussein might only make some noise to impress his fellow Arabs. But the Chief of Staff drove home the important fact: "Don't ask me for anything. You won't get it. Live with what you have."

The Operations Chief, Central Command nodded as he stared at the wall map behind the Chief's head and took in the whole Jordanian area that stretched west of the Jordan River. There were only nine miles from Jordanian Qalkilya to the beach of Herzliyah. The Israeli Corridor that led to Jerusalem was only four miles wide. Less than eleven miles separated

Tulkarm, Jordan, from Natanya on the coast. Less than fourteen miles lay between Gilboa and the Jordan River. And in spite of the fact that much of Israel's population lived between the hills of Hebron and the Gaza Strip, the distance between was just twenty-one miles.

Nodding acceptance of his order, the OC Central Command listened while Lev Hershel told each of the divisional commanders what changes had been made in enemy dispositions. Moshe listened with only half an ear because he had checked this out a few minutes before the meeting started and was aware that the Egyptian 7th Division lay like an abatis across his axis.

Zvi paused in his smoking to make some notes.

Then Lev was saying, "I thought you'd like to know that Nasser's boy, General Murtagi, has announced that . . ."—he glanced at the lined yellow pad before him—" 'our forces are absolutely ready to carry the battle outside Egypt's frontier.' " Lev grinned and added, "The mosques have all been requested to preach a jihad and the head of the Coptic Church has joined in with his Moslem Brethren in declaring this a holy war."

The Chief of Staff was shaking his head. He did not have time for levity. Interrupting, he closed the meeting with the comment, "I'm available if you want to talk. I'll let you know if there is any change in the situation."

It was Moshe, who, as he came to his feet, asked, "Is the Cabinet going to sit this one out?"

The face of the Chief of Staff clouded over. "You will know what the government plans in enough time for you to act."

Zvi winked at Avram while Moshe nodded, and then the three walked out of the war room together.

As they made their way into the night, Avram asked Zvi, "Any problems?"

"Nothing beyond the waiting."

Pausing at Moshe's car, Avram waited to hear if there was anything the brigadier wanted. Moshe stared at Avram for a moment before he looked up at the sky. As much as he wanted to ask Avram if he knew anything about Hannah's whereabouts, he did not want to admit that he himself did not know. "I'll be in contact," he finally said, and then, turning to Zvi, he suggested, "We'd better talk in the morning."

Zvi agreed.

After Moshe drove away, the other two stood looking after him.

"She's driving him crazy, you know," Avram said quietly.

Shrugging, Zvi snorted, "I'm not going to worry about his marriage now."

He thought of the politicians and diplomats talking all over the world and he thought of his men keeping watch in the cold desert.

Then he said softly, "The Egyptians won't get us; the waiting will."

He slipped in beside his driver with the farewell comment, "If we don't move soon, we're going to bog down."

Stopping at the closest phone, Zvi called Dvora. She had already finished dinner. Would she drive out to the house with him while he picked up some things? Silence, and then she agreed. Twenty minutes later he picked her up and gave the driver the address of his house in Ramat Gan. As they drove northeast through Petach Tikva, Zvi half turned in his seat so that he could see Dvora, squeezed in beside his radio operator. The young girl had taken off the earphones and turned the set up so that the General could hear the broadcasts. None of them spoke as the jeep sped through the nearly deserted streets. Glancing about, Zvi saw the sandbags piled against buildings, the windows taped, the houses darkened. An old man standing on a street corner shouted, "Oop the Jews," and Zvi's face crinkled into a smile at the Irish war whoop.

The radio operator switched bands, picking up a Hebrew broadcast from Radio Cairo. It took Zvi a moment to realize what he was listening to.

Snorting, he gestured for the young girl to try another band.

Twisting the dial, she looked at her commander and asked simply, "Are we going to win, sir?"

Zvi looked at her in surprise and then realized that there was no reason why this child, who was probably in grammar school at the time of the 1956 war, should remember it. And he knew, too, that there was no reason why she should not be frightened. "We'll do it the Jewish way," he assured her.

"The Jewish way, sir?"

"A miracle."

The young girl laughed and Zvi could not recall her laughing before. She was small, her face thin, her tiny breasts barely pressing out the cotton uniform blouse. He noticed that Dvora was smiling patiently at the girl. He knew there was at least twenty years difference in their ages, and that Dvora had known worse than war. His eyes dropped to her hand clasping the back of the driver's seat. The tattoo was still readable on her wrist. Wearing a tan cotton tailored shirt and a cord skirt, Dvora looked cool even though the day had been hot. Her head, erect on her shoulders, gave her the dignity she had demanded for herself when they had first met so many years before.

Raising his hand, he pointed to his own street and a moment later the driver parked in the small alleyway. Stepping from the jeep, Zvi helped Dvora down. Before they turned to the house, Zvi ordered the radio operator, "Check with division and see if there is anything we should know, and if there is anything I can bring back." Then, smiling at the driver, he suggested, "There's a shop about two blocks down the street. You can pick up a cold drink there."

Taking Dvora's arm, he led the way across his small lawn. He opened the front door, stepped back and let her in before he turned on a lamp. They were standing in the middle of a living room, two modern sofas facing each other with a coffee table between. Three of the walls were lined with books and windows while a huge stone fireplace covered most of the fourth.

Pointing proudly to a cupboard near the fireplace, Zvi suggested, "Anything you want to drink, feel at home. I've got to get some shorts and socks and another shirt." And he left her standing in the center of the large room. Raising his voice so that she could hear him from the bedroom, he explained, "When they called me down to headquarters, I had just walked out of a classroom and was wearing a business suit. An hour later I was heading for the mobilization point and later I had to send a young officer to find me some clothes and a razor." When he walked back into the living room, he saw that she had not moved from where he had left her.

Tossing the clothes onto the coffee table, he said, "I've a bag some place," and went looking for it. Dvora was folding his undershorts, shorts and socks when he returned. Bending over the coffee table, Dvora's slim figure seemed as young as when he had first met her that day in the shabby apartment in the Old City. Now, nineteen years later, he did not believe he had ever thought of her as lovely then. Impressive, angry, strong. He remembered her that way, but lovely or beautiful, no. And now to his surprise, he thought she was both. And as he stood looking at her, he knew he had to get out of the house and southwest to his division. Wishing he had time to loiter, he set the small canvas bag on the table.

"That it?" she asked.

"I won't be dressing formally," he smiled.

Ignoring his comment, she zipped open the bag and packed it. Watching her, Zvi tried to recall if Zella had ever packed a bag for him, and then he shook his head in disbelief at his own wandering thoughts. This was Dvora, the girl with the thorn in her eyes and ready gun butt. She had shot him.

Crossing to the sideboard, he pulled out a carton of cigarettes, removed one pack and offered the rest to Dvora. She slipped them into the bag while she watched him slit his pack open with a pocketknife and dump the loose cigarettes into his shirt pocket, taking time to light one for her and one for himself.

She stood watching the smoke drift toward the ceiling for a time and he stood watching her. Without looking at him, she asked, "You retired to this house?"

Shaking his head until he became aware that she did not see him doing it, Zvi said, "Bought it a few years before that. I wanted a place for Aaron. The Ministry helped me with the loan."

Nodding to indicate she had heard, she said, "And since then you've been teaching and administering?"

Zvi understood that she was letting him know that she had followed his career. Neither of them moved to the door and Zvi let the bag rest on the table. Dragging deeply on his cigarette, he felt guilty at the time he was stealing. "That's right, I teach," he said.

"You like it?"

Hesitating because he did not know if he should compare it to his military career and because he had never thought about whether or not he liked what he had been doing the past two years, he said, "I imagine I like it."

Slowly she turned to face him. "But you like being a general better?"

"If I had to say something profound about the relationship of knowledge and power, I wouldn't know what it would be right now." He fell silent, watching her bring the cigarette to her lips and he wished it were longer, because as soon as she tamped it out, they would have to leave.

"It's been said," Zvi's voice was soft and almost distant, "that it is really the defenders who start a war because they have reached the point where they won't yield anything more than they have. Somehow I guess in the long run the defender has to evaluate the use of power." He snorted, "Right now I don't feel either profound or powerful."

Her eyes left his face and focused on the wall behind him. Turning to see what she was looking at, Zvi noticed the photograph which Aaron had sent him the day he had been commissioned.

"He's a good boy," Zvi said proudly. "A good pilot, too."

Dvora nodded. "Who was his mother?"

A wry smile twisted Zvi's face. "I don't know her name and I don't know the father's name. Sometime, if you're interested, I'll tell you how he came to me."

For the first time since he had met her, he thought she was smiling because something pleased her rather than because she wanted to taunt him. Bending over, she put her cigarette out and as she came upright, her eyes met his. "I'm not going to say I'm sorry about what happened that time when the city fell. But . . ."

She was bringing her hand up to brush a lock back, when Zvi caught her wrist and slowly turned it so that the tattoo lay between them. "I understand," he said. Then, taking her hand in his, he held it between them. "There was a time when I'm not so certain I did, and then there was the Eichmann trial, and I learned things I wished I had not been there to learn."

Very slowly, her head bobbed back and forth. "I remember during the trial there was an old Hungarian woman who sold newspapers on the corner near our apartment. A young soldier walked up to her and kissed her cheek and said, 'I'm sorry. I just didn't know what it was like.'" Dvora's voice trailed away as she thought of the old woman who had survived the holocaust.

Zvi understood what she was trying to tell him. As far as he was concerned, what had happened between them in the Old City was forgotten.

Zvi started to draw her to him, but she stood firm and shook her head. "I think it's time to go, General."

582

He did not think she was laughing at his rank now. Sweeping up the bag, he took her arm and they returned to the jeep. Zvi waved the driver to the back seat, helped Dvora into his own, and then, taking over the wheel, started back to his helicopter. Crossing Nahal Ayalon, he drove toward Park Leumi. Speaking quickly, he asked the young girl on the radio to contact the pilot and have him bring the helicopter to meet him.

The message sent, Zvi listened to the broadcasts on the military band. Nothing of importance. Then he remembered that he had asked Gabriel Natan if he needed or wanted anything and he checked with the young operator.

"All he said he wanted was about four pounds of gefilte fish."

And then they were at the park. Sitting back and waiting for the helicopter, Zvi turned so that he could see both of the soldiers. "Pick up four pounds of gefilte fish, get some ice for it, and start back to the division tonight." He thought about what he had said and asked, "You know where we've moved to?"

The driver said he did, and Zvi gave the girl several pound notes. "Get some good fish. Miss Kidron will help you shop. I'll see you in the morning." The helicopter was overhead and coming down now. Stepping out of the jeep, Zvi saw that Dvora was doing the same. They met behind the vehicle and stood watching the chopper whirl dust and flatten grass as it touched down a half-dozen meters away.

Drawing her about so that she faced him, Zvi smiled. "I don't know if I'll get back before it starts or not. If I do, can I call you?"

"You still owe me a dinner."

When he started to draw her to him, she shook her head and he let her hands drop. "I'll call," he promised and started running to the helicopter. Dvora remained where she was until the chopper was airborne and lost in the distance.

After he had left his two friends at Hakiryah, Moshe drove to his apartment only to find it empty, as he had the night before. Angry and uncertain what he should do, he closed the door behind him and walked to Ruth's. The streets were quiet. There was almost no moon. A little girl poked her head out of a window and watched him for a time and then she disappeared. Moshe paused to kick a pebble from his path and continued on.

Reaching Ruth's apartment, he stopped to consider what had brought him here. He could have called her about Hannah. There was little reason for him to have come. The night before he had almost kissed his mother-in-law; and though he had not done it, he believed she was aware of what he had been thinking. He had little enough in common with Ruth. Oh, they had fought beside each other nineteen years before, and he had married her daughter, but she would be the first to say that that had not brought them any closer. Sneering at the notion of himself and Ruth, he started to walk away, but almost against his own wishes, he turned back and climbed to the top floor. His reasons, he believed, had less to do with his mother-in-law than his wife, though in a way they had to do with his own image of himself. Much of the day when he had not been thinking of anything else, he had been annoyed at the prospect of Hannah looking for a job. The government would help him into a new career. It had helped others. As he weighed the humiliation thrust upon him by Ruth and her daughter, he banged the door with the side of his fist. He would have continued to bang on it, but Ruth opened it wide and stood looking at him, her hands on her hips and her head shaking its disapproval.

"She isn't here."

The flatness of the statement annoyed Moshe, and he pushed his way into the apartment. "Did you hear from her?"

Ruth shook her head as she closed the door. "If I hear anything, I'll get in touch with Avram and he'll let you know." Then she paused where she was, drew her housecoat tightly about her and cocked her head to one side. "Why didn't you ask him? I told you she went to Jerusalem with Malin."

Growing more frustrated and knowing that he could not explain his humiliation to Ruth, he shouted, "For God's sake, she's your daughter. Don't you care where she is?"

In a very soft voice which set his tone off by contrast, Ruth said, "I agree. I should have paid closer attention to her several years ago. I should have known before you told me that she was seeing you."

Raising one hand for an instant, Moshe let it slam into the open palm of the other. Then he looked at his two hands in front of him and started to chuckle, softly at first and then louder until his tense frame rocked. "I've got four brigades waiting for me in the south, and here I am arguing with you about Hannah." He stopped laughing as suddenly as he had begun. "I'm a fool."

Ruth smiled kindly. "I'm sure that somewhere in the books of wisdom there is advice that no one should argue with a fool."

Moshe read the clock across the room and then, walking to the phone, called headquarters. There were no messages for him. There was no fresh news. They would contact him at this number as he wished. They understood that when he left this number, they would be informed and they would have a 'copter waiting for him at the Arkia airport.

Setting the phone back on the cradle, Moshe saw that Ruth was curled up in a chair, watching him.

"I've got to be going," he said, as though both of them did not already know this.

"Is there going to be a war?" she asked.

"Zvi thinks we could blow it if we don't move soon."

"And you?"

"He's right. The waiting is hard on the men. It's hard on all of us. But I imagine the Foreign Ministry has to go through the motions." He was standing behind a sofa facing her, his fingers spread wide as he braced himself.

"There are only motions?"

Moshe shrugged. "If we move before the formalities of trying to make a peace, then we'll be blamed. If we wait too long, then we could get hit."

Ruth nodded. "Neither of us was here in forty-eight when Tel Aviv was bombed."

Moshe said, "I think I'd rather have taken my chances here."

Ruth agreed. "Somehow, though it was only an old rifle or a submachine gun, there was a kind of comfort in having it in your hand and knowing that you could use it."

"You sound like an old soldier." He stood for a time appraising her. Ruth was no older than he. Probably younger. Her face showed signs of age. There were some lines about her neck which he was certain had not been there in forty-eight. She was a large woman, though not fat. She had been a large girl. He wiped his hand nervously over his face before he asked, "Was it worth it?"

Her head came up sharply. "Was what worth it?"

"What you went through in the Old City?"

Stunned by what she thought was a stupid question, Ruth shook her head in disbelief. "Are you serious?"

Moshe nodded. "But you don't understand. I'm not asking about Israel and questioning the . . ." He tried to find the words and finally admitted, "I think Zvi once called it our own mad dream. I'm asking if you—a young girl who had a face without that white scar over your eye—should have been there when there were so many others who should have been and weren't."

"So many others?"

His hands spread open before him. "Those in the Diaspora, those who stood by and watched us fight."

Placing her hands on the arms of her chair, Ruth pushed herself to her feet. "We didn't do it for them. We did it for ourselves." Her hands still rested on the arms of the chair. "I'm certain it sounds silly, but we did it for Hannah and Aaron and Avram's children and Fishel's, if he had lived to have any, and that crazy girl who shot Zvi. For her children if she ever had any."

He nodded. "You're right. It sounds like something one of the *yeshivah bochurs* would say." He looked at his watch. "There's a dirty, crowded coffee shop at the airport. I'll buy you a cup of coffee."

Ruth considered the offer and smiled enigmatically. "I'll get dressed." She was walking out of the room when she turned back to face him. "You know we had an alternative to war once."

Puzzled, he waited for her to explain.

"Through history," she smiled, "women had two choices when there was a war. They could be noble, ever so noble and keep the British stiff-upper-lip, or they could weep and wail and condemn the fates."

Not knowing what she was trying to say, Moshe decided to wait.

"Israel let women become part of the war. I'm not so sure that was bad." Her voice softened when she added, "You asked if it was worth it. Having lost that option, I can tell you it was."

When Moshe was standing alone, he picked up a delicate porcelain ashtray. Then he laughed softly at himself. There was something incongruous about his standing in the middle of Ruth's living room with a delicate porcelain ashtray in his hand when . . . He looked at his watch, and walking back to the phone, called the communications center again. Nothing. He told them he would leave for the airport in five minutes. They could reach him there fifteen minutes later.

When Ruth joined him, he knew that she was as well-gowned as her apartment was furnished. The dress was sleeveless and slight and blue, and he wondered why she reminded him of his wife, and then he caught himself. "I only promised you a cup of coffee," he reminded her.

Nodding, she told him, "It isn't every day that I'm seen with my famous son-in-law, the General."

Moshe opened the door and stood waiting beside it. She stared at him as she reconsidered going with him. Before she made up her mind, Moshe said in a gentle voice, "You know, I once told Zvi that he and I had lousy luck with our women." And he put his hand out, took her arm and made up her mind for her.

Only when they were in the jeep, speeding north toward the airport, did Ruth wonder just what he had meant by his last comment. She had never been one of his women. And then she knew she should not press him for an explanation because he might have been thinking about Hannah.

Neither of them spoke as the jeep twisted wildly through the streets under Moshe's competent control. When they almost struck a car backing out of an alley, he said, "I could have made sergeant if I had become a driver."

Even though she knew the joke was not very funny, Ruth laughed because she wanted to.

Twenty minutes later, Moshe led Ruth into the large shed which served as an airport building. The bare walls and concrete floor gave the oversized room the look of a warehouse. There were only a few persons inside. The small coffee stand was open and as they went toward it, Moshe noticed Avram seated at a table with someone he did not recognize at first. After he and Ruth had taken their coffee, they joined Avram, who had waved to them. Ruth nodded a greeting to Kineret, who looked both tired and much older than Ruth remembered her. Plump and white-haired now, Kineret sat back and smiled at the two as they sat down.

"You know both of them, don't you?" Avram asked.

586

Kineret nodded. "Though I haven't seen either one in a long time."

Avram's hands closed about his coffee cup as he stared at Moshe. "Shouldn't you be getting south?"

The Brigadier tilted his head to one side. "Avi, are you pointing out my duties to me now?"

The others laughed, though Kineret doubted Avram had found the comment humorous.

Shifting the subject, Avram told Ruth and Moshe, "Kineret just came back from the States."

They waited to hear what had happened there.

With a slight gesture to deprecate what she knew, Kineret said, "I don't think either one of you is a security risk."

"I don't think so," Moshe agreed.

"The Russians are trying to do the same thing the United States is."

"And that?" Ruth asked.

"Get us to wait."

"We may have missed the boat already," Moshe growled.

Kineret smiled. "I always knew you could be counted on as a hawk."

"Have the Russians ever condemned El Fatah?" Ruth asked.

Kineret looked at Avram, who shook his head. "They are in bed with the Arabs and that is a hell of a place to sleep."

"Who kicks a bed partner?" Kineret smiled wryly.

Moshe shook his head in disgust. "You know an Arab who is dirty is colorful; a Jew who is dirty is a dirty Jew."

"You sound bitter," Kineret commented. "And you forget there's a kind of integrity about the Arabs. All of us tend to forget that."

"Integrity?" Avram challenged the comment.

The older woman nodded. "The Americans gave Hussein half a billion dollars, Nasser a billion, and they aren't bought."

Avram chuckled. "You mean they took the bribes and didn't live up to their end of the bargain."

Moshe asked impatiently, "What happened in America?"

Kineret paused to empty her cup, and while Avram, who had already heard her report, went to fetch her another, she explained, "Four days ago two of us were called in by the Assistant Secretary of State for New Eastern Affairs. He pointed out that the President had two choices, and I gather he did not like either of them. He could let us try to settle the problem or he could try himself. It all came down to the simple request that we give them time."

"Anything happen since then that matters?" Ruth asked, and Moshe turned in his seat so that he could see her better. Of the women he had known, Kineret Heschel was the only one who had ever been interested in political affairs. Then he smiled to himself, remembering that he had not picked his women because of their thinking.

"Yesterday we went to see Johnson."

"And?" Ruth was pressing.

Kineret shrugged. "We were about to walk into his office. They call it the Oval Room. If you want to be impressed, you are."

"And?" Ruth repeated.

"The Chairman of their Joint Chiefs of Staff told the Foreign Minister not to worry. United States Intelligence says we can lick the Arabs in four days."

Moshe was aware of the sneer mingled with pride in Kineret's voice. And he was about to say something when Ruth asked, "Did he tell you how we were to keep the Arabs from bombing Tel Aviv while we were licking them?"

Moshe had lost all interest in his coffee now as he stared at his mother-in-law.

Kineret shook her head. "That little detail didn't get answered."

Rejoining them, Avram said, "In short, the trip settled nothing."

Again, Kineret shook her head. "You are also getting impatient. We were asked to give the President more time."

"Crap and corruption," Moshe growled. "We can't stay mobilized and have all our factories closed. We haven't time."

Kineret looked at Avram, who nodded. "I wouldn't put it so colorfully, but let's face it, Moshe's right."

Shoving his chair back, Moshe rose, and standing over the table looking down at the others, he asked angrily, "And so we wait?"

They turned to Kineret who slowly nodded. "We can't afford to lose the only support we have."

Ignoring the fact that Moshe was preparing to leave, Ruth asked, "The only support? In fifty-six there was France."

Snorting, Kineret pointed out, "De Gaulle wasn't there in fifty-six."

"And today?" Ruth asked.

Kineret looked at her and smiled. "Today De Gaulle wants the Arabs to love him." She fell silent while she sipped her coffee.

Ruth shook her head. "And so we're left with the man from Texas."

Kineret smiled. "Don't underestimate." Looking up at Moshe, she said for his benefit, "I've seen a great many wild west movies, and the Texas hero always has integrity and strength when his back is up against the wall and the rodents are shooting."

Laughing, Avram said, "I think you mean *varmints*." Then he looked at Moshe. "Can I drive Ruth home for you?"

"If you will." Half bowing to Kineret, Moshe pleaded, "Get us an answer we can live with and soon." His hand came out and he helped Ruth to her feet, said goodbye to the others and walked outside with her into the night where his helicopter was waiting.

Neither of them spoke for a time, and then Moshe asked, "Do you think she can do anything?"

Ruth smiled gently. "She's trying."

"So's Nasser." Then, turning to her he said, "Will you tell my wife I may or may not get back, but that I hope to hear from her?"

Ruth put her hand on his sleeve and squeezed his arm, saying, "Don't worry about Hannah. She's a very bright girl."

"So's her mommy." Then he strode across the field to where the waiting copter's great blades slowly turned. He paused to wave back and disappeared into the night.

At their table where they were waiting for Ruth, Kineret was asking Avram, "Isn't that a strange couple?"

Grinning, Avram said, "There's a bad English joke Zvi's always telling about 'who was that lady I saw you with last night . . .' "

"I know it."

"Well," Avram said softly, "that was no lady, that was his mother-in-law."

He enjoyed the startled expression on Kineret's face.

IN THE NEGEV

Before dawn, Zvi rolled over inside his sleeping bag and lay listening to the transistor radio someone had turned on. After a short time he unzipped his sleeping bag and, crawling out, walked over to the canvas latrine and then to the command half-track where he shaved. When he was finally ready to face his day's work, he asked the girl if she knew where Gabe Natan was sleeping.

"He got up half an hour ago and went to look at some of the positions."

Zvi smiled, wondering if this was an implied criticism, and strode off to the helicopter.

Ten minutes later he and the Chief of Staff, Southern Command, were on their way to meet Moshe near the Gaza Strip where they surveyed his defense line.

The morning sun was barely climbing the sky now. The dry, loose sand rose in small clouds beside their jeep and settled over the gray cactus. Sitting in the front of the jeep, Moshe pointed out the enemy emplacements he had already located, as well as the possible places where other Egyptian units might be hidden. An hour later they were on their way back to Moshe's headquarters, an old trailer dug into the side of a dune.

Zvi sat back on the bench running the length of the trailer, slipped his hand inside his shirt and stared at the map on the wall opposite where someone had marked Nahal Oz with a large blue star. Pointing out the kibbutz, he asked, "How bad was it?"

Moshe shrugged. "They started shelling from Gaza yesterday, and they hit things. Only a few buildings damaged."

"I'm going to stay wide of you," Zvi told him. "There's no war yet and you've drawn fire in the north and the south."

The C/S Southern Command, a middle-aged colonel from 'En Gedi laughed. "Let's decide how wide you stay," and for the next two hours the three worked over the battle maps. When they were satisfied, Zvi shoved the maps he had brought with him into a web case and smiled. "Now that we've figured out where we're going, when do we start?"

No one laughed, and Moshe told them about his conversation with Kineret the evening before.

The colonel from Southern Command contributed a piece of information. "Johnson is supposed to have told Abba Eban that as president he has his problems with Congress and the Constitution."

Dubious, Zvi shook his head. "All I know is that we can't wait too much longer even to make the Americans happy. Factories are closed, money is pouring out, supplies aren't coming in, and crops aren't being harvested."

The Colonel brushed his small mustache. "Time favors the Arabs. They know it, and so do the Russians."

Zvi was about to rise when they all heard an explosion. They remained where they were while they waited to hear if there were going to be others.

"A mine," Zvi finally said.

Moshe trotted out of the trailer. The other two followed. A quarter of a mile away they could see smoke over a jeep.

Shouting for a helicopter, Moshe started running. When he got to the jeep, two men were already trying to put out the burning fuel. The occupants of the vehicle were lying a few paces away. Spinning on his heel, Moshe gestured for the 'copter to remain where it was. The men were not going to a hospital.

Wiping the dust and sweat from his face, Zvi stared at the three corpses. "The Gyppies got in pretty close to lay that," he said to no one in particular.

Kneeling beside the bodies, Moshe nodded without looking up. "And Avram's preaching patience."

"I'll report this when I get in," the colonel offered, and Moshe jerked his head about to stare angrily at the man—angry at the impotence of the offer. "You do that, and tell headquarters I'm ready to retaliate."

Zvi watched the anger grow on his friend's face and knew that he, too, was just as angry. This was not war. It was murder. Given guns and an enemy, his troops could hold their own. But they were being held back and he did not like it. Without a word, he strode back to the helicopter and pulled himself inside. The Colonel joined him and they returned to Zvi's camp. As Zvi dropped out of the open door to the ground, the staff officer cautioned, "Easy."

Ignoring the man, Zvi walked over to his command post.

The next day—28 May—Avram came south from headquarters. He inspected Zvi's front and then joined his friend at the divisional headquarters.

Knowing that Avram was due, Zvi had contacted Moshe, who coptered south.

The three sat alone in the command half-track. Zvi's boots were up on his table, while Avram, looking comfortable and neat, sat on the vehicle floor with his back against a jerry can. Moshe, who stood looking down at his friends, came directly to the point which had brought him south.

"How much longer? How much more talk? No one can tell me the Gyppies aren't digging their heels in to jump."

With a tolerant smile, Avram looked to Zvi for his complaints. "For a man who isn't supposed to have a reputation for talking, Moshe's expressed it well enough. We can't wait much longer."

Wrapping his long arms about his knees, Avram asked, "Are we just the three of us?"

Glancing about, Zvi nodded.

With a dubious smile, Avram informed them, "The Sudanese mobilized yesterday."

Neither of the brigadiers commented while they considered what this could mean to them.

"And?" Zvi finally asked.

"Yesterday the Soviet ambassador met with Nasser."

"And?" Moshe did not like playing games.

"From what Lev can gather, he told, ordered, directed, warned—or what-have-you—that the Egyptians must not shoot first."

Moshe burst out laughing. "We've told them for years that the closing of the Strait would be an act of war, and from what I heard on the radio that bald-headed ass who represents Egypt at the United Nations has been telling people that 'a state of overt war has been existing.' "

Shaking his head slowly, Zvi disagreed. "That may be fine logically. The Egyptians have a war when they want it because it always exists, but it is one-sided because it does not exist for us. Logically, I agree that is laughable, but who the hell ever said the Egyptians were logical? And more important," his hand came back to rub his neck, "much more important, no one considers it a war unless the shooting starts, and they hope we'll start the shooting so that the Americans will feel the same way they did in fifty-six. The Arabs can hope."

Avram's eyes narrowed as he stared at his friend. "And so can we. There's the line Kineret uses: 'Don't underestimate.' "

Moshe snorted. "I think more battles have been lost because people have overestimated their enemies."

Avram nodded. "We could be expecting too much of the Americans, but they aren't the enemy."

Settling down on the bench, Moshe spat over the side of the half-track. "You think the Arabs are trying to get us to strike first, trying to force us to."

Avram's large head bobbed. "So long as they don't think we're at war with them, and they are at war with us, they want us to go to war."

Moshe turned to Zvi for an explanation.

"Don't look for logic, but that's it."

Then Moshe beamed. "Then, let us cooperate with them all the way."

Shaking his head, Zvi asked Avram, "Nasser was the only one the Russians saw?"

Pleased that his friend understood, Avram smiled. "They called our PM yesterday." He glanced at his watch. "Actually after two this morning."

Moshe and Zvi leaned forward.

"And they asked him if he was going to fire the first shot."

"And?" Moshe remained impatient.

"The P M told him what we all know: 'The Egyptians have already said there was war and they started it at the Strait.' "

Tamping out his cigarette, Zvi folded his hands behind his head and considered the possible reactions. "And our Cabinet met?"

"And talked until five this morning."

Moshe held his temper while he waited for more information.

Glancing at him, Avram shrugged. "Nothing. We pressed. We asked for the go-ahead because of everything all of us know, but . . . . nothing. The Cabinet voted nine to nine to keep the peace for a time."

Moshe slammed one fist into a palm. "What we need is a new PM."

"No!" And Avram half rose from his seat. "He will go if the Cabinet will, but he can't make the decision without support. No man could."

Zvi looked at him wryly as he pointed out, "Ben Gurion would have."

Avram shook his head. "This isn't BG's government."

Staring in silence at his old friend, Zvi wondered if he had shown disloyalty. Then, with a wave of his hand before his face, he shifted the discussion. "Colonel Avram Ben Ezra did not come down here to see my defense line. He did not come down here to tell us that he sat in on a Cabinet meeting with the Chief of Staff last night." Then he smiled, "As much as I love your company, Avi, what brought you here?"

Puzzled, Moshe looked from one to the other. Zvi's generally even temper with his peers was out of balance now, and he was not hiding the fact.

Avram nodded. "I did come for the inspection and your pleasant company. And there was something else. Lev wanted your reaction to the news that Nasser's pulling his troops out of Yemen and throwing them into Sinai. He thought you'd tell me more easily."

"Are the Egyptian troops from Yemen that important?" Moshe was not certain what this meant beyond a larger Egyptian force.

Very slowly, Zvi's graying head began to nod. "They are. Believe me, they are. Maybe as many as seventy-five thousand."

Moshe shook his head. "Right now we need more Egyptians in Sinai the way we need sand in a transmission."

Ignoring the comment, Avram asked, "Then you think Nasser has no place to go except war?"

Zvi's tongue went into his cheek as he thought about this. Finally he nodded. "He's paying too high a price just to keep us off balance. And much too high a price to keep his prestige when he could jerk it all the way up in a year by taking Aden and the oil fields east of it."

Satisfied that he had what he had come for, Avram flew back to Tel Aviv.

As Zvi walked Moshe to his helicopter, he admitted that he was no intelligence specialist: "But I have been teaching the history of the area for the past few years," and as he spoke, he wondered why he was apologizing for his opinion. Looking down at Zvi from inside the copter, Moshe asked, "Did he say anything about Hannah before I got here?"

Zvi shook his head. The drooping blades of the fat bird began to speed up their pace and Moshe was airborne.

Zvi stood for a few minutes in the bright sun of the early afternoon, his hands on his hips, his eyes on the disappearing copter and his thoughts on the letter he had received from Aaron the night before. Shoving his dark glasses closer to his eyes, he felt the sharp glare of the sun off the dunes. Kicking his toe into the loose ground before him, he watched the dust cloud settle. Very slowly, he turned to look at his command post. Moshe had not been good at hiding his impatience. Zvi hoped he would be better at hiding from his men the feeling of despair that was crawling over him.

The next day was little different. With the approval of headquarters, Zvi furloughed ten per cent of his men while fifty per cent were kept on alert. The sun was hot. The slow shift of sand in the late afternoon made very little difference, though those not used to the desert spoke of sandstorms.

JERUSALEM

It was shortly after nine in the morning when Aaron left his room at the King's Hotel and walked over to the Ben Ezra apartment. There were very few people on the street now. He considered stopping some place for breakfast, changed his mind and went on to see Hannah. She met him at the door with the news that Malin had already left for court.

Smiling at the way Hannah always had life arranged to suit her own needs, he suggested they go out for breakfast because even though she might have already eaten, he had not. Her answer was to put her arms about his neck and kiss him fiercely. He was still smiling when she stepped back. In his own mind there had never been any alternative to Hannah. As far back as he could search, he could recall her beside him, and as they matched steps down the stairs and out into the morning light, he took her hand. Even when they had been in school, his friends had laughed to see them together. In America most of the persons they had met took for granted that Hannah was his sister. As they paused at the curb before crossing the street, they looked at each other and smiled. He had never thought of her as his sister. The years that he had been at school near Natanya or in Jerusalem or Beersheba, his father and Ruth had been able to arrange for Hannah and Aaron to be together frequently. Now, as they walked through the bright morning unaware of the slight traffic about them, the absence of men, the few children filling sandbags near an old building, Aaron thought back on those years. He knew neither Ruth nor his father had thought of those arrangements as other than conveniences. Sometimes for his father's affairs—military and sexual—sometimes for Ruth's. And as he reached the age when he knew he was going into the air force, Aaron had taken it for granted that his future would be his career as a pilot and Hannah.

Squeezing her hand, he tried not to remember when he first heard the strange tale over the radio that Hannah had married his father's friend, Moshe Gilead. Moshe Gilead—the lean and angry man who used to visit the apartment in Tel Aviv or Beersheba or Jerusalem. General Moshe Gilead of Sharm el Sheikh fame, of the retaliation raids, and Hannah. Turning as they came to a street corner, so that he could see the gentle lines of Hannah's face against the morning light, Aaron thought about Moshe Gilead and other old heroes like his father. He wondered if his father had ever taken someone else's woman as if by right of conquest as Moshe Gilead had taken Hannah. Then Aaron recalled the woman who used to be about the Jerusalem apartment during the Eichmann trial. Somewhere he had heard that she had gone back to her husband. And as he remembered Libby, Aaron tried to think of other women his father had known. The names were vague now, but the notion that his father was a lonely man came through to him. With Hannah at his side, Aaron did not feel lonely for the first time since she had gone abroad with Moshe. Aaron tried not to think of his father's friend as Hannah's husband, because then all of it made even less sense.

Aaron was glad now that he had written his father a few days before to tell him that he had found Hannah again, and that he did not plan to give her back to Moshe. Now, as they walked silently, hands clasped, they had no need to talk to each other. Aaron wondered how wise he had been to write his father. Even though he remained pleased with the knowledge that his father would read the letter and understand, he felt guilt for the burden he had obviously shared along with his happiness.

Aaron lit a cigarette and dragged deeply on it as he thought about the soldier-turned-professor now somewhere in Sinai. His father was growing old. He was probably forty-five already. Aaron wondered where he would be at forty-five. He reached out to touch Hannah's blonde hair. She would be walking beside him when he was forty-five as she was now. He glanced at his watch. He had four hours left. He had already made two overflights of Egypt. And so long as others were getting short leaves, there was no reason why he should not. His dark face set, his chin lines grew hard, his black eyes narrowed as he thought of the number of times he had taken less than his due to avoid the accusation of *protectzia* because his father was Zvi Mazon. Then he relaxed, knowing that he would have taken this leave if he had had to use *protectzia* to get it.

He felt Hannah watching him and he let his head fall to one side as he pointed to an outdoor café. She smiled, and he felt warm. She was beautiful. The fine lines of her face were classic. The straight nose, the blonde hair, the delicate but full lips. Seeing the question in her eyes, he asked, "Did your grandmother sleep with a Greek or a Swede?" He saw the puzzled expression come into her eyes, and reaching out, he wrapped a strand of hair between his fingers. With his other hand, he offered to share his cigarette with her, and she accepted, blowing the smoke into his face when she exhaled.

Turning away, Aaron flicked the cigarette into the street and then led Hannah to the café where he pulled two chairs together so that the morning sun reached them.

She buried her head in his shoulder; her eyes were closed.

Aaron whispered into her ear, "I don't think I'd have ever called you."

Drawing back so that she could see his face, Hannah smiled. "But you aren't unhappy that I called?"

Then he kissed her, shaking both their heads as he denied unhappiness.

"I love you," he said.

Hannah's voice, always deeper than he remembered it, came through the vague fog of his pleasure. "But you had other girls while I was gone."

Not knowing if this was an accusation, Aaron finally nodded. "There was one from Safed. Redhead. There was another from Lachish. Brunette. Pink nipples that became hard at a touch. There were two sisters in Tel Aviv. One was big and the other was small, but there's a time and place for everything, and they each had their place."

"In bed?" the deep voice was trying not to break into laughter.

"Of course."

Her hands flat on his chest, she pushed herself away and she glared playfully into his eyes. "Were you friends with any of them?"

Trying not to answer too quickly, Aaron played at considering the question. "Friends? With a woman? A most unnatural relationship." His hand rose behind her, drawing her toward him. "Most unnatural."

"And that's all?" she asked as she nestled once more against his shoulder.

"There were in all twenty or thirty, but who keeps count?"

And when she started to bite his ear, he closed her mouth with a kiss.

It was almost eleven when they finished breakfast and cigarettes. Aaron was due back at the field in two hours, and both of them knew there were things they had to talk about. Paying his bill, Aaron took Hannah's hand and they walked back into the street. Now there was a bustle about Jerusalem. Anyone aware would have noticed there were no young men about and few middle-aged ones. Some women stood in front of a market. A small boy ran past Aaron, whirled back at the sight of the uniform and asked what kind of a plane Aaron flew.

"One with wings," Aaron explained while Hannah stifled a laugh. Satisfied, the little boy looked awed and then he ran on.

Hannah and Aaron walked down Balfour Street to Jabotinsky, where they stopped and looked at the street sign on an old building, and both of them laughed, remembering when they had lived in an apartment on Jabotinsky Street. It made no difference if the city had not been the same or the street a different Jabotinsky Street; they had shared the one they knew. Walking back to the rise where Agron slopes down to the east, they stood looking at the Old City.

Hannah pressed close, and slipping his arm about her waist, Aaron drew her still closer. Neither of them said anything for a time as they stared down at the Old City. From the corner of Mamilla, they could see David's Tower.

"I've often tried to close my eyes and wonder what it was like back then," Hannah said softly.

"Then?" But he thought he knew when she meant.

"In 1948—the Old City."

Aaron nodded. He had guessed right. "They lost it. And as my father would say, 'It never pays to lose a battle.' "

They laughed.

"He almost lost another one," she said.

Turning quickly, Aaron shook his head. "No! He won at Mitla. It cost, but he won, and if he had not paid the cost . . . ." His hand came away from her waist and he stood shaking his head. "Where did you get the notion he lost?"

Hannah regretted having upset him at this moment when she knew he would have to leave her. "It's only that Moshe says he didn't really win."

For a long time Aaron's face remained dark at the insinuation that his father had erred. Then he relaxed and, taking her hands between his, asked, "Which one of us is going to tell him?"

Both of them knew he was talking about Moshe.

After a time, Hannah said, "I should."

Pleased that she had the courage, Aaron said, "We'll wait until this is over and we'll both face him." Not having told Hannah that Zvi already knew, he thought he would save this consolation in the event she needed shoring up. Drawing her to him, he kissed her cheek and then her lips. An old woman standing on the balcony of an apartment snickered disapproval.

"You stay on at Judge Ben Ezra's and I'll call you there as soon as I can," Aaron promised.

Hannah started to say something, but he kissed her again and then ran toward Tsorfat Square, where he knew he would find a jeep bound for the airfield.

All the while he sat perched on the back of the jeep, Aaron thought of Hannah. The jeep slammed off the side of the road to let an army truck pass, and Aaron thought of his father and he wondered if his father had ever been in love the way he was in love, and he tried to recall the name of a woman his father had mentioned once long ago: was it Hayah or Chavah? His father had spoken so softly he had not caught the name. Sometime he would ask him, and then Aaron's thoughts returned to Hannah and how she had reacted to the lovely lies he told her about other girls, and the sergeant at his side wondered why the lieutenant was laughing.

TEL AVIV

Sunday 28 May was one of the happiest days for Aaron Mazon, but not for his father or Moshe Gilead, or for the almost three hundred thousand Israelis under arms—for them it was one more day of waiting. And then in the late afternoon, Mitra Glasner ran across the short distance between her communications vehicle and Zvi's half-track.

Zvi, his shirt and shoes off, lying in the heat of the sunbeaten tarp, saw the excitement on her face. Dragging himself to his feet, he waited for her report.

"Hakiryah as quickly as you can."

"That's all?"

"That's all of it."

He started to reach for a cigarette in his pocket before he recalled he was not wearing a shirt. "Find Gabe." Without looking around, he shouted for his clerk. The girl appeared in the driver's seat of the half-track. "Get the helicopter pilot out there to warm that thing up." When she hesitated, he shouted, "Move!"

Two minutes later, Zvi was racing, fully dressed, to the copter. Running at his side, Gabe asked, "Think this is it?"

"I hope so," Zvi said, almost happily. "I hope so. I'll be back as soon as possible. Reach me at Hakiryah." He slapped the tall kibbutznik on the back and, pulling himself inside the copter, shouted, "Don't start anything until I return."

From where he stood in the desert sand, Gabe shouted, "I'll wait for you."

An hour and a half later Zvi reported to the gate at headquarters where the sentry on duty told him, "The others are waiting for you in the War Room, sir."

Zvi made his way to the large bare room where he had spent so much time in recent weeks. Avram and most of the General Staff were already there. None of them was talking, and with a nod in deference, he took a seat behind Avram. The area and divisional commanders were all present but two, and then Moshe arrived, with the Operations Chief Northern Command, following him a few minutes later. No one was saying anything yet. Even though it was already late in the afternoon, the room was hot. The few maps on the wall were easily read from where he sat. There was only one surprise on them. He stared at that newly added China-red marking and tried to relate it to the moves he had planned. Another Egyptian division would complicate matters.

Then the Chief of Staff walked out of the room and the others sat expectantly waiting. A moment later, the Chief of Staff returned with Prime Minister Eshkol. The soldiers rose. The elderly head of government was slightly stooped as he made his way to the large table in the center of the room. Though Zvi had met the man several times in the past, he would not have claimed to know him. The old man's face was lined, and fatigue was in his eyes. Zvi knew the Cabinet had been meeting in around-the-clock sessions for days. At first it appeared the old man was going to say something, and then, as though he changed his mind, he walked around the room to shake hands with each of his commanders. He hoped Judge Ben Ezra was well. And Moshe's charming wife. And another's son, who was racing home from school abroad. He clasped Zvi's hand and smiled. "Your son's flying, I'm told." Zvi nodded, wondering who had briefed the old man so well. And then the prime minister was sitting down behind the large table and waving for the others to sit.

He began to speak very slowly. His voice was tired, his manner weary. He had news he knew they would not like. An honest and simple man, he came directly to the point: the Cabinet had decided to wait. A slight noise behind him and Zvi saw two Cabinet members taking their seats. Both were former generals. Both wore dour expressions.

And the old man talked on in his dull voice, explaining the news Zvi already had heard from Avram. The United States wanted Israel to wait. The Russians. . . . There was no clear-cut certainty that Nasser intended to attack. The Egyptians had been in Sinai before and had not attacked. The Syrians were, indeed, shelling in the north, but after nineteen years of the Syrians as neighbors, what difference did another week or two weeks make? He spoke slowly, he tried to be forceful; he failed to persuade.

And when he was done, he looked at the Chief of Staff, who had been ill the past several days, and said, "I want to hear what the army has to say, and I would like to hear from the commanders." A twisted smile came over the leathered face and Zvi knew he was looking at the last of a breed, a survivor of the Second Aliyah—those men who had arrived in Israel before the First World War, and had lived in the early kibbutzim, had been darkened by the sun and bled by the Arabs while they built a country. The Operations Chief, Southern Command, was talking now, and Zvi listening, had difficulty feeling any empathy with the PM, whereas the OC was saying what he himself would say: the Army was not as eager as it had been days before. A kind of rot set in with waiting.

Then the OC Central Command complained that the army's hands were too tied by the government.

And the OC Northern Command complained that the kibbutzim were being shelled and he did not know how much longer he had the right to ask them to sit still. Their children were sleeping in shelters, their fields were burning, while he and his men merely sat.

And then Moshe in nervous, explosive expletives reported that he had been receiving conflicting orders. He had been moved to the alert for an offensive and then it was called off. His men were being dipped in cold water and hot. He could not promise their performance would be high if this continued.

The prime minister's wrinkled face nodded. His tired eyes settled on Zvi.

Taking his time to decide what really concerned him, Zvi explained respectfully,"I've had a few desertions. Not many. But then, one is too many. The delay is costing us not only in morale, but something more important, offensive strength. The Egyptians are getting stronger, they are preparing to attack, and every hour they have to prepare is going to cost us more men before we are done." He thought for a moment. "I think a case could be made that every day takes an edge off our projections and that edge can be counted in dead." He was silent again and shaking his head. "I don't know where others would place that figure, but I would estimate that we are losing two hundred more than we projected every day we delay." Zvi heard some men suck in their breath at his figure, but he talked on. "We're not going to be able to live with a situation, sir, where our every ship has to be escorted through the Strait by a foreign power. And," he smiled, "in any case the United States *regatta* has not come into being." He had hit the word "regatta" hard, because it reminded him of a boat race.

The old man was not happy with what he had been hearing. He took a moment before he turned to the next officer. But before that man could speak, Zvi said sharply, "It's not Tiran any longer, Mister Prime Minister. It is Israel. Nasser has thrown down the gauntlet, and we either pick it up or we wait until he demands something else."

Everyone was looking at him. All of them knew Zvi and all of them knew that he was not given to talking at staff sessions. This made his words more impressive to his fellow officers, and when he felt the hand of one of the Cabinet officers on his shoulder, he wondered if he had said too much.

The old politician smiled sadly at Zvi. "You sound almost as though you had listened to half my Cabinet. I wish, however, you had heard the other half."

He turned to Colonel Avram Ben Ezra, and there was a note of warm affection in his voice as he asked, "Avi, what do you think?"

Rolling his large shoulders, the staff officer came to his feet, his hands clasping the straight-backed chair before him. His voice was low and the others strained to hear. "We fought in fifty-six. We lost men. We won a war, though some call it a battle. We won, but we did not try for enough. We did not destroy the enemy's army. I believe we should destroy that army now. And by now, Mister Prime Minister, I mean now. I don't want to think we're losing that two hundred extra a day Zvi has mentioned—and I think that estimate is low—I don't want to think we're going to lose because we did not try to win."

The old man seemed small behind the long table as he scanned the faces of his generals. "I am sorry I must ask restraint, but believe me, I shall keep your comments in the foreground of my thoughts. I will take into account your feelings and your advice." He came to his feet with difficulty and stood looking at his generals. Then, like a proud parent, he smiled. Very slowly he started out of the room.

"Restraint!" And everyone turned to look at Moshe, who was not on his feet. "I'll be damned. I've men to consider. We're pushed against the wall, and you're preaching restraint."

The old man nodded tolerantly. "Please be patient, Moshe. Please."

But the lean brigadier was shaking his head. "No." And then to the astonishment of those present, he reached up, ripped off his shoulder insignias, threw them at the old man's feet and stormed out of the room, ignoring the Chief of Staff's "General Gilead!"

For a moment there was a hushed silence, and then the Prime Minister bent down, picked up the insignias and handed them to Avram. "Tell him I understand." Standing before Zvi and Avi, he said, "I think the Americans would call the three of you hawks." His hand went up to silence any protest. "Before this is done, we will need hawks."

And he was gone.

Zvi and Avram waited to learn if there was anything the Chief of Staff wanted to tell them. When he shook his head, they walked out together. It was early evening. The lights of the city hung in the background. Though the sun had set, the air was no cooler than it had been during the day. Zvi stood for a moment in front of the old house and wondered what he was going to do. From what he had just learned, he did not believe he had to rush back to his command post. And if the only thing he had to do there was wait, Gabe Natan did not need his help.

They saw Moshe standing beside his jeep. Approaching his old friend, Avram held out the insignias.

Moshe stared at them.

"Don't misunderstand the old man," Avram warned, putting the insignias into Moshe's hand.

The others waited for his explanation.

"He's not a dove. If he thought the Cabinet would back him, he would give us the orders to move."

Moshe snorted. "If he pushed them . . ."

"The whole coalition government might break up," Avram concluded.

Both waited for Zvi's reaction, but all he would say was, "I don't like being patted on the head."

Moshe almost smiled, and then for the first time he approached the subject he had been thinking about for days. "Avi, is Malin home now?"

The other two relaxed. It was over.

Avram shook his head. "She said she'd be in Jerusalem until the trial she's sitting on is over."

Moshe digested this and understood that Avram had not told him what he had been fishing for. "And Hannah's still with her?"

They were walking toward the staff car which had picked Zvi up at the Arkia airport. "I talked to Malin a few hours ago." The words came slowly and with compassion. "Hannah had gone out."

"Then maybe she's on her way back?"

"Maybe," Avram said, while Zvi avoided Moshe's glance. "There was a message left for you," Avram told Zvi. "Aaron. He just wanted you to know he's back at his base."

Zvi thanked him and, slipping into his jeep, told his driver, "Let's get to my house." Then as they sped out of the area, he asked the radio operator, "Any communications?"

The girl shook her head.

Zvi sat back in the jeep and he found himself thinking of the empty house and of the women he had known since he and Zella had come apart. He tried to recall just how he and the only woman he had ever married had fallen out of love. All he could remember were the small details—a quarrel over his work, her attention to her studies, his own restlessness in those days—the small details which had grown to infidelity. He did not even now know whose came first: his own with Havah or hers with . . .

The sound of his driver honking a car out of the way burst through Zvi's thoughts and he wanted to scream. A moment later, he was thinking of Havah and himself. She was the least pretentious person he had ever known.

And as he rubbed one hand on his shoulder, aware of the insignia there, he hoped he had lost some of his own pretensions.

The vehicle jolted over a break in the pavement, and Zvi listened for a time to the crackle of the radio behind him, and then he thrust the intrusion aside and opened his eyes. There were cars with headlamps coming toward him now and he closed his eyes against the glare.

The driver was hitting the damned horn again, and Zvi's thoughts drifted to Isaac, the silversmith-turned-driver who had also been part of that journey through Yemen and beyond. Isaac had followed him and Isaac had died at Mitla. He could not recall ever having promised the old mori's son anything more than the Holy Land. Of all his guilts, Zvi felt Isaac's death the least among them. And as the noise and confusion of Mitla smashed against the dark side of his lids, he saw Fishel's face in that brief instant when the recce commander had rolled his unit into the Pass.

The radio behind him crackling again, and Zvi's head rolled from side to side as he shook off the intrusion. So many people and so many dead or hurt because they had crossed his path. A bitter smile came to his face, and the young girl sitting in the back of the jeep wondered why the General was smiling. One person in all of those he had known had taken him at face value and played him for a cheap coin, and that had been Libby. Maybe hers was the only honest evaluation of what he was. Maybe, just maybe, Libby, who was little more than a whore, had seen Zvi Mazon for what he was—an ordinary man who could do one job well and that was fight a battle. He was still smiling as he thought of Libby, because somehow she reminded him of Moshe. There was a basic honesty about the pair. Honest, at least with themselves. He opened his eyes and stared at the butt in his hand. Honesty. Maybe that was the quality he had confused with pretension. Zvi let his thoughts drift back to Shoshanna, Zella and Havah. Maybe they had each been hurt in some way because he was not stronger, because he had become involved when he did not have the right. And now he was thinking of Dvora. But there were two Dvoras, the sullen girl on the rooftop and the woman who taught nursery school. The former field whore and the girl whom Fishel must have loved.

Zvi's eyes remained on the road as he started to nod, because for the first time he understood that there was only one Dvora, as there was only one Shoshanna or Moshe or Avram. They had lived to change as he had lived to change. Only the dead had become frozen in time and created a single image. And now he could not compare those who died young with those who had lived to shift and fill and alter, to compromise and learn, to make mistakes and try to do better and sometimes fail and sometimes succeed. Havah and Zella would always be young while he and Ruth and Dvora had to keep on trying, all the while making mistakes and cutting down their options for success. And the words which had come to mind while he thought of Havah came back again without pretension. Without pretensions. To survive in no retreat and keep on trying. His eyes were open now. The girl behind him had picked up some music on her radio, and even though he knew she should be listening for something else, he decided to be patient.

He smiled: to survive in no retreat and keep on trying. Of all the women he had ever known, Dvora and Havah would understand best what he had in mind.

To survive in no retreat and keep on trying.

As he had several times in recent days, Moshe Gilead spent the evening with his mother-in-law. By now both of them had become concerned about Hannah, and Moshe called Malin shortly after dinner to learn if she knew anything which might lead them to her.

The judge, in her apartment in Jerusalem, believed she knew what had happened to Hannah, but she did not think she should even mention the possibilities. While agreeing that she would contact Ruth as soon as she learned anything definite, she realized she was enjoying Moshe's worry and discomfort because she could not forget Zipporah. After she hung up the phone, she called Avram and talked to him about Moshe and her own notion of where Hannah was.

His feet on the chair opposite, Avram sat on the cot which had been brought into his office and listened to Malin's angry attack on Moshe.

"But," he reminded her, "I don't want him upset now." He smiled as he thought how strange the situation had become. "We need him. You may not like Moshe, but right now, we need him."

His wife started to protest, and Avram became firm. "If you hear anything from Hannah, let me know and I'll call Ruth. But don't keep secrets from me now."

They both agreed the situation was ridiculous in view of the important matters at hand.

"Maybe," Malin pointed out, "that's been his problem all along. He's never known what was important."

Not wanting to argue with her, Avram told her that the maid had called to say the children were fine and expecting her home the following Sabbath.

Knowing she was being put off her target, Malin laughed. "You may not be very subtle, but you are nice."

Later, as he thought about their conversation, Avram wondered if he ever got away with anything that Malin might not be aware of, and then he sat back and laughed because he could not recall anything in the years that they had been married that he did not want her to know about himself. A warm feeling came to him as he returned to his desk, covered with work which had to be taken care of before he met with Kineret.

After he had talked to Malin, Moshe returned to the dinner table where Ruth was serving coffee. "She'll let us know," he told her. Then, settling into a chair, he shook his head. "I would hate to come to trial in her court."

For a few minutes they listened in silence to the news over KOL Israel. The Russians were blocking any serious discussion at the United Nations. The Russians were even accusing Israel of Hitlerian tactics. Snapping off the radio in anger, Ruth held her cup so firmly in her hand that Moshe thought she would break it.

"Why?" he asked. "I can remember when they voted to establish Israel in forty-seven and recognized us in forty-eight."

The dining room table lay between them. Ruth's best silver and dishes sparkled under the crystal chandelier she had brought home from her most recent trip to Paris. And sitting opposite Moshe, she watched him slowly turn the small coffee cup.

"Maybe," she said, "this is part of the last mad moments when Stalin thought his Jewish doctors were going to kill him and started the anti-Jewish purge trials."

Moshe shook his head. "I don't think long-term policy comes from anything like that."

Ruth laughed softly. "If I remember rightly, a bomb went off in the garden of their legation here. That gave them the excuse to break relations. But I don't think it was that either." She fell silent as she saw that his white hair caught the light of the chandelier. "I think they used us cruelly. The Arabs have gone socialist for whatever that word means to them, though we are the only country in the Middle East with a legal Communist Party, and yet the Russians arm the Arabs." She watched him sip his coffee while he considered what she had said. None of it was new and none of it was particularly enlightening, but Moshe could not recall if he had ever sat at a table discussing politics with a woman before, and his thoughts wandered back to their last meeting and Ruth prying answers from Kineret.

"What they have done this past few weeks is clever," she pointed out. "They have been accusing us and even the United States of making too much out of what has been taking place." She poured herself another cup of coffee while she talked. "In New York their ambassador said we are dramatizing the situation."

Moshe nodded, waiting to see what she was getting at.

"And at the same time, he claims that we have created a dangerous situation. Just how we can not dramatize a dangerous situation, even though we aren't the ones who created it, I don't know."

Noticing the way Moshe was looking at her, Ruth wondered if she should play the part he expected from women, fawning and innocent; and then she knew she couldn't. "Then the Russian ambassador changed the subject at the United Nations and started comparing the situation with Cuba and Vietnam, and all the time blocking anyone else from doing anything that matters."

Moshe scratched his head for a moment. He was enjoying himself, even though he knew that he should be on his way south. Shoving his chair back, he finished his coffee and shook his head when Ruth started to offer him another cup.

"It would be funny," Ruth said, "if it weren't so tragic. The Russians love modernization and industrial states, and we are the only one here and they make us their enemy."

She was on her feet now, and when he started to rise, she gestured for him to remain where he was.

"I'd like to think it was because we are such good friends with the United States," Moshe said wryly.

Ruth brought out a box of cigars and offered him one. Moshe stared at them and then at her.

"I have to entertain foreign customers," she said, explaining the presence of the box. "I always bring some back from Europe."

Taking one, Moshe held it in his hand for several minutes before he could bring himself to light such a luxury.

Returning to his comment, Ruth asked, "And you don't think we're such good friends of the United States?"

He bit off the tip of the cigar and shook his head. "We're their friend, but I'm not so certain they're ours." He lighted the cigar. "I have visions of little Americans in honeycombs of offices all over Washington who spend their time trying to see that nothing gets done for Israel and living all the time in a state of panic that elected officials are going to make them do something for Israel because of the illusion of a Jewish vote and a Jewish lobby."

"Something?"

Nodding seriously, Moshe said, "Something. Like selling us what they give other countries—guns and wheat and airplanes. Letting us come to the UN table like real *menschen* to talk about the Syrian terrorists. Letting us land an airplane in Los Angeles. Letting us exist—something," he snorted.

Very slowly, Ruth shook her head. "They don't all feel that way."

"I'm only talking about the little men in the honeycomb of offices who work on the levels below feelings, below policy." He was not smiling when he said, "Somehow I can't forget that they kept quiet while six million people were murdered."

Filling her cup for the third time, Ruth paused to stare at Moshe. In all the years she had known him, she had never heard him discuss anything seriously other than women and war.

They fell silent as each thought about the other. Ruth felt a pain she could not quite understand and it had nothing to do with her concern over Hannah's absence, about which she felt guilty.

Walking into the living room together, Moshe paused to admire a painting on the wall and then shook his head, "I don't know about such things," he said. "But if it isn't the wrong thing to say, 'I like it.' "

He stood staring out of the large window that overlooked the street. And Ruth remained where she was by the doorway, trying to understand how she felt about Moshe and trying to understand why she felt anything and if what she felt was different from the way she felt about Zvi and Avram and the way she had felt about Fishel. And she knew there was a difference, and in the instant she knew it, she became frightened.

He turned toward her, his face as always tense, the muscles of his neck firm. Then without a word, he slowly scanned the room as though he had never seen it before. His eyes settled on her face again, and he was about to say something when the phone rang. Ruth let it ring several times, hoping that he would speak, but he finally shook his head and she answered the phone.

For several minutes she listened and then she began to smile at him. He moved closer to her and then their bodies touched and Ruth half stumbled away as she thrust the phone toward him. "Hannah."

With deliberate slowness, Moshe took the phone from her hand, his eyes never leaving her face. Then, as though he were on a parade ground, he came to attention, his eyes shifted to the darkness outside the window, and he began to speak to his wife. He was happy everything was all right. He would see her the next time he came north. Would she please keep in touch? Accepting her promise, he told her he would call her at Malin's the next day.

Setting the phone on the cradle, he turned almost formally to Ruth, who stood with her back against the wall a few paces from him. "She's fine," he told her. "Thank you for dinner." He looked about, located his beret and said stiffly, "I must get back to my command."

Ruth nodded and started to get the beret from a chair for him, but he reached the chair before her, tried to smile at her, and failing, said once more, "I've got to go south."

Then she was alone in the middle of the room. Moving awkwardly, she began to turn off the lights and then stood in the darkness, trying hard not to feel the pain and trying not to feel old, so very, very old.

The morning of 29 May found the armies of Israel and Egypt still facing each other along the Sinai frontier. Outposts from both armies could see the enemy moving along the border. Several times during the bright summer day, Egyptian planes swept out of the south over the Israeli frontier and whirled back to Bir Gifgafa with aerial photos. And as many times that day, Israeli Mysteres dived out of the north, took their pictures and disappeared in the direction of Tel Aviv. Once in the late afternoon an Egyptian artillery battery unloaded twenty shells on a kibbutz near Gaza and then fell silent.

All through the day the Israeli flat-bed trucks hauled two landing craft through the Negev. Just before dusk, engineers floated them at Eilat. Three days before, the same trucks had hauled the same landing craft into Eilat and taken them north again after dark. Now for the fourth time the Israeli navy was going through the same motions, and the Egyptian naval intelligence officer watching the procedure from the Sinai counted two landing craft plus

606

two landing craft plus two landing craft plus the two now moving in and he knew that the Israelis were going to make their move by sea into the Gulf of Akaba from Eilat. Another Egyptian officer who was watching the same operation from the Jordanian side of the border at Akaba counted the same eight landing craft, and for Egyptian Naval Intelligence in Cairo, the information checked out. And so on operational orders, the Egyptian navy was rushed through the Suez Canal to the Red Sea so that its small fleet could be in position to destroy the Israeli navy.

What the Egyptians did not know was that the Israeli navy was almost nonfunctional and that one of the main fears of the Jews was an Egyptian naval attack along the vulnerable, unprotected Mediterranean coast.

The Syrian troops on the Golan Heights and down the craggy length of the frontier sat watching the Jews below. From where they were dug in, the Syrian troops could watch the kibbutzniks working in their fields, driving their children to school in buses and sitting out in the late afternoon sun. The Syrian soldiers could see the Israeli troops from Tiberias and Bet Guvrin. Though the Israeli line was thin on the northern reaches, the Syrian line was probably thinner, because both of Syria's operational divisions were being used for the internal security of a shaky government.

Fifteen Israeli soldiers moving on four weapons carriers along the frontier south of the Dead Sea confronted three Jordanian half-tracks moving in the same direction along the imaginary line. Both units veered away from the border and drove parallel for almost an hour. When the Jordanian column turned east, the Israeli lieutenant waved them goodbye.

Watching from the command post he had set up for his company dug in near Jerusalem, Lieutenant Diyar al Ilm could see the Jewish police on Mount Scopus. The regular convoy which passed through Jordanian territory every two weeks had not made its regular run. Diyar knew the Jews were frightened. The heavy-set Diyar brushed back his handlebar mustache and turned his fieldglasses on the city below. From where his guns were set up, he could reach almost any section of Jewish Jerusalem, and as he selected his targets, he smiled to himself. He had dug his guns in well. His major, the pot-bellied son of a doctor from Amman, would be pleased. Each of the heavy artillery pieces stood either in front of or behind a Christian holy place, and the Jews would not dare offend the Christians. Diyar was proud of himself. For nineteen years and more he had been fighting Jews. And now all those years of training and blood were going to pay off. Walking away from his men, he disappeared into the small house he had commandeered for his headquarters. On the table of the small family room, Diyar's clerk was going over their orders from Amman. Planting his boots in the carpet, the lieutenant looked the house over for the third time that day. He liked it.

When his troops reached Tel Aviv, he was going to find a Jew's house like this and take it over for himself. Striding past the table where his clerk had come to his feet, Diyar swept up the folder with his orders and stalked into the bedroom beyond. With a laugh he threw himself onto the large European-style double bed made up with white sheets and a silk spread. His black boots hooked over the top of the stead, Diyar closed his eyes. This bed needed a wench, and somewhere in the hills over Jerusalem he ought to be able to find one. The vision of a peasant girl with a white gown which was just light enough to reveal her bouncing breasts passed before his eyes and he smiled. Half the Jews on the other side of the divided city were women. He stopped smiling for an instant as he wondered what a woman soldier would be like in bed, and then the smile spread over his face again. Diyar was no fool. They had to be built the same as other women. Having settled the matter in his own mind, he opened his eyes. Looking at the papers with care, he slowly read the last paragraph of the "Jordanian Operational Order to Raid SHA'ALABIM Settlement":

> Task: The Reserve Battalion will raid SHA'ALABIM Settlement with the intent to destroy it and to kill all its inhabitants, upon reception of the Code word "BARAK."

Shaking his head in annoyance, he realized he should have left these papers with the unit which had replaced him. He shouted for his clerk and then yelled at him for being so stupid as to take the wrong orders.

Quaking at the thought of having upset anyone so important as his lieutenant, the youth grabbed the orders and fled.

Diyar lay where he was for a time and then became restless. No man in his right mind lay alone in a bed as fine as this, and he had to find a woman to share it with him.

Shortly before noon Bedia Hassani left her father's stone-and-marble home in Ramallah northeast of Jerusalem and raced her new Dual Ghia into the city. She had been back in Jordan for several days and she was bored. There had been two dinner parties in honor of her father, and she had attended both. The elderly banker was proud of his daughter, but he had complaints.

"Three years in New York," he grumbled. "Then Paris and Cairo. A girl like you should stay home and have children. You married in New York and got divorced in Teheran." He wiped his face with a handkerchief and then blew his large red nose. "I'm not going to have any grandchildren," and, as always when he launched into this accusation, he wept. "I have a beautiful daughter. The Western magazines have her pictures. The newspapers have her pictures. But she marries and has no children—only pictures."

He had paced back and forth through the large drawing room slowly letting his temper rise; and then in frustration, he had slapped the maid who stood just inside the door. "This one has children, litters of them, but my daughter . . ." He slapped the maid again and stormed out of the room.

Bedia, rising from her chair, had handed the weeping maid one of her own silk handkerchiefs with which to dry her eyes and then had taken the car to Jerusalem.

There was no real reason why she had come other than the fact that she wanted to get away by herself for a time. Only after she had let the doorman in front of the Intercontinental Hotel park her car did she remember that there was going to be a war. The four Iraqi officers standing in the white stone entrance way of the hotel brought the war to mind, and she turned to look across the Holy City. The high sun glinted brightly off the Dome of the Mosque. Beyond, she could make out the part of the city the Jews had stolen nineteen years before. Looking at the new buildings on the skyline, Bedia hoped the war would come soon. She wanted to walk through the Jew part of the town. She wanted to see Jew corpses piled as high as their Wall.

She brushed back a lock of hair blown loose by the wind and turned to enter the hotel. One of the Iraqi officers, a young major whose father owned three villages, stepped forward to block her path.

"May I buy dinner for the lady?"

Bedia cocked her head to one side. He was tall, handsome in a plump sort of way. However, when his hand came up to take her arm, she was offended by his neatly manicured fingernails. Then she smiled, "I don't like eating," a pause and she added, "or doing anything else alone."

He took her arm and as they passed the doorman, she said, to impress the major, "Will you kindly call the manager and tell him Miss Hassani will want a suite."

The major half bowed to his companions and followed Bedia.

Entering the hotel, they climbed the narrow stairs to the main-floor lobby. At first Bedia did not know what she was going to do here, but she wanted to see what the hotel looked like. Wandering through the clean marble corridors, they came out to the main restaurant, where she stood for a time looking through the huge plate-glass windows which lined the front of the building. The whole of the ancient city lay before her. She could see a taxi crawling up the road in front of the hotel and she smiled. The Jordanians had had the courage to build the road right through the old Jew cemetery, paving the base of it with headstones. Someone had told her that the grave of the woman who had founded the Hadassah Hospital lay lost under the paving. Raising her eyes, Bedia noticed the artillery dug in near the Greek Orthodox Church nearby. Satisfied that at least one soldier knew how to fight the Jews, she turned away, smiled at the major and told him she wanted a Scotch and soda. If there was going to be a war, she knew the place from which she was going to watch it. Gesturing for a maid to swing a chair about, Bedia seated herself at the window and waited. The plump Iraqi major whose father owned three villages pulled a chair up beside her.

The morning of 30 May looked like any other morning of that week. The troops of both armies continued their patrols. The planes continued their reconnaissance flights. The main body of the Egyptian navy moved swiftly through the Suez Canal to block any Israeli invasion from the south. The Arab soldiers who manned the guns at Sharm el Sheikh were reported to be Algerian, were reported to be Kuwaiti, were reported to be Yemeni. There was no clear indication that Lev Hershel's men actually knew who they were, nor did it make any great difference to the Israeli commanders.

More worried with every hour that passed, General Mazon kept his men on the alert. His patrols covered the long desert line. The hastily dug emplacements were manned against sniper attacks. Those troops not on any other duty reviewed the training they had received years before when they had been drafted. For Zvi and Gabe that Tuesday looked like another long day of waiting. And all the while they knew the Arabs could emerge before them through any gust of sand.

After a long night of checking his positions and reviewing his tactics with his brigade and battalion commanders, Zvi had chucked his boots and was lying curled up on the ground between his command half-track and Mitra Glasner's communications center. The two young women monitoring the messages from headquarters were the first to hear the news. One of them shouted for Mitra. Taking the receiver in hand, Mitra listened as the message was repeated. To the two younger women watching her, it seemed that she took a long time to react. Finally, she dropped the headset back on the radio, said, "Oh, my God," climbed out of the vehicle and walked over to the place where Zvi lay sleeping in the shadow of a tarp. Kneeling beside him, she was about to shake his arm when she saw that he was looking at her. His dark eyes seemed to have crawled farther into his head. He came up on one elbow and waited.

"Hussein has just flown to Cairo where he and Nasser signed a pact."

The two young women watching saw that the General took even longer to react than their lieutenant. All of the possibilities raced through Zvi's mind as he stared unseeing at Mitra. Jordan was in it now. The battle line extended completely around Israel. She was under siege. Shaking his head slowly, he recalled the British military study he had read two years earlier. Israel's armies could defeat Egypt and Syria at the same time. But if Jordan joined with them . . .

Sitting up, Zvi pulled on his boots without saying a word. Then he saw Gabe running toward him and he smiled bitterly. As his Chief of Staff squatted beside him, Zvi said, "Maybe we waited too long."

Gabe nodded. "Maybe."

One of the radio operators climbed out of the half-track and reported, "Hussein is already back in Amman."

Zvi took even longer to react to this news than the other. "Coordination," he finally commented.

"How much longer do we wait?" Mitra asked.

Looking up at her, he shrugged. "*Patience* is the word I've been hearing."

The young radio operator was about to say something, but Mitra shook her head and returned the girl to her work with a gesture.

Zvi sat where he was, his legs pulled up before him, his arms wrapped about his knees. "And they're talking in New York," he said. "And they're talking in London and Paris. In Moscow and Washington. And we wait." He did not try to hide his frustration when he added, "And they are talking in Jerusalem and Tel Aviv. Tomorrow both cities could be destroyed by bombing. But they will have talked."

Before he went to sleep that night, he talked to Moshe on the radio. His friend knew little more than he. The pact had been signed. Nasser, who had been calling for Hussein's head days before, had, indeed, kissed him. The Israeli government was sitting in Tel Aviv so that the Prime Minister could be in close contact with the Chief of Staff. The talking continued everywhere.

"We can't stand down and we can't afford to stay mobilized," Moshe complained.

"Patience," Zvi consoled bitterly. "Patience, old friend. At the rate the shops and factories are closing down, we won't have anything to fight for. Then we can all go home and wait. It's more comfortable there. If there's going to be rape and pillage, wouldn't you rather be home?"

While the Arab world thrilled to the news of the new alignment against the Jews, Israel was alive with rumors if not action. The Prime Minister was going to step down, the old Prime Minister was going to come out of retirement, one Cabinet member or another was going to take over the Ministry of Defense, a former chief of staff was going to take on the Ministry, a still different ex-chief of staff was going to leave his post at the Hebrew University to take over the Ministry, the right-wing party leader was meeting with his old enemy, now in retirement, in search of advice, the religious parties did not want to fight. The Arab Communist members of the Knesset were clamoring for concessions to the Arabs, the Jewish Communist members were condemning the Arab Communists. The former general who was not going to become Minister of Defense would be willing to accept his defeat if he could name the deputy chief of staff who would within months become the chief of staff.

Like rabbits, the rumors ran through the desert and multiplied. The soldiers heard from soldiers who had heard. The civilians heard from civilians who had heard. And the only thing everyone knew for certain was how vulnerable the *demi-tasse* country was.

And all the while the soldiers waited to learn if they were going to attack or be attacked.

The day was long and the shadows short. Zvi wanted to contact Avram to ask which rumor was true and what he could expect. But he remembered his own advice: *patience*, and though he laughed, because he was not a patient man, he waited silently.

It was already dusk when the first hard news was heard.

An Egyptian general was named commander of the Jordanian army with direct responsibilities to the Egyptian Chief of Staff. The coordination so long feared was now a fact. The Arab Legion was now commanded by Egyptians. The small Jordanian air force was now a part of Egypt's larger force. Airfields were now mutually available. An Iraqi armored column had entered Jordan to support a thrust. The long-dreaded pincer movement which could cut Israel in half could now come into play. Not only was Israel under siege, but the siege had a single commander. The Jews could no longer depend upon Arab disunity.

TEL AVIV

Through most of the next day, Zvi waited, hoping that the new, enlarged Cabinet would make decisions the previous one had feared. Though he did not receive the orders he expected, he did receive orders. Mitra Glasner brought them to him shortly after he had eaten a cold meal from a C-ration can, too angry and impatient to wait for something else. He closed his huge hand on the side of the can, crushing it between his fingers while he listened to Mitra.

"They want you in Tel Aviv as quickly as possible."

"Do you think . . . ?" Gabe asked.

Shrugging, Zvi said, "I've stopped thinking."

Ten minutes later the helicopter lifted off the desert to take him north. A staff Lark took him directly from the airport to Hakiryah. The guard at the entrance poked his head in the car, smiled and said, "I've been told you were to go to Colonel Ben Ezra's office, sir."

Without waiting for the driver to park the car, Zvi flung the door open and strode into the old yellow house. Puzzled because there was no sign that any of the other field commanders had been called, he climbed the stairs to Avram's office, and Avram was not alone. Both the Chief of Staff and the Intelligence Officer were sitting with him at the long table. The C/S waved Zvi in, shook his hand and said, "Sit down. There are a few things we have to talk about." Zvi thought he looked tired as he mumbled, "We're both in a hurry."

Zvi hoped his fatigue did not show. Drawing a chair up beside Avram's, he lighted a cigarette and waited to be told why he was there and why they were meeting in Avram's office.

The Chief of Staff put his elbows on the table and spoke quickly. "I didn't think I'd be here. There are some decisions being made tonight, and I have to be with the PM. However, I feel so long as I am still here, I should tell you myself. You are relieved of your divisional command as of now. You will report to Central Command as soon as possible to defend Jerusalem and north to the juncture with Northern Command."

Zvi nodded slowly as he tried to understand what this meant. "And my division?"

"It's already been taken over by Josef," another brigadier both knew well.

"And staff?"

The Chief of Staff shook his head. "I'm afraid there won't be anyone you can take unless it's a driver. Josef will need the others. I assume that Gabriel Natan knows your plans."

"He does."

Shoving his chair back, the Chief of Staff rose and Lev also came to his feet.

"I wish you luck, Zvi," the C/S said. "But don't ask me for anything. I'm counting on Hussein to make very little noise. You will work with what you have."

Zvi shook hands with the two and agreed. "You won't hear from me." As they were leaving, he asked, "Then we are going to fight?"

The C/S paused at the door to look back with an almost detached smile. "When I find out, you'll be one of the first to know."

Then Zvi was standing with his cigarette in hand, staring at Avram. "I could say it doesn't make sense. First a tank division, and I've never commanded tanks or a division before, and now this."

His friend slapped him on the shoulder. "You sound like you're complaining."

Shaking his head more to brush off the comment than to disagree with it, Zvi said, "Let's go down to the War Room."

For the next two hours, Zvi studied the dispositions in the area for which he was now responsible. He knew that Central Command had its own intelligence, but he wanted to think before reporting to Jerusalem. Satisfied that he was not going to learn anything else here, Zvi went to Central Command, where he did little more than report in, read the situation intelligences and leave. Avram was still with him when he boarded his helicopter for Jerusalem.

The two old friends shook hands and Avram told him the same thing the Chief of Staff had. "Here's luck, but don't ask us for anything."

Zvi stood for a moment with his hands on his hips. "It's a bit like going home." What he did not say was that he felt he was being sent home, sent to a place where the battles would be small, if any. He knew what his old friends were too kind to tell him: he was being shelved, placed on the front that was least likely to explode. He knew, too, the C/S was doing what he himself might have done with a Zvi Mazon.

JERUSALEM

Playfully, Avram punched him on the shoulder. "I'll be up tomorrow and go over the land with you if you want."

Knowing that his friend was anxious to get away from the office if there was time, Zvi said, "I want." Then he pulled himself into the 'copter and shouted for the pilot to take it up.

Zvi assumed command of the Jerusalem area and the Jordan line north to the Syrian border shortly before midnight of the first day of June.

In the old barracks which the British had abandoned nineteen years before, he met his new staff. Most of them he had known at one time or another in the past. Two of them had served under him as junior officers in the retaliation raids. One of those was his new chief of staff, Shmuel Givat, who had come to Israel from a concentration camp. The other was his new Communications Officer, David Benari, who had served with the Russian army as a youth. Both were pleased to see their new commander; and together with the intelligence officer, Lieutenant-Colonel Yaacov Brin, a lawyer from Nazareth, they briefed him on the situation as they understood it, adding very little that Zvi had not already learned. However, he listened patiently, because he wanted to know more about them than the information they were passing on. He had two brigades stretched along the full length of the frontier and a third, the Jerusalem District Brigade, within the city. The one thing they did not need to brief Zvi on was the terrain. As he looked at the maps on the wall of his new office, he closed his eyes. Behind his lids he could see every kilometer of ground more clearly than the maps revealed them. He knew where the land turned green, where it would be burned by the summer sun, where it shelved and where it rose. He knew most of the buildings which would serve to cover his movements in the city and every pace of folded hill in the Jerusalem area. He knew the approaches to Hebron and the dangers of Tulkarm. He knew the heights about Nablus and the width of the roads which forked there.

Opening his eyes, he sat quietly at his desk and let Yaacov explain where the Arab Legion had located its guns, where the headquarters of the Legion had been newly established, where the Jordanian tanks had gathered for their thrust to the sea to cut Israel in two, where the Iraqi column would share the front, where the newest airfields had been built, where the Arab engineers had stored their Bailey bridges near the Jordan River, where the Jordanian supply dumps were hidden, where the enemy units were located which would make the dash to cut Jerusalem off near Latrun.

As the Intelligence Officer pointed to each of the enemy's positions, Zvi recorded them in the back of his mind.

Satisfied that Brin knew his job, Zvi turned to Shmuel. The slight Colonel, his withered arm shoved into his belt, had obviously been over all of it before. When Zvi asked him where their own brigade command posts were located, Shmuel pointed to the markings on the map.

"You have a roster of officers?"

Shmuel crossed the room and drew one from some papers on top of his desk. "It's up to date as of this afternoon."

Cocking his head to one side, Zvi waited for an explanation.

"Josef told two of the battalion commanders he was going to take them with him." The Colonel was clearly unhappy.

Zvi considered this. "Did they ask to go?"

"Yes."

"Then I don't want them. Tell Avi we're going to upgrade two officers here unless there are objections." He fell silent and the others waited to hear if he had any other questions. "Contact both of those battalion commanders and tell them they will be sent south in the morning."

Glancing at his watch, he saw that it was already 0300. "David, will you contact Gabe at the division and have him start my driver, Haim Ben Aaron, north? He'll be attached to this headquarters." Shifting in his chair, he asked Shmuel, "Is there anything that has to be done here, now?"

The chief of staff shook his head. "We've been ready to go for weeks."

"Is the waiting done?" David asked.

Zvi shook his head and cautioned, "Patience. If there's nothing to do here, then I'm going north along the line." Coming to his feet, he thanked them for the briefing and then, clapping Shmuel on the shoulder, said, "You will remember that I want to be kept informed. David will be in touch with me at all times." Both understood what he meant.

Ten minutes later, using Shmuel's driver and a radio operator assigned by David, Zvi started north along the frontier line. He felt exhilarated and at the same time calm. To his right lay Jerusalem the Eternal. For much of his life he had dwelled upon the loss of the Old City. And during none of those years had he ever even dared to think that he would command Jerusalem and the hills to the north.

Bouncing northwest along the crooked border created by war and anger, Zvi turned to look at one of the emplacements near the frontier. Gesturing for the driver to stop the jeep, Zvi evaluated the ground from where he sat. Picking up a flashlight from the floor, he made a note to tell the unit commander to move the gun forward and to the left where it would have a better field of fire. Waving the driver on, he let his thoughts drift back to Jerusalem. Through the last hours of darkness and into morning, he checked the line. It was almost noon by the time he asked the radio operator to request that a helicopter meet them at Megiddo in half an hour. When they made contact with the copter, Zvi ordered the jeep back to Jerusalem and explained to the pilot that he wanted to cover the communications lines from Umm el Fahm to Petach Tikvah. It took them much less time to fly over the narrow strip which lay between the Jordanian border and the coast than he wanted it to. Satisfied that he had fully regained in his mind the lay of the roads and rail lines, he shouted for the pilot to take them back to Jerusalem. By the time Zvi returned to his headquarters, he had a pad full of notes. Then word came that Avram was on his way to headquarters.

Zvi went over his notes with Shmuel, and they agreed that they would shift men to meet the possible threat of a Legion thrust south through Ma'ale HaHamisha at the northern edge of the Jerusalem corridor east of Latrun. The corridor had been the main strategic problem in '48. The city had been cut off then. They did not want a repeat of that situation. All Jordanian movements indicated that a drive south at this point was more than a possibility. Sitting on a cot in Shmuel's office, his feet up on his deputy's desk and the pad of notes on his lap, Zvi stared at the large topographical map on the wall where the most recent Jordanian troop movements were marked.

"They have been moving about for days," Shmuel explained.

"When commanders get that restless, I wonder if they actually do have a plan." Zvi shrugged. "When they don't have a plan, guessing becomes difficult. That armored column moving south will probably stop just north of us. Their advance units are already there. I have not the faintest idea where in the hell the Saudis will go into the line if they actually do come in."

"Yaacov says there are seven Jordanian brigades in this area. Does that make sense to you?" Shmuel obviously had doubts.

"That's what I got at Central Command and in Tel Aviv," Zvi confirmed. "We'll go on that assumption."

Shmuel waved his withered arm. "That means Jerusalem will be their focal point."

"I've never doubted it," Zvi told him.

"This Egyptian commander?"

"Adab-el-Mun'an." Zvi added the name. "He may have some power, but that's not been proved yet."

"He served as chief of staff of the United Arab Forces," Shmuel reminded him.

Zvi grinned. "I'm not so certain that makes him either powerful or dangerous." Coming to his feet, he said, "Something's up. I'll let you know what it is if I can." Shoving his shirt tails in, he tossed the last of his notes onto his deputy's desk. "Avram isn't coming up to pass the time of day, though I'm supposed to think so."

Both men smiled. They knew and liked each other. The colonel was a quieter man than his new commander, but he had the same restless energy as Zvi.

"I'll clean this up," Shmuel said, pointing to the notes, "and wait for you to get back."

Nodding, Zvi said, "I think we've got to look over the whole approach to Ramallah again."

They all agreed that whoever controlled Ramallah controlled the West Bank. The Israeli army had come to this conclusion years before when Zvi had been Chief of Operations and the thinking had not changed since that time. Walking over to the map, Zvi stared at Ramallah—a city, a juncture and a height.

Then he left to pick up Avram and drive across Jerusalem to Ramat Rachel, the small Israeli community at the southern edge of the city. Leaving their car and driver behind, they walked up the height overlooking no-man's land. Opposite them near the Mar Elias Monastery, they knew the Jordanians had two platoons. However, both officers were looking at Government House, which had once been the headquarters of the British mandate government and now served the United Nations. The sprawling compound in the demilitarized zone was an easy and obvious target if the Arabs chose to take on the UN.

Turning, Zvi and Avram watched a plane pass over the empty hospital and university on Mount Scopus on the far side of the Old City. "If Jordan fights, that's their first target," Avram warned.

Zvi shrugged. The point was obvious. Then they moved on, inspecting the whole line of the divided city. And after a time Zvi suspected that Avram had come from Tel Aviv to see what his plans would be. However, after they had driven back to Histadrut Headquarters Building, where from the roof they could see most of Jordanian Jerusalem, Avram shifted the subject from defense.

"Have you seen Aaron since you're here?"

Zvi stood with his hands on his hips, staring at the Old City. The high-rise building on which they were standing was going to be perfect for his needs. He shook his head absentmindedly in answer to Avram's question.

"I hate to get into this, Zvi, but there could be trouble." He hesitated and then explained, "The boy and Hannah."

"Don't get into it," Zvi growled. "I know what Aaron's told me." Then, puzzled at Avram's even broaching the subject, he looked at his friend closely.

The tall staff officer shook his head. "I feel foolish, but I'm concerned about what Moshe would do if he knew."

"I could say that we've both got more important matters at hand."

"Then you aren't afraid for the boy?"

Zvi's fieldglasses were on Mount Scopus now as he traced the road that led through Jordan to the Israeli enclave. "Sure, I'm afraid," he admitted without looking at Avram. "Moshe's a killer. Maybe that's why he's a great soldier." His hand went to the back of his bull neck and he kneaded the muscles which had become taut. "Aaron and Hannah," Zvi began, his eyes still watching a Jordanian half-track settling in not far from the base of Scopus. "From the beginning, from the time they were children. I've never quite understood how Moshe got into it."

"Shouldn't something be done now?" Avram asked.

Pulling up the fieldglasses hanging about his neck, Zvi watched two jeeps moving toward the Police School which lay in Sheikh Jarah at the northern edge of the line near the road to Ramallah. When the jeeps finally disappeared into a cluster of trees, Zvi glanced at Avram. "Just what brings all of this up?"

"Moshe's got a terrible job ahead of him. He won't have time to worry about Hannah."

"Then don't let him worry about her." Zvi had no intention of being sympathetic.

"Can you keep those children apart until this is over?" Avram asked.

"All you have to do is see that Aaron is kept busy at his base." Zvi smiled wryly. "You have that kind of authority."

"And you won't object?" Avram apologized: "You know I want no part of this whole thing."

"I won't object while this is on," Zvi agreed. "Go back and tell whoever is worried about Aaron that I'll stay out of it until Moshe reaches Suez." Then he smiled, "Avi, Aaron's a smart boy, and he'll take care of himself when the time comes. I'm assuming Moshe is going to Suez soon."

Ignoring the ploy for information, Avram suggested they drop in on Malin. "She said she would like to see you, too."

Zvi's head came up angrily. "Who told her I was here?"

"The rumor is all over the town and we've decided to let it run its course. If the Arabs pick it up, they'll worry."

Shaking his head, Zvi clasped his friend's shoulder. "Avi, I wonder if time's made you a politician instead of a soldier."

"Don't worry about it," the Staff Officer consoled. "After Moshe retires, the Cabinet will offer him an overseas assignment, and as soon as he's out of uniform, I'm probably retiring myself."

Zvi felt sad at the news. "I'm the old man of the crowd. Aren't you rushing it a bit?"

Avram combed back his thick hair with his fingers as he watched a small detachment of Legionnaires enter the Old City. "In six months or a year my time's out."

"I'm sorry."

"I'm not. If we're here next week, we'll have done what we set out to do."

Zvi was also watching the Legionnaires and he pointed out several machine-gun emplacements on the Old City wall.

"I saw them," Avram told him. Then they left the roof and started for Malin's apartment. Sitting back in the staff car, they listened to KOL Israel on the driver's transistor radio.

"The United States and Great Britain have both released a proposal declaring the Gulf of Akaba an international waterway."

The radio held their attention. "President Nasser has declared that if there is any attempt by alien forces to enter the Gulf of Akaba he will close the Suez Canal. He repeats his warning that the time has come to destroy all Jews."

And then Zvi and Avram were climbing out of the sedan and making their way to the Ben Ezras' apartment on the second floor.

Avram was about to knock when Hannah opened the door. Malin was dressing. She would be out in a moment.

"I think it's all right if I go in to see her," Avram laughed.

Zvi was watching Hannah's confusion and realized how young she really was. Alone with her now, he stood watching while she nervously offered him a cigarette. He accepted, lit it and continued to stare at her.

Smaller than her mother, Hannah had been described by one newspaperman as "lithesome." Zvi thought this was a good word for her. She stood proudly, her head up and her shoulders back. Her short hair reminded Zvi of Ruth's when she was younger. Hannah's face was lovelier than her mother's; and there was a quality about her expression Ruth had never had. Trying to define it for himself, Zvi wondered if Hannah was not the new aristocracy in a country which had shied away from having an aristocracy.

Standing in the middle of the room, obviously disconcerted, Hannah still held the cigarette box in her hands. Her eyes met Zvi's and she waited for him to say something.

"You've seen Aaron?" he asked.

She did not hesitate to nod, and he was pleased. "The other night. He had twenty-four hours."

Zvi wondered why she thought she had to be defiant. "And the two of you made some decisions," he said, not asking a question. "Aaron wrote and told me he was going to."

"Well, we did."

"Good," Zvi said. He dragged deeply on his cigarette. Then, taking her arm, he led her away from the center of the room to the front window where they could see the late afternoon sun. "I'm in a strange position," he confessed. "I never know when I look at you whether I'm looking at the daughter of one of my oldest friends, the wife of another, or the girl my son tells me he's in love with."

Hannah started to say something, but Zvi cut her off. "The relationship with Ruth makes sense. The one with Moshe makes sense. The one with Aaron makes sense. But, I'm not sure the last two make sense at the same time."

"Are you going to fight us?"

He saw that her hand on the window ledge was trembling. "Should I?"

Stepping away from the window, she turned toward him. "Don't," she pleaded.

"Have you told your mother?" he asked.

"Not yet," she admitted.

"Do it as soon as you can," he advised.

A phone rang somewhere in the apartment and Zvi could hear Avram answering. Then the door to the Ben Ezras' bedroom opened and Avram was saying, "They've shelled from Gaza. Killed two more of Moshe's men."

"It's stopped?"

"Yes, but I think you and I had better go some place and talk."

Zvi excused himself to Hannah, asked her to tell Malin he would see her in the next day or two and walked down to the staff car with Avram. After they had settled into the rear seat, the Staff Officer tapped the driver on the shoulder. "Would you please take a walk for a few minutes."

When they were finally alone, Avram said, "I've been waiting for it all day. The Cabinet has just voted. We attack."

For a long time Avram did not think Zvi had heard him or, if hearing, really understood. Very slowly and almost mechanically, Zvi puffed on the cigarette he was holding. He had almost finished it when he asked, "Did they pass any special orders for me?"

The Staff Officer nodded. "You will not go on the offensive without specific orders. Every effort is going to be made to keep Jordan neutral, and that means you can return shot for shot, but you cannot move against them."

Zvi sat back and stared at Avram. "You've been waiting for this all day?"

"All day," Avram admitted.

"And you came to tell me personally?"

Smiling, his friend admitted that was true. "The Chief of Staff said you would know as soon as possible."

Shaking his head, Zvi brushed that off. "Why?"

Avram weighed his answer and then, knowing there was no easy one, said, "Some people think you might react too quickly."

"Mitla?" Zvi asked.

"They want to be certain you understand the ground rules this time. Don't try to pressure for a change in orders. If there's going to be a change, you'll know."

Accepting the fact that he was being put on his good behavior, and at the same time surprised that he did not resent it even more than he did, Zvi asked, "And this trip to the house was for me to settle matters with Hannah for Moshe's sake?"

Shrugging, Avram admitted, "I don't know what you talked about."

"Good," and Zvi grinned. "Worry about that."

Later that evening, Zvi went over the defense plans for the area again. He had not slept for more than twenty-four hours and as soon as he and his staff were done with the review, he went to bed. He fell asleep wondering what Havah would think of the way he had talked to Hannah and what Havah would think of Aaron as a jet pilot, and then he felt sad because he remembered Havah had never learned what an airplane was.

On Saturday, 3 June, Zvi called his brigade commanders together and briefed them on the date and timing of the attack, and at the same time he passed on the words of caution he had received from Avram.

"We will return their fire," he explained, "but we will not go on the offensive." He paused and then warned, "Don't forget that because we've set a time that doesn't mean they won't attack earlier."

For the third time in as many days, he reviewed their strategy. No part of the city was to fall, no invasion would be permitted. Beyond that . . .

"All of you know me," Zvi said. "There aren't going to be any formalities among us. Let me know what you need, and if I can, I'll get it for you. Let me know what is happening so I can make the decisions I have to make. I won't bother you for reports unless I have to."

He thought a moment. "As long as possible, let's maintain radio silence. Let's keep them confused as to what we are going to do, but don't keep silent if what you have to say is important." He glanced at Shmuel. "Is there anything I've left out?"

The deputy commander shook his head.

Zvi walked the others to their jeeps and wished them good luck. He hoped to talk to all of them on Sunday. If there were going to be any changes in the dispositions, he would come to see them himself.

Then he was alone with Shmuel and his own staff. "Will you see the mayor?" he asked Shmuel. "Just have him lean on everyone to dig in."

Shmuel nodded and left.

Standing at the door of the old barracks, Zvi turned to look at the sky. The sun was high. There were few clouds. He wondered if Aaron were on patrol. If he had time later, he would write the boy a note. The others were waiting for him to enter the building, but he lingered outside, trying to remember if there was anything else he could do now.

"Yaacov," he said, calling for the young Intelligence Officer. "When did we last get an airphoto of the area?"

"Not since the thirtieth."

Sighing, Zvi decided not to ask for another one now. His orders were not to irritate the Jordanians and an overflight would. His eyes still on the horizon, Zvi asked, "The Jordanian Sixtieth Armored has eighty tanks?"

"Pattons," Yaacov said.

"And that Iraqi Division, one hundred and fifty?"

"Russian and American."

Zvi's hand closed on the back of his neck, his eyes still on the northeastern horizon. "Let's hope they don't know how to use them."

No one laughed.

Across the frontier Zvi was staring at, the large Russian bomber that was bringing Colonel Yusef el Sindi from Gaza to Jerusalem was putting down.

While the door of the plane was being opened, Yusef leaned against the side of the plane and peered out. He had told the Signals Officer at Gaza to contact Bedia to let her know he was coming. But she was nowhere to be seen. Taking a deep breath, he restrained his anger. The Signals Officer might have been slow in sending the message, and then there was no way of depending on the Jordanians—tribesmen from the desert and little more. He would have to contact Bedia on his own.

On the ground, he looked around. There were soldiers of the Arab Legion standing about, but there were no men walking sentry duty. Raising his hand, he waved a Jordanian colonel over.

"See that those men are given sentry posts and that they have a regular schedule of duty. There will be no sloppiness hereafter."

"If you're Colonel el Sindi, we were expecting you," the Jordanian officer said. "General Riadh has asked me to say that he will see you in Jerusalem either later today or tomorrow morning. He says that you will be responsible for coordination among the troops coming in."

Yusef smiled, knowing that the young Jordanian had not yet been informed of the great support and surprise in store for him. "What is the best hotel in the city?" he asked.

The younger officer thought for a moment. "The Intercontinental."

"Good," Yusef said. "You will see that a suite is reserved for me, and you will contact Miss Bedia Hassani and inform her that I shall be waiting for her there."

And without another word to the young man, Colonel el Sindi followed the fawning officer to a new Chrysler parked near the edge of the strip. Half an hour later they were being led into the hotel by the doorman and two clerks.

"I will call Miss Hassani," the Jordanian officer said again, while the clerks led the way to a large suite overlooking Jerusalem. Waving the others out, Yusef looked the suite over with care. He had had few nicer. He was certain Bedia would enjoy it. Taking off his coat, he sat back to wait for her and for General Riadh.

That night, as Bedia lay in bed beside Yusef, she wondered if it were true that the Egyptians were sending two commando companies to Jordan, and if they thought they were going to be able to defeat the Jews by adding two companies to the Legion. She had not expressed her doubts earlier when Yusef had introduced her to his commander, the fat-faced Riadh, who had difficulty keeping his hand off her bottom when she walked past him or his eyes off her breasts. Neither Yusef nor his general would have understood her explanation that General Mazon was not going to be beaten by two Egyptian companies, but by the Iraqi and Jordanian tanks. Lying in the dark, she touched Yusef's hairy chest. The problem with General Zvi Mazon was that he had never needed her. She wondered if he had ever needed the plump Jew-bitch with the big tits whom she had met in New York. She smiled to herself. When the war was over and the Jews defeated, Yusef and his general would think that they were the ones who had beaten Mazon and the Jews in Jerusalem. They would never take into account the hatred she and a million other Palestinian refugees felt for the Jews, the hatred which would bring the victory she knew was finally going to be won.

When Zvi reached his office on the morning of 4 June, there were two pieces of intelligence waiting for him. Each was funny in its own way: the first confirmed the arrival of two Egyptian commando companies on the Central Command front; the second reported a warning by Nasser: any declaration by the maritime powers asserting that the Gulf of Akaba was international waters would be considered by him, "a preliminary to an act of war."

Checking the first item with his Intelligence Officer and deputy, Zvi agreed that fewer than three hundred Egyptians would not seriously change anything. After Shmuel had read the second item, he asked Zvi if there were any possibility the United Nations could be asked to send a psychiatrist to Cairo.

Zvi failed to see the humor. "Don't forget the story about the little Arab in his village. It was lunch time. He wanted to eat, but some children were playing under the only shade tree. And so he told them that on the far side of the village some merchant was giving away figs. When the children ran off to get some figs, the little Arab settled down under the shade tree to eat his lunch. But he could not, because all he could think about was the merchant on the far side of the village who was giving away figs. And a moment later, he abandoned his lunch and was running to the far side of the village for his own share of those figs." He shook his head as he added, "And therein lies the danger."

Walking over to the barracks window, Zvi read the sky: few clouds, the sun had just risen. Checking his watch, he said, as casually as he could, "See that all units furlough at least twenty per cent of their men." He thought a moment and added, "They have to be back before dinner."

Ignoring the startled expressions on the faces of his staff, he walked down the corridor to the Communications Center, where David Benari was checking out his contacts with all the units along the front.

Along the Sinai border the three Israeli divisions were ready to move. In his command post near the Gaza Strip, Moshe stood at a large sand table on which his route had been laid out. His hands shoved into his pockets, his hair wild on his head, he stared at the miniature of his march. He picked up the clipboard which lay on the edge of the sand table and reviewed his schedule once more. As in the race to Sharm el Sheikh, he was again fighting time. Time was supplies, fuel, ammunition, and most of all it was men. He did not have a strong enough reserve to let his men rest. He had to pick up momentum and keep on moving with the men he had.

He wondered if anyone had made a study of how long a soldier keyed to perfection and motivated by family and history could stand on his feet. Moshe did not know, but he was certain that he would have the answer by the time he saw Suez. He hoped he would have better judgment than Zvi had had when he drove his men to Mitla only to watch them fall asleep while he was talking to them. Moshe thought of Zvi in Jerusalem. The chances were that Zvi would not fight there. Moshe hoped so, because he believed that Zvi was getting old. Then he shook his head in disgust. Only two days before, Avram had told him the government had found a job for him now that he would be retiring, a job that everyone thought he would like. Maybe Zvi was not too old at that. Moshe hoped Hannah would like the new job. It held some prestige. The salary and his pension totaled more than he made now. And they would travel. He thought she liked traveling. He was thinking of Hannah now and he was happy, knowing she was with Malin. He was still thinking of his wife when his Intelligence Officer reported that there was reason to believe the Egyptians were shifting their weight toward the south. Moshe nodded. He had heard this report earlier from Tel Aviv. He was not worried. They would not have time to move against Eilat while he was moving toward Suez. The real question was who would make the first move. Glancing at his watch, he knew that he was ready. The sun and the loess rose and settled. The day was long and for the men waiting in the desert seemed to have no end.

TEL AVIV

Avram Ben Ezra spent most of the day with the Chief of Staff. There was very little more they could do now. If the plans they had prepared over the years were not ready, no last-minute makeshifts would serve them any better. Twice Avram met with Lev Hershel. The Intelligence Officer had nothing to say that was new. The latest air photos showed what was expected. A few more MIGs in the lower Sinai than there had been a few days before. The weather forecasts were favorable: the Sinai in summer offered few surprises. There were indications UAR Intelligence had heard the army was furloughed. He hoped that they believed the Jews would not fight. Lev Hershel was keeping all his men busy. He wished he had more. Avram listened and was sympathetic; a staff officer for almost nineteen years, he had learned that no officer ever had enough men. Waiting at Hakiryah, he remembered the nights spent in his office standing by for the report that Moshe or Zvi had completed a retaliation raid. He remembered, too, the long night when Zvi's brigade had dropped into Mitla and the one when Moshe had dashed for the Strait. Years had passed and in its own way his career had passed. Angrily, he snapped the pencil in his hand and, resting one hand on his shoulder, he leaned back in his desk chair and admitted that while life had been good to him, he wanted what Zvi and Moshe had had. Then he thought of Malin and the children and knew that he would not have traded them for his friends' anguish and loneliness. Staring at the small alarm clock on his desk, he thought of calling Malin. He rarely did so on Sundays when she was in Jerusalem. A call now might be misunderstood. She might become concerned, believe something was going to happen.

SINAI

In the late afternoon the troops were all back at their posts. By early evening they were all briefed on their missions. And then they waited.

A barber from Haifa rolled under his tank to avoid the setting sun and waited.

A truck driver from 'Omer sat in the shade of an old Bedouin fence of straw and waited.

Two brothers who owned a butcher shop in Beersheba sat under a Mystere and waited.

A young secretary from the Jewish Agency in Jerusalem, sitting in the back of a half-track, combed the desert sand from her hair and waited.

A lawyer from Eilat scanned the field of fire of his heavy guns and waited.

Only the Cabinet, the General Staff, and the top commanders knew when they were going to attack, and for them it was no easier to wait.

The desert cooled. The transistor radios broadcast from Cairo. The young Egyptian rock singer ended his song with a shout: "We are going to war. Oh, we are going to war, to war!"

The small transistors from Japan, Germany and the United States vibrated as the Cairo crowds echoed the shout: "We are going to war!"

The Israeli soldiers sitting in the Negev evening nodded in agreement.

Darkness still covered the Middle East. There was a low mist over the edges of the sea, the Canal and the Nile Delta. Though the day to come would be hot, the night was still cool. The Israeli pilots were dressed and ready. They knew their targets. Though speeches had been made, they were not needed: the pilots knew the importance of what they were about to undertake. Sitting in the lounge at the airbase near Tel Aviv where he had been moved two days before, Aaron Mazon watched two of his companions play Ping-Pong while a third sat smoking a cigar given him by a Spanish tourist. Aaron's lean face was relaxed. Before he had gone to bed, he had written his father. He had wanted to phone Hannah, but he knew that would not have been wise. Stretching, he waited. His soft almond eyes were half closed while he listened to a transistor someone was playing in the lounge.

There had been many songs over KOL Israel this past month. Most of them had been serious. Many had been old folk tunes. Aaron knew little about music. There had never been a record-player in his father's house. Now, as he listened, he knew that he had missed something. Making a mental note to see that there was a record-player in his own home, he decided that one day he would ask his father why there had been so little music about them. Vaguely in the back of his mind he remembered that both Ruth and his father had once known a violinist. He could not recall if he had ever met the man. The music changed to a somber piece of orchestration which lost Aaron. The pilots at the Ping-Pong table gave up their game. One of them offered Aaron a cigarette, but he shook his head. What he wanted was another cup of hot coffee. Dragging himself out of the old gilt chair he had been resting in, he crossed over to the stove where a girl in uniform was pouring herself a cup. She offered hers and Aaron accepted. She asked how he felt.

He weighed the question and shrugged. "I don't know how I'm supposed to feel."

The girl was no shorter than he and almost as dark. "You're Lieutenant Mazon, aren't you?"

Knowing what was coming next, Aaron said he was.

"I've heard about your father."

It had been what he had expected, and even though it had happened often, he still felt proud.

"Is it true, he's in Jerusalem?" The girl was only making conversation, and Aaron was not worried about security.

"I honestly don't know. I had a letter from him the other day. I think it came through Tel Aviv."

They turned to listen to KOL Israel's report that two Israeli soldiers and one Syrian saboteur had been killed in the Galilee. Aaron looked at the clock on the lounge wall: 0700. He finished his coffe and thanked the girl.

"We'll win, won't we?" she asked.

Smiling at the ingenuous question, Aaron assured her, "We'll win."

Then he picked up a couple of chocolate cookies lying beside the coffee urn. Since the mobilization he had seen too many cookies and cakes. These two crumbled in his hand as he ate them. Brushing off his palms on the side of his flying suit, he grinned at the girl. "Imagine having no other way to fight except making cookies."

The girl did not smile. There was a folded newspaper lying on the chair beside her, and picking it up, Aaron scanned the headlines. On Sunday the Cabinet had discussed, "the Security situation, Israel Bonds, defense taxes, defense losses, a cultural accord with the Belgians and a scientific accord with the Peruvians." There were pictures of soldiers playing on the beaches. Tossing the paper back onto the chair, Aaron grinned.

"Do you think they know the field's here?" the girl asked.

Aaron shrugged again. "They overflew from the Dead Sea to El 'Arish twice this past two weeks."

"And we couldn't stop them?"

"Three MIG-21s at about sixty thousand feet going Mach 1.7 made the pass in less than four minutes."

Nodding to indicate she understood, the girl said, "Maybe we should have a larger country."

Both of them smiled.

Aaron walked over to the window. It was dawn. He should have known that from the clock. Thinking back on the girl's question, he wondered where his father was. "A dirt soldier," Zvi had always called himself. Maybe he was in the desert. Maybe. Aaron did not know. For a nervous moment, he wished he had thought to ask his father what the waiting was like. The answer, he knew, would not make much difference soon. The waiting would be over before long and then he would be able to answer the question himself. One of his companions came over to stare out of the window.

"Coffee?" he asked Aaron.

"When I make my turn-around."

The other pilot smiled. He was about to say something when the sad wail of a siren broke the morning air.

Grabbing his helmet, Aaron spilled out of the shack along with his companions. Within minutes four Mirages were flying west toward Egypt. Their radios were silent. They swept low over their own troops and on toward the west. The desert lay only thirty feet below. A slight swell on the ground and the four Mirages with the white and blue stars rose and settled with the desert's contours. The only sound was their engines.

Aaron Mazon, his white helmet pulled down, the morning sun behind him now, tested his guns. They worked. The ten bombs below were steady.

The plane handled easily to his touch. Day after day he had flown the Negev, dropping his bombs on target and flying on. Now the training was done. Now the training had to prove out as he had to prove out.

The ground lay brown and gray below. Scattered scrub brush. An Egyptian truck on a lonely road.

The four Mirages flew on.

There was the vague line where the land wedded the sea, and they raced on. Water below and mist. For ten minutes they sped silently over water and then there was land under the jets and villages.

Somewhere behind them lay the Canal. Ahead, their target.

There were tongues of muddy river delta shimmering in the morning mist. More villages. The surprised and upturned faces of fellaheen early in their fields.

Then a city with buildings sprawled in a murky haze below them. The lead pilot took his plane up now and the others followed.

"On target Number One," and the radio silence was broken.

Banking swiftly, Aaron recognized Cairo West below. The Illyushin bombers rested like tired birds at the end of a strip just as the photos had shown. Four MIG-21s were taxiing down a runway. Two MIG-17s rested at the end of a second runway. Checking his clock, Aaron read 0745. Twenty-two minutes from base. Only seven and a half minutes over target and he was coming down on it now. Over the MIG-21s and coming in too fast. He jerked his flaps down and then his wheels. The Mirage slowed and the target lay below. Half the bombs were gone.

The plane jerked high and Aaron brought up his flaps and wheels. The plane behind him was after the MIGs and a reddish-brown flower exploded. Then, as Aaron banked for another pass, the field burst into flames like roses in the morning light. The fourth plane had made its first pass. Unable to count all the Arab planes, Aaron scanned the field. Two bombers intact and he was raking them with his cannon. The Mirage seemed to chug and jerk. Then he went high once more as a second Mirage made its pass. Then the third and fourth. Wheeling tight, Aaron could still see Cairo and minarets and to the east the Nile. A pass at a fuel tank now. His cannon cracking like a giant's knuckles. Then the flames climbing the sky. A wild steep rise as he read the field. His companions were making their passes and there were more flames as more fuel tanks flowered red.

Sweeping low for a final pass, Aaron saw a dark cloud break beside his wing. They were firing at him now. Lower and still lower until he could have touched down in a second. He laid the last of his bombs on the runway. Even as he rose, two of them exploded. A smile crossed his face. The other bombs would explode in time. Higher now and the four Mirages formed once again and headed straight east toward home. They were not talking. The only sound was the screeching engine.

Glancing at his clock, Aaron knew they had come off target on the quarter minute. None of the planes looked damaged. The Egyptians were throwing up flak before them. Rising, they flew on.

Far to the southwest of where they had just struck, Israeli Vatour bombers had finished their work over Luxor, Egypt's largest bomber base. Mysteres and Mirages were all completing their tasks and on their way east toward Sinai. By this time another wave of Israeli planes was already striking. Aaron hoped the other ten fields were as completely damaged. He saw the plane in front of him wiggle its wings and he smiled. He was not the only pilot pleased with his own performance. The Canal and then Sinai. Below crawled several Egyptian trucks and a tank.

The Israeli formation raced east without pause. The third wave was already flying west, the second east, and Aaron's formation was only ten minutes from base.

Then the formation rose and swinging tight, came to rest on its own field. The ground crews closed in on them. More bombs were set in their racks, the twin cannon and machine guns reloaded. The oxygen tanks were replaced and a mug of coffee was thrust into Aaron's hands.

His Commander walked the length of the four planes answering the same question: "It's all good news."

"Luxor?"

"Even Luxor."

Then the canopy was closed and the four planes were rolling down the runway to repeat the attack begun less than an hour before.

Aaron's clock told him they had turned around in seven and a half minutes. No better and no worse than he had expected.

Now as they raced back over Sinai, they could see the fire of heavy guns and the movement of tanks. The radio crackled with the quick orders of dirt-troop commanders. Aaron and his companions kept their silence. Twenty-two and a half minutes to target. Sinai burned in the morning sun. The Canal muddied south like a thin blue cord into Bitter Lake. Brown-roofed villages, and then Cairo splashed wide along the edges of the Nile. Ahead were pillars of smoke, and once more the Mirages swept across Cairo West. Four small training planes were touching down on a far strip. Aaron cannoned three of them in a single pass. The fourth exploded as the Mirage completed its sweep. And now they were after the remaining fuel tanks. Smoke continued to crawl wildly over the morning sky, smoke mixed with ack-ack fire and fresh oil flames. The air was thick. The four pilots read the field as they passed over it, leaving the runways pocked, the seven choppers looking as though someone had plucked their blades. And then rising toward the sky, the Mirages started home again.

Less than half an hour after the Israeli Air Force struck at Egypt's eleven fields, the Southern Commander ordered Moshe Gilead: "Move out and good luck."

For over two hours while the Egyptians had been shelling the kibbutzim along the Gaza border, Moshe had restrained his men. Now he told his communications officer, "Let's go," and the message was passed on to the brigades. Stretching north and south across the route of the division lay eight miles of enemy fortifications, concrete bunkers, trenches, mined approaches, strung and concertina wire and infantry manning the defenses. The Egyptian artillery sat behind all of it. And in front were the large Stalin-3 tanks and American Shermans. Spread almost evenly along the Egyptian front were anti-tank batteries waiting to bruise and blunt the Israeli thrust. Moshe joined his advancing column in his command half-track, ordered two tank battalions to drive directly north into the enemy bastion at Khan Yunis. The tankers raced over the last stretch of Israel, crossed the frontier within half an hour and moved straight at Khan Yunis. The radio chattered and, turning where he stood, Moshe listened. They knew he was coming. He had never expected to keep his attack a secret.

Then suddenly, shockingly, the Egyptian heavy guns opened fire. The large shells slammed into the tank column, hurled loose dirt over the men, ripped treads off rolling tanks, excavated holes large enough in which to lose a tank. Moshe watched from his half-track. The column raced on, his heavy Centurion tanks rolling across the Egyptian road while his lighter Shermans lumbered through the planted fields. A smile crossed his burned face. The pincer was closing. Khan Yunis was going to be the first victory. But he had soldiered long enough to know that there had to be more victories and that he would have to pay for what he won. Calling for air support, Moshe watched the small Fougas pass overhead to bomb and cannon the Egyptian positions.

The Arab artillery continued firing for several minutes. Then, as though someone had turned off a spigot, the firing ceased. The first report to reach Moshe from the air claimed that over sixty per cent of the enemy heavy guns were silenced. He nodded, asked his communications officer to thank the air force, urged them to keep coming, and then he told his own driver to move forward. At the same time he ordered his Pattons to start probing the enemy's southern flank. Behind him, mounted on old trucks and half-tracks, rolled the mechanized infantry.

A column of smoke sprouted to his right when a tank blew up and burned. From where he stood, he could hear the brigade commander shifting his Pattons south to avoid the mine fields. The Shermans and Centurions locked with the enemy's giant Stalin tanks. For several minutes the Stalins, well dug in, and the approaching Israeli tanks poured point-blank fire at each other. The noise of guns and screams and exploding mines and aerial bombardment shattered the desert air. Then the Stalin tanks fell still. Pushing forward, Moshe's Shermans rolled into the artillery emplacements and quickly silenced the remaining Arab guns.

To the south the Pattons raced west and then north to cut off the

Egyptians. The whole desert shook under the impact of tank against tank, tank against emplacement. Loosing his paratroopers, who had been with his northern column, Moshe directed them toward the center of the Egyptian line. Smoke covered the field as bunker-hidden machine guns laid down a beaten zone so wide it caught the oncoming battalion and pinned it down. Ordering his other battalion to forget their assault on Rafa, Moshe sent them south to break out the trapped battalion. At the same time he loosed his own heavy guns and those on his tanks. They struck at the enemy bunkers, ripped the ground, shattered concrete, rolled over wire and spun it into webs of twisted steel.

Everything was confusion.

The men with Moshe waited for orders, and he spilled them as quickly as he could speak. There was a detached calm about the brigadier. He did not seem to hear the guns or the tanks or the Fougas dropping their loads over the enemy emplacements. His fieldglasses tight to his eyes, his ears tuned to the radio beside him, he made his decisions. The Patton column would have to swing back to help the men who were pinned down. Creating a new pincer of the men moving from the north and those from the west, he hoped to crack the nut of Khan Yunis. While these two elements were moving into position, he turned his attention to the column which had smashed its way past Khan Yunis. Urging the brigade commander on, Moshe said he wanted the tail up, the momentum maintained. His attention turned on El 'Arish to the west where he thrust his reserve battalion. Then the Patton column was moving east and joining with the trapped battalion and the one coming from the north. Moving in as closely as he could, Moshe followed the action on the radio and in less than an hour and a half, he knew his men had destroyed an Egyptian brigade. Without giving his troops time to rest, he shoved them west while he met with several of his commanders at a crossroads south of Rafa. The enemy guns broke the earth about them. Mortars whined high, splashing steel splinters across the open desert and dunes. Kneeling in the sand, Moshe laid out the next move against the enemy brigade to his south. The commanders returned to their battalions and started moving once more. The air smelled of cordite. There was no wind to clear it. The hot sun brazed the sand. The heat of burning vehicles warped the view. Choppers came in for the wounded, and enemy guns reached into wadis and over the open ground.

Coming erect, Moshe watched his battalions move out. Returning to the command half-track, he listened to the reports. The movement south was taking shape. The mop-up at Rafa was almost over. The men who had been pinned down were moving now. The column of Centurions which had broken through at Khan Yunis was racing west.

Puzzled at it all being so simple, Moshe called for a report from the Centurion commander. He had brushed Khan Yunis. He had passed right through the fortification at Sheikh Zuwedi and Jerardi and was continuing along the road to El 'Arish.

Moshe pulled two battalions out of his reserves—one armored and one infantry—and ordered them west to Jerardi. "Tell them to move their butts and fast," he snapped angrily. When his orders had been passed on, he could see that his staff was questioning his decision. Taking a deep breath, he explained, "The Gyppies let us through Jerardi. They'll slam the door on the Centurions and roll them up from both sides if we don't protect their rear."

Then the word came through that the Sherman column which had been slow in catching up with the Centurions had passed Jerardi and had not been stopped and Moshe began to worry. Two of his strongest armored battalions were approaching El 'Arish and they moved between two strongly fortified enemy positions. Crediting the Egyptian officers with out-thinking him for the moment, Moshe grabbed for his map. The road between Jerardi and El 'Arish was paved and open. El 'Arish lay at the end like an anvil. Behind his two battalions, Jerardi's defenses spread wide for six miles in depth along the road and two miles wide. At the width's end deep in the desert lay dunes which no tanker could flank under fire. Between lay his men. They were trapped and he knew it. Tossing the map aside, he decided to lead his two reserve battalions directly into Jerardi to destroy the enemy hammer poised over his tank columns. To do that they had to move right through the six miles of enemy bunkers, dug-in tanks and fortifications. However, he had no choice even though he did not know what it would cost. And as his half-track sped down the road, Moshe Gilead knew he did not have time now to count his dead. And when the fortifications at Jerardi rose before him, he tried not to compare his drive to that of Zvi to free his men to Mitla.

JERUSALEM

Shortly after the first wave of Israeli planes battered the Egyptian airfields, the Israeli Prime Minister sent a message to King Hussein of Jordan by way of the United Nations Commander in the Middle East. The message was brief: We shall not initiate any action whatsoever against Jordan. However, should Jordan open hostilities, we shall react with all our might and King Hussein will have to bear the full responsibility for all the consequences.

Standing on top of the Histadrut Building in Jerusalem, Brigadier-General Zvi Mazon read the copy of the message which had been sent to him. He knew the air force had already struck at Egypt. He had alerted all of his units. He was still hoping that he would not have to use them when the first Jordanian shells struck Jerusalem. The radio operator who was standing at his side spoke quickly. Sporadic firing along the entire perimeter. Zvi nodded while he watched the shells landing in New Jerusalem. Two buildings nearby were struck. A wall collapsed. Looking down, he could see people scurrying through the streets. An old man hugged a wall, slipped into an entranceway and disappeared. More shells were falling now. Then the radio operator reported that shells were falling on Tel Aviv. In the north the Jordanians were trying to reach the airfield at Ramat David with Long Toms.

Zvi listened and watched. Picking up the phone he had had pulled out onto the roof, he ordered an immediate air raid alert. A moment later he could hear the cry of the sirens. Still holding the phone in his hand, he asked the operator to get through to the mayor of the city. "It's war," Zvi said. "We can control it here."

He handed the phone to a sergeant and pulled out his fieldglasses. The shelling continued. The phone rang and the sergeant answered.

Zvi waited to hear the report.

"They've hit the Hadassah Hospital at Ein Kerem."

Cursing under his breath, Zvi scanned the approaches to Mount Scopus. So far he could see there was no movement toward the enclave.

Then the radio operator told him that Radio Amman reported an attack on Jordan.

Trying not to smile, Zvi nodded. "Turn it up." He listened for a moment.

"The hour of revenge has come . . ."

The little king wanted war. Zvi waited for the Jordanians to invade. Without looking at the radio operator, Zvi snapped, "Get more radios up here. Tell David Benari and Shmuel Givat I want them here."

He could see more shells landing in the city now. South of where he stood a fire started.

The radio beside him chattered and the operator handed him a phone. Central Command. There were some tanks now. Did Zvi want more tanks? He did not think so yet. So far he had committed nothing. Yes, he knew he might have to take Government House. He was looking south toward the former mandate headquarters in the demilitarized zone as he talked. Abdul Aziz Hill? If he had to take it, he would. Handing the phone back, he asked the operator to contact the Chief of Staff. Two shells passed over the roof and Zvi wondered what the Arabs were trying to reach. The phone in his hand again, he said, "I'm ready to move out." Turning where he stood, he looked to the west where there was the trace of smoke in the air. "I'll go for Latrun if it's all right."

It was not.

Zvi waited while shells fell over Jerusalem. David was at his side now and a moment later Shmuel joined them.

"There," Zvi said, pointing toward Ammunition Hill. "They've got a battery over there." His hand went up again, and he pointed to a monastery. "And several guns over there."

"We could knock them out," Shmuel offered.

Zvi shook his head. "I made it clear at the briefing. We will not strike any religious site. I don't care what it costs us, but we . . ." His voice trailed off as he shook his head.

The operator was listening to something now. "Nasser says he has destroyed our entire air force."

Looking at the man balefully, Zvi waited a moment and then turned his attention to the Jordanian guns once again. They were picking up tempo now.

He was looking at the Old City. There were machine guns on the walls sweeping the empty streets nearby. Now Zvi recognized the sound of rifle fire. From where he stood, he could see few people anywhere.

"Shmuel," he snapped. "Contact the brigade commanders. I don't want them to do any more than answer the firing."

The small deputy with the withered arm was rephrasing the order and passing it along.

A flicker of red on the Old City wall caught Zvi's attention: sandbags burned where the Jordanian guns were firing. A wry smile crossed his face.

Then David Benari told him, "The Syrians claim they have attacked in the north. The Galilee is theirs. They have captured the villages and are marching toward Haifa."

Again, Zvi looked dubiously at someone passing on so questionable a report.

"It could be true," the Communications Officer said sadly.

Zvi could not dispute the point. His fieldglasses focused on Government House. The Northern Command's division would have to fend for itself now. He could not help it. There were more shells falling. More rifle fire. Zvi half closed his eyes and the old sounds passed through his mind. Mortars and twenty-five-pounders instead of 105s.

A shell landed nearby and his head came up sharply.

"Are the wounded being taken to the hospital?"

Shmuel had already checked. They were.

Down the length of the frontier now his men were answering sniper fire with sniper fire. The *swoosh* of a bazooka broke over the city as Israeli gunners tried to knock out Jordanian positions. Then there was more bazooka fire. At the sound of firing on his right, Zvi swung toward Ramat Rahel to the south. Mortars now.

"Return that," he snapped, but before Shmuel could contact the local commander, they heard more mortars and knew the fire was being returned in kind.

"Zvi," David Benari called, and when Zvi nodded to indicate he was listening, the Communications Officer reported, "They are shelling the length of the front. Me 'Ammi has been struck.

Trying to recall the small settlement, Zvi nodded again. A noise overhead and he watched planes sweeping west.

"Find out where they are going," he ordered, and a moment later he had the report.

"Jordanian Hunters have attacked Natanya, Kfar Ya'betz, Kfar Sava, Ra'anana and are bombing the Kfar Sirkin area."

"Where the hell . . . ," Zvi started to say and then he saw the Mirages overhead. A pause while he listened to the chatter on the radio. The Israeli air force was striking at the Jordanian fields at Amman and Mafrak.

Shmuel smiled, and kneeling, flipped open a large map. Marking the fields with a pencil, he listened for further reports. The Syrian airfields had already been bombed. Marking these, too, he came to his feet.

For the next several hours, Zvi kept close track of the Jordanian heavy guns. So far no troops had invaded. It was 1130 hours when he asked Shmuel to reach headquarters again. When Zvi had the phone in his hand, he winked at Shmuel and said flatly, "We're ready to move out."

From the firm "No" on the other end, he knew he was talking to Avram.

"They've started firing on Mount Scopus," Zvi explained.

"The answer is no," Avram repeated.

Shmuel was tapping Zvi on the shoulder, and so he rang off. Looking at Shmuel, he waited.

"Odd Bull from the UN wants to know if we will accept a cease-fire."

Zvi nodded. "Tell Central Command to pass the word on. We'll accept."

The Jordanian big guns continued slamming shells into New Jerusalem.

"There are over forty civilians in the hospital now," Benari informed him.

Zvi's hand slipped into his shirt. His own artillery was striking back where they could, but most of the Arab Long Toms and 105s had been placed behind or directly in front of religious sites.

"Are they hiding behind only the Christian holy places?" he asked Shmuel.

"As far as I can tell," the deputy admitted.

Swearing softly, Zvi asked to speak to Avram again.

When they had the staff officer on the phone, Zvi said flatly, "We're taking a heavy shelling. I think we have to move. Hussein would probably like to be able to call it quits now that he's blustered, but there's that Egyptian commander."

Avram said there were no orders to attack.

"I could move into the positions discussed earlier."

"No." And Avram was off the phone.

Wiping his face with a broad palm, Zvi lit a cigarette. It was almost noon. "Get a rundown on the situation elsewhere," he told Benari, "and find Yaacov."

Five minutes later the Intelligence Officer emerged on the roof. Zvi knelt where he was and prepared for the news by flipping his cigarette over the roof and lighting another.

"We've knocked out the airfields in Egypt, Jordan and Syria. There's even been a strike on the Iraqi field near the Jordanian border."

"And our air losses?"

"Fewer than twenty-five."

Dragging deeply on his cigarette, Zvi thought of Aaron. People had told him the boy was a good pilot. He hoped so.

"We've knocked out over three hundred planes. We control the air," Yaacov said proudly.

"That should help Moshe and the others," Zvi admitted, thinking of the division he had left in Sinai.

Coming to his feet, Zvi watched the Jordanian guns strike at Mount Scopus. They were out to destroy the old university and hospital. He watched for a moment and then told Shmuel, "Have the brigade ready to move directly north if the Arabs attack Mount Scopus."

When his deputy hesitated, Zvi assumed his responsibility. "It's on my head."

Yaacov was taking a report from the radio now. Making a note of it on his pad, he told Zvi, "They're moving their armored brigade—the Sixtieth—up from Jericho. Their Twenty-seventh is moving out toward Jerusalem."

Zvi sucked in his cheek and chewed it while he decided what this would mean. "The Sixtieth has Pattons?"

"Eighty-eight of them," Yaacov told him.

"And the Twenty-seventh is infantry?"

The Intelligence Officer nodded.

Kneeling beside the map, Zvi traced the route from Jericho with his finger. The Arabs would be moving on Mount Scopus from the east. "Where the hell is that Iraqi brigade?" he asked.

Yaacov squatted beside his commander. "Right where they were as far as we know. The Damiya Bridge."

Smiling, Zvi did not think the Iraqis were going to be an immediate problem. He was coming to his feet, when Benari reported, "Jordanian Hunters struck at Tel Aviv."

Zvi glanced at Yaacov, "We don't hold all the air yet."

He was about to turn toward the Old City again where the machine-gun fire had become more insistent, when one of the communications sergeants turned up a radio.

"Mount Scopus has been captured." The words were Arabic.

Worried, the others looked to Zvi for an explanation.

"Now we know where they think they're going."

"But . . ." one of the young girls manning a radio started to say.

Zvi smiled at her. "With the Arabs, words are almost as good as action; and besides, no one gets hurt that way."

The others laughed, but all of them were looking at Mount Scopus.

An operator handed Zvi a phone. Central Command. Zvi listened and smiled. Setting the phone down, he told the others. "We may move yet. Start

636

them rolling toward Kastel and move up the armor. I'll let them know when they're to cross the frontier."

He swung about at the sound of heavy guns and, bringing up his glasses, focused on the Police Barracks to the north of the city. "Shmuel," he said softly. "I want the infantry in position to take that Police School if we have to."

For the next several hours Jordanian shells fell without regard to target across west Jerusalem. And Zvi waited for orders to attack. He lit another cigarette and waited.

TEL AVIV

In the War Room, Avram sat listening to the Egyptians. The military radio network was completely confused and confusing. There were Egyptian generals sending reports to Cairo claiming that they had taken Beersheba and Eilat, and were marching on Tel Aviv. There were Egyptian generals screaming for more supplies and men. There were Egyptian generals who claimed they had just destroyed five hundred Jewish tanks. There were generals who said they were beating a strategic retreat, hoping the Jews would follow so that they could cut them off in the desert. The Israeli staff officers with Avram listened quietly, wondering what Nasser would make of the confusion. Then, slowly, one at a time, the Arab military stations began to drop off the air.

Avram's attention turned to Radio Cairo which was now claiming the destruction of Tel Aviv, reporting that Jerusalem was in flames, that the bold Egyptian army had sliced the Negev in two, that there was already a juncture with the Jordanians and that together the Jordanians and Egyptians were marching north to capture Haifa and join with the Syrians moving south.

Kneading the large muscles of his shoulder while he listened, Avram wondered what the Arabs would do to recover from this series of claims.

SINAI

Deep in the desert where the remnants of his division had been driven, the Egyptian General listened to the reports of victory over Radio Cairo. He wished he knew which of the divisions had been so successful as to have sliced the Negev in two, which had junctured with the Jordanians, which were marching north to meet with the Syrians. Looking about his half-track, he could see columns of smoke rising toward the sky. He could hear the heavy Israeli guns battering at his last defenses.

Turning his head slightly, the General continued to listen to Radio Cairo. The President was on the air now, telling the Jordanians and the Syrians that Egypt's air force had already destroyed the Jew air force. He was claiming that his 7th Division was already battering at the gates of Tel Aviv. The General standing in the desert sun looked around for his division—the 7th— and bitterly wondered how his men had got so far so fast without his knowing anything about it.

Radio Cairo continued to claim victory. The refineries in Haifa were on fire. The city of Beersheba was flattened. The port of Eilat no longer signified. There were few buildings left in Tel Aviv. The Egyptian commandos attacking from Latrun had cut the Jerusalem road. For a moment the General thought the hot sun had baked his brains. Then he heard someone on Radio Cairo announcing that the military network had been abandoned because there was no longer anything to fear from the Jews. Direct orders would be broadcast in the clear over Radio Cairo. And someone was telling the General to swing his division southeast, to bypass the Jews so that they would expire in the desert or be caught between his 7th Division and the five Egyptian armored divisions rolling east from Kantara and El 'Arish.

The General glanced over his shoulder toward El 'Arish, which was already in Jewish hands, and wondered how he was supposed to take orders from Radio Cairo which was now proclaiming victories and which only moments before had placed him at the gates of Tel Aviv. Then he heard the clatter of tanks coming toward him and from the silhouette, he knew they were Centurions and he had no Centurions in his command.

He was about to walk away from his half-track when Radio Cairo informed the world that he had just defeated the Jew General Gilead far to the east of Khan Yunis. Taking a deep breath, he walked out into the road and awaited capture.

TEL AVIV

Listening to the confusion over the Arab radio, Avram picked up the phone and called the Office of the Army Spokesman. Speaking in the name of his superior, Avram ordered, "Don't tell the press anything. Keep all information to yourself. The enemy has no idea where we are or how badly he's been hurt. And I have no intention of telling him."

The Army Spokesman laughed and at the same time asked, "Do you want to tell the correspondents that we don't know anything?"

"Let them wait," Avram suggested. He thought a moment and added, "And when you tell them we will be talking to them later, don't look so damned happy."

JERUSALEM

Judge Malin Ben Ezra listened to the closing argument of the prosecution and gaveled a recess. No one in the courtroom could keep his mind on the trial because of the shelling in the streets, and the decisions could wait for another twenty-four hours. Ten minutes later she was driving through Jerusalem.

She had almost reached her apartment when she saw the ambulance parked in the street and the police blocking the road. Swinging the car to the curb, she jumped out, and as she ran she could see Hannah on her knees beside the ambulance, her head bobbing back and forth as though she had been struck. The rubble of a stone wall covered part of the street. The explosion of Arab shells broke over the city. Malin brought herself up short, trying to decide what she should do and at the same time trying very hard not to panic. She knew it would not be in keeping with her status as a judge and the wife of Colonel Avram Ben Ezra. It took great effort to control herself. However, when she heard a child screaming through the rear door of the ambulance, she screamed.

Hannah rose and put her arms about Malin and told her, "She will be all right. She will be all right. She will be all right."

When Malin realized her baby was injured, she screamed again. Only when she was done screaming was Hannah able to tell her that the doctor had said the baby would live. Several minutes later, the door slammed; and with Malin inside, the ambulance sped away.

NORTHERN AXIS, SINAI

Standing in the back of the lead half-track, Colonel Gabriel Natan wiped the dust from the rubber-rimmed glasses which clung to his face. The sun was bad and the enemy fire was worse. Only two hours before, his column had junctured at Gebel Libni with one of the columns of General Gilead's division. His new commander had pointed westward and Gabe had joined the first of the brigades moving west. The desert lay white and hot. Enemy tanks burning by the side of the road created their own whirlpools of flames and smoke. Ahead, he could make out the emplacements at Bir Hamma, but he was not thinking of these as much as he was thinking of Mitla, where the division was supposed to block the enemy flow of reinforcements to the east and the enemy retreat to the west. He wiped his hands over his glasses again, thought for a moment of Zvi Mazon's comment that no battle went according to plan and that this fact had to be part of the plan. He was thinking of Zvi when the Egyptian shell struck the half-track, ripped out the front and hurled the heavy vehicle on its side. Two soldiers in the rear jumped free before the ammunition and fuel caught fire. Neither of them could reach the division's deputy commander, even though just before the half-track blew up one of them was able to hear the colonel say, "This wasn't part of the plan."

JERUSALEM

For hours the Jordanian gunners had been pouring their fire into Israeli Jerusalem. Jordanian jeeps mounted with recoilless rifles swept along the frontier, firing point blank at buildings and villages.

Standing on the roof which overlooked East Jerusalem, Zvi knew he could not wait much longer. The damage was extensive, and yet he knew he could not move a man across the frontier until he had orders. Several times during the morning he recalled his own work on the problem of Superior Orders and wondered if any of it applied now. How remiss was a commander who did not take it into his own hands to protect the people who lived within the area he commanded?

Zvi's staff waited with him. Some few were already grumbling, though none within earshot of the stocky brigadier who was known to have a short temper.

Several times Zvi reviewed the intelligence he had on the Jordanian emplacements. They were good, well-located, well-dug-in, solid entrenchments. Selecting the units he would use in the event he was allowed to move, Zvi waited. There was little else he could do.

Then David Benari brought him a note. The Jordanians had taken Government House. Zvi read the message again and told Shmuel to pass it along to Tel Aviv. Ten minutes later Zvi heard that the parachute brigade which was waiting to be dropped into Sinai was going to be split and one of its battalions shifted to Jerusalem. Sighing with relief, Zvi smiled. He and Moshe had created these shock troops. Acknowledging the information, Zvi turned his attention to the square white building called Government House which lay in no-man's land. The only occupants of the building before the Jordanian attack had been the UN commander and his staff. Realizing that none of the Arabs gave a damn about the United Nations except to call upon it when in trouble, Zvi waited impatiently for his orders.

They reached him at 1425 hours. Passing them on to the commander of the Jerusalem District Brigade, Zvi set out to meet with the troops who were going to retake Government House. By the time he arrived at Allenby Barracks in southeastern Jerusalem, the unit was already formed: a small force of half-tracks, tanks and jeeps. Zvi and the force commander conferred briefly, and then Zvi told him to go at it.

The detachment moved out slowly, paused to let the half-tracks batter the Jordanians dug into the grounds of Government House, and then all the vehicles opened up with everything they had. As the column started to roll on, heavy mortar fire broke over it. Once more the column halted while one of the tanks moved forward to knock out the Jordanian mortars.

Returning to a height from which he could watch the action, Zvi saw the force moving once more. Its heavy fire kept the Jordanian soldiers down and away from the windows. And then suddenly a detachment of Israeli soldiers made a frontal attack on the building. The door gave way and the men ran inside. Zvi waited impatiently for news. Being a commander had its drawbacks. He was still waiting for word from Government House when he was told that Avram was on his way to Jerusalem. Nodding to acknowledge the message, Zvi kept his fieldglasses on Government House. The remains of burned-out jeeps and half-tracks could be seen on the grounds. Heavy rifle and machine-gun fire could still be heard. Without looking around for his deputy, Zvi said in a quiet voice, "Shmuel, keep that force on the move toward Sur Bahir."

Sur Bahir, the small Arab village near the Israeli village of Ramat Rachel, stood on a height which covered much of the surrounding area and straddled the road from Jerusalem to Bethlehem.

Zvi began to smile as a white-and-blue flag rose above the UN Headquarters. Then he turned his attention to the tanks and half-tracks moving on Sur Bahir. The Jordanians were dug in on top of the hill where the village stood. Zvi watched the fire fight between the two forces and then he saw one of his detachments start running toward the Jordanian stronghold. Cursing under his breath at whoever the fool was who had thrown forty men against a battalion, Zvi waited to see what would happen. The radio beside him was making noises and a communications officer reported that the UN staff in Government House had been found locked in a room, that now they wanted to withdraw toward Jordan, and that one UN officer had been found with the Arab Legion at Sur Bahir when the forty men had taken that village.

Knowing that his men were waiting for orders, Zvi decided quickly, "The UN personnel will not be allowed to withdraw to Jordan. I don't want them under fire again. And as for the UN officer at Sur Bahir, he will be brought back here with the others."

Shmuel passed on the orders and then asked, "Why the devil would the commander and his people want to go to Jordan?"

Zvi shook his head. "There could be two reasons: the first is they think we will lose and they don't want to be trapped in Israel. The second is probably even more logical—Christians hate Jews more than they hate Moslems." However, he was no longer thinking of the UN staff. "Ask Tel Aviv if we can take Latrun now. I want to keep the road open. I don't want Jerusalem cut off."

His attention was on Sur Bahir again. The detachment was moving in and he gave orders for the unit to keep rolling east. "Tell them not to lose momentum," he urged.

Then Shmuel reported: "They are sending us another battalion of the paratroop brigade. No authority to attack Latrun now. Government House cost us eight dead."

Sucking in his breath, Zvi fumbled for a cigarette, lighted it and then snapped, "Let's get back to the roof."

Twenty minutes later he had returned to his headquarters. From where he stood, Zvi could see the damage the Jordanian guns were creating in Jerusalem. Several fires had broken out. Several buildings revealed holes. He knew there was much more that he could not see. He drew up a plan for the movement of the second battalion of the paratroopers into Jerusalem and for the attack on the plateau to the north of the city over which passed the Ramallah road. He had just completed his plans when David Benari brought him the news that headquarters was sending him an additional armored brigade. Zvi grinned and nodded. "Thank Tel Aviv, be certain Colonel Ben Ezra knows where we are, and . . ." He hesitated and decided not to ask about Aaron. Other fathers had to wait and so would he.

Picking up the sentence where he had broken it off, Zvi shifted his thinking and explained that he wanted the two paratroop battalions to form in the more protected area of the western part of the city before they moved to the frontier area north of the Old City and the Mandelbaum Gate. Zvi was happier than he was willing to admit that the paratroopers had come under his command. Long having recognized that the parachute was only a means of transportation, he knew from his own experience that this brigade was possibly Israel's best—its commandos, its shock troops.

Within an hour Zvi was even happier to learn that he had been given the last of the three battalions of the paratroop brigade. At about the same time, Avram joined him. They walked down into the building where the General Staff officer briefed the commander.

"You know they claimed taking Government House an hour before they took it?"

Zvi had not heard this and wondered what it meant.

Shrugging, Avram said, "It may have been a warning to the UN staff. It's hard to say."

"Am I to understand Government House was the only reason I got permission to move out?"

"No. They were pushing at one of the airfields near the border and Northern Command was told to knock them back. Once we had made that decision to move into Jordan, there was no sense in keeping you fettered."

Wryly, Zvi smiled. "In short, we're fighting here because they started fighting in the north."

His friend laughed. "I think there was pressure to start down here." And both of them were remembering Zvi's requests. "Now that you have two more brigades, where are they going?"

Zvi eyed Avram. "I want the armor across the Ramallah—Jerusalem road by morning and the paratroopers to swing northeast, taking the Police School, the hills there, and then, if they can, swing them back to enter the Old City from the east."

Avram nodded. "That's the way headquarters sees it."

"Thanks," Zvi snapped, angrily. "How are the paratroopers getting here and when?"

"By bus in a few hours."

Zvi smiled at the thought of his shock troops being brought to the front in civilian buses. "What is a few hours?"

"By seventeen hundred."

Nodding, Zvi accepted this and they returned to his command post on the roof of the building. Calling his staff together, he told them he was going to meet the armored brigade west of Jerusalem. Shmuel and the staff were to remain where they were. Zvi looked to Avram for his decision, and the General Staff officer said that he would remain in Jerusalem.

Forty minutes later, Zvi met the commander of his armored brigade in the Jerusalem corridor. The two sat in the back of one of the trucks and went over their plans. The armored column was strung out for more than twenty miles. Over a thousand trucks, half-tracks, jeeps and tanks were now moving toward the front. Though most of the tanks were old Shermans which had seen action in the Second World War, there was one company of Centurions.

"How soon will you be in position?" Zvi pressed.

The tanker glanced once more at the map before he committed himself: "Seventeen thirty."

Zvi read the map again. "You've two routes to the Ramallah road: Radar Hill and Sheikh Abdul Aziz."

The tank commander agreed. "I'll strike at both, break and move on toward the high ground between the City and Ramallah."

Zvi said, "Remember, they've had twenty years to build defenses in those two passes."

For the next two hours Zvi watched while the tanks arrived and were positioned. Beyond the frontier lay the fortification: concrete bunkers, pillboxes, blockhouses, and deep trenches all behind well-laid mine fields.

Leaving the armored commander to handle his own battle, Zvi moved back to the tank brigade's communications center, where he requested air strikes on the wandering Jordanian 60th Armored Brigade.

Ten minutes later than he had promised, the tanker began his bombardment of the Jordanian heights. Zvi could hear the guns rumbling as he sat back in his jeep. The Jordanians answered. The tempo rose and then slowly began to fall as the Arab defenses crumbled.

Twenty-five minutes later, Zvi heard the heavy fire stop, and he knew the tanks were moving forward now. Knowing there was work to be done elsewhere, he started back to Jerusalem to meet the paratroopers who had already arrived at their first rendezvous.

While he rode, he was briefed on the successes and failures of the armored attack. Radar Hill was difficult. The Arabs were fighting hard. It was hand-to-hand for more than a quarter hour. Sheikh Abdul Aziz was no better.

Darkness had helped very little. Almost all the Centurions were out of the fight. Bogged down on the ridges, bottomed on rocks, most of the large tanks were almost useless. For a moment, Zvi considered returning to the armored brigade. However, deciding the commander knew what he was doing, Zvi raced back toward the western edge of Jerusalem where he had ordered the paratroopers to assemble. Meeting with their commander, he reviewed the plan of attack. It was simple enough; a direct thrust across the border at the Police School by the first battalion. From there, part of the battalion would drive southeast toward Sheikh Jarah and the Ambassador Hotel. The other part would attack Ammunition Hill to the north. The second and third battalions would take the Rockefeller Museum in a pincer movement, move up the Mount of Olives and back westward to enter the Old City from the east. At the same time the first battalion would break open the road to Mount Scopus and with help move on to Augusta Victoria Hospital and the height it commanded.

Sitting in a corner on the floor of an apartment kitchen, Zvi accepted a cup of coffee from the family living there and asked the paratroop commander, "How well do your men know this ground?"

The younger officer shook his head. "Many of them have never seen Jerusalem before, and those who have never looked at it as attackers." Both men knew what this meant—a point of view, a way of looking at terrain for cover and routes, for dangers and exposure. Zvi half closed his eyes while he considered this. Finally he asked bluntly, "Do they know what they're getting into here?"

The paratroop commander assured him they did. "Urban warfare. None of us has fought this way before."

Zvi grunted. "It's different, but we haven't time to go into it now. See that they are told that much." He smiled as he apologized, slapped the younger officer on the back and said, "You know all that."

The paratroop commander nodded. "You fought inside in forty-eight?"

"Inside." Somehow, Zvi had never heard it put that way before. The word was descriptive. "How soon can you be in position to move out?"

The younger officer weighed the question, the terrain and his transportation. "O-two-hundred."

"I'll depend on that." And Zvi came to his feet. "I'll see you before the attack," and then he went outside to where his communications truck had caught up with him. His armor was still fighting for the heights. Standing in the street listening to the report passed on to him by Shmuel, Zvi weighed returning to the hills west of the city. And once more he decided that he should not. Picking up the radio, he told Shmuel, "I'd like the armor to capture the heights by O-two-hundred." The timing made sense in view of what he had just approved.

Then he found he was talking to Avram, who had remained at the area headquarters; "When are the paratroopers attacking?"

Zvi considered the question. It was obvious to him that Avram was not asking for himself. "I'd like midnight," he admitted, "but they will attack at O-two-hundred."

"No," Avram protested.

"What?" and Zvi found that he was shouting in the street. Before anything else could be said, he snapped, "I'll meet you in a few minutes." Jumping into the jeep, he told his driver that he wanted to get back to the Histadrut Building.

While they raced through the almost empty streets of the city, Zvi listened to the radio. The action in Sinai was still chaotic. Twice during the day he had been told there were breakthroughs, but he did not know any details as yet. The Northern Command was moving toward Jenin. No one needed to tell Zvi about his own front.

Reaching the building, he found Avram waiting for him in the lobby. The two walked off by themselves.

"You had better hold the paratroopers until morning," the General Staff officer advised.

Shaking his head angrily, Zvi held his ground. "No." And he pulled a cigarette from his pocket and lit it so that he would have time to control his temper. Dragging deeply on the cigarette, he explained as though to a child, knowing that Avram was becoming impatient. "These men are trained to fight at night. The Arabs are never good at that. The terrain doesn't mean anything to men who do not know it to begin with, and so daylight has less advantage than you might imagine."

"But, Zvi, we can give them air and artillery support."

For a moment Zvi weighed the offer, and once again he shook his head. "Go tell headquarters that we are fighting too close to the city to attempt an air strike. One bomb drop on a holy place and we will be saying *mea culpa* through history; and while we are doing it, every good Christian nation which is standing by to wring its hands over our corpse will be spitting on it."

With great effort, Avram restrained himself as he thought of Zvi's decision to move on eleven years before.

Knowing what his friend was thinking, Zvi lightly slapped the taller man on the arm. "Explain to Tel Aviv I think I'm right." His grin was broad and ingenuous.

It took Avram a moment to laugh. They were about to separate when they saw Kineret Heschel standing alone in a corner of the lobby. Looking at each other, they shrugged and started toward her. For an instant it seemed as though she would draw away. Then she smiled and came forward.

"I'm not going to take your time," she apologized. "I just thought that I would like to be near where it was happening."

"Avi's bound for the roof," Zvi explained. "I'm going to be traveling most of the night." He did not want to tell anyone how worried he was about the armored brigade's lack of success so far.

"Join me," Avram invited her, and after a brief apology, Zvi fled the building while the other two went to the roof.

Outside, Zvi contacted the armored commander. The tanks were moving slowly. The mine fields were the main problem. The engineers were helping.

"The Centurions?" Zvi asked.

"Twelve bogged down and the other eighteen barely moving."

"Kick them in the butt," Zvi growled. Then, "I'll be looking for you on the Ramallah road by dawn."

Without waiting for an answer, he had Haim drive him to Shmuel Hanavi, the road from which the paratroopers would move out into Jordan. The city was bright with tracers of Arab guns and the fires begun by the bombardment. Streets shook and buildings collapsed. Haim told Zvi that he heard more than a hundred persons were in the hospitals already. Zvi knew there had to be more than that. A shell slammed into a building several yards from where they had slowed at an intersection, and both of them turned to watch stones fall into the street.

Ten minutes later they rejoined the commander of the paratroops, who had moved his men to the frontier line. The approach of his trucks had brought Arab fire into the area, and both of them stood against a wall while the battalions took their positions.

Zvi checked his watch with a flashlight. 0140. A smile came across his face as he thought about Kineret. She was the one woman who would appear in the middle of a war. Then, as he rested his head against the building, he thought of Dvora and in the same instant he wondered why she had come to mind. Maybe it was the reminiscent sound of twenty-five-pounders striking stone. Maybe . . . Shaking his head as though to clear it, he suggested to his companion they try the roof of the building. When they emerged above, Zvi let his head drop back. "It's a good sky for a dirt soldier."

The young Colonel nodded.

"I hear that the chaplain says we are making history."

Zvi chuckled. "I hope he remembers to bring his shofar."

Then they were pointing out what they thought was the best route for the three battalions. Both of them knew the city. Zvi was about to check the time again when a shell struck the parapet of the roof, tearing the stones away and scattering debris over them.

"I never thought things like this happened to generals," Zvi's companion said, and they laughed.

Leaving the roof, Zvi contacted Shmuel. The armored brigade held both the heights at Radar Hill and Abdul Aziz. Sighing with relief, Zvi demanded, "What did it cost?"

"Twenty dead and eighty-one wounded."

Half closing his eyes, Zvi visualized the rocky roads that led into the hills where he had sent his men. "Can they get the wounded out?"

"By hand, but they are doing it."

"Give them any help they need." Then, taking a deep breath, he asked, "What's the plan from there?"

"He wants to move the armored brigade out to the height after taking the fortification at Biddu and leave one battalion behind to cover his rear."

Zvi agreed. "Congratulate the tankers. Tell them they're doing fine."

"Zvi," Shmuel's voice was tentative.

"Yes?" Glancing down the street, Zvi could see sparks where shell fragments struck stone. The noise of the Arab guns seemed louder now and he knew it was the night air.

"Miss Heschel, she went out and we don't know where."

Smiling to himself, Zvi comforted his deputy. "She's one woman you don't have to worry about." He looked at his watch: 0200.

Then he heard what he had been waiting for—the shock of his own artillery and the crunch of his own tanks as they struck across the frontier toward the Police School, Ammunition Hill and the area known as Sheikh Jarah, where the Ambassador Hotel was a large landmark.

SINAI

The battle which Moshe Gilead began in order to take Jerardi and keep the door from slamming shut on his two columns racing toward El 'Arish lasted more than ten brutal hours. His tanks penetrated the defenses along the six miles of fortifications and then peeled off to attack each of the enemy positions. They closed with the Egyptians and fought from bunker to bunker, from trench to trench. Uzis burned hot and grenades exploded in the midst of the Arab strongholds. Slowly, yard by yard, they battled to open the highway, and finally the van of the division came to El 'Arish. Skirting the city, Moshe planted a detachment of Shermans to the west of the city and waited for his long column to collect. His men stretched all of the way back to Khan Yunis.

Tired and wanting to rest after more than eighteen hours of continuous battle, Moshe decided he had to move on. Behind him lay a mauled Israeli division, still fighting at Khan Yunis and Rafa, but he did not know this. Aware of the strength of the Egyptian position at Bir Lahfan, he ordered his men to keep their distance while trying to pick off the enemy's positions. The gun duel lasted almost two hours, and then Moshe sent a battalion eastward around the enemy's defense line. Pouring its fire parallel into the enemy trenches, the Israelis battered the Egyptians until they broke and fled.

Wheeling another battalion about, Moshe led it into El 'Arish from the west and smashed the enemy stronghold there. Fatigue covered him and his men like damp clothes. Few could think well. And yet all of them knew instinctively that they had to maintain the momentum they had gathered. Splitting his forces in two, Moshe pointed one of them straight west along the coast road toward the Canal while he led the other southwest. The desert sun was rising now. The skyline flickered with the smoke and flames of burned-out tanks, trucks, and depots. The bodies of Arabs and Israelis lay almost casually dead along the road.

Standing in his command half-track, Moshe wiped the grit from his glasses and sucked in the air as though he could not get enough of it. The radio behind him crackled and he waited for word that the rest of his division was catching up. However, the only news he heard was that the battle for Khan Yunis had started up again and that the cost of Gaza was going to be higher than anticipated.

Knowing he could not turn about to help his men, he moved on into the desert. Ismailia and Suez still lay ahead. And he could not allow the enemy time to think and regroup.

JERUSALEM

The Israeli artillery began to soften the Arab positions, and the paratroop commander moved over to Yoel Street to wait for the attack to begin. The few available tanks moved swiftly into position down the slope of the street facing the frontier. And their clanking steel treads alerted the Arabs, who started a barrage down the length of the line. The whole border came to life as the Arabs returned the Israeli fire and attempted to block the invasion they knew was coming. With all their ponderous clumsiness, the tanks poured direct fire into the Arab positions. Slowly the heavy fire began to take its toll. One after another the Arab guns fell silent as the tanks rolled toward them and over their positions.

Zvi waited for the paratroop commander to lift his barrage, knowing the tanks were moving into the fire of their own artillery and all the while he admired the coolness with which the young colonel held his order until the last safe moment. The enemy artillery had already taken its toll as soldiers were struck before they even crossed into Jordanian territory. There were hushed screams of men who were trying not to scream, the sudden gasps of men struck and the race to pull back the wounded. Finally, the young colonel gave the signal, and the Israeli artillery fell still. Taking a deep breath, Zvi watched, knowing that now everything depended on the infantry already closing with the enemy.

The Arab trenches were well constructed and well defended. The Israelis leaped into them, firing as they came. The battle was rough, brutal and without quarter as both sides knew that the issue would be settled here.

The Police School before them, the ground between broken, the Legion fire heavy and the gray bayonets blooded, grenades exploding and the wounded hiding in corners of concrete or lying in the open, guts showing while the bunkers flung death and the paratroopers kept running, their wounded passing back wounded and the cries for medics and ammunition and a farmer from Galilee dying with an Arab knife in his chest and an Arab from Amman falling behind him and the trench strung over with wire, the sharp steel barbs knifing the skin and the floor damp with blood.

And screams where a bayonet slashed and the sigh where a man's breath burst through his open chest, and the driver from 'Omer lying on his face with a paratrooper's boots on his back with Jews passing from trench to trench over wire or under it, and all the while the Uzis pumping, the mortars whining, exploding with fragments and shock, and men shouting for more cover and more ammunition and never a moment to rest or catch breath long gone, with the wounded and winded gasping and a medic spreading white pads over red-flaring wounds, and all of the time the officers moving forward and the men trying to follow and some of them making it while others died or lay where they were hit trying to crawl on and dying or not dying and hearing the noise and the officers calling.

And over it all the Long Toms, the 105s, the twenty-five-pounders, while in the sky seeking targets were the Fougas and choppers, but the targets were few and from a thousand feet looking down a running man is a running man and none wants to kill his own and the dirt soldier dies in the dirt while the pressure grows with fire and noise and more men running with grenades and guns, and the Arab yields one street and then another, leaving his dead on the cobbles, the houses behind him silent, the windows smashed or shuttered and somewhere a muezzin praying and an officer shouting.

And all the while there are the wounded passing back wounded, the helmets gone, the yarmulke bloodied, the fingerless hand trying to close the open wound while more men move on.

The streets taken, the bunkers blasted leaving pieces of men, and the next street taken, the next block falling, the next hill stormed and more bunkers and grenades and wounded lying dead among the cobbles. The Jewish dead beside the Arab dead and only the uniforms different, while the lines flowed east where the objectives were marked on maps by commanders.

Zvi walked over to his communications truck to contact his command post. Shmuel, on the rooftop, trying to keep pace with what was happening along the front, reported that the armored column was already moving toward the Ramallah Road.

Zvi walked back to the paratroop commander, whose men had moved out of the trenches now to the streets. They were moving too fast, leaving pockets of Arabs sniping at their rear.

Zvi listened to the young colonel issuing his orders to one of his staff. "Hold the pace until we clean up behind them."

Satisfied, Zvi said, "I'll be at headquarters."

The busy young colonel merely nodded. He did not need a kibbitzer now.

For the next several hours, there was little Zvi could do. The enemy fire continued heavy, and though the soldiers tried moving through the streets, they were driven back to cover. Finally, after hours of fighting, the paratroopers moved on.

When Zvi impatiently contacted their commander, he, too, was waiting for more information. All he could say was the whole thing was costing him men, a great many men. As he stood on the Histadrut roof, Zvi closed his eyes.

Then the young colonel reported, "There's a civilian woman helping with the wounded. I've given orders to get her out, but she won't go."

Zvi considered sending someone to remove her from the battle area. However, he decided she knew what she was doing and ignored the report.

Two large searchlights mounted on the top of the Histadrut building cut broad wedges of light over the battleground. From where he stood, Zvi called for artillery support from the heights of Kastel to break the ground in front of his attacking paratroopers. The colonel thanked him, and Zvi grunted. Pulling out his fieldglasses, he tried to make some sense of the battle below. He could see tanks and men moving, but he had no way of knowing which way the battle was flowing.

It was almost dawn when Zvi heard that the paratroopers had taken the Ambassador Hotel and that the ground at Sheikh Jarah was his. Quickly distributing the tanks he had already pulled from the Jerusalem District Brigade fighting to the south and bracing for a counterattack on the hill beyond Government House, Zvi turned the tanks over to the paratroopers.

Light was breaking over the city. The great searchlights were no longer needed and the men who controlled them withdrew from the roof.

Dissatisfied with the time one battalion was spending near Mandelbaum Gate, Zvi asked the young colonel when he was shifting it.

"I gave them orders to move on to Herod's Gate. You said we might try breaking in there. You got your Police School, but it cost us forty men dead. So far, I'm told we've lost seventy-five."

Zvi had nothing to say.

The commander of the armored brigade reported that he was astride the Ramallah–Jerusalem Road. His remaining Centurion tanks had caught up with the main body. He stood on high ground. A company of armored half-tracks which Zvi had scrounged for him during the night had joined the brigade. Telling the tanker to stay where he was, Zvi contacted Shmuel. "Where is the Jordanian Sixtieth Armored?"

The Chief of Staff was able to report that part of the enemy's heavy armor was approaching Jerusalem from Jericho to the east.

"Part?" Zvi demanded. "How many and what?"

After contacting air liaison, Shmuel reported that "part" was twenty U.S. Patton tanks and a column of motorized infantry moving almost due west from Jericho.

Making contact with his armored commander, Zvi ordered an ambush. "Is there anything you need?" he asked.

"Fewer Arabs and more tanks."

Not yet ready to laugh, Zvi tried to reach Avram, but David Benari told him the General Staff officer had disappeared sometime during the night. "Get me headquarters in Tel Aviv," Zvi requested.

"We took Latrun on the way to Ramallah," he reported to the C/S, trying to sound casual.

There was laughter on the other end of the phone, and Zvi was told to stop showing off.

He was about to turn away when a signals officer handed another radio phone to him. The armored commander thought he would want to know they could see Jerusalem from where they were.

Considering what this might mean, Zvi asked snidely, "Have you picked up any picture postcards?"

"No, but if you want some . . ."

And then over the radio Zvi could hear the large tank-mounted 105s begin to fire. "They're here," the armored commander shouted, and Zvi was left holding a dead radio line.

Then he gave orders to shift men from the Jerusalem District Brigade to the paratroop brigade which had suffered heavy losses. From where he stood, Zvi could hear the tank battle being fought to the north of the city where the enemy's Pattons had closed with the Israeli armor. Ten minutes later he was in a copter on his way to the tank battle.

As the copter settled down, Zvi saw that his own armor had the advantage of the better ground. The battle seemed to be one-sided in spite of the huge enemy Pattons. Though the Jordanian tankers tried fighting from house to house, keeping their cumbersome armor as well hidden as possible, the Israelis would not let them avoid a fight. Tanks were already burning on the road, and as Zvi emerged from the chopper, he saw two Arab tanks catch fire. One exploded, taking up part of a house as it blew.

From where he stood in the command half-track, he counted nine burning Pattons. Then another exploded. Two more probed forward from behind high stone fences and were knocked out before they could return to cover. The eight remaining Arab tanks turned about and lumbered off the field, heading back the way they had come. Making radio contact, Zvi asked the air force to keep track of the Pattons if they could not knock them out. Calling the armored commander over, Zvi ordered, "Move south toward the city and make contact with our own men just north of Jerusalem." He thought a moment and added the warning, "Don't get caught fighting each other. Coordinate."

The two stood on the height from which they could see the minarets of Jerusalem. The city lay small to the south, covered by a haze of battle smoke. "It looks pretty from here," the armored colonel commented.

Zvi looked dubiously at the other officer. "I'll arrange a guided tour when this is all over. Meanwhile, get to Mount Scopus, the Hill of the Split Road and French Hill. And believe me," he warned, "they're dug in deep." Then he explained, "From Mount Scopus we can take Augusta Victoria Hospital. I don't want to leave that high ground in their hands." He thought about what he had said and advised, "Remember, you are going against a hospital, and you aren't going to hit it."

The tank colonel nodded. For an instant he almost said that he resented the unnecessary warning, but then he remembered the pressures Zvi must have been under and nodded. "We aren't there yet."

Zvi made his way back to the helicopter and returned to his own command post in Jerusalem. He could still hear the fighting and as he stood looking down at the battlefield, he asked Shmuel to find Avram. Then he himself contacted the armored brigade. The battle to reach Mount Scopus had already lasted two hours. Ten men were dead, thirty-one wounded. Two Shermans were scrubbed and three half-tracks. "And the ground?" Zvi asked.

"We're on top," the armored commander explained. Then, reproach-fully, he added, "Zvi, a cemetery is a hell of a place to fight a battle."

He was thinking ahead, but he had no intention of giving the orders yet.

Squatting on the roof, Zvi rested for the first time in more than twenty-four hours. He tried to remember if he had eaten, could not, and asked one of the girl soldiers standing nearby if she could find him a can of something. Another of the girls brought him a cup of coffee, and he slipped to the floor, holding it between his hands. "What time is it?" he asked her, too weary to look at his own watch.

"It's thirteen hundred, sir."

"Will you find Shmuel?" he asked, seeing that his deputy was not on the roof now.

Zvi was drinking the hot coffee in large gulps when David Benari came over to tell him they had located Avram. With great effort, Zvi pulled himself to his feet and picked up the radio phone. "Avi, where the hell are you?"

Listening for a moment, Zvi shook his head. He wanted to weep, but he knew he would not, not yet and certainly not here. "I'm sorry, Avi. Tell Malin I'm sorry."

"What can I do for you?" Avram asked. "I'm leaving the hospital now."

Deciding it would not hurt to keep his friend busy, Zvi suggested, "Get in touch with Tel Aviv and explain that it would be a mistake not to let me move into the Old City now." And then he said what he had been thinking since the moment he had heard he was to command in Jerusalem. "We can take the Old City, Avi. Tell them we can take the Old City."

The first girl who had gone for some food, handed him an open C-ration can and Zvi thanked her. Turning, he stared down at the Old City. He had meant it. He could take the ancient walled town.

Then he saw Shmuel coming toward him. "The armor and the paratroopers have linked up," his deputy informed him.

Zvi nodded.

The Colonel brought his withered arm up and pointed toward St. Stephen's Gate. "That's your short cut into the Old City."

Zvi agreed.

A clerk brought Zvi word that the armor held all of Mount Scopus. Resting his back against a table, he closed his eyes. It would have been simple enough for him to fall asleep at this moment. He wished he had word of Aaron, but he decided not to ask for it. Avram was going to be joining him soon. Maybe Avram would know something. Zvi felt ill about the news Avram had given him on the phone: their youngest child had lost an arm in the shelling. Wishing once more that he knew something about Aaron, Zvi opened his eyes and asked a startled girl, "What day is it?"

The girl, a slight blonde with dirt on the front of her uniform, thought the General was joking. Then she could tell by the way he was waiting for an answer that he was not. "It's Tuesday, the sixth, sir."

"Thanks." Calling for Shmuel, who was standing by a radio, Zvi said, "I'm going to Mount Scopus. If Avi has not gone back to Tel Aviv, I'd like him with me."

Shmuel said that he would try to locate the staff officer and then told Zvi, "That woman who was helping with the wounded last night . . ."

Zvi tried to remember what Shmuel was talking about, and then he recalled having decided it had to be Kineret. "Well?"

"She's still with the paratroopers. They're afraid she might get killed."

It took Zvi a short time to bring himself to focus on the problem. "You tell Kineret Heschel I said she should get the hell back to the Foreign Ministry. Just tell her I've got enough problems."

"It isn't Kineret," Shmuel told him.

"Then who the . . ."

Shmuel shrugged. "Do I forcibly remove her?"

"I don't give a damn. Get Avi and arrange for a half-track with communications." Shaking his head, he stormed off the roof, annoyed at being bothered.

Half an hour later Avram joined him on Mount Scopus. The police who were part of the regular guard were sent back to the city, and Zvi made up a force of paratroopers and armor to hold the height. When he was satisfied the place was secured, he and Avram stood looking down on the two Jerusalems which they were determined to make one. Then the sound of shelling brought Zvi back to the moment. Looking around, he found the paratroop commander.

"We are going to cut these hills off from attack," Zvi explained, "I want you to move from here to Augusta Victoria and then to the Mount of Olives. From there try to move on to Izaria," and he was pointing to a small Arab village on the lower edge of the slope.

The colonel weighed the task and said, "If I had another tank company . . ."

"What would you do with it?"

The younger officer explained, "Use one for cover and send the other down the main road toward Augusta Victoria." Before Zvi could ask the next question, the colonel added, "And I'd send an infantry battalion with it."

"You've got it," Zvi promised. Contacting the armored brigade, he shifted a company to the paratroopers and left with Avram for his own headquarters.

When he arrived, he learned his attacks were completely stalled and the move toward Augusta Victoria was coming under heavy fire from two ridges overlooking the route.

Raising his fieldglasses from the thong about his neck, Zvi carefully read the terrain his men were to cross. "Shmuel," he called, and waited until his deputy joined him. "What's wrong?"

"Sheer exhaustion. These men are tired, Zvi. They've been at it too long."

Avram, standing with them, looked to Zvi for a decision.

Pulling a cigarette from his shirt pocket, Zvi lighted it while he stared off toward the Old City. He was remembering a brigade at Mitla which had fallen asleep while he talked.

"Time's a factor now," Avram told the two. "I just talked to Kineret, and she says the United Nations is trying to close us down."

Zvi weighed the problem, and then to the surprise of the others, he said, "Tell the paratroopers on the move to Augusta Victoria to wait. We'll try it after dark."

"And the Old City?" Shmuel asked.

"Cancel the order for now."

"But . . ." Avram started to object and stopped when he saw Zvi shaking his head.

"We'll have the heights before we are forced to stop," Zvi promised.

"You can tell headquarters that." He flicked the cigarette over the side of the building and accepted the cup of coffee one of the girls was handing him. "Tell them we'll have the heights and the Old City."

Below, he could see a tank and several jeeps burning on the slope of Mount Scopus. The Arab anti-tank fire was heavy, the snipers were still at work. He looked at his watch. 1715. "Tell the tankers to take Ramallah tonight," he ordered. "That we can secure." And while he and Avram watched, they heard Shmuel pass on the orders. A few minutes later they saw the remains of the tank brigade peel off the hill and roll north toward Ramallah.

"Tell the paratroopers they can rest where they are," Zvi directed Shmuel, "but I want them moving by twenty-three hundred."

The staff officer understood and left to take the orders to the field himself. A few minutes later Zvi turned to Avram. "We'll move out tonight."

The Israeli artillery swept low across the base of the Mount of Olives, avoiding any buildings, but keeping the heads of the Arabs down. Watching from the window of the Intercontinental Hotel, Bedia wished she had driven home earlier. Her Egyptian colonel had left the hotel in the morning to explain to the Arab Legion officers how a Egyptian would use artillery and he had just returned, angry and disappointed. "The Jews are holding the road to Ramallah."

Bedia sneered in disbelief. "What are you going to do?"

Colonel Yusef el Sindi shrugged. "These Legion bastards don't know how to fight and I haven't time to teach them."

Knowing that she had received a kind of answer, Bedia was tempted to ask if he had taught the Egyptians how to fight, and decided against it. Yusef el Sindi was going to have a difficult time, and she did not want to add to his troubles. She did not love him, but she enjoyed his company and he was as clever as any Egyptian she had met. Looking out of the hotel window toward that part of Jerusalem held by the Zionist gangsters, she wondered if the Jew Mazon was actually headquartered on the tall building, as one of the waiters had told her. She watched her colonel light a Cuban cigar while he tried to make up his mind what he was going to do.

Finally, drawing himself up full height, Yusef took her arm, "We'll take your car and try to make our way to Amman."

Jerking herself free, Bedia shook her head. "I'm a Palestinian. I'm staying here."

Startled that she would dispute the point and at the same time not wanting to offend her because her father could be of help to him in the months to come, Yusef said, "You certainly don't expect me to stay and be captured."

Putting one hand on his cheek, she came to tiptoes, kissed him and offered, "Take my car. Maybe sometime we can find another bed."

The bluntness with which she bade him goodbye and put their

relationship into perspective annoyed Yusef, but he did not have time to argue with her. Opening her purse, he took her keys and a heavy wad of money which he pocketed with a smile.

Bedia laughed softly as he ran, leaving her at the window watching the enemy tanks deploying to attack the Mount of Olives.

Ten minutes later, wearing pajamas instead of his uniform, Colonel Yusef el Sindi drove out of the broad parking space at the side of the hotel. A burst of machine-gun fire splashed over the Rolls Royce, sent it into a spin, and rolled it over the side of the Mount. The Israeli paratroopers did not see anyone emerge before the car began to burn. Watching from the hotel window, Bedia saw the petrol tank explode and she sighed. She had liked that car.

The southern road from Tel Aviv to Jerusalem had not come under the heavy fire that the northern road had, and so Ruth found the drive easier than she had expected. Twice she had had to pass road blocks, using Zvi and Avram's names as her pass. It had been late Monday night when Hannah had called to tell her about the Ben Ezras' child. Never having been very close to Malin, Ruth knew that she was making the trip because of Avram, who had fought beside her in the Old City.

Entering Jerusalem, she was aware just how heavily the Arabs were shelling. A jeep raced past her and two large trucks rolled through a cross street. Ruth watched the young reserves in the back of the trucks as they slept, leaning against each other's shoulders. She wondered how it would feel to be so young again and then she smiled to herself. The very young never know they are young, never know that they will become tired, become old.

Stepping out of the car, she looked up at the building. One wall had been badly damaged. There was debris on the ground. After climbing the stairs to the second floor, she knocked.

Hannah opened the door, and the two looked at each other, and Ruth thought her daughter was beautiful, and she wondered how she had ever come to have a beautiful daughter, and then in that instant she knew she was not going to say anything about Aaron or Moshe because Hannah was the one who mattered.

Then Hannah was kissing her mother and drawing her inside where she explained that Malin was still at the hospital and that Avi was somewhere with Zvi Mazon and that she had not heard from Aaron since the war began though people had told her Moshe was on his way to Suez and did her mother know if that was true and had her mother heard anything about Aaron?

Standing in the center of the Ben Ezras' living room, Ruth smiled because her daughter wanted not only the best, but everything.

SINAI

The desert sun slipped low and the sands seemed to turn from shining white to a purple-gray. Five thousand feet below, the column of Israeli tanks battered their way through the defenses east of Kantara. Looking down, it appeared to the pilot that someone was trying to draw white and red lines between the small tanks and the smaller bunkers. Then, off toward the horizon to the west, he made out a column of tanks moving east. Swooping down, he radioed the Israeli column below that the enemy was approaching. Then passing on, he began his run down the length of the Egyptian column. His first bomb struck a target and he felt the blast as a tank exploded almost beneath him. The second missed, but he knew he had struck with the third. Whirling high and around, he set his sights on the mammoth Stalins rolling defiantly east. One in his sight and he cannoned it. The next and he missed. Another miss. Then another strike and he was pulling high and circling once more. There were half-tracks and motorized ack-ack below and he saw that the Egyptians were trying to draw a red line or a white one from the ack-ack to his plane. Then he saw the tracers reaching upward from several half-tracks as they too sought to draw the line, but he was coming down now for another run and as he slammed over the column his own cannon drew lines to one half-track, to another, to a group of fleeing soldiers and then a petrol truck. And then he saw a white line extend out to his wing, felt his Mirage jolt and falter and he tried to seek the sky, but the plane would not respond and the ground was coming up fast and the wing fell away and he knew the Arabs had drawn well and he was skimming over the column now at more than six hundred miles an hour. A flash of light blinded him as the jet ripped through an Egyptian truck killing ten soldiers. Then both the truck and the plane exploded. A pillar of white smoke, reaching skyward, marked the place where he died.

JERUSALEM

The Zionist gangsters from the other side of Jerusalem had already swept through much of the area east of the frontier in spite of what Lieutenant Diyar al Ilm and his men could do to stop them. The swarthy lieutenant and his men had withdrawn to the Valley of Kidron to cover any Jew attempt to take the Old City from the rear. Having fought them all of his life, Diyar felt he knew how the Jews fought. He set his guns where they could not be approached except over open ground. If there was one thing Lieutenant al Ilm did not want, it was a surprise. Except with women, he did not like surprises.

When the Jews came, he would start the great counterattack and after it was over, he would find the girl who had come down from the hotel with the Egyptian officer days before, the girl who had walked as though she never needed to squat and whose thing was always clean. He crouched beside his detachment, one hand resting on the heavy machine gun and recalled the look of the Arab girl in the thin white cotton dress who showed her legs to a man and wore the rigging he had seen in a shop window by which a woman slung her breasts forward. Diyar had never taken one of those rigs off a woman, but he was willing to try. The sun of the late afternoon was hot. There was smoke over the Old City where the Jews had dropped mortars on the Moslem Quarter. His thoughts drifted from the woman in the white cotton dress with the legs sheathed in silk to the woman he had taken the night before the fighting started.

One of the men behind Diyar al Ilm slapped a machine-gun barrel and pointed toward an Israeli half-track moving along the ridge above them. Diyar brought one hand to his lips. He was going to wait until the Jew infantry moved over the open ground, and then he would make them pay for the way his shoulder ached at night from the wound he had received above the Wall of the Jews so many years before. Until the Jew soldiers came he would ignore the half-tracks and tanks. He was a seasoned soldier, and the men with him felt confident that their lieutenant knew how to defeat the Jews.

Taking a deep breath, Diyar al Ilm watched the half-track disappear off the ridge and his thoughts drifted back to the two women he had seen since the long waiting began: the one in white cotton who looked as though she were waiting for a man to take her and the one whom he had tilted on her father's bed the night before. As always with the middle-aged lieutenant, decisions came hard. He was trying to make up his mind which of the women he would honor the night the war ended, when the Israeli half-track swung up behind the machine-gun emplacements and pumped six shells into them. The first knocked out two of Diyar's four guns. The next four killed or wounded all of the men in the detachment except the lieutenant, who rose to his feet, a grenade in hand, and charged the half-track. The Israeli gunner watched, fascinated, for an instant, and then he let go a short burst from his fifty-caliber machine gun. The lieutenant from the Arab Legion felt his chest break apart and then he smiled because he would not have to decide between the two women, because in Paradise he would have them both.

The Israeli soldiers in the half-track looked at each other, shrugged and moved on over the emplacement.

For the past hour, Zvi and Shmuel had been reviewing the situation.

Satisfied that the men had been fed, that ammunition had been distributed, that the armored brigade was ready to take over Ramallah and that the Jerusalem District Brigade was ready to reach out for Bethlehem, Zvi relaxed. Leaving the office where they had been conferring in the Histadrut Building, he walked out into the night by himself. In all his years as a soldier he had been under strain. That was part of being a soldier. But in the past he had been part of the action, he had known the battle, he had seen the enemy, had locked with him, had talked to the dirt soldiers himself. Now he was a commander and he felt too far removed from the battle because he had to keep his eyes on so very much.

Pulling a cigarette from his pocket, he lighted it and stood looking down on the Old City. How much of his tension came from the fact that he was fighting for the Old City now instead of Mitla Pass or Suez or a police station in Jordan or the Gaza Strip? His eyes closed as he tried to recall the conversation he had half a dozen years before with Moshe and the girl called

658

Tamar and Aaron. Then, he had had his doubts about so many things—the future of Israel if the Jew gave place to something new—an Israeli who did not care—or if the generation of Tamar and Aaron had come to the point where the Old City meant nothing to them.

A flare broke over the land and his head came up. Now he was going to find out what it all meant to these young people. As the flare skidded down the sky, throwing mad shadows over the Old City, he laughed at himself and flicked the cigarette away. What he had been thinking about had to be something more than a sense of history. It was, in some way he could not explain to himself, linked with that thing he had never really known or understood—the religious part of being a Jew.

When he arrived at the entrance of his headquarters, his head went back and he looked at the sky. The night was black. A soldier's night. Somewhere he heard a plane overhead. He wished he could ask someone about Aaron, but if anything had happened to the boy, he would have heard. Looking at his watch, he decided it was time to move. His driver and a communications sergeant were waiting for him at the jeep.

"Let's get around the Old City," Zvi ordered, and they were driving through the line held by the Israelis. From the walls of the Old City, the Arab Legion was still firing at anything that moved. Twice, flares burst over them and the driver brought the jeep to a stop. Once they were silhouetted by a still-burning tank. Zvi noticed it was one of his. Then they were stopped by two paratroopers. Zvi identified himself and the grizzly-bearded men moved closer to the jeep.

"Zvi," one of them said, "we'll take it for you." And they all knew the paratrooper was talking about the Old City.

Waving, Zvi tapped Haim on the shoulder and they drove on. A short distance away, they were stopped again. A medical officer had problems. "I've five men wounded, sir, and I need some help."

"What?"

"A truck."

Zvi asked his radio operator if he could carry his equipment. The sergeant thought he could.

"Let's go then," Zvi ordered. Turning back to the medical officer, he explained, "I'm short of trucks, but a jeep should do it for now."

The driver understood and started to help the medical officer carry the wounded from where they lay behind a wall to the jeep. One paratrooper emerged, helped by someone Zvi could not see clearly in the dark, and then he knew it was a woman.

His hands came to his hips as he watched her and when she reached the jeep, he snapped, "Lady, what the hell are you doing here?" He reached out and helped the soldier, whose leg was heavily bandaged, while he waited for an answer to his question.

The woman was walking away without answering him, and he trotted after her, took her arm and brought her about. "I can't afford any dead women here," he explained, trying not to show his impatience, and at the same time proud of any woman who had come to help his men.

In the almost total darkness of the night, she said, "I think you've got other things to do, Zvi."

His head came up and, reaching out, he put his hands on her arms and drew her closer so that he could see her face. When he recognized her, he smiled. "Don't you know better?"

He could tell she was staring at his hands, and then he thought he saw her smile.

"I'd feel better if you were somewhere else," he told Dvora.

Again, he thought she was smiling. Stepping back, she glanced at the high wall of the Old City. "You're going in there?"

"I'm going to try." He thought she nodded before she turned away.

Shrugging to indicate he had no more time to argue, Zvi walked toward the Mount with his radio operator until the half-track he had radioed for caught up with them.

When he joined the commander of the paratroop brigade, it was already 2200 hours. The young colonel explained where his men were, and Zvi approved the positions. A few minutes later, the armored companies, which were in reality the remains of battalions, started for Augusta Victoria. Suddenly the sky became bright as flares burst above them and slowly slid from side to side down the night. Then the anti-tank guns near the Old City walls opened up, firing across the valley between the walls and the Mount, and Zvi could see one tank burst into flames and two recce jeeps hit. His casualties were rising.

The paratroop commander looked to him for permission to call off the attack, but Zvi did not meet his eyes. This operation had to succeed. He could not afford to count his casualties now. Then several paratroopers came running over to tell their commander that tanks had been heard coming down the road from Jericho.

"Call your men back," Zvi conceded.

And the sky above became a sickening white as the Arabs lighted it with flares.

Angry with what he was watching and knowing that there was nothing he could do about it, Zvi said flatly to the brigade commander, "Do what you have to do to get out the wounded."

Then Zvi radioed Shmuel. "What's on the Jericho Road?"

"Maybe twenty Jordanian Pattons. Maybe more."

Zvi watched more men crawling out under the flares to bring back their companions. "Ask the air force to strike those tanks. We're caught up here."

Crossing over to the brigade commander, Zvi ordered, "Bottle up for the night. If the air force can't stop those tanks, you'd better prepare for a counterattack."

Zvi was still watching the attempt to bring out the wounded from the burning jeeps and tanks when Haim rejoined him with the jeep. Climbing in, he started back toward New Jerusalem.

At the Histadrut Building, he received the first report of the air strike. The pilots had hit a column on the Jericho Road. Whatever they had struck had turned back. Then Zvi explained to Tel Aviv that the attack on Augusta Victoria and the Old City would have to wait until morning.

Half an hour later, Avram joined him.

"What about the Jerusalem District Brigade?" the staff officer asked.

"They start for Bethlehem and Hebron and will need everything they've got that rolls. I want Bethlehem by tonight."

Less than two hours later, Avram took a call from Tel Aviv. He listened for a moment and then waved to Zvi. It was already dawn when Zvi took the phone. He listened and nodded. When he handed the phone back to the girl who was monitoring it, he looked at Avram, who smiled. "You promised, Zvi."

Zvi nodded and, turning on his heel, he faced Shmuel. "We have to take the Old City and the heights now. There's pressure in New York for an immediate cease-fire." He thought a moment and said, "I'll be with the brigade." He looked at his watch. 0515. "I want an air strike to soften up these points," and he was walking over to a table where a detailed map was spread out. His finger went to the Legion emplacements which had battered the paratroopers the night before and to the Augusta Victoria heights. "Tell them to hit anything that moves but to keep clear of any roads we have to use and any religious sites. Other than that, just break down the doors so we can come in."

"When?" Shmuel asked.

Zvi considered what had to be done before the brigade moved and what the message from Tel Aviv had meant. "O-eight-thirty to O-nine-hundred, and then we'll move."

Then he was down in the street waiting for the command half-track. Pulling himself inside, he told the driver, "Let's get to Mount Scopus."

Less than half an hour later he and the brigade commander were reviewing the plans which Zvi had brought with him and the plans which the colonel had prepared the night before. They were almost identical. One regiment was to attack straight up the hill from Mount Scopus to Augusta Victoria. A second regiment would attack with the Old City wall behind it. The third regiment was to shift from Herod's Gate along the wall and break through at Lion's Gate, which the Christians called St. Stephen's Gate. The regimental commanders understood their assignments. All of them looked at their watches.

Crouched in the shadow of his half-track, Zvi looked at the faces of these officers. Most of them he had met at one time or another in the past. All of them were brave men. If he had been called upon to name heroes, these men would have been among them. Coming to his feet, Zvi looked over the field. It was morning. The sun was bright and the day was going to be beautiful. The paratroop commander, standing at his side, said, "It's been a long time, sir."

Zvi nodded. "I'd like to get this day done."

And as he spoke, the first air strike blasted the Jordanian Legion emplacements near the entrance of Herod's Gate and in a second pass took out some of those located along the ground in front of the wall of the city. At the same moment in which the jets swept on over the Old City, rising high to return and strike again, the artillery opened up. For the next half hour, Zvi watched the precision of the bombardment. Some few stones on the wall seemed to rock. The very ground shook. Then he saw a stone from the wall crash below. He recalled the pathetic air drop which failed to reach him in '48 and appreciated the support he was getting now. The planes overhead were small training planes for the most part, but the sky above them was protected by Mirages. Zvi wondered if Aaron were in one of them. The half-tracks, tanks, trucks and jeeps of the three regiments were in place now ready to move. From where he stood, Zvi thought he saw a woman in the rear of one of the half-tracks. He was tempted to ask if he had seen rightly, and then decided that if he had, it was none of his business. At the same time, he recalled that the night before he had felt proud of Dvora Kidron, as he was feeling proud of her now.

The ground seemed to shudder as the aircraft made another pass. Zvi looked at the time. 0859. Then the airplanes rose once more and disappeared in the distance. At almost the same moment, the artillery stopped firing.

The attack began.

From every Israeli tank, the heavy guns seemed to be firing in every direction. The half-tracks raced across the ridges. Jeeps spewing machine-gun fire sped over the bridge which had been blocked the night before.

Arab fire from the Old City wall struck the second battalion, but the troops, ignoring it, moved on toward Augusta Victoria. Time, Zvi had said, was the problem. The men seemed to feel both this and the importance of their mission. Where there had been ennui the day before, there was a mad vitality now. A detachment of half-tracks and jeeps with recoilless rifles swept the ridges, overwhelming any Arab fire. The brigade commander was already in his command half-track and moving out.

Zvi remained on Mount Scopus to receive the report from the armored brigade. It had entered Ramallah, raced from one end of the city to the other and, confused as to how one took a city, the tankers had whirled about and blasted their way back to their starting point. Wherever they found resistance, they blanketed it with heavy fire and once it was silenced, they moved on. All resistance in Ramallah was ended now. Listening to the report and enjoying the wild innocence of the approach to city fighting, Zvi had to admit to both the armored brigade commander and Shmuel that this was as effective a way to take a city as any. Then Shmuel was telling him Northern Command had taken Jenin and was moving south. Ordering his deputy to make contact with

Southern Command and seek permission to move on Jericho and Nablus, Zvi congratulated the armored commander and turned his attention once again to the battle unfolding in front of him.

His half-tracks had already overrun their objectives and were beginning to regroup. Tapping his driver on the shoulder, he told him to get to the Mount of Olives. Once there, Zvi stood in his half-track, from which he could make out the Old City and beyond it the New. Jerusalem looked like a city newly risen. And before them, what seemed only paces away, rose the Temple Mount topped by the silver-and-gold domes of the Arab mosques.

The Old City waited and within it the holy places. What else mattered to a people who had not visited their holy sites for almost two decades? Surprised at the extent of his own bitterness over the way the Jordanians had flaunted the treaty to allow the Jews access to their holiest site, Zvi felt his anger turning toward the Christians who were now worrying about the future of the Moslem holy places.

Then the artillery attached to the brigade broke loose, battering the northeastern quarter of the Old City and everything in it north of Lion's Gate. Under the barrage, the tanks, half-tracks and jeeps rolled up toward the walls, where they paused to begin firing with their own heavy guns and recoilless rifles. For ten minutes Zvi watched the fire continue, and then he heard it stop. There was almost no fire returned and the field became suddenly quiet. The tankers moved close to the walls which they could not breach, and Zvi saw a half-track roll into the city. Tapping his own driver on the shoulder, he shouted, "I want to get in there."

The scattered firing from Arab snipers caused a momentary halt to the infantry before Lion's Gate and Zvi sped through. An Arab soldier stood near the gate, but the man did not seem ready to do anything. Paratroopers were flowing into the city now, their weapons at the ready, prepared to fight from house to house if called upon.

All they discovered was a profound silence.

Zvi's driver brought the half-track to a halt and waited for directions. To the surprise of those with him, General Zvi Mazon was as silent as the city. For a long moment all he could think of was the sound of twenty-five-pounders breaking the walls and the shattering explosion of mortars and the smell of cordite and burning buildings and the face of Dov Tervisky as the bullet struck him and the way the old sailor, Ben Ezekiel, who had commanded, walked proudly through the Quarter as though he were on a battleship and the way the radio in a battered apartment had reported that a State had been declared and the way Avram Ben Ezra, a much younger Avram, had smiled, while he himself had asked, "Why in my lifetime?" and he now knew why in his lifetime.

Zvi heard the shouting brigade commander reorganize his men in the event the Arab Legion was in hiding, and then Zvi remembered that neither of them had taken into account the strength of the Arab forces inside the Old City. And he smiled because he knew it would not have mattered what they had known, since both of them had accepted this without discussion.

Seeing two Arabs approach, Zvi dismounted from the half-track and Haim came off, protecting his general's back with an Uzi in his hand.

Zvi and the brigade commander decided to let the Arabs cross the ground between, and then they were facing each other.

The taller of the two, a man in his late fifties with a red scar on his cheek and a red necktie under his collar, introduced himself as Governor of the Old City, and his companion, a reedy elder with a brown beard and fierce eyes was the Qadi, or holy judge.

"There will be no fighting on our part," the Governor said simply. "The Legion has withdrawn, and we have decided that we will not fight you here."

"There is too much that is holy to us," the Qadi explained.

Zvi let the young brigade commander talk. The victory was his and he had paid dearly for it in dead.

The colonel came to his full height and stood looking at the two Arab dignitaries before he said, "We have come in peace. We will not do any shooting within the walls unless we are fired upon."

The Governor nodded. "I understand. However, I do not think I can be responsible for the actions of any fanatics."

Somewhere a rifle shot was heard and the colonel looked to Zvi, who said quietly, "We will not hold the Governor responsible for fanatics, but we will not lose any men if we can help it. Snipers will be killed."

Nodding to his men, who had been held in quiet restraint until the discussion was over, the paratroop commander did not have to tell them what they were to look for. And hundreds of Israeli soldiers began racing through the narrow streets of the Old City.

Zvi smiled as he watched them go, wishing he could be with them and knowing he had other things to do.

Both the Governor and the Qadi stood at his side for a moment. "Are there any synagogues left?" Zvi asked, trying to sound casual and finding it difficult.

The two Arabs looked at each other. It was the Qadi who shrugged and the Governor who said, "I think there is one left." Then as if it were possible to apologize, he tried to explain, "What with the poverty and our own holy places needing repair, we never had time for the synagogues."

Zvi stared coldly at the man. "If I recall, there were more than twenty when I was here last."

The two Arabs looked at each other again, and again the Qadi made no attempt to apologize for the destruction of Jewish holy places, but the Governor did. "People had to live and they took what building material they could. It was a roof for one man and the need of a stable for another."

With great restraint, Zvi walked away from the others.

The heavy boots of the paratroopers still rang through the cobbled streets of the Old City. Walking after them, Zvi could see his men darting down one alley and then another, all of them hunting. An Arab boy stepped out of a nook and spat at the Israeli general, and Zvi stared at the boy until the child turned and fled. The windows of most of the apartments were closed. The shops and niches were all shuttered.

Down the street, coming toward him, Zvi saw a number of Arabs dressed in striped pajamas, their hands over their heads and a single paratrooper walking, Uzi at the ready, behind them. One of the Arabs was wearing a gown with a red cross marked on it and he stopped and smiled at Zvi. "I am a man of peace, sir. I would like to be allowed to go my own way. About these others here, I know nothing." The expression was benign. Zvi watched as the man's palms came together in a gesture of peace as he paid homage to the Jewish officer. Zvi nodded and before anyone else could move, he reached out, grabbed the front of the gown with the red cross on the back of it, and with a jerk tore the length of the gown. Beneath he could see a blood-stained uniform of an Arab Legion officer. Zvi's two palms came together in mockery as he shoved the Arab deserter back into the column of men in pajamas.

Somewhere, someone was shouting that they had found it, and Zvi could hear the paratroop boots on the pavement as his soldiers started running once more.

Following them through the Via Dolorosa, Zvi made his way to the narrow steps which stood between two buildings and emptied out to the Wall. Most of the paratroopers were already there. Some had flung their helmets aside and were standing with their heads against the great stone wall which rose high above them. Others were silently staring in disbelief. A few wore skullcaps, and one was climbing to the top of the Wall with a flag in his hand. After a moment, with the help of his companions, he raised the flag, and several of the paratroopers fired their guns in salute. Then Zvi heard the men fall silent about him; and turning, he saw the bearded Chief of Chaplains, his uniform neat, his brigadier's rank clearly visible, move toward the Wall and do what most of the soldiers were doing. He bent over and pressed his lips to it. Zvi smiled, and moving in, found that he was doing the same. Then he heard a strange sound behind him and, turning, saw the Chief of Chaplains was blowing a ram's horn, the shofar. From where he stood, Zvi could see that many of the men were weeping. Then he heard more people coming, and looking over his shoulder, he saw a Hasid. There were two companions with the old man, and after they had kissed the Wall and prayed, they put their arms about several of the soldiers and began to dance. Watching the hora, the Chief of Chaplains at his side, Zvi told the rabbi, "You blew the shofar!" There was awe in his voice and tears on the other man's cheeks.

Then one of the paratroopers, wearing a skullcap, ran into the narrow area before the Wall with two stools in his hands. Zvi did not ask him where he had found them. It did not matter. Both Zvi and the Chief of Chaplains sat down on the stools and looked at each other in disbelief. Neither the Turks nor the British had allowed a Jew to blow the shofar or sit on a stool by the Wall, because it meant possession, and for almost two thousand years mighty empires had decided that the Jews would never again possess the Wall that had been a part of Solomon's Temple.

Zvi was still sitting on the stool when he saw Avram, Malin, Ruth and Hannah coming down the stairs. The word *protectzia* passed through his mind, and then he brushed it aside. Who had more right to come than Ruth and Avram? There was a stir among the Hasidim who had already arrived as the women approached the Wall along with Avram, but one of them saw the firm look in Zvi's eyes and held his companions back for the moment. They would have plenty of time to see that the women did not profane the sacred Wall by worshiping with the men.

Zvi looked up at the blue-and-white flag which the paratroopers had raised over the Wall and he smiled. Then the Chief of Chaplains was intoning a prayer and the men and women at the Wall fell silent.

" 'If I forget thee, O, Jeruslaem, let my right hand forget its cunning.' We have not forgotten thee, O, Jerusalem, and it was your hands, the right hands of your men that did so valiantly."

Avram threw his arms about his old friend, and Zvi drew Ruth to him and held her affectionately. Looking beyond her shoulder, he saw a middle-aged Arab woman in a white cotton sheath and silk stockings staring at him from the top of the steps. For a moment he thought he knew her. Then Ruth was stepping back and Zvi saw that Moshe had arrived. "We flew him back," Avram explained, and Zvi placed both of his hands on Moshe's shoulders and he wished he knew how to weep as others were weeping. Malin stood beside Avram with tears in her eyes, while Moshe closed one hand on Zvi's arm and said, "It is good."

The Chief of Staff and the Minister of Defense were coming to the Wall now, and people parted to let them approach. About to pass Zvi, they paused. The Chief of Staff embraced him. They stared at each other for a moment, then the Chief of Staff asked, "What did it cost?"

"One hundred and twenty-five dead from the brigades," Zvi reported.

The senior officer nodded, was about to say something, shook his head sadly and walked on to the Wall with the Defense Minister. Then Zvi saw the old Prime Minister, whom he had resented so profoundly less than a week before, and he smiled at the old farmer who looked at him and said, "I told you then 'patience,' " and Zvi nodded and agreed. The Prime Minister was placing a slip of paper in a crack in the Wall where so many others had left their prayers for so many centuries, and when Zvi looked up at the old man, he saw Kineret Heschel beside him, and the paratroopers stepped away, knowing who she was. After she had prayed at the Wall, she approached Avram and Zvi and put her hands out to them, and raising her voice to be heard over the singing of the paratroopers, she said, "I'm happy for both of you and for Israel." She smiled, and beaming at Zvi as though she were his parent, she added, "I'm so proud of you." Leaning over, she whispered in

666

Zvi's ear, "I think he saw the Wall." Zvi, too, at that moment was thinking of the old judge Kineret had loved, and smiling, he agreed, "I'm sure of it." She was about to say more when Zvi stepped out of the circle of his friends to bring in Dvora Kidron who had just appeared with one of the paratroop medical officers. He was about to speak to her when he heard several rifle shots and, looking about, became concerned for the safety of the officials.

But it was the Chief of Staff who came up to him and said, "The snipers are the paratroopers' problem. After all, it's their city too." And he smiled and told both Avram and Zvi he was happy.

After he walked away, Zvi whirled about, looking for Dvora, who was still standing apart from the others and staring at the Wall in disbelief. Reaching out, he took her hands and pulled her to him, and placing one arm about her, he asked Avram, Ruth and Kineret if they remembered her. Ruth smiled. She remembered Dvora. She looked about for Moshe. He was standing a few paces away, holding his wife's hand. Zvi followed Ruth's glance and his face took on the same puzzled expression as Ruth's. Without taking his arm from about Dvora's waist, he turned to Avram, "What have you heard about Aaron?"

The General Staff officer looked at his friend in pain and surprise. When, after a time, he raised his eyes, he said simply, "I thought you knew Aaron was killed yesterday over Sinai."

Zvi was barely aware of Dvora's hand closing on his and Ruth's gasp as she stared at her daughter and knew that Hannah had already heard the news because she was clasping Moshe's hand and smiling at him through tears anyone watching would have thought were related to the Wall. Ruth stood lonely and closed her eyes and prayed for the first time in her life.

Very slowly, Zvi approached the Wall and leaning forward, he pressed his lips against it in love and despair and in prayer. Behind him he could hear the soldiers singing as they danced themselves into exhaustion:

> *Our ancient hope will not perish*
> *Hope from ages long since past.*
> *To live free in the land we cherish,*
> *Zion and Jerusalem at last.*

Stepping back from the Wall, he tried not to weep before his men. He felt Dvora's hand clasped on his, and his head shook from side to side as he stared at the high gray wall with the moss and plants growing from its cracks. A young woman standing not far away was weeping; and when she raised her head, Zvi recognized the girl Moshe had called Tamar, the girl who had not believed in being Jewish and in all the fantasy she had called religion. And then Zvi did not see her any more as his eyes misted over with grief. And nearby he heard the Chief of Chaplains intoning in a clear loud voice, "Comfort ye, comfort ye, my people, saith your God."

And Zvi's hand, holding Dvora's, reached out to touch the Wall, and somehow he knew he was comforted.